Praise for
REGRETS ONLY

"A sexy insider's Washington novel...a highly readable work of fiction."

The Washingtonian

"One juicy read...a solid, engaging, and gossipy tale."

Pittsburgh Post-Gazette

"A stylish cast...the real story here is about female survival tactics in a man's world."

Newsweek

"The perfect book for a lonely fall evening. Glitz and glamour have never been better."

Rave Reviews

(more)

"A juicy blockbuster . . . the action never flags."
Erica Abeel, *New Woman*

"She makes us care about the vulnerabilities her characters share, and the outcome of their relationships is suspenseful until the novel's close."

Publishers Weekly

"There's plenty to keep the pages turning . . . lavish Georgetown parties, torrid love affairs, life inside the boudoirs and drawing rooms of the capital's rich and famous."

Cosmopolitan

"A piece of fine popular fiction...the most exciting and refreshing debut in the world of popular fiction since Judith Krantz gave us *Scruples* way back in 1978...a juicy inside saga of Washington politics and sex, and very rarely in that order...one of the most incisive recent renderings of just what is it that makes some men and women tick very well together in the bedroom but absolutely bomb-bomb-bomb when it comes to competing with each other at work."

New York Post

"Fast-paced, sexy."

Chicago Sun-Times

"The compelling tale of a woman in the painful grips of trying to figure out who she is—who she is in relation to her own past, present, and future...You will keep turning these pages to see what happens next."

Houston Chronicle

REGRETS ONLY

Sally Quinn

BALLANTINE BOOKS • NEW YORK

This novel is a work of fiction. Names, characters, places, and incidents either are the product of the author's imagination or are used fictitiously. Any resemblance to actual events or locales or persons, living or dead, is entirely coincidental.

Library of Congress Catalog Card Number: 86-6705

ISBN 0-345-34459-6

This edition published by arrangement with Simon and Schuster, Inc.

Manufactured in the United States of America

First Ballantine Books Edition: September 1987

For Ben

CHAPTER 1

LORRAINE HADLEY WAS PLEASED WITH HER guest list. Finally. It was getting harder and harder to get a good group together. Thank God there was a new Administration. New blood. She didn't think she could bear another month of those dreary Republicans. Yet one couldn't be a successful hostess in Washington without them. It was risky to have a party so soon after the election. There was always the chance of making a mistake when a new Administration was being formed. One risked getting associated with people who claimed to be close to the candidate, only to find that the candidate wouldn't recognize them if he met them in their own living room.

There was that Sherman couple from Colorado everybody was fawning over. They had just bought a big house on Kalorama Road and suddenly they were everywhere, introduced as close friends of the President-elect. Lorraine was ready to bet her husband's fortune that they were phonies. They had been dining out on Roger Kimball's name since August, certain that Kimball would win, establishing a beachhead before the herds hit town. Lorraine had to admit it was clever of them. She had just the tiniest suspicion that the Sherman woman had ambitions as a hostess.

Lorraine dismissed that unfortunate thought. She was confi-

1

dent that she and she alone occupied the role of The Hostess in Washington. When she had come eight years before, she had filled a role left vacant for nearly a decade. She had money, perseverance, dedication, style, nerve, and most of all, she cared. Being a hostess was her profession. She loved the nuances—one *has* dinners, one *gives* parties; she loved the power that went with being able to attract the most important, powerful, sought-after men and, lately, women in Washington.

And now Lorraine happened, by heavenly coincidence, to know slightly the parents of the Vice President–elect, William Rosewell Grey III. Not only that, but she had been cultivating Allison Sterling, White House correspondent for *The Daily*, for the past couple of years, simply because she was an attractive and influential extra woman. The President-elect and his wife, the Kimballs, were Allison's godparents. It had paid off.

Lorraine whispered a prayer of thanks for what she believed were her God-given premonitions. She believed that she was meant to be the leading hostess of the century in Washington and she felt that her role would be recognized by the historians, once she got her salon going. A great Washington hostess, long dead, had once said that to get people to come to your parties in Washington, all you had to do was "hang a lamb chop in your window." This had not escaped Lorraine.

She looked at the clock. It was quarter after six. Her social secretary was still downstairs with the Secret Service. She might as well go downstairs and say hello, check the kitchen, get Miriam back up to go over the party list. She still had to take a bath and rest before she dressed. Besides, she needed a cup of tea. She slipped on suede loafers and straightened her smock, her trademark. It was important, in everything, to have one's own style, to be different, though one had to be careful in Washington. You couldn't be too strange here, because so many of those in power had to toe the line . . . but they adored just a bit of eccentricity in their hostesses. There was a slight mystery to Lorraine. Her accent was unplaceable. Though mostly British, it held a hint of New York, even a hint of the Midwest. Her dark hair, pulled back from her face, gave her an ageless look. Though she was just over fifty, she could have been anywhere between forty and sixty. She was not beautiful, or even pretty. She was what the French called *belle-laide*—beautiful-ugly.

* * *

As Lorraine went down the wide circular staircase to the first floor she looked out the window on the landing. The terrace was almost dark; she could barely see the few leaves left on the November trees. The wind was blowing. A wonderful night for a fire.

The Secret Service were just coming in from the terrace shivering when she walked into the living room. One of them was a tall, blond, pale young man with a cool smile, cool eyes. A killer, observed Lorraine to herself. Just the person I would want guarding me.

"Toby Waselewski, ma'am," he said. "Sorry to disturb you."

"We were just finishing up," said Miriam. "Toby will be working for the Vice President—elect from now on."

"Well." Lorraine smiled winningly. "I do hope we'll be seeing a lot of you."

Her expert eye passed over the flower arrangements in the living room: the chrysanthemums in fall colors, some pussy willows on the mantel, a little pyracantha in her Chinese vases—appropriate, understated. In the dining room her round table which would serve as a buffet was draped in country-print tablecloths and laid out with contrasting napkins. Baskets lined with paisley fabric would be filled with homemade breads. A pasta would be the main course, with a salad of arugula and cherry tomatoes, another of mixed vegetables, and, of course, a ham. She always served pork—either crisp bacon as an hors d'oeuvre, a pork roast with dinner or at a buffet, a country ham. Country ham was very salty and the guests always drank more. If they drank more they relaxed more and had a better time.

The guest of honor tonight, Lawrence Devon, had a bestseller, a satirical novel about the persecution of a white Anglo-Saxon Protestant minority in a faraway country where the blacks ruled and the whites were all the laborers, servants, and untouchables. It had gotten marvelous reviews. Washington was the first stop on his book-promotion tour. Lorraine had been lucky enough to snag him because she had befriended him in London when he was a little-known novelist.

Devon did not move along the usual New York—Washington axis. He lived somewhere in northwest Connecticut and hardly ever appeared on the social scene. So everyone was always curious about him, curious about the series of female writers whom he seemed to run through at a staggering rate and who seemed not to interrupt his writing, except as subjects.

As Lorraine walked into the kitchen to say a last word of encouragement, the servants bombarded her with questions. What time did she want to eat, how many were finally coming, did she want both white and red wine?... all questions she had answered before. This was last-minute stage fright. Ezio, the chef, was going into his final sulk before the dinner.

"Ezio," she lied, "the Vice President's Secret Service agent said he had heard about your famous pasta and hopes to taste it."

Ezio brightened perceptibly, puffed up his chest, and continued to roll out the tortellini as Lorraine assured them that everything would go splendidly. She ordered tea with lemon, no sugar, and beamed her approval.

But it was she who had worked them up into a fever to begin with. Tonight was crucial. The Vice President and his wife would be on display for the first time at a Washington party, and her handling of it and them could advance her or set her back.

Lorraine Hadley rated her guests by numbers, and when the list was complete, she tallied the numbers to see whether the party got a high-enough score. If not, she would add or subtract a few numerically rated guests to get the right one.

The highest one could get was a 5, except for the President. The President was a 10. One really didn't like to have the President come to a party, at least not for the whole time. It ruined things because nobody else got to shine.

The ultimate coup was to have the President come for a half-hour before dinner. He should sweep in, shake hands around the room, make everyone feel important, make the hostess look stupendous, and then leave. Lorraine had not yet managed that, but there was a new Administration and anything was possible.

The Vice President rated a 5. Most 5's made their number because of their positions, though Lorraine did try not to invite deadly bores even under those circumstances. Top White House and Administration people, Cabinet officers, Senators, and out-of-town celebrities such as authors, movie stars, producers, directors, or magnates and a few star journalists could be 5's if they were also attractive.

Fours might have the titles but no personality. Congressmen were 4's. On rare occasions they made 5 if they were fabulously attractive. Ambassadors could also be 4's, as could undersecretaries, people who had something to do with the arts, the top journalists, and lesser authors, though Washington had very few authors.

Middle-rung bureaucrats were 3's, as were Congressional staffers, attachés at embassies, lobbyists, and those "formers" who made up the rest of the population of Washington.

Twos were those who weren't terribly attractive but had some reason to be invited. An out-of-town celebrity has a relative or old family friend who must be invited, or the party requires an expert on something or other. Ones were the unavoidables. Unfortunate spouses who came with star guests—husbands or wives; it was not sexist. No matter how depressing, there was nothing one could do about them. Lorraine would never have anybody lower than a 1, and if her guests did not work as hard as she did, unless they were a 4 or 5 they were not invited again.

She had never told her secretary about the numbers. Miriam Schlesinger was not a kindred spirit. She did not share Lorraine's passion for entertaining or social life. Nor did she particularly care that much about politics or power. She was simply the most efficient human being Lorraine had ever known. She just wasn't any fun.

Together, though, they were always pulling little surprises out of the hat. A guest of honor's favorite, if obscure, dish; a special hard-to-find vodka for a member of the President's staff; a spontaneous compliment for the wife or child of a powerful member of the Cabinet.

Lorraine's signature writing paper, pale pink onionskin with her Dumbarton Street address in bright scarlet, was already the most recognizable stationery in town. With Miriam keeping tabs, Lorraine sent little congratulatory notes to everyone she'd met of any significance on the occasion of favorable news, either personal or professional. The trickiest ones were to journalists. One had to be sure to choose the right pieces to praise, never to send off little notes at random. Journalists knew when they had written a bad piece, and you could be labeled a climber if you seemed not to distinguish. Miriam helped Lorraine on this matter because it was sometimes hard to tell.

Lorraine detested buffets. In London she had refused to have anything but seated dinners, insisting that the other guests come afterward for her salon. That was not done here. There was no way one could drag any of these politicians or Administration types out past ten. It was dinner or nothing. Compared with London, Washington was dull and provincial, even now. But Archie had lost his post at the Embassy and had refused to stay on unemployed. And it was, after all, Archie's money.

Another thing Lorraine loathed was the custom of writing "Regrets Only" on an invitation. It simply gave people an excuse not to respond at all, particularly the younger journalists who were sorely lacking in elementary protocol. Lorraine always insisted on R.S.V.P.

Washington parties were working events. People came first to work, and seemed to have a good time. They came to learn; to exchange views, ideas; to persuade; to lobby; to explain.

The mix, the balance was everything. It was like casting a play. Being a hostess was being sociologist, psychologist, choreographer, and director.

Newcomers in any administration were deceived by the evening clothes, the settings, the drinks in people's hands. They misunderstood. They were used to expense-account lunches, but they found it difficult to relax with journalists at private dinner parties.

It had taken Lorraine almost no time to learn the ropes. She had made very few errors. She had to be told only once. She learned that many people in new powerful positions would not accept invitations because they felt they couldn't pay back. They didn't realize that they were paying simply by accepting.

Lorraine kept a record of each party in one of her scrapbooks, a new one each year. They contained the seating charts, the menus, the flowers, the linens and china, the dress she had worn, and her comments: an especially boring or rude guest; someone who made a particular effort, or was delightful. If two people didn't get along, she would make a note so as not to seat them together another time. She despised the habit some Washington hostesses had of putting people who hated one another next to each other, or inviting all enemies. The whole point of a party was for interesting, amusing people to get together, to learn something, accomplish something.

A well-known statesman and diplomat had once remarked to Lorraine that there were "safe houses" in Washington and "unsafe houses." A "safe house," he explained, was a place where one could count on seeing the powerful and the important, having a good seat at dinner, and not encountering too many undesirables.

Lorraine's was a "safe house."

There were pitfalls, of course, in being a Washington hostess, and Lorraine had not escaped the most dangerous one of all. It had nearly wrecked her career before it started. Lorraine Hadley had made the hideous mistake early on of having an affair with a member of the Administration. It had been a casual outlet for her sexual energies. Poor Archie certainly didn't fill that bill. It turned out to be not so casual when the man's wife had found out. Many of the Republican wives in the Administration wouldn't touch Lorraine after that, and even some of the journalists were surprised at her bad judgment. She hadn't had time to establish herself with them. Had Archie found out, she might have lost him as well—and that would have meant losing Archie's money, and that would have meant losing her profession.

In Washington serious hostesses did not have affairs. As one had to be ideologically neutral to be a successful hostess, so one had to be sexually neuter. Giving up her extracurricular sex life meant relying on Archie. But it also meant that she had a shot at greatness. Greatness required sacrifice. To be a great hostess required concentration. To be a great hostess required celibacy.

Miriam was waiting in Lorraine's little office with her yellow pad on her lap, tapping her nails on the desk. She was ready for the final rundown—the political quiz—before she made the last-minute check on the kitchen and left.

Lorraine flopped down on her chaise, slipped off her shoes, and snuggled up among her Porthault linen baby pillows like a schoolgirl waiting to be drilled by her roommate on the eve of an exam.

Miriam was tough on Lorraine, but Lorraine was a dedicated pupil. Now, though, just as she had pretty well mastered the old Administration, there was a whole new group coming in. Names were popping up in the paper each day. Lorraine read the papers avidly as she had breakfast in bed. First *The Daily* with a fine-tooth comb; then skimming over *The New York World* for anything the Washington paper might have missed and also to keep her New York hand in. Miriam brought her the financial journal, marked. Evenings she checked the gossip column of the New

York afternoon paper; Mondays she read *The Weekly* and the other newsmagazines.

Once a week Miriam quizzed her. "Name the new Secretary of Commerce . . . What were the reasons behind the latest teamsters' strike . . . Did the price of oil go up or down yesterday . . . Name the British Foreign Minister . . . What was the cause of the riots in Chile . . . Who is the President's new Appointments Secretary and why was the last one let go . . ."

When Lorraine was giving a party, Miriam put her through a spot quiz on the guests and what they had been involved in that week. If the Secretary of Defense had been testifying on the Hill, Miriam clipped the accounts of his testimony and Lorraine read through them. If Lorraine had invited a visiting star from the Kennedy Center she would have tried to see the performance and make sure she didn't invite any critic who might have panned it. With Miriam, nothing ever fell through the cracks.

Lorraine's tea was brought up by Irma, maid-housekeeper, confidante, adviser, a black woman in her late fifties or early sixties—she wouldn't tell—who had worked for Archie's family for thirty years. Irma knew everyone in town. Before Miriam came in the mornings Irma would bring Lorraine's breakfast upstairs on a tray with the paper and the two would hash over the last night's party. Irma understood the importance of the Washington social scene in a way Miriam never would.

In London, of course, they'd had a butler. But a butler in Washington, she quickly found out, would look ridiculous. Even the richest and most elegant Washingtonians didn't have a proper English butler. It was just too ostentatious in a city where most people lived on government or newspaper salaries. Irma was as good as three butlers.

Everything now had been reviewed except the guest list.

"The Vice President–elect and his wife."

"The Vice President and his wife," repeated Lorraine as she swallowed her egg sandwich. "William Rosewell Grey III, 'Rosey' to his intimate friends, 'William' to his colleagues and the press. Governor of Virginia, conservative Democrat from Richmond. One of the First Families of Virginia. His parents are friends of Archie's. Bores."

Miriam raised an eyebrow.

It amused Lorraine to irritate Miriam.

"Patrician, tall, good-looking, drinks Glenfiddich. His wife is

Sara Adabelle, 'Sadie' to her close friends. Attractive, thirty-eight, auburn-haired, bright, outspoken, from Savannah, drinks champagne." Lorraine wondered whether she would live up to her publicity. She sounded divine. Lorraine might hate her. On the other hand, they could become best friends.

Though she'd have to be careful about Allison Sterling. Allison was the most successful and glamorous reporter in Washington. Allison covered the White House for the powerful *Daily* and she would be put off if Lorraine appeared to befriend Sadie Grey too obviously. Allison would be suspicious of Lorraine's motives and Lorraine certainly didn't want to lose Allison now that her godfather was going to be President. Besides, not that it was important in the scheme of things, but she liked her.

Unlike Allison, Sadie Grey didn't know anything about Washington. Lorraine could teach her. She decided to cultivate Sadie Grey.

Sadie was having trouble with her hair. And she really wanted to look good tonight. It would be her first real Washington party. Not one of those official things. This one was going to be fun and glamorous. There were going to be all sorts of fascinating and exotic people. Lorraine Hadley was one of the great hostesses of Washington. Lorraine had been in Washington for only eight years, Sadie knew, but already she was constantly in the fashion magazines and dailies for her parties and her style. After all those stifling years in Richmond, now suddenly Sadie was reprieved. She was the wife of the Vice President-elect and she was going to make the most of it.

She brushed her auburn hair forward, then back. Finally it looked the way she wanted it, full and sexy. Rosey was beginning to get impatient. He wanted to go downstairs, look around, have a drink with their hosts. Vice President and Mrs. Hall—George and Audrey—had been gracious to let them stay with them for the weekend. They were in the guest room of the Vice President's House this time, but it wouldn't be long before it was their home.

Rosey had been appalled at the idea of coming up to Washington for a party two weeks after he had been elected. But Sadie had begged him and he had relented, mainly because he had work to do in Washington. He wasn't crazy about Lorraine Hadley, either. He thought she was a gossip and an opportunist, the kind of person Washington inspired, encouraged, bred. She represented everything he did not want to be a part of. And it was, he feared, everything that would appeal to Sadie.

Sadie was about to make her debut. And she feared she might have to carry them both. It was not exactly Rosey's crowd. She would soon learn that the Vice President didn't have to do anything but just be there. In Richmond, Rosey knew everybody and felt comfortable with his country-club friends. And as a member of a First Family of Virginia, he was always socially desirable. So Sadie, though an outsider, was acceptable too, barely.

Washington, she knew, was a very different scene. She had heard that the fast social track was dominated by the press and by the liberals, though that had begun to change with the last Administration. They were the glamorous ones, they were the ones she read about. They were the ones she wanted to get on with. And that was the one crowd, she was afraid, that would not so readily accept her husband, who was a Southern conservative, a bit serious.

When Lorraine had called her in Richmond last week to invite them to the party, she had gone over the guest list with her.

"Darling, this is not one of those dreary official parties I'm sure you've been to when you've come up from Richmond," Lorraine had announced in her grand and slightly British accent. "This one is just for fun. It's for Lawrence Devon—you know, the author. He's adorable, absolutely divine, and I'm having a lot of the younger crowd tonight, journalists and writers. Archie calls them the troublemakers."

"Is it seated?" Sadie had asked, with some trepidation. She was unnerved at the idea of a buffet where she didn't know anyone.

"Heavens, no!" cried Lorraine. "One would have to be certifiable to even contemplate a seated dinner with these people. They're much too undependable. And I'm talking about Senators, too. You'll learn, my dear. They're always at the Capitol until midnight voting and one is constantly stuck with their dreary little wives all evening. Archie hates buffets, but there's nothing I can do about that. It's the world we live in now. Do wear something comfortable. You may end up on the floor."

Sadie liked the casual way Lorraine talked to her. There was something cozy and female about Lorraine. She felt she could be friends with her.

"I have to tell you I'm a little nervous about this," said Sadie.

"I don't really know a soul in Washington very well. I just don't want to make the wrong friends, if you know what I mean."

"I know better than anyone. I've seen it happen too many times. Particularly to ambassadors who don't bother to weed out their predecessors' lists. One can end up with guests who went out four administrations ago. All it takes is a little patience, a little research, a little study."

"I've, uh, I've had some problems with the press too," said Sadie.

"Darling girl. It's trial by fire. You've had the worst of it. It can only get better. Besides, you're a celebrity now, an object of interest and fascination. In Washington one couldn't wish for anything more. As long as it doesn't hurt your husband."

"Well, it's just that I didn't have that much exposure to the press because I was sick during so much of the campaign. And in Richmond nobody ever socialized with reporters. They just weren't in the same circles."

"The whole point of entertaining is that politicians and the press mingle, they use each other," assured Lorraine. "It's part of the game. You'll enjoy it once you get the hang of it."

"I don't know whether I'm clever enough for them," she said.

"You'll be just fine. The Vice President can go anywhere, and if he has a beautiful, bright, amusing wife then it's beyond anyone's expectations. Rosey and Sadie Grey are going to be the toast of Washington. Trust me."

Sadie had found her best friend in Washington. And just knowing that Lorraine was there and that Lorraine was giving the party made her feel more secure.

She had thought carefully about what to wear. She didn't want to be overdressed. Finally she had chosen a turquoise silk-and-wool dress with a boat neck to show off her turquoise eyes and long, slim white neck. It was a ravishing color, the perfect frame for her auburn hair and pale skin. The knit waist showed off her figure, and the skirt was full and ankle length. That would be comfortable for sitting on the floor, and she could still look dignified. She would wear turquoise earrings and no other jewelry.

She really did look good. And Rosey (she was going to have a hard time getting used to calling him "William" in public) was being very sweet. He walked into the room, saw her standing in front of the mirror, and whistled. He knew how nervous she was. What he didn't know was how concerned she was about him and how people would react to him. She looked at him with affection and despair. He was so handsome in his tailored English suit, tiepin, dark tie, and clean haircut, yet he did look so proper. Well, he was her husband. There was nothing she could do about it. She kept looking at him in amazement thinking that he was soon going to be Vice President of the United States.

"Sugar," she said. Her normal Southern accent was a bit husky. "You ready, darlin'?" He came over to her, smelling of lemon after-shave, leaned over, and, ever careful not to mess up her makeup, gave her a gentle kiss, touching her lightly on the shoulders.

"You look ravishing, as always," he told her. She smiled up at him, putting her hand on his.

Rosey was so polite. In the early days she had had fantasies that he would come bounding into the bedroom just as they were getting ready to go out to a party, throw her down on the bed, rip off her clothes, and take her.

Right now she was reluctant to give up the old fantasy. She was hoping that the new job, the new city, the new power would rekindle what they'd once had. She had been so in love with him once.

Beneath that stiff, mannered F.F.V. demeanor there was a good ol' University of Virginia boy. She had seen glimpses at his St. Anthony Hall reunions, at the goose hunts on the Eastern Shore, at the parties after football games where the boys told stories of past conquests, wanton women, lost weekends.

It was this side of Rosey that had drawn her to him. Most of the time, even in the old days, he was contained, reserved, always perfectly mannered; a true reflection of the somber family portraits that hung in the hallway of his parents' Richmond manor house.

They reminded her of Rosey, those ancestors in their gray Civil War uniforms, the wild Southern boys trying to break out of their country-gentleman upbringing, only to be reined in by their obligations to their families and to their heritage.

And as Rosey became more and more involved in politics he suppressed his other side and buried himself in his tradition.

It had been hard for Sadie to watch the man she had fallen in love with emerge as William Rosewell Grey III, eminently respectable citizen, husband, father, politician. It made her sad.

She had felt bored and trapped in Richmond, and now, even though the children were older and away at school, she would be even more trapped. To be the Vice President's wife dashed any thought she might have had of going back to her writing.

But this was not the time to give up. If there was ever a chance to revitalize her marriage, this was it. Besides, what choice did she have?

"I think I ought to tell you now," said Rosey, "that I have no intention of spending my time in Washington going out to parties designed to give hostesses like Lorraine Hadley something to do and build up the egos of pompous politicians and journalists. It's not why we're here."

Sadie's first reaction was to get angry, as it usually was when Rosey made one of his pronouncements. But she was not going to fall into their old pattern this time. She was going to change the rules on him and force him to change as well.

She wanted the old Rosey back, and for her own salvation she was going to get him.

"That, my darling husband," she said, "is exactly what we are here for. That may not be written in the job description for Vice President, but you tell me of a better way you could help and support your President than massaging egos." He looked surprised for a moment, taken aback. He had never thought about it that way.

"And you tell me who better to do it than you, the most devastatingly charming man in the South."

She could see him smile reluctantly. He straightened his tie and lifted his shoulders.

She walked over to him, put her arms around his neck, and kissed him lightly on the cheek.

"You are, you know," she said softly.

He smiled again, flushed with pleasure.

"Okay," he said, patting her behind gently, "let's get this show on the road."

She took one last look in the mirror after he left the room. She suddenly felt good about herself and about how she would do tonight. She had the feeling that something important in her life was about to happen.

As she walked out the bedroom door and down the stairs to the hallway, she looked around at the dreary colors, the tacky furniture. She couldn't wait to get at this house. That would be her first project. She would get Lorraine to help.

The limousine was waiting, the driver standing at the door.

Sadie sank back into the plush seat and shivered from the cold as well as from excitement. She could see Rosey's distinguished profile in the darkness.

She rested her hand on his thigh and stroked it.

She could see him soften. "I'm so pleased to be able to show you off tonight at this party. Wait till the ladies get an eyeful of you! They'll be scratching and clawing their eyes out . . . you ol' handsome devil."

Rosey beamed.

It would be all right. At least for now.

"Claire and Worth Elgin," Miriam said for the second time with a touch of irritation. "We don't have much time."

Lorraine loathed Claire Elgin. If there was anyone in Washington who was a bigger phony and climber, she would like to know. But Worth was editor of *The Daily*'s Sunday "View" section and wrote a controversial column. Claire featured herself a singer and held musicales at her house. Worth was a power. Claire was an embarrassment. They were one of the most sought-after couples in Washington.

"What were the outstanding pieces this week in View?" asked Miriam. "Can you guess which editorials Worth wrote? Don't be specific unless you're sure it's his. Just compliment the page."

"There was an amusing column Sunday about the differences between Grey and Roger Kimball, a play on 'Everything's Comin' Up Roses,'" said Lorraine. "Probably Worth's. A salute to his wife's musical talents. That's in her repertory. And *The Daily* comes out against Kimball's rumored choice for Defense as too dovish—rather surprising for *The Daily*."

"A-plus," said Miriam. "That will be a big topic tonight. Especially because of our next guest on the list . . ."

"Who?"

"Bud Corwin."

"Chairman of the Senate Armed Services Committee, less dovish than Kimball's man, and he wants to be Secretary of Defense."

"Bingo. Why are they being invited to a literary party for Lawrence Devon?"

"Corwin's wife, Helene, is Washington correspondent for *Fashion* magazine and she has just done a spread on Devon." Corwin was possibly the sexiest man in Washington. Never mind that he knew it. Bud Courtin' was his sobriquet. Poor Helene.

"Okay, let's go down the list fast to make sure you've got the wives and escorts. Who's June Levitas?"

"All right, you've got me. Who in the name of Heaven is June Levitas? Are you sure she's invited?"

"June Levitas"—Miriam beamed—"lives with your guest of honor on weekends. She is a free-lance writer in New York. She had a piece in *Moment* last month on the backlash against the women's movement."

Lorraine sighed. June Levitas was probably another one of those little sharp-tongued snippets from New York who had an opinion on everything and didn't mind saying so. One of those loathsome feminists. Thank the good Lord they were becoming passé. One didn't have to have at least one feminist at a party anymore. They terrified her and she always said the wrong thing around them. The worst problem with them when they were writers was that everything they saw or heard was fair game. Lorraine liked to be in control of her publicity.

"Michael Addison."

"Divine book reviewer, *The Daily*." Even more so since he had given Lawrence a good review. She shuddered to consider what she would have done if he had panned the book.

"Rufus Turner."

"Novelist friend of Lawrence's, Southern novels." He drank too much. Hadn't written in several years. Told good stories. Had a wife named Sue Ellen or Ellen Sue.

"Harry Saks."

Kimball's campaign manager was the hottest pol in America. Wry and mean as hell. His wife, J.J., was a lawyer with no sense of humor.

"What job will he get?" Miriam asked. This was a trick question.

Lorraine was ready. She hadn't seen anything about it in the papers, but Allison had hinted that Harry Saks would not ask for the expected post of media coordinator or White House adviser. Nor Chairman of the Democratic National Committee. Saks wanted London, and that was going to create an enormous stink, especially among Kimball's rich contributors—not to speak of State. A lot of people wanted London, and Harry Saks' was hardly the name that came to mind. Too Chicago. His wife had the social graces of a porcupine. Nobody denied they were smart, hardworking, loyal, and there was nobody to whom Roger Kimball owed more than Harry Saks. Personally Lorraine thought it the most appalling idea.

It annoyed her that Miriam knew about it somehow. But it would annoy Miriam that she knew. So they were even.

"Craig Marsden."

"Outgoing Republican White House domestic adviser. Will write a syndicated column." He had a fairly attractive wife, Buff, who was interested in the arts.

"Warburgs."

"Allen and Amy. National Editor of *The Daily,* rumored to be the next Editor." Allen Warburg was in a power play with the managing editor for the top job about to be vacated by Wiley Turnbull, the long-shot out-of-towner who was a disaster.

It was one of the toughest problems the Washington party-givers had faced in years. The meek of heart simply decided not to invite either of them and just wait for the shakedown. But Lorraine Hadley was an old roulette player. She had placed her chips on Allen Warburg.

Allen was tough, a brilliant political infighter, shrewd, calculating, ruthless. Amy was exactly the opposite.

Lorraine loved having Amy. She could always count on Amy to take care of the number 1's, the spouses who came with their star husbands or wives. Allen lent an atmosphere of power, of competitiveness, of energy. Amy mopped up the leftovers, the dead weights. They really were the perfect couple to have at a dinner.

"T. R. Travis."

"Feature writer for *The Daily.*" Travis was a mere child of twenty-five, acerbic and a bit sophomoric; interviews and bitchy reviews. He had profiled Lawrence, not entirely flatteringly. Travis might or might not show up, depending on his mood, and he might be wearing blue jeans, short shorts, or possibly a kilt if he felt like it. She would not dream of inviting Travis to a seated dinner, but she did like having him to buffets because he livened things up. He usually insulted someone, but he knew how far to go, and deep down he was a social climber. The iconoclasm was just to establish his independence. His wife was the giveaway, a mouse who never left his side. He knew she held him back. Lorraine felt sorry for her.

There was a knock on the door and Archie poked his head in. "Are you girls still at it?" he chuckled. Archie never had understood. He was patronizing about her parties, as she was patronizing about everything *he* did.

"Archie," said Lorraine, ignoring his tone. "I've had Irma lay out your clothes. You're to wear your navy blazer. I wish for once you wouldn't wear a tie, especially a bow tie—just one of those Turnbull and Asser silk shirts with the collar open. It would look so much more casual, especially with this group. I've told the men no ties."

"My dear," said Archie. "You know perfectly well I wouldn't be caught dead without a tie. In fact, you know how I dislike buffet suppers. No place to sit, nobody proper to talk to, balancing one's plate on one's knees, spilling wine."

Archie was beginning his preparty whine. Archie was such an old maid, sometimes she didn't see how she could bear it another moment. On the other hand, she suspected he realized he was nothing more than a prop, not to mention the bankroll. She really ought to be grateful. Even though Archie had barely turned sixty, he dressed, looked, and acted as though he were in his mid-seventies. But there was nothing she could do about it. Even an ascot . . . no, forget it. Just pretend he wasn't there.

"Jane Fletcher," said Miriam.

"Jane Fletcher, NBC correspondent." She was fairly nice, not bad-looking, better than most, smarter than average. She had been assigned to cover the Vice President during the campaign. Her husband, Blair, was an attractive lawyer for the SEC.

Lorraine didn't know Jane Fletcher, and she was a little leery of having a television person in this crowd of writers. These print people were so snobbish about the TV people, particularly those who hadn't started on papers. The politicians, however, liked having TV people around, and they felt safer with them. Also, Jane was national, not local.

"Jerry Mendelsohn."

"Allison Sterling's friend." This was not a romantic involvement. He wrote for the political section of *The Weekly* in New York.

"Desmond and Chessy Shaw."

"Oh, for God's sake, Miriam. Chessy is one of my oldest friends."

"Allison is a friend of yours too, and the last time she came you got her escort's name wrong."

Sometimes she really couldn't bear Miriam. She wasn't in the mood for this tonight.

Desmond Shaw had been head of the political section at *The Weekly* in New York and had just been named columnist and Washington Bureau Chief. "Chessy is about to kill herself to break into the Washington scene, but my guess is she won't have time before Des dispatches her back to New York in spite of her money and connections. The only question is . . . who is the lucky lady?"

Miriam perked up at this one in spite of herself. She detested Chessy. And Chessy couldn't stand her. They were rude to each other when Chessy called once a week from New York. Lorraine didn't really like Chessy either. Their friendship went back years to New York, when Lorraine was working for a fashion magazine and Francesca and Desmond Shaw were the young couple about town.

"If you breathe a word of this, Miriam darling, I will strangle you."

Miriam was indignant. She was, as Lorraine knew perfectly well, a sphinx. They could torture her to death before she would give out the menu. And that was probably the number one reason Lorraine kept her around. That and the fact that she was both fascinated and appalled at anyone capable of total discretion.

"I'm quite sure," said Lorraine, lowering her voice conspiratorially, "that it is Allison Sterling . . . but I can't get a thing out of her."

It was bad enough that Chessy was coming down from New York to go to the party with Des; now, to make matters worse, he was twenty minutes late for drinks. Allison felt like walking out, but she wanted a confrontation. She had left an unscheduled briefing at the White House at six fifteen to meet Des at Nora, a small restaurant away from the White House where they wouldn't be seen at this hour. She didn't much care, but he did. It hadn't been a problem during the campaign, when they were both traveling, and when he was in Washington they had been happy to stay at her house and cook and make love in front of the fire.

But the election was over last week. Des was now officially the *Weekly* Bureau Chief in Washington, and he had already rented a sparsely furnished house on Twenty-first Street near Dupont Circle. He still hadn't told his wife he was leaving her, and now Chessy, who had originally planned to stay in New York, was making noises about moving to Washington.

Since they'd started seeing each other at the convention, Allison and Des had been going to parties separately but without dates so that they could meet afterward. Journalists often traveled alone.

Allison wondered if she hadn't made a mistake in not confiding in Lorraine. The truth was that she wanted people to know. When Des had asked her to wait until after the election, it had seemed reasonable. He wouldn't have to deal with Chessy while he was trying to cover a Presidential election. Besides, he said, they would both be traveling and it wouldn't matter.

Now Des was going to this party with his wife, and Allison had had to resort to having her old buddy Jerry fly down from New York to spend the weekend with her and take her to the party. Jerry knew, so he was safe, and she needed someone who could get her through this evening.

She was appalled that she was in this situation. Allison had vowed long ago that she would never get involved with a married man. Another five minutes passed and she succumbed to the waiter's second request for a drink order. What the hell. It was Friday. She didn't have to file before the party, and she needed a glass of wine to get up her courage. She was going to tell him that the time was now. Either he told Chessy this weekend or she would end it.

Allison felt like a reluctant skydiver. She was in love. She had fallen totally for Des the first night. But she had had lots of attractive, successful, interesting men, and she wasn't prepared for this. She had no intention of slinking around, hiding in corners. If Des wanted her he would have to have her openly, on her terms. She was working herself up. That was all right. It would be convincing. She knew he would be alarmed about this drink.

Now he rushed in out of breath and she almost burst out laughing. He looked like a schoolboy who had been called into the principal's office. As upset as she was, Allison couldn't help thinking how marvelous he was. His curly black hair was disheveled; his Burberry had the requisite stains and rips ("bullet holes"); his shirt collar was unbuttoned; his tie was loosened and there was a tiny spot on it. The last time he had worn that tie she had told him there was a spot on it.

"Sorry, baby," Des said, leaning down to give her a kiss. Though she wanted to, she did not lift her mouth to him. She let him give her a peck on the forehead.

He sat down self-consciously at the small table next to the bar, smiled, avoided her eyes, and turned to signal the waiter. "One Beefeater martini, dry, no vegetables." He turned to Allison rubbing his hands together, indicating that it was cold outside.

"Well," he said.

Just the sound of his deep voice turned her on.

She said nothing.

"Goddamn, I had trouble getting away from the office," he tried. "We've had real problems with this cover story on Kimball's Cabinet. Every source is giving us a different story. I don't suppose you have insights you'd like to share." Teasing. He was trying to jolly her up. He knew having the President-elect for a godfather was a problem for her. He had taken the tack early on to tease her about it, get it out in the open rather than pretend it didn't exist. If he could josh about it in front of her colleagues it would make it seem more acceptable. Allison was not in the mood to discuss Uncle Roger today, or the cover story, or why Des was late. She was not about to help him out.

Des practically grabbed the martini from the waiter.

"So," he said. "So I guess you're pretty pissed?" When Des was nervous, what was usually the slight trace of a Boston Irish accent became pronounced. Even now it amused her.

"Do I have a right to be?" She was determined not to raise her voice.

"I can see I'm in a shit sandwich already," he said with resignation.

Allison was rather enjoying the scene. It was a new experience. In the three months or so that they had been seeing each other they had not spent that much time together. They had had disagreements but never really a fight. This was their first serious fight. If she could detach herself, she might learn something about him. And about herself. She just had to stop thinking about his strong brown hands on her body.

"I only asked a question," Allison said. "What would make you think I was angry otherwise?"

"Look, sweetheart, I know this is a tough deal on you. But try to see my side. What am I supposed to do when Chessy calls and tells me she is coming down for this party? She had already accepted for both of us. I haven't had time to talk to her. I just can't get into a hassle until I've finished this story. C'mon, be fair. What do you want me to do? Tell Chessy she can't come down because I'm taking the woman I love to the party?"

He was talking too loud.

Allison shushed him, shaking her head slightly and motioning toward the people around them.

Des looked embarrassed. "I'm sorry," he said, looking quickly around.

"That's fine," said Allison. "I understand perfectly. We agreed you wouldn't tell Chessy until after the election. And I realize you haven't seen her since then. I also understand that you had no way of knowing Lorraine would have a party and invite Chessy as you were finishing a cover. You were trapped."

"Oh, Sonny," he said, practically gasping with relief. He signaled for another martini and looked at her with his winning, normally devastating smile. "Baby, you are sump'n else. I didn't think you would be nearly so understanding. What a doll." He was almost chortling.

"You don't give me enough credit, darling," she said quietly.

She asked him about the cover story. He said there was some stuff in it he obviously couldn't talk about. She understood. She didn't push.

"So," she said, crossing her arms and leaning on the table. "How was it with Chessy last night?"

His face fell. "Do we have to?" he pleaded.

"Just curious," she said pleasantly with a little shrug. "I am interested, you know."

"I'm sorry. You know how it was with Chess last night. It was the usual. She talked about how she was going to start looking at apartments in the Watergate and in the meantime put this needle-point carpet here and that Coromandel screen, or whatever the hell it is, there, and silk curtains, and I don't know. I just sat there getting deeper and deeper into the tank. Then she called me a drunk, accused me of ruining my daughter, and went to bed. That, for your information, is how it was with Chessy last night."

"Well, then, it shouldn't be so hard for you to tell her you want a divorce this weekend."

Des looked up from his glass as if he had been slapped.

"What?" His black eyes pierced hers.

"You heard what I said." She was trying to sound calm, in control, though her heart was beating and her lips were dry.

"Wait a second," said Des. "I never said anything about telling her this weekend. I mean, Jesus Christ, I've got this cover and—"

"*I* did."

"What are you talking about?"

"I'm talking about the fact that if you do not tell your wife of twenty-five years, the mother of your child, that you are divorcing her because you are in love with me, then it's over. That, my friend, is what I am talking about."

She hoped her voice held conviction.

"Jesus, Sonny"—his voice was soft—"you're the first woman in twenty years I've wanted to change my life for. There've been a lot of dames, but you're the only one I've loved. It's just that—"

"Just that it's hard to make the break? Des, do you think I don't know it? What do you think I'm telling you? I love you. More than I've ever loved another man."

Her eyes were dangerously close to welling up.

"This is not going the way I had planned it," she said, laughing, trying to hide her emotion. "What I'm saying is, I had better get out of this relationship before I can't. I have the strength to do it now. I care too much about myself to let myself get fucked over. I also care too much about you to lose respect for you."

He looked so miserable that it was all she could do not to throw her arms around him. But she knew if she did she would lose her edge. And she had to admit that being able to have this effect on him did give her a certain thrill. She decided she had better leave while she was still in control . . . those dark eyelashes, that mouth, that firm jaw . . . and he knew it too. He'd seen his own effect on too many women.

They hadn't finished their drinks, but Allison stood up to go. "Call me Monday morning—if you've done it."

She leaned down before he could see what she was doing and quickly kissed him on the cheek in a last burst of mischief.

"See you in a few hours," she said almost gaily, and waltzed out the door, leaving Des clutching the edge of the table.

* * *

"Finally," said Miriam, "Sir Rodney and Lady Edwina Abel-Smith."

"Always save the hardest till last." Edwina was Lorraine's closest friend, the wife of the British Ambassador. They had been friends in London during the years Edwina and Rodney were there between posts. About Lorraine's age, Edwina had masses of tousled brown curls creating a jungle on top of her head, sloe eyes, a thin nose, and pouty lips. Eccentric, very English, she was also the most talented professional gossip Lorraine had ever known. Edwina had taught her the subtleties, and Lorraine bowed in deference. She had made a name in fashion magazines all over the world as a stylish hostess, decorator, conversationalist, appreciator of the arts, and—not least—one of the most famously promiscuous women on four continents. Anyone who knew anything knew that Edwina had had affairs with half the richest, most powerful and famous men in the world, though that may have been a slight exaggeration which Lorraine enjoyed perpetuating.

Sir Rodney, terminally boring, rather like Archie, was from a well-known and titled family and was as rich as he was dull. Edwina, who came from a rather modest middle-class background, was generally credited with helping her husband to success. She was a legend in the diplomatic corps, and upon their arrival shortly before the election all of Washington was poised to see just exactly whom she might go after in the new Administration.

Lorraine was almost certain Edwina would make a play for Rosey Grey. Just a guess, but Edwina had been asking a lot of questions about the Greys. It was not by accident that they had both been invited.

Lorraine had barely reached the foot of the stairs when Irma opened the door and let in Desmond and Chessy.

"Lorraine darling," said Chessy eagerly. "I hope you won't think us gauche to arrive on time. But I told Des I never see you and we had to come early so we could visit."

The two women kissed, brushing the air.

"Chessy, how marvelous to see you. You look positively divine. You've cut your hair. Des, my angel, I'm angry with you. You never call. You've given your heart to another hostess."

"Knock it off, Lorraine. You know I've been out campaigning." Des gave Lorraine a hug, then looked around for the waiter. "What do you have to do to get a drink around here?" He spotted Archie, hovering near the foot of the stairs.

"Hi, Arch, how goes it?" he said as he moved in to grab Archie's hand, then, seeing his attire, let out a long low whistle. Archie had worn his Chevy Chase Country Club blazer and velvet slippers, despite the fact that Lorraine had laid out a cashmere jacket and loafers.

Lorraine hurriedly led the way into the living room, ignoring Archie, and the four circled around the fire. The waiter appeared immediately with Desmond's martini, soda for Lorraine, a Scotch-and-soda for Chessy, a gimlet for Archie.

"You always do everything so well . . ." said Chessy. "But darling, let's not waste a second. Tell us who's coming. I feel like a tourist."

"Well, of course this is just a simple buffet for Lawrence. Everyone will be on the floor."

She was eying Chessy's black silk dress. There was no way Chessy would end up on the floor. She was overdressed for Washington, Lorraine was pleased to note.

"Lorraine, who's coming, for heaven's sake?"

"Well, the Vice President—elect and his wife," said Lorraine, and let the words sink in.

"Where did you meet them?" Chessy asked, eying Lorraine suspiciously.

"Well, I haven't met them personally," said Lorraine. That was just the information Chessy wanted.

"Oh?"

"Well, Rosey Grey's parents are friends of Archie's. He's known them for ages. In fact, we entertained them in London when they came over once a year, the senior Greys, while Rosey was Governor of Virginia. But I thought—we thought it would be nice to have the new Vice President and his wife over to make them feel welcome in Washington."

Lorraine was a bit embarrassed. It was so obviously a coup to have them. It killed her that they had been Archie's acquisition. She knew that Chessy knew that it was pretty hard-core social climbing. Chessy was in a hostile mood, too. Des was ordering his second martini. They must have had an argument.

"How thoughtful of you to invite the new Vice President and his wife over," Chessy said.

Lorraine stiffened. Chessy was playing hardball tonight. "Wouldn't you like to hear the rest of the guest list?" she asked.

"Of course," Chessy answered a bit tartly. Something was coming.

"Allison Sterling. I'm sure you've heard of her. Desmond, you know her."

Des, who had been leaning against the fireplace with his martini, enjoying them going at it, bristled slightly. Now he sensed that he too was going to get it as a weapon against Chessy.

"She's *The Daily*'s White House correspondent *and* the goddaughter of the new President-elect, in case you haven't been reading the columns. I know you'll like her. . . ."

Silence. Lorraine had scored. And by the look on Des's face she was sure that Allison was the one. Lorraine had heard the campaign gossip. She had made the right guess.

The doorbell rang. It was the opinion-page editor, Worth Elgin, and his wife, Claire.

"Lorraine," said Claire Elgin, "the house looks divine. You always outdo yourself. And what a cozy fire." She handed her coat to the waiter, ordered a glass of white wine, and raced over to the fire to stand with her hands behind her back making small shivering noises. "Oh, it's marvelous; I think I'll just stay here all night. Hello, Archie dear," she said as she brushed his cheek with her heavily powdered one. "And Chessy, I haven't seen you in ages. I hope you've decided to come down to Washington and keep an eye on Desmond." She gave Des a warm smile. Chessy was not going to like this evening, she could tell. And Des was acting odd. He wouldn't argue with her. It was disconcerting.

"Well, Des," said Worth Elgin, reaching for his drink, "what do you think the new Cabinet will look like? It seems to me Kimball's going pretty fast. It's only been two weeks."

"Oh, no, don't tell me you two are going to start right out," Chessy said. "That's all anyone thinks about in this town. I was hoping we could get in some good gossip before everyone arrives."

"First of all, Chessy, politics is gossip, as I'm sure you'll learn when you move to Washington." Claire watched Des's expression carefully.

Claire had looked quizzical when she heard Chessy say she hoped they weren't going to talk politics all night. She would never have said that. One read the papers and tried to seem interested. Only when it got too boring did one fall back on sex. But it was risky and it usually didn't work.

Des and Worth talked about the Administration. Archie rocked back and forth from his heels to his toes in that annoying way he had.

Lorraine wished somebody else would come. This was always the hardest part, when a few of the first guests arrived and everyone was half-standing, half-sitting.

"Claire," she ventured, "how did your recital go?"

Claire brightened. "Oh, actually it went quite well. The *New York World* critic thought I was underexposed."

Someone was coming in, and Lorraine couldn't get away fast enough.

It was the Warburgs, looking eager. Thank God. They gave their coats at the door, ordered drinks, and came breezing in. Allen, ever the newsman, greeted the women perfunctorily and joined the men. "I bet I'd never guess what you are talking about." He laughed the male-camaraderie laugh that accompanies good political discussion. Archie continued to tip back and forth on his heels.

It did not go unnoticed by Lorraine as the doorbell rang again that Des glanced up each time the waiter went to answer it. Chessy watched him out of the corner of her eye.

The Sakses, the Marsdens, and Michael Addison were the next to arrive. Still no guest of honor, still no Vice President, still no Allison. Lorraine was glad that the Vice President was a little late. She wanted the party on its feet when he arrived so that she could take him around. He will do well here, Lorraine decided. He understands how to make an entrance. It was now fifteen minutes after eight. He'd wait another ten or fifteen before getting here. She was annoyed about Lawrence. He should have been here at least a few minutes after eight.

Another group. The Elgins, Rufus Turner and his wife, Jane Fletcher and her husband. Bud and Helene Corwin.

She would never speak to Lawrence again if he didn't arrive before the Vice President. If he arrived at the same time she'd have to murder him.

Just then she heard a small shriek and turned to see Edwina Abel-Smith gliding through the door, arm in arm with Lawrence, who had clearly had something to drink. The Ambassador followed with a resigned look. They must have met at the foot of the stairs. Edwina had known Lawrence in London and had always had a slight sneaker for him. But tonight, tonight it was fairly obvious that Edwina had made a decision. It was also fairly obvious that the dark-haired young woman standing next to Rodney glaring at the two of them was June—Oh, God, what was her name?—Lawrence's friend.

Everyone in the room looked up at Edwina and smiled. She knew how to make an entrance. A hostess could count on Edwina.

"Darling Edwina, you have saved the evening," Lorraine said gaily. "You have brought my guest of honor. Now do me a favor and take him around the room, will you, while I take care of Rodney and—oh, God what is that girl's name?"

"Levitas. June Levitas," said Edwina. That meant Edwina was serious. She had made the effort to learn the lady in question's name. This meant that she was not going to make a play for the Vice President unless she decided to switch horses. Lorraine was disappointed.

Most of the men had fallen into little clumps. Senator Bud Corwin had staked out a spot in the center of the room. This way he was available for any journalist who wanted to ask his opinion or any woman who might want to flirt. Claire Elgin had had her eye on him since he arrived. As she walked over she smoothed her hair, licked her lips, and unconsciously touched her ample breasts.

But as Claire got to Corwin, Maria Marsden, wife of the outgoing Republican domestic adviser, approached him batting her eyes. "Tell me, Senator, who do you think the President has in mind for State?"

"Well, of course, there are a number of fine possibilities," said Corwin, winding up for his spiel as though he were sitting down to a good dinner. Claire was going to have none of this. She knew it was almost a toss-up between sex and politics with Bud Corwin as long as the attention was on him, and she also knew he didn't give a damn what Mrs. Marsden thought about his opinions on anything.

Usually Claire played the astute political journalist's wife, nodding, listening, bringing out whomever she was speaking to. But Corwin was different. Claire had gotten Corwin's signals before. His voice was fading out as he watched her approach. "Oh, let's not talk about anything as boring as this Administration," said Claire, risking the ploy. "It's Friday night. Let's relax. Let's talk about sex."

Mrs. Marsden nearly dropped her drink. Claire, prompted most likely by Chessy, had just broken the sacred Washington rule. Never bring up sex obviously. Mrs. Marsden backed off quietly.

Lorraine ran over the guest list. Allison still hadn't come, and they were missing Travis. She busied herself making sure everyone had a drink and that the *crudités* and cheese puffs were being passed. She couldn't concentrate on conversation until the Vice President arrived. Allison was usually so prompt; where was she?

Lorraine glanced toward Des. He was still talking to the men. She reminded herself that she would have to break that up. Chessy had not budged from the sofa. She had cornered a few women and was regaling them with tales of the jet set, celebrities and fashion personalities she ran with in New York and Europe. They had all followed her in the fashion magazines. They thought she must be pretty spectacular to be married to someone like Des.

The doorbell rang. Lorraine, chatting with the British Ambassador, made a move toward the door when Allison appeared in the hallway, Jerry Mendelsohn behind her. She drew her breath. She had never seen Allison look so beautiful. Her silver-blond hair, usually pulled back, was loose around her shoulders. Her dress was pale blue-gray cashmere. She looked elegant, confident, and untouchable.

Most of the room had turned to look at her. Allison was not theatrical, but she was aware of the effect she had on people and she seemed to take it in stride. Lorraine was watching Des. She saw Chessy with a look on her face that was nothing but fear. She knew.

"Sorry," Allison whispered, kissing Lorraine on the cheek. "Jerry's shuttle was late getting in and I decided to wait for him."

The waiter brought her a glass of white wine and Jerry a whiskey.

"Oh, there's Des," she said, as if she were surprised. "C'mon over and say hi to him, Jerry."

Before Jerry had a chance to say anything, Allison excused herself and strode over to where Des was standing with Worth Elgin, Harry Saks, Craig Marsden, and Allen Warburg.

"Des, how are you?" She leaned over and gave him a friendly kiss—just enough to disturb, not enough to arouse suspicion.

Allison turned to the other men, leaving Des holding Jerry's arm.

"Hello, everybody," she said. She kissed the journalists, shook hands with Saks and Marsden. Allison did not like to be on kissing terms with politicians.

"Well, Sonny," said Saks, "what do you hear from Uncle Rog?"

Allison flushed. It was a cheap shot, not uncharacteristic.

She smiled sweetly. "So far I haven't heard who the President is going to appoint as Ambassador to England."

Saks grimaced. He had thought it was his little secret that he wanted the Court of St. James's.

"Speaking of appointments," continued Allison, "I notice that Senator Corwin is running for Secretary of State."

"If it were a beauty contest he'd certainly have no trouble winning," said Warburg dryly. They all turned to see Claire Elgin draped over Senator Corwin's arm. The two were perched on opposite arms of a chair. It was a coup for Claire to have lured him out of the center of the room.

Saks took the opportunity to go speak to them. Corwin jumped from his perch and put his arm around Saks, leaving Claire balanced alone on her side of the chair and very much annoyed.

She moved over to Allison's group and took her husband's arm. He was unable to suppress a tiny smirk. Didn't she understand that ego massage was what really turned them on?

"Hello, Sonny," Claire said, leaning over to peck Allison on the cheek. She did not particularly like Allison, but Allison was a good extra woman at dinner—attractive, and now, of course, so close to the President. "You look heavenly. And that dress! Whose is it?" The hint of a fashion talk and the men began to turn away.

Allison had no intention of spending time talking to Claire Elgin about clothes or anything else. But Claire was pressing her.

"I whipped it up myself on my sewing machine, Claire," said Allison.

Des laughed. Good.

"Jerry," she said, "we haven't seen Chessy. Is she here?" She was watching Des.

"Why don't you two go over and say hello?" said Des. "I think I'll just stay here and talk to Claire. Claire," he said, "come over here and tell me everything." Then to Worth, "You don't mind, do you, pal?"

Allison made a beeline toward Chessy on the other side of the room.

Jerry took her by the arm to slow her down. "Are you sure you want to play it this way, Sonny?"

Jerry knew everything. He was the only one who did. He cared about her. He was worried that she would blow it.

"Relax, Jerry. I know what I'm doing," she said.

"I just don't want you to get hurt, kid."

"I know. But I also know Des. I know what turns him on. Balls, for one thing. I'd much rather be at home with you watching *The Late Show* and having a pizza. But I've got to show him that I will not back down. Believe me, Jerry, if she isn't gone by Monday morning, Des can go to hell."

"Okay, okay. Calm down."

Jerry was right, and Des would hate a scene. From the looks of Chessy, she was ready for one. It was obvious she was not having a good time.

It made Allison feel stronger. She was sure now she was going to win. She saw Chessy look up and notice Jerry with relief.

"Jerry, Jerry, Jerry," she said in her husky lockjaw accent. "Christ, I thought I wouldn't see a soul I knew here, and now, dear boy, you swoop down to rescue me."

As she reached over to give Jerry a kiss, she saw Allison a few steps behind. She was slimmer, more beautiful, cooler than she'd imagined. After all these years, and all those women. Normally she was a fighter, but tonight Chessy felt tired. She looked across the room and found Des sitting on a sofa with Claire Elgin and caught his eye. He looked as though he were awaiting a terrible eruption and had sought the farthest spot to avoid the hot lava.

His face told Chessy only what she already knew. She wouldn't give him the satisfaction of causing a scene. For once she would surprise him.

She moved away from Jerry and turned to Allison. "You must be Sonny Sterling," she said softly. "I've heard so much about you. I'm delighted finally to meet you. Lorraine talks about you all the time and Des has mentioned you many times. It must be exciting to be a woman in such a powerful position, to have so many men at your feet."

Allison was caught off guard and disappointed. It would make it easier if she could hate Chessy. But she really wasn't up to a giant catfight tonight either. Her bravado of a few minutes ago had drained her energy.

"Aren't you nice to say so," Allison said sincerely. Jerry looked amused.

"I've seen you many times in *Fashion*. Your pictures don't do you justice."

"Oh," said Chessy. Her face softened. This girl wasn't after blood at all. There was no trace of sarcasm in her voice. None. Maybe she had been wrong. No, she knew the truth. Well, maybe it was just as well. Though it would have made things easier if Allison had been a bitch. This girl didn't seem like one. She seemed nice.

The doorbell rang and Irma moved toward the door. This time there was an electricity in the room that only happened when the President or Vice President was about to arrive. This was perfect timing. They would make an entrance to a full house. Brilliant. Many of them had only read about William and Sara Adabelle Grey. And many who had met or covered him hadn't necessarily met his wife. She'd had pneumonia during the last six weeks of the campaign. But everybody knew that Sadie Grey was reputed to have a smart mouth. There had been hints that she was not the demure and dainty Georgia Peach they had expected at the beginning. There had been that incident in Oregon. The room reverberated with excitement.

Lorraine tried not to hover too anxiously. The others all tried to concentrate on their conversations.

Four Secret Service agents walked in and fanned out. That gave everybody a thrill. The Secret Service meant power. No matter how many times they experienced it, it always made them feel special, closer to the power themselves.

Sadie looked fabulous. She stood there framed in the doorway and for a moment everything stopped.

It was a moment unusual for Washington. Here were beauty and glamour as well as power. Somehow Sadie looked larger than life. She seemed slightly unreal in that already glittering group. She was vivid. She was clear. She was more than they expected.

Rosey moved in from the hallway a moment later, just long enough, although he wasn't aware of it, for Sadie to have had the stage to herself. They stood there together for another moment, suspended.

For years afterward, everyone who had been at the party would remember that moment, the moment when Sadie and Rosey Grey had first entered Washington, when Washington had got the first glimpse of the Vice President—elect and his wife. For years afterward, Allison Sterling would remember too how, for reasons she would be able to explain only much later, she had felt suddenly sick.

Lorraine broke into the silence as though she had just experienced ten seconds of TV dead air. There was a burst of activity. "Bud, you know the Vice President—elect and Mrs. Grey," she said a little too stiffly.

"And, of course, you know Harry."

They shook hands politely.

Before Sadie had a chance to say anything Lorraine was leading her on to the next guest. "Edwina Abel-Smith, the wife of the British Ambassador. One of my dearest friends. I'm sure she will be one of yours too."

Edwina took a long look at Sadie, a look that a man might give her, assessing her immediately as competition. In London, Edwina would have set out immediately to undermine Sadie. Washington was not a city known for its beautiful women. She had never really been able to quite figure out what happened to women who came here. Even attractive and glamorous women came to Washington and immediately went dowdy. She had vowed that that would never happen to her. Though she had less motivation here to keep up her looks, she had really made an effort not to flag. And except for Allison, there was no competition. Now here was competition, but it was competition she could not take a whack at. Rodney, as Ambassador, depended on his close association with those in power. They would need to be in tight with the Greys. Edwina would have to find another approach. They would have to become friends. Lorraine would arrange that.

She had been so busy with Sadie that she failed to notice Rosey, just to her right.

She turned her dazzling smile to him and made him a mock bow. "Governor," she said, as she curled up the corners of her mouth. "What an honor."

Rosey was taken aback. If there was one thing that made him uncomfortable it was any kind of approach from a woman that smacked of something sexual. Not that he wasn't interested; it was just that he didn't know how to handle it. Years as a politician had convinced him that men who fell for passes by political groupies got into trouble.

Edwina raised her eyes from her little bow and looked up at Rosey, expecting to find a smile or a glint in his eyes. Instead she saw embarrassment and a slight unease. He covered it with a gentlemanly bow. "The honor is mine."

From that instant Edwina felt a certain kinship with Sadie. Sara Adabelle Grey was not in love with her husband any more than she was with hers. Making friends with her would not be so hard after all.

Sadie barely had time to think about Edwina, though she noticed that she had come on a little to Rosey. That made her chuckle. The one thing Sadie never had to worry about was that her husband would go after other women.

Rodney was telling Rosey that he was a friend of his parents' and saw them often in England. They fell into conversation about mutual friends, much to Lorraine's chagrin.

She made a brief effort to pry them apart, until Sadie grabbed her hand.

"Oh, let them talk, Lorraine," she whispered. "Everyone seems to be having such a good time. We'll meet them all. Rosey's found a friend. Why don't you take me around? I'm dying to meet everybody."

Lorraine didn't enjoy leaving her prize behind, but it did seem that Rosey was enjoying himself, and people had resumed their conversations. She reminded herself that this was not a protocol evening. Better to let the Vice President-elect chat and keep an eye on him than drag him all over the room and then leave him standing alone. He'll remember that it was relaxed and pleasant here and look forward to coming back. Besides, she could spot Allen Warburg heading toward Rodney and Rosey. It was after eight thirty, too. She wanted to start the buffet at nine. That would give everybody time.

Sadie told Worth Elgin that the View section was the first thing she turned to Sunday mornings. She mentioned a particular column. She had heard about Claire's singing. Sadie had seen Jane Fletcher on TV and had enjoyed a recent piece she had done; she was looking forward to seeing Craig Marsden's column; she had seen Helene Corwin in *Fashion;* she had read and liked Lawrence's novel.

Lorraine took Sadie over to June Levitas and Allison and Chessy. "You know," said June, "I had been assigned to do a magazine piece about you during the campaign. But when you got pneumonia your press person canceled it. I'm pleased to see you have recovered."

She was referring subtly to an incident at an Oregon airport in September. It had been cold and rainy, Sadie was coming down with a cold, and a refueling vehicle had splashed mud all over her suit.

"Oh, fuck," she had said.

The press had played it big; Roger Kimball had expressed his disapproval to Rosey; and Sadie had taken to her sickbed, not to emerge until election night.

"Probably just as well we couldn't do the interview," Sadie said, laughing. "I'm sure my husband was not heartsick at the thought of canceling my interviews. In fact, I think if I hadn't gotten sick he would have chained me to my bed for the rest of the campaign and told the world I was dying of some rare and mysterious disease." She drawled out the last words.

"I wouldn't worry about that," said June. "We need a woman in your position who says what she thinks and feels."

Sadie beamed.

Allison, who had not yet been introduced to Sadie, remembered being a little shocked when she'd first heard the story although she certainly wasn't morally opposed to politicians' wives swearing.

"Sonny Sterling," she said now, holding out her hand.

"Yes, we met at the convention. I'm glad to see you again. I didn't know at the time that you were Governor Kimball's goddaughter."

"I'm afraid I'm as sensitive about being Roger Kimball's goddaughter as you are about that story, Mrs. Grey."

Only afterward did Allison realize she might have sounded unfriendly.

Sadie blushed. Chessy coughed. June looked surprised.

Lorraine, usually vigilant, had slipped off to check on the Vice President and make sure the waiters had the drink situation under control. Jerry Mendelsohn sociably came to the rescue.

"Mrs. Grey," he said. "As one outsider to another, what is your impression of Washington?"

"Well," said Sadie. She was relieved to be drawn out of this tension. She felt depressed by what had just happened. It shouldn't have happened. She remembered liking Allison at the convention, though she thought Allison had been a bit cool then as well. She had talked about adversary relationships between press and politicians as though she were warning Sadie they could never be friends.

"It's all so new, there are so many people to meet, so much to learn," said Sadie. "I imagine it will be somewhat more exciting than Richmond. Not to denigrate my home state, of course," she added with a laugh. "This is my first unofficial Washington party."

"Actually it's mine too," said Chessy, pleased to be able to have something in common with this lovely person. She had felt uneasy about the way Allison had jumped on Sadie. She wanted to be on Sadie's side. "I always thought of Washington as formal dinners and political receptions."

Lorraine was sweeping over, and before they had a chance to continue the conversation she was telling Sadie that dinner was being served. Off they went.

"Sadie dear, you are such a hit," confided Lorraine as they were walking across the room. "Everybody is talking about how glorious you are. You do look heavenly. You may become more popular than the Vice President." She squeezed Sadie's hand delightedly.

"Now, I've asked Desmond Shaw to take you in to dinner, so you two can get a place and find a cozy spot in the living room to chat."

"Did I meet him?"

"No, darling, the rogue was off in the corner talking to some of the ladies. You met Chessy, his wife. He is the one man in this town who doesn't automatically end up talking politics with the men. He's the new *Weekly* Bureau Chief. He's divine. Or at least, he would be if we could find him." Lorraine had spotted Des in the central hallway behind a staircase where she had set up a bar. He was pouring a glass of wine for Claire Elgin.

Des had found a haven in Claire. He was so absorbed by his predicament that he could hardly concentrate on anything. Claire would natter on about sex and music and relationships and he could let his mind wander, occasionally giving her one of his knockout sexy looks just to keep her interested.

"Claire, my dear, I'm going to have to break up this romantic little scene," said Lorraine, realizing too late there was acid in her voice. Des was attractive to women. Sadie would adore him, and Des would not be bored. If he got bored he might leave. It would also annoy Chessy, who was not making an effort tonight. One always made an effort at one's friends' parties. This would serve her right. And Lorraine had not missed the look on Allison's face when Sadie walked in the door with Rosey. She would not forgive Allison for not confiding in her about Des. She was positive now there was something between them. They had been avoiding each other all evening. She would smoke Allison out.

Claire looked ready to kill, but before she could get in a word Lorraine had deftly moved her toward the dining room and turned to Des.

"Des, I want you to meet—"

"I know who you are," said Des, ignoring Lorraine. "You're much more beautiful than your pictures."

"Ahhhh," Lorraine sighed the hostess' contented sigh as she swept off to find the Vice President.

Sadie focused on Des for the first time. She was captivated at once. He was wearing a tweed sports jacket and open-necked shirt. His hands, she noticed, were still clutching the wine bottle. He gazed directly at her.

"What do I have to do to get some service?" she challenged, holding out her glass.

Her breath became short; she felt embarrassed, as if she had been caught daydreaming.

"You've already done it," he said, smiling at her. He began to pour wine into her glass. She looked down at the glass and watched it fill slowly with the pale liquid.

"I thought you drank champagne."

"How did you know?" She seemed genuinely surprised.

He laughed. He knew he had made an impression on her. Bastard. He was playing with her.

"Oh, I read it somewhere. You love champagne, you smoke only occasionally when you get angry or nervous, you prefer informal dinners to formal seated things, your favorite color is coral, you have trouble making decisions, you like John Cheever's short stories, you speak French with a Southern accent, and"—he paused for effect—"when the going gets rough, you say 'fuck.' "

She just looked at him.

"I thought it was terrific," he said quickly. "I thought, 'What a sensational dame!' I've been wanting to meet you ever since."

"You and about four hundred other journalists. I was forced to take to my deathbed to get away from them. Tonight is the first time I've been out in real company, and everyone here seems to think it was amusing."

"Then let's say it's a plus for candor and openness, a sorely missed trait in this town."

"Not anymore," she said, and she giggled. She was having too much wine. She had better hold it down.

"That's the spirit," said Des. "Now, may I escort the lady to dinner?"

Many of the guests had begun to serve themselves as they entered the room. Lorraine had paired Rosey with Amy Warburg —small, delicate, and gentle, the opposite of her editor husband. She was asking him all sorts of questions as she led him around the table, and he seemed more relaxed than Sadie had seen him in months.

Des saw Allison sitting on the sofa next to the fireplace with Worth Elgin. She never stopped working. Sadie was halfway there when Des took her arm and steered her to a smaller sofa on the other side of the room, where they were immediately joined by Jerry and Senator and Mrs. Corwin.

"I thought that by taking you all the way over here," he said, "I wouldn't have to share you."

Jerry, in fact, after chatting politely with Sadie for a few moments, immediately engaged Des in a discussion about office politics. Des apologized to Sadie every five minutes; he'd been away so much during the campaign, he had lost touch with what was going on.

At first Sadie was having a perfectly good time talking to the others, though most politicians, she had long since decided, were bloody bores. She kept forgetting she was married to one.

She talked to Helene Corwin about her job at *Fashion*. That distracted her for a time. How could she get Des's attention again?

Allison Sterling kept glancing in her direction. That scene earlier had puzzled and depressed Sadie a little. It had been the only bad note of the evening. Everyone said Allison Sterling could be scathing. If Allison was going to be around and if she was going to be writing about them, Sadie wanted to make friends. She would have to talk to Lorraine about that. Perhaps they could all have lunch. Maybe she ought to try to talk to Allison again this evening.

She saw Edwina Abel-Smith coming toward her group and watched almost helplessly as Edwina plunked herself down between Des and Jerry. "It is an absolute travesty," she said in mocking accusation, "that you two delectable creatures have been sitting here talking to each other all evening." Then, gesturing toward Sadie: "My dears, it wouldn't be so bad if you had a plain Jane next to you. But with this ravishing lady sitting here it really is inexcusable."

"I just couldn't get them interested in decorating," Sadie teased. "Or flirting, for that matter." She had had just enough wine.

"All Washington men should be sent to the stocks," said Edwina. "Mrs. Grey, you are only getting the first bitter taste of life on the Washington social scene. I haven't had a single proposal since I've been here. But I'm about to change all that," she said, and squeezed Des's shoulder with her hand which she had conveniently rested there. For a second Sadie felt proprietary about Des, then realized how ridiculous that was. Des seemed to be responding rather favorably to Edwina's approach. He was laughing with delight.

"Well, I can see it's time to leave you two lovebirds alone," said Sadie, trying to act like a good sport.

Des looked genuinely upset. "Please don't leave," he said. "I've hardly had a chance to talk to you." For a moment Sadie saw him lose his bravado, but then he turned on his winning grin.

Edwina looked at both of them for a moment, then laughed a bit too merrily.

"Well, I can see I'm too late," she said, cocking a mischievous eyebrow at Sadie. "I think I'll do my magic on this delicious morsel." And much to Jerry's surprise she turned her full attention on him and within seconds had involved him in a conversation about his love life.

Embarrassed, Sadie looked down at her plate and pushed her food around, trying to think of something to say.

"Edwina's right, you know."

"About what?"

"We're much too preoccupied with politics in Washington. We don't ever really talk about—"

"Sex?"

She hadn't meant to say it, and she could feel her face heat up.

"That and the fact that we don't really know each other, any of us. I could ask you about the campaign. But I know about the campaign. I don't know about you."

"You know enough to make me uncomfortable," she said, laughing.

"But not enough. For instance, why—"

"Help, Des, get me out of this; I'm being eaten alive!" Jerry had interrupted and was laughing, a slightly desperate look on his face. "The lady wants to know about the women in my life. I told her you were a much more interesting subject."

Des looked helpless.

Sadie was relieved. "I think," she said to Jerry, "I'd like to go over and join your friend Allison. They seem to be having a rather spirited conversation over there."

"I enjoyed our talk," she said, not looking directly at Des, and made her way across the room to Allison and Worth Elgin and Warburg. Harry Saks had joined them, and Allison and Harry were arguing.

When Saks noticed Sadie coming toward them, he waved her over and pulled up a chair. "Mrs. Grey," he called, "come over here and join us. We are always privileged to have another lovely lady in our midst."

That irritated Allison. She knew exactly what Saks was doing. He was trying to put her in Sadie's category: another pretty lady.

They all turned to Sadie as though Allison had disappeared. Sadie was not displeased. She was never one to let another woman intimidate her. Allison Sterling was an accomplished professional. She had an identity. She was respected for her opinions; the men treated her as an equal. Sadie wanted to make her pay, and the only way she knew was to take the men away. That was her only weapon, and it was not beneath her to use it.

Allison was annoyed that a woman like Sadie would use her sex. Here was this woman, with just a little bit too much wine, playing on the men's egos, and they were eating it up.

Sadie mentioned Elgin's column in which he'd said he hoped Kimball would appoint a strong Secretary of State and downplay the National Security Council. Sadie thought it "interesting"—a word she had long ago learned to use when she was unsure of her position or wanted to avoid controversy. She was uneasy with her political opinions.

This opened the way for the men to get involved in a discussion of U.S. foreign policy.

Now Sadie cursed herself for bringing it up. She looked around for her husband. Both with Des and now with these men, she had attracted their attention with her looks and her sense of humor. And she was certainly bright enough. But in the long run, these men weren't interested in flirting.

Suddenly, she felt alarmed. She didn't want to become like those political wives. She had no way to be an Allison. But she was not a loser. She would be the wife of the Vice President. Washington would have to pay attention to her. She would make it worth their while.

Sadie saw Des coming toward their group looking at his watch, but Lorraine stopped him.

"Just where do you think you're going?" she crooned. Sadie did think it was quite early. It wasn't even eleven yet, and people were beginning to get up, mill around, make noises about leaving.

"Christ, Lorraine," whispered Des. "I've got a cover story. I've got to be at the office at the crack of dawn. Besides, I'm half in the bag. If I have another drink you'll have to roll me out."

He was, Sadie noticed, a bit high, but even high, only his smile was a little more crooked.

Lorraine protested that the Greys hadn't left, but she got nowhere and Des moved toward Sadie. When he got to her group he looked only at her, reached down, took her hand in both of his. "Mrs. Grey," he said softly, his Boston Irish accent stronger with a little booze, "I'm glad you're here."

Allison just stared at him.

For a second Sadie considered the fact that perhaps Allison was interested in Des, then dismissed the thought. Allison was too ambitious to get involved with someone like Desmond Shaw.

Allison stood up and without a word walked over to Jerry, who was talking to Edwina, took his arm, and announced they had to leave. Immediately. She saw Lorraine by the door, watching Des and Sadie delightedly. Her party was going well.

"I've got to sneak out before the Vice President. Beautiful party," said Allison as she sailed by.

"But Allison," Lorraine called after her, looking worried. The Des thing had gone too far. Allison was obviously upset. That had not been her plan. "Allison?" A placating look on her face, she moved to the door, where Allison was putting on her coat. Allison was stony.

"I'll call you tomorrow," she said, and barely giving Jerry a chance to say good night, she was out the door.

Rosey, seeing Allison and Jerry leave, jumped to his feet. He knew that protocol dictated that no one leave before he did. If someone had left, it meant he was staying too late.

He walked over to Sadie, who had stood up. The others were already on their feet. "Sadie, I think we are keeping all these nice people; we ought to be going."

"Oh, of course. I'm so sorry; I hadn't realized," she said, genuinely alarmed that everyone had been waiting for them to leave.

Elgin and Warburg rushed in to reassure her. At informal parties, people left when they felt like it.

But the party was clearly over.

Des quietly took Sadie's hand, though he didn't shake it. She was about to say something she might regret when Rosey said they must leave.

Des straightened up and offered his hand. "Desmond Shaw, sir," he said, very officially, the way people do when they're trying to act as though they have not been drinking.

"Oh, yes, Mr. Shaw," said Rosey. "We didn't meet earlier. I trust you have enjoyed talking to Mrs. Grey this evening."

Des searched for a trace of sarcasm, a hint of a challenge, but there was none. He was just making polite conversation.

"How could I not?" he replied. "She is lovely. You are a lucky man." He felt like an ass. Like somebody trying out for a part in a period movie. Yet something about Rosey compelled him to talk like that.

Sadie burst out laughing. "Come on," she said to Rosey, "I think we all need a breath of fresh air," and she raised one eyebrow. Then she turned and was gone.

Chessy had had too much to drink. She walked carefully over to Des to get him to go, and he put up little resistance. They both went to Lorraine, who except for Allison's abrupt departure was ecstatic over the way her party had gone.

"My, my, Des," said Lorraine, "you were a hit with the ladies tonight."

He smiled.

"So what else is new?" said Chessy as she grabbed her husband for support, and the two went somewhat unsteadily out the door. It wasn't until the house was empty that Lorraine realized that Archie had disappeared upstairs halfway through the evening.

Lorraine's line was busy the next morning.

She was in a state of total bliss. Flowers, hand-delivered notes, and phone calls had been coming in since 10 A.M.—all accolades; all received with great grace. She lay in bed on her Pratesi sheets, her breakfast tray at her side, not even glancing at the paper. It was her day off.

"You did it again," said Allison, when she finally got her. She had decided to flatter her rather than apologize for leaving early. "If you keep this up you'll be on the cover of *The Weekly*."

"You looked wonderful, Sonny," Lorraine told her. "But you did seem a bit distracted. Was something worrying you?"

"Actually, you guessed it. I'm having a serious decorating problem and I need your help. I just couldn't get it out of my head last night."

"Okay, Sonny." Lorraine was not amused. "By the way, how did you like Chessy?"

"How did I like Chessy? I think I would like Chessy a lot better in New York. In fact, I think Chessy would like New York a lot better than Washington."

"Is this an announcement?"

"Nothing of the kind. I'm trying to be compassionate."

"I'll be sure and pass that along. She's coming for a family dinner tonight. Des is working late on his cover story."

"Really? On what?"

"Sonny darling." She sounded exasperated.

Allison laughed. "Okay. Truce."

"I'm going to ask Sadie Grey too. The Vice President is busy as well."

Allison was taken aback. She didn't know why it irritated her.

She wasn't going to let herself think about it. She would just be casual. There was no reason not to be casual anyway.

"Tell me," she said. "Tell me about Sadie Grey."

Sadie called a little later, and Lorraine wasted no time in inviting her for that evening. "Archie told me the Vice President has a working dinner tonight and you would be alone." Sadie accepted immediately.

She had had such a wonderful time the night before. The party was great fun. Rosey had had a good time too, and had confessed to her that Washington parties weren't so bad after all. The house was marvelous. Lorraine would have to take her in hand, give her advice on redecorating the Vice President's residence. Edwina was smashing and such a character. Edwina must be quite a pistol. It was nice to meet writers. She had had such interesting conversations. And Allen Warburg and Worth Elgin had been so cordial to her, had made her feel so at ease. She had enjoyed seeing Harry Saks; he had been so good to her during the campaign. The pasta was extraordinary. How long would it take her to get up the courage to have a party herself? There were so many interesting people in Washington.

"How did you like Allison Sterling?" Lorraine asked carefully, aware of the glaring omission.

"We had met before," Sadie answered. Then, casually: "Tell me about Desmond Shaw."

CHAPTER 2

WHEN ALLISON ARRIVED AT *THE DAILY* LATE Saturday morning, things were heating up. President-elect Kimball's Denver office had announced that the first Cabinet officers would be named on Monday. Allen Warburg was in a fever to get them into Sunday's paper. Several of his reporters had been with some *New York World* reporters the night before. They had implied that the *World* had the names in the bag.

Allison was the obvious one to turn to. Not an unusual situation for her. She had learned how to make herself indispensable long before her godfather was elected President, and she had long since gotten used to the idea that she was one of the most valuable reporters on the paper.

Despite her misgivings that morning about Des and their relationship, the minute she walked through the doors of *The Daily* she regained her self-confidence, her composure. She was a consummate professional; cool, fast, thorough, tough. There wasn't a man in the newsroom who could touch her—personally or professionally. She was the best. She knew it. So did everyone else.

Warburg saw her walking toward her desk and came charging over. "Jesus," he said, "am I glad to see you! We've got to get the Cabinet appointments; otherwise we'll get our asses beaten by the *World*."

Walt Fineman, the national editor, was standing nearby. She glanced at him for support, noticing the trace of a smile on his lips. Walt was one of her closest friends. She knew she could count on him. It was Warburg who was making the case that Allison should be pulled from the White House beat after the inauguration. Nobody could disagree ethically.

"Allen," Allison began, then noticed that a number of her colleagues on the national staff had stopped typing or telephoning. "Allen, could I speak to you in your office?"

Warburg nodded and escorted her into his glass office on the editors' row. Everybody followed with their eyes. They were waiting for her and the editors to do the right thing, and everybody had a different idea of what the right thing was, from having her quit the paper to having her assigned permanently to the President-elect as Court reporter.

Once he had closed the door, Warburg went behind his desk and sat down, motioning to Allison. She preferred to stand. If you were a woman, and if you wanted to make a point to your superior, you stood.

"So why are we behind closed doors?"

"Allen," she said, "I believe it was you who decided I should have nothing to do with the President-elect, that I should be taken off the beat. Now you want me to find out who's going to be in the Cabinet, just like that. They have an embargo on the story."

She hadn't realized how angry she was until she started talking, and she had to strain to get the sarcastic tone out of her voice midway through. She didn't particularly like Warburg, but she didn't want him to know it. She suspected he would be editor if they dumped Wiley Turnbull, and that was inevitable.

And she respected Warburg. He was a brilliant journalist and a brilliant editor. He was also arrogant and full of himself. He was short, wiry, black hair, black eyes, bushy black eyebrows, a five-o'clock shadow. His smile was more a ruthless grin. He did not like to be bested, but he did enjoy intelligent people. He respected Allison and he didn't much like her either. He thought she was full of herself, and he resented her sexually. He was attracted to her, and that pissed him off. He hated to be confused. Allison knew she had this effect on him. She knew it and she took advantage of it. He knew she knew it. That irritated him.

Now Warburg was confused. Allison was right. He was mad. She could see that. She sat down and smiled at him.

"Okay," he conceded. "I have to admit we've got a more complicated problem here than we thought."

"Allen, that's been my whole point all along. This is not an easy problem. In fact, Walt and I had planned to have lunch today and talk about it. I guess that's out. We don't have time with the Cabinet story. But look, Kimball is family to me. I am a reporter; he will be President. I have been covering the White House. I know that story. *The Daily* is a competitive newspaper. We want to win out. I have the sources to do that. So we have a problem. We've known about this since New Hampshire. We've all agreed I should not stay on the White House beat. The role I can play is on some sort of overview beat I can carve out for myself and still stay available for the inside stories. I am also going to have to have a talk with the Kimballs. There hasn't really been any time since he was nominated. Besides, nobody thought he would win."

Warburg knew Allison was making some sense. He also knew that she would end up being one of the most valuable reporters on the staff. If she wasn't already.

"I think when Kimball comes here next week I should go have a long talk with him and maybe Manolas too, if he stays press secretary. I will ask him not to tell me anything that will compromise me if I can't use it or at least pass it on as background, and I'll tell him that I hope we can do this without compromising the integrity of either one of us or the people we work for. The most important thing to me here is that I cannot, nor will I, jeopardize either my integrity or my relationship with this man. I'd quit journalism first."

"Sounds good to me." Warburg laughed. "We should have that in writing." He paused. "Now will you find out who he's appointing to the Cabinet?"

"You prick," she said.

They both got up and walked out of the office smiling. The rest of the reporters turned back to their typewriters.

Allison and Fineman went down to the cafeteria to get a sandwich, where he advised her to call the President-elect. "Explain the situation to him," he said. "Tell him you need to talk to him when he gets here about the ground rules and ask him if he could give you any guidance on the Cabinet. Talk to the reporters who are working the story and get their long shots. Tell Kimball those are what we are going with unless we're wrong. So how goes it with Shaw?" he asked, changing the subject abruptly. Allison had told him about Des even though she knew Walt was one of the few journalists in town who had never really liked Des. Des was too brash and tough-talking for him. He respected Shaw, he just didn't like him. Allison also suspected that Walt was a little jealous of him. For one thing, he had grown jealous of Des's new relationship with Allison. For another, Des had a reputation as a ladies' man, and Walt had never had much luck in that department.

"Well," sighed Allison, "who knows? He's got Chessy down here for the weekend. He's supposed to tell her. I just don't know whether he's going to get up the courage. I'm trying not to think about it or it will drive me crazy. I've given him an ultimatum."

"Isn't that a little risky? I mean, what if the timing just isn't right? He's got a big cover story. You know that that's pretty rough after twenty-three years. I went through it. I ought to know. You just don't walk in and say 'Sorry, toots.'"

"Oh, Walt. You sound just like Jerry. You don't even like Des."

"I never said I didn't like him. What makes you think I don't like him?"

"Walt, it's me, Allison. You know you can't hide anything from me. I can just watch your skin go sallow when I mention his name."

She loved Walt. He was tall and lanky, with dark brown hair and the kindliest face she had ever seen. He reminded her a little bit of Abraham Lincoln. He always seemed so wise and so good. He had been going through a painful separation for the last year and a half, and it had left him with a permanently sad expression. He was a devoted father to his children and spent a good deal of time worrying about his wife. In the agreement, he had given her practically everything.

"That's bullshit," he said, offended. "I admire and respect him as a journalist."

"Exactly. That's just what I said. You don't like him."

He looked at her for a long time, then lit a cigarette. He started to say something.

"You're right," he said finally. "I don't like the son-of-a-bitch."

"That's better. Don't you feel good now, having gotten it out?"

"No, I feel worse."

"Why are we talking about this?" she said suddenly. "I don't want to talk about him. I was perfectly happy agonizing over my godfather problem and you have to bring up that bastard." Her eyes seemed to wander off for a moment. At last she said, "It's kind of like that old Japanese hospital treatment for pain. They brand you with hot irons so you'll forget the pain you're feeling from your sickness. I'm worried about how to deal with Uncle Rog so you bring up Des to take my mind off my other pain."

Walt looked at her quizzically. "What are you talking about?" he asked.

"Never mind. Let's get back upstairs. I have to make a call."

The conversation with Roger Kimball went more easily than she had expected. He understood her problem. He did say he would make sure the staff was accessible to her. But he wouldn't play all the way.

"I'm announcing it on Monday, Allison," he told her. "But I will tell you which ones are wrong."

This information pleased everyone. *The Daily* decided to go on Sunday with the names Uncle Rog had not denied.

Walt and Allen decided that she should *not* get a byline. "Let's not tip everybody off right away that you're a conduit," joked Allen. She stiffened before she saw him smiling.

It was agreed that her name would be put in an italic box at the bottom of the story along with those of several other reporters who had contributed to the article.

By the time she was finished it was nearly six thirty, and she called Jerry at *The Weekly* to see if he was ready to leave for the *Boston Express* party. She didn't ask whether Des was going to be there, though she knew he hung out with a lot of the *Express* types.

"There's good news and bad news," said Jerry.

"Lay it on me," she said.

"The bad news is that Shaw's coming to O'Grady's tonight. The good news is that he's not coming until late because he's still working on his story. I think I'm about ready to leave. I just have to give my number to the desk. Can you pick me up?"

As Allison went out into the fall twilight she pulled her jacket around her closely. It wasn't cold enough for her teeth to be chattering the way they were.

"Maybe he won't come at all," said Jerry as she was driving him back to Olive Street to change. "Chessy is having dinner with Lorraine and Archie. I can't imagine that she would want to go to a party with Des's drinking buddies. She also doesn't like him running around without her. I bet they won't come."

"Did you tell Des we were going?" She hoped Jerry didn't hear the nervousness in her voice.

"Well, yeah. I just asked him casually if he was going. I thought you might want to know."

"Now that he knows we're going he's bound to show up, and he'll bring her. I know him. He'll want to show me he's not afraid of me."

"Gimme a break, Sonny. He is scared shitless."

"Not me. I'm totally under control." She laughed. "Nothing like work to take your mind off your problems."

"Oh, yeah. Work go well today?" He said it a little too casually. "What are you working on?"

"Nice try, fella," she said, laughing. "If you think I'm going to tell you so you can call the office the minute I've disappeared into the bathroom, you're crazy."

"But Sonny," he said in mock innocence. "We're all partners in crime."

"Fine. Then you can tell me what Des's big story is about so I can call it in and *The Daily* can beat *The Weekly* by a day."

"Well, you can't blame me for trying. Besides, you have better sources."

He was still joking, but she was suddenly angry.

"Not fair, Jerry."

"Look, Sonny, I'm sorry, but it *is* fair. If you think for a minute this isn't going to give you access to privileged information, or if you even think everybody else doesn't think so, you're crazy. I can't believe you've been around this town as long as you have without understanding that. Christ, I do, and I don't even live here."

"Oh, I know. I'm sorry, Jerry. The irony is that we're not all *that* close. Yes, we saw each other in the summers with my father. God, Jerry, you know how I tried to stay away from him during the campaign."

She found a parking space in front of the house. She turned to look at him. Then, in an uncharacteristic gesture, she put her hand on his.

"I'm sorry that I've put you through this weekend. I know I'm being a pain in the ass. So if I'm a little edgy, it doesn't mean that I don't appreciate you a lot. Okay?"

He was moved. He knew how hard it was for her. His voice, when he spoke, surprised him, it was so husky.

"Okay, Sonny," he said. "Listen. Don't worry about it." They were both embarrassed. He put his hand on her head and rubbed the back of her neck. Then they both opened the car doors and stepped out into the brisk November twilight.

O'Grady's party was relaxed and intimate, a typical Saturday-night gathering of Washington journalists. Allison hadn't even bothered to change. Saturday night in Washington was the night off. People worked political receptions, cocktail parties, and dinner parties during the week. On the weekends, Congress left town, usually to go home. The President often went to Camp David or to his own hometown, and the rest of the city collapsed to rest up. Nobody with any sense scheduled an important social event on Saturday night.

The O'Gradys lived in a small house just inside the District line near Chevy Chase Circle in a relatively suburban neighborhood. It was comfortable, if a bit drab—sofas and unmatched chairs, an old rug, lamps that seemed to have nothing to do with each other. Two small children and a large dog would occasionally interject themselves.

There were about a dozen people there. A couple from *The Express*, a guy from the L.A. paper and the woman he lived with, a British journalist, a network reporter and his wife, another network reporter and the man she lived with, an editor at *The Democratic Review*. All the women worked except Patricia O'Grady, who always seemed to apologize for her existence.

Allison was not particularly sensitive to women who didn't work. She thought them boring, the ones who stayed home and watched babies all day. They were unlike the wives of older journalists, the women of another generation who had some money, who dressed and entertained well and knew how to gossip. These women hung in the background, never had anything interesting to say, and hurried back and forth to the kitchen fixing dinners as if they were servants.

Allison liked O'Grady. He was the wittiest man in Washington. He knew everybody, and everybody knew him. He was the quintessential boy if you wanted to be one of the boys, and Allison did. You picked up a lot of good stuff that way, passing information, trading it. If you were doing a story on the head of the Federal Reserve all you had to do was mention it at O'Grady's and you'd go home with five anecdotes and a list of whom to call. People were always working on each other's stories, climbing all over each other, and once somebody had filed, they were more than happy to share the information they had gathered, knowing the favor would be returned.

Most of the people in the room suspected that Allison had been seeing Des. He had traveled with the Republican incumbent too often, as had she. O'Grady was one of Des Shaw's closest friends. They had grown up together in Boston in the same neighborhood, had gone to the same parochial school, the same college. O'Grady was Catholic the way Shaw was: lapsed. And they were both male chauvinist pigs.

Most of the people in the room also knew that Des was a ladies' man and that Allison was hardly the first. Nobody ever mentioned one to the other. When O'Grady had invited them to dinner separately he hadn't known that Chessy was going to be in town because Shaw hadn't known. O'Grady was surprised that Shaw was even considering bringing his wife. But then, Shaw was full of surprises.

The way he figured it, that was their business, Allison's and Des's. He just hoped it wasn't too awkward or that it didn't cause Allison pain. Des Shaw had broken a lot of hearts. Allison might seem pretty cool and pretty tough on the outside. Everybody in Washington thought she was. She was putting on a good front, but O'Grady could see that she was nervous and that she kept glancing at the door.

Dinner was a big lamb stew with heavy homemade bread and salad. It was delicious, and Allison felt a twinge of jealousy toward Pat O'Grady, who had seemed to put it on the table so effortlessly. Everyone toasted her effusively; too effusively. Sometimes journalists could be terribly patronizing. Pat beamed and blushed, uncomfortable with praise, then heard one of the children crying and was relieved to escape. It touched Allison to see how different she was from the rest of them who lived with their egos exposed, who demanded recognition and praise, the fix of the byline, the rush of the most beautiful phrase in the English language: "Great piece!"

As she had known it would, the conversation came around to how Allison was going to handle it. It was Hemmings, from *The Democratic Review*, who brought it up. He had wanted the White House job when she got it and had left *The Daily* shortly afterward. Hemmings had a reputation as a killer. So did Allison. He was as judgmental about his colleagues as she was. Live by the sword, die by the sword. But God, sometimes it hurt. His date, a reporter at *The Weekly*, winced. She did not want to see Hemmings get into a match with Allison.

"So," he had begun. He had had too much to drink. It was going to get ugly. "So tell us. We're all waiting to see how you will handle this situation. No doubt it has been discussed in the halls of *The Daily*."

She decided to let him set himself up.

"Naturally, you will quit the beat. Will you stay in Washington?"

Hemmings' date tried to joke. "Down, boy," she said nervously.

"Actually, I thought I'd ask everyone here," said Allison. "What would you all do if you were in my position?"

He hadn't expected her to return it to him that way. He was quiet for a moment or two.

"Well," he said, stalling, "I would certainly take myself off the White House beat."

He was saved by Pat O'Grady.

"Dessert, anyone?" she said, bringing in two apple pies and a bowl of ice cream.

"How timely!" joked O'Grady. "Anything to sweeten up this discussion."

After dinner there were mugs of coffee. Hemmings was brooding in his armchair. Allison was seated on the sofa across the room.

"Now, where were we?" he said. "What would I do if I were Allison Sterling? Well, I would demand a foreign post." (Only the more affected reporters talked about foreign "posts"; everybody else said foreign "assignments." And nobody on newspapers demanded anything; reporters requested to be sent abroad.)

"Why would you do that rather than stay in Washington?"

"Well, obviously having your godfather as the President poses conflicts of interest. There is nothing the President does that doesn't touch on every part of this city. How could you report on any aspect of government and expect to be objective?"

"Fairness and objectivity being the goal?" she asked.

"Exactly."

"And being favorable toward an administration would preclude me from being objective or fair about any facet of Washington?"

"Without question."

"Then," said Allison, "can you and I expect to be colleagues in some foreign capital together?"

"What do you mean?"

"I assume that in the interest of ethical behavior, you too have demanded a foreign post." She emphasized "demanded" and "post."

"Just what are you getting at?"

"Well, Hemmings, really. There you were being very pro the Republican Administration and writing favorable pieces some even thought apologetic. Then you quit *The Democratic Review* to go to work for the Republican Administration on the National Security Council. Now that a Democratic administration is in you are back writing very unfavorable pieces against them. Surely by your own definition you should have disappeared in your safari jacket. Isn't the conflict of interest tearing you apart? Aren't you having a moral crisis?"

"Let the poor S.O.B. go home and sleep it off. Have you no mercy, woman?"

The sound of his voice. She had forgotten.

Allison didn't dare look up. She couldn't bear to find out whether Chessy had come with him.

"Hi, Chess," O'Grady said. "Glad you could make it." He lied. Allison could feel the coolness in his voice.

She composed herself, then caught Jerry looking at her, a strong, confident, supportive smile on his face.

"You creamed him," he whispered across the room, covering his mouth and pointing to the departing Hemmings. "Now do it again, killer." This time he pointed to Des.

Everybody in the room had brightened when Shaw came in, and they were all curious to meet his wife.

They were deliberately avoiding looking at Allison. They didn't want to seem to be curious. But Allison had put on her public face, and she was smiling as she turned to greet Des.

"Christ," he yelled to O'Grady, "could I use a drink!"

"What'll it be, me boy?"

"Ah, just a wee taste o' Jameson neat will do me fine." Des and O'Grady nearly always talked in brogue when they weren't insulting each other or talking politics or sports.

Allison got up from the sofa and walked around it to where he was standing.

"How are you, Des?" she said, surprised at the sound of her voice. It was deeper, sexier, almost suggestive. It still amazed her, what happened to her when they were in the same room together.

She leaned over and kissed him on the cheek the same way she would have kissed Jerry. Very friendly, buddy-buddy. Then she patted him on the arm. "So. Cover story, huh? Gimme a headline."

"You know Chessy."

"Of course." She turned to her. "How are you?"

"Marvelous," she said, beaming. "I'm having a simply marvelous time. You all must just adore living here."

"Chess is used to New York," Shaw said. "The gossip and intrigue there is nothing compared to Washington."

O'Grady beckoned to everyone to sit. Chessy went for the nearest chair.

"Well, I just came from Lorraine Hadley's. Sadie Grey was there. Her husband had a working dinner and she joined us. She's just as new to Washington as I am and just as intrigued, particularly by Lorraine's stories. I can't wait to move here. Although" —she laughed—"my idea of comfort and Des's are different."

Allison had become silent. Jerry nudged her with his foot. She was depressed by the mention of Sadie Grey.

Hemmings' departure and Shaw's arrival had greatly improved the company. Shaw had launched into a story. There was considerable laughter and joking and yelling. Chessy had gotten into a deep conversation with Pat O'Grady.

She pretended to listen to Des's story. Finally, she excused herself and went quietly up the stairs to the bathroom. She shut the door, pulled the lid down on the toilet seat, and sat there wondering what to do.

The bathroom looked like what you would expect the bathroom of a couple with small children to look like. It gave Allison the shivers. It represented everything that marriages stood for. It made her throat close to look at the room. It wasn't the first time Allison had thought this. She always had that same claustrophobic feeling, that same sense of entrapment. To Allison marriage was a frightening thing. The idea of children was beyond even thinking about.

She got up from the toilet seat and stared at herself in the mirror. She felt as though she were looking at a stranger. She smiled. She could see squint lines around her eyes. They seemed dead and lifeless. She had left her purse downstairs. She grabbed a little of Pat's old eyeliner, licked it with her tongue, and smudged it around her eyes to give them more expression. They just looked smudged. She took some of Pat's lipstick. It was bright red. She tried it anyway. It made a garish slash across her face.

She took a little of the red lipstick now with her fingers and rubbed it on her cheeks to make rouge spots. She had made herself up to look like a clown. She could not look at herself now without embarrassment.

There was a knock on the door. "Sonny? Are you all right? Sonny!" There was a worried tone to Des's voice. "Sonny. Can I come in?"

Without thinking, she said yes in a soft whisper.

He pushed the door open slightly, then opened it quickly and stepped in, closing it behind him.

She didn't turn to look at him. She was still staring at herself in the mirror, almost in shock. He walked over to the sink and stood behind her, putting his hands on her shoulders. Only then did he see what she had done.

"Sonny, what the fuck have you done to your face?"

She didn't answer. She seemed surprised. She couldn't figure it out. She wasn't drunk; in fact, she had hardly had anything to drink at all. She had just lost herself for a moment. She shrugged. She still couldn't say anything. There wasn't anybody else in Washington who was as confident as Allison Sterling. She had made it. She was untouchable. Why would she want to change herself?

"I don't get it," he was saying. "I thought maybe you were sick or something. I got worried about you. You've been up here for nearly half an hour. What's going on?"

He was genuinely disturbed, and of course, there was no explanation, since she didn't understand herself what she was doing. But she had snapped out of it sufficiently to get hold of herself.

She started to smile, then burst into a grin. They were both staring at her face in the mirror, he behind her. She stuck out her tongue. Then she put her fingers in her ears and waved her fingers at him. She started to giggle, then to laugh. She couldn't stop laughing. Des started to smile tentatively. He still wasn't sure she was okay. She was hysterical now, laughing so hard she couldn't breathe. She was leaning over and clutching her sides. Des was caught up in the hilarity but still not convinced. She was falling against him, grabbing him for support.

"Help me, help me," she gasped, going off into another fit of laughter.

By now, Des had decided that she really was laughing, though tears were beginning to stream down her face. He was laughing too, a quizzical laughter, begging her to tell him what was going on. She couldn't possibly explain until her laughter had subsided, and she had fallen up against the back of the door, holding her sides and gasping for breath. Des went over and grabbed a handful of toilet paper and came over to her. He stood in front of her for a moment, waiting for her gasping to subside. He dabbed at the tears on her cheeks. Then he began to wipe the lipstick off her cheeks with the damp toilet paper. Next, he took the paper and blotted the scarlet lipstick from her lips.

He moved the tissue away and leaned closer to her, breathing a little faster. He put his lips on hers, touching them lightly, brushing them with his.

He kept doing this in a slow, rhythmic motion. Back and forth he moved his lips, brushing her so softly that he was almost not touching.

Allison had just gotten her breath, and now she lost it again. She saw him close his eyes and she closed hers, slumping now against the back of the door. She whimpered—half a whimper, half an attempt to breathe. He was pressing up against her harder now, as if he knew he had to support her, and indeed she felt as if she would slide to the floor if it were not for his strength pinning her against the door.

Finally she flicked out her tongue at him and grabbed his lower lip with her teeth. He let out his breath as though he had been struck. She could feel him harden, and she felt as though she were perched on a ledge when he reached his hands around behind her and hoisted her up just a few inches so that the lower halves of their bodies met. He was kissing her now; they were both nearly frantic.

"Hey, Shaw, is everything all right? Hey, Shaw! Are you up there? Is everything okay?"

O'Grady was whispering from the top of the stairs.

"Are you guys all right?" There was a pleading note in his voice.

"Oh, Jesus. Oh, Jesus," moaned Des. "What are we going to do? Jesus Mary and Joseph. Holy Mary Mother of God. I can't leave you now. What will I do?"

He glanced downward. "Oh, Jesus," he said again. "Look at me. Jesus. I've got to calm Junior down. Oh, my God."

He was making little sense as he pulled away and more or less staggered around the bathroom muttering to himself. "Oh, Christ. Oh, my God. How are we going to get out of here?"

Allison was leaning against the door. Her body was trembling, and she felt as if she knew what it must be like to have a hot flash. Unconsciously she moved her hand down her body and put it between her legs, leaning over as though she had the bends. Des was staggering and muttering. "Shit, I haven't had this happen to me since I was in high school and Maureen O'Dougherty's mother caught us necking in the living room."

"Answer him," Allison said. "Answer him or we'll really be in trouble."

"Everything's okay," he called to O'Grady. "Sonny's just a little nauseated. She's been throwing up, but she's okay. I've put some cold towels on her forehead. We'll be right down."

"You shit," she whispered. "Now they'll all think I had too much to drink or that I got upset over the argument with Hemmings or that I'm upset that you brought Chessy. They'll all think I'm the asshole instead of you."

"How else do you figure on explaining all that red stuff all over your face? Have you got a better idea?"

He wasn't really irritated; his voice was teasing.

She looked at his crotch and started to giggle again.

"Listen, Miss Smart Ass," he said, "you better hope things quiet down. If I were you I'd splash a little cold water on my face and hope I looked presentable enough. Look at your hair; you better pin that up."

Now Pat O'Grady was walking up the stairs. "Allison, is there anything I can do to help?"

"No, thank you, Pat, I'll be okay," moaned Allison in her most pitiful voice. "I'll just splash some cold water on my face and be right down. Des's been terrific."

Allison did her best to look pale and washed-out as she got herself down the staircase slowly, only to find that the crowd was waiting at the bottom of the stairs to see the little drama. Jerry was wearing a suspicious look, but he rushed over to her oozing sympathy just in case.

"Sonny, what in the world . . . ?"

"I made the fatal mistake of eating lunch in the *Daily* cafeteria," she said weakly. "It must have been the mayonnaise in the egg salad. It looked a little yellow, but that wasn't anything new."

Pat O'Grady looked relieved and everybody was sympathetic. Allison glanced at Chessy, who seemed to sympathize once she saw how pale and bedraggled she looked. "Where's Des?" she asked.

He came hurtling down the stairs, grabbed his coat, and shepherded Chessy to the door. As he was leaving he turned to Allison, who was still standing there leaning on the staircase.

"Hey, Sonny," he said, his eyebrows mischievously arched. "What's it feel like to be the goddaughter of the President of the United States?"

"Bastard," said Allison.

In bed later, with the lights out, she masturbated. It made her feel lonely and sad. It embarrassed her. She had no choice. She had never felt such sexual desire in her life. No man had ever made her feel the way Des did. She hated him for it. She was also in love with him. What would she do if he didn't leave Chessy? She was beginning to think that she might not have the courage to stay away from him even if he didn't leave his wife. It was hours before she drifted off to sleep.

Only the sound of the telephone woke Allison, and only after several rings. She was still half-asleep; she didn't know what time of day or night it was. She felt drugged as she fumbled for the phone. But before she could speak, she heard Jerry's voice answer Des's call.

"Jerry," said the familiar voice.

She realized she had been dreaming about him. It was her usual dream. People were racing after her trying to kill her. She kept trying desperately, frantically to find Des, but everywhere she looked he had just left. She could see him far ahead but she couldn't get his attention and the people with the knives were getting closer and closer.

"Listen," Des said. Allison continued to eavesdrop. "Is Sonny around? I've got to talk to you."

"She's still asleep," said Jerry. "You saw the story?"

"Saw it? Jesus, are you kidding? I didn't pay all that much attention until I saw her name at the bottom. That's what worries me." There was a note of exasperation in his voice.

"I was just getting ready to call you," said Jerry. "We've only got a few hours to make the changes. You don't disagree that we make the changes? We've gone pretty strong with some names *The Daily* says are definitely out. Sonny must have talked to Kimball himself, for God's sake. No way we can change the cover, though." He was trying to sound calm. "New York is going to go bat-shit when they hear about this."

"I don't blame them," said Des. "This makes us look like assholes. Even though *The World* has the same stuff we do. We have it solid on the three we went with, or at least on two, with Defense an almost sure thing. We talked to Holloway, and he's Kimball's coat carrier. Holloway said we could count on it. He must have talked to *The World* too. But shit, I talked to Rosey Grey myself yesterday."

"Okay, look," said Jerry, "we don't have much time. I'll call New York and tell them we've got to make some changes. We have four hours. I'll meet you at the bureau. I'll leave Sonny a note and tell her I've gone down to the office to clean up some last-minute details.

"I better get off the phone now. Damn, we sure don't need this."

"Hey, Jerry," said Shaw.

"Yeah?"

"This sure as hell complicates my life . . . You know what I mean?"

"Yeah, Des. I know what you mean."

Allison put the phone back on the hook. She stared at the ceiling. A crack was developing in it; it looked as if something were buckling. Probably water damage. The paint around the crack had begun to yellow. She would have to get the contractor. There was always something going wrong with the old house. It was at times like this that she thought about selling it and moving into a condominium. But she always decided against it. It was where she had been born. This house was her only remaining tie to her family.

This diversionary exercise kept her mind off the telephone call.

She had only suspected that *The Weekly*'s cover story was on the Cabinet. They had been really close-mouthed about it. Why hadn't Des or Jerry told her? She knew why, and she was glad they hadn't. If she had known, what would she have done? Tried to save them? Now they were going to look silly with cover pictures of guys who were not going to make the Cabinet. Suppose she and Des had been living together and this had happened? Suppose it happened again? Her allegiance was to her paper and to herself.

The hardest thing to think about was what Des was going to do. From the sound of his voice, he was plainly not happy. And there was something chilling about the way he had told Jerry that it complicated his life.

The other thing that gnawed at her was that she knew the leaks now. That little creep Derek Holloway was a leak. The President should have fired him long ago. He'd been peddling information to *The Weekly* since he'd been with the campaign.

So now what was she supposed to do about Holloway? Should she tell Kimball? That certainly wasn't her role as a journalist. Her role was to report stories, not to tell the President-elect how to run his staff, and surely not to inform on leakers. She was supposed to *use* leakers, not squeal on them. She was sure that the *Daily*'s reporters had gotten their inaccurate reports from Holloway as well. He was probably leaking to everybody.

No wonder Ray Bradshaw, who had the byline on the Sunday

story, wouldn't tell his source. He probably thought Allison would tell her godfather and dry up one of his sources. She couldn't figure out, though, how Holloway had gotten so many names wrong. Could it be that Uncle Rog was testing him?

Her other problem was the Vice President. Des had told Jerry he had talked to him. How could Rosey Grey have gotten things so screwed up? That didn't make any sense either. They obviously weren't trying to test him. The only thing Allison could think of was that Des had run the names by him and he hadn't wanted Des to know he didn't know so he had just nodded or shrugged or had said something noncommittal.

Allison had to get out of bed and get to the office. They would probably all be gleeful when they heard about *The Weekly*. The only thing she could hope for was that Holloway had gotten to the other newsmagazines as well. It wouldn't hurt either if he had had a little chat with *The New York World*.

It was close to noon by the time she got to the office, and all the others were already there, bitching and griping. They were standing in a circle near the national editor's office eating from a platter of Danish pastries. Allison was amused to see them all moaning about giving up their weekend. There wasn't a reporter who wasn't thrilled to be there. Working Sunday made you feel important. There was a big story and they were on it. Working in blue jeans was a little like camping out. It created a sense of camaraderie.

Allison slung her jacket over the back of her chair, dropped her bag on the desk, and walked a few steps to the group gathered around the national editor. Allen Warburg and Walt Fineman knew she had made that call the day before and the rest guessed.

Bradshaw, who had written the Sunday lead, was annoyed. "*The World* went hard with the three guys we say aren't going to make it." He took a sip of coffee and gazed at her.

Allison glanced at Walt.

"What edition did you read, Bradshaw?"

"The early. I got someone to read it to me last night from New York. I hope we know what we're doing." He was staring at Allison. He didn't like her. She had brushed him off years ago. He had wanted the White House assignment before she got it, and now that he had a shot at it again she was outsourcing him.

"Then you didn't see the later editions?" Walt didn't like Bradshaw.

"No."

"They've softened their story; they must have gotten a look at our first edition. They must have beaten their guy around the ears a little between ten and midnight."

"Wonder who the newsmagazines are going with," said Warburg.

"Well, *you* must know, Allison," Bradshaw said. "Isn't Jerry Mendelsohn staying at your house this weekend?"

"Just get off my case, will you, Bradshaw?"

"Relax, Sonny," said Walt gently.

"Okay, Al. I'm sorry," said Bradshaw, half-scared, half-pleased that he had struck a nerve with Allison. She was usually so cool.

"Can I talk to you a minute?" Allison asked Walt.

"Absolutely. Step into my office." He showed her into his little glass room and shut the door.

She told him about the phone call between Jerry and Des.

"Look, you've got to forget Des Shaw for now. I think you've got to get Roger Kimball on the phone and find out what the fuck is going on. Somebody is playing some kind of game here, and I don't like it. If that Holloway creep is trying to use the press to further his own career, his plan is going to backfire."

"Walt?"

"Yeah?"

"What should I tell Kimball about Holloway?"

"Just put it in the form of a question. Tell him that certain names are all over the press corps here and ask him if there is somebody on his staff who could be passing out bad information."

"But what about Grey?"

"I think I'd ask him straight out if Grey knows. Don't tell him why. Just see what he says."

He looked at his watch. "You better get on it. We've got a lot coming in today and the desk is short a couple of people. If we're going to lead the paper with this, I want to get it down early."

He left his office so she could use his phone in private.

Kimball's secretary answered the phone. She sounded harassed and irritated.

"Oh, hi, Sonny," she said. Her voice was at once confidential and cozy. It made Allison a little uncomfortable. "So you want to talk to him too. Get in line, m'dear. So does everybody and his brother. He's tied up in a meeting right now. How urgent is it?"

"Well, I'll need him before my deadline. He knows what it's about. I'd certainly appreciate it if you'd have him get back to me when he has a minute. I've got to run. Talk to you later."

It was almost five when Kimball called.

Bradshaw had written the lead for Monday, taking a few guesses, but they couldn't do much without the names. Other reporters had been assigned individual Cabinet officers and were waiting too. Though they hadn't been told it was Allison who was going to supply the names, they had a pretty good idea.

"Hi, honey," said Kimball. "I'm sorry it's so late. Loretta just gave me your message. I've been in meetings all afternoon."

Allison mentioned to him that other journalists were all getting the same wrong information. He didn't answer her question about a leak, simply indicated that he'd isolated the problem. She asked him if the Vice President knew who was going to be appointed to the Cabinet.

"He does now," said Uncle Rog.

"Uncle Rog," she said gently. She didn't want to seem too eager, and she did feel a little guilty about taking advantage of their relationship. "I am on deadline. You were going to confirm the Cabinet nominations for me."

Walt peeked in through the glass office. He gestured thumbs-up.

She motioned to him to wait.

"Confirm. That's a clever word," said Uncle Rog, chuckling.

She laughed too, though anxiously, as she looked at the clock. "Just force of habit, I guess."

"All right. I shouldn't do this, but I'm going to give you the list of appointees which will be announced by me at a press conference in the morning. I don't want you to think I'm going to make a habit of this, Sonny. But it burns my ass that somebody on my staff would mislead major news organizations, and at least somebody should get it straight. But you can't use it for your early edition. I don't think I made that clear yesterday."

"Okay. Thanks, Uncle Rog."

He gave her the list. They had most of it already. The bombshell was John T. Hooker, the irascible conservative Southern

Democrat who was head of the Senate Foreign Relations Committee, as Secretary of State.

As she was about to hang up, Kimball paused. "Oh, and Sonny," he said. "I have one more announcement, for publication."

"What's that?"

"As of this afternoon I have accepted Derek Holloway's resignation."

Allen and Walt were frustrated that Allison couldn't get Kimball to let her go with the story for the first edition. "This is chicken shit," said Warburg. "What difference does it make to him? I can't see his reasoning. One edition. Why would he think all fingers would point to you if we had it in the early edition and not if it was in the later?"

"He's giving copies of the Cabinet names to his staff around nine to start preparing bios. There's no way they could leak it in time to get the first edition, so if we had it early it would be obvious that it had come from him to me. Besides, it's moot. I promised. Let's look at the bright side. Now *The New York World* won't be able to recover. They won't be able to get it from our first edition. We'll beat them all night."

"Well, fuck this," said Allen. "What the hell are we going to lead the paper with for the first edition?"

His face brightened.

"Hey, Walt, have you got any bus accidents in Peru? Maybe there's an earthquake in Turkey—and get art. Maybe a great picture of rubble and huts. C'mon—we've got a newspaper to put out."

He started to head out of his office to break the bad news to the desk that they were going to have to fill for the first edition. He turned to Allison. "Hey, Brenda Starr, do you think you could give Bradshaw a hand with his lead for the late editions? You might get the clips on some of the appointees. Why don't you put together a sidebar on John T. Hooker."

This was not a request. Allison could hear the groans from the news desk as they heard the bad news. She walked slowly back to Walt's office, where she had left her notes. She took them over to her desk, then turned to go to the library to get the clips. She glanced over at Warburg, who had turned away from the desk and was looking at her. She smiled. He smiled back, a little puzzled at how cooperative she was being.

Then, softly, through clenched teeth, she addressed him, still smiling, under her breath.

"Prick," she said.

Jerry had called from the office to say that there were some last-minute details on the story. He would go back to her house after he finished and read the papers and watch the game. He had tried out the idea of going back to New York, but she had protested. She didn't want to be alone this last night of the weekend. Jerry didn't resist too much. Now that the cover was closed he really didn't even have to be in on Monday.

She tried to call home before she started on the sidebar, but there was no answer. She tried again at seven thirty. She was beginning to get worried. Walt and Allen kept coming to her desk to stare at her computer. She felt so exposed with these computers.

She had written what she thought was a pretty good story:

He had amassed the kind of power and prerogatives it takes thirty years to do in a town like Washington, D.C. And still that elusive, most desirable of all positions evaded his tenacious grasp.

Until today.

Today, John T. Hooker, controversial, colorful, powerful Chairman of the Senate Foreign Relations Committee, was named Secretary of State by President-elect Roger Kimball in a surprise move which . . .

"Bullshit," said Warburg, standing behind her reading her screen. "This isn't the fucking Living section. Knock off the first paragraph and lead with 'Today, John T. . . . '"

"You asked for a sidebar," said Allison. "This isn't the lead story in the paper."

She couldn't figure out why Warburg was mad at her, but she was certainly angry with him. Why was he picking on her? She had gotten the damn story for him. It was more than Bradshaw had done. What was his problem?

"Allen, I'll handle it," said Walt. "We're all a little tired."

Warburg looked at Fineman for a minute, then shrugged and turned away. "I didn't ask for the great American novel, for Christ's sake."

Walt could see how annoyed Sonny was.

"Look," he said, "Warburg just sees this case as the beginning of a long series of problems for all of us. He's trying to work it out. He doesn't like being told he can't have the story for the first edition. It screws everything up and the desk is out of sorts and they blame him. He probably thinks you could have soft-talked Kimball into letting us go with it if you'd really tried."

"But, Walt, I—" she protested.

"I know, I know. Look, let's just get to the story. Tone down some of the adjectives and it'll be fine."

Jerry called about eight thirty. He sounded as if he'd been drinking. He was at the house.

"Are you coming home anytime soon?" he asked. "I'm starving."

"I didn't expect you to say you were thirsty."

"What kind of nasty crack is that directed at your most trusty and reliable friend?"

Allison was amused. Jerry's drinking always amused her. He could not hold his liquor.

"So who you been drinking with, ol' buddy?"

"Just an ol' buddy," he said. "Nobody you'd be interested in." She tensed again.

"Des?"

"Let's have Chinese tonight."

"Did he say anything about Chessy?"

"Do you want me to go and get carryout or shall we eat at the restaurant?"

"Do you think he's told her?"

"Why don't we get carryout? You can pick it up on your way home."

"What did he say? Damn you, Jerry, this isn't funny."

"Get moo shu pork with six pancakes, and don't forget the hoy sin sauce. It's nothing without the hoy sin sauce."

"You know I'm going to get it out of you."

She was partly terrified, partly amused, partly exasperated.

"And don't forget the chopsticks."

She burst into the house an hour and a half later, dumped the Chinese food on the kitchen counter downstairs, then ran up the narrow little stairs to the second-floor study to find Jerry listening to records, half-dozing over the *World* crossword puzzle. The fire was almost out.

"Wake up, wake up," she said. "Now, what's going on? Not one bite of moo shu pork until you come out with it."

Jerry woke up immediately and laughed.

"Okay, okay, I'll tell. But not before I've eaten. I can't rat on my best friend on an empty stomach."

After she had spread the food out on the floor on newspapers, serving Jerry his plate and watching him eat a pancake, she pounced.

"Jerry, please."

He could see she was serious, that he had pushed her far enough.

"He's going to tell her tonight."

Allison gasped. Jerry put out his hands as a warning.

"Assuming he isn't too drunk."

"How drunk is he?"

"Pretty drunk. But," he said brightly, "you know Des. Most people can't tell when he's had a few too many."

She moaned.

Jerry grabbed her hand. "It'll be okay, Sonny. I promise you."

She didn't seem appeased.

"Listen, Sonny, the guy's really in love with you. You're the first. It's gonna be hard for him and a lot harder for you. Basically he's just a Harp, and to him women have always been whores or Madonnas."

She was staring into the fire.

"Are you hearing what I'm saying to you, Sonny? It's important."

"I hear you," she said finally, her gray eyes lifting up to his filled with either fear or gratitude, he couldn't tell which.

It was about nine thirty Monday morning when the phone rang. Allison had just gotten her tea and had carried it upstairs to the living room with the paper.

It was sunny in the living room, a beautiful early-winter morning, bright and clear. A slight wind was blowing the branches outside her window, the last dead leaves whipping past as if they were calling to her to come outside and play.

He sounded pretty awful.

"Hi" was all he said.

Suddenly she couldn't swallow, she couldn't breathe properly.

"Hi," she said softly.

"Well, I guess congratulations are in order."

"What?"

"On your Cabinet story. Kimball hasn't announced them yet, but his office has confirmed that the names are accurate. John T. Hooker. That was a real curve. Who would have thought Kimball would have the balls to appoint old John T.? At least we have you to thank for softening our own cover story."

"It wasn't my story. It was Bradshaw's." She said it carefully. "I did the sidebar."

"Hey, Sonny?"

"Yes?"

"We're both in the same business. We're competitors. This is fair game. But you better understand one thing."

"What's that?"

"I'm not a fool. If you and I are going to make it together, don't ever take me for a fool again, okay?"

She could feel her stomach drop. She couldn't speak right away.

"*Are* you and I going to make it together, Des?" she asked finally, her voice barely audible.

"Yeah, Sonny. We are. We are going to try."

She didn't say anything. She just let out her breath. There was silence on the line.

He broke it.

"I'll come over about seven tonight. We'll eat at Nora Okay?"

"Okay."

CHAPTER 3

SADIE'S DREAMS WERE TROUBLED AND FILLED with strange faces and names.

She was at a party where she knew no one. As she walked into the room, the faces loomed. They were big, much bigger than the bodies, and they laughed and leered at her, whispering and telling jokes which she did not understand. There were two women, one with black hair and bright red lipstick. The hair was pulled back tightly against her head; the face was white, geishalike. When Sadie shook her head, the giant red-and-white face would shriek and look back at the rest of the guests, and the guests would gasp and sigh and laugh and hiss.

Then the dark-haired woman would move away and the next one in line would step forward.

This woman had a narrow face with thin lips and see-through eyes. Her hair was long and pale, silvery. "Of course, you understand," she would say, menacing. "She doesn't even know anything." Again the crowd would gasp and crow. Each guest in line; bulbous heads and faces leered. She kept looking for Rosey, but he wasn't there. She kept reaching her hand behind her back, grasping empty space. She was riveted, wanting to leave but unable. Her feet were too heavy. "Please help me; show me how to get out of here!" she cried. They laughed.

Then she felt a strong hand. At first she thought with relief that it must be Rosey. She turned away for a moment and saw another face, this one huge too but not ugly. The hair was dark and the eyes sparkling with laughter. She couldn't understand why he was laughing. He didn't seem to take the other people seriously, and as he laughed at them and pointed his fingers at them they began to get smaller and smaller.

"Surely you can't be afraid of them?" he asked. "This is the circus and these are the freaks and the clowns. Do you want some cotton candy? I'll get you some."

He started to pull her hand.

"No, no, please don't let go. Please don't leave me alone with them."

"But they won't hurt you. Look at them. They're so small."

She realized that she had gotten larger as they had diminished.

"Aren't you uncomfortable in those concrete shoes?" he was saying. "Here, let me help you off with them; you'll feel much better and you can move around. We can take a walk around the whole circus; the sideshows are what I like the best."

She was beginning to feel calm. He reached down and pulled her feet out of the shoes with no trouble. Once her feet were free she started to walk around.

"They look so funny."

"We look the same way."

"What do you mean?"

"We're part of the circus."

She stared at him as he held a mirror up to her.

She clapped her hands to her face in horror. "But I don't look like that!"

"You look pretty to me," he said. "Now do you want to see the high-wire act?"

"Oh, I don't think so. I think it's too scary. I can't watch."

"Just wait," he said, laughing. "Pretty soon you'll be doing one of your own."

When she finally woke up on that same Saturday morning, she was soaked with perspiration. She opened her eyes and looked around. It looked like a hotel room. The twin bed next to her was

"Yes," he said. "It was nice."

She could tell he wasn't interested in talking about it. He was already involved in his work. She didn't want to give up.

"Well, I couldn't help noticing that the wife of the British Ambassador made quite a play for you. She couldn't keep away from you all night."

He perked up a little. Rosey responded to flattery.

"Yes, well, I did notice that a little bit." He smiled.

"I can't imagine how she could be married to that boring old fool Rodney," said Sadie. "Money and position, I suppose."

She hesitated, wondering whether Rosey would take that amiss. No. For one thing, he had no doubts about his attractiveness. Rosewell Grey was a very secure man. First Families of Virginia: F.F.V. He was secure in the way people are when they have been brought up to believe that they are superior. Even when Rosey was depressed, and that was rare, he never doubted himself at the core as some people did. When he had had bad moments during the campaign, had made mistakes, he had always put it off to bad luck or at worst a temporary failing. Sadie wanted just once to have Rosey bury his head in her lap. In seventeen years, she had never seen him falter. She imagined that somewhere inside his body was an endless reserve. She couldn't crack it. Nobody else could either. That was why his response to flattery amused her. It was his one weakness, and it was a weakness she capitalized on. She had used it to get what she wanted for as long as they had known each other.

"What does she look like, the wife of the British Ambassador?" Vonelle asked.

"Well, I think Mr. Grey ought to describe her to you," Sadie drawled. "What would you say, darlin'?"

"I'd say that she was pretty fine-looking," he said, looking at Sadie while answering Vonelle. "A pretty fine-looking woman. Very exotic, you know, the way those Englishwomen can be who've lived in India. They have a sort of Oriental twist to their way of thinking, even their way of dressing."

Sadie was surprised. He had paid more attention to Edwina than she'd thought. She wasn't sure that that didn't annoy her. She had been so preoccupied with Chessy and Desmond Shaw and Allison Sterling that she hadn't paid much attention to Rosey. It wasn't that she was jealous of Edwina or that she thought she would steal Rosey away. It meant that Edwina might have underestimated Sadie. And that was a very stupid thing to do. Especially now. She could be, although most people didn't know it about her, quite vindictive.

This amused Rosey, particularly because, as he pointed out to her, people made so many enemies in politics that it was impossible to hold grudges. You wouldn't have the time or the energy.

"Sadie," Rosey said in his patronizing way, "I happen to know you weren't paying all that much attention to your husband last night. You were busy taking in Washington. If you had been, you would have noticed that I spent most of the evening with the Ambassador. And you also would have noticed that Lady Abel-Smith flirted with everybody in the room. Besides"—and he smiled—"I noticed you weren't having such a bad time yourself with that fellow from *The Weekly*."

She blushed. "Actually, I spent most of the evening talking to his wife. I think he's got a crush on that reporter—what's her name?—the blond one."

"You mean Allison Sterling, Roger's goddaughter."

Rosey didn't see through her pretense. "No wonder they were all fawning all over her."

Rosey just laughed, but Sadie was surprised and pleased that he had gotten as involved as he had in the conversation. There had always been a part of the Southern boy that liked gossip. It had turned her off a little bit when they were living in Richmond. She had always thought of men who gossiped as slightly unmanly. But somehow in Washington most conversation was gossip. She was pleased to learn that the men here gossiped, and that it was considered clever, and that Rosey was warming to Washington so readily.

"Now, listen, sugar," he said, "I've got an awful lot of work to do and I can't very well get it done if you sit here and gossip with me all day—can we, Vonelle?" He looked at his secretary and winked.

"I'd just as soon sit here and gossip, if it's all the same to you, Mr. Grey," she said, and cackled with laughter.

Dear as she was, Vonelle was very country. She had a country accent and country taste. Sadie was not at all sure how she would do in Washington. She could never figure out how Vonelle had lasted all these years with Rosey. But she was glad of it in a way. It made Rosey more likable, more human.

"Darlin'?" He turned to Sadie. "Will you excuse us?"

He was the Southern gentleman even as he was throwing her out of his office.

She had been sitting on a hard little chair. She made a note to herself that she would replace it with a comfortable armchair. After all, this office would be for the house manager, someone who was theoretically on her staff. She would have to start thinking about her staff. She probably ought to find Audrey Hall and start talking about her own business.

"Oh," Rosey said, as she was halfway out the door. "Desmond Shaw is coming over this afternoon at four to interview me. Why don't you join us for tea afterwards?"

It was more an instruction. She knew he wanted her to come down and soft-soap Shaw for him. She had defanged many a reporter for Rosey.

"I'll be delighted," she said to Rosey. She felt her stomach tighten. But Rosey had asked her. She would be there.

"Don't you have some things to discuss with Audrey?" he asked.

Why did he always have to push her as though she were a little girl? "Don't you have some homework, dear?"

"That's exactly where I'm going."

She hadn't meant to sound so testy.

Audrey Hall was coming through the dining room as Sadie walked out the passageway and into the entrance hallway.

"Hello, darling," she said. She gave Sadie a maternal kiss.

"Did you have a nice time at Lorraine Hadley's? She usually has interesting parties. They've got your 'breakfast' all heated up. The head steward was rolling his eyes. Why don't we sit down here in the dining room, and I'll chat with you while you eat? I've gotten most of my chores out of the way for this morning. Then, if you like, I'll give you a tour and explain how the house is run."

The dining room was large and airy, and Sadie and Audrey Hall sat down at one end of the long table. Audrey patted Sadie on the hand and smiled. "You look so pretty today," she said. "That color green becomes you. But you must know that."

Audrey had snow-white hair and a round, sweet face. She had a mischievous sense of humor, and there was nothing she loved better than a cozy gossip herself. She had given way to her age gracefully. There was no attempt to dye her hair or indulge in face lifts. Sadie felt she had to be careful around her, not to slip and say anything outrageous. She was a good Episcopalian lady who did needlepoint kneeling pads for the cathedral and tried to make her husband's life as easy as possible. She was delighted to be leaving Washington and the job and going back to New York and their country house in Connecticut.

Audrey joined her in a cup of coffee and a piece of corn bread. She giggled with delight after the steward had left.

"They're awfully touchy, the stewards," she warned Sadie. "They're Navy and they think this house should still belong to the Chief of Naval Operations. They really resent having it turned over to the Vice President. They get upset if George or I ask for anything after hours, and the head steward threatens to quit at least once a week. But we manage to get along. I'm sure they'll like you, and maybe you can find a more workable solution. It's just that if we get home late and George wants a cup of coffee or a snack if we've been traveling they take it as an insult, as though we thought they were indentured servants. Honestly, one would think that the Vice President of the United States wouldn't have to put up with that kind of thing. But what is there to do?" She sighed a deep sigh.

Sadie was eating her stew and listening to Audrey with one ear.

"Isn't there a cozier place to eat?" she asked.

"Unfortunately not. With the kitchen in the basement, all the stewards spend their time down there."

"Do you ever use the kitchen yourself?" asked Sadie. "I love to cook, and I wondered . . ."

"Well, we do sometimes. On weekends we can go down there and cook. But George detests kitchens, and I'm hopeless. Besides, it's not terribly attractive."

Sadie had noticed a little service area off the dining room. "Couldn't that be made into a little private dining area?"

"Oh, well, now, that's another question," said Audrey. "You see, for years we've had a plan to build a new kitchen off the pantry on this floor, extending it over the garage in back. Unfortunately, the money had to come from Congressional appropriations, and it just doesn't seem to be in the cards." She smiled at Sadie. "Perhaps, my dear, with your charm you might be able to convince a few Congressmen that it would be for the good of the country for the Vice President to have a new kitchen."

Sadie had finished her corn bread. She took a linen napkin and delicately wiped the butter off her chin. That would be another hundred calories right there. She was going to have to watch it.

"Now, dear, I think we'd better do the house."

It was a wonderful, graceful Victorian house, surrounded by a veranda and set high on a hill in a parklike enclosure overlooking Massachusetts Avenue. It had big, sunny windows and large, open rooms. There was a coziness about it that demanded it be decorated informally.

Audrey showed Sadie downstairs to the kitchen in the basement—which was, she decided, unacceptable. She inspected the china closet and was shocked to see such cheap china for the Vice President's house, and so little of it. Audrey explained that people stole souvenirs so it didn't make sense to have good china. Back upstairs, and down the hall where Rosey was working, was the office of Audrey's staff person.

"You'll surely want to bring in your own person for that job," she said. Oddly enough, this was something Sadie had not given much thought to.

She had never, first of all, expected Rosey to be picked, and then she hadn't thought that they would win. She had imagined they would go back to Richmond and settle down, that Rosey would take up his law practice or maybe run for the Senate. She was walking around in a dream world.

"The office where your staff person will be is also used as a holding room for V.I.P. guests. We call this door here at the end of the hall the V.I.P. entrance so we don't have to call it the back door." She laughed. "You'll learn that that kind of thing is very important in Washington. Always remember that it is not what things are that matters, it is what they appear to be."

Upstairs, Audrey showed her the master bedroom. Sadie noticed that there were twin beds against the wall next to the bathroom. Over to the right where the turret was, there was a rounded end of the room with a small desk and a chair. "This," said Audrey, "is where I do most of my work. The view is lovely from here, and it faces south, so you get the sun all day long."

"It must be nice in the spring and summer when you get a cross breeze," said Sadie.

"Oh, no, the windows are sealed. The Secret Service insists. We have to have air conditioning in here, even in the winter."

Sadie felt sick. "I can't live that way," she said.

"That's what I thought too—but no matter how much we complained, they wouldn't relent. I'm afraid you'll have to try to get used to it the way we did."

A tiny bead of sweat had appeared on Sadie's upper lip as they continued their tour.

The third floor was perfect for the two children, with large bedrooms and a sitting room, though they were both away at school for now.

"I hope that gives you some idea," said Audrey after the tour. "Feel free to roam around. Now I must be off. My plane leaves at one o'clock. I understand George and Rosey have a working dinner tonight. I hope you won't be too lonely. I've told the head steward to prepare something for your dinner tonight. You will forgive me for leaving, my dear? I shan't be back until Monday, and I know you're leaving then. But we're only a phone call away. You know you and Rosey are welcome to stay here any-time you like." She smiled a mischievous smile. "I think the President was a little irritated when he heard I'd invited the two of you to stay here. Of course, he and Roger Kimball are poles apart politically. Not like we are." She kissed Sadie on the cheek and disappeared into her room to collect her things.

Sadie walked back into the guest room and closed the door. She flopped down on the bed, which had been made while she was downstairs, and lay there for a few minutes.

"I, Sara Adabelle Grey, am the wife of the Vice President of the United States." She let the words out slowly, then waited until they drifted away, then said them again. "Oh, my God, what have I got myself in for?" It was not unusual for Sadie to talk to herself. She seemed to be doing so more and more lately. "Well, now what am I going to do? I suppose I could start thinking about decorating."

She wasn't really in the mood. She was restless. She didn't want to lie around the bedroom all day, and she really didn't want to stay home by herself that night. She couldn't take a walk without the damn Secret Service.

Maybe she could call Lorraine Hadley.

* * *

Sadie got through on the third try. Lorraine Hadley was thrilled. Sadie was full of praise.

"My God, my phone's rung off the hook this morning," Lorraine said. "I must say I've heard nothing but compliments for you, you and your handsome husband. That's all anybody's talking about. Particularly the women. You may find that gets you in trouble here. Attractive women are not always welcome."

Lorraine was somebody she could learn from. Sadie already felt comfortable talking to Lorraine.

"So you and William had a good time?"

Sadie wasn't used to Rosey's being called William, though she knew Rosey had asked Lorraine to call him that. They had changed his nickname from Rosey to Bill after he became Governor, though nobody in Richmond ever called him Bill or William. Everett had insisted that William Rosewell Grey III was an unacceptable name for a politician, and that Rosey was out of the question.

He had been introduced to the national press as William Grey, and that was what most people in Washington would call him unless they knew him well. Now that he was about to be Vice President, people were going to call him Mr. Vice President. But Rosey wanted to be referred to in the press as William Grey.

Sadie assured Lorraine that they had had a splendid time. They chatted. Finally she asked about Desmond Shaw.

There was a slight pause, and Sadie was embarrassed for no reason. Why had she asked? Why was Lorraine pausing?

"I'm asking," she said, "because he's coming over here this afternoon to interview Rosey. Well, I just want to know if he is all right."

"Oh, certainly. It will be fine. I wouldn't worry about it. . . ." Another awkward pause.

Sadie was furious with herself.

"I wouldn't get too interested, darling," said Lorraine.

"Anyone you're interested in interests me," said Sadie, trying to sound casual.

"That's right, darling, and your husband is the Vice President—elect of the United States. Don't forget about that. No one else will. And he's very attractive. All I'm saying is that just because you're married doesn't mean you can't have a little flirtation now and then, does it?" Lorraine could hear Sadie breathing.

"All right, dear, I know I'm being mischievous. I'll tell you why. There's nothing I love better than a little intrigue, especially a little romantic intrigue, and we almost never get that in this city. My God, everybody's so power-mad, and they wouldn't dream of doing anything to jeopardize their political situations. But every now and then . . ."

Sadie was more relaxed now. And Lorraine was putting out the bait. It amused her.

"What are you talking about, Lorraine?"

"Ohhhh, nothing much. It's just that I . . . Can I trust you, Sadie?"

She had her now. All she had to do was reel her in. Sadie knew it too.

"Of course you can."

The magic words.

"Now, this is strictly between us, darling. You mustn't breathe a word to a living soul."

"I wouldn't think of breathing a word," said Sadie, repeating what was to become a catechism.

"Well, I suspect there might be something going on between Des and Allison Sterling. Of course, I don't think poor Chess has a clue, though I must say she and Allison did not hit it off at all last night. Were you noticing any of that?"

"A little," said Sadie. She didn't want to admit that she had paid much attention. "I did notice that Chessy and Allison didn't exactly seem like best friends. But they're so different. They don't really have anything in common."

"Except Des."

They laughed.

"Do you know anything or are you just guessing?" asked Sadie. "I thought Allison seemed relaxed and cool, completely in control, as though nothing could faze her."

Sadie wasn't really aware of the frost in her own voice.

"So you didn't like her?"

"I thought she was nice. I didn't really have much of a chance to talk to her. She seemed to be involved with the men."

"Oh, you *really* didn't like her."

"Lorraine, you are being mischievous. What are you up to?"

"Oh, nothing. It's just that I noticed that Des was being very attentive to you. If he and Sonny do have something going between them, his interest in you would account for her behavior last night. I think Sonny wants him, and if she does she can get him away from Chessy easily, even if she doesn't know it."

"Would he just leave Chessy? Is that what you mean?"

"In a flash. He's ready to go. I've seen Sonny when she gets her mind set on something. She's ferocious. Whatever Sonny wants, Sonny gets."

"Poor Chessy," said Sadie. She meant it. She felt suddenly afraid.

"Speaking of Chessy, she's coming for dinner tonight with Archie and me. Would you like to join us? Your husband mentioned last night that he had a working dinner this evening. We'd love to have you. Very informal. Ezio would adore a chance to show off for you."

"That's nice of you," said Sadie. "I think I would like to, actually. I was dreading the idea of eating all alone in that big dining room. I'd be happy to come."

Lorraine was clearly delighted. Sadie was a catch, and she had her firmly in her grasp. Not that she didn't like her: Sadie realized that. But she understood that by going there twice on the weekend she was giving Lorraine a leg up on the social scene. She didn't want to belong to anybody. But she knew that a relationship with Lorraine could benefit her as well. Lorraine was a good tutor. She would be an excellent guide through the minefields, and if she helped Sadie she would be helping Rosey. Besides, she was fun. And Sadie needed a friend.

Rosey had said that Shaw would arrive at four. Sadie phoned the kitchen to remind the stewards that she would be taking tea with the Vice President, and instructed them to ask him what time he would want it. She feared Rosey would forget that he had invited her.

When the steward came and knocked on the door it woke her. It was almost dark outside, and she saw from the clock that she had slept for almost two hours. It was after five.

She jumped out of bed, called to the steward to tell him she would be right down, then ran into the bathroom. She splashed water around her eyes so as not to disturb the mascara, brushed her hair quickly, and ran out the door.

Rosey had taken Shaw into the back sitting room off the living room downstairs.

Desmond Shaw had on corduroy trousers, a crew-neck sweater, an open-necked shirt, a tweed jacket, and loafers. Sadie was used to seeing Rosey in a coat and tie, no matter how informal the occasion. Shaw had an Irish barroom look to him.

He was laughing a deep low laugh, as though he were really enjoying himself. He had just lit a cigarette with a gold lighter, which he put back in his pocket, and was taking a deep drag. Rosey was standing looking at him, both hands in his pockets. There was an air of masculine camaraderie which Sadie could feel as she stood in the doorway watching them. She liked men and she liked seeing them together; she liked watching them sniff around each other to get the measure of each other's worth and power.

Rosey had never been a man's man in the truest sense of the word, but he was tall and handsome and intelligent, good at sports, and successful. Des Shaw, on the other hand, was the kind of man men flocked to. They always ended putting their arm around him, jousting with him, calling him a son-of-a-bitch, a prick, a bastard, in the most affectionate way. Rosey commanded men's respect. With Shaw it was something else. It was an immediate attraction.

She had asked the stewards to light the fire. Jackson, the head steward, had taken an instant liking to her and was bustling around trying to please her as best he could. He had brought in a tray with tea and cookies. Somehow to Sadie, Des, standing there, didn't exactly appear to be the tea type.

"A little Irish whiskey in your tea to take the chill of the day off?" said Sadie, a slightly husky tone to her voice.

Both men looked up. Des smiled.

"Why, Mrs. Grey," said Des, not moving. "What an unexpected pleasure."

She could see that Rosey was a little taken aback by his familiar tone. She was a little, too, for that matter. Yet he had done it with such natural ease, such confidence, that she felt a little foolish for being surprised.

She smiled at Jackson, who had been listening, and gave him a nod. He scurried out of the room for the whiskey.

"Looks like you've got poor Jackson under your thumb already," said Rosey, laughing. "Poor fellow never had a chance."

Rosey was proud of her, she could tell. He liked having other men think she was attractive as long as she didn't do anything to provoke their attention, like being overtly sexy. It made him feel good to have other men give him admiring looks when they met her.

"I daresay, Mr. Vice President," Shaw offered, "that this entire city awaits the same fate as poor Jackson."

She had walked over to the coffee table near where they were standing and sat down to pour the tea. She could feel Shaw's eyes on her as she walked. She could feel the blood rushing to her face.

"Did you have a nice interview?" she asked quickly.

Both men started to answer at the same time, then stopped, deferred to each other, then laughed.

"I'd be interested to hear what you have to say, sir," said Shaw.

It amused Sadie to hear Des call Rosey sir.

"It was a very informative interview for my part," said Rosey, laughing. "I can't remember when I got so much information out of a reporter who was interviewing me. Very educational. This is going to be an interesting four years."

"What did *you* learn from the interview, Mr. Shaw?" asked Sadie.

"I learned that your husband is not going to be my best source for leaks in the new Administration."

Jackson was back with the Jameson, which Sadie poured into Shaw's teacup.

"And please call me just Des, not Mr. Shaw. It's much too formal."

He looked directly at her.

She looked away.

Rosey had surprised her.

The light went on.

"What in heaven's name are you doin' lying here in the dark, sugar? Are you awake?"

"Uh-huh," she said. "I was just lying here thinking."

"Well, I just talked to Kimball in Colorado. That's what I've been doing for the last half-hour. I must say I feel something of an idiot."

"What's the matter, darlin'? You look so upset. Is there anything I can do?"

He seemed agitated. He was pulling off his tie. He always showered and changed before dinner, even if it was just the two of them, which it often was.

"Well, I had just finished with Shaw. He asked me about a number of Cabinet appointments he is going to report this week. They were all the names Roger had discussed with me last week. So when Shaw brought it up just now I didn't confirm the names, but I certainly didn't deny them."

"Well, are there many changes?"

"Three."

"Why did Roger wait so long to tell you?"

"I suppose he was trying to minimize the leaks and he probably hadn't gotten them all to accept until just now."

"Well, if he can't trust his Vice President, who in the world can he trust?"

He stopped and looked at her. "I guess he's just going to have to learn who to trust. He doesn't know me. He doesn't know yet exactly what kind of a player I am. I can understand."

"What about Shaw? He's going to write this story."

Rosey was sitting on the edge of the bed in his undershorts, taking off his shoes and socks. He turned to look at her, his eyes wide with amazement; then he laughed. "We were just talking about trust. How can I convince the President that he can trust me if I go running to the nearest reporter every time I learn something? I told Shaw nothing. He told me that these were the people he had heard were going to be named. That left room to confirm or deny. He shouldn't take my lack of denial for a confirmation. He knows better. He'll have to get a substantial source. He's a big boy."

"Still, it could be embarrassing for him. It's going to be on the cover."

"Nonsense," said Rosey. "These reporters get things wrong all the time. They're used to it. They'll have another story, another magazine, another cover. Nobody will remember. These guys play hardball. They're after us every time they get a chance. Good news is no news. Bad news, page one. Let me goof, get a fact wrong, disagree with Kimball, forget somebody's name and by God I'm guaranteed page one headlines. And that goes for you. Everything you say or do is fair game. We shouldn't trust anyone, even Desmond Shaw."

Lorraine had said informal. Sadie had brought a pair of dark brown wool-crepe pajamas and simple heavy gold clip-on earrings with cat's-eyes in the center.

She dusted her pale cheeks and gave herself the once-over before she went downstairs to the waiting car. She did look pretty good for thirty-eight. Brown was not her favorite color, but it was a good fall color, it worked with her hair, and Rosey liked it. He had picked it out for her at Bergdorf's, where she shopped mostly when they went to New York. It was perfect for this evening. She wanted to look elegant tonight, not sexy.

Cocktails were in the library, a beautiful room done in deep gray velvets and soft reds. The bookcases were lined with leather-bound books, and the Louis Quinze desk, suede chairs, dark red paisley chintz, and a blazing fire made it seem both glittering and cozy.

Chessy was already there and had settled in. Archie, in his smoking jacket, was fixing drinks.

Lorraine was in one of her famous caftans, this one a simple burnt red. No jewelry. Her black hair sleeked back, her lipstick matching her caftan. Perfect.

Chessy, again, was a little overdressed. A few drinks had taken the elastic quality out of her face, and gravity was definitely her enemy.

Now, giving her full attention to Chessy, Sadie could detect a slight Oriental cast to her eyes. Face lift. A beautiful job, no doubt, but one could always tell. Nothing wrong with that. Sadie had every intention of doing the same thing when she was a few years older. She wondered how old Chessy was. Probably about forty-five. She looked forty-five, at least. Sadie wondered who her plastic surgeon was. She could probably find out from Lorraine. She didn't have to worry about that now, but there would come a day . . . Everybody said this job would take its toll. The press was always running Before and After pictures of politicians and their wives, and they always aged tremendously in those jobs. Stress. That was what they said. Sadie wondered if she could handle the stress. She really would have to learn to keep her mouth shut. Anyway, "Thirty-nine and holdin'," as the country song said. That would be her motto soon enough. Well, she didn't see any *reason* why she should worry about it, only that was easier said than done.

"Don't you look nice," said Sadie. She simply could not put Chessy together with Desmond Shaw.

Chessy turned to Lorraine. "Really, Lorraine, I don't see what it is in this city that fascinates you. Especially after London. Now, there's an exciting city. Washington is filled with dreary politicians and journalists and the women they married when they were twenty-two."

"That's an old cliché, Francesca dear," said Lorraine a bit testily. "Look again. This has become quite a glamorous town. Nothing substitutes for power, not even money."

"I haven't noticed you divesting yourself of all your worldly goods, darling," said Chessy.

"Money only matters in Washington if you haven't any power," said Lorraine. "Things have changed considerably since you spent any time here, Chessy. When Des was in the *Boston Gazette* bureau it was a very different world. Now they're writing movies and books about those dreary politicians and journalists you talk about. And those dreary little wives they married when they were twenty-two are gone. The new wives are all anchorwomen and Cabinet officers. You have no idea what a strain it is to try and seat these dinners. It's enough to break even the most dedicated hostess' spirit. I've really given in to having only buffet suppers."

"When one is called to a higher purpose, one must sacrifice," said Chessy. "My hat's off to you. That was quite a little group you put together last night." She glanced sidewise at Sadie. "Quite a coup."

There was an edge to the conversation that was making Sadie a little uncomfortable. The two women had to have known each other very well for a long time to be talking to each other like this. Although Lorraine was visibly embarrassed by Chessy's reference to Rosey and Sadie's appearance at her party, Sadie knew perfectly well it was a coup for Lorraine. She was only just beginning to understand how much of one.

Irma appeared to say that dinner was served. The dining

room, which had been arranged for a buffet the night before, was set up now as a dining room. In the middle of the room was a polished wood table; the other one had been folded away. A large antique Italian hand-painted folding leather screen had been pulled across the room near its entrance to shut off part of it and make it cozier. A fire was blazing, and the table was set with beautiful traditional china and silver and crystal. There were embroidered white organza placemats on the table. The four silver candelabra glistened from the candlelight, and in the center of the table had been placed a crystal bowl of fruit.

Small cups of soup were already at their four places, with lids on them to keep them warm.

"Have there been any surprises about Washington yet?" Lorraine asked Sadie once they were seated.

Sadie took a moment to think. The only sounds in the room were the tinkle of silver spoons on the china and the crackling of the fireplace.

"Of course, I'm always surprised at how well-known people are so human. Even though I'm one of them and shouldn't be surprised by it, in public they take on a sort of larger-than-life quality."

"How do you mean?" asked Chessy.

"Well, you never see a First Lady with a hair out of place or a run in her stocking or perspiration stains. How do they do it? Do they never fight with their husbands, never have to go to the bathroom in the middle of a motorcade, never have too much wine and throw up all night long, never get cramps? Nobody has come to give me perfect pills or the proper inoculations. I still have days when I can't do anything with my hair. Somehow my skirts never seem to be the right length. I perspire like a washerwoman when I get nervous, which lately has meant all the time."

Sadie was laughing at herself. She had had more to drink than she'd intended. But she felt safe with Lorraine. Lorraine was her Apache guide through Indian territory. She knew all the footprints, the color of the beads, the meaning of the feathers, the importance of the smoke signals, and could she ever play the tom-toms! Normally she would never have talked this way around a man, but Archie had a way of fading into the background.

When Irma came around with more wine, Sadie did not put her hand over her glass as she should have. She was having a good time and she was getting some things out of her system. Why not? This was the beginning of a new life.

Ezio had made a glorious stuffed wild duck with a persimmon sauce and spectacular crisp green vegetables, some heavenly *pommes soufflées*.

"That's another thing," she said. They were all fascinated. No one had said a word after she began talking.

"Weight. I am constantly on a diet. No other Vice President's wife has ever had a weight problem. They always look thin and svelte. First Ladies and Second Ladies always have marvelous projects that they work on from dawn until dusk, and when they're not doing that they're taking foreign-language courses to improve themselves. Sometimes I get the lying-down disease for days. It's all I can do then to get out of bed and get dressed to go to a party."

By now they saw the humor in what she was saying, and they were beginning to laugh.

"Y'all go ahead and laugh," she said playfully, "but I haven't even got to the worst part yet. Sometimes you get the impression these political couples are surgically joined together, the way they hang on to each other for dear life. But there's something about the adoring-wife role that just isn't suited to me. And Rosey is not demonstrative. He thinks it's kind of tacky to hold hands in public."

"Riveting," muttered Archie as the crème brulée was passed. "Riveting."

It was a rare experience these days for her to be the center of attention in any group when Rosey was there, and she was very wound up.

"One thing I have noticed—I mean compared to Richmond: that there are an awful lot of Jewish people. I mean I think that's fine, but it did seem to me that that was unusual socially. I guess I'm just not used to it."

"Don't get me started on that," said Archie, clearing his throat.

"Now, Archie," said Lorraine with a harsh tone in her voice. "Please."

Archie seemed not to hear her.

"You're a very wise girl," said Archie to Sadie. "Very wise indeed. Very observant. There *were* a lot of Jews here last night."

Sadie flinched at the word "Jews." Where she came from it

was not polite. One said Jewish or Jewish people. Jews sounded so harsh.

"There are more and more Jews every time we have a dinner party. Soon there will not be a single Christian left at any of our parties. It's not chic to be a Christian anymore. Did you know that, my dear?"

Archie was now peering over his glasses at Sadie, who was sorry she had brought it up.

"They're taking over the media, they're taking over the government," continued Archie. "Look at all those *Washington Daily* people. Jews, every single one of them. It's the new thing now. Good Yankee Puritan stock is passé. Just add 'stein' or 'feld' on the end of your name and you've got it made. We're supposed to be ashamed of our heritage, our families, our background. Lorraine apologizes for me all the time. I don't see you apologizing for the good Yankee Puritan ethic that made the Hadley fortune —eh, my dear?"

"Archie, this conversation is getting ugly and I won't have it. We were having a perfectly nice talk until now."

"I'm so sorry," whispered Sadie.

"I'm going to the loo," said Archie. He winked at Sadie as he got up from the table. "You're a very smart girl," he said approvingly.

Sadie could see that Lorraine was having a hard time keeping back the tears.

"Come on, Lolo," said Chessy, her voice soothing and sympathetic. "Don't let Archie get you down. You know he does it just to get your goat. Now, let's not let a silly thing like this ruin our lovely evening. Why don't you ring for the coffee? I think we could all use some of Ezio's fabulous espresso. Let's move into the living room and have our coffee there. The fire is already lit."

Lorraine rang for the coffee, then steadied herself as she got up from the table. Sadie excused herself to go to the bathroom.

Lorraine and Chessy were speaking softly when Sadie came back.

"Let's settle back and have a little girl-talk," said Chessy. "Sadie, what are your observations about the women at the party last night?"

"I felt that the women had not decided yet what role they wanted to play. They were confused. One minute they were trying to act more professional, tough, smart. Then the next they were trying to be sexy and feminine. . . . Part of the problem was that the men seemed confused too. Does that make any sense?" asked Sadie. "The reason I felt confused is that one minute people were responding to me on a female level, another minute they were ignoring me. Half the time they were eating out of my hand and the other half their eyes would glaze over. So by the end of the evening I felt as confused as the other women in the room were behaving."

"Was there any woman in particular whose behavior you were referring to?" asked Chessy.

Sadie couldn't help herself. She quickly looked at Lorraine for her reaction. Lorraine wouldn't play. She stared impassively ahead as though she hadn't heard the question.

"There was one." Sadie hesitated.

"And who might that have been?" inquired Chessy, now glaring at Lorraine.

"The blond one—the one with long blond hair. I can't remember..." She did actually seem to have a mental block against the name.

"You couldn't possibly be referring to Allison Sterling, could you? The national reporter from *The Daily*?"

There was such an edge to her voice that it was obvious to Sadie that Chessy knew; or if she didn't know for sure, then she surely suspected.

"Yes. Yes, that's the one. Allison Sterling." Sadie said her name, made herself say it. There was a bad taste in her mouth after she did.

"What a coincidence," said Chessy. "That's exactly who I was going to say. Allison Sterling," she repeated slowly and deliberately.

His voice was sudden and sharp and startling.

"What about Allison Sterling?" he said.

They all whipped around to see him standing in the doorway to the living room. Irma had obviously let him in the front door and they hadn't seen him.

"Desmond, darling," said Lorraine, jumping up to forestall any potential fireworks. "We were just having a little girl-talk. Won't you come and join us?"

Sadie was surprised. She hadn't known he was coming by. She automatically put her hand up to her hair to make sure it looked all right, licked her lips. She was blushing. It embarrassed her that he had caught them talking about Allison. She wondered how much he had heard. She said nothing.

"I'd love to, Lorraine, but Chess and I have got to go stop by a *Boston Gazette* party. I promised them I would have one drink with them. One of my oldest friends. I can't let him down. Ready, Chess?" There was no warmth, no fondness, no love in either his voice or his gaze.

In a very uncharacteristic move, Chessy jumped up and went to get her coat without a protest, although Sadie could see that she really wasn't eager to go. When she came back she kissed Lorraine and Sadie on both cheeks, thanking them for a most enjoyable and absolutely fascinating evening. "And tell Ezio he outdid himself once again," she said. Then she took her husband's arm almost shyly and they left.

As he was leaving, he turned at the door and looked back at Lorraine and Sadie, a sassy grin on his face.

"G'night, Lolo," he said, then nodded to Sadie. "G'night, Miz Grey."

He shut the door behind them.

"Poor Chessy," said Sadie underneath her breath. She felt a shiver run all along her body, and it was not just from the cold November night air let in by the door.

"Poor Chessy is right," said Lorraine.

She had just gotten into her nightgown when Rosey came upstairs and into the guest room. She was brushing her hair and feeling a bit woozy. The coffee had sobered her up a bit, but she had had a lot to drink and eat, and she really didn't feel at all well. She was embarrassed and annoyed at herself. And she was fighting the most horrible feeling that she might throw up.

Sadie stood at the bathroom door and looked at her husband. He was handsome, she had to admit. He was very distinguished-looking. He also looked in control. When she drank too much, which was rare, she felt weak. She was wearing a long white satin nightgown with wide sleeves and a lacy neck.

For a moment Rosey stopped at the door and stared at her. He had that look in his eye. She couldn't bear it. What was she going to do? The longer she stood up the dizzier she got. She started toward him and found herself not exactly on a straight course.

She threw herself into his arms and hugged him, curling up against his chest for balance.

"You look awful pretty, darlin'," he said to her as he held her in his arms. His voice was husky, and she could tell that he had had a couple of drinks. He began to rub his hands up and down her back in a soft stroking movement, up and down gently, his soft hands sliding down over her behind, then back up again to the small of her back, then her upper back and around to her breasts. That was always the way he began. There was never any deviation in his lovemaking. She was not aroused tonight, but she wanted to be held and loved. Their lovemaking for her was mostly like that. She enjoyed being caressed and held and whispered to. It made her feel good to know that Rosey loved her so much.

Now he was kissing her. He held her head in both his hands and kissed her firmly on the lips, his own lips only slightly parted.

She wrapped both her arms around his waist to steady herself.

He kissed her several times as they stood there toe to toe. She could tell he was feeling more passionate than usual. Perhaps it was his newly acquired power. Being driven around in limousines, being in this house, having people defer to him, being followed by Secret Service agents; it was all a bit heady, like living in a movie. It was that way to her; it must be that way to Rosey too.

"Do you want to make love?" he asked in a husky whisper. Even in passion he was shy and polite.

"Yes," she answered back softly. In truth she would have been just as happy to lie down and go to sleep. But her mother had told her long ago never to deny a man, and in fact she never really felt like denying Rosey. She always felt more secure and more loved after they had had sex even if it wasn't the most exciting thing in the world.

Rosey pulled away from her, took her gently by the waist with both his hands, led her to one of the beds and helped her down. Then softly he walked over to the closet and began to undress. He took off his coat and hung it in the closet.

Then he took off his vest and his tie and hung them up. Next came his shoes, which he placed neatly on the shoe trees; then his shirt and socks, which he rolled up and placed in a dirty-clothes bag. Finally he was in his shorts. He turned out the light on the table next to the chair, walked over to the bed smiling at Sadie, turned off the light on the bedside table.

She could hear him slip off his shorts as he slowly lowered himself on top of her. She was still so dizzy, even worse lying down, that she slowly moved one leg off the bed and put her foot on the floor to steady the room. Rosey had pushed her nightgown above her breasts and had buried his face in them, kissing them, first one and then the other, fondling them both in his hands as he rotated his kisses.

Suddenly, Sadie felt ridiculous. There she was, tight as a tick, with one foot on the floor and her nightgown bunched up around her neck and her husband hunched over her in the dark fondling her, and it was all she could do not to giggle. It wasn't that she thought Rosey ridiculous; it was just that everything seemed funny.

The only thing she could think of was a story Rosey's father had told her.

An elderly British friend of the Greys had told them that when she married, her mother had told her to make sure her winter nightgowns had fur around the hems.

"Why?" asked the perplexed young lady.

"Because," answered Mummy, "you'll want to keep your neck warm."

Sadie bit her lip. Rosey was still kissing her breasts and her neck and shoulders. He would never understand if she burst out laughing. He would think she was laughing at him.

"Oh, Sadiebelle, I love you so," he moaned softly as he raised his body on top of hers.

It only made her feel like giggling. She bit her lip even harder, made a slight choking noise which she disguised as part cough, part moan, and relaxed her body.

He took first one knee, then the other and pushed her legs apart, putting both his knees together in between hers. Then he entered her gently, thrusting methodically as he did so.

"Ohhhh, God, that's so good," he said.

"Uhhhhmmmmmm," she responded. If she kept making noises it would be easier not to laugh.

Now he was kissing her on the lips, his mouth opened wider. She pulled her mouth away from his and began kissing him on his shoulder, biting his shoulder. It stifled her laughter.

He was leaning his face over her shoulder now, thrusting in and out determinedly.

Finally she could feel him begin to pant heavily, and as his whole body gyrated he cried out. Then his body shuddered and fell relaxed and heavy on top of hers. She was surprised to find that there were tears coming out of her eyes, trickling down her cheeks and onto the side of his face.

"You're crying?" he half-asked. "Oh, Sadie sweetheart, I do love you. You know that, darlin', don't you? I don't know what I would do without you. I really don't."

What was she crying about? One minute she was drunk and dizzy and giggling, the next minute she was in tears. She didn't feel sad really. Well, maybe a little. Mostly she was frightened and confused. Glad that she had Rosey and that he loved her. So glad and so grateful.

"I love you too, angel," she whispered, as she wiped her wet cheek on his and stroked the side of his head.

A dream woke her again. This time it was only three in the morning. Rosey had gotten up and moved to the other bed.

It had scared her. She and the dark curly-haired man were lying in a van with a glass dome watching the fireworks. They were naked and she could feel his body pressed up against hers as they watched the sparkles and flames and plumes shoot through the air. Her limbs felt hot; her body was trembling. He reached over and lightly brushed her abdomen, up upon her breasts. The desire was overwhelming. He leaned over to kiss her, his lips forcing her mouth open, his tongue finding its way between her teeth. "I can't," she said. "Please, no, stop. I can't do this to Rosey. I can't do it to him."

When she woke up she was trembling, and she found her hand between her legs, still sticky. She moved her hand up and down, caressing herself until she found herself breathing faster. Her body trembled, and she quickly drew her hand away and closed her legs, satisfied.

Immediately she drifted off into a deep sleep.

It hurt when she opened her eyes. Her head ached from behind her eyeballs. Her mouth was like the inside of a dry sock. She felt she couldn't swallow or she would throw up. Rosey was sitting on the edge of the bed shaking her.

"Darlin', it's time to get up. We'll be late."

"Late?" she muttered. "Late for what?"

Through the squint in her eyes she could see that Rosey was already dressed. He was wearing a crisp white shirt and a black-and-white-striped tie. His hair was slicked back and still wet from the shower.

He leaned over and kissed her forehead, pushing back her tousled curls from the pillow.

She remembered before he reminded her.

"Oh, shit," she said. "Don't tell me. Church."

"Sadie."

"Sorry, angel," she said.

She tried to sit up, then flopped back.

"Oh, God, I don't believe it. I feel awful."

"Could it be, my sweetheart, that you had a bit too much last night?" He didn't seem angry. Even vaguely amused. He was always in a pretty good mood after he had gotten laid. They weren't very active sexually, but Rosey thought he had a great sex life. He was always very loving afterward.

"What makes you say that?" She was lying on her back, her hand placed over her eyes to block out the light.

"Because you could hardly stand up without falling over when I came in and because you had to put your foot on the floor to steady yourself when we got into bed."

She raised her hand and looked straight at him. She never gave him the benefit of the doubt. He was always surprising her.

He was laughing now, standing at the foot of the bed and grinning at her.

"You thought I'd be mad at you, didn't you, darlin'? So I just played along as though I thought you were perfectly all right. You should have seen yourself. You were something. Trying to act all sober and coy, curling up in my arms."

"You didn't say anything because you wanted to be made love to, that's why," she accused.

"Well, missy, you may just be right. Now come on and get out of the bed, 'cause we've got to go to church. I have spoken to the good bishop and he is expecting us. Apparently they're going to have a small reception for us afterwards."

"Ohhhh, please," she moaned. "Please don't make me go to

church. Please. I'll do anything to get out of going to church. Besides, I'm about to get the curse. 'I'm so very sorry, Bishop, but you see the Vice President's wife was unable to make the services this morning because she had menstrual cramps.'"

"Nice try, darlin'," he said, laughing, then looked more serious. "I do believe you are in worse shape than I thought. What did you girls drink last night, anyway?"

"Don't worry," she assured him. "This is a very expensive hangover. Only the finest wine."

He pulled her reluctantly out of the bed.

"I'm terribly sorry, Bishop, but you see the Vice President's wife was unable to attend because she had a bloody awful hangover this morning."

He thought it over in mock seriousness. "Nope. I just don't think it'll work, darlin'. I just think you'll have to get dressed and walk proudly and with dignity on my arm down the aisle. How 'bout if I call downstairs and get the stewards to whip up a mess o' grits for my sweetheart this morning? It might absorb some of those fumes."

He was in his jesting, St. Anthony Hall mode this morning. She couldn't remember him being this playful in a long time. It was too bad that she felt so awful or she might have enjoyed it.

Instead, all she could do was to stagger to the bathroom and grab the bottle of Tylenol and splash cold water on her face before she got into her bath.

Now it was time to start being perfect.

The idea of a Bloody Mary after church was the only thing that got her through. She really didn't like the National Cathedral, and she did not look forward to spending every Sunday morning there for the next four years. But Rosey was insistent. He was a serious Episcopalian and had been religious about going every Sunday in Richmond even before he got involved in politics. The National Cathedral was the High Episcopal church in Washington, the obvious choice for him. It was too big, with all that gray, cold-looking stone inside, to please her. She liked cozy little Presbyterian churches with sun pouring in.

She kept her head down in church and barely got through the reception afterward until Rosey took mercy on her. It was only once they were in the limousine that she realized she was perspiring, that her forehead was damp and the curls around her face had begun sticking to her head.

"Score one against Miss Perfect," she mumbled to herself out loud.

The stewards had prepared a light lunch after church as the Halls had asked them to do, but they were clearly not very happy. They were even less happy when Rosey told them that as soon as they moved in they would be having a large Sunday dinner in the middle of the day and invite people over. In Richmond they had always had Sunday dinner at G and Miz G's, much to Sadie's chagrin. But it was family, and usually they had a big group, so it was never too bad.

She resisted the idea of having another Bloody Mary as she picked at her omelette.

After lunch she excused herself and went upstairs for a nap, leaving Rosey to disappear with Everett Dubois, his right-hand man, into the back office. It was just as well, since Sadie despised Everett. Besides, she needed a rest if she was going to be able to get through dinner with George Hall later that evening. She couldn't remember having felt this awful in years. Sunday, she decided, was a lost day. As she drifted off to sleep she made a note to call Lorraine and thank her for the dinner. Lorraine would have talked to Chessy about the party afterward with Des. She would be full of news. Sadie would definitely call Lorraine later. In fact, she couldn't wait.

"My dear, you certainly were in top form last night."

Sadie was barely awake when Lorraine called.

"Lorraine?"

"Oh, Sadie, did I wake you up? You sound sleepy."

"No, no," she said quickly. "I was just dozing."

"I'm sure I could have used a little nap too." Lorraine laughed. "I had a dreadful headache this morning. In fact, I still haven't got out of bed. Sweet Irma brought me an ice pack for my head and some Alka-Seltzer. I did glance at the front page of *The Daily*, though. I noticed that Allison Sterling had the lead story on the new Cabinet. It doesn't have her byline on it. But she wrote it."

"If it doesn't have a byline, how can you tell?" asked Sadie.

"Her name is in the box at the end of the story. It's just a matter of learning how to read the paper. I'll teach you how to do that. You'll be an expert in no time. But just a little primer for now. Allison, as you are well aware, is Roger Kimball's god-daughter, which means that she has now got the ear of the most powerful man in the world. If a story this definitive appears in *The Daily,* you can be sure that they had Allison check it."

"Then why wouldn't her byline be on it?"

"Because then everyone would know that she got the story and it would look like conflict of interest."

"But they know anyway, if you're right."

"Ah, yes; but this way they can't really point the finger and *The Daily* is safe on accuracy."

Sadie was still a little groggy, but what Lorraine was saying didn't seem to make a whole lot of sense to her.

"I don't get it. Why would her being Roger's goddaughter"—she would have to start saying "the President"—"make her guilty of conflict of interest? She hasn't done anything wrong."

"You're dealing with tribal shibboleths, Sadie. Journalists have their own set of values and customs and ethics. The public doesn't really care that much. But you watch. Allison is going to be in for a very tough time. Much tougher than she thinks. And it's going to be her colleagues who will give it to her, not the public. She can't appear to be flacking for Roger Kimball; she can't afford to look as if she favors the President or is in his pocket in any way. I suspect they'll take her off the White House immediately. And I imagine that if anyone writes tough stories about the new Administration it will be Allison, just to prove something. I can't wait to see what Des has written for *The Weekly.* I hope for their sakes he doesn't have a Cabinet story. It could be very difficult for them if they are both covering the Presidency. You don't have to be stupid to figure out which one of them will get the most inside stories."

Sadie hadn't thought about that. She couldn't imagine any-thing worse in the entire world than to be in direct competition with the man you loved. The idea of having to lose and lose deliberately all the time would be terribly demoralizing. And to Sadie's mind, there could be no alternative to losing.

"Do me a favor, darling," said Lorraine to her pupil. "As soon as we hang up I want you to go and read the paper. Look at Allison's story. You'll understand. Then read Worth Elgin's col-umn in the View section. It's a valentine to John T. Hooker."

"The head of the Senate Foreign Relations Committee?"

"That's right. He has been wooing Hooker for years. John T. is one of his best sources. He is Worth's candidate for Secretary of State. A long shot, since he is so controversial. But if he gets it, Worth will be set up for the whole Administration—and so, I hate to say, will be his adorable wife, Claire. Claire is probably addressing the envelopes for the invitations to the first party in honor of John T. just in case."

"Lord," said Sadie.

"It all goes with the territory. Now, darling, I know all this is a little much, especially on a Sunday afternoon when one is trying to recover from a hangover, so I'll give you one juicy morsel. Then I really must hang up. Archie will expect me to put something on for our supper."

"What?"

"Well, I absolutely swore not to breathe a word to anybody."

Sadie laughed. That was Lorraine's code for "It's not all that confidential."

"I swear."

Lorraine lowered her voice. "I hear that Claire Elgin is having an affair with our own Senator Bud Corwin. And as far as I'm concerned they deserve each other. Bud Corwin has never been in love with anybody but Bud Corwin in his entire life. And Claire is such a fool. . . . It is absolutely impossible for anybody to have an affair in Washington without getting caught. Period. This is Lorraine's Law. Ah, it certainly is going to be an interesting fall. And what with that one and Sonny and Des . . ." She paused for effect. This was the first time Lorraine had acknowledged that one so openly.

Sadie for some reason did not want to discuss Sonny and Des. She changed the subject. "Are you a good friend of Claire's?"

"Of course I'm a good friend of Claire's. I'm one of her closest friends in Washington. Unfortunately, she wants to be a great hostess and have an affair. I am Claire's friend as I am everybody's friend. One cannot be a great hostess in Washington and have enemies."

"But if you think she's a fool . . ."

"Most people in Washington are. There must be some who think *I* am. Claire just happens to be a worse fool than most. Nobody's perfect."

"Oh, Lorraine, you make me laugh; you really are funny."

Just then Rosey came into the bedroom. Sadie hated talking on the phone when he was around. She apologized to Lorraine, telling her she had to get off the phone.

"Not before I tell you one thing," Lorraine said. "I want to warn you of something, Sadie." Her voice had suddenly grown serious. Sadie sat up a little more in bed.

"Claire, like many others in this town, will try to befriend you. She can be very seductive and very cozy. Take my word for it. I wouldn't trust her as far as I could throw her."

"Lorraine, you've been so helpful. I really can't thank you enough."

"Oh, yes, you can, darling. We'll talk."

Dinner with the Vice President was quiet and pleasant. George Hall was supportive and encouraging to Rosey. He seemed calm and relaxed. And Sadie felt reassured.

"How is it that you look younger than when you came into office?" asked Sadie.

"Governor, I have to say your wife is not only lovely but very intelligent as well."

"But I'm serious," insisted Sadie. "Neither of you has that desperate look that outgoing Presidents and Vice Presidents usually have. You look happy and relaxed. Please tell us your secret. I'm already beginning to feel the tension and I've only been here for a weekend."

"Well, Sadie, you are asking a serious question and there is a serious answer."

"Well said," said Rosey. He was very quiet, taking it all in.

"This is directed more to you, Sadie," said Hall. "This is a fascinating and tantalizing place. And there are some really expert game players. Some people feel there's no point to being here if you're not going to get in there and play. I'm just too old for all that, so I never got into it the way some do. Because it's a dangerous game. Careers and reputations can be made or destroyed by it, and if you want to be dramatic, lives can be saved or lost; countries can be destroyed or built. If you're going to be part of it, it's like playing blackjack at the highest stakes with the most brilliant opponents. And in Washington nobody stops to pick up the wounded. The most dangerous part is the gossip. It's considered fun and exciting, and it's deadly. I don't mean to

frighten you, but I think it is terribly important for both of you—
particularly you, Sadie—that you understand. The gossip is seductive, and I apologize for saying this but I couldn't help but
overhear that Lorraine Hadley had called you this afternoon. I
want to tell you that she is one of the cleverest and most ambitious players in Washington. She won't want to lose you. She can
be great fun; her parties are the best in Washington. But the most
important thing to know about this city is who to trust."

The next morning she saw the *Daily* story about the Cabinet.
It was all over the radio as they took the limousine to the airport
to return to Richmond. That afternoon she saw the *Weekly* cover
story. Shaw had three of the Cabinet names wrong. It made her
feel sick. It also made her feel excited. She couldn't figure out
either emotion.

CHAPTER 4

THIS WAS NOT HER MILIEU. NEVERTHELESS, IT was a coup for Lorraine to be involved, even if Des Shaw had insisted on having the party at Nora, a rather dreary little restaurant near Dupont Circle, an iffy neighborhood. But it was "in" because journalists hung out there. You had to pretend to adore it. It was everything Lorraine hated. As far as Archie was concerned, it was out of the question. "You eat there and I'll eat at the Metropolitan Club," said Archie firmly, "and frankly, my dear, I think it is reverse snobbism and highly hypocritical of you to pretend to like it. It has nothing to recommend it. And that includes the patrons."

It had been an eventful eight months since the election even by Lorraine's standards.

The Greys had taken Washington by storm, and she felt some of the credit was hers. Sadie was proving an excellent protégée; her grasp of the city in such a short time was impressive. As for Rosey, he had managed to inspire the confidence of the President and his staff—no mean feat for a Vice President—and with no apparent effort had established himself as a figure of power. Their skills, their looks, and their money made these two a combination to be reckoned with.

Des Shaw was ending his twenty-five-year marriage with Chessy. She hadn't had a chance against Allison. Now Des was the flamboyant and aggressive Bureau Chief of *The Weekly* and Allison the famous and controversial *Daily* reporter and goddaughter of the President. The two of them were the stuff of legends.

And they were all Lorraine's best friends.

As if that weren't enough, the honeymoon was over in Kimball's Administration. The President was an amiable professor who couldn't have organized his way out of a paper bag. When his staffers feuded, Kimball went off to his family quarters and locked himself in his study, leaving word that he was not to be disturbed unless the Russians were coming. The press was off and running. Scapegoats were sought out, victims chosen, sides drawn. The whole thing made Lorraine shiver with pleasure. It was the beginning of July—normally a time when things start to get dull in Washington—and there was the smell of blood in the water. People were in a state of lustful anticipation. What perfect timing for a party! Everyone would be in great spirits. What luck. Something ghastly just before the party.

This time it was the President's Chief of Staff, Addison Marbury, formerly on the faculty of the University of Colorado with Roger Kimball before Kimball had gone into politics. He was of good old New England stock, an excellent mind but short on balls, as they say in the trade.

Anybody who had lived six months in Washington knew that it was essential for the President's Chief of Staff to be a killer.

Addison Marbury had proved a disaster. One of Marbury's assistants, and a Harry Saks protégé, Kurt Weyhauser, had even gone into Marbury's office at lunchtime and moved his desk out into the hallway.

Now, in the week before the Fourth of July weekend, the whole town was waiting for the ax to fall. *The Daily* had had stories on the front page every day, and the Living section had reports of parties where the talk was of nothing else. How could anyone compete with Lorraine when she had this kind of luck?

It was a coincidence that Sonny Sterling and Sadie Grey had the same birthday, though they were four years apart.

Lorraine had had an idea for a joint party more than a month ago, and she had gone to Des Shaw and the Vice President to help her plan it. She was rather surprised when they both agreed. She had assumed it would be at her house, but Shaw wanted the party on neutral ground, and he had insisted on sharing the cost. Rosey had gone along in a rather distracted way. "I'm sure whatever you all decide will be fine."

The guest list, of course, was a problem. Lorraine and Des struggled over it. This would be one of the most sought-after invitations of the season. Lorraine had a lot of people she owed. Shaw insisted on having all those dreary *Boston Gazette* people who drank too much. Lorraine wanted a good mix of politicians and Administration types; Des wanted to keep that to a minimum. Lorraine wanted to sprinkle an ambassador or two. Des vetoed that. So she compromised except on a few crucial points. And she found that all she had to do was say that Sadie liked somebody and he capitulated.

So the guest list was eclectic. Des would have Sadie on his right. Rosey would be between Lorraine and Sonny. Des told Lorraine she could do the rest; he would just like to be sure she didn't put any of her friends next to his buddies. Lorraine practically drew names from a hat for the seating.

There was one thing troubling her which she had not discussed with Des. Sonny and Sadie had not exactly developed a great mutual fondness and she had never really been able to bring them together. Lorraine suspected that they were jealous of each other.

It had been clear to her from the beginning how the two felt about each other. Yet here were the men in their lives leaping at the idea of this party. It was probably as simple as the fact that men never really knew how to celebrate the women they loved and were happy for an idea when it came up, no matter what it was.

The question of the President had arisen. Lorraine had brought it up, trembling with anticipation. She had yet to have a President of the United States. Granted the party was not being held in her house, but she was doing the arranging and the organizing. She would be dealing with the White House appointments secretary, the social secretary, the press secretaries. From then on they would all be sure to know her. This entrée would make it easier for her to invite them at some later time.

She always hated those awkward moments at the door when you had to introduce yourself to your guests—or worse, they had to introduce themselves to you. Everyone did it; it was perfectly acceptable. Still, it was preferable to be acquainted with one's guests.

Rosey and Des had agreed that the President should be invited.

Lorraine was still working on the logistics as Leo, her driver, took her over to Nora that evening. As he drove the sparkling brown Mercedes up past Massachusetts Avenue and the grand old Cosmos Club, Lorraine thought how much Washington had changed. There was this impressive old white stone building, once an imposing private residence in the best part of town. Now it was a private men's club for "intellectuals" who were long since out of fashion with the important and powerful elite of Washington. It seemed ironic that the new "club" in Washington, only a block away on the corner, would be so different. A tiny little red brick building with a glass front, Nora had a makeshift frame of railroad ties on the sidewalk in front, enclosing a small kitchen garden.

Inside, its exposed brick walls, large bar, quilts hanging from the walls, shelves of country artifacts, and small tables covered with French country prints were a testament to its studied informality.

Most of the luncheon customers had left, and the Secret Service was swarming over the place to ready it for the President's visit. The waiters had begun rearranging the tables.

Everything was humming along to Lorraine's satisfaction. And the best part was that Archie had already gone to his family's summer house at Fishers Island. It was going to be a good party.

Allison couldn't figure out why Des was behaving so oddly all day. She had called him several times at the office and he seemed distracted. Was he fighting with Chessy over money? The divorce seemed interminable. It had been a year since he'd told her he wanted out and she had moved back to New York, yet they still weren't speaking. It made her wonder about marriage. Marriage was something she hadn't contemplated seriously for a very long time, not since Nick. Only now that she and Des were living together—though he still kept the house on Twenty-first Street—did she occasionally start thinking how easy and convenient it would be if they were married. She usually brushed those thoughts away. Listening to Des's tales of hassling with his lawyers and her lawyers made the whole idea of divorce demeaning. After twenty-five years, two dignified people were haggling over petty details of money, and it had nothing to do with what they were haggling over at all.

He had been acting mysterious and secretive, and she thought it must be about her birthday. He was obviously going to give her something special. He was not a great present-giver. For Christmas he had gone to Bendel's and bought her a big hand-knit mohair sweater. It would have been perfect for Chessy. She had managed to wear it a few times when they were at home alone together. She had bought him a new Burberry which had set her back six hundred dollars. Naturally he was embarrassed.

She was preparing herself to be disappointed tomorrow. One thing she was relieved about was that he wasn't going to give her a birthday party. "No surprises," she had warned him. "I loathe surprises. They are a hostile act."

"Baby?"

"Yep."

"You up for tonight?"

"Not particularly."

"Now, come on, Sonny. Don't be such a downer. It'll be fun."

Allison signed her story off on the computer and cradled the phone. "I still don't believe this. I can't believe you really want to do this. It's so uncharacteristic."

"Keep 'em guessing. It would be awful to have you always know exactly what I'm thinking and doing. A little mystery is important."

"Don't you have some work to do at your office? It's Thursday. There is a magazine to get out."

"Oh, I'm not worried. It'll get out without me."

"That's not what you usually say. How come you can get Thursday night off? I thought you had to be there until midnight every Thursday. Or have you been staying late so you can get a blow job from your secretary?"

"Poor Mabel. She would faint to hear you say something like that. She's a good Christian."

"Poor Mabel."

"Sonny, I can't understand what's gotten into you."

"Go screw yourself."

"I am getting the impression that you're not exactly thrilled with the prospect of tonight's dinner."

"What would lead you to conclude that?"

"Intuition."

"Look, Des, I've agreed to go. I just don't understand what we're doing taking the Vice President and his wife to dinner at Nora. It seems phony. Nora is no place for them. In fact, just why *are* we doing this? Sadie Grey will probably be dressed to the teeth. I have a good mind to wear jeans. And it looks like we're sucking up to them."

"I told you. When I was talking to Sadie at the Elgins' she told me that all she heard about was Nora, that she would love to go there. So I said why didn't they join us for dinner there one night and she said 'Great, when?' Well, what was I supposed to do?"

"You didn't have to come up with a date."

"I didn't. She said they were going to have to be here for the fireworks on the White House lawn tomorrow and then they were going up to their house in East Hampton. The Vice President had been traveling a lot and this was one of their few free nights. Gimme a break. I was caught."

"And I bet you hated every minute of it, too."

"What's that supposed to mean?"

"I don't suppose you've lost your senses of sight, smell, hearing, taste, and touch?"

"I give up. What are you talking about?"

"I am talking about the fact that Sadie Grey has the hots for you."

"That's ridiculous."

"God, men are so dumb sometimes I just don't believe it. When she bats those great big turquoise eyes at you and tosses that mane of auburn curls and implies that you're just the 'handsomes', stronges' ol' devil theah evah was in this great big ol' world,' you go limp."

"Better limp than hard," said Shaw, laughing.

"Funny."

"Look, I think she's an attractive woman. In case you've forgotten, she happens to be married to the Vice President of the United States, who also happens to be a pretty attractive guy."

"I think he's a wimp."

"She obviously doesn't."

"I'm telling you she is not in love with him. I bet she hasn't had a good lay in her entire life. She's hungry and she's got the sign out. And she's got it out for you."

"Hey, darlin'."

"Uh-huhhh."

"What's the matter, Sadie?"

"Oh, nothing. I just wondered if we really had to go to this restaurant tonight. We've got a big day tomorrow with all the fireworks, and then we'll be leaving for East Hampton the next day."

"But you've been dying to see Nora."

"I know, but . . . we don't really know Des and Allison that well. I'm not sure that they aren't using us in some way."

"I think they're trying to be friendly."

"Friendly?"

"I told you how it happened. I was talking to Sonny . . ."

"Sonny? Since when do you call her Sonny?"

"Oh, for God's sake, Sadie. Everybody calls her Sonny. That's her nickname."

"*I* don't call her Sonny."

"Well, I can't help that. I was giving her an interview several weeks ago and she suggested it would be nice if we could get together."

"It just seems that nobody in Washington ever does anything for no reason."

"Oh, for God's sake, that's Lorraine talking. She is turning you into a very cynical person, and I don't like it one damn bit."

"I don't think it's cynical to recognize it. I heard your conversation with Allison at the Elgins'. She was asking you confidential things about the White House."

"Listen, Allison is a good reporter. But I'm not exactly stupid either. Besides, I don't think she's after information for the paper. I think she is worried about her godfather."

"If you believe that, you'll believe anything."

* * *

Des had agreed to invite the British Ambassador and his wife. "Rodney Abel-Smith bores my ass," he told Lorraine, "but Edwina is a piece. No other ambassadors." Lorraine wanted John T. Hooker, the Secretary of State. Des thought that was excessive, but Lorraine had prevailed. "Okay," said Des finally. "He's a rogue. I like the old son-of-a-bitch. He's going to keep things lively. Sure, let's have him." To Lorraine's delight, Des wanted Malcolm Sohier, the attractive junior Senator from Massachusetts, and his wife, Abigail. The Sohiers were old Boston—Beacon Hill, Somerset Club. Des had covered Sohier when he ran for the House, then for the Senate. Lorraine had not really gotten to know the Sohiers. She had invited them in the past but they had never accepted. Lorraine suspected that they didn't want to get involved. The Sohiers picked and chose.

The guests, who had been told to arrive promptly at seven thirty, included a slew of Allison's and Des's friends whom Lorraine did not know. But Rosey's list was almost identical to hers. That didn't surprise Lorraine, since she had introduced Sadie to almost all her new friends. It had been decided by all that they would not invite out-of-town guests. This was to be a simple evening.

Des and Lorraine met at Nora early to go over the final arrangements. President Kimball was arriving at eight. Nora looked like a stakeout for a mob drug bust. Lorraine's heart beat faster as she saw the police and agents. She was part of the real thing tonight. This was power. This was the stuff of life.

"Here comes the Vice President," said Des.

William Rosewell Grey walked through the double swinging doors of Nora and into the brick front room. He smiled politely when he saw Des and Lorraine standing at the top of the short flight of stairs.

"Well," he said. "Well, everything certainly looks fine. My congratulations, Lorraine. It looks splendid."

"You look about as nervous as I do, old man," said Des. "I guess I'm just not cut out for the role of hostess with the mostes'."

"I must say," said Rosey with a sympathetic smile, "you're pale as a sheet. You look the way I feel."

"You think this is a good idea, huh?" said Des to Lorraine.

"If you two don't cut it out you're going to start making me nervous."

One of the waiters approached Des and Rosey and asked if they could advise on the bar. After discussing the bar arrangements and complimenting Lorraine, Rosey and Des kissed her goodbye and headed out the door.

They stepped out onto the sidewalk and looked at each other. They both wore summer suits. The temperature had to be nearly a hundred degrees, and the humidity was unbearable. Though it was almost seven thirty, the sun was still shining, and the perspiration began to appear on both their brows—and it wasn't just the heat. They took out handkerchiefs and wiped their foreheads, put their handkerchiefs back into their pockets, and burst out laughing.

"What do you think, Mr. Vice President?"

"I think this could be a disaster."

"I'm with you."

They shook hands solemnly like soldiers going into battle together. The Vice President stepped into his waiting limousine. Des walked around the corner to the house on Twenty-first Street and got into his old white Thunderbird convertible. "Get more pussy with this baby than you can get flies with honey," he muttered routinely to himself as he patted the car on the dash and turned the corner into Florida Avenue.

Allison was in a grim mood as they drove over to Shaw's house. He took the long way around Dupont Circle and up Nineteenth. "Traffic jam on Florida," he said.

They parked in front of Shaw's cream-colored town house and walked slowly around the corner to Nora.

When they got to the door it was clear that something was going on.

"Jesus," said Allison, "what's going on here?"

The President and Mrs. Kimball stepped out of the crowd where they had been waiting with their backs turned, and everyone shouted, "Surprise, surprise, surprise."

Allison put one hand to her hair, the other to her skirt. She was wearing a pale blue linen skirt and matching knit top—

pretty, but not necessarily what one would wear to a party in one's honor. The President came over to her and put his arms around her. "Happy Birthday, honey," he said in a voice loud enough that everyone could hear. "We love you."

"I don't believe it," said Allison finally. The President seemed pleased.

"It's a surprise party, babe," whispered Des.

"You bastard," whispered Allison as she smiled radiantly.

She saw Jenny Stern, her best friend on the national staff.

"Do I look all right?"

"You look gorgeous, as usual."

"Well, there's nothing I can do about it. I might as well have a good time. This is better than dinner with Rosey and Sadie Grey."

Before Jenny could ask what she was talking about, the door opened to the Greys.

"Oh, noooo," said Allison.

"Surprise, surprise, surprise," shouted the crowd.

The President turned toward the door and walked over to kiss Sadie Grey. "Happy Birthday, Sadie," he said.

She put her hands to her hair.

"Oh, my God, I don't believe it." She looked up at Rosey. "Did you plan this?"

"I sure did."

"You sweet thing."

As Roger Kimball was greeting her, she looked up and saw Allison Sterling on the landing, Des beside her, his arm around her waist.

Lorraine was next to Sadie.

"So we really are having dinner with Allison and Des?" she said.

Des and Allison were pushed toward the Greys. Allison was smiling. Sadie maintained her grin. Her cheeks hurt.

"Hey, Des!" the *Weekly* photographer shouted. "Can I get a picture of the birthday girls with the President?"

"Relax, Gonzalez."

Sadie looked stricken. "Birthday girls? What do you mean, birthday girls?"

"Well," said Rosey, "it's Allison's birthday as well. So we thought . . ."

Sadie stared at Lorraine. "Why, what a wonderful idea.

Did you know it was my birthday too, Allison?" she asked sweetly.

"It's as much of a surprise to me as it is to you."

"Well, then, the party is a success," said Roger Kimball. He put his arms around them as the photographer snapped. Some guests clapped.

"My two favorite girls in Washington," said the President. "And the two prettiest girls I know."

"Girls!" said Allison, rolling her eyes.

"I don't mind being called a girl," said Sadie. "At our age, Allison, we ought to be flattered."

Allison knew she was four years younger than Sadie. She bit her lip to keep from asking Sadie her age in front of everyone.

Nobody approached them. They appeared to be deep in conversation, and people were hesitant to interrupt.

Allison, who had been nervous all day about a story on the power play at the White House, had been hesitant to try to speak to the President. But now she couldn't resist this opportunity. Pulling him aside, she whispered, "What's going on, Uncle Rog, with Marbury and Weyhauser?"

Kimball sighed and looked visibly tired, clearly reluctant to answer. His face suddenly looked a mass of wrinkles, and his shoulders sagged. Allison was instantly sorry she had mentioned it.

"Oh, poor man," said Sadie, and turned to the President. "Let's not bring up something unpleasant when the President's here to have a good time and celebrate our birthdays."

The President looked at Sadie with gratitude.

Kimball spotted Howard Heinrich coming toward him.

"Howard!" he called out.

Howard Heinrich strode over. The two men shook hands. Clearly Kimball liked this tall, dark-haired, elegant-looking man with the graying sideburns and the perpetual smile.

"Mr. President." He bowed his head slightly.

"Where the hell have you been the last two days? You're supposed to be the Special Counsel to the President and you're never there when I need you."

Kimball was smiling, but there was a serious tone in his voice.

"I've been out on the Coast looking into a certain project we discussed last week, Mr. President."

"Oh, yes."

"I only just got off the plane. In time to wish these two lovely ladies Happy Birthday." He beamed at the women and quickly turned back to the President. He had spent enough time on the "ladies." He spoke more frankly than he normally would at a party, but he knew he could trust the Vice President's wife. He knew too that he could trust the President's goddaughter: he was one of Allison's best sources. Heinrich was also one of the most powerful men in Washington, a survivor in a city where that was a number one attribute. Those who survived in Washington beyond two administrations were automatically part of the Establishment, whatever their party. The Establishment was a club in which everybody got along, a club where ideology was never a priority. Those who burned with political passion when they arrived in Washington left whatever administration they had come in with tempered and mellowed. Even reporters mellowed over the years. Those who'd been in town longest had watched their moral outrage turn into healthy cynicism.

Nobody knew what Heinrich's politics was or whether he had any. Women liked him because he was fun to flirt with. Men liked him because he could talk locker-room politics, knew how to play the game. Nobody trusted him, nobody who was a member of the club. Roger Kimball, obviously, was not a member of the club. He was only the President.

"Mr. President," said Heinrich. "I don't think you have a damn thing to worry about. I think you just handled the Marbury thing beautifully. You'll get a couple of bad days in the press. There'll be some fallout, but not much."

"Yeah, yeah," said the President, nodding. Heinrich was telling him what he wanted to hear.

"The only thing that's too bad is that it happened when it did. Fourth of July week, middle of the summer, slow news. These guys will go with anything in the summer—right, Allison?"

Allison was annoyed but admiring. Heinrich was talking to the President about exactly what she had just tried for, only to be rebuffed. She had asked; Heinrich had offered.

Sadie was amused. She adored sitting next to Howard Heinrich at dinner parties for this very reason.

Before Allison could answer, Senator Bud Corwin and his wife, Helene, had approached the President. "Mr. President," said Corwin, an adulatory grin on his face.

"Mr. President," cooed Helene. "What fun to see you at such an informal gathering. And how lucky these two are. What an honor!"

"Unfortunately, I can't stay," said the President. "In fact"—he glanced at his watch, then looked up at his chief agent and nodded—"it's just about time for me to be going. I have to speak to the National Education Association in about half an hour."

"Oh, no, you mean you're not staying," said Sadie. "What a disappointment!"

"Well, if you, uh, women could get your boys"—he grinned —"to plan ahead, I might have been able to fit it in."

"I'm just kidding," he said apologetically. "I've had this one on the books since right after the inauguration. Now I've got to find Molly."

He left Allison and Sadie standing there with the Corwins while he quickly went to the bar and got his wife and brought her back. "Sorry I have to go and miss this good party."

He leaned over and kissed Allison on the cheek, then gave her a big hug. For a moment it seemed that his eyes were misting over.

"I remember when you were just a tiny girl. Now look at you! Sometimes I just can't believe it. I'm real proud of you, Sonny. You know that, don't you?"

Allison felt her throat constrict.

"Sadie, you're a beautiful thing. Don't let that husband of yours forget it. Now, I want you to have a happy birthday too, you understand?"

He leaned down and kissed her on the cheek, then took his wife's hand and departed with his phalanx of Secret Service agents.

There was a general sense of relaxation after the President left. Though the Vice President's Secret Service agents were there, it wasn't the production it was with the President. And the agents hung back more or less discreetly.

Rosey walked over to Sadie. "It's time to see some of your guests before we sit down to dinner in a few minutes. The President stayed longer than we expected." He grabbed her hand and took her over to the Sohiers.

Des saw Allison standing there as Rosey and Sadie excused themselves, and he came to take Allison up the stairs to O'Grady and the *Boston Gazette* crowd.

"Jesus H. Christ," said O'Grady, "I'm really surprised the President came. He's been keeping a low profile all week. He could have pleaded the banquet. He looks terrible. He's really hurting, so my sources tell me."

"Did you see Heinrich working him over?" said Allison. She wanted to change the subject.

"Jesus," said Des, "that Heinrich fries my ass."

"You gotta give him credit, though. He knows how to deal with the big boys," said O'Grady.

"Yeah, I suppose. But I still don't see why anybody trusts the son-of-a-bitch."

"Well, shit, Shaw, you trust him," said O'Grady. "He's one of your best sources."

"How do you know that?"

"Because he's one of mine," said O'Grady, smiling. "And I'll bet you a lunch at the Maison Blanche that he's also a very hot source for our own Miss Sterling."

"He's yours too?" gasped Allison in mock horror. "My God, is there nobody in this town we can trust?"

"Uh-oh," said O'Grady. "Look at the Corwins kissing the Greys' ass. They're giving Heinrich a run for his money."

"Why don't we edge over there and see if we can hear what they're saying," said Allison. "I'll bet it's enough to make you gag."

"Well, sir," Senator Corwin was whispering, "what do you make of this week's little episode at the White House? Rather unfortunate, wouldn't you say?"

"Well," said Rosey carefully, "there's always a little settling in to do, as you know better than anyone. I think it will work out."

"But don't you think it affects the President's appearance of capacity for leadership?"

Heinrich put his arm on Corwin and leaned over to his ear. "This has hurt the President, between you and me. You just can't have people behaving as if the White House is some sort of day-care center, now, can you?"

Corwin looked properly flattered that Heinrich had chosen to confide in him. Rosey had not heard what Heinrich was saying, but Sadie had. Even though she thought she had a clear fix on Heinrich, this surprised her. He had told the President fifteen minutes ago that he hadn't been hurt at all. But it was clear that

Corwin wanted to hear that the President was hurt. Corwin had Presidential ambitions. Heinrich didn't want to hedge any bets.

Lorraine was looking frantic. Hooker's office had called to say the Secretary of State would be detained. He was to sit on Sadie's right, and Des was signaling that it was time to eat. "I'll need time to redo the seating," she said. "Can't we just wait five minutes? We're still waiting for Hooker and Harry Saks. I can't understand where they are."

"The hell with Saks," said Des. "I don't like the bastard anyway."

"Well, he *is* the President's domestic adviser. It wouldn't be polite to just sit down now. He's probably tied up with something at the White House."

"Bullshit," said Des. "He just didn't want to get here until the President left. He's still smarting over getting caught in that childish maneuver this week. I'll be surprised if he shows up at all, frankly. He knows if he does he'll never get out of here alive. Let's eat."

"I'll just put Howard Heinrich next to Sadie," Lorraine was saying, and having solved the Hooker problem, she recovered her composure.

Des, however, was agitated. "There is a distinct freezola going on between the 'birthday girls,' and I'm not at all looking forward to the toasts," he said.

"You'll make it, Des," said Lorraine. "I refuse to waste a minute worrying about you." Her eyes darted over his shoulder to the entrance. "Oh, thank God, here come the Sakses! Looking a little sheepish, I might add." Lorraine went off to greet them.

Allison came over to Shaw.

"The host with the most has decided it's time to eat," said Des. "I'll go and start getting people rounded up."

"I suppose we're not going to be able to sit together," said Allison, slipping her arm around his waist.

"Talk to your friend Lorraine—she did the seating," said Des. He was perspiring. Even though the air conditioning was turned as high as it would go, the evening sun pouring in, the heat and humidity, the crowd, and the tension were beginning to get to him.

"Are you all right?"

"Yeah, fine. It's just so bloody hot in here."

"What do you mean, Lorraine did the seating?"

"I mean she put you next to the Vice President and me next to his wife, that's what I mean."

"Oh, great."

"Well, it wasn't my idea. She said it would be tacky to do it any other way."

"I can't believe this. Happy Birthday, Allison."

"I wanted this to be a great surprise and a great party. I can see I've blown it."

"Forget it. It's not your fault. But don't think I'm not going to have my eyes on you every minute."

Des looked relieved even though she was only half-kidding.

"I'll be sure to be on my best behavior."

"Well, I'll just be forced to vamp our fine Vice President tonight."

"Lots o' luck."

"What does that mean?"

"It means that you will be so busy pumping him you'll forget, that's what it means. It also means it would be too humiliating. It's not liberated behavior."

"You don't know your ass from liberation, my love, so let me be the judge of that."

As Allison approached Rosey and Sadie, she noticed that Claire and Worth Elgin had moved in tight so that nobody else could get near them.

"Mr. Vice President," Worth Elgin was saying, "I really would like it if you would consider doing a piece for our Sunday View section. You could write on anything you wanted to. For starters, how about the scene at the White House this week?" This was his attempt at humor. Rosey responded with a weak smile.

"I must say, Sadie, you look heavenly," Claire Elgin was saying. "So fresh and cool and . . ." She giggled. She didn't say, ". . . so sexy."

Sadie's flowered-cotton bodice showed off her ample bosom in a most discreet way, though her uneasy husband had tugged at the top on the way to the restaurant.

"You're just so sweet to say so," Sadie said.

"Claire darling," Lorraine said, "I'm terribly sorry, but we're about to sit down for dinner." Claire glared at her. Lorraine's tone had not escaped her.

"Mr. Vice President, will you take Allison to dinner?"

"It will be my pleasure," he said.

As soon as he had said it he glanced nervously at his wife. She leaned over so that Lorraine could not hear and whispered to him, "Be careful what you say to her."

"Oh, Sadie, for goodness' sake."

"I mean it."

"Oh, good Lord," murmured Rosey to himself, "I knew this party was a bad idea."

Des was coming over to fetch her.

"Mrs. Grey," said Des, "I believe I have the honor."

"I don't know why it sounds cheeky when you call me Mrs. Grey," she said.

"But I am cheeky—that's part of my charm."

"Is that what all the girls tell you?"

"In the old days, before I became monogamous."

He had been leading her to their places at the table. There were two long tables running the length of the restaurant. The two guests of honor were seated in the center of the tables with their backs to the walls so that they could see each other directly across the room face to face. As Des and Sadie got to their places, Des glanced up to see Allison making a face at him.

Des said to Sadie, "You were supposed to be seated next to John T., but his office just called to say he'd be late. I wish to hell I knew what's keeping him. Must be something up. Lorraine replaced him with Heinrich."

"That's fine," said Sadie. "I adore watching Howard in action."

"Ah, you've noticed?"

"How could anybody be in Washington more than a week and not catch on to Howard?"

"You're not just a pretty face, Mrs. Grey."

Sadie turned to Howard. "I understand I'm lucky enough to have drawn you. Now, you behave or I'll call Mr. Shaw, here, to my aid."

"Well, I'm just as pleased as I can be to be seated next to the guest of honor," he said. "I had no idea Lorraine would give me . . ." He stopped.

"Such a plum?" asked Des.

"Well, Des, I'm not sure I would put it exactly that way. . . ." Howard seemed relieved when Claire Elgin found her seat on his right and turned to him.

"Now, Howard," they heard her say, "you haven't paid any attention to me all night. Have I lost *all* my looks?"

"Claire, you're still the most beautiful lady in town."

Des and Sadie looked at each other and smiled.

"Made in heaven, the two of them," he said.

"Isn't it sad they couldn't have found each other earlier," said Sadie.

"Oh, I don't know—as a couple they might well have been too overpowering. I think Heinrich does better as a single man. He's got more moves that way. Have you been invited to one of Claire's musicales yet?"

"No. She wants me to come when they get back from the Vineyard in the fall. What are they like?"

"I wouldn't think of spoiling it for you. Besides, there are no words. You won't want to miss one. Watching John T. Hooker snoozing in the back of the room is one of the great sights of Washington. They all show up."

"Why?"

"They all come because Worth is the editor of the *Daily*'s View section. The last time they had a musicale and John T. went, Worth ran a big piece several weeks later saying what an effective Secretary of State he was. You can buy that kind of publicity if you play the game right. You must have observed that."

"Of course. And it's more fun for me. I feel sorry for people who have to put in long hours and then spend the evening working. Because it's hard work. Everything you say or do is watched and recorded. And if you've had a few drinks it can be dangerous. So Rosey has found out. He has enough of a hard time trying to relax, have a Scotch or two, and still be on his guard. And he has to keep an eye on me. I have this unfortunate tendency to be candid from time to time."

"Don't change."

He had said it more seriously than he intended.

Sadie had been sipping her soup, but she looked up. He was looking at her directly. "Well, thank you. It's nice of you to say that. I mean I hope I won't disappoint you." She was flustered by his sincerity. So was he.

"Now do me a favor, will you, and give me a fill on Chessy," he said, changing the subject. "You probably think I'm a real bastard, don't you?"

"No, of course I don't."

"Well, Chessy sure thinks I'm the world's greatest louse."
And Des proceeded to describe to her the reasons he had left his
wife.

There was something about her that made men want to tell her
things. She did not discourage this. She was fascinated with the
way men's minds worked. They were so different. She loved to
listen to men talk about their feelings because Rosey never did.
And because she had never really lived with any man but Rosey,
he was the only example of male behavior that she had observed
close up. She often felt very lonely. Des intrigued her. She was
drawn to him. There was something challenging. She had
thought she would never attract a man like Desmond Shaw; a
man like that would never be interested in someone like her, a
wife. Yet he obviously was in some way. Maybe he was just
playing up to her because of who she was, but she didn't think
so. She had stayed friends with Chessy because she wanted to
know more about him.

"Chess and I hadn't been in business for years," he was saying. "We never should have gotten married in the first place."

"Why did you?"

"Oh, Jesus, we were both so young. I was knocked off my
feet by her. She was the most beautiful thing I had ever seen in
my life. I was an Irish Catholic kid from the South Side. She took
my breath away. She had class, and she liked *me*. My roommate
from B.C. fixed me up with her. He was a dumb rich boy who
couldn't get into Harvard. But he was Catholic, so they took him
at B.C. He spent most of his weekends—and nights, for that
matter—driving around Radcliffe and Wellesley and taking out
rich girls. Then one weekend he invited me down to New York to
his place for the weekend. He took me to my first coming-out
party. Chessy was the debutante, ebony hair and pale skin and
white satin. She was some kind of goddess."

Sadie felt jealous.

"She paid attention to me, and all the guys in their patent
leather shoes with bows and their mid-Atlantic accents were jealous. 'Who's the Mick?' they kept asking Charles, but I didn't
give a damn. Chessy had singled me out and they couldn't stand
it. I was twenty-one years old and in love. The fact that she
wanted to marry me was a miracle. I still don't understand it. We

fought from the moment we said our vows. Her parents were outraged. My parents weren't delighted either.

"We settled in Boston to be away from her parents. I got a job as a reporter on *The Gazette*, where my old man was a printer. I had worked there as a delivery boy and a copy boy. It was a washout. Chess had money, so we could afford an apartment in Back Bay. I was not accepted by her fancy friends. I was not even allowed in the Somerset Club or the Myopia Club or any other club."

"What made you stay together?"

"Sex."

The conversation was making her nervous. She changed the subject.

"Do you have brothers and sisters?"

"One's a priest and the other's a nun."

"Your family was religious?"

"No more, no less than other Irish Catholic families in Boston. Which means yes."

"Now it's beginning to make sense to me why the divorce is not so easy for you."

"Well, I'm glad somebody understands. Allison thinks I should have been divorced yesterday. This is a hell of a thing for me. It's the most difficult thing I've ever done in my life. And I'm not religious. I haven't been to confession since I was twenty-one."

"Why did you stop?"

"I went to confession. I told the priest I'd slept with a virgin. He chewed me out and I lost my temper. I told him, 'You're here to forgive sins, not to lecture.' He told me I was impertinent. I said, 'Hey, Padre, go fuck yourself!' and I walked out."

Sadie was visibly shocked. "Did you feel guilty? I mean aren't you supposed to feel guilty for something like that?"

"I never went back. I'd flunked redemption. Yet I don't feel less Catholic. That's what Sonny doesn't understand."

So, all was not perfect in paradise. She had envied Allison. She stared at him for a moment. He was looking down, taking a bit of food. He seemed vulnerable, and she felt like touching him.

"Jesus," he said. "I've done nothing but talk about myself. Sonny would say I am the typical Washington dinner-party bore. And I want to know about you. How you keep yourself interested in being the Vice President's wife. What are you doing for yourself? I can't believe your historic preservation projects or even Planned Parenthood keep you all that stimulated."

"I have a secret project."

"Aha. I knew I wasn't just guessing."

He was pleased. He looked gorgeous when he laughed.

"You're blushing," he said. "I like that about you. It's an attractive trait. One of your many, I might add. . . . What's the project?"

"I can trust you not to tell?" She almost added: "Allison."

"You can."

"I write."

"You what?"

"I write."

"What do you mean? I mean, what do you write?"

"I write short stories. I've been doing it for years. I used to write for the Smith College literary magazine. You probably know that I went to work for *The Gotham* after college. I was a researcher, but I wrote for Around the Town once in a while, and I wrote stories but I never submitted any. I was there two years when I married and moved to Richmond and had two children and I didn't do much for a while. But ever since Rosey's been in politics I've been writing things. Usually I tear them up. I'm working on one now that I sort of like. I got the idea because of a friend of mine in Savannah . . . I suppose it sounds silly to you. You're a professional and all your friends are. . . . They're probably hopeless—the stories; I've never shown them to anyone."

"Would you let me see them?"

"I shouldn't even have told you I wrote anything."

"Look, I think it's terrific. Why don't you let me have a look? I'm an editor. I could help you. Wouldn't you like to have something published?"

"I couldn't do that. It would embarrass Rosey."

"Under a *nom de plume*."

"I never thought of that."

"Then it's solved. So when do I see this *chef d'oeuvre*?"

"Look, you're already making fun of me."

"I swear I'm not."

"Let me look at it first. I'm not sure . . . But I must admit I've been longing for somebody to see what I'm doing. If it's hopeless I'd like to know. Then I won't waste my time anymore. I'm a little too old to be writing short stories to hide away in a drawer. We all did that in college with our poetry. If I'm not any good at all, I want to scrap it and go on to something else."

"Do you have something else in mind?"

She blushed agáin.

"Forgive me," said the voice on Sadie's right. "Forgive me, my dear lady, but I'm afraid that the table is being turned by our hostess."

Heinrich was leaning toward Sadie with a smile.

"Howard, I apologize."

She could tell that Howard knew she was one down. He would pay attention to those things. Nobody wanted to be one down in Washington.

"Howard, old man, Mrs. Grey deserves better," Des was saying, "but protocol demands that I hand her over." And he put his hand on Sadie's arm lightly as he turned away from her. It made her catch her breath.

"I hope I will be able to captivate you half as much as that pirate Shaw," Howard was saying. "You better watch out for him. He has a way with the ladies."

She decided not to show her annoyance. She glanced across the table—she had forgotten to keep an eye on Allison and Rosey—and caught Allison watching her in return. For a moment they gazed at each other; then Allison turned to Rosey. It was Sadie's turn to be uneasy.

"I saw Bud Corwin working you over," Allison said to Rosey. She had hardly been able to concentrate on her conversation with Worth Elgin the first half of dinner. Sadie and Des had seemed enraptured until the table had turned. Des had never even greeted the woman on his other side. And he had done almost all of the talking, looking solemn. If he was talking about her, she would not forgive him.

The only way she could recoup now was to get Rosey's full attention. She was pleased to see Sadie's glance as she turned toward Rosey. She decided Rosey was pretty attractive. She found herself drawn to him.

Rosey had a certain military bearing about him. He had been in the Marines. He respected authority. He relished his own position and sought more responsibility. She could easily see him as a successful President. He was a leader of men in a different way than Des was. Men followed Rosey automatically. They wanted him to tell them what to do. Des was a man other men envied. They imitated Des. They wanted to be like him.

With Des, she always had the sense "You're on your own, kid." He gave them rope, and if they hanged themselves, well, so be it. Des was nobody's keeper. He didn't want other people hanging over him. He was independent, his own man. He had zero respect for authority. And he had no desire to tell anybody else what to do.

In fact, he spent more of his time as Bureau Chief writing and doing the column on the White House and letting his deputy handle the day-to-day duties.

Rosey was more of a father figure. There was something about him that made one feel secure. She knew what appealed to the voters about him. He seemed to have things quietly in control. He was not a grandstander or a hotdogger. He just had a reserve that gave the impression that he was in command. He didn't have quite the same charm that Des had, but he had something else. Allison could see where he might be sexy. He was good-looking enough, but he wasn't enough of a bastard to be really sexy. She wondered what it would be like to go to bed with him, and she decided that it would probably be a pretty dry screw. Des was the best lay she had ever had in her life. Rosey was definitely a missionary-position man. On the other hand, there was a certain challenge there. She was sure she could turn him on, and the possibility intrigued her.

And like all men, he was not impervious to a compliment.

She had found that out in their first interview. She had said she admired his speeches and the rest of the interview had been a piece of cake. Allison didn't like to do that. It made her feel a bit of a whore. But it worked.

She had seen Rosey stiffen when she made the crack about Bud Corwin. She knew he didn't know quite what to expect. And he seemed to be on his guard this evening. Had Sadie warned him against her?

"How do you mean?" he asked her.

"Oh, you know," she said with a challenging smile.

"Allison, surely you don't want to put me in an uncomfortable spot," he said, returning her smile.

"I wouldn't think of it. It's just that the Senator never fails to amaze me."

"Are you trying to get me to say something negative about the Majority Leader?"

"Why are you so suspicious tonight, Mr. Vice President?" she asked.

He seemed at a loss for words—an unusual reaction for a politician. Allison was sure Sadie had said something to him.

"If I didn't know better, I would say somebody warned you off of me."

Again he was on his guard. He certainly wasn't going to tell her the truth.

"Well, Allison, you know you have a certain reputation."

"Unlike Shaw?"

"Shaw has a reputation for being tough, but it's not the same thing."

"Why isn't it the same?"

"People are scared of you."

"And not of Des?"

"Well, no, they're not."

"They respect him but they're not afraid of him?"

"Yes."

"And they're afraid of me but they don't respect me?"

"Don't put words in my mouth."

"But that's what you meant to say?"

"No, but—well, you print different kinds of things."

"Untrue things?"

"No, but things that are on the edge, personal things—you get people to say things. . . . I mean, nobody knows what you're going to print, so they don't feel as comfortable around you."

"So what kind of a journalist do you think that makes me?"

"Certainly a very good one. . . ." He hesitated.

She saw that he was struggling, and it amused her. "What you are trying to say is that it's different for men and women. It's not just your perception. It's true. There is a kind of Good Ol' Boy school of journalism and politics. Des understands it. It's a pact, an unspoken agreement. We're all in this together. The problem for women journalists in this town is that we don't get to hang around bars or go out drinking with our sources without having everybody question our reputation." She had his attention now. "The men in Washington belong to a club, no women allowed.

So I don't have to abide by the rules of the club. Frankly, I think that makes me and my female colleagues better, more independent journalists."

She paused for a moment, then laughed. "I usually get paid a lot of money for that speech," she said. "And you're getting it for free."

"To what do I owe the honor, ma'am?"

"Just buttering up a source."

"Well, you're a damn sight more honest than most of the men I've dealt with. It's just that I'm an old male chauvinist pig and I don't know the new rules. I have to keep being reminded. Thank you for that." He grinned. "It's true what you say about the club. It's something I've honestly never thought much about. But it's not only men who don't trust women journalists. Why . . ."

He stopped and looked almost stricken for a moment. He had almost told her he had been warned by his wife. Allison knew it, and she waited to see how he would get out of it.

"Uh, earlier today some people were talking about you and teasing me about watching out," he said. "I said I wasn't afraid and they said if that was true, then I was the only man in town who wasn't. I'd take it as a compliment."

"It sounds like one coming from you."

"You've interviewed me enough times. I'm not unaware of your devastating technique. But you've always been fair and honest with me, and I appreciate that."

"You've always been fair and honest with me. That's why. May I say something, Mr. Vice President?"

"Rosey, please."

"William or Bill in public, Rosey in private—right?"

"Yes. My campaign manager told me a long time ago I could never get elected with a name like Rosey. But I've never really felt comfortable with William, though most people here call me that. Except the ones I'm closer to."

"Well, then, I'm flattered."

"It's the least I can do after insulting you."

He looked her directly in the eye and she could see he was being playful. He was intrigued. That was clear. Yet what amazed her was that she found herself attracted to him, and it made her blush. He pretended not to notice.

"As I was saying," she said finally, clearing her throat.

"Yes?"

"You must understand that you could trust me under any circumstances because of my relationship with the President."

"You mean because he's your godfather?"

"Of course. Because of that I can't very well write ugly things about him. It's the worst conflict I've ever encountered in my career."

"So how does that affect *my* relationship with you?"

"Because you are the Vice President and you are also a trusted confidant of the President. It would put a terrible strain on my relationship with my godfather. Secondly, I think you can help me." She couldn't help smiling at his surprise.

"I'm serious. I'm worried about Uncle Roger. I know something about him that you may not know. And certainly the rest of the country doesn't know. He has a heart condition."

Rosey looked genuinely shocked.

"He had a small stroke about ten years ago. God knows how he managed to keep it out of the press. It was just before my father died, and he swore my father to secrecy. Now you can see the problem. But it's something I simply cannot reveal."

Rosey was almost grim.

"Why are you telling me?"

"It's hardly the place or time, is it? I apologize. He needs somebody to watch out for him."

"What can I do?"

"I'm sure you have noticed that Roger Kimball's worst failing is that he is overly trusting of people. He doesn't have a cynical bone in his body. He has managed to surround himself with some real fools. They are leaking to the press, fighting with each other, and making him and his Administration look ridiculous. These people are going to eat him alive unless somebody does something. Some of them have to be got rid of."

Rosey was staring at Allison. She had said she was going to be honest, but this was something he had never seen before.

"I see you're surprised at what I am saying."

"Stunned is more the word," he said.

"What surprises you—my candor?"

"That too, but your accuracy in sizing up the situation."

"The only way the President will ever really know what is going on and how bad it is is by reading it in the paper."

"And that's where I come in," he said.

"This nonsense is taking a heavy toll on him," she said. "I'm afraid the stress of all of this could cause him to have another stroke."

"My God, I don't know what to say."

"Say you'll help me."

Rosey just looked solemn.

"Look," she said finally. "It's not all that bad. I'm only saying that he has to be careful, and those jerks around him aren't helping any. I'm speaking now as someone who loves this man."

When he didn't respond, she turned teasing.

"We'll need to meet and talk occasionally. We could even meet in underground garages at night—all very clandestine."

"I must say you're making it sound very attractive. You know you really are an evil girl, Sterling."

"Person," she joked. "I'm an evil person."

"That too. I'd be fingered as a prime leaker. I wouldn't be trusted ever again."

"I'd disguise you in print . . . 'a source second only to the President'?"

"Yes, but will you respect me in the morning if I agree to be your source in the White House?"

The conversation wavered in and out. They were walking a tightrope. Allison was a little surprised at herself, at how bold she was being. Yet he was encouraging it.

"I just can't tell if you're serious or not. You've had a mischievous look in your eyes on and off all evening, Allison."

"Sonny, please."

"Thank you. I'm flattered."

"I've just been trying to keep the conversation going," she said. "I thought you might be amused."

"I'm not sure amused is the right word," said Rosey. "Fascinated, maybe." He paused. "How did we get started on this, anyway? Oh, yes, we wee talking about Corwin. There was something in your tone of voice when you mentioned him that made me think you weren't crazy about him. What is it you don't like about him? Please be candid. None of your usual wishy-washy answers."

"When Des and I first started seeing each other we went to a party at old Mrs. Randolph's, shortly before she died. It was a very high-powered group. We followed the Corwins and overheard the Senator saying to his wife about us, 'You take him; I'll take her.'"

Just then Lorraine came over to Rosey and leaned over his shoulder.

"We're about to bring out the birthday cakes and sing 'Happy Birthday,'" she said. "Then I'd like to ask you to begin the toasts."

"Toasts?" moaned Allison. "Please, no toasts."

"Now, Sonny, just relax."

The toasts, as Allison later told Des, were a litmus test of the various guests and the degree of their raised consciousness.

Rosey was the perfect Southern gentleman, referring to Allison's and Sadie's beauty, wit, charm, and intelligence.

Allison thought it was a rather uninspired but safe toast.

As the toasts went forward, Allison and Sadie sat with frozen smiles.

When Rosey sat down, Howard Heinrich stood up.

"I'm making this toast by proxy," he said, after having tinkled loudly on his wineglass with his fork.

"The President asked me to toast the two birthday girls for him, and I told him I would be delighted."

Amazing. Howard had maneuvered himself into speaking for the President. He had managed to one-up everybody.

"Although," he said with an overdone chuckle, "the President specifically wanted me to make sure that I toasted the birthday 'persons.'" He waited for the laughter, then looked up and nodded at Allison. She forced a laugh.

"And to say that he would like everyone in this room to stand up and join him in a toast to, and I quote, 'my two favorite women in Washington, after my own Molly.'"

The guests all stood and lifted their glasses to the glassy faces at opposite sides of the room, murmuring, "Hear, hear."

Bud Corwin couldn't stand it. He had to get up and say something.

"I'd like to drink to two great gals," he said. There was a perceptible moan from the group at large.

Lorraine stood. "I may be the only female here to stand up and speak, but I thought there should be one of us. I just want to say that I can't remember when in Washington there was a gathering of this magnitude, of this many successful, powerful, and influential people to honor any woman. And tonight we are honoring two. That there are two such women to honor speaks well for

Washington, for our times, and for the women themselves. To Allison and Sadie."

There was some cheering, and people relaxed a bit more.

O'Grady stood up. There was much hooting and jeering from the journalists.

"Shut up," said O'Grady.

"Oooooooooh," shouted the journalists.

"None of you has the guts to get up in front of all these big muckety-mucks and toast your friends. But no one can say that Francis O'Grady is chicken. Now, I don't know Mrs. Grey as well as I do Sterling, and much is the pity, and here's hoping that I will soon, but I will say the two of you darlin' things look like you've kissed the Blarney Stone and I'd like ye all to drink to that."

Things were getting raucous, and the politicians were beginning to feel a bit uncomfortable. Up until now the journalists had been on their best behavior. Now they were getting rowdy. The party had definitely changed hands.

Des finally stood up. He put two fingers in his mouth and whistled everyone to order. Nobody wanted to come to order. Des whistled again. "This will be short."

A round of applause and more cheering.

"I want everybody to drink a toast to two spectacular dames," said Des. "That's it."

The guests all stood and raised their glasses again.

It was the first time all evening that both Sonny and Sadie had genuine smiles on their faces.

Suddenly there was a small commotion at the door and then a flurry of excitement. Everyone looked up as John T. Hooker, the crusty old Secretary of State, strode in. Lorraine jumped up from her seat as though she had been shot. She could tell immediately that he had been drinking. Business at the State Department had been the reason why he couldn't be at the dinner. Lorraine had heard about John T.'s private bar in the Secretary's office. And she could see by his jolly expression that he had managed to weather the crisis fairly well.

"*I* want to make a toast," John T. told Lorraine in a voice loud enough for all to hear. He was standing at the top of the stairs, his hand on the rail.

He was an amazing-looking man: in his early seventies, still straight and over six feet tall, with a mane of beautiful sweeping white hair that he wore almost shoulder length. His face was usually flushed red, his silver-blue eyes changed to steely gray when he was angry, and his beaked nose seemed to reproach anyone who looked askance. He always dressed in black three-piece suits with a black bow tie.

Lorraine hit a glass on the side with a piece of silver to get everyone's attention. She needn't have. They were already rapt.

He began with an oration. He was known for his fine rhetoric on the Senate floor, though it was considered florid and windy.

"I would like to drink a toast to the President of the United States."

There was a low mumble among the crowd. This was not the toast to make to a group of journalists.

Howard Heinrich was the first on his feet—a little too fast, everyone noticed. "To the President of the United States," reiterated Howard, raising his glass.

"To this great country on the eve of our celebration of Independence," said John T.

Howard was kind of stuck. He continued to stand while everyone sat down and then was left there as the cheerleader. Most of the journalists were letting him stand there out of pure meanness until Bud Corwin jumped up and repeated John T.'s second toast.

Finally, after waxing eloquent about the Fourth of July and Independence Day and what it meant to Americans, Hooker paused for effect, his voice taking on a histrionic roll.

"And now, distinguished ladies and gentlemen," he said, "I would like to propose a toast to the two fine women here tonight who are the embodiment and the personification of what this country's womanhood should be all about. They represent the independence of spirit and soul that this great country was founded on. And so, I ask all of you, in the name of our President and our great nation, to stand and drink a toast to these two noble women."

Everyone rose. Nobody wanted to provoke Hooker. At first everyone drank silently, but Des, who was now feeling no pain, shouted, "Hear, hear; I'll drink to that. Not bad, Mr. Secretary, not bad, not bad at all. I'd like to propose a final toast of the evening to John T. Hooker's entrance tonight. May it never be surpassed in our nation's capital."

It was the perfect thing to say. John T. beamed. He knew he

had made a brilliant entrance. He was pleased to see it appreciated. The group roared its approval.

Some of the guests began banging on the table. "Response, response," they chanted, looking at both Allison and Sadie.

They both closed their eyes. Finally, Sadie stood up. It was not such an unfamiliar thing for her to do. As a candidate's wife she had had to speak often, and she was perfectly comfortable with it.

"I'll be brief, because Allison is the public speaker here," she said sweetly.

"All I want to say is that this 'little gal' [She got a few laughs] has certainly appreciated all the generosity and kindness displayed here tonight. And frankly, I haven't seen anything else since I came to Washington. Everyone said this was a tough town to make friends in, but I haven't found it that way at all. And tonight is just another example of the kind of warmth and friendship I have come to expect here. I want to thank you all and to tell you how much I have come to love your city in such a short time."

There was enthusiastic applause. Des smiled at her when she sat down. She hadn't realized she was shaking. Rosey looked over at her and winked his approval.

It was Allison's turn. She stood up.

"I would like to toast modern times," said Allison. "Only in this liberated age could two women be celebrated at the same party and be amused."

Everyone laughed, though there was a slight edge to the mirth.

Allison raised her glass. "And I would like everyone to drink a toast to Sadie Grey. For being such a good sport tonight, and to welcome her to Washington. May the rest of her stay here be as happy as the beginning."

CHAPTER 5

SADIE HAD BEEN HOLDING OFF GOING TO MILLI-cent. Rosey was against it. "How would it look for the wife of the Vice President to go to an astrologer? And don't think she wouldn't use it. It would be in every magazine and paper in the country. You would be her prize client. That woman is danger-ous. I understand she is the most indiscreet person in Washing-ton. You'll confide in her and our personal lives will be all over town."

They were having a drink in the upstairs sitting room one evening in late September.

"I think you're making up all those things about Millicent."

"Suit yourself. If you want to believe that, it's fine with me. But just keep away from her. Frankly, I don't understand how Lorraine could have given you a reading with Millicent as a birthday present. I suppose she gave Allison Sterling one too?"

"That's what she says. I haven't talked to Allison lately."

"Well, I surely can't imagine her going. She's got too much sense for that."

"And I *don't* have any sense."

"If you go to that quack."

"And I suppose you would say the same thing to John T.? You

do realize, of course, that our Secretary of State has gone to Millicent for years?"

"What are you talking about, Sadie?"

"Hooker has been having readings by Millicent for many years and still does."

"That's preposterous. I don't believe it."

"Suit yourself. If you don't want to believe it, well, that's fine with me. Claire Elgin goes and so does Helene Corwin, and for that matter, so does Jake Weston. Millicent told Jake he was going to get the big network anchor job long before he was ever even talked to about it. Jake was stunned."

"So Jake Weston is a fool."

"I thought you liked him. You always say he is your favorite anchorman."

"He was."

"I suppose you feel the same way about Hooker."

"If you're going to try to get me to jump on the Secretary of State, you can forget it. But if what you say is true, I am genuinely shocked. I don't want *you* to do it."

"Rosey, where is your sense of humor? You used to have one. . . ."

He stared at her.

"Well, I am going to Millicent. And I will venture that your political reputation will not be destroyed because of it."

She got up to pour herself another drink. Rosey didn't say a word.

"Oh, God, what am I going to do about this thing with Millicent? Lorraine has been after me for the past month about it. I think she's already paid her two hundred dollars."

"So go. What's the big deal?"

"Des, it's ridiculous. Besides, I don't want Millicent to be able to throw around my name the next time somebody comes to interview her. 'Among her clients is reporter Allison Sterling. . . .' "

"Don't take yourself so seriously. All it is is a joke. Of course it's a pile of crap. But Millicent is an institution. A lot of people in this town go to her. I would think as a reporter you would look at it as a little sociological investigation. Observing the Washington scene."

They were sitting in Allison's house on Olive Street, upstairs in the little chapel, having a drink after work.

"Of course, then there's another problem."

"What's that?"

"Well, the problem of gifts. Do I allow Lorraine to give me an expensive present? It makes me uneasy."

"Look, Lorraine is a friend of yours."

"True, but she's still a public personality."

"Have you ever written about her?"

"No. But—"

"Do you think you might write about her?"

"I can't think why. Oh, I might quote her, but I wouldn't write specifically about her."

"Do you ever exchange gifts? Have you ever given her a present?"

"Christmas presents. Not much. I mean, I'll give her a wicker basket and she'll give me some batik cocktail napkins. But nothing of importance; nothing that costs two hundred dollars."

"Look, Sonny, I think you're agonizing over nothing. If you don't want to go to Millicent, then don't go. But you can't put it off on conflict of interest. A good friend of yours has given you a birthday present. It might be a little more than you would spend on her, but it's not out of the question."

"What if people found out that I had gone to Millicent? I would be laughed at."

"Of course people will find out. Because you're going to tell them. Or I will."

"What are you talking about?"

"I mean where is your sense of humor? You could dine out on it for weeks. People are always titillated by astrology. I'll bet Sadie Grey will go. She gave her a reading too, I presume."

"So she said. And, I might add, Sadie Grey's going is a very good reason for me not to go. 'Oh, Mistah Shaw, Ah went to this little ol' astrologeah and she tol' me that I had a great big ol' crush on a big ol' strong handsome journalist with curly black hair and the most devastatin' smile.' You turn into a complete half-wit when you get around that woman."

"Now, Sonny, calm yourself." Des was amused. It did turn him on to see Allison get so aroused about Sadie. "We were, after all, talking about Millicent. We were not talking about Sadie Grey. Are you going to go?"

"Yes. I am going, and I am going to take your exact moment of birth, and I will get her to read for you as well, and I will tell everyone in Washington about it. That's what I'm going to do."

"Millicent darling. I want you to take it easy on Sadie Grey. Don't tell her a lot of horrible things. She's a very fragile girl, though she may not look like it. She's also a dear. You'll love her. And she will be a good client of yours. But you must understand her husband is very much against her coming to you. He is furious with me. And I must say, for a very good reason. He has heard, my dear Millicent, pained as I am to tell you this, that you are not the most discreet person in Washington. That you are often tempted to pass along a little delicious nugget or two from one client to the next. Now, don't say a word, Millicent; what I am saying is the God's truth. I'm not making any judgments, I'm not being critical. I'm only saying that if you want to keep this client you'll keep your mouth shut. And by the way, old girl, I know you can do it because you've done it with Hooker. You've never breathed one word. Of course, I suspect that is because there's been a little more to your readings with John T. than astrology. But . . . that's just instinct. Don't bother to deny it. I'm never going to say a thing about it. Besides, I think it would be marvelous if you and John T. had something going. I've often wondered how you could stand such a lonely existence. But then, that's something we all have to face sooner or later.

"I've really got to run, Millicent darling; I'm desperately late for lunch. But do promise me that you'll be sweet and gentle with Sadie. And for God's sake, don't tell her anything gloomy like Saturn is retrograde. Upbeat, upbeat, that's our word for the day. I'll call you this evening for a full report. Ciao."

Millicent was excited. Sadie Grey! She had heard and read a lot about her. She devoured every morsel of gossip as though it were her last meal. One of the things that were so satisfying about her work was that she picked up so much gossip during the readings. People confided in their astrologers. It was like being a combination hairdresser, doctor, and shrink. And you didn't have to take the Hippocratic oath, though certainly she tried to maintain the illusion of being discreet.

Millicent stepped from her living room into her dressing room to check one last time to make sure she looked all right. Her silver hair was set perfectly, curled and swept back off her face in a slight bouffant that gave her the definite look of a *grande dame*. Her smooth skin belied her sixty-eight years; her pale, watery blue eyes only helped to add color to her face. Her beaked nose and defined jaw kept her from being the great beauty she had always longed to be, but her carriage gave her an aura of importance. When people first met Millicent, they knew they were in the presence of somebody to be reckoned with.

Millicent was from someplace in Mississippi, so the story went. It was said that she had been tragically widowed and had sold her possessions and had come to Washington to make a new start. She was young then, in her early thirties, childless and with enough money to buy an apartment in The California House, an old building that was only just now becoming the fashionable place it had been during the turn of the century.

Millicent had started reading palms first at parties, then, when her funds began to run low, for money.

From there she had studied astrology and had begun doing charts for friends. She had managed to present herself to the right group when she first came to Washington and soon developed a devoted clientele: the Georgetown Establishment, the Congress, and a few new people every time an administration changed. Middle Eastern and Latin American ambassadors were among her most noted clients and the most willing to talk about her. She was a favorite dinner guest on Embassy Row and in the more established houses in Washington.

And what so many people often forgot when they went to Millicent, for whatever social or political reasons they went, was that she was a very good astrologer. The downside was that she had a mean streak, and when she felt clients were getting a little out of hand or a little too cocky, she would whack them down. In fact, her power over them was the most appealing part of Millicent's job. Which made her no different from anybody else in Washington.

Sadie Grey was only a few minutes late. Millicent thought how much prettier she looked in person. She still had a little tan left from summer, which made her blue-green eyes sparkle, and her auburn hair had a few sun streaks through the top. The minute Millicent heard Sadie's Southern accent, she knew they were going to develop a good working relationship.

Millicent reminded Sadie of her grandmother Pamela, and Millicent's apartment, with its fifth-floor view overlooking the Capitol and the Washington Monument in the far distance, was decorated exactly the same way as the living room was decorated at Horace Hall, where Sadie had grown up, in Adabelle, Georgia.

The grand piano had an embroidered, fringed flowered scarf hanging from it. The velvet armchairs were worn and frayed, with doilies to hide the arms and back. Over in one corner, away from the light, stood a card table with a pretty cloth, where Millicent had set her charts.

Sadie felt as if she had come home.

"Why, Miz Grey," said Millicent with a warmth in her voice Sadie had not been led to expect. "I can't tell you what a pleasure it is to finally meet you. You're much prettier than your pictures, you know."

"I'm happy to meet you too," said Sadie. "You can imagine I've heard a awful lot about you. There are a lot of people in this town who say they won't make a move without consulting you."

"Well, well, I'd say they're exaggerating a little," said Millicent, smiling, but she was pleased. Things were definitely getting off to a good start.

"Why don't we have a little tea before we begin?" Millicent knew most clients were eager to get to the readings and that she shouldn't hold off too long, but she always felt a cup of tea relaxed them, made them feel less self-conscious.

She had set up her silver tea service, one of the few things she had brought with her from Mississippi, on a table next to a love seat, and she prided herself on freshly pressed linen napkins, perfect little cucumber sandwiches, biscuits with honey and jam, and some little fruit confection. Today's were strawberry.

"Oh, my, doesn't everything look just lovely," said Sadie as she sat carefully on the edge of the love seat and crossed her ankles demurely.

They cooed at each other for a few minutes in the way only Southern women know how to do as they exchanged small talk about Washington, the weather, and Lorraine.

Sadie finished her tea, delicately wiped the corner of her

mouth with her perfectly pressed linen napkin, and put it back on the tea tray. It was her signal that it was time to begin.

Millicent led the way to the corner table and gestured to Sadie to sit in one of the four brocade armchairs that encircled the table.

Millicent had put a large silk folder on the table, and she opened it up with great authority to produce two charts. They were beautifully drawn, with exquisite detail. The circle was large, and the lines through it delineating the various aspects of the chart were painted in watercolors in very delicate shades. The charts could have been framed and hung.

Sadie told her so, and Millicent nodded in agreement, mentioning that many of her clients had done just that.

"I was going to be an artist before I got married and gave up my career, and I dabble here and there," she said.

"Why are there two charts?" Sadie asked.

"Why, one for you and one for your husband. I have been looking at the Vice President's chart ever since Roger Kimball chose him for his running mate. My, oh, my, he certainly does have a lovely chart."

"Thank you," said Sadie.

"Don't thank me, my dear. Thank the stars. And you should too, with your chart. You have one of the luckiest charts I've seen in a long time."

Sadie was visibly relieved. "Oh, God, I feel glad to hear you say that! I was nervous. I was sure you'd have nothing but predictions of death and destruction."

"You know I never do predictions. I leave that to the quacks," said Millicent, a bit annoyed. "What I do is tell the aspects. There are good and bad aspects to a chart. I can tell people when the bad aspects are coming and they then can try to be careful or to take charge of their charts. I am not a fortune-teller."

Sadie decided to let it pass. She certainly did not want to get on the bad side of Millicent before she did the chart.

"Now, I assume you've had your chart done before. A good Southern girl like you."

"Many times," said Sadie. "My grandmother did charts, and I'm always attracted to astrology. I've had it done maybe four or five times by different astrologers. Usually they say pretty much the same things about my chart. I always expect, though, that sooner or later someone is going to tell me something terrible."

"Nonsense. Now, you know, of course, that you are a Cancer and that your rising sign is Pisces."

"Yes."

"The other important aspect of your chart is that your Mercury is in Leo, but we'll get to that later. Let me start by telling you about the combination of Cancer and Pisces. It's so perfect for you. And now that I see you I think it is even more perfect. Cancer with Pisces rising is a charming, seductive, sultry, beautiful woman with a touch of the actress in her. There's a lot of Scarlett O'Hara in you. Isn't there? And that's not because you're a Southern girl."

"At least you didn't say I was a Melanie. I would have hated that."

"All Southern girls are either Melanie or Scarlett. You are clearly a Scarlett, though there are those who may not realize it right away. You have such a soft, feminine exterior and approach I would imagine that some people are easily fooled. I feel sorry for them." Millicent let out a gleeful cackle. "Especially in this town. There will be some who think you are a pushover. Oh, that sweet little Southern belle. Oh, will they be surprised!"

"I wouldn't go that far," said Sadie, giggling.

"Of course, with that chart, I don't know, I just can't figure out how you came to marry Mr. Grey." Her tone was suddenly serious, and Sadie's face dropped.

"You see, you have Virgo in the seventh House, which is marriage, and Mercury rules that House. That would give your marriage a certain masochistic aspect."

She looked up to see Sadie's shocked expression. This was not at all what she had expected. She didn't miss a beat.

"You see, the mind rules most aspects of your marriage. Emotion plays a smaller part. Your marriage has a great deal of sacrifice in it."

Millicent watched Sadie. Sadie said nothing, but her lips tightened. She hadn't put in for this. What was she supposed to do or say?

Millicent could see that she had started out too strong.

"Let's get back to the Pisces rising. This is a most important aspect. It gives you a certain glamour, an artistic bent. Are you creative? From your chart I would think you might be a writer. Maybe an actress."

Sadie loosened up. "I do write short stories. I've never done anything with them." She seemed shy but pleased.

"This could be very important to you and becoming more important. Do not let this talent go. You could do something important with this talent. The Pisces rising. Yes, it makes you soft; you are a kind person, I can see that from your chart—kind, softhearted, but you have a tendency to wrap yourself around you, to cushion yourself from outside emotions, influences. Yes?"

Sadie could see what she was doing. She was clever. She would make an educated guess, then look for confirmation. It was the way Washington reporters talked to you. They would make a statement which showed that they knew a little something about a subject, then wait for you to confirm their information. Rosey had pointed it out to her and had saved her from finding out the hard way.

But Sadie was not going to play. She surely was not going to give away anything about her marriage.

"You have very beautiful eyes—those blue-green, shimmering eyes; they look like the sea. Definitely Cancer-Pisces eyes." She paused. "I noticed you stiffened when I mentioned your marriage. You don't have to respond. For you power is important. It is necessary for you to be married to someone in power. The way you love is by nurturing, mothering. You can mother your husband, or the men in your life. And you have a great love of children."

Sadie said nothing. She wondered how accurate that was. She adored Outland; but Annie Laurie, her own daughter—she felt happier when Annie Laurie was not around. It made her guilty. She should love her more. Millicent was being too glib, telling her what she thought she wanted to hear. Life was more complicated.

"Mercury in Leo. In your case," Millicent continued, "this adds to the sexy, attractive aspect. You are very attractive to men because of this. You will always have lot of lovers..." She looked up and smiled. She paused. "Or potential lovers, I should say."

What was she implying?

"To men you seem seductive. Let me see. What is the word I am searching for? Giselle, that's it. Your chart is foggy, smoky, silent, like a Southern city with moss hanging over the trees.

You're from Savannah, aren't you? That's perfect too. You are the personification of that city. Soft, feminine, weeping trees, pools of water. That's all part of the Pisces personality. Mysterious, deep. I can smell it in your perfume. Sortilège? I knew it. My favorite. Nobody wears it anymore. There is a strong side to you, too. Cancer is always deceptively strong. There is an outgoing side. Wherever you go, you leave not only a trace of your perfume lingering behind, but a trace of yourself which people find difficult to get out of their minds. It is hard for you to understand this power you have over people. You are very powerful. You just don't know it yet. You don't understand how strong and how powerful you are. You are probably the kind of woman who thinks that because she doesn't have a job, a career, she isn't worth anything. Well, don't fool yourself. You are a force, and you will become even more of a force in this city before you are through. You need really to see yourself for what you are. Your chart can help. It can elucidate for you who and what you are."

"What do you see for the future? I'm sorry—I know you said you're no fortune-teller—but what aspects do you see?"

"You have Cancer in your fifth House. That Cancer is afflicted. With Jupiter about to enter your fifth House, which rules children, there is a chance that you might get pregnant."

"I'm almost forty. That's totally out of the question."

"All right, darlin'," said Millicent. "But don't say I didn't warn you."

"I stand warned."

"I want to talk to you about your sexuality. Men will always be taken in by your femininity, what appears to be your pliable nature, your soft seductiveness. But you are never totally able to surrender. It's like the fog. No man can ever conquer the fog. You will always elude him. That must be partly because you want it that way. You feel more secure when you are never totally possessed."

Sadie was uncomfortable. For one thing, she was not crazy about the idea of discussing sex with this woman, and for another, what she was saying was too close for comfort. It made her nervous. Like being possessed by a man, she did not like the idea of being understood completely. She didn't like it. There was something sinister about Millicent. About this reading. She wanted to change the subject.

"And what about my husband's chart?" she asked brightly.

"You mentioned that you had seen his chart. What does it tell you?"

"Of course, he is a Capricorn. Capricorns, though they can be highly sexual, never romanticize. And since he has his moon in Virgo, he will never wholly satisfy the romantic in you. For Capricorn and Cancer, the emphasis is on home, family, stability. He has ambition and drive, but no romanticism. You need to be seduced. Capricorn will not do this."

Rosey had been absolutely right. She shouldn't have come. Even if she, Sadie, never said a word or acknowledged anything that Millicent was telling her, Millicent would still tell everybody that she and Rosey had a mediocre sex life. And the tragedy was that she would be right. How could any chart tell her these things? The woman was a witch. Sadie wanted to get up and run out of the room. She could feel the perspiration forming on her forehead. She didn't know what to do or say. Finally she pulled herself together.

"All right, now, Millicent," she said with a casual laugh. "Enough. Any more and this session will have to be X-rated. Let's talk about future aspects. Tell me something wonderful that's going to happen."

Though she was speaking lightly, there was an underlying tone which Millicent did not miss.

It was Millicent's turn to get nervous. She didn't want to lose this client. Nor did she want Sadie bad-mouthing her. She could be hurt by her. She had gone over the line with Sadie. She was absolutely serious about this reading. There were extraordinary things on this woman's chart, and somehow she had to be prepared for them. Millicent realized, though, that she had better bring the reading back to the realm of social astrology or something terrible was going to happen. Sadie was shaking.

"Now for some fortune-telling," said Millicent lightly, making fun of herself. "As I said to you earlier, there is a chance you may get pregnant. And"—she looked Sadie in the eye and did not flinch—"there is a strong possibility that there is a love affair on the horizon."

Sadie sat back in her chair in disgust, let out a sigh, then gave Millicent a warning look.

"I really don't think this is what Lorraine had in mind," she said. She hadn't meant to get angry.

"I'm sorry, Mrs. Grey," said Millicent very softly. "But I'm not a carnival act. I am a professional astrologer. I read the charts. This is what the charts indicate. You don't have to believe it or take it seriously, and the interpretation of the charts is not always right. I am only telling you what I see."

Millicent was serious. Sadie could see that she was upset. Then why did she go on in this vein? Why didn't she just tell her she would take a long trip and come into a lot of money? But Sadie knew why. Millicent was telling her what she saw. She decided to let her finish. Her curiosity had gotten the better of her.

"All right, I understand, but you must realize this isn't all that pleasant for me. And I don't have much time. Could we get on with this?"

"Of course," said Millicent softly.

"If you had an affair..." She paused, took a deep breath. "... it would shake you to the roots. You would wish for all your life that it had never happened. I do not know whether it would culminate in marriage or not. I do not see your own marriage broken, but it is not clear to me. I don't understand what I see. Maybe you don't get pregnant but would treat your new lover as a child. I just don't know. But there is something very important which happens to your chart at that time. And to your husband's chart. There are changes in status, and you are thrown into prominence. Something happens with your husband. Prepare yourself. There is another aspect in your status, both of you. Around the same time."

"Millicent," said Sadie, standing. She was white now with fury and with indignation. "Millicent, I think I have heard enough. I am terribly sorry. This is not at all what I had in mind. You will excuse me."

With that, she turned and walked to the front door, which she opened and let herself out. The door slammed behind her.

Millicent sat in her chair for a long time without moving. She could not believe she'd done what she had just done. She had ruined things. Finally, as the room was filling with the shadows of dusk, she got up. She walked over to the telephone by the window and watched the sun setting over the Capitol dome. "It's so beautiful," she said to herself as she had done many times. She picked up the phone and dialed. "Hello, Lorraine? Millicent. I think I went too far."

* * *

Millicent was not "whistling 'Dixie,'" as Sadie might say. Lorraine was shocked. She had listened with some sympathy as Millicent described the session to her, but of course Millicent had managed to leave out the worst parts, such as Rosey and Sadie's sex life, or Sadie's affair.

"I was only speculating in an amusing way, sort of having fun with the charts" was the way Millicent had put it.

"Vile woman" was the way Sadie had described Millicent. "Telling me that I would go off with another man and that the whole thing would cause a great scandal. Even if she thought she was just having an amusing little afternoon. What was I supposed to say? I couldn't believe it. How could anybody ever go to that woman? What gives her the right to impose herself like that into other people's private lives? It is an outrage. And I simply don't understand how you could subject me to it. I really don't, Lorraine. If Rosey ever found out about it, he would be wild. For God's sake, don't ever mention it to him. I'll just tell him she said I was going to take a lot of trips and that I had good aspects. He would positively go crazy if he found out what she had told me. And there is not one shred of doubt in my mind that that woman is now telling her next client that the Greys have a terrible sex life and that I'm about to take a lover."

Lorraine had tried to calm her down. It hadn't worked. Lorraine was trembling as she got off the phone from talking to Sadie. She was so upset with Millicent she didn't know what to do. She also did not know what to do about Allison. She had better warn her. She knew that Allison, unlike Sadie, had not been too crazy about the idea in the first place.

She called Allison to tell her about it, though she edited the specifics. To her surprise, Allison burst out laughing.

"How silly of Sadie to take anything that ol' phony has to say seriously! I think astrology is nonsense, and I'm looking forward to seeing Millicent as a part of Washington sociology. Besides, I think it could be funny. Don't worry about me, Lorraine. I promise I'm not quite as fragile as our Second Lady."

Next Lorraine spoke again to Millicent. She tried to keep her voice calm. She knew Millicent was upset, but more than that, Millicent might turn mean and give her a bad reading. She had to stay on her good side so that Millicent would interpret her chart in the most positive way.

"Now, Millicent, we don't want to dwell on this unfortunate occurrence, but you must know how upset Sadie Grey was. In fact, I don't think you quite know how upset she was. So I don't need to tell you that this will remain just between us. I can count on you to keep the details to yourself. I know Sadie Grey is not going to talk to anybody about it. I wouldn't be honest if I didn't tell you that I forewarned Allison. As I mentioned to you earlier, she has absolutely no faith in astrology. You are dealing with a different kettle of fish here. My feeling is it doesn't matter what you tell Allison because she won't believe any of it anyway. But I just wanted to speak to you about it because Allison Sterling is not someone you would want as an enemy either. You could damage your reputation and your business, Millicent. Now I must run. Good luck with Allison, dearie."

Millicent never worried much about her clients who were skeptics. All she had to do was tell them one thing that struck vaguely home and they would leave saying they didn't believe in astrology but Millicent really was amazing. She didn't think she would like Allison, either from what she had heard about her or from what she'd read of her pieces. The real tragedy was that she had been instantly drawn to Sadie. She had wanted to help her. Now, it seemed, she had ruined that possibility forever.

The doorbell rang. She had put out tea for Allison, but she hadn't gone to nearly as much trouble with the tea sandwiches and cakes this time. Store-bought chocolate-chip cookies would do very well.

Allison looked cool and reserved in a gray-and-beige silk blazer, a gray skirt, a pale gray silk blouse. She had her hair pulled back and her sunglasses perched on top of her head. A large satchel was slung around her shoulder, filled, Millicent could see, with a tape recorder, notebooks, pencils, papers, press releases. It was a mess, that bag—the only messy thing about this totally pulled-together young woman. Seeing her tape recorder reminded Millicent that Sadie had left in such a rush that she had not taken the tape recording which Millicent routinely made to give to the client as part of the reading. She had left the recorder whirring as she slammed out of the apartment. Millicent wondered if Allison planned to tape her own session.

Allison had a vague smile on her face as she took in the ornate

Victorian room. "Perfect," she said. "Just what I imagined an astrologer's apartment to look like."

"Right out of a stage set, you mean?" said Millicent.

"Something like that," she said. "I would have been disappointed if it had looked like a psychiatrist's office. You want atmosphere when you have your chart read."

"Have you ever had your chart read before?"

"This is a big first for me. And I'm counting on you, Millicent, to make it memorable." There was something a little contemptuous in her tone, but Millicent chose to ignore it. She could not ignore her next comment: "Although I'm not so sure I want it to be as memorable as the reading you gave Sadie Grey."

Millicent decided it best not to respond. Instead she offered Allison some tea and cookies and motioned her to the love seat.

Allison shook her head.

"If you don't mind, I don't have all that much time today. I've got to get back to the office to prepare for an interview tomorrow. Do you mind if I just take a cup of tea to the table with me?"

Millicent didn't like that, but she acquiesced. This woman was too professional, too businesslike. Nevertheless, she walked to the table, sat down, and pulled the charts from her folder.

Allison observed Millicent's artwork, but said nothing.

"Of course," Millicent began, "you know you are a Cancer?"

"So I've been told," said Allison.

This was going to be a tough customer. Millicent took in a deep breath.

"A Cancer with Aries rising."

Allison shrugged.

"Aries rising is an important aspect of your chart. Aries is dominant here. Aries wants everything now, immediately. Aries is a child. An Aries is open, childlike in its demands for instant gratification. Aries wants to know everything. Tell me, tell me. They can be very demanding."

Millicent glanced at Allison to see how she was reacting. She was smiling with what seemed to be delight. Millicent went on.

"The Aries rising can be very perceptive; they pick up the emotions of others. They have the sheer curiosity and impatience of a child.

"As you know, I have done the chart of Mr. Shaw. It is a very interesting combination, this Cancer with Aries rising and his Scorpio. There will always be, between the two of you, a big clash of wills and a clash of personalities. Usually Aries will break down Scorpio. Aries wins, but sometimes with Scorpio that can mean that she loses. Both Aries and Scorpio are ruled by Mars. Therefore they are both very combative, although they have different styles of combat. The Aries in you will be very straightforward, while Scorpio goes sideways. You are both very aggressive, I see by your charts. Though you go after what you want openly, he will go after it quietly."

Allison had lost her smirk and was staring at the charts. "Where do you see that?" she asked, almost in spite of herself.

Millicent pointed to several pale red lines on the two charts which made no sense to Allison.

"I also see that there is a great deal of physical attraction between the two of you and always will be."

There was a long silence as Millicent stared at the charts. The only sound in the room was the slight squish of the tape recorder: Millicent's.

"You have a lot of conflict in you, I see," said Millicent. "Cancer is right on your fourth House. There will always be a tremendous pull in yourself."

"What will I be conflicted about?"

Her voice was challenging and quizzical. The sarcastic tone was gone.

"For one thing, your relationship with other women. You will envy other women, both professionally and when it comes to men, but you will suppress it. You will also be conflicted in other ways. With Mars squaring the sun in Cancer, there will be a tremendous drive of self, a conflict between wanting to show off, wanting to forge ahead, break new ground, take risks, reform things, and the other side of you, which is timid—the Cancer side, which hates to take risks, avoids danger of any kind. Your Cancer side is in constant conflict with your Aries rising. Cancer wishes only that she could have a peaceful life."

"Ha!" shrieked Allison. "That's a laugh. Where's my Cancer side been all these years? I must have been completely dominated by my Aries side. No wonder none of those astrology columns about Cancerians ever made any sense to me. I could never identify with any of that moon-maiden stuff. They always seemed to me to be wimpy. I hated my sign. Well, Millicent, you may have made me a convert. Just telling me I had Aries rising perks me up enormously. I can't tell you."

Millicent couldn't tell whether she was putting her on, but at least she was enjoying the reading. That was the best she could hope for.

"You have your Mercury in Leo," said Millicent. "So does your friend Sadie Grey. It is a very unusual aspect and a highly desirable one."

"What does it mean?" Allison was getting more interested.

"It means that you are attractive to men, that you will have lots of lovers, that you make people want to make love to you. There will be a 'Here I come' rather aggressive, forward sexual approach to men."

"That certainly doesn't sound like Mrs. Grey," said Allison carefully. "I mean, she's such a Southern lady."

Millicent was not unaware of the disdain in Allison's voice. She knew she should keep her mouth shut and move on with Allison's chart, but as with Sadie the other day, something compelled her to keep talking.

"You are both Cancerians, as you know, but she has Pisces rising. That is different from Aries in approach to sexuality, but no less strong or insistent. She will make the man think it is his idea. It would be my opinion from looking at the two charts that you two would not get along well. I would advise you to keep your distance from each other."

Why was Millicent saying this? She obviously realized that Allison would listen and be fascinated, not offended. Aries rising.

Sadie, with her Pisces rising, would want her feelings about Allison to remain murky. She would not want to face the truth. Allison was looking at it head on.

"Aries and Pisces rising, both in Cancer, cannot stand each other. The adjoining signs, Aries and Pisces, irritate each other. Forget any friendship there. With Mercury in Leo, you both understand each other, so much so that others may be startled from time to time because of it."

Millicent sensed that Allison was tensing a little. She decided to change the subject.

"But now let's get back to your chart. It shows that you can be quick, witty, sarcastic, cutting, satirical. You can seduce men with your charm, your sex, and most of all, your brain. You are like a bee or a spider. With your Scorpio male the sex will be totally satisfying to him, totally pleasing, satiating. For Scorpio, sex has a need for totality of feeling: he must feel that nothing has been missed, and the Aries in you will do that. Because when the Aries in you surrenders, she really surrenders; she is openly sexual. There is an old Southern saying that the more queenly a woman is, the more she desires to be a slave. Because you are aggressive, when you surrender and give all of yourself, it will be irresistible to a Scorpio."

Allison could feel the blood rushing to her face. This was not something she had planned to get into with this woman. She was astounded that Millicent could sit there in her little frothy pastel lace dress, with her curly hair swept back and her whispery Southern accent, and talk like this.

"You see," Millicent was saying, peering matter-of-factly at the chart, "Scorpio needs an animal sex life. You can give him that."

Suddenly Millicent could feel the heat from Allison's face, and she looked at her.

"Oh, I'm sorry, dear. It's just that it's all here on both of your charts. And Lorraine did say that you were a direct person who would want only the truth . . ."

"It's all right, it's all right," said Allison; "it's just that it's a little surprising to hear someone talk about your sex life to you like this. Not that anything you have said is necessarily true, you understand." She caught herself quickly.

"Of course, my dear. Well, we're pretty much finished with that section of the reading anyway. I would like to do a few projections for you, see what your charts look like over the next few years."

"Oh, yes, good," said Allison. "Let's look into the future. Give me some good predictions."

"I can't very well do that, but I can tell you what the aspects are and possibly give you some advice as to how to deal with some of the things I see looming up in the chart."

"What do you see?"

"I see that you will be sorely tested in the next few years and that you will need all the energy and the stamina and self-confidence you can muster to sustain yourself over this period. You will come out of it, but it will be hard for you."

Allison could feel a quickening of her pulse, and she began to perspire. It was fear and nothing else. She was annoyed with herself for letting this fortune-teller get to her, but she was too curious to make her stop. So she just waited for Millicent to tell her the specifics.

Millicent sighed. Allison became more nervous. Her impulse now was to get up and walk out; but she couldn't do that because it would look as if she cared, as if she believed. She couldn't tell whether Millicent was indulging in histrionics or whether her sighs were genuine.

Finally Millicent spoke.

"Well," she said slowly, deliberately, "I'm sorry to have to say this, but I think you should prepare yourself for a breakup with your Mr. Shaw. It looks like there might be a breakup which comes unexpectedly to you. It could be about one year in coming."

Allison felt slightly faint. She put her hand up to her forehead to wipe her brow and tried to smile. She felt as though her stomach were falling in.

"It seems to be the result of what you may do because of your personality, something that you may indirectly precipitate. If I may give you some advice . . ."

Allison said nothing.

"I would not be so competitive. With his Scorpio, your combative forces go after each other. What could cause a breakup is that Scorpio cannot be pushed too far. If he is pushed, he will finally not be able to stand it and he will walk away. I would try the mellow approach. I would try to be more cooperative, less combative."

This was making Allison furious. "I didn't come here for a lecture," she said, her voice rising more than she would have liked.

"I'm not giving you a lecture, dear," said Millicent. "I am only giving you advice based on what I see in both of these charts. You may follow it or not. But the consequences are not to be avoided."

Allison was less hostile when she asked her next question: "But how can I change my personality? I have my own identity. I'm my own person. I can't just acquiesce. I don't know what you are advising. It's not clear."

"Dearie, if you love this man and want to hold on to him, then you will take my advice."

Allison was stunned at the hard edge in Millicent's soft Southern speech.

"If you whistled all the time and he hated it, would you continue to whistle?"

Allison just stared at her. Millicent saw that she was upset and confused. Her face softened.

"Look, Allison, I don't mean to sound harsh. But I hate to see someone mess up something good in her life. Your two charts are karmically linked. There may be a lesson to be learned here and you will have to learn it."

She could see Allison's puzzlement. "Karmically linked means that the two charts may have been linked in another life or may be linked again. It means often that people are destined for each other. But it may be that you will have to find out what is more important to you. Where do you draw the line?"

"Why should anyone have to make that choice?" said Allison. "That's outrageous. That is something I simply cannot accept. I will not accept it."

"I am not telling you how I believe things ought to be in this world," said Millicent with another long sigh. "I am only trying to tell you how they really are. You are still young. I have had my share of compromising. And maybe I haven't done enough of it. I'm still alone, as you can see. All I can tell you is that if you can work out a compromise with yourself on this issue with your Scorpio, the break may not be permanent. The question I want you to ask yourself is this: Would you be as competitive with a woman friend you were living with? Would you be as uncompromising? Would you be as combative? If you were competing for a story, for instance, would you let a woman friend fall on her face? I am not asking you to answer these questions for me. I am only asking you to think about them. Only you will know when you have gone too far."

"I thought I was going to get an amusing little reading," Allison said. "I'm not sure I'm up for this. I particularly don't like the part about how I'm going to be tested in the next few years."

"You are a survivor," said Millicent. "You will make it. You are someone who gets up when she's knocked down. You have the energy and the determination to transform your pain into something productive. You will always have that."

"Oh, great," said Allison. "That's a relief."

Millicent had a somber look on her face again. But this time she hesitated, then held back. "I can't say if it is just a breakup with your boyfriend on the chart or if there is something more.

There could be illness—a sudden illness, even sudden death involving members of your family."

Allison laughed. "Well, at least I know that can't happen. I don't have any family left. They're all dead."

"I don't know," Millicent was murmuring. "It all comes pretty much at the same time. It appears to be simultaneous. All I can say, my dear, is I would prepare myself."

"So, on that happy note, I think I had better get back to the office." Allison's voice was much gayer than she felt. She said goodbye quickly and disappeared down the corridor of the apartment house. Millicent closed the door and walked to the phone.

Lorraine answered right away.

"I'm glad," Millicent told her. "I'm really glad she doesn't believe in astrology."

"So how was it?" Des asked on the phone that afternoon. She was calling to say she would be late.

"Oh, it was amusing. Kind of fun, actually. But it was all bullshit. Total, ridiculous, unadulterated bullshit."

CHAPTER 6

DES HAD CALLED SHORTLY AFTER THE BIRTH-
day party to see if she still wanted to show him her story.

Sadie had not returned his call but had asked her secretary to
tell him she wasn't quite ready yet for him to read it. She would
call him when she returned from East Hampton in September.
Even then she had put off calling him for weeks, and he had not
pursued the matter.

Finally, even though something told her not to, she called him
at the beginning of October.

"Lorraine Hadley says I'm crazy to trust you," she said. "She
told me never to trust a reporter. They'll even destroy each other
for a good story."

She heard her own voice get lower, huskier. She hadn't meant
it to. She hadn't meant to tell him what Lorraine said. She
wanted him to tell her it wasn't true.

"It's true," he said. "Finally, it's true. We have no gods. We
have no God unless it's the First Amendment. In the end, I would
betray you if I had to for a story. You should understand that."

"Why are you telling me this?" Her voice caught. She didn't
want to hear it.

"Because I want you to trust me."

"I don't understand."

"You will never trust me if I don't tell you the truth. I'll tell you something. One of my colleagues, a very good and decent reporter, once went down to Savannah to do a profile of your friend Senator Grayson Spence. They hit it off right away, got along like smoke. Senator Spence took him in, showed him around, introduced him to his friends, confided in him. They sat up late at night drinking and telling each other secrets. Senator Spence told my friend he felt like he was his son. They embraced and cried and told each other they loved each other. Later, my friend went back to his magazine and wrote a hatchet job on the good Senator. Really sliced him to ribbons. The Senator approached me in Congress one day, asked me back to his office. He was devastated, he said, by this piece. He was almost in tears. He'd never been so hurt, felt so betrayed. He asked me to find out what had happened. He said he didn't understand, that he thought they had trusted each other. I went to my friend. I told him about my conversation with the Senator, and I said, 'He thought you liked him.' My friend nodded and smiled, then sighed. 'I like 'em all till I sit down at my typewriter,' he said. That's a true story."

"How am I supposed to feel about that?"

"You're supposed to know that I understand and sympathize with my friend and colleague."

"I don't know what to say."

"You're not supposed to say anything. You're just supposed to hear."

"Is there no such thing as a reporter one can trust with anything? Or is that a contradiction in terms?"

"Pretty much."

"How about your friend Jenny Stern at The Daily? People say she's trustworthy, that you can tell her things and she won't write it."

"Don't let that get out. It will hurt her reputation."

"Are you saying Jenny is not a good reporter?"

"If people think they've got Jenny in their pocket, then she's probably not a good reporter. And there are people who think that about Jenny."

"You're not very loyal. I thought she was Allison's best friend."

"She is. That's because she's trustworthy. She's the only reporter Allison would ever trust."

"I don't understand what you're saying. You can't be proud of that."

"Who said proud? It's just a fact of life. It's not a matter of pride or shame. If you live your life as an adversary you can't belong to anybody."

"Who said belong? And besides, what's so bad about belonging to somebody?"

"If you belonged to somebody it wouldn't be."

"Desmond, are you going to read my short story?"

"Do you still want me to?"

"Why else would I ask you?"

"How can you be sure I won't write about it in *The Weekly*?"

"I'll just have to trust you, won't I?"

"That's like putting me in bed with a naked woman to test my celibacy."

"Something like that."

"Somebody's going to get screwed."

"It won't be me."

"How can you be so sure?"

"Trust me."

Des was on his way over. He had read her story. He wouldn't discuss it over the phone. She hadn't thought it a good idea for him to come to the house. How could she explain to Rosey about the short story if he found out? But she set a time, finally, when Rosey was out of town, and she arranged to have Tilda do some errands for her at the Executive Office Building. Only the household staff were around. She debated where to meet him. The office would be more appropriate, but if the secretary came back and found them there she'd have to explain. She decided on the upstairs sitting room. It was quiet, there was a fire, they could have coffee or tea and discuss the story. It would be more private.

It was a dreary October morning, cold and damp outside. She would wear a sweater and pants. She tried on practically everything in her wardrobe. Gray was too dreary on a day like this. Her salmon sweaters looked too frivolous, her white too elegant, the rust and greens too fall-fashion-coordinated. What would a writer wear? Black. That looked serious and professional. She rarely wore black, only when she didn't know what to wear. She put on a black turtleneck and black pants, just a touch of Laszlo Light Controlling Lotion, a tiny bit of eyeliner, a little mascara. She brushed her hair.

She patted her chin. It did seem that it was less taut than last week. She had always thought she would have her first face lift at fifty. Only in the last few weeks had she determined that it would have to be earlier than that. She would just have to hold her chin a little higher than she had before. These were not the thoughts or actions of a serious writer. She slipped on a pair of black leather shoes and looked at herself in the full-length mirror in her dressing room. She could still feel the chill from the night before in that room. It was the only room where the Secret Service would allow her to open a window at night to get some fresh air, so naturally when she went to get dressed in the morning it was always freezing. She would have to get a space heater.

She had asked the steward to lay a fire and to take all incoming calls. Shaw was coming at ten. Her palms were sweating. She didn't know whether she was more nervous over the fact that she would be alone with him or that he was coming to talk about her story. She hadn't realized how much she cared about this story. If he didn't like it, it would crush a dream she had cherished for more than twenty years. If he did, well—if he did, she didn't know. That was scary too.

She had given him only one. It was a new one she had written about her friend Dolly in Savannah. It was called "Fay's Last Chance" and it was about a middle-aged married woman who has an affair with the tennis pro at the country club. Contentedly married to a doctor, living in the suburbs, she has noticed the crow's-feet around her eyes and the bulge around her middle and has determined to break out of her rut before it's too late. The tennis pro, tall, handsome, and muscular, asks her to leave her husband for him. Unlike Dolly, though, Sadie couldn't bring herself to have Fay take the step. She had decided to leave the ending ambiguous, even though she thought her friend's decision was a more modern ending and had more literary value. Every time she sat down at the typewriter to write the part about Fay leaving her husband, she had cold feet. Finally she had to let it slide. She wasn't satisfied with the ending as it was and had written Des a note to that effect when she sent him the pages. Perhaps he could give her the conviction she needed to change it.

The steward was buzzing. It was just a few minutes after ten. Prompt, but not early. She took a last look in the mirror over the bar in the sitting room and walked over to the mantel to wait for him. She had decided to have him shown upstairs.

The minute he entered the room she could feel his energy. The room seemed to vibrate as he walked over and leaned down hesitantly to kiss her on the cheek. Neither one of them was comfortable with that, yet it seemed too stilted to shake hands. He sort of grabbed her hand as he kissed her. They both laughed and pulled away a little too quickly.

"Electricity," they said simultaneously, and laughed again, even more self-consciously. They both reddened a little and laughed again. They felt that giddiness which comes from being attracted to somebody before the attraction is acknowledged.

"Would you like some coffee or tea?" she asked, and burst out laughing.

"No, I don't think so . . . well, yeah, sure, why not?" He was laughing too. There wasn't anything funny to laugh at. She was relieved. Pouring would give her something to concentrate on.

He started to say something, then laughed, this time almost in a giggle. "Where should I put this?"

He was holding the manuscript.

"Oh, uh, just set it down anywhere—unless, of course, you want to put it in there."

She gestured toward the fire.

"Ah, fishing for compliments." He smiled.

"No, just giving you an easy out." Her teeth were sticking to her lips. She kept licking her lips, hoping he would not take that gesture as deliberately provocative. How had she ever gotten herself into this charade?

She handed him a cup of coffee and saw that his hands were shaking.

She sipped her tea, looking down at the cup. He needed a haircut. She rarely saw a journalist who didn't. Either that or their hair was too short. She surmised that it was because they hated to get haircuts and hated even worse to pay for them so they practically had their heads shaved every three or four months and then waited till their hair was much too long to go back again. Politicians were religious about haircuts. Every two weeks. Trim. He wore a rather shabby-looking tweed jacket, a wool tie, a wool plaid shirt, khaki trousers and loafers. His face was ruddy from the cold. She could smell his smell again, even though they weren't that close. Rosey always wore some kind of lemon shaving lotion. It wasn't bad. She didn't even know what he smelled like.

She was thinking how handsome he was when he looked up over his cup and caught her eye. There was a twinkle in his eye when he looked at her, but when they caught each other's glance they both became serious.

"Let's get down to business," he said.

"Why don't you give me the bad news first?" she said, her voice rising nervously.

"I don't work that way; it's not good for morale."

"How uncharacteristic of a journalist."

"Don't give me that."

"So-or-ry."

"Okay. Now, what I'm going to do is to tell you the good points and then get down to criticisms."

"Then you don't think it's totally hopeless?"

"Of course I don't. If I did, I would have told you on the phone to forget it. Could you do anything that was totally hopeless?"

"You haven't experienced my singing."

"There's a lot about you I haven't experienced." He laughed.

She blushed and looked down at her cup. He cleared his throat.

"The good points of the story are these: the characters are clear, vivid; they are real people. That's good. You made them believable and we have sympathy for them right away. The dialogue is pretty good—no, I would say very good. The story is interesting. I wasn't bored; I didn't want to put it down. It moves along nicely. It's not prize-winning fiction, but it's a good read. It is nothing to be ashamed of. It's a brave story."

"Now for the bad news."

"Listen to the good things. This is good work, really, much much better than I expected. Now for the bad. The subject matter is trite. I've heard the tennis-pro story too many times."

"But it's true. It actually happened to my friend in—"

"That's what trite is. How do things get to be trite unless they're true too many times? Nevertheless, that's the story, and you can't very well change it unless you make him a swim coach or the postman, and that's even more trite. So we'll stick with the tennis pro for now."

"Whatever you say, Coach." She hadn't meant that. She hadn't realized its implications until she said it. He didn't seem to notice.

"The writing is not brilliant. Good at its best. It's amateurish in places, but it is natural. It's too long. It needs to be cut. That's not a big problem. I could do that. A mean red pencil and it will be fine."

"There must be more."

"There is no ending. You've got this woman who has just turned forty. She's bored in her marriage; the sex isn't great or isn't there anymore. The kids are away. She loves her husband, but she's not in love with him. He is a prominent doctor and they have an important social position. She falls desperately in love with the tennis pro, the sex is fabulous, he loves her and he wants her to leave her husband for him, start a new life. Then it stops. She doesn't do anything."

"I know."

"You've built this great case for her to leave the husband. In fact, you've given us no reason to believe she will stay, and then she doesn't leave."

"I know."

"Well, why?"

She had been poring over her own copy of the story while Des was talking to her.

"Would you like some more coffee?"

"Why does she stay?"

"I could ring for—"

"Sadie?"

She looked at him again. Neither one of them smiled. He had a questioning look in his eyes. She couldn't look away this time. For some reason, she wanted to cry. They kept looking at each other. She was unable to break the gaze. Instead she heaved a large sigh, then whispered, "I don't know."

"Well, you've got to think about it," he said finally, his own voice little more than a gruff whisper. "Otherwise the story doesn't work."

* * *

"Baby, you realize this thing is going to be a giant Rat Fuck tonight."

"No question."

"Then why are we going?"

They were whizzing past the Washington Monument en route to the Castle at the Smithsonian Institution. The Woodrow Wilson Center was having a dinner for a visiting Russian delegation, in town to negotiate with Roger Kimball over his policy on Soviet political prisoners and human rights. Kimball had been putting a lot of pressure on the Soviets ever since taking office, and the Russians were balking.

"We're going because we might learn something. We're called reporters, remember? Besides, you sit up in your office all day staring out at the White House and the Capitol dome and sucking your thumb. You need to get out more and see some of the people you write about. It's important, Des."

"Thank God I have you to run my life."

"Oh, knock it off. You'll have a good time. Maybe you'll get to sit next to some cute little translator."

"No way. I'll get some fat wife of a minor Soviet diplomat at the Embassy here. I'm too important for cute translators anymore. There are times when it pays to be a junior reporter. Like at Washington dinner parties, for instance."

"This is the most pathetic thing I've ever heard. Let's try to be positive. Maybe we'll get a good story out of it."

"*You* might. You always get to sit next to the men. I have to sweat it out making conversation with their wives."

Des was slumped down in the seat of his Thunderbird, his left hand on the wheel, his right hand casually draped over the back of the other seat.

"No more pussy for old Desmond now that I'm a big-shot bureau chief."

"You got La Divina at the birthday party. That should be enough to hold you for at least a year."

"Jesus, will you knock that one off? You're beginning to sound like a broken record on the subject."

They were silent for a while as he stepped on the gas crossing Fourteenth Street, which he knew would annoy her.

"Well, at least there'll be plenty of vodka tonight," she said finally. "You can always get drunk while I'm scooping you."

"Not you, Sonny. Never. Why, beating the man you love out of a story would never cross your mind. You're much too loyal for that."

"Just watch my smoke, ol' buddy."

"Be careful you don't self-immolate."

Inside the Smithsonian Castle was a great hall where drinks were being served before dinner. The hall was filled with hundreds of gray-faced, gray-haired, gray-suited men and a few women in dowdy suits. In the center of the room stood a handful of celebrity politicians, Administration officials, and journalists swarming around each other like bees pollinating flowers. The standard configuration of Washington parties. The bar was a few feet away from the power center, and those celebrities who couldn't find an academic to fetch them a drink broke out of the nexus at their own risk.

Des took the risk and was back in the circle within what seemed like seconds, a double Irish-on-the-rocks in hand.

"Thanks for getting me a drink," said Allison.

"Oh, sorry, baby," said Des. "I forgot."

"You just didn't want to wait for a glass of wine."

Allison spotted Malcolm and Abigail Sohier a few feet away listening intently to a former Ambassador to Moscow expound his theory of Soviet–American relations. She strolled quickly over to where they were standing and nudged the Senator forcefully in the ribs.

Consummate politician that he was, Malcolm never even flinched, but Abigail let out a delighted giggle and came around to hug Allison, escaping the person she was talking to.

"Thank God you're here," she whispered. "How did you manage to drag Des along?"

"Kicking and screaming. He claims anyone who can decipher Washington invitations could tell from a glance that it was going to be"—she lowered her voice—"what the late Mrs. John T. used to call a Philadelphia rat fuck."

"Speaking of Hooker," said Malcolm, "he's meeting with the Godless Commies tomorrow before they go in to see Kimball. We've all tried to persuade the President that this is not a good

NOT FOR US

006855   0001628   A50

BOARDING PASS

NAME OF PASSENGER

DICHTER/CAROLE

FROM
X   WASHINGTON

TO
PHILADELPHIA 30TH

CARRIER
AMTRAK

CARRIER	FLIGHT	CLASS	DATE	TIME
A3	118CM		14JUN	300P

GATE   SEAT   SMOKE

PCS   WT   UNCKD   BAGGAGE ID NUMBER

2 554 1109688493 0
131502542

idea, but Hooker seems to have the President in his pocket on this one. We can just hope he hasn't started World War Three before they get to the White House. I can't figure out what's going on over there."

He was looking to Allison for information, but she didn't want to get into a discussion of Uncle Roger's problems with Malcolm, at least not at this dinner.

"Who's Des talking to?"

"Oh, Mr. Smoothie," said Abigail, following Allison's gaze. "Malcolm and I met him in Moscow. He's the spokesperson for the Central Committee. Very, very well oiled. Speaks perfect English. He's quite Americanized. He was at the U.N. a few years ago. He's become a big TV personality recently and writes a column for a prestigious weekly, I can't think of the name. He's a good source. He's one of the few who manages to play both sides. He gets away with it somehow."

"I'm surprised he's talking to Des and not you," said Malcolm. "He has quite an eye for the ladies. Like Abigail, for instance."

"Oh, God, Malcolm. Malcolm got all upset because he flirted with me at the dinner they gave for our delegation in Moscow. He told me I was beautiful and that he thought he could fall in love with me. Malcolm was so annoyed that he got up to make a toast and said there were good Americans and bad Americans just like there were good Russians and bad Russians, staring right at Vasily. It was ridiculous."

"Well, for God's sake, the man makes a pass at your wife, what would you do? I have a good mind to change my position on Star Wars."

They all laughed as the guests began to move toward the paneled banquet hall for dinner.

Allison found Des up ahead in the crowd and moved quickly to join him, whispering in his ear as they entered the dining room, "So what did you learn from Vasily Antonin?"

"Nothing *The Daily* needs to know," he said, smiling.

"You mean he didn't tell you about his meeting with John T. tomorrow?" She pretended to look shocked.

"How the hell did you know about that?" He looked genuinely surprised.

"Just a little crack reporting. Stick with me, baby."

"I'm trying, I'm trying, but you're moving too fast for a poor little Irish kid from the South Side."

"Save that one for the Russian translator." She laughed.

"I should get so lucky."

"Mr. Shaw, Mr. Shaw?"

A thick Russian accent interrupted their exchange, and as they turned they were greeted by a short, stocky woman with an enormous chest, a rather heavy mustache, a mole on the end of her nose, and her mousy gray-brown hair pulled back in a bun.

"Mr. Shaw," she repeated, tugging at Des's sleeve, "I am the translator for the delegation. I have the honor of being your dinner partner."

Des took one look at her and rolled his eyes as Allison turned away, doubled over with laughter.

They were both seated at the same round table—unusual for a Washington dinner—but on opposite sides. On Des's left was a minor Russian Embassy official who spoke poor English, and he glared at Allison.

She, on the other hand, was seated next to Vasily Antonin, and as she saw him approach her she looked up at Des, saw the outraged expression on his face, and again burst out laughing. On her other side was the former head of the CIA Russian Section, now head of the Russian Studies department at Columbia University.

Altogether, a terrific seat. She dared not look at Des again for the rest of the evening.

"What a lucky fellow I am, to be seated next to someone as beautiful as you."

She and Vasily had sat down together, he perched sidewise on his chair, facing her, his cocktail glass in hand, filled, she assumed, with straight vodka.

"Oh, no," she insisted. "I'm the one who is lucky."

"Charming as well as beautiful," he said, laughing as he leaned closer to her. "I can see we are going to have a very good time tonight."

He didn't mention Kimball or *The Daily*, so she had no idea whether he knew who she was.

Vasily was not conventionally handsome, but he had a Slavic elegance that appealed to Allison. High cheekbones, a faint slant to the eyes, pale hair, pale skin, pale blue eyes, a pale smile. She imagined he would be sensuous, maybe a little cruel in bed.

They made conversation about Soviet—American relations, full of *double entendres*, as the first course was served. He had turned his back on the drab little woman on his other side, a silent announcement of his intentions with Allison. When the waiter came with the wine, he put his hand over his wineglass, gesturing for more vodka. His conversation was loose and easy—too much so for such a high-powered Russian, though he did not appear to be drunk. If she hadn't heard Abigail's story, Allison would have believed that he was genuinely smitten, but it annoyed her a bit to think that he was doing a number on her. Particularly such an effective one.

"Is that your husband?" he asked finally, gesturing toward Des.

"My lover."

There was a glint in his eye. He said nothing.

"Are *you* married?" she asked.

"Of course." He took a swig of vodka.

"Do you have a mistress?"

"Yes."

"What's her name?"

"Viktoriya."

"Do you love her?"

"She's the only person I have ever been able to talk to honestly in my life. I can say whatever is in my mind, my thoughts, and she will understand. And I don't have to be afraid. She is the only person I have ever known who is not afraid to say anything."

"What does she do?"

"She's a journalist, like you."

So he did know who she was.

"Is she married?"

"Yes, to a member of the KGB."

"Does he know about the affair?"

"No."

"How did you meet?"

"She came to interview me in my office. The attraction was immediate. We wanted each other. We talked of many things besides the interview.

"When it was over," he continued, "she asked me to walk her to her car. It was very cold, midwinter. We got in her car, very tiny. We made love. I can't remember anything except that I had to have her."

He stopped, stared into his glass, took a sip, then looked up at Allison.

"What do they call you?"

"Sonny."

"Sonny. Beautiful Sonny. I would like to make love to you too."

He seemed so serious, she was just vain enough to believe he meant it. It didn't matter. She was going to go in for the kill in a few minutes.

"The other day," said Vasily, suddenly changing moods, laughing, "she asked me to make love to her again in her car, the way we had the first time. I told her, never again. I had never been so cold, so uncomfortable in my life. She accused me of losing my passion for her."

The waiters had cleared the soup, then the fish course. He hadn't touched a bite.

"Well?"

"It's not true. She's the only thing that keeps me from committing suicide. But I don't want accusations, recriminations. I get that at home. I despise my wife. She is crazy. And our son. He has a serious neurological disease. We have had to go outside Russia for treatment. Everyone on the Central Committee does when they need first-class treatment. We just don't let it be known."

Now she was getting something out of him.

"Why don't you leave her and marry Viktoriya?"

"It is not possible. Viktoriya's husband would destroy me. And my wife. We have too much. In our position we have cars, television, hi-fi, shopping privileges, country dacha. We live like capitalists. Nobody wants to give up the good life."

"It doesn't sound so good to me."

"To tell you the truth, it isn't. Every night I have to take three sleeping pills just to fall asleep.

"I think of killing myself every day. I want to die. Do you have any idea what life is like in Russia? Nobody is ever allowed to say what they think or feel. If you did, you would be put in an institution for the mentally ill or sent to Siberia. Everyone is afraid all the time. Everyone lives in fear. I am in constant fear. Fear that my wife will report me for something. Those on the

Central Committee, those high up in government are more afraid than the rest because they have more to lose. It is a horrible life. Death has to be easier."

He had to be drunk, Allison decided. He couldn't be talking to her this way if he were not. He knew she was a reporter. Could this be a setup? But he didn't appear to be drunk.

"Well," said Allison cheerily, "think of it this way. At least you have Viktoriya. That's more than most of the men on the Central Committee have."

"Don't be naive. They all have mistresses."

"So what will you do? *Will* you commit suicide?" She was only half-joking. It did seem like a reasonable alternative.

"I don't think I have the courage. I think I'm daring somebody to kill me. I'm writing messages to Viktoriya in my column each week. This week I wrote about Star Wars. 'Let the Americans have their Star Wars,' I said. 'As for me, I prefer to gaze at the stars and think of love.'"

"What sort of reaction did you get to that column?" asked Allison in disbelief.

"No one took it seriously. They all laughed about it, winked and nudged me in the ribs. But it's true. I do prefer to think of love. And I cannot think of anything else when I am sitting next to you. Will you meet me tomorrow? I have to be on television tomorrow morning at seven. Then we don't have to be at the State Department until eleven. You could come to my hotel room."

There was a frantic tone to his voice and a look of desperation, not lust, on his face.

Allison couldn't quite make out what it was he wanted from her. He had his hand on her thigh now under the table, gazing at her, beseeching her almost. He seemed oblivious when the former Ambassador to Moscow stood up to speak and the room became hushed.

"What would *he* say about us?" he said, gesturing toward Des, who had been rolling his eyes at her most of the evening, not realizing what was going on. "Would he be jealous? Would he want to kill me?"

"I have to go to the ladies' room," said Allison. People had begun to stare.

The conversation had gone too far; this man was out of control. Her reporter's instinct told her to keep him talking, but she couldn't allow his advances to continue, and she didn't know how to stop him without staying away and missing the head of the delegation's speech.

After five minutes in the ladies' room, she returned to the table. She sat with her back to him, pretending to concentrate on the speech. The head of the delegation, a large, muscular man with a red face and leonine mass of white hair, reminded her more than a little of John T. She regretted she wouldn't be a witness to their scheduled confrontation the following morning.

"You are ignoring me."

She could feel his breath on the back of her neck. He had his hand on her arm.

"Why are you ignoring me? I love you. I have fallen in love and I want you. You have become cold and distant. Where is my warm, sensual Sonny of a few moments ago?"

She turned to him, putting her finger to her lips in a shushing motion.

"Don't do that to me, Sonny. I have something you want to know."

She looked at him and he suddenly looked very sober. The speeches were over and there was applause and everyone was standing to toast Soviet–American friendship.

"Our Premier will be dead in three months at the longest," he whispered to her. "He has a terminal lung disease. Nobody knows this. This man, Ivanovich, our chief of delegation, will replace him."

Allison looked stunned, but he stopped her before she could say a word.

He reached over and kissed her hand quickly. "We would have been lovers in another life. Do not betray me, Sonny."

And before she knew it, he had disappeared.

Des slammed on the brakes and nearly drove the car into the Tidal Basin by the Jefferson Memorial.

"Jesus, are you serious? That son-of-a-bitch was propositioning you the whole time I was sitting at the table?"

"That's not the point. The point is that I got an incredible story."

"I don't care what you got. That guy has some balls doing that to you. I'm going back there and beat the shit out of him."

Des turned the car around, nearly colliding with several cars as he did.

"Des, for heaven's sake, calm down. This is not a big deal. Just listen to what he told me."

"No big deal? Some bastard propositions my woman in the middle of dinner with me sitting right there and it's no big deal? It's going to be a big deal when he finds his testicles in his throat."

"You wouldn't be so annoyed if you'd gotten to sit next to some gorgeous piece."

"Maybe."

"He didn't have an ounce of sex appeal."

"Who?"

"Vasily. He was a joke. You can't take a man seriously who pulls something like that. In fact, I don't really like men who make passes at women at all. It's much sexier to have to make a pass at the man you want to make love to than to have him come on to you."

"Yeah?" There was a hint of a smile on his lips.

She put her hand on his thigh and began rubbing it slowly, letting her hand move upward to his crotch, where she felt him swell almost immediately.

"Get your hands off me," he growled.

She rubbed at him harder, then leaned across the gearshift and kissed him lightly on the ear, taking his earlobe between her teeth and gently chewing on it.

"Cut it out," he said, his voice huskier than before, and he halfheartedly pushed her away with his elbow. "What do you think you're doing?"

"I'm going to fuck you," she whispered.

"It won't be the first time," he said, putting his foot on the gas.

"And probably not the last," she murmured.

"Are you serious?"

Allen Warburg and Walt Fineman were both standing in Allen's glass office as Allison recounted her conversation with Vasily.

"I'm telling you, the guy unloaded on me."

"I'll say," said Walt. Allen hadn't said a word. He was just listening.

"So what do you make of it?" he asked Allison, finally.

She stopped for a moment as though she hadn't thought that far.

"Well, it's a fabulous story."

"So how do you write it?"

"The way it happened."

"No, I mean, do you write it as a news story for the A section? 'Yesterday, Vasily What's-his-name said that blah-blah-blah . . .'"

"Of course not."

"Then it's a Living story. 'Sipping his third vodka, he pushed back a lock of silver-blond hair and mumbled in his husky Slavic accent . . .'"

"Come on, Allen. You're acting like I've just come back from covering the Folk Life Festival on the Mall."

"Were you covering this event?"

"Not officially."

"So the guy didn't know he was speaking on the record."

"Oh, please. He's talking to a national reporter for *The Daily* and he thinks he's off the record? This is a very experienced man. He's a journalist himself."

"That's what worries me."

"Look, let's get Berger and Cutler in here," said Fineman. "They've both lived in Moscow, they both know Vasily, they've covered the CIA. Let's see what they have to say."

"Berger was there last night," said Allison. "He was raising his eyebrows at me all night."

Moments later the two reporters listened as Allison went over the previous evening for them.

"Jesus," said Cutler.

"I knew the guy was having problems," said Berger. "But this is something else again. I can't believe it."

"The Soviets are up to something," said Cutler, the conspiratorialist. "The guy's a plant. They know about Allison's relationship with the President. The question is, What's the point? What do they want to prove?"

"Listen. I was there. I'm telling you the guy was for real. I think he was close to a nervous breakdown."

"What about this stuff on the Soviet Premier's health, Berger?"

"We've had rumors but nothing definite. If he were that sick I can't imagine we wouldn't have heard about it."

"So what if he's a CIA plant? What if the spooks are up to something?"

"You guys have been reading too many spy novels," said Allison. "We have an incredible story here. What are we going to do with it?"

"I would think very carefully before I wrote it," said Berger.

"Why?" asked Allison.

"Because even though he was incredibly stupid and you have no obligation to protect him from himself, you are signing the guy's death warrant. He will either be killed, sent to Siberia, or be forced to commit suicide. They play hardball over there. I'm not kidding."

There was a long silence in the room.

"But you've got yourself a hell of a story."

"Thanks," said Allison, as she picked up her notebook and left the room.

She didn't sleep well that night. What disturbed her most was that normally she would have. A story to most journalists was like Mount Everest. You climb it because it's there. You print for the same reason. Let the editors worry about the consequences. It was almost like a game of Chicken. You challenge your editor to print, then argue if he refuses, but acquiesce. Now they had thrown it back at her. And now she had to examine the consequences. And the consequences looked very different when it was her responsibility. For some reason she didn't discuss it with Des that night. She waited until she had made her decision before calling him the next day at his office.

"I just can't do it," she said.

"Why not? You don't owe the guy anything. What did he think you were going to do with the information—write it in your diary?"

"Because, Des, it could—no—would endanger his life."

"Not even if we were talking Pulitzers?"

"No story is worth a person's life."

"What kind of journalist are you, anyway?"

She knew he was half-joking, but it annoyed her anyway. It was killing her not to at least follow up on the story.

"I've tried to think of some way to do it without identifying him. Maybe for the Sunday Magazine with fictitious names. Or maybe even fictionalize it."

"Forget it. You could never do that."

"Why not?"

"Because nobody would ever believe it."

"The whole thing just bothers me. I feel like the guy made an ass out of me. Telling me all this stuff he knew I couldn't or wouldn't use. He was almost daring me to write it."

"Hey, Sonny. Y'know what?"

"What?"

"I love you."

"Why?"

"'Cause you're tough."

"Oh, yeah?"

"But not that tough."

"Is that a compliment or an insult?"

"You guessed it."

"I'm stuck."

"What do you mean?"

"I can't get the ending. Blocked."

Des had called Sadie back after not having heard from her in several days.

"So what do you want to do?"

"I think I'd like to scrap it for now and try something else."

"Any ideas?"

"I was kind of fantasizing about the idea of my leading a double life. Veep's wife by day, cat burglar by night. How would I do it, what would it be like—that sort of thing."

"It's a great idea. Working out the logistics would be a challenge."

"I haven't worked it out. I mean I was just thinking about it yesterday, what a prison this is and how hard it would be to do anything without anyone knowing."

"I've got an idea."

"What?"

"Let's have lunch."

"What's that got to do with my idea?"

"Alone."

"I still don't get it."

"I'm talking about absolutely alone. No Secret Service, no stewards, no secretaries. Alone."

"It's not possible."

"So we can scrap your fantasy. No literary value there. Moving right along . . ."

He was daring her, and she didn't know whether she wanted to play or not. If she did, she wasn't ready to admit it.

"No, no. You're right, of course. It's just that I can't think now."

"Call me when you can."

It was Hugh, the gardener, who finally gave her the idea. She was talking to him about the spring planting. She had been consulting with him constantly since she got back in September, and their talks were the highlight of her day; the decisions she would make about the grounds would be so much more permanent than any to do with the interior, and she was taking it very seriously.

Hugh was tall and carrot-topped, with an innocent freckled face which made him look younger than he was. He was so friendly and sweet that she could hardly keep herself from patting his head. He was one of the few people she dealt with who seemed totally oblivious to her position. He appeared to like her for herself, and that made her feel comfortable. And since he was always the expert about gardening, he treated her like an equal. There was something about Hugh that made her want to confide in him, and they had developed a cozy, teasing relationship. Some days she was so eager to talk with Hugh that she would meet him in his van as it pulled into the garage off the kitchen to unload whatever surprises he had picked up for her that day at the nursery.

By the kitchen door to the garage was one of the many TV monitors that recorded the comings and goings of every member of the household. It was impossible to leave the house from any exit without being seen by the Secret Service.

The next time Hugh came, shortly after her conversation with Des, he brought her an especially prized Japanese maple, and she rushed out to meet him. They had walked the length of the yard discussing where to plant it.

"You're getting so good you really should think about going into gardening," he said.

"I would if I weren't planning to be a best-selling novelist," she said.

"You're writing a novel, are you?"

"I'm thinking about it."

"What's it about?"

"It's still a little vague, but I have this thought that it might be about a Vice President's wife who leads a double life. A kind of spoof. But I've been trying to think how to get her out of here logistically, and I just can't figure out a way short of being smuggled in and out in a trunk."

"How about a garbage can?" Hugh grinned.

"You think that's more appropriate," she teased.

"More unlikely."

"You have something specific in mind, I presume?"

"Actually, madam, I do. Come with me."

They were enjoying their little jest as Sadie followed Hugh up the sloping lawn and over to the garage, where he kept his supplies. He opened the door to his van and pulled out two very large new green plastic trash containers.

"I brought these along today to collect the fall leaves. May I?" and he bowed.

Luckily she was wearing slacks, so she let him help her into the garbage pail and put the lid on. Then with seemingly little effort he lifted the pail up and slid it into the back of the van and closed the doors.

"Brilliant!" she cried, laughing, as she peered out the doors of the van.

She would dismiss the stewards early, or give them the day off on a holiday; have Hugh bring a garbage pail inside the house, where she would climb inside in the pantry; then he'd carry it out to the van. The Secret Service wouldn't see her leave on the TV screen and they would assume she was in the house. Then Hugh would just drive out of the grounds and to her secret destination.

"Do I dare?" she asked, extricating herself from the garbage can.

"Now that you know it's possible, how can you not?"

"Columbus Day. It's next Monday. I'll let the staff off and . . .

oh, Hugh, could you possibly do it that day? I didn't even think that it might be your day off too."

"Are you kidding? For this I'd come back from vacation."

"Okay, then: see you Monday. If it falls through I'll call you."

She raced upstairs to her second-floor sitting room and still out of breath, called Des at *The Weekly*. She was amazed at the physical reaction she had to him, to his voice.

"Let's have lunch," she said.

He was silent on the other end.

"Alone."

L'Auberge Chez François was closed on Mondays. Des knew François from the old days when he had had a restaurant a block from the White House and near his office. It had been his hangout when he was working for *The Boston Gazette*. Now François had moved out into the Virginia countryside, past McLean, past Great Falls Park. Des didn't get there often, but they were still buddies.

François would open the restaurant for them Monday; he would cook the lunch personally, and his wife would serve. No staff. All very discreet. They agreed that Hugh would take her to the Potomac overlook at George Washington Parkway and, dressed casually and wearing dark glasses and a hat to conceal her hair, she would get out and join Des in his car for the drive out to the restaurant. Everything was set.

The night before, Sadie lay awake, her mind racing. Every possibility for disaster arose.

The President would drop dead and Rosey would be President. They would look for her everywhere. It would be a major scandal. She would have Des ask François to keep a radio on.

Des would have a heart attack and they would have to call an ambulance. How would she get back?

She would have a heart attack. What would they tell Rosey?

By morning she was exhausted and desperate to get out of the whole scheme. It was insane. She couldn't call Des. He was at Allison's. She tried to call Hugh. He had probably gone to the nursery to pick up some plants. She went down to the kitchen. The house was empty. She couldn't eat. She tried to read the paper. She couldn't concentrate. She turned on the morning television shows. She turned them off.

She had a little talk with herself. What am I doing wrong? Nothing. I am just going to have lunch. Big deal. With somebody who's going to help me with my writing. Privately. I'm trying out a plot angle. I am a person. I am not a slave to my country. I am not the Vice President. Why can't I have a little freedom? Where is it written I can't try to sneak out? I am testing the Secret Service. If I can fool them, then they're not very secure. Anybody could. That's it. I am testing their effectiveness. They will get in such trouble if I am found out. Toby, at least, is on vacation. He won't get into trouble. I won't get caught. If I do, it will be lucky it was something like this, not a serious breach of security. Besides, it's not illegal. So why not?

It was a brilliant day. Bright and clear. And cool for mid-October. Indian summer hadn't hit yet. She wore a deep blue-green suede outfit. The top was a sweater jacket which zipped up the front; the skirt, suede.

No jewelry.

She decided on rust leather flats; they might take a walk after lunch. And she took along a paisley shawl in case it got colder later in the afternoon. Not that she planned to spend that much time.

His car was waiting on the overlook. He was standing by the front, his foot on the fender, looking down at the view of the Potomac. The leaves all around were beginning to turn, with bursts of yellows and reds among the green. It was her time of year. He had on his corduroys. His hair was mussed as usual. They were both still tanned from the summer. There were no other cars. She saw him turn casually toward the van as it pulled in. She had stayed in the back during the trip.

Hugh helped her out. He and Des shook hands solemnly, like a father handing over his bride; then he drove away.

It was a little after twelve thirty. Their reservation was for one. She was wearing large dark glasses and an old rust-colored slouch fedora, wide-brimmed, which she pulled down even lower over her eyes. She tipped her head up slightly and smiled. He leaned over to kiss her cheek and the hat nearly fell off. They both tried to catch it, then both laughed, embarrassed.

She wanted to put off getting into his car, as though that were the final commitment. She suggested they look at the view. It was too risky, he said. She still made no move for his car, and a brisk wind caught her hat and blew it off, so that they both lunged for it and hit their heads together. They laughed again, and she sheepishly took her hat and climbed into the T-Bird, positioning the brim even lower over her eyes than before. Maybe she could just make herself disappear.

They pulled out onto the George Washington Parkway and headed toward the restaurant, driving in silence for a while. They were both awkward. Like teenagers on a first date. Sadie kept trying in vain to think of something to say.

He was the one who finally spoke.

"Well, you don't look as if you just stepped out of a garbage can."

"I should never have told you."

"You had to. There can be no secrets between us."

She blushed.

"Do you realize the power I have over the Vice President of the United States at this very moment?" he asked.

"Is that important to you?" He couldn't tell if she was teasing.

"I suppose it must be. Otherwise it wouldn't have occurred to me."

"So now your fantasy is realized."

"I thought this was *your* fantasy."

"So it is."

They drove along the winding roads, up and down hills, occasional patches of sunlight almost blinding them after they came up from a shaded part of the road.

"What's Great Falls Park?" she asked finally, desperate for conversation, as they drove past a large sign to the right.

"It's one of the most spectacular places you've ever seen. Beautiful river views. There's another one, River Bend Park, which is beautiful too. But dangerous. There are a lot of drownings."

"Why does anyone ever go there, then?"

"I guess danger excites."

"Well, I certainly don't understand it."

"I think you do."

He looked at her and smiled. She looked at him and felt her stomach drop.

The Auberge was enchanting and unexpected in a place so close to Washington. Close your eyes and you are in France. The entrance and the front room were dark, with little tables, red-flowered curtains, a large wheel lamp, plates on the walls, pine cupboards, and a large fireplace. A newer wing was glorious with large windows where sun splashed over the green pottery, the flowerpots, pretty lamps, and checked tablecloths. A table next to the window overlooked a lovely garden and the woods beyond.

François deliberately did not notice who she was. It was as if his family had been serving French monarchs and premiers and their famous mistresses for centuries. With a Gallic flourish, accompanied by dancing eyebrows and a profusion of compliments, he kissed her hand and led them to their table. He already had a bottle of dry white wine on ice next to the table, and after he had opened it he bowed deeply and sailed away. The *chef d' oeuvre* he was whipping up for them in the kitchen required his full attention.

Sadie giggled as he disappeared.

"*Voilà!*" said Des, with a sweeping gesture, imitating François.

She was touched by his vulnerability as he said it. He wouldn't have learned French where he grew up. Rosey, of course, spoke excellent French.

"Do you speak French?" he asked, tentatively, when she didn't say anything.

"A little. I learned it in school. But I'm self-conscious about my accent and I rarely try."

"Chessy's French was perfect," he said. "Sonny's isn't bad."

Why had he mentioned her name? The clouds covered up the sun for a moment. Not that he shouldn't. But somehow, just for today, she wanted to believe they were alone.

Des poured the wine. She was surprised to see, when she took her glass, that her hand was shaking.

"Cheers," he said, as he clicked his glass to hers.

They made small talk. He told her all about the good old days when they used to hang out at Chez François.

She didn't hear a word. She kept watching his hands as they played with the bread crumbs on the table, watching his eyes as they sparkled when he laughed: mocking? serious? she couldn't tell; his lashes as they swept his cheeks when he looked down. His lower lip was full and curved down at one end, so that he always had a sort of wry look about him, ready to smile or grimace. His jaw was square, and he worked it when he was silent as though he were chewing his thoughts.

She tried not to think what his mouth would feel like on her mouth, what his hands would feel like on her body.

She began playing with her bread crumbs.

"Washington isn't the same anymore," he was saying. He had put his in a pile, brushing them together.

"Why is that?" she forced herself to respond. She did the same with hers.

"Things aren't as much fun. I don't know. Maybe I'm just older. But there's no excitement."

As he said it he looked at her. Their eyes caught. He reached over and brushed her crumbs onto his. She was helping him put the piles together. Their fingers touched.

"Excitement is where you find it," she said, and reddened.

"More wine?" Their hands pulled apart as he reached for the bottle and they both sighed.

"I don't know," he said finally. "I feel bent out of shape. Maybe I'm just older. Or maybe it's the Washington tilt."

"All right," she giggled. "What's the Washington tilt?"

"Well, the Washington tilt is what happens to a person's neck after he or she has lived too long in this city. It comes from going to too many dinner parties and tilting your head in a listening position to hear the important words of whatever important person you happen to be talking to. It usually begins innocently with something like 'Tell me, Mr. Secretary,' and then you tilt your head forward to listen or to appear to be listening. Before you know it, after so many evenings of tilting, you find that it's difficult to hold your head up straight. Then wherever you go, people can tell right away that you're a Washingtonian by the slight tilt to your head. It's not great for the balance either. Too much tilt and walking a straight line becomes difficult. Tilting and slanting go hand in hand. It's a dangerous disease for a journalist. It's as dangerous as Potomac fever is for a politician."

Sadie laughed. It wasn't that she had forgotten how funny and sexy he was. It was just that she hadn't allowed herself to remember.

"Have *I* got it yet?"

"No, and I hope you don't. You have too pretty a neck to have it ruined that way."

She could feel her face flush and her pulse beat a little faster. Her lips had gone dry. She licked them. She tried not to smile, but heard herself giggling again. She didn't know what to say.

"You're terrible," she said.

He laughed.

"Have *you* got it?"

"Got it?"

"The tilt."

"Only when I talk to you."

She blushed again.

"You haven't complimented me on getting out of the house," she said. They were both concentrating very hard on his wine pouring. She wondered if his heart was pounding the way hers was.

"I would have expected nothing less. Besides, I'm a demanding editor. I want a story out of it. You have the Vice President's wife out of the house to lead a double life. But what does she do?" He knew what he wanted her to say.

"I guess I didn't really get that far," she lied.

François brought a delectable fish mousse for the first course, followed by a veal roast in chanterelles. Salad and cheese. They had switched to a Beaujolais. The conversation was going slowly; both were uncomfortable and stilted, two people on Novocaine, numbed by desire. There were great pauses as they ate or stared out at the park and commented once more on the beautiful day. All the clever things Sadie had imagined they would talk about seemed to escape her.

All of the witty things he was supposed to say did not materialize.

The pear Hélène was superb. The wine was light and smooth, the sun bright, the espresso strong.

They lingered over the espresso, talking in starts. A little of her school years at Smith, his in Boston; a little about the South; something about journalism, travel, food, friends. Pleasant but disappointing.

Then it was three thirty. She had told Hugh to meet her at four at the overlook. That would give them time for a walk, she'd thought, but now it was too late. They thanked François profusely. Des fought gamely for a check, and François presented one in the end. She didn't feel as guilty leaving as she had coming in. Nothing had happened. Des, who had been almost impudently suggestive in their conversations before, had not even once intimated anything.

She felt let down as they drove back down the hilly roads. The morning had been full of promise. Of what she didn't know. Now the day was over, the promise unfulfilled.

"This has been so pleasant," she said halfheartedly, as he stared ahead. A knot in her stomach was tightening. She had somehow let it—let him—get away.

"We must do it again sometime," he said.

"Oh, no. I don't think so. It's much too risky."

"I don't see why. All we did was have lunch."

It sounded like an accusation. She could feel herself sinking into a depression. "Alone," she said in self-defense.

Just as she spoke, Des wheeled the car so quickly that she slid over to his side, falling against him.

Then they were careening down a dark, bumpy narrow road toward the river, past houses and tennis courts peering out from the woods, then past thick oak and hickory trees which shaded the road into dusk. He seemed so grim and so determined that she was afraid to speak.

The patches of sky, which had been so clear and pure and sunny, suddenly seemed ominous as clouds wafted over the sun and a wind swept up from nowhere. The road was deserted as they pulled into an entrance to a park with a small guardhouse and drove down to the edge of the river facing several tiny islands that were being assaulted by the rough, swirling rapids.

Her mouth was dry and her throat closed. There was something violent about the way he pulled the car into the space, slammed on the brakes, and turned off the ignition.

"What?" she finally managed.

He reached over and took her mouth in his, and then everything was a swirl of arms and hands and her skirt was up and she was moaning and he was inside her and she was grasping at him and he was coming and so was she and she stopped breathing.

They sat silently in the darkness afterward, breathing now, heavily at first, then more slowly.

"Jesus" was all he said finally as he looked at his watch and turned on the ignition.

She didn't move as they pulled out of the parking place.

Driving back up the road, she tried to repair the damage. Luckily, it was dark. She prayed Rosey wouldn't come home early. It was after five.

Neither of them spoke until they were at the overlook.

Hugh was standing by the van looking worried.

Des maneuvered his car as close to the van as possible and waited for Hugh to open the back door. He leaned over across Sadie to open the door for her to get out. She looked down at his hand. They had not looked at each other since the river.

As she was getting out of the car, Des reached for her hand in what seemed like a belated farewell as he mumbled, under his breath, "I'll call you."

When she finally took his call, it was more than a week later.

"I'd like to see you again," he said softly.

"I've decided to give up the idea of writing for now," she said, as though she were talking to an editor. "I've really got so many responsibilities. The National Trust for Historic Preservation, Planned Parenthood, and there's so much entertaining. And then the children will be home for Thanksgiving—"

"Sadie."

"Yes."

"I want to see you."

"No."

"I don't understand."

"Yes, you do."

"Look, I know it's risky but—"

"Des."

"We could work out a way—"

"No."

There was such a firmness in her voice that he knew it was pointless to argue.

"Well, then, let me know if you decide to resume your writing."

"I'll call you."

CHAPTER 7

S HE COULD HEAR DES'S KEY IN THE LATCH downstairs. Now the tree was lit, the fire was going, the wine and caviar were out, she looked beautiful, and she had a choice, she told herself. She could start a fight and ruin the evening. Or, she could make it a happy evening.

She decided she would not let him know how angry she was. Better to say nothing.

Des came bouncing upstairs full of good spirits, his face flushed from the cold; no packages under his arms—empty-handed, she noted. It annoyed her to see him so gay. Something in her wanted to give him some bad news.

"Baby, don't you look gorgeous!" he said.

He walked over to the sofa, pulled her up in his arms, looked lovingly down at her, and began to kiss her, first in little bites on her lips, then her cheeks, then her neck. "Jesus, what a piece of ass you are."

His hands ran down her back. He squeezed, then moved his hand up and around her waist and kissed her again, a long and loving kiss.

She could feel herself giving in. God, she loved him so. Her acquiescence made her angry at herself, then at him. She felt helpless. She wanted to keep her eyes closed and just never think about anything again. He was kissing her and she was moving her body into his, warm and supple; she was giving in. How could she be mad at him? Wasn't this better than those other empty Christmases?

"Don't you want some caviar?" she murmured in between kisses.

"Caviar! Why didn't you say so? And here we've been wasting all this time kissing."

"Your choice: caviar or me?"

"The hell with that; I'm having both. But I think I'll save the best till last. Where's the caviar?"

He went over to the bar, poured himself a glass of Irish, then sat down and dug into the caviar.

"How do you like the tree?"

"Oh, it's gorgeous, sweetheart." He barely glanced at it.

"It was a nightmare out there on the streets, trying to buy things today."

"Ummmm." He was munching another spoonful of caviar.

"The lights got tangled. I almost called you at the office and asked you to come home and help."

"Probably a good thing you didn't. I was tied up with the cover story on the Middle East. Seems like everything went wrong at the last minute. Some of our files from different correspondents didn't jibe. We had to get all of them back to check. The State Department is stonewalling, really laying a load on us. That John T. is a shrewd fucker. But I'll tell you, there're going to be some unhappy people around the White House come Monday. Christmas or no Christmas. They are so confused. The right hand doesn't know what the left hand is doing."

She was interested in spite of herself.

"I hate to say it, babe, but your Uncle Roger is not handling this one very well. He can't seem to get control of his people. The factionalism at the White House, especially among the top-level staff, is the worst I've ever seen. If he doesn't call all those guys in and read them the Riot Act, and soon, he's going to be in deep shit. People just don't feel he's in charge. And he won't get rid of the losers. They're the ones who are causing the most dissension. Naturally, John T. Hooker is making the most of it. He's throwing kerosene on the situation every chance he gets."

"I know, I know," said Allison. "I just don't want to hear it, I guess. As if it weren't bad enough, I think Aunt Molly is drinking too much. She hardly even goes out of the White House now, and every time she does the staff is half crazed that she'll do or say something wrong."

"That's a story, isn't it?"

"It's all yours, sweetheart," she said with some sarcasm. "It would make a great lead story for *The Weekly.* You could even put your byline on it. I give it to you. And believe me, it's accurate. You don't even need to verify your sources."

"Now, don't get huffy. All I said was it's a story."

"It sounds a little like you expect me to write it."

"Hey, why are you so defensive? I only made an observation. You've got a real hard-on tonight. What's your problem?"

"Do you really want to know?"

"Sure."

"I'm angry, that's what."

"No kidding. Why don't you give me a break and let me know what it is that I've done? That way maybe I can feel guilty."

"I'm pissed off at you."

"You just said that. Why are you so pissed off at me is the question."

She poured herself a glass of wine before she spoke.

"I am pissed off at you for several reasons."

He decided to wait. Obviously she had an agenda.

For some reason she was most annoyed with him for not going with her to get the tree. It baffled her that it mattered so much. It was, after all, no big deal. It was just a stupid tree. Maybe it had something to do with domesticity and his not really being involved in her life. If it was about something like that, she didn't want to deal with it. She would wait to mention the tree. She would bring up the Kimballs. That was something he could understand. For that matter, it was something that she could understand.

"I am annoyed at your attitude toward Aunt Molly and Uncle Roger," she said finally.

"And just what is my attitude toward them?"

"You're always making fun of them. I have to tell you it really upsets me. They are my family, you know. In fact, they're really the only family I've got now that Nana and Sam are gone. I'm not all that close to them anymore and he is the President and we are journalists and he hasn't been a smashing success. But there are ways you could criticize them without somehow making me feel personally responsible. I mean, what if *your* parents were in the White House?"

"Oh, come on, Sonny, that's ludicrous. You can't possibly equate the two. Jesus, I hate to argue with you. My parents are irrelevant. I don't want to talk about them."

"These people are the closest thing I have to parents in my life. I can criticize them, but it hurts when you do. Especially the way you do. Uncle Roger may not be the greatest President the country ever had. But he is not an evil man. And he is a lot better than the one we just got rid of."

"Sonny, I'm sorry if I have seemed to ridicule the President. But I'm not even sure you are right that he is better than our last President. Roger Kimball is really hurting the Democratic Party. I like Kimball. You know I do. I like your Aunt Molly, too, for that matter. But I do not particularly admire Kimball as a politician or as a leader. He has terrible judgment about people, he has the worst Cabinet ever picked by any Democrat in history, and he is not a leader. He may have been a brilliant professor of history and government at the University of Colorado. He was obviously a popular Governor, but he just doesn't cut it as President. Now, I think he has a wonderful sense of humor and he is a kind and decent man. He has been good to you, and for that I love him. But I can't go any further than that. It also makes me a little nervous for you professionally. I don't like the situation you're in. I feel uncomfortable for you about it, and for me, if you want the truth. Even though you've been taken off the White House, you're still covering pressure points. It's too close. I'm not sure you wouldn't be better off on some other beat. Maybe you should take off and write a book while he's in office. I don't know. It's tough, I admit. I sympathize with you. But you put in for it, kid. You can't ask me to live with you and be truthful and then not tell you how I feel."

Allison had not bargained for this lecture. He had put her on the defensive now.

"Listen, Des," she said. "You're not hearing what I'm saying to you. I don't mind you criticizing the President of the United States. I don't even mind that you criticize my godfather. What I mind is the way you do it. The incessant put-downs and wise-cracks. It hurts my feelings when you do it in public. And the thing that outrages me is that you do it half the time by telling stories that you wouldn't even know unless I had told you or unless you had been around him."

"That's bullshit, Sonny. He's a big boy. We're both journalists. He knows perfectly well that nothing the President of the United States says or does is off the record. That just goes with the territory. Everything is fair game. He's not a stupid man. If he thinks that what he says to us isn't out on the streets in twenty-four hours, then he's dumber than I think."

"Is everything *your* parents say to us fair game?"

"For Christ's sweet sake, will you leave my poor parents out of this! They have nothing to do with what we're talking about."

"Well, you're just not fair or realistic."

"It's you who's not realistic. The President is the President. He is different. It's open season. Ask any journalist in this town."

"Oh, am I ever sick of all these pious journalists! Every single one of them has got some conflict of interest. I could sit down and name them all. Some politician from their home state, somebody's wife's best friend who is now in high office. And the worst are these guys who've fucked every secretary of every candidate and every politician in town and then cry Conflict when I cover the Presidency. We both know three guys for sure who screwed Uncle Roger's secretary during the campaign, not that that takes a whole lot of talent. I'm sick of standards that apply to me as if I were some special case. But what am I supposed to do? Leave town? Well, I don't care what they say, I'm goddamn well not going to. I'm going to stay here and do what I do."

"Calm down, baby. You know perfectly well that a lot of it has to do with jealousy. You're too much. You've got it all. They can't stand it."

"But Des, you're one of the ones. Even if you don't always say so, you're always implying that I should have written something negative about Uncle Roger. Even Aunt Molly. And yet none of you does it. Most of the White House press corps just do nothing but suck up to the President all the time. *The Daily* has probably been tougher on him than any other paper, and partly that's due to me. I don't just get handed stories on a platter either. Those guys over there are terrified of me. They're afraid if they talk to me I'll tell Kimball that they're leaking to the press. I have to tell you, Des, that I resent the fact that you think my job is a piece of cake because I've got access. Every time I've gotten a good story you've managed to raise your eyebrow just a little."

He knew perfectly well that she was right. He did resent her access. And it had been a little embarrassing for him occasionally when *The Daily* had come up with one good story after another that *The Weekly* had had to credit to it. He had taken his share of kidding from the guys about being beaten out by his girlfriend. The kidding was tinged with a little hostility, and the implication was always there. He felt conflicted about his own reactions. On the one hand, he resented being made to look silly. He didn't want to have to compete with Allison, and he really didn't want to have to lose out to her or to answer to the New York office for not having stories she had. On the other hand, it upset him when people implied that she had a conflict or that her credibility was in question at all. He knew how careful she was, and how diligent. He had to spend a lot of time defending her, which he did willingly and with some ferocity, but once they were alone together, his frustrations got the better of him and he lashed out. He never told her about the arguments. He didn't want her to feel any more torn than she already did, but he took it out on her. He didn't mean to.

He didn't want to discuss it anymore. Besides, it was time for the seven o'clock evening news broadcast, and since they had come home from work early they could watch it together, something they almost never had the chance to do.

He got up from his seat, poked at a log, went over to the bar and poured himself another Irish whiskey neat, and flicked on the TV set.

"I gather that is your way of saying you don't have anything more to say on the subject?" she said.

"It is my way of saying I want to watch the news," he said. "I always watch the news at the office, and I'd like to see it now."

"There's hardly ever anything on the news that they don't pick up from the paper that day except for breaking stories."

"Not to mention that everybody's on deadline at the paper at that time anyway." He laughed. "Jesus, you newspaper people are such snobs about TV."

"Good evening," said the anchorman. "Today President Kimball responded to reports of a staff shakeup at the White House. In a statement issued by his communications adviser, President Kimball denied that there was any truth to the persistent rumors that he would replace his Chief of Staff with his domestic adviser. He also denied any evidence of a rift between the two men. . . ."

"Martin Spence reports from the White House," the anchor continued.

"The communications adviser insisted today that President Kimball has no intention . . ."

"Well?" asked Des, looking at Allison.

"Well what?"

"Is it true? Are they going to dump the Chief of Staff?"

"How should I know?"

"C'mon, Sonny, let's not fight. We're going with it pretty hard for next week. From everything we've learned, it looks like Addison Marbury the Third is about to bite the dust. That Harry Saks is a real prick. Not that Marbury deserves to stay. But Jesus, I have never seen such maneuvering over there as I have from Saks. He really wants to be Chief of Staff in a bad way."

"I have to tell you that I haven't talked to Uncle Roger about this at all. So our sources are no better than yours. I will talk to him when we get ready to go with our story. But I have a feeling that Saks has leaked this to try and plant the idea, to create a groundswell to get rid of Marbury. Harry is such a shit. But I'm afraid Harry is a lot swifter than Addison. I just don't think Addison is tough enough for the job. He can't seem to keep Harry under control. And even if he does have the power, he isn't perceived as having the power. I think the networks are going with this a little early. I think they're being used. But then, what else is new?"

"Why haven't you run anything about it? *The Daily* is usually the first to go with leaked rumors under some analysis column, just to get them on the record. I would think you guys would be all over this story."

"We talked about it this morning. Walt feels that it's a Saks plant, and so does everybody else. We just didn't feel like letting Harry use us to get Addison. Anyway, it was a vague leak. It came from one of the secretaries in the White House Press Office. I guess Harry couldn't find anybody else to do his dirty work except for that little tart he's been screwing. It just smells, that's all."

"I agree, but what we don't know is whether it's true or not. I don't understand why you haven't asked Kimball."

"I thought we could ask him in person tomorrow night. It will be your big chance to interview him yourself. See what you can get out of him."

She had waited until the middle of the broadcast to drop that one. She took a sip of her wine and pretended to be watching the news.

At first he wasn't sure he had heard her right. He was looking at the TV set as well. Then he turned to her. "Tomorrow night? What do you mean, tomorrow night?"

"Well, Aunt Molly called today. They noticed that we didn't show up at the White House Christmas press party night before last."

"Oh, Jesus," said Des. "I guess we should have gone. Were they upset?"

"Not really. Not when I explained to her why we didn't go. I told her these things are mob scenes, so crowded that nobody can move, and that they always run out of booze halfway through the reception and that the receiving line is so long you have to stand outside on the South Lawn in freezing weather waiting to get in the door."

"What did you just say about my being able to ask Kimball myself in person?"

"That was what Aunt Molly was calling about. She wants us to have dinner with them in the family dining room tomorrow night, a sort of Christmas dinner before they take off for Aspen. I told her I would love to and I knew you would love to as well unless you were too busy putting the magazine to bed. I did leave you an out."

"Who else is going to be there?"

"I think it's just the four of us."

"Jesus Christ. They've never done this before."

"I guess before they've felt more comfortable seeing me alone for tea on Saturday afternoons. They don't really know you, and I don't think they've really known whether or not we're really living together or what. Aunt Molly knows you're still married to Chessy and that you have your house on Twenty-first Street. I guess they haven't felt all that comfortable embracing you into the 'family' without really knowing whether or not they could trust you."

"So what's changed?"

"I don't know. I guess the last time I was over there she was asking me about you and I said we were pretty much living together. She said she was always a little shy around you because she didn't think you liked her and she never knew quite what to think of us. I guess it was a big enough step for them to ask us to that one dinner this fall."

"Holy shit. Dinner with the four of us. I don't know, Sonny. I just don't know."

"I've also told them how difficult my relationship with them has made things for me, and they don't want to put me in an awkward position. I told them it would be easier for me if my name or our names weren't always on every White House guest list. Not that you would necessarily have gone along with it."

Allison was thinking out loud, listening to the TV set with one ear, Des with the other. He was shaking his head.

"I don't know whether this is a good idea. I mean, I could really be locked into a hell of a compromising situation if he said anything really important."

"Oh, come on, Des. You're big buddies with Malcolm and Abigail Sohier. Malcolm's a Senator. You spend a lot of time with them. You don't quote everything Malcolm tells you. I've heard him tell you dirty jokes, even racist ones, the way only one liberal can tell another liberal. You could devastate him if you printed those things. So could I, for that matter. You've never seemed to have a major crisis of conscience over that situation. What's the difference? They're both public officials. They're both close friends. I just don't think you can make that much distinction because one of them is the President."

She had embarrassed him. She had a point. He was a close friend of Sohier's and Sohier was the junior Senator from Massachusetts. He wouldn't think of betraying a confidence of Malcolm's, and he knew Malcolm knew that. They also had an implicit understanding about ground rules. If Malcolm were ever to say anything that smacked of a good news story, Des would immediately tell him to tell it off the record or for attribution or warn him that he was going to try to get a second source. Malcolm planted stories with Des that way. They were useful to each other. Des was always a little worried about the appearance of the friendship and the fact that sometimes things Malcolm told him in private were just not fair game for print. It made him feel guilty and a little ashamed in light of what Allison's tough situation produced. She was probably a lot more careful and a lot more diligent about her relationship with her godfather than Des was about his with the Sohiers. Happily, Allison had the class not to rub this in. She didn't have to. She had made her point.

"Don't tell me you're considering not going," she said. She couldn't help smiling. She knew he would never be able to resist. It was an invitation from the President of the United States. One never turned that down. Not unless the man was a fascist criminal. This was clearly not the case.

"Jesus H. Christ," mumbled Des. "Holy Mary Mother of God. I guess I don't have any choice. But I better tell the magazine."

She jumped up from her spot on the sofa and went over to the chair where he was sitting on the other side of the fire. "Oh, Des, thank you. I would have been so depressed if I'd had to go alone. Besides, I don't think Uncle Roger is feeling great these days and I know Aunt Molly worries about him. I don't know what I would have told them. It would really have hurt their feelings." She climbed up on his lap and buried her head in his neck, hugging him as tightly as she could. She hadn't realized how relieved she was and how important it was to her that he go. There was a definite element of commitment in his acceptance. They sat still holding on to each other for a while, listening to the newscast in the background. Finally Des pulled away and looked at her.

"Okay," he said. "Out with it. You were mad at me about something else too. We might as well get the whole thing over with tonight. I don't want you sulking around all of Christmas and seething at me about something I don't even know I did wrong. What is it?"

"Oh, it was nothing."

She really didn't want to fight with him now. Now that he had agreed to go to the White House. Besides, now it didn't seem all that important.

"Sonny, don't do this to me. I know you too well. You can't hide it from me, and so you might as well tell me what you were so pissed off about. It didn't start out to be about the Kimballs."

She debated for a moment, saw that he was serious and that he was probably right. She should get it out of her system. She did feel depressed about Christmas and about missing Sam. It had been ten years since her father had been murdered in this house by robbers. Des was the only person she had really cared about since then. She felt very close to Des now. She should tell him.

"I was depressed that you didn't help me with Christmas at all. I had to go get the tree and carry it in here, and set it up.

Then I had to decorate it by myself. And hang the wreath and put the holly and poinsettias around."

"Oh, shit," he said. He eased her off his lap, got up to turn off the TV, then fixed himself another drink. He leaned against the mantel and looked down at her for a minute, then over at the beautiful tree, the pretty holly in vases on the mantel, then back down at her. He made a funny sucking noise with his mouth, as if he were trying to decide what to say. Then he spoke at last.

"Baby, you know I hate Christmas. I've told you a hundred times I hate Christmas. I can't stand anything about it. It's a nightmare to me. When I was little my parents never had enough money. They were always sad and apologetic on Christmas morning. You know what Santa brought us? Shit. That's what Santa brought us. And we were good kids. We went to Mass on Sundays and said our Hail Marys and went to confession and did our homework. We had been good. And Santa brought us shit. And after we learned that there was no Santa it was almost worse because then we understood that it was our parents who couldn't do for us. So we had to spend our Christmases making them feel like we didn't care if we didn't have ice skates when all the other kids would go out skating, or that we didn't have a sled when the other kids went sledding. It was a pathetic little ritualistic farce. Even with a large Catholic family which should have been merry, it was hopeless. So we would go to Mass and pray that next Christmas would be better."

Allison had rarely seen Des wound up. She was stunned by the emotion in his voice, by the genuineness of his feelings. She wanted to tell him she was sorry, but she didn't want to stop him. He wanted to talk more. She let him.

After all, she had asked him to tell her his feelings, something he'd never done.

"Well, it got better, all right. For me, anyway. You see, I married a New York debutante, a little socialite, and my first Christmas with her was a nightmare. She had gone down to New York to Cartier's and bought me the most expensive watch in the place. She had gone to Abercrombie and Fitch and bought me the most expensive game table in the place. She had hit Tripler's and bought me cashmere bathrobes and cashmere sweaters and Bonwit's for Turnbull and Asser shirts, and oh, God, it was awful. I had gone down to the nearest department store and I had bought her, in the costume-jewelry department, what I thought was a pretty crystal necklace. I don't know, it cost maybe fifty bucks. That was all I could scrounge in those days on my salary. We were living in Back Bay in Boston on her dough, but I didn't have any money. That was a lot for me then. And I wanted to get my parents something nice, too. You can imagine how embarrassing it was for me on Christmas morning. Her giant pile and my box of fake jewelry. You should have seen her face. I just kept opening and opening my presents, getting madder and more humiliated by the minute, and she didn't see it.

"You ask me why I don't help you with Christmas?"

He didn't want an answer.

"The answer is that I hate Christmas and I don't want to have to be a part of it. I've been dreading this weekend. I can see you have such great expectations for Christmas and I know I am bound to disappoint you. If *you* want Christmas, then do Christmas. But don't expect me to get involved."

He had been standing in front of the fire looking down. His face was flushed, not only from emotion but from the heat of standing next to the flames. She couldn't remember being more in love with him than she was at this very moment. He looked so earnest. His black hair was curled over his forehead. She wanted to jump up and put her arms around him, but she couldn't. Something made her feel as though she should be angry with him. Pride—something—made her unable to move.

Des turned and placed both his hands on the mantel, stretching his arms out and hanging his head in between his arms, staring down at the fire. He stood that way for a long time, the silence creating a strange nearness between them rather than a gulf. Then he stepped over to the side table and poured himself another Irish neat. He took a long swig of it, swallowed it, and leaned back against the mantel, staring at her this time. She could feel the heat from the fire beginning to ruddy her face. Suddenly she became afraid of what he was going to say next.

Finally, he smiled a little half-smile. "Why," he said slowly, "couldn't we be making love under a blinking tree?"

Relief made her nearly faint. She had braced herself for the worst. She let out a deep breath. She hadn't breathed, she realized, in over a minute.

"Oh, Des!" she cried. Then, as in a trance, she got up from the sofa and went to him. She buried her head in his chest, her arms wrapped around his waist. She could feel the tears of relief streaming down her cheeks and she didn't even try to stop them.

Des had one arm tight around her waist; with the other hand he stroked her head.

"Baby, baby, baby," he kept murmuring as he stroked her, trying to soothe her. "It's all right, baby. It's all right."

"Oh, Des . . ." But she couldn't get any more words out. Her body was racked with sobs she couldn't control. It had been a long time in coming.

"What is it, Sonny? It couldn't be what I said that's making you cry. What is it?"

"It's Sam. My Christmases with Sam. They were so wonderful. I loved him so. I miss him so much. I just wanted to re-create with you what I had with my father. You're the first one I've ever done that with since he died. I just wanted a Christmas like the ones I had with Sam. Don't be mad at me. I'm sorry. I expected too much from you. I should have explained." She was choking on her words but it seemed deeply important to her now to get them out, to let him know how she felt, to finally tell him about Sam. She had kept it in so long, afraid to let Des see her vulnerability.

"Did Sam always go with you to get the tree?"

She nodded.

"Oh, Sonny, I didn't realize."

"It's all right," she said in a soft voice.

He lifted her face up to his so he could see it in the firelight. He kissed her gently on the lips, then licked at her tears.

"Do you understand how very much I love you? You are the most important thing in my life."

She stared at him for a moment. He had told her before that he loved her. It had always seemed a little perfunctory. She knew now that he meant it. She really knew. She was embarrassed. She looked quickly down at his chest.

"I've got tears all over your shirt," she said, laughing in shyness. "And I need to blow my nose."

"You really are an asshole, you know," said Des, embarrassed himself, as he reached for a Kleenex on the end table. "I can't believe this scene. Now can we cut the crap and have some caviar? It is Christmas, after all."

* * *

"Christ, this is embarrassing."

Desmond Shaw was standing at his desk in his shirt sleeves, his top button unbuttoned, his tie askew, his sleeves rolled up. The journalist's dishabille. No self-respecting journalist would ever think of sitting at his desk with a coat on or a tie neatly tied. Behind him the glass panes were frosted over so that it was difficult to see the lights from the Washington Monument, the Lincoln Memorial, the White House. His office had the best view in town. Sometimes he just liked to sit at his desk in his black leather swivel chair and lean back and look at the view. It gave him such a sense of place. Most of the time he felt so hassled he could have been working in Toledo for all the location mattered. It was only occasionally, when he was writing his column or something spectacularly newsworthy happened or the magazine had just been closed and he had opened up his little bar and poured a taste of Irish, that he got sentimental about Washington and the history and the moment of it all. Those times were fleeting and rare, but they kept him going. Even when he was most frustrated, even the times when he felt world-weary or just plain burned out he felt the exhilaration when he glanced out at the city below, watched the limousines with their flags careen in and out of the White House gates, saw the sun set over the Capitol building in the evening.

Tonight, however, was not one of those nights. It was Thursday night, and normally he would be there until midnight going over last-minute files, sending out for Chinese, arguing with New York to get his reporters' stories in, taking queries, fighting over space, doing last-minute checks. He had rarely missed a Thursday night at the bureau. The staff counted on him. At any given moment there were two or three people in and out of his office, sticking their stories on his spike for him to read before they were telexed to New York. They counted on him to lobby for them with New York. They liked to schmooze, hang out, hash over stories and pool Periscope items. This would be the first Thursday night he had missed in a long time. And he was missing it because he was having dinner at the White House with the President and his wife upstairs in the family room. He had telephoned the editor of *The Weekly* that morning to tell him. Even though he had said he wasn't going to. Gordo Franklin had been ecstatic.

He was enough of a stargazer to be overjoyed at the news. He was always a little annoyed with Des anyway for his seeming lack of interest in playing the high-powered social game of Washington. Des was a dedicated player, but Gordo had no understanding whatsoever of Washington social life and had no way to distinguish between which kind of parties were important and which were not. He thought if there was a party covered by the press and it ended up in all the gossip columns filled with the names of the powerful, then it was an important party. That was often the mistake made by outsiders who didn't realize it was the smaller private parties where the business was really conducted.

"That's not the way it used to be in my time," Gordo would insist when Des tried to tell him how things had changed. "In my time we went everywhere. The press never missed a good party."

Those days were over, Des had told him. Smart hosts and hostesses knew it was too dangerous to have reporters hovering around trying to catch their guests saying something indiscreet. The stakes were too high these days. Whereas the press had been docile and passive fifteen years ago, now they were carnivorous. Nothing and nobody was sacred.

Des was thankful that Gordo was his boss this time when he had to tell him about the White House invitation. Gordo must have called Des back three or four times that day to discuss topics of conversation, suggest questions, propose a cover story. Doing the cover story would demand a high-level session with the President with the editors of *The Weekly*. That way Gordo could fly down, take his usual suite at the Hay-Adams, and probably suggest an intimate dinner upstairs at the White House with the various *Weekly* editors. He was driving Des crazy, but at least he wasn't giving him a hard time.

"Gordo, you know this is really a private evening," he said in exasperation after the third call. "I'm not sure a heavy grilling or interrogation is in order here. That's what bothers me about the whole evening." Then, in a mischievous mood, he added, "You know, Gordo, I've been thinking about this all day and I thought maybe it wouldn't be such a hot idea if I went. I mean, it's really going to put me in somewhat of a compromised position. Don't you think from the point of view of the magazine's credibility I ought to regret?"

Gordo did not disappoint him.

"Jesus Christ, are you out of your mind? You would turn

down an invitation to dine with the President of the United States in the family dining room alone? Des, I don't often do this, but if I have to I will order you to go."

"Well, Gordo, if you feel that strongly about it, I suppose I have no choice."

"I'll decide what's best. Now you get your ass over to the White House."

Des was still laughing when Allison walked in the door of his office and flung her fur coat and gloves on his black leather sofa.

"Hi, kid," she said. "What's so funny?"

She walked over to where he was sitting at his desk, leaned over, and gave him a kiss, another kiss, another kiss.

"Oh, it's that asshole Gordo. He's so excited I'm going to the White House that he's about to expire. I decided to have a little fun and told him I didn't think it was good for my credibility to go and maybe I should regret. He went bat-shit."

"You bastard," she said. "Poor old Gordo. The energy it takes to be such a power fucker."

"Did you walk over?"

"No, it's too cold. I treated myself to a cab. I left early. There's not a hell of a lot going on. Very slow news day. I've got my instructions from Walt and all the other editors about what to ask Uncle Rog. I figured I'd better tell them. It'll be all over town tomorrow. Have you informed your illustrious bureau yet?"

"I'll leave that to Gordo. I haven't had the guts. I've tried to tell them a couple of times and the words got stuck in my mouth. I'm just not up for all the shit I'm going to have to take."

"Oh, Des, you've got to tell them tonight. They'll all know about it by tomorrow morning and then you'll look worse. It will look like you were taking it too seriously and that you were holding out on them. Besides, it's Thursday night. You never miss Thursday night. What excuse do you have?"

"I hadn't figured it out. I was thinking of having a small stroke and having you carry me out to the hospital."

"What's your cover story?" she asked, ignoring the suggestion.

"We're going with the battle between the Chief of Staff and the domestic adviser. We'll have several pictures of White House staff on the cover, including the President's, with a cover line asking 'Who's in Charge Here?'"

"Oh, Uncle Rog will love that."

"We're not going to tell him, though, are we, sweetheart?"

"You know he'll ask."

"You're right. Well, fuck it. I will tell him. I just won't tell him the cover line. I'll say we're doing a piece on the White House staff."

"You better tell your own staff. For one thing, you'll probably get stuff you can use. You know Uncle Rog isn't going to let you go with that cover without trying to have some input."

"Okay. Okay, you're right." He got up from his chair and moved around the side of his desk. He leaned over her where she was sitting on the sofa and kissed her on the mouth.

"What time are we supposed to be there?"

"They suggested seven thirty. But it's only six thirty now. I came over early."

He walked over to the door and yelled down the hall: "Cal, Milt, Mary. Can you come into my office? I need to talk to you."

Mumbles erupted from the line of little glass cages down the hall, and minutes later a group of people trooped into Des's office, bitching and moaning and complaining about New York, those stupid writers up there, mauled copy, fact checkers' mistakes, dumb queries, and various other things.

Allison sat on the sofa and picked up a copy of *The Weekly*.

"Sonny, I hate to disturb you now that you've gotten so comfortable, but do you mind disappearing for a while so that we can have our secret and important conference unhindered by the ears of competition?"

"Who would I tell? Besides, by next Monday it will be all old news anyway."

"Boo, hiss," shouted the others as she turned and walked down the hall.

Des broke the news to the troops. He had decided how to head them off.

"Eat your hearts out, gang," he began. "But I'm about to move out of the small time and into the fast lane."

"Don't tell me you're moving to New York?" asked Milt in horror. "Not just when we've gotten accustomed to your face."

"Not so fast, Milt," he said. "Your shot at my job will come soon enough."

"Des, you know that I am happy to serve you for as long as I am needed."

"So what's the fast lane, then?" asked Mary.

"The White House."

"You're going to run for President?"

"Christ, what a bunch of wise-asses. No, I'm going there for dinner tonight. Just me and Rog. I thought you great reporters might like to know about your chief's access so you'll be able to fend off your colleagues' questions tomorrow when they want to know what went on."

"What's going on?" asked Mary. "Is it some big party? I don't remember—"

"No, it's just Allison and me. And Gordo is in seventh fucking heaven. He's already getting out his dinner jacket in preparation for an invitation to the next White House dinner."

They were mollified by his nonchalant attitude and his putting the brunt on Gordo.

"Now, it is obviously off the record, but we'll no doubt talk about the White House staff, so if anybody has any thought on an approach, any specific questions, let me have it."

Allison came back when his office was empty.

"Well?"

"I think the natives are mollified. I made it sound like a big joke and put it off on Gordo."

"Well, it's not going to be funny if we're late. Can we go?"

"I guess so. But I've got to tell you I'm not totally comfortable with this."

"Are you kidding? You wouldn't miss it. You just have to go through this tormented soul-searching to ease your pure journalistic conscience."

Des looked at her for a moment, deciding whether or not it was worth it to get mad. Finally he stood up, rolled down his shirt sleeves, buttoned his top button, straightened his tie, ran his fingers through his hair, put on his suit jacket, and motioned to her to go. As they walked through the door of his office, he reached down and goosed her.

They walked to the White House from Des's office, a block away on Pennsylvania Avenue. They crossed Seventeenth Street in the dark and the swirling snowflakes and walked past the Executive Office Building to the West Wing gate. They showed their White House press passes to the guards, who buzzed them in through the metal gate. Then they walked up the slope toward the pressroom, turning just before they got there to the door of the business entrance. They didn't want to go through the pressroom. At the lobby of the main entrance, a White House guard at the desk called to check on them; then a Secret Service agent appeared to lead them through a narrow hallway, through several passages, and into the glass-enclosed portico that led to the first-floor diplomatic entrance. They walked past the portraits of First Ladies to the elevator that would take them upstairs to the family quarters.

It was odd for both of them. Des had never been in the family quarters. Allison had been there several times, but each time she felt awed. They were standing in the hushed silence waiting for the elevator door to open. Des reached over and took her hand. It amused them that they both had sweaty palms. The White House, after all, was the White House, no matter how jaded one was about Washington.

When they got to the second floor and the door opened, the Secret Service agent excused himself and went back down. An elderly butler led them over to the sitting area at the west end of the long hall. Aunt Molly had decorated it in her own Western style. Everything was done in reds and yellows; there were Indian artifacts around and lots of family pictures. It wasn't Allison's taste, but it was as friendly and warmhearted as the Kimballs themselves.

Both Aunt Molly and Uncle Rog were sitting having a drink. Both stood up expectantly. Molly was wearing a long pale green wool caftan, and the President had on a turtleneck and a sports jacket. He looked pale and tired.

Allison walked over to Aunt Molly, kissed her on the cheek, then turned to Uncle Rog, who kissed her, then gave her a big bear hug.

"Hello, honey," he said warmly. "Gosh, I'm glad to see you. You look wonderful." Then to Des, "You must be taking good care of my girl."

"Well, sir . . ." Des began.

"She's obviously got her hooks into you. Don't tell me she's responsible for your being all dressed up tonight. God Almighty, you look like you're going to a fancy dinner party. Here, take off your jacket and loosen your tie, and I'll get you a sweater."

"Oh, no, sir, this is fine. . . ." Des was not his usual cool, confident self.

"The hell it is. We're going to relax tonight. We're just family. Here, I'll go and get a sweater myself."

With that the President disappeared into the bedroom next to the family sitting room and came back a moment later with a pale green crew-necked sweater. Des dutifully took off his jacket, loosened his tie, and pulled the sweater over his shirt.

"There—that's better. Now I can relax. You looked like some goddamn journalist ready to get out your tape recorder the other way."

"As a matter of fact, sir," said Des, reaching for his pocket.

He was regaining his sense of humor, Allison was pleased to see.

"Oh, no, none of that," said Kimball, laughing. "This is strictly off the record tonight—unless, of course, I say something brilliant, in which case I will instruct you to write it down. Now," he said, rubbing his hands together, "what'll it be? Allison honey, you want white wine, right?"

She nodded.

"Scotch neat will be fine, sir," said Des.

"Actually, he drinks Irish whiskey, Uncle Roger, if there is any."

"This is the goddamn White House. They have everything here. Ernest," he said, turning to the butler, "surely there is Irish whiskey here, isn't there?"

"Yes, sir, I believe there is, sir," said Ernest as he turned to get the drinks.

"Sit down, sit down," Uncle Roger said, motioning to Des. Allison was suddenly getting the feeling that Uncle Roger was playing the role of the father interviewing the prospective son-in-law. She hoped he didn't carry it too far.

"Done all your Christmas shopping?" Uncle Roger asked Des.

God, next he'd be asking how much he made and was he going to be able to love, honor, and cherish.

"Well, *we're* not having much of a Christmas this year," piped up Aunt Molly. "I just couldn't fight the crowds, being stared at and having umpteen Secret Service men trailing around behind me. I always used to get Roger socks and underwear to stuff in his stocking. But I just couldn't see walking up to the counter at Garfinckel's and saying, 'I'd like ten pairs of underpants for the President, please.'"

"Aunt Molly, why didn't you ask me? I would gladly have gone out and done some shopping for you."

"Oh, Allison, you're a darling, but I got one of the girls in my office to do it for me. Anyway, we're leaving for Aspen tomorrow. That will be Christmas present enough." With that she took a rather large gulp from her glass.

"Now, Molly, let's not start with that," warned Uncle Roger. "There's no point in subjecting these two to your laments."

"Well, why not? Who else am I going to talk to about it? Locked up here in this tower like Rapunzel, getting constantly criticized if I even cross my eyes, or worse, if I don't, and watching my husband get crucified every day in the press, not to mention seeing his staff going at each other. All I said was, I'm glad we're going to get away."

"It must be tough as hell," said Des, interested in keeping the conversation alive, though he could see that the President was getting irritated. "I don't think any of us, even covering the White House, have any idea how little privacy you have and how hard it is to try to lead a normal life."

"Normal?"

"Now, Molly, they're not interested in our little problems." There was a warning note in his voice. It fascinated Allison how she always managed to bring this out in them. When Allison was around, they turned into the Bickersons. It was almost as if they were competing for her approval. It was like watching one's parents fight. It annoyed her that Des seemed intent on prodding Aunt Molly. She could see his eyes light up when Molly mentioned the staff. That was the kind of confirmation he needed for his cover story. She wondered whether this dinner had been a good idea after all.

"So, Desmond—I hope you don't mind my calling you that."

"Not at all, Mr. President."

"Tell me about yourself. You're from Boston, aren't you? You used to work for *The Boston Gazette*. Tell me, do you like working for the magazines better than the newspapers?"

Des launched into a discussion of newspapers versus newsmagazines to be polite, though Allison could tell he didn't have much enthusiasm for the subject, while she and Aunt Molly talked about what they were going to do in Aspen, whom they were going to see, and exchanged gossip about their friends out there.

It was shortly after eight when dinner was announced.

They moved into the family dining room to the left. Des had seen pictures of it, but it was prettier in reality. The wallpaper was murals of old battles, and the sideboard was a beautiful old American desk which had once belonged to Daniel Webster. Roger Kimball proudly pointed out the desk as one of his favorite pieces in the White House. The table was set for four, and candles were burning brightly. Bowls of consommé were served as they sat down, and Uncle Roger directed that the butler serve white or red wine to Des and Allison. Aunt Molly stayed with her Scotch.

"I know it isn't chic, but I've never been much of a wine drinker," she said. "I have to drink it when we go out to official functions or when we entertain. It would look terrible if I kept my Scotch with me at the table."

"What are you boys planning for this week's cover?" Kimball was trying to change the subject.

"We're planning a cover, as a matter of fact, sir, on the White House staff. We've done a lot of interviewing and talked to many of the staffers over the past few weeks. We thought it would make an interesting study."

"What the hell," said the President, obviously perturbed. "Nobody told me about it. And nobody's tried to interview *me* on the subject. Why not?"

"You, sir?" Des seemed taken aback.

"Yes, me. I'm the President, as I recall. Wouldn't I know more about the staff than anybody?"

"To tell you the truth, sir, we put in a request for an interview, but your press secretary turned us down. We always put in a request to interview you on all of these stories, but it's rare we can get to you unless it's some special year-end roundup or a cover on you personally, and even then it takes weeks, even months of arranging."

"God damn, Molly, you see what I mean? Now, why wouldn't Manolas tell me about these things? They think they're protecting me from all of this and half the time they're simply keeping me in the dark. I'd like to make up my own mind about these interviews. I ought to fire the lot of them, by God. Just get rid of the whole bunch. A little housecleaning. We've been here a year now. Maybe I'll surprise the world and announce in my State of the Union Message that I'm getting rid of everybody."

"If you'd listen to me every once in a while, these things wouldn't come as such a shock to you, Roger," said Molly a bit caustically.

"I have a good mind to get that press secretary on the phone right now."

"Don't, Uncle Roger," said Allison quickly. "It will only cause trouble. Manolas knows we're here tonight and it will look like we're complaining about him behind his back. That won't be helpful to us and he'll spread the word around. Besides, he's only trying to do his job."

Kimball sat silently for a moment, then turned to Des.

"What time can you be here in the morning for an interview with me, young man?" he said. "It's not too late for that, is it? I mean they won't have put the magazine to bed yet or anything, will they?"

"No, sir. We can get stuff in as late as Saturday night or in an emergency as late as Sunday morning. It is certainly not too late for an interview with the President. Would nine o'clock be too early, sir?"

Allison couldn't help smiling at how quickly Des jumped.

"Good. Then nine o'clock it is. I'll be damned if I'm going to have those sons-of-bitches run my life and tell me who I can and cannot see." He turned to Des again, this time a look of suspicion on his face. "I don't suppose this is going to be a very favorable story?"

"I'm not sure I'd use that word, sir. It is going to be a fair and accurate story, and more fair and accurate since we will be having your point of view in it as well as those of your staffers."

"I guess you're going to make something of the feud between Addison Marbury and Harry Saks."

"To be honest, we can hardly not write about it. It's pretty much open warfare between the two, as I'm sure you know only too well."

"I know, I know," said Kimball, a dejected look on his face as he rang for more wine. "But God Almighty, I have called those two in a hundred times. I've even threatened to fire both of them. I talked to them about it yesterday. I don't know what more I can do. Then I pick up the news summary every morning and they're going at each other in the press tooth and nail. I expect I'll see even more in your story. I have a good mind to get rid of both of them—and I'm serious."

"Amen," said Aunt Molly from the other end of the table.

Allison was beginning to get panicked. This was important stuff they were talking about and Des was getting it all. He was going to have an on-the-record interview with the President tomorrow. *The Daily* hadn't been able to get one. Now she was in a jam. Her editors knew she was here tonight with Des. Des would get the interview. They would at least expect her to set up an interview with the President with somebody else from the paper. She could probably talk Kimball into giving *The Daily* an interview, but then *The Daily* would have it for Sunday and beat out *The Weekly*, and Des would be furious. He would have some right. She wondered how much the President would tell Des on the record. It didn't matter. He could use a lot of it as background. She would have to report everything *she* had learned as well. Still, unless *The Daily* rushed into print with a new story on the staff, it didn't really have any outlet for this information, without having it look as if it came directly from the President.

The conversation had drifted away from the staff. Uncle Roger was clearly saving what he wanted to say until tomorrow, and Des, she could tell, was delighted.

"Am I wrong," Uncle Roger was saying, "or am I getting more hell from the press than my predecessor?"

Here it comes, Allison thought. She hadn't seen Uncle Roger once since he'd been in the White House that he hadn't railed about the press. Not that he was different from any of his predecessors.

"It seems to me that you guys are giving the Republicans a free ride."

Venison and puréed chestnuts were being served.

"Actually," said Des, "I think you have a point, sir. It may well be that the press tends to be harsher on Democrats. For one thing, we have a tendency to bend over backwards to be fair to the Republicans. We see Democrats as more our own. I think there is something in that old song 'You always hurt the one you love.' It's just more comfortable criticizing your wife than your neighbor's wife. You are more conscious of the flaws of people you sympathize with."

"That's a helluva note," said Kimball. "We get crucified for trying to do the right thing. It just doesn't make any sense."

"There's even more to it than that," said Allison. "The press has a definite sense of survival. And the Republicans are very good at stirring up antimedia sentiment around the country. It's their favorite theme. I think the press runs a little scared when Republicans are in power."

"By God, I think they've got the right answer," said Roger. "Put the fear of God into you. Maybe we've been going about it in the wrong way. Maybe we just ought to complain more every time somebody prints something untrue. When you're sitting where I'm sitting it doesn't seem like such a bad idea. You know, nobody can run the country nowadays. It's impossible to be an effective President anymore. I don't think there should ever be another two-term President. And I'm not sure I'd like to run again even if I thought I could make it."

"Gosh, you sound discouraged. Is it really that bad?" said Allison. She was worried. She hadn't ever seen Uncle Roger without his usual ebullience. She knew him well enough to see he was seriously depressed.

"Oh, don't pay any attention to me. I'm just in a philosophical mood tonight. What's that old saying? Even paranoids have enemies? I'll be all right tomorrow. And I'd be a lot better off if I had a staff I could trust."

"What's stopping you, Uncle Roger?"

"He's too nice for his own good," said Aunt Molly. "He's too loyal. Everybody is innocent until proved guilty, and guilty and guilty. If somebody's been with him for a long time he doesn't have the heart to get rid of them. Addison and Harry Saks will be here three years from now. Even if they destroy the Administration."

Allison and Des both looked at the President. He didn't lift his head or refute his wife.

"The only person worth a damn in the whole inner circle is the Vice President," continued Molly. "He hasn't made a single slipup. And he's loyal to Roger. Hasn't done any backsliding or made any stupid power moves. He's managed to get along well with both Harry and Addison. And with our esteemed Secretary of State, John T. Hooker, which takes talent, let me tell you."

"That's another story," sighed the President.

"Seriously," said Molly. "I don't know what you'd do without Rosey Grey. I think he saves us from a lot more embarrassment and bad publicity than we know."

Kimball brightened. "Yes, and that wife of his is a real peach. What a honey she is!" He whistled at that one.

"I have to admit," said Molly, "that even though Roger is gaga over Sadie Grey, I'm just as mad about her. She's a wonderful girl. Don't you think so?" She looked at Allison, then Des.

"I can't argue with either one of you," said Des, almost in a whisper, as he looked down at his plate.

"That husband of hers better realize what a lucky guy he is, that's all," said Kimball.

Allison had been enjoying herself in spite of everything, but now she felt scared. She hated the sensation, and she hated the fact that it had become familiar. There were very few times when Allison Sterling lost her cool. Sadie Grey made her do it every time. And she couldn't go anywhere without hearing about Sadie. Every man in town, including the two she most cared about, had gone completely nuts over her. And though she didn't want to think about it, she was afraid Des was more than a little attracted to her. She wanted to say something, but she was afraid her true feelings would show. She had to muster her sense of humor.

"And what a mind," she said finally.

"My, I do believe we've struck a nerve," said Uncle Roger.

"Don't be silly," Allison said, more sharply than she had intended. "It's just that I find it interesting that all of you intelligent men can go into the tank for a woman just because she tells you you're strong and handsome. What if she were a man?"

"But she's not a man," said Des. "That's the point."

"There's no mistaking that," said Roger, and he laughed knowingly at Des. Des was clearly uncomfortable. He cleared his throat, took a sip of wine.

"You put such stock in intelligence and competence and achievement in men, but when it comes to women the standards are never the same."

"Well, your Aunt Molly has never had a career and she's smarter than most men I know," he said.

He was throwing her a bone, but Allison suddenly felt embarrassed and ashamed that she might have insulted Molly.

"I didn't mean you had to work for a living to be taken seriously. I only meant that—"

"It's all right, sweetheart," said Molly, reaching over and putting her hand on Allison's. "You don't have to explain. I know what you meant."

She loved Aunt Molly at that moment. Molly was the only

one there who had sensed her pain. Molly could identify with that helpless feeling. She had obviously been there. You couldn't be a politician's wife and not have felt that. Clearly Sadie Grey was no threat to Aunt Molly. For one reason, Sadie wasn't interested in Roger Kimball. So it didn't matter if he lusted after her a little bit. But Molly could tell by Des's tone of voice that he really did think Sadie was something special. And for some reason she sensed that Allison was afraid.

"Allison's right," said Molly, a little more forcefully. "Sadie's a sweet girl, but there's not a whole lot going on there. I never did trust those Southern women anyway. They'll kill you with kindness and stab you in the back any day. You two are lucky you have more forthright, strong women to deal with. Isn't that so, Allison? Now, why don't we all go back into the living room and have our coffee there?"

With that, she got up. As Allison was getting up, Molly came over to her, put her arm around her shoulder, and walked her into the living room, muttering on about what silly asses men were and how they never would change. The men followed behind, only a little chastened.

The butler brought brandy. Allison declined, but the President and Des and Aunt Molly all accepted. She was getting a little nervous at the amount of drinking. She was afraid Uncle Roger would talk too much, afraid that Des would get belligerent and Aunt Molly, bless her soul, would start drifting.

Molly was talking to Allison about something while Allison was trying to keep tabs on what Des and Uncle Roger were saying. They were talking about foreign policy and Capitol Hill, but she could hear only snatches. Finally, frustrated, she put her hand on Aunt Molly's arm and whispered that she wanted to hear what Uncle Rog was saying.

It was only then that she noticed that Molly's eyes were filled with tears.

"What is it?—what's the matter, Aunt Molly?"

"Oh, Sonny, I'm so worried," she whispered, and Sonny had to lean toward her to hear. Molly looked quickly at Uncle Roger to be sure he was not looking. "I don't know how much more he can take. You mustn't tell anyone, but he had another small stroke last week. It wasn't serious, but his left side was a little numb and he really couldn't move his arm for a few hours. He's been in a terrible depression and I just can't get him out of it.

He's on all kinds of medication and I don't know how much longer we can keep it quiet."

"My God, Aunt Molly! I can't believe it. What can I do? Is there anything I can do to help?"

Allison was having trouble fighting back her own tears. Much of the time she wouldn't let herself think about how much she loved and depended on these two people.

A quick glance at Uncle Roger in light of this new information confirmed what Aunt Molly had said. She hadn't really noticed how he was favoring his right side. She suddenly felt heavy with grief. This man might die.

"You've done so much just being here for me," Molly was saying. "But I need you to do more. I need you to get them to downplay all of these problems here. They'll listen to you, Sonny. You've got to tell your editors everything is fine. And your colleagues. Even Des. The bad publicity is just the added burden that is going to break him." She started to cry, partly from despair, partly from drink. "I can't bear it, I just can't bear it. I hate this place so, Sonny. I want to go home. I want to take Roger home."

Sonny could feel her own tears coming. She had to get Molly out of here.

"Why don't you go to the bathroom?" she said. "I'll cover for you."

Molly quickly got up and disappeared into her bedroom without the two men noticing. Allison took a few minutes to compose herself, then joined their conversation.

"Christ, I can't seem to get anything out of those bastards," Uncle Rog was complaining. "That Senate Foreign Relations Committee is full of the biggest jerks in Congress. I'll tell you, Desmond, there's only so much a President can do if he doesn't have the Congress on his team. You boys in the press just don't realize how hard it is trying to be a Democratic President and deal with a Republican Senate and a House that though nominally Democratic is filled with a bunch of sissies. With a few notable exceptions, of course. And as if that weren't bad enough, I've got Hooker. I thought it was a coup to get the Chairman of the Senate Foreign Relations Committee over to be the Secretary.

"I thought he would know how things worked, would be able to deal with those guys, would really know how to manipulate his colleagues. Well, I'm not saying he can't; he just won't. The ornery son-of-a-bitch has done everything in his power, it seems to me, to alienate them. He refuses them top-priority information, he thumbs his nose at them, he is arrogant and vain and self-centered. He has managed to annoy every single goddamned one of them, even those who were on our side. I think naming John T. to State may have been my biggest mistake. And the irony, the real tragedy of the whole situation is that he is brilliant at it. He is a true statesman. And so far he has managed to keep relatively smooth relations with my National Security Adviser. I really want to avoid going through what every other President has gone through with the political infighting. Christ, I've got enough of it on my domestic staff."

Des was sitting quietly and Allison watched him taking mental notes, trying to sear these quotes on his brain. She knew he would be up all night revising his cover story, and she would be up all night trying to decide how she should deal with this information—not get scooped by *The Weekly*, not betray Uncle Roger, not try to beat Des on his story. It wasn't going to be easy.

She was edgy. Uncle Roger was way out of school. She was sure he was allowing himself to be so free because he felt it was all in the family. He should know better. A journalist is a journalist, and a journalist is always working. He should have learned that. And there was a certain reckless quality about the way he was talking. She wondered if it had to do with his health. Des did not have the same strictures or the same sense of loyalty as she had. The President would be fair game. Not that he would directly quote him, but he would query him hard tomorrow, try to get him on the record, refer to much of what he got out of him as "high government sources (or "officials") said" and go with it much more strongly than she would be able to. If she wrote it, Des would be angry at her for scooping him, and Uncle Roger would never forgive her because it would be clear to all where the information had come from. She was truly screwed on this one. Uncle Roger would probably be annoyed with her for not making the ground rules clear to Des, but he wouldn't really be furious with Des.

She had to get them out of there. They had had enough.

"I hear John T. is having an affair with that astrologer, Millicent." Aunt Molly had quietly slipped back into the room. Except for a false cheeriness which only Allison seemed to notice, she looked fine. "In fact, I hear he may even leave poor May and run off with Millicent. Even shut up in this place I hear things now and then."

Allison had heard the rumor, but she was surprised to hear it from Molly. Des hadn't heard it at all.

"Is that true?" he said.

"Molly, you don't know what you're talking about," said Kimball. "You shouldn't be spreading rumors."

Molly smiled at him. "Even the President deserves to hear some good gossip now and then," she said. "It's very distracting."

"It's true, Uncle Roger," said Allison. "Or at least, it's true that that's going around."

"Christ, Molly, why didn't you tell me this before?" He obviously did not see the humor in it. "My goddamn Secretary of State having an affair with a goddamn astrologer. He probably tells her everything, and she tells everybody else in town. How did this happen? How could he be so crazy? That woman is a known kook. This is preposterous. Jesus, I knew I had made a mistake, but this is really terrible. You don't think he believes in all that nonsense, do you?"

"Millicent is Allison's astrologer too," Des said. "We should be careful what we say about her. Allison is very protective."

"Oh, be quiet," said Allison. "Lorraine Hadley gave me a reading as a birthday present, and I went once just for fun. Actually, she gave the same present to Sadie Grey, who does believe in all that. I think it's quite a delicious piece of gossip, and now that it comes from a very high White House source, I feel inclined to pass it along to our very own gossip columnist, who I'm sure will roll over and die when she hears it."

"You will like hell," said the President. "That's all I need. He'd be the laughingstock of Washington, and we'd be the laughingstock of the world."

"In that case, Uncle Roger, I strongly suggest that if I've heard it and Aunt Molly has heard it, it won't be long before it's all over town and in print somewhere. And we might as well have it first. I'll tell you what: You talk to John T., and if he denies it, I won't give it to the gossip column. If he doesn't, then I will. You'll be on the honor system to tell me whether it's true or not."

"My, my, you certainly drive a tough bargain, little lady," said the President, relaxing a little.

"I have no choice, Mr. President. You wouldn't want me to subvert my own paper by suppressing the news, would you?"

"You really want to know?" There was an edge to his voice.

"Well, I must say this has certainly been some bombshell, Mrs. Kimball," said Des. "Great piece of gossip. World-class. You win the prize."

"Call me Molly," she said, beaming.

"I think we'd better go, Des," said Allison suddenly, standing up. "This has been more excitement than I can take in one evening. And I think we've kept Aunt Molly and Uncle Roger up. What time are you leaving for Aspen?"

Des and the President got up too.

"Not until the afternoon. So don't worry about keeping us up," said Aunt Molly. "You're the first honest-to-God company —I mean, real friends—we've had to dinner since I can't remember when. It's nice." She went over and gave Allison a warm hug. Allison was afraid she was going to cry again.

"Now, Molly, don't go maudlin on them," said Kimball. "It's just that what Molly means is that you get to feeling so besieged here, and you begin to feel as if you have no real friends, that everybody is out after a bite of your ass. It's nice once in a while to be able to sit and talk with people you trust." He walked over to Des, took his hand, and shook it hard.

"It was great to get to know you," he said. "You take care of that girl of mine there. She doesn't like me to say this, but she has a soft side to her. Underneath all that toughness, there's a real pussycat."

Des looked down at the floor. He was genuinely embarrassed.

"Oh, for God's sakes, Roger, next you'll be asking him when he's going to make an honest woman of her."

"Well, when are you?" asked the President jovially.

"Okay, it's time to go. Good night, everybody," said Allison. "This has gone far enough, folks. Now I want you both to have a wonderful Christmas and great skiing. Try to keep your minds off Washington. You need a little diversion. I'll check in with you when you get back." She hugged them both a little harder than usual as they walked to the elevator.

Neither Allison nor Des said a word as they reached the diplomats' entrance, met the Secret Service agent, and walked through the garden terrace and out the door on the West Wing side, up the driveway in the snow, and out of the gate, waving good night to the guards as they went.

Finally Des spoke. "I feel like total shit," he said.

"I know."

"I don't think I ever quite realized how tough a position you're in, Sonny."

She didn't respond. She wanted him to talk.

"They really are nice people, aren't they?"

She didn't say anything.

"I mean, Jesus, why would anybody want to be President? What a crappy job. Who needs it? You're never going to win. You're never going to please everybody. You're destined to four or eight years, assuming you don't get shot or die of a stroke"— he didn't notice when she flinched—"of taking nothing but criticism for everything you do or even think."

He was talking rather loudly the whole time as they crossed Seventeenth Street and automatically headed toward his office.

"I feel particularly bad because I really don't think the guy is well. He looked like warmed-over death, and did you see the way he was walking? He was kind of bent over or something. It was weird."

"Isn't that funny?" she said, hoping to keep her voice light. "I was going to say just the opposite. I thought he looked so much better than he did a few weeks ago at his press conference. He was more relaxed than I've seen him in a long time. He has an amazing way of compartmentalizing. He just doesn't let things get to him."

"Well, you know him better than I do."

They walked in silence for a few minutes. Suddenly he turned to her, reached down, and took her hands in his. It was still snowing lightly, and the white flakes were settling on her eyes and nose as she looked up at him in the darkness.

"I want to apologize."

"Oh, Des . . ."

"Not 'Oh, Des.' I've been a jerk. And for the first time I see how hard it must be for you to love those people and have to write about them at all. And by the way, I love you a lot, in case I didn't make myself clear last night. You're one hell of a dame; you know that."

He reached down and kissed the snow off her eyes, her nose, then kissed her lips.

Finally, when he pulled away, she looked up at him soberly, then smiled.

"I know," she said. "The cover story. You have to go back to the office."

"Yeah." He grinned. "I'm afraid I do."

"How long will you be? Should I come in with you and wait?"

"I may be here for hours. I'm going to have to re-create the whole conversation for background and prepare for tomorrow's interview. And I'm going to have to struggle to keep the President's confidence without looking stupid. And Sonny?"

"Yeah?"

"I'm not going to scoop you or make you look bad to your paper. I could see what you were thinking at the table. But now I'm in the same bind. I feel the same strictures. So don't worry. Okay?"

"Thank you," she said. "I appreciate that."

"Okay, baby, here comes a cab. Let me put you in it and send you home. Lord knows what time I'll be back. And then I've got to be at the White House at nine o'clock. I'm going to be a zombie by the time this weekend's over. See you later, sweetheart."

They kissed goodbye, she got into the cab, and he watched as the taxi pulled slowly out on Pennsylvania Avenue and disappeared in the snow toward Georgetown.

Then he turned and went inside his office building, taking the elevator up to his office.

Most of the staff were still there, poring over files and copy coming down from New York.

They followed Des into his office and stood while he took off his coat and jacket and tweed cap, rolled up his sleeves, loosened his tie, and sat down at his desk, deliberately putting his feet up on the desk before he spoke.

"Well?" asked one. "How was it?"

"Did you like them?" asked another.

"I like 'em all," Des said with a grin, "until I sit down at my typewriter."

She was tired when she got down to the paper. It didn't really matter that much. She wasn't writing, and it was Friday, the day before Christmas. Everybody was in a holiday mood. People were going out for long, wet lunches and planning to leave the office around four. Allison took off her coat and went down to the cafeteria to get some hot tea and a Danish. She knew she had to talk to Walt Fineman about last night and probably Allen Warburg too, and she wasn't looking forward to it.

Des had tumbled into bed about three, his adrenaline pumping. He wanted to get laid, and even though she had moaned and made a joke and generally not turned on to him, he had finally had his way. It wasn't that she didn't enjoy it. There was something kind of sexy about making love when you were half-asleep, letting him do all the work, then drifting back to sleep. Des had awakened her again at around seven, kissing her gently, then caressing her, then making love to her before he crawled out of bed.

"Jesus, I don't know why I'm so horny all of a sudden," he said. "I guess nothing turns me on like a good story."

"That's flattering."

"You know what I mean," he said, biting her lip. "You're exactly the same way. It just gets your blood going."

"Unfortunately, I think I do," she said.

Now she was sitting at her desk, staring blankly at her computer. She couldn't get the specter of Uncle Roger and Aunt Molly out of her mind. Maybe the rest in Aspen would do them both good.

She put her feet up on the desk, a position she felt comfortable in when she was wearing pants, picked up the paper, and began reading as she sipped her tea. She was hoping for a little while to wake up before anyone came at her about last night. It was almost eleven, and she was waiting for a phone call from Des. She was still debating whether or not to tell Fineman that Des had got an interview. She decided she had better. They would know it when they picked up the magazine on Monday. The paper was pretty thin this morning. The town closed down over Christmas. It was dead the minute the President left and Congress called its Christmas recess. She was just as glad. It gave everybody a respite. The only problem was the boredom.

"Well, well, well, if it isn't Sonny. We're so pleased you decided to come in this morning. When you have a little free time, you might want to share last night with us."

She looked up and saw Allen Warburg and Walt looking down and grinning at her, and she relaxed.

"Feel free to bring your tea and Danish into my office if you like. We just thought it might be kind of fun to debrief you."

"Sonny, you don't look so hot this morning," said Walt with a little more sympathy than Allen had managed. "Was it that late an evening?"

"Merry Christmas, boys. And many happy returns to you."

"We've got some Christmas cheer in my desk, if you'd like a little spike to your tea," said Allen. "Strictly forbidden except for medicinal purposes. You look like you could use a little something to bring you back to life."

"Since when do we have booze in the newsroom? Does Wiley know about this transgression?"

"Relax," said Allen. "It was a Christmas present from my brother-in-law."

"That's all I need," said Allison. "Besides, wouldn't that look great, me tipping the ol' bottle in your glass office for the entire newsroom to see at eleven o'clock in the morning? 'BOOZE PROBLEM AT THE DAILY OUT OF CONTROL.'"

"Okay, so do without," said Allen. "We're dying to hear about your evening. I suppose your friend is back at the office hard at work rewriting his cover story."

"*The Weekly* likes to keep its cover confidential."

"Believe it or not, we have high White House sources."

"Oh, shit, is it all over the pressroom over there?"

"Your friend spent a little over an hour this morning with the man himself. Now, how did that happen? Are you going to tell me they already had that thing set up before last night?"

"Jesus, what is this, the Inquisition?" she said. "I can't believe this. I told you yesterday we were having dinner over there. I can't control Shaw or what he writes, even if he had told me what he planned to write, which he did not. Nor can I stop the President from doing an interview if he wants to. It came out at dinner that *The Weekly* was planning a cover story on the President's staff and Kimball more or less demanded an interview with Des to talk about it. They had requested an interview weeks ago and Manolas had turned them down without consulting the President. But I didn't have any reason to ask for an interview. I'm not doing any special story right now. I didn't feel I could jump in and say, 'You can't give him an interview and not me.' I'm sorry about it. I just didn't think I should do it. But I don't think Des is going to get much out of him this morning, and I also don't think he's going to be able to use much of what he heard last night. It was off the record."

"So let's hear about it," said Allen. He was testier than usual this morning. "I was afraid this kind of thing might happen."

After she had told them the headlines from the night before, both Walt and Allen sat looking at each other.

"Well," said Allen finally. "How much of that stuff do you think Shaw will use?"

"I told you," said Allison, "I don't think he will use anything on the record. I think it mainly depends on what he got out of the interview this morning. Why don't I go call him and find out?"

"So what are you waiting for?"

Allison put in a call to Des at the bureau.

"Well? How did it go?" she asked.

"You can tell Allen and Walt that they can relax." He laughed. "I got blanked. Totally, one hundred percent blanked. If I hadn't actually had you at the dinner last night as a witness, I would think I dreamed it. This morning it was all honeymoon and roses on the record and Kimball refused to go off the record and he had his press secretary sitting in. He sat there and looked me in the eye and told me that there was no problem between Harry Saks and Addison Marbury. I gotta hand it to your uncle. He plays hardball. He knew that I knew, and there was no give at all. Just those cold blue eyes staring at my bloodshot green ones."

"What are you going with?"

"I'll have to use his quotes in the story. What I'll do is write it as 'Although high White House sources close to the President say he is considering getting rid of both Saks and Marbury, the President denies it and says, quote, That's absurd; they're the two most valuable people in my Administration. Period. Unquote.'"

"Did he really say that?"

"I swear to Christ."

"I've never known him to play that way."

"Well, there it is, sweetheart."

"Okay. I better go back and jolly them up. They were pretty unnerved when they heard about your interview. It was all over the White House this morning, of course. And by the way, that prick Manolas told the entire press corps what *The Weekly*'s cover story is about. Our guy was over there this morning."

"I'm going to get his sorry ass for that one."

"Yeah, well, good luck. Listen, I've got to go. What shall we do tonight?"

"I don't know. Do you feel like Chinese?"

"Des, it's Christmas Eve!"

"Oh, God, you're right. I'm sorry. Look, I should be finished with this thing by about eight or nine. Why don't I surprise you? We'll go out somewhere, okay?"

"Okay. Are we going up to the mountains this weekend?"

"Absolutely. We may have to wait until tomorrow afternoon. But I really want to get out there. I've got to get some exercise or my muscles will atrophy."

"I haven't noticed any signs of that."

"Oho, are we in top form today! I can see I've had a bad influence on you. Maybe we can continue this conversation later."

"It's not the conversation I'd like to continue."

"All right," said Warburg when she came back. "Let's get our guy to put together a rumor story—you know, all the stuff Allison picked up last night. Then he can routinely ask the press secretary for a comment, Manolas will deny the whole thing, and we'll carry the denial. We can run it Sunday. Below the fold. Maybe even inside, depending on what kind of news hole there is tomorrow. But unless there's a natural disaster or an assassination, we'll use it out front. I hope this won't compromise you with the President—or your boyfriend, for that matter."

"He's a real shit, isn't he?" said Allison to Fineman. "You know, I didn't even have to tell you about dinner last night. It is, after all, my personal life."

"Poor Allison. One of the gang, just like the rest of the reporters. Why single her out?" said Warburg.

"C'mon, Allison," said Walt, steering her out of Warburg's office as she glared at him. "Let's go get some lunch. How about Chinese?"

"Merry Christmas," said Warburg.

Allison decided to go back to the office after lunch to clean off her desk and answer some mail. She was reading press releases when the phone rang. It was Jeanette Radford, the producer of *Meet the Media*, one of the network Sunday talk shows.

"Allison, you've got to help me out. We've just landed Harry

Saks on the show this Sunday. We need you to interview. You know there are all these rumors that he is trying to ease Marbury out of his job. We've been trying to get Saks for weeks and suddenly his office just called and offered him to us on a platter. I know I'll have trouble getting family types because Sunday's the day after Christmas. I thought maybe you would be free."

"Oh, Christ, Jeanette, I was planning to go up to the country. I want to say yes. How late can I let you know?"

"You can let me know no later than one hour ago. I'm desperate. And you know that whole scene. I need somebody who can nail Saks down."

"Which means, translated, you really need a woman." Allison chuckled.

"All right, already. Now that we've dispensed with the formalities. I need a woman. You're it. You've got to help me out. You'll do it, of course."

"Just let me make one phone call. I really did promise Des I'd go away for the weekend."

"What if the sisters heard about this? The great Allison Sterling has to ask her boyfriend if she can go on *Meet the Media*? I hope it doesn't get out."

"Up yours, Jeannie. I'll call you right back."

She put down the phone and pondered for a few minutes. She knew Des would be furious. He would probably go without her. No. He wouldn't do that. Not on Christmas. Yes. He might well do that. The real question was, What would he do if he were in her shoes? No contest. He would stay and go on the show. It was good exposure. He liked doing TV from time to time. He was good at it. He got paid. It didn't hurt *The Weekly*'s image. He would stay and do the show. That was it. Well, then, she would stay. She really wanted to do it, and she couldn't keep Jeannie waiting. She picked up the phone.

"Yeah," Shaw answered.

"Hold the line, please, for the President of the United States."

"I'm sorry," he said solemnly. "This is Desmond Shaw, the *Weekly* Bureau Chief."

"You jerk," she said, breaking up.

"How could you do that to me? Here I am exhausted, trying to tie up this story, hung over, frantic . . . you'll pay."

"Listen, angel, I've got a huge favor to ask you."

"Anything."

"Could we possibly stay in town this weekend? I've been asked to go on *Meet the Media*. They've got Harry Saks and they want me on and I would like to do it. I think it could be a good story."

"Oh, damn, Allison. Listen, sweetheart, get out of it, will you? You don't need it. It's just a bunch of hacks blathering on at the mouth anyway. Don't screw up the weekend. I really want to get away. I'm just beat. I need to get away. Okay, sweetheart?"

She paused.

"C'mon, baby?"

"What would *you* do?" she asked.

"What do you mean?"

"I mean if they asked *you*, what would *you* do?"

"If I promised you a weekend in the country, I'd go to the country. It's no big deal."

"Des, I'm sorry, but I promised Jeanette that I would do it. I want to do it. I think it would be good for me. I hope you'll try to understand."

"What am I supposed to do? Cool my heels all weekend and then pick you up at the studio Sunday so we can go for a day? That would blow the whole thing. There would be no point in it."

"Anyway, I have to be back for the eleven A.M. White House briefing on Monday. I've got the duty. Everybody else is off and our regular guy is in Aspen."

"The hell with it, Sonny. *I'll* just go. I'll try to understand if you stay here. You try to understand if I go. All right?"

"All right," she said finally.

"Look, I can't talk any longer. I've got New York on the phone. I'll see you later."

"Okay. I'll be at home when you're through."

She hesitated only a moment before she called Jeanette back.

She was sitting by the fire with a glass of wine, watching the news, when he came in. She was surprised by the expression on his face. Instead of the locked jaw and steely gaze she expected, Des looked chastened.

"Hi, angel," he said, throwing his arms around her. He kissed her on the lips, then sighed and kissed her again, rubbing his hands over her behind.

"Ummmmmm," he said. "I'd forgotten how good that felt. I

haven't knocked off a piece since this morning. How can I still be horny?"

She didn't say anything. He fixed an Irish and came over and sat down next to her on the sofa, not his usual seat.

"Where would you like to go tonight?" he asked. "I'm feeling in a good mood. I'm having my usual postcoital experience after I've finished a major cover."

"Why don't we just stay here? It's so awful outside, and we've got some steaks and some of that caviar left over. We could have dinner by the fire."

"Perfect," he said. "I knew there was a reason I was in love with you."

It wasn't until dinner that she brought it up. She was still surprised at his jovial mood.

"So what are your plans tomorrow?" she asked as casually as possible.

"Well, I thought we could get laid. Get up. Open our presents. Then maybe go over to O'Grady's for Christmas dinner. Then we could come home and get laid, then maybe go out for supper and a movie later or just stay in bed and watch television, then get laid, then go to sleep. How's that sound?"

"Maybe I missed something," she said, "but I could have sworn that you were planning to go up to the country for the weekend."

He smiled. He had had enough to drink so that his lip curled, and one lock of hair fell over his forehead.

"Oh, didn't I tell you?"

"What?"

"I've been asked to go on *Dateline: Washington* this Sunday."

"And?"

"And I said yes."

She could have rubbed it in; she decided against it.

"Who're they having on?"

"Addison Marbury. His office called and offered him up. I have a feeling that our dinner last night and my follow-up interview this morning with the President precipitated this. They're anticipating a story in *The Daily* and a cover story in *The Weekly*. They know perfectly well that we're going to say that they don't get along and they both may be on the way out," he said. "I'm sure the White House has cooked this one up to get them to say they love each other and have no intention of leaving. The show knew that I was working on this cover. Your show didn't ask you by chance. I guess the White House put that one out over the wires. They'll want us to counter whatever Marbury and Saks may say. They're going to try to refute everything we've got. I added a footnote to the story about how the White House was sending these guys out to put a lid on the rumors, just to cover my ass."

"I'm glad you're staying even if it's not for me. I was going to miss you over Christmas weekend. I wasn't looking forward to being alone."

"I'm glad too," he said softly, taking her hand across the table. "I felt as though you were abandoning me. I was hurt, Sonny. I've got to admit that to you. I wouldn't if I hadn't been into the sauce a little tonight. But I feel like there ought to be times when a woman puts her man first before her career. And I always know with you which comes first. And it ain't me, kid. It's okay; I can live with it. And I know you think I do the same. But I've gotta tell you that it just doesn't feel good. There are times when I want to be number one. I can't help it. If that makes me a male chauvinist pig, then so be it."

She knew he was right. She gave the impression that her work came first. But it was only out of instinct for survival that she always chose her career first. It had never occurred to her that he even noticed, or that he might be hurt. She didn't think he cared enough to be hurt by her. She was so preoccupied with her need, so afraid of her dependence that she had never really dwelt on what he might feel.

Now she felt almost like weeping. She couldn't let down her defenses even when it was safe. And here was Des telling her it was safe. Did she believe him? Could she trust him? She would try. She promised herself. She would try.

"Now," she said, getting up from the table and walking around to the back of his chair and putting her arms around his neck. "Now look who's being an asshole."

The two Sunday interview shows had not gone equally well. Allison had made news. Des had not. Addison Marbury had been his usual upper-class, boring self. He was a master at evasion and had turned every question, no matter how tough, into a compliment for the reporter. Des had tried to get something out of him;

so had the others. They had tried to goad him and Marbury had made them seem like bullies.

"Of course, we all have different styles and methods of operation," he said. "That includes Harry Saks and myself. There's bound to be friction from time to time because of that.

"But as far as any out-and-out warfare, I'm not aware of that. Regardless of what the inevitable rumors are, isn't it S.O.P., Mr. Shaw, that about this time in every administration, *The Weekly* comes out with a cover story on how the staffers are fighting with each other? I seem to recall one in every administration in the past, and as far back as I go, that's a long way."

"Charming, evasive, infuriating," Des said in disgust later that day.

Allison had had better luck with Saks. Harry was irascible and given to outbursts.

While she was being made up, Saks had stuck his head in and seen her. "Ah, Allison," he had said sarcastically, "what fun to see you here this morning. I suppose now I should prepare for a little blood on the floor."

"Harry, what are you talking about?" They were both smiling, but the edge was there.

Allison's turn to question came last. The others had brought up the rumors of the infighting with Marbury and rumors that they both would soon be out, mostly because they had read the third-page *Daily* story that morning.

"Why do you have so much trouble getting along with people, Mr. Saks?" she asked. "During the campaign you were always fighting or reported to be fighting with somebody. Since you've been in the White House there has hardly been a week when you weren't engaged in some form of combat with some colleague or staffer. If it's not having somebody's desk moved, or leaking damaging information about someone, then it's something else. Do you think there is something about you which provokes these kinds of reports, and in the end, is this kind of behavior really helpful to your President?"

The reporter next to her gasped under his breath, "Heavy stuff," and everyone sat rapt, waiting for Saks.

"Well, Allison," he began, his voice oozing with sarcasm, "leave it to a woman to ask a question like that."

Everyone gasped again. Saks realized he had made a mistake.

"But seriously—" His face had reddened and she could tell he was about to let loose, although nobody was prepared for his outburst. "In campaigns and even in the White House there are people who don't know what they're doing. If you're in a highly pressurized situation every day and dealing with the immense kind of power and making the kind of decisions we are making every day, you often don't have time to be polite the way some people think you do. Maybe upper-class accents and Old School Tie manners are in order. But it is just not the way I see getting things done effectively. So if I appear abrasive or difficult to get along with at times, or some touchy staffers have their egos bruised, then I'm sorry, but that's just the way I operate. I always have and I always will. And if the President is displeased he has the prerogative to let me go. So far, he has not seen fit to do so."

"A follow-up question, please," said Allison. "I assume you're referring to Addison Marbury when you speak of Old School Tie and upper-class accents?"

"I'm not mentioning any names. I'm speaking in general."

Allison thought she had probably gone too far. Saks was practically apoplectic. The moderator was getting a little nervous. "Thank you, Mr. Saks," she said, and let the moderator ask about the economy. By the time the show was over Saks had cooled down. He left without saying goodbye to anyone.

Jeanette came barreling out of the control room, her face beaming.

"Great television, Sonny," she said. "And boy, did we ever make news! We were monitoring *Dateline: Washington*. Marbury was a bomb. Boring. They got nothing. They'll make page eighteen of the A section tomorrow. We're page one."

Allison felt a twinge. Des had hoped to get something out of Marbury. She decided not to bring it up. Des got home first and was reading the paper in the dining room when she got back.

"Well, I see you really got that son-of-a-bitch to open up," he said casually, then went back to the paper and his Bloody Mary.

"I'm not sure," she said. "I don't think it will get much play tomorrow."

"Yeah," he said.

Allison decided to walk to the White House for the eleven-thirty press briefing. It had stopped snowing, though it was still overcast. Even though it was Monday, it was the week in between Christmas and New Year's and there wasn't much going on. The President and his retinue were in Aspen, and Congress was in recess. This week would be one long Saturday.

She trudged down to M Street from her house, turned left, and headed downtown toward Pennsylvania Avenue. The press adored Roger Kimball for at least that one thing. The vacation White House was in Aspen, so it was a great place to hang out. Many of the correspondents had taken their families with them, so for once there were no cries of anguish from those assigned the Christmas watch. In the past, there had been some Presidential hometowns that were dogs. This was a dream come true, and their organizations were paying for it.

The walk gave her some time to think.

Des hadn't said a word about the rumor article when he read the paper that morning. Monday was a slow day for him. Often he didn't even go into the office. If she didn't have to file, they could have lunch together. As she approached the White House she reached into her purse, fished around for her wallet and pulled out her White House press pass on its metal chain, grimaced at last year's picture, and flashed it at the guard in the window.

"Hi, Allison," he said as he pushed a buzzer and the metal gate to the left swung open for her. She slipped the pass over her neck so that it was visible, then poked her face into the guard box to say Merry Christmas.

"Any action today?" she asked.

"Are you kidding? The most exciting thing going on is that some of the network guys are chasing poor Mabel around trying to kiss her under the mistletoe. Last we heard, she had burst into tears and was hiding in the ladies' room."

The guards all cracked up, and Allison laughed in spite of herself. She felt sorry for Mabel, a tall, stooped-over spinster who had worked for a small-town newspaper in upstate New York and had been covering the White House for nearly forty years. She was definitely the veteran White House correspondent. She was plain, boring, pushy, and obliging, and she was there from dawn every morning until midnight every night.

Allison marched up the curved driveway toward the pressroom. Some TV cameras were already set up on tripods in the snow for the reporters' stand-uppers.

She shivered thinking about it. Thank God she didn't work for television. The way those people had to hustle around, putting on makeup and memorizing lead-ins, standing out there in the cold and rain, redoing spots—it was such a bore. One thing about writing for a newspaper was that you could phone your story in if you had to.

Allison could hear the laughter before she stepped into the pressroom. There was a mike set up at one end, where the briefings took place, and a TV reporter stood bellowing out a description of what was going on as though he were announcing a horse race. At the other end of the room the cameramen were standing on the platform screaming and cheering while one of the male reporters from quite a reputable newspaper was chasing Mabel up one side of the room and down the other with a piece of mistletoe held high above his head, shouting, in a deep Texas accent, "Pucker up, Miss Mabel; I'm a-comin' to get ya."

"Ladies and gentlemen," said a voice from the mike. "If I may be so bold as to use that term loosely. Is it possible for us to put an end to this merriment for few moments so that we may reflect for a bit on some of the overriding problems of this nation? I realize that that is not why you are here. Immediately following the briefing there will be apple dunking and Pin the Tail on the Elephant and we will be serving punch and cookies for those of you who have behaved. . . ."

The press secretary was just getting warmed up.

"Boooooooooooooooo. Hisssssssssss. Get the hook. Sit down. . . . Bring on the clowns. . . . We want Santa. . . ."

"Please, boys and girls. We will be forced to call your mommies if there is not more appropriate behavior. Now, does anybody want any news? Everybody who wants any news please raise your hand."

"Yeahhhh, news," said one reporter, raising her hand. Even the women had begun acting like jerks at the White House press briefings. Equality.

"What about the Saks stuff on *Meet the Media* yesterday? How has the President responded to that, and what does Marbury to say about it?" They were all looking at Allison. Some shouted congratulations at her.

All the reporters were clamoring with questions until the press secretary could quiet them down.

"All right, all right, one at a time. I only have two brief statements. The President is satisfied that both of his two top aides have made it clear that there is no conflict between them and is pleased to announce that they both have his strongest support and confidence and that both of them will stay on."

Another clamoring of questions and comments. "Can you believe that horseshit?" "It's Kafkaesque." "Tough it out." "Fantastic."

"What about Marbury?" someone shouted.

"Marbury said that happily he has been assured by Saks that he was not referring to him during the broadcast because if he had been he would have been forced to challenge him to a duel."

"Is that it? Christ," mumbled another reporter. "Leave it to Marbury. I can't decide whether he's the stupidest bastard I ever heard of or the smartest."

The press secretary refused to entertain any more questions about Saks and Marbury and insisted on telling the surly crowd what the First Family had exchanged for Christmas presents.

"Now, boys and girls," said Manolas, "I'm going to tell you what Santa brought President and Mrs. Kimball. Isn't that fun?"

"Hey, cut the shit, buddy," yelled somebody from the sofa over on the sidelines. Edmond Smythe. He was new to the White House press corps. At some point, the circuslike ritual of the press briefing would be brought back to reality by somebody who was relatively new to the group and who was appalled by the abominable behavior of so many of the reporters. There were so many nut cases who called themselves White House reporters that they often outnumbered the real reporters from reputable news organizations. On a bad day the cries could get to the real people, and then the entire briefing resembled something closer to Mondo Bizarro than any kind of serious vehicle for the dissemination of news to the American public.

After disclosing what the First Family had exchanged (new ski outfits) the press secretary made a few brief news announcements which amounted to nothing and then ended the briefing. "That's all for now, boys and girls."

Allison walked to the back room past the bulletin board, scanning it for any news items, checked through the holders for press releases, and then went to *The Daily*'s booth to call the office.

"Whatd'ya get?" said Al, who was on the desk for the holiday shift. "Any hot breaking news?"

She laughed. "You want a list of gifts the First Family exchanged?"

"I don't think so. Somebody's just put a wire story on my desk with the list. I'll shoot it back to Living. No need to file. What are you up to today? Are you working on anything?"

"I'm supposed to be doing that piece Walt wanted on the economic program and the dissension between the White House and Congress on how to play it. But I'm kind of hung up because everybody's out of town so I can't get any interviews this week."

"There's nobody here. The place is really dead. Why don't you knock off for the day? If there's an emergency I'll give you a call, but there are enough shleppers around here I can work with."

"Make it a real emergency, okay?"

"Okay. See ya."

Allison put down the phone, then picked it up again to call Des. His secretary answered the phone.

"Hi, Shirlee," she said. "Is Des there?"

"He's awfully busy right now."

"It's Monday, Shirlee. You want to put him on for me?"

There was ice in her voice.

Des picked up the phone.

"Yeah?" His voice was cool. He was still upset about blowing it with Marbury. She could tell.

"I love you," she said. "I love you a lot." He didn't answer.

"What do you want?"

"Actually, I want lunch. And then I think I want a little nap with you afterward. It's Monday, so I know you don't have a thing to do over there."

He didn't say anything, so she tried again.

"Hey, Shaw, whatd'ya say? My treat?"

Another pause.

"Jesus Christ, do you have any idea how many men in this town would kill to have me ask them to lunch, not to mention offer them my body afterwards? What *is* this?"

"Okay. How about Mel's?"

"I'll meet you on the corner of Seventeenth and Pennsylvania in fifteen minutes and we can walk down. I don't think we need to call. It'll probably be dead today."

"See ya."

She met him on the corner in the snow and they walked down Seventeenth Street, making small talk about what a slow news day it was and what a bunch of jerks some of the White House reporters were. At Mel's they walked down the circular staircase into the center of the underground room, all brown velvet and plush. Mel showed them to one of the front tables he reserved for his more illustrious customers.

He ordered a martini. She ordered a Bloody Mary. They said nothing until their drinks had arrived.

Meanwhile, everybody who came down the winding staircase had to acknowledge their presence, it was such a conspicuous spot. Almost everyone mentioned Allison's appearance the day before.

"Hey, Allison, great performance yesterday."

"Jesus, did you ever nail Saks."

"What a show! You really had him going, didn't you?"

Hardly anybody mentioned Des's show, and if anyone did, it was "Marbury's a crafty son-of-a-bitch."

One reporter, an older man who had always been envious of Des and had his eye on Allison, took the opportunity to tuck it to Des.

"Hey, Shaw," he yelled out in a joking manner from a nearby table. "You guys really let Marbury off the hook yesterday."

Several people chuckled. Saks was Topic A at Mel's that day. Des was trying to keep his cool. If it had been another reporter on her show who had gone after Saks, Des would have given as good as he was getting. But he couldn't. He couldn't come back at the Saks interview without putting Allison down. So all he could do was to sit there and try to be a good sport. But she could tell he was hurting, and it made her hurt too.

She was getting absolutely no pleasure out of her triumph at all. It would have been better if nothing had come out of her show and Des had cracked Marbury. She would have felt good sitting there, listening to him accept compliments. And nobody would have put her down or made cracks at her about not doing well with Saks. This, she decided, was a dangerous train of thought. She would have to get over it. She changed the subject.

"God, there are a lot of people here today. I thought the place would be dead over the holidays."

He didn't say anything.

"How's the cover look? I didn't get a chance to read it, but I saw a few copies of it over at the White House."

"Frankly, I think it's terrific. It may be one of the best things we've done out of this bureau since I've been here. I'm very proud of it." There was a defensive tone in his voice.

"I have the afternoon off. I'll read it."

"You don't have to."

"But I want to. I'm sure I'll learn something. You've probably got some great quotes from Uncle Roger that you didn't tell me about, you S.O.B."

She was trying to tease him out of his slump.

He shrugged but said nothing. They sat in silence for a while, looking at the menu, then ordered the crab cakes when the waiter came around again.

"So," said Allison, finally. "I gather the Greys had a party for John T. and it was a big success."

"Oh, yeah?"

"Lorraine says our names were put on and taken off the list about ten times. Apparently Sadie just couldn't make up her mind about us until the very end. Or I should say 'me.'"

"Well, she obviously did, didn't she?" He was trying to sound noncommittal.

"If she had invited us at the last minute I wouldn't have gone."

"Why not?"

"Because I think it would have been goddamned insulting, that's why."

She hadn't meant to sound that upset.

"I'll bet it was a good party. *I* would have gone."

She just glared at him. Neither seemed to realize how childish they were being.

"Why?"

"Because," he challenged, "I think she's a dynamite dame."

CHAPTER 8

IF SHE COULD GET THROUGH THE NEXT FEW weeks, Sadie decided, she would deserve a medal. The children were coming home, and at the President's suggestion, she had foolishly agreed to have a huge party for the Secretary of State before Christmas. Also, her office had scheduled an interview the following day with *The Daily* which she had been trying to avoid for months. The director of the National Trust had told her that to get final funding from Congress on some projects they had been planning, he needed a meeting with her. And work was to be started on the new kitchen after the first of the year and there were men all over the place measuring and surveying.

She was sitting upstairs in her bedroom, in the lovely round alcove she had made into her private work space. From her window in the turret she could see the British Embassy and the park and she could watch the sun move around the house. It was a bright, cozy little hideaway where she had a desk, her files, her phone books, and an easy chair with a footstool and her cashmere throw. And, her telephone. Her telephone life was her most active social involvement since she'd come to Washington, a fact she was not planning to reveal to the reporter from *The Daily*, a rather harmless creature, relatively new on the staff.

It was ringing again. During the day the stewards were supposed to answer it. Occasionally, she answered it herself when they seemed to have disappeared, though you never knew whom you were going to get. The number wasn't listed, of course, but it was one of those things that just got around fast. It was hooked up to the White House switchboard, which took their calls if nobody was home.

The phone had now rung at least eight times, and Sadie picked it up.

"Can I speak to Jarrell?" said a child's voice.

There must be a conspiracy of children in Washington, a lobby set up to drive the occupants of the Vice President's house crazy with wrong numbers. She patiently told the child he had the wrong number. When the next call came through a few minutes later she let it ring three times, then picked it up again.

"Hello," she practically barked into the phone.

"Ah," said the vaguely familiar voice, "I would know the sound of your voice anywhere, even after all these years. Though you have lost a little of that Southern accent. Yankee exposure, I presume."

She was tempted to ask who it was in a brusque voice, but then she had to remember who she was, always. A servant of the people.

"May I ask who I'm speaking to?" she said softly, only the slightest edge in her voice.

"You don't recognize my voice. And I thought I had made an impression on you."

She had stiffened when she first heard his voice; now she weakened. She could feel her face redden. She felt a rush of bitterness, sadness, even longing.

"Is it . . . ?"

"It's me—Tag. Remember?"

Remember? Was the son-of-a-bitch kidding? After nineteen years. How could she forget the one man she had fallen madly in love with? Who had jilted her, broken her heart, made it hard for her to love again.

"Of course, Tag," she finally said. Casually.

"Well, that's better. You had me worried there for a minute."

There was the old cockiness.

"How are you and where are you?" she asked.

"I'm right here in our nation's capital and I couldn't be better. I'm calling, in fact, to see if you would consider having lunch with an old flame. Any restaurant of your choice. Just for old times' sake. I'll bet you're even more beautiful than when I last saw you."

"Well, let's just say I've changed, Tag. It has been nineteen years."

"It seems like yesterday."

He might have done better than that. She was furious at herself for being undone and furious at him for springing up out of nowhere. Why now? Taggart. How she had loved him! He was tall and handsome and sophisticated and he knew everything and he had made her feel he understood her better than she understood herself. Romantic. Sexy. He was every girl's fantasy in college. And he had loved *her*. Or so he had said. He had taught her about sex and given her her first orgasm. He had taught her the difference between making love and fucking. Tag had made love to her and he had been the object of her sexual fantasies even much later, even when she made love to her husband.

She blushed. He had always been so clever at knowing what she was thinking that she was afraid he might guess even now. Lunch was out of the question. She was too nervous for that. She was still so traumatized by her lunch with Des that she almost didn't want to leave the house, and she refused to allow herself to think about it. Besides, it wasn't so easy for her just to take a jaunt out in public for lunch anymore—legally, anyway. It was like a goddamned state occasion. She would need two reservations, one for her and one for at least two Secret Service agents. She'd have to have her car with the two agents in front and a follow-up car. They'd all want to know whom she was lunching with. She'd have to tell Rosey. He hated Tag, hated the fact that he had walked out of Sadie's life. He had seen how sad she was afterward, and how long it had taken him to bring her out of it, to respond to him, to agree to marry him. The press would make a federal case out of it. An old friend from college days? They would know from the way she looked at him. And no doubt from the way he looked at her.

Tag would most certainly try to turn on the charm. He couldn't help it.

Maybe that was what he wanted: to be seen with her, to be mentioned in the gossip columns. Wasn't it convenient that he would call her only after her husband was Vice President! Maybe he wanted something from her. How stupid not to have thought of that right away. He needed something. Didn't everybody, these days? Nobody in Washington didn't want something. Friendship was a rare thing—pure friendship, at any rate. God damn it, why hadn't she guessed? He wasn't any more interested in her than he had been nineteen years ago when he just walked away. Never to call again. Until her husband became the second-most-powerful man in the country. Well, he wasn't going to use her this time to get himself in the columns. Should she invite him to the house for lunch? As a matter of fact, she really didn't have time. Tea. She would invite him for tea. That was safe. If she enjoyed it, whatever that meant, she could always invite him again. If not, tea was fine. She had the perfect excuse.

"How long are you going to be in town?"

"Oh, a couple of days. I'm here on business. It depends on how things go. I'm pretty open-ended."

"You know I would adore to see you." The voice was sweet.

"Great," he said before she could finish. "Just name the time and place. I'll be there."

"Oh, Tag, this is such a hectic time, with Christmas and everything. The kids will be home, I've got several interviews, I've got a crisis involving one of my projects, and we're getting ready for a large party for the Secretary of State." That'll get him. "I just don't see how I can possibly get away for lunch. It's not simple for me to do that, as I'm sure you know. Why don't you come by here for tea this afternoon? Around four."

He hesitated on the other end of the line, but she knew that he had not missed the firmness in her tone. He debated, then dropped the issue.

"Great, sounds great," he said. "I'm disappointed I can't take you out. I'll come for tea if you'll give me a rain check."

"We'll see about that," she said with a tinkly little laugh. "I've got to run now. See you at four."

When she put down the phone, she noticed that her hands

were shaking. "Shit," she said out loud. "Shit. Shit. Shit. I don't need this."

She jumped up from the desk and walked over to the dresser in the bedroom. She looked into the mirror and gasped. Her hair was a disaster. Ivan wasn't supposed to come until the next day to do her hair for the dinner.

She picked up the phone and dialed her hairdresser's private number. "Ivan. I have an emergency. I'm having my picture taken this afternoon and my hair is a mess. Could you possibly come over now and do it instead of tomorrow? Maybe tomorrow I could get away with a comb-out. Please?"

"Oh là là! I'm going to lose all my business here if I have to keep cancelling my clients." She heard him sigh. "But for you, Madame Grey, it would be worth it."

She had her special hairdresser's chair and dryer all set up in the bathroom when he arrived, fluttering about the room, complaining about how busy he was. The more she thought about it, the madder she got at herself. She couldn't understand why she had even agreed to see him. She hated him. She always would hate him. It had taken her almost six years before she had stopped feeling sick to her stomach at the thought of him. Now he was intruding into her life again. Would she still be attracted? Would she feel anything? She had to appear completely in control.

She rang downstairs to tell the stewards to have tea ready in the small living room off the main drawing room, to lay a fire, and to use some of the cookies and cakes they had received as Christmas presents.

By four she had done her nails twice and had changed her clothes several times, settling finally on a winter-white cashmere cowl-necked sweater and white wool pants. Casual. Just running around the house and stopping for a quick cup of tea. The white sweater set off her turquoise eyes and her auburn hair. One quick dab of moisturizer around the tiny crow's-feet. At four sharp the doorbell rang.

She had decided to be upstairs when he arrived. She grabbed some tissues, pressed them against her palms, which were perspiring, and wadded them into her pockets. With one last toss of her hairbrush, she went down the curving staircase and sailed into the back sitting room, where Tag stood, his back to the door, gazing at the collection of books on the Vice Presidency.

"Pretty obscure, some of them, aren't they?" she said too brightly.

He turned to look at her. They both drew their breaths.

He hadn't expected her to be so beautiful. His expression told her so. Though he had obviously seen her in countless magazine pictures, still, there was something luminous about her which cameras never managed to pick up. She was terribly unphotogenic—at least, she thought so.

He didn't say anything, just looked.

She stared back. His face was a little fuller, his dark hair was wispy, curling down around his neck, and he was tanned and windburned, as though he spent a lot of time sailing. He was less taut, more relaxed than he had been as a young man. And he was still beautiful. His long eyelashes veiled his mischievous eyes; his grin was challenging. He was still an upper-class rogue, a bandit, a bad boy in Guccis, carelessly and elegantly turned out. Only the slight shift in bearing spoke of any pain or disappointments.

In one of their last conversations, he had told her that there were too many women out there he wanted to know, too many things to experience, which was why he couldn't marry her as he had promised. It was such trash, such hypocritical trash that it made her furious even now. Except she wasn't staying furious. She was succumbing again to his charm. It was obvious to her that he had experienced those things, those women. It just made him more attractive.

She reached out her hand and stiffened her arm just the slightest so he would not try to bend it or pull her over to kiss him. There was another flicker of surprise in his eyes. Did he still think he could have his way after all these years? She looked at him, determined. The outrageous sex appeal was still there. He knew too. Or did he?

She gestured to him to sit by the fire. There were two chairs pulled up facing each other by the fireplace, where she and Rosey sat before dinner at night. Better that than sharing the sofa, she decided. Jackson brought the tea and placed it on the ottoman between them. As he stood waiting, she nodded to him that he could go. She poured the tea without saying anything, then handed Tag his cup.

"So," she said finally, "tell me everything. Catch me up from when . . ." She didn't finish. "Well, you know everything about me, I suppose. Tell me about yourself." She didn't want him to know she had been following his adventures in the movie magazines.

"I'm producing films. Just like I always wanted to. But I've been in Europe. In fact, I've been doing so well that I decided the time might be right to venture into the nation's capital and see if I might pick up a little action here."

Between the lines it became clear that he had been less successful than he had hoped, which explained why she rarely heard of any of his work. The publicity about him was almost always involving his love life. One of his problems, she suspected, had always been money. He had too much of it.

He had made a number of films in Africa, he told her, a few features in Italy, and a couple of documentaries in London. One on drugs, which he seemed particularly proud of, had had some success and had gotten some good reviews. In between he had been married and divorced twice, once to a woman whose name was well known in New York society, then to a French movie star.

He indicated with a chuckle that both had left him. Other women was the implication.

"What is it that interests you about Washington?" she asked finally. She was afraid of his answer.

"Ah, well, I was hoping you'd ask that," he said.

Here it comes, she said to herself.

"Actually, I was thinking now was a good time to start making some political films, some campaign films, possibly even moving to Washington and setting up my headquarters here. There is so much material here in Washington and so many people who could use a little help. Most of the campaign films I've seen are pretty rotten. In fact, I didn't think much of your husband's, to tell you the truth. Very amateurish, I thought."

How dare he? Who the hell was he, anyway? She didn't have the nerve to say that to him. If only she could be more direct— but it just wasn't in her.

"Nonetheless," she said softly, "he didn't do so badly, did he?"

"Oh, his winning didn't have anything to do with those films," he said in an authoritative manner. "Nobody could have beaten Kimball. He was golden. But your husband needs a better image. He comes across a little stiff, you know, too formal. He needs loosening up. These are just my personal observations, you understand."

If it hadn't been true she would have been less angry. And it wasn't Rosey's image Tag was talking about. It was Rosey himself. Tag knew her, knew what turned her on. He always had. And he would know that Rosey did not. At least sexually.

"I'm afraid you'll have a hard time convincing him of that," she said, seething. "He quite likes his image. So do I, for that matter." Would he believe her?

He didn't seem to hear. "Anyway," he continued, "this is a great town, if"—he paused at the "if"—"if you've got contacts."

She said nothing. Why didn't she have the guts to throw him right out of her house? Once again she was furious with herself. It was her Southern upbringing. "A guest in my house can do no wrong," she could hear her father saying. "I may not ever invite him back, but while he is here he is entitled to the best hospitality I have to offer." She knew that that was in part why she couldn't speak back to him. It didn't seem to matter, though. He was smart enough to realize she was still confused about him, if nothing else.

"Sadiebelle," he said finally, softly, "I can't tell you how fabulous you look. I hadn't expected to see you looking so beautiful. But then"—and he lowered his eyelids in a way he had clearly done hundreds and thousands of times before with some success —"you always were a spectacularly beautiful woman." The emphasis, in a low, guttural, sexual tone of voice, was on the word "woman." She could feel it between her legs.

"I've always thought," he continued, "that a woman was never really at her most attractive until she reached thirty-five. At thirty-five, women begin to blossom, to ripen. The French have always understood that. *'Un certain âge.'* You women are so silly. You all think you are over the hill by the time you're thirty-five. I say that's when you become worth paying attention to."

God, he was using the same old lines, yet when he had told her that in college, alluding mysteriously to all the older women he had had in his past, she had been faint with desire and numb with awe. And even now, she couldn't help herself from still being attracted to him.

"You know, I did you a favor, Sadiebelle, when I left." He said it with such pride. She wondered if he dined out on that one. "I walked out on the Vice President's wife. Sweet girl, but so naive.

"When I left, you weren't ready for marriage any more than I was. You needed experience too. I can see that you got it. And you've become the kind of woman I knew you could be, the kind of woman you had the potential to be. I'm proud of you, kid."

She could barely swallow, she was so outraged. How did he think he could just appear on her doorstep like this and talk to her as though she were some broad he had popped once in his life? He was trying to seduce her even now. What was it about her that made him think he could treat her this way? Suddenly she was filled with the same sense of insecurity and failure she had felt nineteen years ago.

Except for Danny when she was sixteen, and that was hardly what she would call experience, the men in her life had consisted of Tag, Rosey, her brief and near-disastrous affair with Stuart Cortwright when Rosey was Governor of Virginia, and Des. They were all of a type except for Rosey. She was inexorably drawn to rakes and bastards.

Tag was rattling his teacup. She could tell he was angling for something.

"Got anything a little stronger than this?" He obviously wanted to prolong the visit. It was nearly five thirty. She contemplated saying no. Then, caught up by her upbringing once more, she stood up, walked over to the bar, and took out a glass.

"Scotch neat; Glenfiddich if you have it."

She poured the Scotch—Rosey liked Glenfiddich—and carried it over to him. She saw his approving gaze. She was suddenly overcome with humiliation. Somehow he knew she was not as fulfilled as she would like him to think. She was insulted by his presumption, after all these years, that he could flatter her, entice her into allowing him to use her and her husband's position to further his pitiful little film career. It did not occur to her that he might really be attracted to her. And it made her wonder again, as she had many times since her encounter at Great Falls, whether Des was using her as well.

She handed him the glass and grasped the crumpled-up Kleenexes in her pocket.

"I'm sorry to make the drink so short," she apologized, "but we're getting ready for a Christmas party. I've got so much to do I don't even know where to begin. I still have to go over the seating with my secretary."

She was rubbing it in now. She wanted to feel superior. She wanted to diminish him.

"I've never been to one of these formal Washington do's," he said. "Of course, I've been to every kind of party in New York, on the Coast, in Paris and London, but Washington is a totally different scene."

"Totally. Entertaining for fun exclusively isn't done here. Every party has a reason. People work at parties. Parties are a wonderful place to make contacts, see people you wouldn't be able to get on the telephone, have informal conversations with people, pick up or exchange information. They are really invaluable to people who want to do serious business, political or otherwise, in this town."

She was painting a picture that he would find irresistible.

"I'd love to see one firsthand," he said. The way he said it, so matter-of-fact, reminded her that he was a man used to getting what he wanted from women.

"I'm sure you will, especially if you plan to spend time in Washington. But think it over carefully before you do. This is a very rough place to break into. Unless you are in a position of power either in the government, in politics, in journalism, or in law, it is difficult. People won't be interested. There are so many people who move here with high expectations. . . ."

"Well, if you know the right people . . ."

"If you know the right people. But not everyone does. And now, Tag, I'm just sick at the thought that we have to end this delightful visit, but I really must get back to business."

Her palms were perspiring. She had to get him out.

Jackson appeared at the door.

"Excuse me, ma'am," he said, "but the White House is on the line."

That was his way of telling her she could get out of it. "The White House" could be the switchboard calling back with messages. Jackson was so clever. He had sensed something. And this was a no-fail way to end a conversation. Nobody ever questioned the White House. She glanced at Tag and saw that he was properly impressed.

"Tag, dear"—she stood up—"I'm going to have to run now. I do hope you will understand."

She began walking him to the front door.

"I certainly hope your project will be a success." Sweet, polite, noncommittal. He couldn't complain, couldn't pressure. Nothing about calling again or lunch or do drop by.

As she turned in the central hallway to go back to Tilda's office to take the phone call, Tag stopped her.

"Oh, by the way," he said. "I forgot to mention to you that I'm seeing a close friend of yours. She asked me to give you her love."

Why did she flush? Why did her stomach flip over?

"Oh?" she asked, almost to herself.

"Chessy Shaw. The soon-to-be-ex–Mrs. Desmond Shaw."

She caught her breath. She had been avoiding Chessy's calls since the incident with Des.

"How nice for you. You and Chessy would be perfect together."

He winced. Sadie smiled. "Goodbye, Tag. Let's promise to meet again in nineteen years."

Before he could answer, she had turned her back. The door slammed with a bang, and she leaned against it and took a deep breath.

She had exacted her revenge. Yet why did she feel so unnerved? Even now, after nineteen years, she wanted to make him pay, wanted to hurt him. Even now that she knew she was no longer in love with him. Was it Tag who had a hold over her, or her fantasy? She suddenly felt depressed. If only he hadn't mentioned Desmond Shaw.

"Have you made up your mind about Desmond Shaw and Allison Sterling?" Tilda was asking as they went through the guest list in order to do the seating.

Tilda Traina had given up her business in New York to come down and take the job of Sadie's social secretary and special assistant. On the government payroll. For less money, she liked to point out. Tilda was from California and had been one of Sadie's best friends at Smith. Her business in New York, Services Rendered, handled parties, gave advice on social problems, did special shopping for people, and essentially catered to the whims of the rich. She had money herself and had been longing for a break from her business. When Sadie had asked her to come to Washington she was thrilled to get away and glad to be able to turn her business over to her assistant.

Tilda was wonderful. Though she had never really spent any time in Washington before, she had dealt with the rich enough to know how to deal with the powerful. After a month one would have thought she had been there her whole life.

Tall, with blond hair, horsey-looking, slightly overbearing, some might have said bossy, Tilda had adapted to Washington's played-down, low-key style despite the fact that she had not abandoned her New York upper-class, Fifth Avenue mannerisms. She had understood from the first that money was not the bargaining chip in Washington. She began reading the papers and studying the scene like an anthropologist. Sadie had been tutored by Lorraine, but Tilda had acquired Washington expertise by osmosis. It was the smartest thing Sadie had ever done. For one thing, she had a good friend she could trust, someone who was good at organizing and entertaining, who had taste and had helped her redecorate, and someone, as well, with whom she could hash over problems.

Sadie had taken up Rosey's generous offer of three people from his own staff slots, and she had rapidly claimed the office space of the former Vice President's wife at the Executive Office Building. But she had reorganized things. Instead of having a housekeeper at the house, an assistant for her projects at the office, and a secretary, she had made Tilda a combination assistant and executive housekeeper, though she wasn't called that.

At the office, Sadie had hired a woman who had been a journalist and who had covered feature stories for a local paper which had folded. She was not a specialist but had written extensively about city projects, urban renewal, ghettos, local communities. She was invaluable because she took the onus off the potentially frivolous aspect of historic preservation—Let's redo all the pretty houses—and made it a substantial concern. She was also astute at handling the press. "Don't talk to them any more than you have to" was her advice, "and then limit the interviews to the topics you want to discuss. Historic preservation, the role of the

Vice President's wife. No personal stuff. They'll kill you. You're too candid. Just keep your mouth shut."

Nan Tyler was a strong-minded, hardworking, efficient sort, rather tomboyish in dress and actions, a no-frills person who got along well with everyone and was respected by the staff and the press. She was not exactly Sadie's type, but that was good. Nan and Tilda complemented each other. Sadie was satisfied with her team. They also both prodded her out of her lazy moods and got her "off her ass," as Nan was wont to say.

Tilda seemed a bit more harassed this day than usual. She had been on the phone with the State Department protocol office half the day trying to work out the seating arrangements. "Those half-wits at Protocol," she said. "Veronica, the woman I usually deal with, has taken a Christmas leave, and nobody over there knows what the hell they are doing. I can't believe this. We'll have ten international crises over seating in this town before the holidays are over with. God knows who we're going to insult. And your husband's office has just added more names to the list. They say that because the Saudi prince is in town, we have to invite him—Hooker wants him too—and because we've got him we're going to have to invite those air-conditioning people. Now, I know it is good business for the United States to sell air conditioners to the Arabs. But it is bad party planning. They are such bores. Where are we going to put them? We can only seat seventy-two, and that's if they're packed in like sardines. We've got three tables in the front hall. This could be a disaster, Sadie. I don't want to be downbeat about this party, but I'm getting very bad vibes."

"You know what you need?" she told Tilda. "You need a good stiff drink. You're letting this party get to you. It's not worth it. It will be fun no matter what."

"What's gotten into you? I can usually work you into a state in no time. You're not going to play tonight?"

"Nope. Sorry. I'm not in the mood. Why don't I fix you a Scotch? I'm afraid to ring for it. Jackson has just about had it. They're in a frenzy in the kitchen too."

She went back into the living room and fixed Tilda a Scotch, poured herself a glass of white wine, added a little cassis, and went back down the hall to Tilda's office.

"You never answered my question," said Tilda. "Did you decide on Des and Allison yet? All the other invitations have already gone out. It is a little rude."

"I don't think so," she said.

"I've said it before. They're part of that crowd. It will be strange in this group if they're not included. It's such a large party. And John T. likes Allison."

"I said, I just don't think so, Tilda."

"Hmmmmm," said Tilda, raising an eyebrow. "You really don't like her, do you? Or is it that you really do like him?"

Sadie's face turned flame-red. "I don't know why you say that. I don't see why I should have to invite her just because her godfather is President. Especially since he's not coming. I can't exactly recall having been inside her house. I don't owe them."

"Come on, Sadie. You know it's not the same. People are shy to invite the Vice President."

It did startle Sadie how strongly she felt about Allison. She felt threatened by her in a way she had never felt since little Stephanie with the golden curls in Statesboro, Georgia, when they were six. She had actually tried to kill Stephanie. She had covered her with leaves and tried to light a match. It shamed her more than she could bear to remember even now.

"Of course," said Tilda, "you could always invite just Des Shaw."

Sadie ignored her.

"What about your old flame? Or have you decided not to confide in your old roomie Tilda?"

"Tilda," she said, surprised at her own cool, "seeing Tag again may just be one of the highlights of my year."

"Oh, no. He's still that divine? Don't tell me. You're going to have an affair with him. We simply can't have that kind of scandal, Sadie. It won't do. I refuse to allow it to happen."

"Relax, Tilda. He's still attractive, I have to admit. But the glamour has definitely faded." She was trying to sound noncommittal.

"Oh, how disappointing. I can't bear it. He used to be so gorgeous. I thought then that he was the most divine man I'd ever met. And you were the luckiest girl."

"Let's put it this way. He's not the same person I wanted to commit suicide over . . . but then, neither am I. Do you know why he called me after nineteen years?" She was surprised to hear her voice rising, and she noticed that Tilda was surprised too. "I guess I am a little upset about seeing him, even now," she said, smiling a little in embarrassment. "He came here because he's doing political films, or wants to, and he's trying to get me to let him do some of Rosey's campaign films next time around. He wants to change Rosey's image."

"You should get him together with Everett," snickered Tilda.

"Well, he didn't exactly say that's what he wanted, but he hinted rather broadly. And then he started hinting at being invited to the party."

"Speaking of the party, my dear, we do have to make some decisions here. Wait a sec. Let me go to the little girls' room first, before we get to the fascinating subject of flowers."

She jumped up from her desk and slipped into the bathroom next to her desk. When she came out, she was fuming. "You know, I'm sorry to bring it up again, but this office is simply not suitable. The fact that you have to come through here to get to the only powder room on this floor is simply unacceptable. Every time we have a party I have to completely clear off this desk and hide everything so that your illustrious guests don't snoop. It's a hideous bore. Can't we do something about it?"

"Stop whining, Tilda. I've asked Rosey and he says no. We've already hit up the Navy for a hundred thousand dollars for the new kitchen. There isn't more money to add on another anything."

"Well, the setup stinks; I just hope you realize it."

"Weren't you saying something about flowers?"

"The garden-club ladies are just swarming around. They're thrilled to do the Christmas decorations for the reception hall and the rest of the rooms downstairs. Apparently they do it every year. It's a tradition. They'll be all over the house tomorrow, so watch your mouth. We've got plenty of greens from the greenhouse, but they'll be bringing mistletoe and poinsettias and things like that. Red ribbons."

"I don't want a bunch of blue-haired little old ladies tacking up my house. I can't stand most Christmas decorations. Tell them all fresh greens and no ornaments unless I approve. And no flower arrangements. That last group for the Thanksgiving decorations was the most hideous thing I ever saw. Better tell them beforehand what we like so we won't hurt their feelings."

"Okay, Coach. Oh, good, here's Jackson. We need to talk to him about the booze."

Jackson came in in his white starched steward's jacket and regulation black pants. He was rubbing the back of his head, a scowl on his face.

"What's the matter, Jackson?" she asked. "As if I couldn't guess. Don't tell me. You hit your head on the ceiling above the stairs." Sadie was trying not to laugh.

"Yes, ma'am. I'll tell you, I'll be the happiest person alive when we get that new kitchen and we don't have to traipse up and down those dollhouse stairs. They were made for Filipinos."

"It won't be long, Jackson. You're terrific to put up with so much." She really meant it, too. Jackson, for one thing, had agreed to move into the house from the Navy barracks. Before he had, there had been no staff living at the house, and the stewards had wanted to serve dinner at 6 P.M. so they could clean up and get out by eight. Since Sadie and Rosey never ate dinner until nine o'clock, this had caused serious problems. And Sadie hadn't liked being in that big house all alone when Rosey was away, even though there were guards at the gate outside. It just seemed crazy. Jackson had volunteered before Rosey had had a chance to order anyone to do it. He was wonderful. Tall, balding, funny, a Southern renegade, Jackson had become indispensable to Sadie and to Tilda. He ran the house like a dream. Rosey loved him too, and his abilities had freed Tilda to do more restoration work and to travel with Sadie.

"I've had to order more booze for the official locker," he said. "We were almost out. I had to borrow some the other night from your own personal liquor locker. And the Democratic Committee liquor locker is almost out too. We're sure drinking a lot of liquor around here these days."

"I'll notify the office about the other two," said Tilda. "But don't forget to put some back in the personal locker. No point in having the Greys supply half the government with booze on their own dime."

"Which china do you want for the party?" asked Jackson.

"What's the least chipped?" asked Tilda.

"Let's use the white-and-gold," Sadie said. I'm not crazy about the navy-and-gold with the Vice Presidential seal anyway, and the white will look prettier with the Christmas decorations. I don't suppose there are enough goblets with the gold edge left."

"I'm sorry, ma'am," said Jackson. "They've most of 'em been taken as souvenirs. We'll have to go with the new plain ones."

"Can you imagine just stealing a glass out of the Vice President's house? I mean, what kind of guest would do that? It's just unthinkable," sputtered Sadie.

"The air-conditioning people, that's who," responded Tilda, which sent the three of them off.

When the phone rang, Sadie opened her eyes and peered at the clock on the bedside table. It was exactly 10 A.M. Nobody made a social call before ten in Washington. She was sorry to note that the sound of the phone gave her a pain in her head, and it was clear as she became more fully awake that she had a hangover. She hadn't intended to drink so much at the party, but it had been so festive she hadn't been able to resist. The house really had looked marvelous. The English chintzes, bright colors, and pretty antiques she had added made it a dream. And of course, the decorations and the tree itself, with her beautiful Bavarian feather angels, tiny white lights, and the great big velvet angel on top, were splendid.

She had dimmed the lights, put candles everywhere, and had the fireplace blazing. A combo from the U.S. Marine Band had played Christmas carols, and everyone had joined in. John T. had gotten smashed and said it was the best time he'd ever had in his life. Rosey had followed Sadie around all evening removing glasses of white wine from her hand, but she had still managed to get a bit tipsy.

Sadie knew before Jackson buzzed her that it would be Lorraine on the phone.

"It's Mrs. Hadley—don't tell me," she said as she groped for the phone, moaning over her hurting head. "Jackson, do we have any spaghetti left over from night before last? Good. Could you bring me some up on a tray, please. And could I have a Coke too. Thanks. I'll take the call now."

She pressed the button on the phone and picked up the receiver, propping herself up in bed. She plumped up the pillows around her, turned on the bedside light, and generally got herself comfortable for a long chat.

"Well?" she said.

"Darling, it was a triumph. An utter triumph. Best party of the year. I had a simply marvelous time. And so did Archie. Thank you for my seat. You do look after your old friends, don't you? Now, admit it, aren't you pleased? Oh, the house is simply to die. Darling, you've really done such a magnificent job decorating it. Now, who were those dreary air-conditioning people?"

An hour later, they were still hashing it over. "Could you believe," asked Sadie, "that Claire would dare wear those knickers? I was shocked. She's much too old for those things. With legs like that she should live in caftans. I was amused to see the way she fell all over the Saudi prince. Buttering him up so that Worth will take her on his next trip to Saudi Arabia, no doubt. She left dear Senator Corwin high and dry."

By this time Sadie had finished her spaghetti and her Coke and had sent Jackson back downstairs for some tea.

"Now, Sadie, I couldn't help but notice that the Secretary of the Treasury was not in evidence last night, though half the Cabinet was."

"Rosey and I had a big argument about it. I told him if we didn't invite Gower that everybody would notice. But he says that the President hasn't decided whether to fire him or not, and Rosey didn't want it to look like he was making a political statement. He felt if we invited Gower while he's under investigation for stock fraud, it would look like a vote of confidence. I said I didn't see how we could leave him out. Besides, I kind of feel sorry for him. I mean, they've just let him hang there dangling for the last two months."

"Darling, the man is a crook. Everybody on Wall Street knows that. Roger Kimball should never have appointed him in the first place. But then, what Roger Kimball knows about the financial world you could put in your hat. I do agree that it's perfectly ghastly that this investigation has dragged on so long. But it's the President's fault. Why doesn't he just end it and keep him or fire him? Just another example of how badly managed the White House is, I'm sorry to say. Now, if your husband were the President, things would run on time."

"Oh, stop, Lorraine. You know these conversations make me uncomfortable. I like Roger Kimball. I think he's a decent, wonderful man. And I think he's a good President. Obviously there are problems. But what administration doesn't have problems? I blame the press. If they didn't get onto a story and bleed it to death it wouldn't end up being such a major incident."

"Well, I certainly agree with you there, dearie, but don't say I said so. I certainly wouldn't want to alienate any of the little darlings."

"But they're always trying to find a fault, to find flaws in everyone. Do they ever look for anything nice? Good news isn't news at all. Look at the way they've tried to make poor Molly Kimball into a staggering nitwit. She's a bright, interested, active woman. She isn't very chic, to be sure. . . ."

"Darling, let's not overlook the tiny little drinking problem. . . ."

"Okay, so she likes a little nip now and then. She's not the President of the United States. She didn't put in for this."

"My dear, I've never heard you so wound up on the subject of the press. Where did all this come from? You certainly don't show it when you're around them. You had half the Washington press corps there last night."

"I don't know, Lorraine. I'm sorry to launch a tirade. It's just that it's been building up in me. I haven't ever really talked to anybody else about this. It's not that I don't like them personally. You know I do. Individually I like a lot of them very much. I think they've got too much power, and I don't see any way to rectify it. I shouldn't be talking about it. Let's change the subject."

"You know, just to continue this conversation for another moment," said Lorraine, "I once asked Des Shaw about the power of the press, and about the arrogance of so many of the reporters we know. And he said that you have to compare the press with any other profession; there are some lousy journalists, some rotten reporters, some really dishonest, hypocritical, self-righteous people in journalism. Just as there are in politics, or medicine or law or business. But how on earth did we get on this heavy subject when we were right in the middle of a delicious gossip? I can't think."

Just the mention of Des's name made her breath go short.

"Let's talk about something else," she said. "I've gotten myself all worked up and it's not good for my hangover. Though I do feel better after the Coke and spaghetti. An old Southern trick."

"Okay. Speaking of Des Shaw, where was he last night? Didn't you invite him and Sonny?"

"As a matter of fact, I did not." Sadie's voice suddenly turned cool.

"Oh, Sadie. That's so silly of you. I just don't understand this. Why have you got such a scunner on Sonny? She's such a darling girl. And Des—well, Des is the dreamiest man in all of Washington. It just doesn't make any sense."

"I don't have anything against Des. I think he's quite nice, though I'm afraid I don't see his charm the way you do." She hoped she sounded convincing to Lorraine. "But Lorraine, I have to be honest with you. I'm really not crazy about Allison. Claire Elgin doesn't like her either, and neither does Helene Corwin."

"Yes, and they're both so jealous of her they could spit. They all have sneakers for Des. But it's too late. I have a suspicion that Des is going to propose to Sonny this Christmas. Just a hunch."

Why did Sadie suddenly feel nauseated? The spaghetti and the hangover must have been too much of a combination. She didn't feel like talking anymore.

"Listen, Lorraine, I've adored talking to you, but we've been on the phone for over an hour now and the kids are driving up from Richmond this morning. I've really got to get up and get dressed."

"All right, dearie. I'll talk to you later. . . . Oh, Sadie?"

"Yes?"

"I didn't say anything to upset you, did I?"

"Not at all. What could possibly upset me?"

"Good. I was just worried, that's all. Talk to you soon, lovie."

"Goodbye, Lorraine."

"Miss Landry is here from *The Daily*. She's in the back sitting room."

"Okay. Thanks, Jackson. Is Nan here from the office yet?"

"She should be here any minute."

"Look, why don't you offer her something to drink and tell her I'm on a telephone conference with the White House office or something."

Jackson disappeared downstairs, and Sadie fiddled around with her makeup waiting for Nan to show up. She was probably late because of the snow. It had started just before noon and was coming down hard. Nice for a white Christmas, but not great for trying to get around. Washington stopped dead whenever there was the slightest bit of snow.

She decided to put on the same white cashmere sweater she had worn the day before but with a green Irish tweed skirt, a wide leather belt, and boots. It was simple enough and not too dressed-up. She couldn't bear all those photographs of First Ladies and Second Ladies dressed for interviews as if they were going to church, as if they always dressed that way to sit around at home.

The phone buzzed. Nan had arrived and they were both waiting for her in the sitting room sipping orange juice.

She had had Jackson light the fire, and the sitting room looked beautiful, done mostly in greens and browns to pick up the green-and-red chintzes in the living room. It seemed made for Christmas with the greens, the poinsettias and cyclamen.

"Hi," said Sadie in the bounciest voice she could summon. She didn't want the reporter to notice that she was under the weather. If she just raised her voice, then her body would be uplifted as well, she hoped.

Nan looked at her somewhat in surprise.

Carol Landry stood up politely to shake hands. She was probably no more than about twenty-five, with pale brown hair, freckles, and a wide grin. She was trying to look in control but was obviously scared to death. This relaxed Sadie. She would be able to handle this. She had read the girl's stories since she had begun writing less than a year before. She wrote perky little party stories and an occasional harmless profile. She'd done some stories on the National Trust for Historic Preservation which were fair but boring. Obviously none of the big guns wanted to do them. She had been assigned to this story because, on the advice of Nan, Sadie had approached her one evening when Carol was covering a party and told her that she had considered the paper's request for an interview and had decided that if Carol wanted to do it she would be willing. Nan explained to Sadie that people are not allowed to pick and choose which reporters they want. But if they know that one of the tougher reporters is after an interview they can stall it and promise the interview to a lightweight. An editor would be reluctant to take the story away from whoever got it first.

It had worked. Nan had learned from the grapevine that every-one in the Living section had been furious when Landry came back with the interview. But Landry had made a case that she had been cultivating the Second Lady at these parties and had won her confidence. "Isn't that why we cover parties?" Landry had asked. It had paid off. As Nan had predicted, nobody would take it away from her.

The only problem then was that Sadie was stuck with it. Nan had also suggested that she do it right before Christmas so the house would look wonderful. They could talk about the Christmas decorations, and people would be in a holiday spirit, not the usual vicious frame of mind that seemed to take over Washington in the spring and fall.

Nan had been right on all counts. So here she was now, face to face with this trembling creature, wondering why she had to do this sort of thing in the first place and wishing she could be upstairs in her bed with an ice pack. She also wished she hadn't eaten the spaghetti.

"You don't mind if I tape-record the conversation as well as take notes, do you?" said Landry, setting up her tape.

"I don't suppose so—do I, Nan?"

"No, I'm here to act as your witness, God forbid," said Nan, laughing.

Landry then took out her notebook and crossed her ankles in a very ladylike manner, leaning toward Sadie in a confidential way.

"Tell me," she asked, then cleared her throat. "Excuse me, I guess I'm a little nervous. It's just that I've admired you so and I hadn't expected to get the interview."

Sadie relaxed even more. This was going to be a piece of cake. Nan, however, raised a suspicious eyebrow.

"How do you like being the wife of the Vice President? Is it different from being a Governor's wife?"

That one was easy enough.

"I like it very much. It's fun and interesting. More than the job, though, the difference is living in Washington. Washington is the most fascinating place I have ever been. And so compli-cated. Just learning about the city and the people and how it works has occupied a great deal of my time."

"What about Washington is it that you find so fascinating?"

"Would it be too much to say everything? I love the politics—

the stakes are so much higher on a national level than they are on a state level. I love the different groups, the different power centers, the mix. You never go anywhere that you don't see people from several areas—the diplomatic, the journalistic, the Congressional. It's never boring."

"When you say power centers, what do you mean? Do you think, as so many people have contended, that power is the motivating factor for most people in Washington? Who was it who said that power is the greatest aphrodisiac? Do you agree with that?"

"Well, of course, it does seem to me that power has some motivating influence on some of the people in Washington." She laughed. "To say the least."

"Would you say that *you* are motivated by power?"

She hadn't really noticed how the conversation had been veering, but Nan was by now sitting on the edge of her chair. "Certainly from Mrs. Grey's point of view the office of the Vice Presidency has given her a greater platform on which to espouse the things she cares about. She is able to accomplish a lot more for the National Trust for Historic Preservation in this position than she would if she were the wife of a Richmond lawyer, or for that matter the wife of a Governor. Here in Washington she can get a national focus. Isn't that right, Mrs. Grey?"

Nan was smiling, but through her teeth. Sadie might have said she was glaring. She pulled herself up. She had been too relaxed. Thank God Nan had insisted on sitting through the interview.

"Oh, yes, very definitely," she said. "I can get people to pay attention to these projects that I'm interested in, these areas that we are trying to revitalize all over the country. We want people to focus on the active role of historic preservation and get away from the house-museum concept."

She could tell that Carol Landry was not pleased with Nan's intervention. She had been scribbling furiously as Sadie talked about power. Now she seemed less interested. Yet Nan had specifically told her they were to talk only of historic preservation. That had been agreed upon. Nan had been perched on the edge of her chair. Now she leaned back. Sadie knew her answer had been okay. Nan had told her to keep talking, to offer things rather than wait for the reporter to ask another question; that way she could keep her writing about preservation and not trying to get in a personal question. Landry had been pretty

clever starting off on Washington like that. She would have to
be more careful.

"You see," continued Sadie before the reporter could get in
another question, "in the last fifteen years or so historic preservation has moved from the concept of the historic shrine to inner-
city rehabilitation."

She paused.

"How do you respond to the charges of some black leaders
that you are supporting gentrification only in their areas, that this
is upgrading their buildings and their real estate taxes and forcing
out poor blacks?"

Nan was on the edge of her seat again. She was behaving like
the worst kind of stage mother, but Sadie was amused.

"Our job is to work with them, to show people this is not the
case," said Sadie. "Certainly that would be a lot more true with
private real estate dealers who would be likely to buy up everything in one neighborhood and simply evict everybody. HUD
now puts money into these projects so that we can rehabilitate the
old houses, and we are getting housing subsidies from both federal and private funds. Part of my job is to help raise private
funds for this very purpose. If the people own their own houses
through the subsidies, then they will live in much more stable
neighborhoods. And of course, with the Tax Reform Act of 1976,
there are new tax incentives for people to rehabilitate their own
houses." Sadie couldn't believe this was she talking. She
sounded like a soundtrack. Obviously Landry thought so too.
Only Nan looked pleased. "It has a wonderfully stabilizing influence in people's lives, in their communities. And when you see
some of the horrors of urban renewal like miles of empty parking
lots, you can see why it's so important. We want to help the
communities preserve their roots in their pasts. It's terribly exciting."

She could see that Landry was about to interrupt again. She
wasn't taking many notes. She didn't exactly look riveted.

"Europe," continued Sadie, "has accepted the idea for genera-
tions of preserving the past; why can't we? We have so much to
be proud of in this country."

"What do you see as your biggest problem?" asked Landry
hopefully.

"New Orleans is a perfect example," said Sadie with confidence. "There is a situation where historic preservation has come full circle, unfortunately."

"How do you mean?"

"If you look at the Vieux Carré—the French Quarter—you can see that it was a great success, and there's the problem. It has been too successful. There is unrestricted tourism, and now what was a delightful residential area has begun to go downhill. There is crime and prostitution, so that people are beginning to move out. Charleston is about to have the same problem. So you see that success can breed problems. But I wish those were the main problems we had to deal with."

"How did you get interested in this subject—in this project?" asked Landry.

"As you know, I'm sure, I'm from Savannah, Georgia, originally. We have one of the most fabulous historic-preservation projects in the country. We have just acquired the old Victorian district, which is spectacular. I got involved on and off in the thing when it was first starting, some twenty years ago. Some of the most beautiful houses were going to wrack and ruin. Now it is a living, vibrant integrated downtown area."

"Does this project occupy most of your time, or are you involved in anything else?"

"As you know, I've been involved in redecorating the Vice President's house—with some funds raised by the public, with some of our own money. And I've started a collection of memorabilia from other Vice Presidents. We thought it might be interesting to have a little museum here. We've found some amazing things."

"Weren't you involved in Planned Parenthood in Richmond before you went to the Governor's Mansion?"

"Oh, yes, I was active in that. It was one of my major interests besides writing."

"Tell me about your writing."

She hadn't meant to talk about that.

"Oh, it's not important. You know I worked for *The Gotham* before I married. I would occasionally do things for the Around Town column. When I moved to Richmond I obviously couldn't keep my job, but I did try to keep writing. It's mostly short fiction, stories and things like that. I've never had anything published."

"What sort of things do you write about?"

Nan was stiff again. She was shaking her head slowly in warning.

"Now, what writer would reveal his story ideas?" she said with a smile. "Somebody might steal them."

"What happened to your interest in Planned Parenthood? Do you still do anything with that?"

Nan was about to come out of her chair.

"Mrs. Grey," she said, a firm warning in her voice. "You didn't tell Miss Landry yet about the Harlem project or any of the other projects you are working on."

She had almost let herself get lulled again. Nan had always told her the most important thing about giving interviews was never to lie, but that didn't mean you had to tell everything. Somehow, Sadie had never managed to find the middle ground.

"Oh, yes," she said, trying to make it seem as if she had forgotten something. "You know one of the things I'm trying to do is draw attention to the fact that historic preservation is not the pastime of the well-to-do. I want to call that to attention, particularly by visiting various sites around the country.

"Here in Washington, which has a different set of problems, one of my major involvements is in rehabilitating Union Station, which is one of the great bureaucratic disasters of the century. That should be an alive, active, bustling commercial spot in Washington. Instead, it has been a dangerous, crumbling eyesore and a national humiliation."

"Ummmm," said Carol Landry, "that's fascinating. Will you have time to work on your Planned Parenthood project with all these preservation projects going on?"

Not too subtle that time. Landry probably sensed that her time was running out, and she was right. Nan was looking at her watch.

Sadie was a little annoyed at the idea that she was too stupid to conduct her own interview, though she knew Nan was there only to protect her.

"I'll certainly do some work with them," she said. "If only to support them. I think they are a very worthwhile organization and they do a lot of good."

Nan was standing up now.

"You are prochoice, I understand," said the reporter.

"Yes, I am."

"Have you had any problems with the right-to-lifers?"

"No, none. But I'm not exactly on the soapbox, either. Choice is the law of the land. And I don't make the laws."

"Well, I'm sorry, Carol," said Nan, a slightly frantic tone to her voice. "I'm afraid our time is up. Mrs. Grey has got so much to do for Christmas. I'll walk with you to the door."

Landry was standing up too, but she wasn't moving, and she was writing fast. Sadie had stood up too, but she wouldn't look at Nan, who was desperately trying to signal her to shut up.

"How do you feel about amniocentesis—the test to determine Down's syndrome and other birth defects? It's become a focus of the conflict lately."

"I feel it is their choice."

"If you were pregnant, would you have amniocentesis?"

"Yes, I would."

"Would you have an abortion if the test showed the fetus to be defective?"

"What's the point of amniocentesis? I think women are fortunate that there are those tests now that they—"

"Thank you, Carol," said Nan, interrupting as she took Carol's arm and firmly led her toward the door. "Mrs. Grey, I'll be back in a just a moment."

Sadie sank back in her chair, put her hand over her head, and sighed. Her hangover was really killing. It wasn't helped by the dreary day outside and by the pressure of giving an interview. She had already taken two Tylenol, which had done no good at all. She had eaten spaghetti, which usually helped, had drunk a Coca-Cola, a glass of milk, and some tea. There was only one more thing she could think of. More booze. She got up and rang the bell for Jackson and asked him for an ice-cold beer.

"That bad, huh?" said Jackson. "I mean, yes, ma'am."

"Jackson, could you please stop talking and hurry up with the beer? This is a crisis."

She was sipping on her beer when Nan walked back into the sitting room. Nan's jaw was set. She stood in front of the fireplace and placed her hands on her hips.

Sadie slunk down in her chair and took another sip of her beer. Nan didn't say a word.

"Okay, okay, I know. I shouldn't have said it. You are right. You did everything you could to protect me and I went through all the red lights and I'm sorry."

"I'm afraid," said Nan, "you don't realize how sorry you're going to be. Do you realize the right-to-lifers are going to be out here picketing on Massachusetts Avenue the minute that story comes out? Do you realize how much grief this is going to cause your poor husband? I just can't believe this has happened."

"Oh, come on, Nan. It's not the end of the world. She seemed pretty naive. Maybe she won't use it."

"Are you kidding? That's the lead. That's the headline. 'VICE PRESIDENT'S WIFE WOULD HAVE AN ABORTION.' Jesus. And all this from an interview about historic preservation. We'll be lucky if we get one word in about historic preservation."

Sadie was beginning to feel sick, and it wasn't her hangover. In fact, the hangover was subsiding with the beer. She knew Nan was probably right, but she didn't want to admit it. "You got me into it. I told you I didn't want to do this interview. So it's the headline. It is the truth. I believe it. So why shouldn't I say it? Why should I be afraid of something I believe in so strongly? Frankly, Nan, I am sick to death of these right-to-lifers trying to push everybody around. And don't forget the polls. Eighty-five percent of the population believes the choice should be up to the woman and her doctor. The antiabortionists may be vociferous, but they are very much in the minority. Let them yell. It kind of amuses me, if you want the truth. I'm tired of being Miss Goody Two-Shoes."

"I wonder if it will amuse your husband as much as it does you." Nan was practically in tears.

"Nan, you're really upset, aren't you? Just calm down. It's not your fault. You did the best you could. It's my big mouth that's going to get us in trouble."

"But it *is* my fault. I did get you into it. You told me you didn't want to do it. I thought we could contain it to preservation. You were right. I should have listened to you. It's my fault."

"Well, just let me worry about it, okay?"

Nan had just left and Sadie had gone upstairs, climbed into her wrapper, and gotten into bed with a decorating magazine when the phone rang. It was Rosey.

"Hey, sugar," he said. "I just called to tell you I'm going to be a little tied up here until about eight. How'd your day go? Did you have that interview?"

"Yeah." She held her breath.

"And?"

"It was fine. We talked about historic preservation. I think it went all right. Nothing exciting."

"Good girl. Well, listen, I've got to run. I have to go see the Chief about something. I'll be home as soon as I can."

"All right, darlin'. Don't worry about me. I'll be just fine."

This Christmas Eve was not going exactly the way Sadie had planned it. Particularly her first Christmas in her own house. She had tried to plan a nice family Christmas, but with only the two of them and the children it didn't seem like much of a crowd—certainly not compared with the Christmases in Richmond, where the Greys' house seemed to be filled with family and friends for a solid ten days. Everyone was out of sorts. Sadie had been the one to insist on staying in Washington, but then, faced with rather dull prospects, she had tried to rally some friends around. It was interesting to realize finally that they didn't really have very many close friends in Washington. They were feted and admired and invited and sought after, but when the crunch came, on special holidays when you wanted to feel close and kind of cozy with your friends, there just wasn't anybody around. The Sohiers had gone up to Boston, and Lorraine and Archie Hadley had taken off for England, where they always spent Christmas.

"Darling, you certainly don't want to stay in this dreary place at Christmas," Lorraine had said when Sadie first told her they planned to stay in town for the holidays. "It's too depressing. There's simply nobody in town. The entire Congress goes back to their home states. The President goes off to Colorado and takes half the press corps with him. The lawyers and Establishment types either go skiing or go to the Caribbean. Who else is there? There aren't any parties to speak of. The restaurants are completely empty. If you do stay, don't tell anyone. Just hide. It's better that way."

Sadie did not tell Rosey what Lorraine had said, but she had the sinking feeling that she was telling the truth. Still, she had made such a point of the fact that this was her home and she wanted to spend Christmas in it. She had taken the confrontational route with the Greys, deliberately inviting them to her house knowing perfectly well they would never budge from their castle in Richmond. Miz G could rule the world from there. Outside of Richmond nobody cared about them, and so they simply never went anywhere except to visit old friends and family in London and Scotland once a year. G and Miz G would come eventually, but it was going to kill Miz G to see Sadie get all the glory.

Rosey had realized that Sadie was taking a stand on the issue, and as usual when she did take her rare stands, he went along. He understood that she was trying finally to establish her independence from his family, who had dominated their lives in Richmond, even when he was Governor of Virginia. He sympathized with her need to make her own nest, create her own environment. Yet he was miserable about it, and his misery showed. He had never spent a Christmas away from his own family before. Annie Laurie was being a giant pain. She had done nothing but sulk and go out shopping with a few of her friends from St. Tim's.

Outland was trying to be a good sport, and he certainly held no great affection for the Greys. Yet there was something rather festive about an old-fashioned English Christmas with carols and punch and eggnog and lots of servants around in their best uniforms and people dropping in and garlands of evergreens and candles. They always went to services on Christmas Eve in Richmond, then came home to a midnight supper.

Half of Richmond came back to the house with them, and they stayed up until all hours, sending the little children to bed to await Santa Claus.

Christmas morning was festive and exciting, with stockings and all of the cousins and uncles and aunts arriving for a huge feast in the middle of the day. It was truly the perfect Christmas, and even Sadie had to admit that try as she might, there was absolutely no way that she could re-create it.

The stewards had prepared dinner so that they could leave early on Christmas Eve. Except for Jackson they were an impersonal lot, all Filipinos who had their own families and were hardly devoted to the Grey family. Rosey came home from work in time for a drink with Sadie and the children in front of the fire in the downstairs sitting room. Sadie had turned on all the Christmas lights and lit candles, but still the house seemed big and empty with just the four of them. Rosey decided to play some Christmas carols on the baby grand in the reception hall, and they stood around the piano singing Christmas carols rather listlessly. They were all a bit embarrassed at the forced nature of their little ceremony and grateful when Jackson called them to the table.

Dinner was solemn. Sadie tried to get the children to talk about their schools, but they had long since learned that such conversations were fraught with danger. Outland could never get through a discussion of his school experiences without some kind of criticism from his father. Annie Laurie's interests were so involved with clothes and parties and who was from which family that Sadie invariably got angry with her.

The minute dinner was over, Outland excused himself to go watch television and Annie Laurie engaged her father in a game of backgammon, a game Sadie despised. She found herself sitting alone in front of the fire while the two of them played, then excused herself to go upstairs. Rosey insisted they all go to Christmas midnight services at National Cathedral, which nobody was very enthusiastic about but they did anyway.

Christmas morning was no better.

The opening of the presents was dull and perfunctory. Sadie gave Rosey the VCR he had been asking for. They each had asked for specific presents, which they got. Sadie was treated to the one surprise. Rosey had had a small replica made of the Vice President's house, all newly decorated the way she had done it. It was perfectly and exquisitely made, and she couldn't have asked for a more wonderful present. It was clever and imaginative. Exactly what a present should be.

She burst into tears. Rosey was plainly delighted.

"Hey, sugar," he said. "It's not all that terrific. It's just something I thought you would like."

"Like? I love it! It's beautiful, and so thoughtful. I feel so embarrassed. You obviously put a lot of time and effort into planning something like this. I feel so guilty. I didn't get you anything nearly as nice."

"You got me just what I asked for. Don't you see it's much more of a pleasure if I can get you something you really love? That's the best Christmas present I could have."

He got up and came over and kissed her, brushing away the tears from her cheeks. He was pleased and touched by her reaction. He loved her, too, she could tell. Just looking at his adoring gaze, she felt the tears coming again. Out of guilt this time. She felt like a true bitch. She had kept him away from his own home and a much jollier Christmas, really ruined her whole family's Christmas actually, and Rosey was giving her this wonderful present.

The children were a bit embarrassed by this show of affection. They rarely saw it between their parents. Outland seemed pleased. Annie Laurie was miffed by her father's obvious devotion to her mother. She wanted to be number one with her daddy.

Sadie had given all the stewards the day off; she planned to cook Christmas dinner herself. After the presents, and coffee, orange juice, and croissants which she had ordered the night before, Rosey and Outland turned on the TV set to watch the football games and Sadie reluctantly headed downstairs to the basement kitchen.

"Annie Laurie, sweetheart, do you want to come down and help me with dinner?"

"I don't think so, Mother, if you don't mind. I have things to do. I'm going out tonight and I have to wash my hair."

She hadn't expected her to, but somehow she felt let down and disappointed. It was cold and gloomy all alone in the kitchen, and it was so big, so uncozy.

She put on an apron and turned on the radio to some station that was playing kitsch Christmas music. She suddenly felt terribly lonely. Here she had what most people would consider a wonderful family— two beautiful, intelligent children, a handsome, loving, successful husband—and it wasn't enough. Her life seemed empty. After seventeen years of marriage with Rosey she still didn't even feel as though she knew the man. She knew he loved her, far more than she loved him. That was for sure. But more than that, she knew little. He was an extremely intelligent man, a man of integrity, dignity, honor. A man she was proud of. A good leader, a man who was respected and admired by everyone who knew him well. He was a gentleman, a kind and decent person. He was an exceptionally devoted father and a solid, faithful husband. That was the problem. He was too good. Only bastards had sex appeal for her. Yet she could barely allow herself even a fleeting thought about Des without breaking into a panic attack. She couldn't even fantasize about him now. It was too dangerous.

So here she was standing in the middle of the kitchen with a white apron around her wrapper and tears rolling down her face as she listened to "O Holy Night" on the radio. How many people in this city, this country, this world envied her, thought she had everything? How many people would be stunned if they could see her now, her hands greasy from stuffing the poor goose, no makeup on, her tousled red hair barely combed, her nose running, her eyes bloodshot as she sobbed, allowing the music to incite her even further? The more the music played the sadder she got. Here it was the end of a year, and what did she have to look forward to? Three more years being the Vice President's wife, a ceremonial figure.

Planned Parenthood and the National Trust, what little she was really able to do in her ceremonial role, was hardly the answer. She would love to write, to put down her thoughts and ideas on paper and actually have them published. But her pitiful little short stories lay yellowing in her underwear drawer. Des had allowed her to hope something would come of it, but now that was impossible. As the Vice President's wife she really couldn't be published, despite what Des had said. Not the kinds of things she would write. It would be a scandal. And the idea of living a sexually unsatisfying life for the next forty years seemed almost intolerable to her if she allowed herself to think about it.

The whole time she was thinking these thoughts she was trying to make dinner. She sniffed and sobbed, blowing her nose intermittently as the Christmas carols encouraged her melancholy mood, chopping the mushrooms for the wild rice casserole, running the Cuisinart to puree the peas. Was it possible that she hadn't really done her share in their sexual relationship? It had never really occurred to her to actively make love to Rosey, or even initiate sex with him, in all of these years. As she stuck the goose in the oven she made an early New Year's resolution. She was determined to improve her sex life with her husband.

There was, she had to admit, a certain grimness to her thoughts. If she didn't do it, if she was unable to improve it, what was she going to do?

Christmas dinner was a disaster. The goose was dry and overcooked. The wild rice casserole mushy. The pureed peas too thick. Either the stewards had forgotten the lingonberry jam or she couldn't find it, so that there was no condiment to eat with the goose.

Rosey was sweet. He kept trying to make her feel better.

"Ummmm, very good, darlin'," he kept saying. "I do love a goose at Christmas." For some stupid reason she had tried to re-create the Greys' Christmas dinner instead of having her own. Her mama had always served a turkey at Christmas, with corn-bread dressing and mashed turnips. Why hadn't she done what she knew how to do? The Greys' servants had always cooked the dinner in Richmond. Miz G, as far as Sadie knew, had never boiled water.

"A little dry," Annie Laurie snipped, making a major produc-tion out of trying to cut her goose.

"Perhaps you could have done better?" Rosey looked at her. She looked down at her plate.

Outland broke her heart. "Great, Mum," he said with an en-couraging smile. But he hardly touched his food, just pushed it around on his plate.

Dinner was over in about twenty minutes. Both kids got up and announced they were going ice skating at the Chevy Chase Country Club.

Though the Greys were not members—Rosey couldn't join a restricted club, even though he had belonged to the country club in Richmond—most of the parents of their kids' friends be-longed. They would probably stay out at the club with the other kids and have supper at the Winter Center.

Rosey could see the look of utter disappointment on Sadie's face. Neither of the children had made any effort at all. Not even Outland, who normally was so solicitous of his mother's feelings.

"Nobody's going anywhere until you ask to be excused," Rosey said fiercely.

"May I please be excused," they chimed in unison, standing before their places at the table.

"Yes," he said finally with a resigned sigh.

Sadie went to get coffee, and by the time she had come back upstairs the kids were on their way out of the house, and the door slammed as cold air came blasting across the reception hall and into the dining room.

"Shall we go into the sitting room for coffee?" she suggested. They moved into the sitting room. Rosey stoked the fire. The tree lights were still on. He went over and turned up the radio, which was playing classical Christmas music. For a few minutes they both sat silently, staring at the fire.

Finally Rosey looked up, and to his surprise there were tears rolling down Sadie's face.

"What is it, sugar? What's the matter?" he asked, a worried tone in his voice. She rarely cried in front of him.

"Do you think we could go out to eat tonight?" she asked in a barely audible voice. "I mean, it's so depressing just sitting here in this great big house all alone."

"Sure we can, darlin'. But what's open on Christmas night?"

"I know." She brightened. "We can go to the Jockey Club. I'm sure it's open because of the hotel. It's their only dining room. Let's do that—okay?"

"I wonder if I could get Marlene at home to make the reservation for us," Rosey mused. He picked up the phone and asked the White House operator to get him his scheduler. The phone rang a number of times and there was no answer.

"Hell's bells," he said, finally putting down the receiver. "Now what are we going to do?"

"We could call ourselves," suggested Sadie.

"Oh, I'd hate to do that," he said. "I would feel like an ass saying, 'This is the Vice President of the United States. Could I please have a table?' They'll never believe me. Some wise guy will say, 'Yeah, sure, and I'm the Pope.'"

"I know," said Sadie. "I'll call. I'll pretend that I'm your secretary. Then when the Secret Service calls to advance it they'll know it's for real."

Rosey laughed. He was clearly amused by the complication over something so silly as getting a dinner reservation.

"People will think the Vice President and his wife ought to have something better to do on Christmas night than go out to a restaurant to eat," he said. "But go ahead. Just be prepared to read about it in the gossip columns."

"Hello. May I have the Jockey Club?" Sadie asked in her most officious voice. "Yes, how are you today? Fine. That's good. This is Marlene Johnson, from Vice President Grey's office. I'm calling to see if you have a table for the Vice President and Mrs. Grey for eight P.M. tonight. If you do, we will have the Secret Service call to confirm and arrange to advance the restaurant. And we will, of course, as you know, need an extra table for them. Yes, that's right: Vice President Grey. Of the United

States. Right. Tonight at eight. For two. Yes. The Secret Service will be calling shortly. You can? How marvelous. You're so kind. They'll be very pleased. You're very welcome. Thank you. Goodbye."

They both collapsed in giggles. Sadie was very proud of herself. Then she looked worried. "Oh, God, what if they try to reach Marlene to make sure it's not a hoax? I'll be caught impersonating a White House staffer and go to jail."

"I better get the Service on the phone right away," agreed Rosey, still chuckling.

He rang the Secret Service post. Toby Waselewski, Sadie's favorite, was on duty that day.

"Waselewski," said Rosey in a firm voice, "Mrs. Grey and I have made reservations for dinner tonight at the Jockey Club. We have a table for eight o'clock. Will you boys take care of it. Righto."

He hung up. "Done, madame," he said. "And now I have a small stocking present for you which I was saving to give you a little later. I think I'll give it to you now. You won't feel bad when you see what it is," he said with a smile.

He went over behind the bar and pulled out a small wrapped box. The tape was badly stuck on and the ribbon wasn't properly curled. He had obviously done it himself.

"Here," he said. "There is no doubt in my mind that you will like it. I have never been so supremely confident about any present in my entire life."

She tore the package open and found, to her delight, a videotape of *Gone with the Wind* to fit the VCR.

"I was pretty sure of what you were going to give me," he said, smiling.

"Oh, Rosey," she said.

"Let's not have any more tears. It's only three o'clock. The movie is four hours. Why don't you go upstairs and watch it? I hooked up the VCR in the upstairs sitting room while you were fixing dinner. I bet that will improve your mood."

"That's exactly what I'm going to do," she said. "I haven't seen *Gone with the Wind* in almost two years. If I don't watch it again soon I'll forget all my lines."

"All right, Miz Scarlett, honey. But you best get on upstairs and watch it so we don't miss our supper."

She grabbed the tape and started upstairs, only to turn around and come back, put her arms around his neck, and kiss him lightly on the lips. "I love you," she said. She meant it.

There was nothing that put Sadie in a better mood than *Gone with the Wind*. It set her up for weeks. She always got over her depressions after seeing that movie. "Tomorrow" was, after all, another day. Naturally she identified with Scarlett. She *was* Scarlett. No question. She knew every line, every word, by heart. She could start to cry in the sad parts before they even happened. She was, of course, deeply in love with Rhett. How could Scarlett ever have been in love with Ashley Wilkes, or even have thought she was? That was the only thing that never made sense to her. And yet, she herself had not married Rhett Butler. Rosey was more like Ashley. He wasn't weak like Ashley, but he certainly was not the dashing, masculine, debonair lover that Rhett was. Maybe she was more like Scarlett than she knew.

She chose his favorite green silk dress with the long sleeves and put on the pearls he had given her and a lovely small emerald-and-diamond pin which had been in his family. She would please him tonight.

The Secret Service had checked out the Jockey Club, and the four of them took their places at the table next to the Greys. The front room, with its red-and-white-checked tablecloths, was a little more than half-filled; still, there were more people than they had expected. All eyes were on them as they walked in. People were stunned to see them there on Christmas night, but their entrance immediately picked up the place, and Sadie could feel the electricity shoot through the room. Nothing like a little glimpse of power to give the old town a shot in the arm.

"We want this to be a very special occasion," said Rosey to the maître d'hôtel. "We would like a bottle of Roederer Cristal to begin with. We may even have another." He smiled.

She could tell he was as determined as she was to make this a nice evening. He probably didn't have the same thing in mind as she did. Well, maybe he did. He was looking at her with real appreciation, something he sometimes forgot to do, particularly since they had come to Washington. He just never had time and he always seemed to be preoccupied with his work.

The waiter brought two glasses and poured the champagne. Rosey had ordered caviar—a real extravagance for him. Rich as he was, he had a thrifty puritan side that was baffling to Sadie. He knew she loved caviar more than life, though, and he had obviously struggled with this grand gesture. She adored him for it. He was being so gallant.

When the waiter had left, he lifted his glass to her.

"To a wonderful year in Washington," he said.

She lifted her glass to his without saying a word and took a sip. It felt good going down. It put her in an even more buoyant mood, if that was possible, than she had reached by watching *Gone with the Wind*.

"And to us," said Rosey.

She looked into his eyes. He lowered his. He was so shy with her, even after all these years, about anything sentimental or romantic. He was almost blushing.

"To us, angel," she said softly. Impulsively she leaned over and kissed him on the cheek.

Immediately he pulled away. "Not here in front of all these people," he whispered. She had forgotten his aversion to what he called PDA. Public Display of Affection. He found it tacky and crude. He had opposed it even when they were first married and completely unknown. Now he was adamant about it. He shunned the usual First Couple's public displays for political reasons even more. He felt it was hypocritical and in poor taste. She actually agreed with him, and generally it didn't bother her much, since she rarely felt like making a display anyway. But tonight was different. Tonight it had been spontaneous. He could see the hurt on her face even as he recoiled from her affectionate gesture.

"I'm sorry, honey," he said. "You know how I am."

"I know," she said. "I'm sorry too."

She could have gone into a pout, but she decided she was simply not going to ruin this Christmas night. It was too important to her.

"Tell me about the reaction to the piece in *The Daily*," she said, changing the subject. "Have you heard from the President about it?"

Rosey brightened. He should have. *The Daily* had run a year-end piece about the Vice President's first year in office and how he was doing. It was by one of the paper's biggest hitters, an assessment by the press and members of the White House staff as to how effective Rosey had been. It had run the day before Christmas—a wonderful Christmas present for Rosey, and probably the reason he had been in such a good mood despite their depressing Christmas celebrations. She had read the piece and commented on it briefly, but there had been so many last-minute things to do for the holidays, and with the staff let off they really hadn't had a chance to discuss it.

There was also another element. Though Sadie was genuinely proud of her husband, there was a certain resentment too at his seemingly easy success at whatever he did, in contrast to what she saw as her hopeless inefficacy. Nothing she ever did seemed to be a grand success, and as she approached middle age she felt more and more useless. Sometimes she wished privately that Rosey would just fail a little at something. That she might just once have a feeling of being superior instead of inferior. Even equal would do. If it weren't for the fact that she knew he loved her more than she loved him—which gave her whatever power she had—she didn't think she could bear it.

It wasn't that she wished him ill. In fact, she felt horribly guilty even admitting to herself that she would like to see him falter. But she felt he needed some kind of equalizer. Her own image and self-confidence were completely wrapped up in him. She was measured by the world by how well her husband did because she had nothing of her own. The projects were not enough. Her writing was not enough. Her taste and style, her charm, her attractiveness as a woman were nothing. Everything she was she owed to this man. That kind of power over one's life was so complete that it couldn't help creating a certain resentment in any woman with any brains. So she couldn't wish him to fail. His failure would be her failure. She wondered if he understood any of this. She guessed he did not.

"What a Christmas card that article was!" he said. "The staff was ecstatic over it. Randy said that in all the years he had been press secretary he couldn't remember a more favorable piece. I was a little amused at how he was vaguely trying to take a little credit for it. He kept mentioning how he had been taking Riley, the reporter, to lunch and how he had been softening Riley up for the last year, and how it had really worked. Well, hell, if the news is good let's spread the credit around."

"But what about the President? Surely he saw it. Did he say anything about it? I must admit I was a little worried about the part where it said you would be a formidable candidate for the next election if Roger Kimball decides not to run again because of his lack of popularity in the country."

"I know. That worried me too. But I talked to him about it."

"What did he say?"

"Well, you know Roger. He's a big man. He's not a petty or small person. Still, it must have stung a little bit. And I was worried about creating any tension at all. It's not that he would take it out on me. It's those S.O.B.'s on his staff I worry about. They're all so busy jockeying for position and trying to figure out who's on first that they don't pay any attention to running the country. That's one of his big problems to begin with. He seems not to be able to control them. I just can't figure it out. So I got a few digs, going into the Oval Office, about how I was going to really like it there in a few more years, and that kind of thing. But Roger was all class. He just said he'd seen the piece and that he was proud of me for outfoxing those press bastards, not letting myself get chewed up by them. Then he nodded toward his door and said something like 'Unlike others on my staff I could mention who seem to have a penchant for bad publicity.'"

"I told him that my loyalty to him was one hundred percent—which, as you know, it is. He told me he was grateful to me for bringing it up and that he hoped that I would stick with him. He said it hadn't been the easiest of years for him but that my presence had made it easier than it might have been."

Sadie was listening with rapt attention. Rosey hardly ever shared his conversations with the President with her. He was leaning toward her in a confidential manner and stopped talking only when the waiter came to bring their venison and pureed chestnuts.

"Did you mean it?"

"Mean what?"

"Mean that you wouldn't break away and run against him."

"Of course I meant it. Why would I say it if I didn't? And what would make you even ask such a question? Have I ever indicated to you that I would do anything like that?"

"No, darlin', you haven't; but then you never told me you wanted to be Governor either for the longest time, or Vice President, for that matter. We've never discussed it. Would you like to be President someday?"

She didn't know what answer she wanted to hear. It was odd

that they had never discussed it before. Nobody would believe it. She glanced around the restaurant as though they had all heard what she was saying. She wondered with amusement how they would react if they knew what she had just asked her husband, the Vice President, in all seriousness. Her question had the solemnity of a proposal of marriage. It was one of the most intimate things she had ever asked him. She felt embarrassed. So did he. He didn't answer her for a while. He leaned back against the red leather banquette and took a sip of champagne. Then he sighed.

"You would think that would be an easy question for somebody in my position," he said finally. "But it isn't. Of course I've thought of it. At times I've thought of nothing else. This year, in particular, when I see so many mistakes. There are so many things I would like to do, so many things I would like to change. I have the ideas but not the wherewithal to change things. Roger Kimball respects me and my ideas. I know that. I know he thinks I am bright, and he listens to what I have to say. But he is totally in the power of those idiots on his staff. They have a hold over him I just can't understand. I can't imagine he believes that they are the most knowledgeable and the most expert men he could have. Yet they hold the key to his office. They can block anybody and anything from getting to him. They isolate him and cut him off from valuable sources of information and advice. It's not that I want to run, but I sure as hell don't want to go down in flames with him either because of a bunch of half-wits that he hasn't the guts or the will to get rid of. Those people are incompetent, and malevolent, some of them. I believe they are actually dangerous. It is driving the liberals crazy, and I must admit I do enjoy seeing that part of it."

"You still haven't answered my question. Do you want to be President?"

"Oh, Lord, Sadie, I don't know. I came out of the White House the other day after talking to the President about various crises. The level of tension and stress in that place was so high you couldn't jump over it. From the President all the way down to the guards at the gate. The burden hangs heavy over there. And though I see mistakes being made on every score, there are questions I don't have the answers to. There are situations I don't know how to handle. There are some things that are just too hard to solve. So I don't know what to say. In some way, I feel that if I've come this far, it is inevitable; I feel that I don't have the option anymore, that it goes with the territory. I've put in for it, in a way. It's the top of the ladder. What's the point of going this far and stopping? And yet, for the life of me, I can't see why any normal, rational human being in this world would want that job. And would want it for four years—or, God forbid, eight years. It just isn't worth it in terms of what a toll it takes on your life. On the other hand, it is the only game in this town, the only job worth having, the only place where you can really make a difference. And if you are a patriot, if you care about your country, about the world, about your fellowman, then how can you not take the opportunity and run with it? How can you deny yourself this power to change things for the good?"

"And the answer to my question?"

"I may not have any choice."

"How do you mean?"

Rosey sighed, and his shoulders sagged. Suddenly he looked very tired.

"I went to see Molly Kimball Thursday afternoon. She invited me for tea."

"Why didn't you tell me?"

"She asked me not to."

Before she could register her surprise, he continued: "She made me promise I wouldn't say anything, especially to the President. But she told me . . ." He hesitated. "She told me Roger has had another stroke."

"Another?" She was shocked.

He realized he had never told her what Allison had confided to him at the birthday party. He tried to brush over it.

"Apparently years ago he suffered a very mild stroke. Nothing serious. No paralysis or anything. It never came out in the press."

"My God," said Sadie. "How did they manage to keep that a secret?"

"Only their family doctor knew. And it's the same this time. He had a very mild stroke. They've got the White House doctor on orders to keep quiet. Nobody on the staff knows. Roger had some numbness and a mild loss of the use of his left arm. They just said he had a lot of reading and paperwork, and he just stayed in his private quarters for a few days. I saw him then. It's certainly not noticeable unless somebody brings your attention to it. I never would have guessed there was a problem."

"So how does this affect you?"

"Molly says the doctor says it could be more serious next time around. She would love it if he would resign, but she says there's no chance of that. I don't think there's much I can do except be prepared."

"For what?"

"To be President."

She felt as though somebody had knocked the wind out of her.

Even though rationally she had always known that a Vice President was only "a heartbeat away," she had never dealt with the possibility in any real sense. Now it was upon her and the only thing she felt was overwhelming terror. But she didn't want Rosey to know that. And so she took her time, gathered herself together before she responded. She reached over for her champagne glass and took a long sip. Somehow the icy bubbles soothed her and she was able to speak without losing her control.

"Do you want to be?"

"Have you ever thought of being a reporter? You're awfully persistent."

"Well?" She smiled.

"Oh, God, Sadie. I guess the answer is yes. Yes, I would like to be President."

The kids weren't home yet. They said good night to their agents and went upstairs to the bedroom. Sadie was feeling warm and cozy about the evening, even a little excited. She had had a good time with Rosey that night. Her husband had even been flirtatious with her. She could tell that he wanted to make love. They were both slightly tipsy from all the champagne. She went into the bathroom and got ready for bed, putting on a long-sleeved white satin nightgown that she knew he liked. When she came out of the bathroom he was carefully getting undressed, as usual putting his shoes on the shoe trees, hanging up each piece of clothing.

What would the shrinks say about that? she wondered. But then, one would sleep better at night knowing that somebody like Rosey was Vice President. Or President. That was one she would have to start getting used to. It was something she didn't much want to think about at the moment, though. There was enough pressure on her now that she didn't need that. Besides, she was feeling rather sexy.

Rosey took off all his clothes except for his shorts and disappeared into the bathroom to brush his teeth.

When he came out, she was still sitting propped up in bed. She smiled at him. He smiled shyly at her. He climbed into bed next to her and reached over to turn off his light.

"Turn off your light too, will you, sugar?"

There was no getting around it. He would simply never make love to her in the light. She turned off her lamp, then took a deep breath and plunged into the conversation she had been wanting to have with him all evening.

"Do you ever think about our relationship?" she asked.

"What do you mean?"

"I mean do you ever think about us, about how we get along, how we communicate, about our sex life."

"Well, to be honest, honey, I don't think about it much. I mean, after you've been married as long as we have, what's there to think about? I do think about how lovely you are sometimes—like tonight, for instance. You looked beautiful tonight."

He had moved closer to her in the darkness and had put one hand on her breast. There was always something tentative about the way he did it, as though he were never quite sure she wanted him to. He had always been that way. Maybe it was because *she* was never quite sure.

"No, but do you ever wish we could be more frank about things?"

"What things?"

He was caressing her breasts now in a soft, sweeping motion.

"Like what pleases us in bed. Things like that."

"Everything you do pleases me in bed," he said, moving his body over so that it was halfway on top of hers. He reached his hand for her chin, turned her face toward his, and began to kiss her softly on the mouth.

"But sometimes, do you wish we could be more adventurous?" she tried again, in between kisses. She felt slightly aroused, and yet she could almost feel her ardor dampen at the thought of another routine session.

"I like things just the way they are," he said.

He had moved on top of her now. He was still kissing her, and he had begun to move his hands down her sides. She had felt him tense just the slightest bit when she brought up the subject. She had tried so many times before and he couldn't deal with it. She had thought about every conceivable way she could broach the subject without making him feel defensive or inadequate. Love-making was not the area where he felt most secure anyway. It was terribly hard for him to let out his feelings, to talk about any emotions, and sex was even more taboo. It was difficult for him to discuss sex, and it always ended unhappily for both of them. He considered himself a very private person, whatever that meant, and a very special person in some ways. He was an inter-esting contradiction in that respect. He felt superior to most peo-ple, no doubt because of his upbringing and his background, yet there were doubts about his own adequacy as well. His way of hiding those doubts was to prevent people from getting to know him well. Including his wife.

She thought he felt deep down inside that if she really knew his fears and his anxieties she wouldn't love him anymore, and he felt it not without reason. Sadie required his sense of confi-dence, control, and superiority for her own sense of self-worth. Though she asked him to reveal himself, she really didn't want him to. She knew that to some he seemed arrogant, and to those who didn't read his superiority, which was really reticence, as arrogance, he just seemed very self-confident.

Bed was the only place where he didn't. She wished, just once, he would take her. Push her up against the wall, say, "Come here, woman," push her down on the bed, and thrust himself at her. Just once she wished he would seem really hungry for her; just once she longed for him to lose control. But he was incapable, she thought. So why did she still try to arouse that in him? Sometimes she thought of those women championed by the feminists who were taking their husbands to court for raping them, and she couldn't help thinking how nice it would be to have Rosey so inspired.

Rosey thought his sex life was terrific. He always enjoyed making love to Sadie, even if it was usually every two weeks or not even that often. Twice a month and he thought he had died and gone to heaven. He didn't see any reason why he should try anything fancy as long as they both were satisfied, and he was. It never occurred to him that she wasn't. He thought the business of oral sex was unappealing. He had told her long ago that before they were married he had once had a girl perform oral sex on him and he had to admit that it had felt pretty good. But she was a cheap woman, not the kind of woman he would have married, the kind of woman he could love. That kind of thing, he told her, he could do without in his marriage.

For some reason she had not given up hope. She kept thinking that at some point he would feel so close to her that he would want to do it to her.

She had felt so close to him this Christmas night that something about the way he talked to her and flirted with her at dinner had made her think maybe he would try, or at least let her try.

His hand was moving up and down on her thigh now, and she softly took it and gently guided it down between her legs. He let her move his hand up and down the way she wanted, but when she stopped he probed around awkwardly, then moved his hand back up where it was safe—around her breasts.

She pulled slightly away from him, then whispered as softly as she could, in a reassuring way, "Rosey, I love you." She began to kiss his chest, making soft biting motions as she worked her way down his body, occasionally licking him and kissing him alternately. But as she got to his abdomen, her head buried beneath the covers, he grabbed her hair and pulled her back up.

He pulled his body on top of hers and slowly entered her. She closed her eyes. This was where she usually fantasized.

Rosey was breathing heavily, and she knew that if she wanted to be satisfied herself before he came she would have to quickly come up with a fantasy that would turn her on. She closed her eyes as tightly as she could and made her mind a blank for a moment. Then *his* face appeared before her. His black curly hair was touching her forehead. His eyes were dancing, his mouth bent in a smile.

"Oh, God, how I want you. How I've wanted you since that day in the car," he was saying. He had her hands pressed back against the sheets so that she was pinned against the bed. "I'm going to take you now."

"Oh, no, please, we can't, we must not. Not again. It isn't right," she was saying; breathless from passion, she could barely get the words out.

"I've got you here at last. I'll never let you out of my grasp again," he said, and his mouth was over her body, caressing her everywhere, until she thought she would faint. Yet still she had to struggle, to cry out against what they were doing. It was wrong, she was married, he had to stop. But he wouldn't let her go, and now he thrust himself into her mouth and she took him gratefully, lovingly. Finally he embraced her and took her, and she felt herself lose control.

She was trying to call to him, to tell him to stop. "Oh, please . . ." But her voice faded into a deep moan and she whispered to herself, "Please, oh, yes, please, Des, take me again, please."

The phone rang. It was after 10 P.M., late for the phone unless it was a crisis. Rosey answered it.

"This is the Vice President speaking." He paused. His face darkened.

"Damn," he said. He glanced over at her. She was curled up in front of the fire on the sofa in their upstairs sitting room, doing her needlepoint. He was reading a stack of foreign-policy briefing papers which the White House had sent over earlier that evening, in preparation for the first meeting of the National Security Council after the holidays. Normally Rosey did not sit in on NSC meetings, but in this case the President had asked him to because of the nature of the crisis—North Vietnamese incursions into Thailand—and because he wanted Rosey to watch John T. Hooker. John T. suspected that the President didn't exactly trust him, but Rosey had cleverly mitigated any hard feelings that might have arisen between the two of them by having that Christmas party, at the President's suggestion, in honor of John T.

In fact, he had been thinking how well he had been handling things and how well everything was going until this phone call.

It was Everett Dubois, his personal Chief of Staff, aide-de-camp, right-hand man, confidant, troubleshooter. Rosey had brought Everett with him from Richmond.

Everett was an uncouth slob and someone totally opposite to Rosey. He was a self-made man and a consummate politician. He had been the mastermind of many a conservative Democratic campaign ever since he'd left the PR business in Louisiana and gone to Oklahoma. There he had fallen upon hard times after his candidate for Governor had to drop out of the race because of a scandal. Sadie despised Everett. She thought he was an unscrupulous and loathsome man. The feeling was mutual. Sadie had every right to hate Everett.

It was Everett who had discovered her affair with Stuart Cortwright in Richmond. It was also Everett who had covered it up. Nobody except Rosey had ever found out about it. It pleased Everett no end to have something over her. And particularly in the months after he found out, Rosey was much closer to Everett than he was to his own wife.

Now Rosey could hear the pleasure in Everett's voice as he called to tell him the bad news.

The first edition of *The Daily* had come off the presses, and Everett, as was his habit, had had a copy brought to his house. The Feature section led with a story on Sadie with a picture of her standing in the downstairs reception hall by the Christmas tree. The headline read, "SARA ADABELLE GREY: PLANNED PARENTHOOD AND PRESERVATION. A Prochoice Vice President's Wife Speaks Frankly."

"As the snow fell outside in the dusk, a serious Sara Adabelle Grey stood up to walk a reporter to the door. The interview was over but there was still something on her mind. She brushed her hand back through her auburn   in a thoughtful gesture. The subject was amniocentesis, a test procedure for pregnant women over 35 which determines Down's syndrome and other birth defects. Would she have it if she were pregnant today at the age of 39?

"'Yes, I would,' she said, without hesitation. And an abortion if the test showed the fetus to be defective? 'What's the point of amniocentesis?'

"If the tests determine that the fetus has Down's syndrome," the article went on, "then the woman can have an abortion. Unfortunately, the tests are not administered until the 16th to 18th week of pregnancy and take two to three weeks to develop, so that an abortion would be essentially a premature labor.

"Sara Adabelle Grey's position on amniocentesis should come as no surprise. She worked for Planned Parenthood while she was the Governor's wife in Virginia. Planned Parenthood has a decidedly prochoice position.

"Mrs. Grey also discussed her work with the National Trust for Historic Preservation and the renovation and redecoration of the Vice President's house, mostly done at the Greys' private

expense as a donation to the country. In a frank interview which
lasted over an hour . . ."

"Don't read me any more," said Rosey. "I've got the picture.
Now what do we do?"

"Hunker down, boss," he said. "There ain't a whole lot more
you can do. I would get Nan over here first thing in the morning,
though, so we can figure out how to answer the right-to-lifers
when the shit hits, which I predict will be about eight A.M.

"And we'd better get Randy geared up for this too. They'll
want to know how you stand on the whole thing. In fact, I think
you better call a breakfast meeting at the house about eight A.M.
with me, Nan, Randy, and Mrs. Grey so we can get this whole
thing figured out."

"Yeah, I guess you're right."

"Oh, and boss—"

"Yes?"

"Make sure she said it, first. You know how the press is. They
could have distorted the quote or got it out of context or something. This is a new reporter."

"Do you think so?" There was too much eagerness in Rosey's
voice.

"No. But make sure anyway."

"Okay. Thanks, Everett. I'll see you at breakfast. Make it
seven thirty. Get hold of the others for me?"

"Sure. See you tomorrow."

Rosey turned to his wife. His lips had disappeared into a thin
line. His face was pale, his eyes narrowed. He was in what Sadie
called "one of his white rages," she could see that. What she
didn't know was that it was directed at her.

"What is it, sugar? You don't look too happy. Who was that
on the phone anyway at this hour?"

"Everett."

"Oh. And what happy news did he impart?"

"It was not happy news. Actually, it should come as no surprise to you."

"What do you mean?"

"The interview you gave *The Daily*. It's in tomorrow's paper."
She could feel her heart drop into her stomach.

"Oh?"

"Yes. Oh?"

She said nothing. She didn't know what to say, so she decided to wait and let him say it.

He was controlled, controlled the way he got when he was trying not to let his fury show.

"I thought," he said, pronouncing his words with care, slowly —"I thought we had agreed that you would discuss your historic-preservation project and nothing else, Sara."

He called her Sara only when he was angry. Sara Adabelle he reserved for teasing, Sadiebelle for passion and tenderness. "The whole point of not having you talk to the press in the first place was that you were unsure of yourself, you were afraid you would shoot your mouth off. It was you who were afraid. So why did you do it? We have talked about the abortion business over and over, and we had decided, I thought, that it was too controversial for you to get involved with."

He was beginning to lose his temper, yet the steely composed voice still prevailed. She rarely saw him angry, and it frightened her, especially when the anger was directed at her.

"Well, I didn't mean to get on that topic. I mean, she brought it up at the end of the interview. I couldn't just stare at her and not answer the question. What was I supposed to do," she asked, "say 'No comment'? Then I'd really look like a fool."

"Why couldn't you just say that your private life was yours and that others would have to make their decisions for themselves? Why couldn't you say that your husband was against abortion and that you were not the person in office and that what you thought was a private matter."

"Because I am not a private person. I am a public person. I have ideas and thoughts and feelings of my own. I am my own person. I think those right-to-lifers are vile, despicable people. I believe a woman has a right to her own body. And I want to tell the truth about it because I think if I do it will have influence over some women in this country, and for me that is the most worthwhile thing I can do while I am the Vice President's wife." She was warming up to her subject, exhilarated by the idea of standing up to her husband. "Besides, it is the truth. Never lie to the press, remember—you are always telling me that. Never cover up. I am surprised that you want me to lie for you. And as for you being against abortion, that is a pile of shit. Yes, Rosey, dear, I said shit." She could feel her face flush, but she kept on. "You can goddamn well bet if your precious daughter Annie Laurie got raped by a nigger—yes, I said 'nigger,' which is what your genteel parents say in the privacy of their home—you can goddamn well bet she'd be on the abortion table so fast you wouldn't believe it." She paused for effect. "And you can goddamn well bet that if I happened to get pregnant, which, believe me, I will not, and I decided to have the baby, which I might or might not, you can surely bet that I would have amniocentesis and that I would abort a child, as painful as it would surely be, if that child had a major birth defect. And when you have your little strategy meeting tomorrow morning you can tell them all that the official line is that Sadie Grey is her own person and speaks for herself and not the Vice President and that he is the one in the office and not she. And now I am going to bed."

It was only after she had left the room that she began to tremble and she realized how much courage it had taken to talk to her husband the way she had.

Rosey was so dumbfounded by her reaction that he couldn't speak. He had never seen an outburst like this from her.

After a while he went into the bedroom. Sadie was undressed and on her side of the bed. He decided to let her pretend she was asleep. He got into his pajamas, then crawled into his side of the bed. The two of them lay awake, not speaking, most of the night.

Everett was the first at the breakfast. He drove up to the house in a White House car. He loved the perks. Sadie had thrown on a pair of slacks and a turtleneck sweater for the early-morning strategy meeting. But as she had lain awake all night, she had determined to stick to her guns. It hadn't escaped her that Rosey had been impressed by her stand. She was a little stunned at her own reaction, but quite proud when she thought of it. Now she was going to tell them all they had a choice. Either she would be his wife and nothing more, not a public figure, or she would be her own person.

If he wanted just a wife, then she could be that. But that meant no independent trips, no projects, no official late things—nothing. She knew he wouldn't settle for that. If he wanted her to be her own person, it might be a little frightening for him, but probably a little better for his image than he knew. People, especially women, would respect him for letting her do what she wanted, or for not trying to hold her back.

She waited until Everett, Randy, and Nan were all downstairs in the dining room. Let them get their heavy sighing and eyeball rolling out of the way before she came in. She had decided to be strong.

Their voices lowered as they heard her walk down the staircase, and they stopped talking as she walked into the room and took her seat at the long table, her back to the kitchen.

Jackson had brought out her tea and put it in front of her, with skim milk and honey, the way she liked it.

Still nobody said a word.

"Well, good morning, everybody," she said with a smile. "Let's not all have such long faces; it's too depressing with the weather outside."

Rosey wouldn't look at her. Everett had a sneer on his face. Nan looked as though she were about to commit suicide, and Randy just looked exasperated.

"Before everyone rushes to speak," she continued, pleased with the way she had taken control of things, "why don't I make a few suggestions about the way we should handle this 'snafu,' I believe it's called."

"Well, we've been discussing that," Randy started, "and we thought—"

"Wait a minute," said Sadie. "Let me just say one thing. This is a crisis only if we let it be. It doesn't have to be at all. Furthermore, it can be turned to our advantage if we are smart." She paused and chuckled. "God, I don't know why I say 'our.'"

"Sadie," said Rosey.

"Darlin', if you don't mind," she said, as politely as she could, "I would just like you all to ponder my role for a moment. Rosey and I went over this last night, but I would just like to reiterate to you my thoughts on the subject. Being the wife of the Vice President is not the most fun job in the world, unless, of course, you happen to be a mindless half-wit, which, in all modesty, I don't believe I am. So I've been a pretty good little girl for the past year playing the role of dutiful wife. I do everything you tell me to do, all of you. I go where you tell me to. Well, I guess the other day when that reporter was here I just had had it. I was sick and tired of it."

She could see Rosey wince, probably more in fear of what she might say than in reaction to what she had said.

"I'm tired of not being able to say or do what I want to say or do."

"Sadie," said Nan, "nobody's asking you to do that. But it's not too much to ask that—"

"Nan," interrupted Sadie, an unexpected firmness in her voice, "I know you mean well. And God knows you tried hard enough to get me to shut my mouth that day. I hope you are not taking any of the blame for this on yourself. I hereby testify to all of you that Nan practically bound and gagged me while this was going on. She did everything but pick up the reporter and carry her out of the house. I've been thinking this one over since it happened, giving it a lot of thought. It wasn't that I had planned it. It was that I wanted it to happen. I needed to assert myself. And I'm not sorry I did it. I also don't think that I made a mistake, either for myself or for my husband, and that is the matter I think we should discuss this morning as we try to determine our strategy."

Everett had been silent. "Well, now, Miz Grey," he said, that tone in his voice which made Sadie want to pop him one in the face. "With all due respect, I beg to differ. I'm afraid that your remarks have put the Vice President in a terribly difficult position. He has, as you know, come out against abortion personally during the campaign, and it has not been a big issue. We all understand your desires and needs to be an independent woman and to lead your own life. But we can't be naive enough to think that because you want your own identity it doesn't reflect on the Vice President. This could hurt him, particularly when—or, uh, if he should ever be in a position to run for the Presidency. This could be a liability."

Rosey was still. He had decided to listen instead of interfering. He was almost curious.

"That's exactly what I wanted to talk to you all about," said Sadie. "On the contrary, I think people will respect my husband more and it will redound to his credit if I am perceived as someone who is a strong, thinking person in her own right. It will look like he had enough self-confidence to have a strong, independent wife. I think women will buy it. Have any of you all bothered to look at the polls on abortion? Eighty percent of the people in this country are prochoice."

"That may be," said Randy, who was always a little deferential to Sadie. "But you know how vociferous the right-to-lifers can be. And how publicity-conscious they are. They can make your life miserable. It's more in the Who Needs It? department than anything else."

"Randy, I appreciate what you say. But what I want you all to know is that I feel very strongly about this issue. I don't think anyone here has addressed that fact. I care a lot about it. I have felt bad for a long time about not speaking out. I think I can make a difference. Now, I know that the Vice President"—she said this looking directly at her husband, but carefully, without any trace of sarcasm in her voice—"has come out against abortion. But he has said he is against it personally. He has never said he is against it for others. He can now say that he is against any Constitutional amendment. He can say that it is one issue upon which he and his wife disagree, and he can also be humorous about it and make some remark about how it would be old-fashioned and unliberated to try to control his wife's thinking even if that were possible, which it is not. What man in this country would not identify and sympathize with that? What woman wouldn't respect his stance?"

"But what if they ask him the obvious question?" asked Nan, a pained look on her face. "What if they asked him what he would do if you were pregnant?"

"Yeah," echoed the others at the table. They hadn't thought about that one.

"That's very simple," said Sadie. "You say that we've had our family. And if they really pressure you, you say that you would be against it if it happened but that there would be no way you could physically stop me, if I were determined to have an abortion, because you are not the keeper of my body."

"Oh, Jesus," muttered Everett.

"Look, Everett," said Sadie in her toughest voice, "if this is all too much for you, you can leave now. If you think this is going to ruin my husband's political career, now's your chance to bail out and latch on to a winner."

"Sadie," said Rosey. It was a reproach. Still, he was impressed with the new person he was seeing. He knew she was independent, but he had never seen her like this. He couldn't figure out where it had come from, this assertiveness. She had never gone after Everett in public before, or at least not that he had seen.

Everett seemed stunned. He looked at Rosey, who avoided his glance, then down at his plate.

"Anyway," finished Sadie, "I just want to sum up my thoughts. I am sorry for the fact that I have not spoken out on this issue before. I feel guilty because it is something I believe in devoutly. My husband and I disagree on this subject—at least politically." She had to get that one in. "I respect his views. I will not make a crusade out of this. And I will not make it my project and I will not take on the right-to-lifers.

"But I will say what I think if I am asked. I will make a point of saying that Rosey and I disagree, but I will tell the truth."

With that, Sadie pushed back her chair and got up, walking to the door of the dining room. As an afterthought, she turned to the assembled, who were staring at her as though she were the latest victim of the body snatchers.

"Now," she said with a mischievous smile, "if I were the wife of the President, it might be a little different. But I'm not. So you can all thank God—for the first time, I suspect—that Rosey isn't the President of the United States."

And so do I, she said to herself as she turned and went up the stairs.

CHAPTER 9

T HE VICE PRESIDENT'S PLANE CIRCLED An-
drews Air Force Base on its approach, and Allison regretted that
the campaign swing was over. It had been fun as well as profit-
able. Rosey Grey had seemed to come alive and relax on the
campaign trail.

The midterm elections were almost upon them, the Democrats
had been lagging in the polls all fall, and Kimball's strategists
were using William Grey to push a positive view of the Administration. There were rumors that Kimball might not run again—
rumors about the President's health—and the press was
beginning to size up the Vice President.

Allison had signed on for this trip early, sensing that a good story
was getting better. She had put in a routine request for an interview
with the Vice President—it was normally no big deal—but now
Grey was besieged. All three networks had crews on board, and
reporters had taken turns moving to the front of the plane for fifteen
minutes with the Vice President. Allison had the last interview, two
hours before landing, with nobody scheduled after her. The others
had concluded that it was because of her relationship with Kimball.
The interview had gone well. Grey had not denied that he wanted to
be President—the first time that he had not done so vigorously.

"I could use a drink," he said finally to signal that the interview was over. "How about you?"

"I'd love a beer."

"Let's not talk about politics anymore," he said after the steward had brought their drinks. "Tell me what's going on that I should know about."

"Have you heard about Corwin?"

Rosey looked blank.

"There's talk that Bud Corwin has been going to some health spa which turns out to be a massage parlor."

"Oh, no," said Rosey. Then he paused and looked at Allison carefully. "We are off the record now?"

"I'm glad you mentioned that," said Allison. "Do you want to be off the record?" She couldn't help smiling.

"What do you think?"

"I think nobody is ever off the record in an interview unless they say they want to be off the record."

"You play hardball, if I do say so, ma'am," said Rosey, returning her smile, then becoming serious. "Is it agreed that we are off the record from here on out?"

"Agreed," she said.

"How reliable do you think this rumor is?" He was trying to be casual.

"Nobody is taking it very seriously. Most people think it's a Republican rumor started to get the Democrats in trouble right before an election. You know—'head of the Senate Armed Services Committee in massage parlor'—but I've certainly never heard anything of the kind about Bud Corwin before. I don't think his marriage is in great shape. But that's nothing new for a Washington politician."

"If you had to guess, what would you say?" asked Rosey.

"If I had to guess? Oh, I don't know. You know, after you've lived in Washington any length of time you'll believe anything. And anything is always true. If I had to guess . . . I'd say I think it's probably true."

"So what do you think your colleagues will do with this?" He was more intent now.

"Chase it down, of course. But nobody's going with a story like this unless they've got it nailed. And it will be tough to nail. It is an election year, though. It would be great copy."

"Good God. This is all Roger needs, with his other problems." He shook his head and stared out the window for a moment.

"Other problems?"

"Molly told me you were the only other person she had talked to."

"I just didn't know how much you knew."

"I'm deeply concerned. Roger could have another anytime. I know it's been almost ten months, but he doesn't look well, and the pressure seems to be getting to him more and more. And I don't see how we can keep it quiet forever. I must say the doctor certainly managed to keep his mouth shut."

"Well, he is the old family doctor from Colorado. He kept his last stroke a secret too. I've been agonizing since last Christmas. I've never had such a conflict. It was an interesting moment when I realized that when the crunch came my first loyalty was to Uncle Roger and not to the paper."

"I have a more serious problem. Whether my loyalty is to Roger or to the country."

The plane was beginning to descend, and Rosey fastened his seat belt. He was ending the conversation.

Allison was trying desperately to squeeze her feet back into her shoes and put her notebook away at the same time.

"Mr. Vice President," said one of his aides as Allison was getting up. "The limo will take you directly to the Vice President's house. You will only have a few minutes to change before the dinner party at the British Embassy. It's black tie, sir. Mrs. Grey will be waiting for you there."

"Righto," said Rosey, looking slightly distracted as an aide handed him his schedule for the next day.

"We'll see you later, then," said Allison as she slipped beyond the curtains into the back of the plane toward her seat. "And I understand that the Corwins will be there too."

He suddenly looked up, alert.

"And remember what they say," she added. "All gossip is true."

The Vice President's house was next door to the British Embassy on Massachusetts Avenue. The limousine pulled up under the arched driveway, and a doorman stood waiting to let them out. He waited in the foyer at the foot of the massive circular stairway as Sadie slipped into the ladies' room to leave her coat and take a last look in the mirror. She was pleased with what she saw—a long boat-necked black silk dress with long sleeves and a three-strand pearl choker with a diamond clasp. Elegant. Quite British. Except that they never dressed that way.

Edwina Abel-Smith was got up like a circus tent as usual. She stood at the top of the staircase amidst the grand portraits of British monarchs and hailed her guests with great swoops and shouts and expressions of pleasure as Rodney stood stiffly by her side, greeting his guests as if they were arriving at his funeral. Sadie did quite like Edwina, even though she was a bit of an ass.

The Greys moved into the large reception room where guests were sipping cocktails among the marble columns. The party was in honor of Lord Trittenham, the publisher and owner of one of London's largest newspapers, so there were more journalists than usual.

Sadie had been around long enough to know that this was a relief. Edwina, like most wives of British Ambassadors, had never really gotten the hang of Washington guest lists. They relied on hand-me-down lists, some as much as ten or fifteen years old, and consequently there were always an alarming number of climbers, "formers" (former ambassadors, former Senators and Congressmen, former administration types), and B's and C's— aging Washington cave dwellers. British Ambassadors' wives seemed to have a weakness for the fashion press. Even members of the Georgetown inner sanctum, who held to the idea that the British Embassy was the icon of social diplomacy, had to admit that the guest lists were often unsettling.

As Lorraine had sighed to Sadie earlier that day, "One is never safe at the British Embassy."

Allison and Desmond were among the last to arrive and Sadie and Rosey were standing directly in their path as they entered the main reception room.

It was not the first time that Des and Sadie had run into each other since the "incident" at Great Falls. But both had chosen to pretend that it had never happened. So when they were thrown together socially they simply avoided each other. If they ended up in the same group they rarely spoke and averted their eyes. This night was no exception.

Allison was wearing a pale pink silk, and she knew she looked good. She was feeling terrific.

"I see you made it before I did, Mr. Vice President," she said. The tone was vaguely intimate.

"Not by much," said Rosey in a friendly way.

The teasing note was not lost on Sadie, who was irritated by the familiarity. She was about to say something when there was a slight hush and people began turning toward the receiving line. There, the last to arrive, were Helene and Bud Corwin, flushed and out of breath, but aggressively there.

"Oh, Edwina darling, you must forgive us," said Helene in a loud voice.

Edwina beamed. What fun to have the latest *scandale* at one of her dinner parties. The British greatly admired those who toughed it out in public.

"Scandal or no scandal, one simply keeps a stiff upper lip and faces the bloody buggers down," she had once remarked to Lorraine. She deplored the American custom of going into seclusion or retreating from disaster. There was nothing people liked more than seeing others retire in shame and defeat. It was much more effective just to go about your business and defy people to challenge you about it. She had half-expected that Helene and Bud would send their regrets.

So the evening was made. All she had to do was sit back and watch the party take off. It had been a little stuffy up until now. She felt like hugging Helene. In fact, she did hug her. Helene was too flustered to realize that it wasn't sympathy but gratitude.

"Balls," said Des. "The guy's got balls."

"Either that or he's more of a jerk than we thought," said Allison.

Rosey and Sadie were standing apart.

"Poor Helene," whispered Sadie. "Even if it isn't true, it must be horrible for her. I don't see how she manages that brave face."

"Stupid," said Rosey out of the corner of his mouth. "The man is stupid to have allowed himself to get involved in something like this. And recklessly irresponsible, not only to himself but to his party."

Lorraine Hadley was approaching both couples. "And I thought we would have to be contented with Addison Marbury and Harry Saks and their boring little feud this evening. I feel a little tingle up and down my spine. Oh, my dears, and here they come. They've spotted us as an appropriate sanctuary. I can't imagine why."

Lorraine opened her arms to Bud and Helene as they headed their way, looking for a harbor.

"Helene darling," said Lorraine. "I want to congratulate you on that marvelous piece in *Fashion*. It was a triumph. And here we have your two stars. Don't you both agree?"

"It's lovely," said Sadie quickly. "I only got my copy today. I lied about doing my exercises every day, of course." And she laughed.

"Sadie," said Helene, "you mean you don't really jog on that trampoline each morning? We have misrepresented the Vice President's wife to our readers?"

"I lied about everything. I am a lazy slob. It's all I can do to do Miss Craig's facial exercises each day without collapsing from exhaustion."

The men laughed, and Allison was annoyed. She waited until Sadie wasn't listening before she said quietly to Helene, "It was my understanding that the piece was to be about Washington's working women."

"But Allison, it is. Certainly no one could deny that the wife of the Vice President is a working woman."

Helene knew she was on dangerous ground, taking on Allison, especially when she was not exactly dealing from strength.

But Corwin caught the tension in his wife's and Allison's voices.

"So," he said loudly, turning to the Vice President, "how did the trip go? From what I read, it was a great success. You seem to have captivated the press. Even Ms. Sterling. I'd like to know how you managed that fancy trick."

There was a small awkward silence.

"It's not so hard," Allison remarked. "All you have to do is flatter the reporters, give them exclusive interviews, let them ride in the front of the plane, and serve them drinks. Good stories will naturally follow."

"I suspect," said Sadie, "that being a woman is often to one's advantage, especially when dealing with Southern gentlemen."

"Of course," Allison continued, "nobody should ever trust a reporter. Just when you think you've got them charmed, they strike."

Just in time, Edwina swooped over to the group and linked her arm with Rosey's. "Come, dear boy," she said, then turned to Sadie.

"Rodney is in seventh heaven at the idea of having you for a dinner partner. I've had to restrain him all during cocktails from talking to you. And Rodney is usually such a stickler about things like that. A seating chart at the door is a fundamental of civilized behavior as far as he is concerned."

She guided Sadie to Rodney and whisked Rosey away, not without a flirtatious glance at Desmond.

Des took Allison's arm and led her toward the dining room. "That was a little heavy," he said. "What were you trying to prove?"

"What do you mean, what am I trying to prove?"

They were whispering in hisses.

Rosey managed to extricate himself from Edwina's grasp long enough to lean over to Sadie. "Don't you think you overdid it a little?"

"I don't know what you're talking about."

"Ah, my dear Mrs. Grey," said Rodney, taking Sadie by the arm. "It is my greatest pleasure to have you sit next to me at dinner."

The dining room was dimly lit, with one long table where the forty or so guests were to be seated. There were footmen behind the pink leather chairs to help the ladies, and the heavy silver and crystal and china glistened in the candlelight.

Allison's heart sank when she saw that she was seated between two men she had never heard of. Sadie, of course, was on the Ambassador's right, and on her right was Allison's dinner partner. Allison was not in the mood for competition. She was tired and wanted to sit back and have a gossipy conversation with somebody she knew. Now she would have to draw these men out, whoever they were.

On her left was a British book publisher, Lord Bumbry, who was traveling with the guest of honor and on her right a New York investment banker. The banker had turned to her at the beginning of dinner and asked what her husband did.

"I'm not married."

"Oh," he said. "I'm so sorry."

"It's quite all right," said Allison, smiling. "I'm sure my life will take a turn for the better."

"Yes," he replied.

"And what does your wife do?"

"What do you mean?"

"What does your wife do?"

"Oh, well, we have three children. And she's taking art

courses. And, of course, she does a great deal of charity, and, well, she has her hands full."

Allison was sympathetic.

"I'm sure she's a very worthwhile person."

She settled back to have a boring conversation with him, dribbling out bit by bit what she did until he finally realized who she was and was embarrassed. It gave her only marginal satisfaction.

The publisher was worse. She asked him endless questions about his publishing house, what books he was putting out this season, what his opinion was of the New York publishing world and of some literary agents they both knew. He answered perfunctorily. He never bothered to look at her place card.

Sadie looked bored too. Rodney was not the most scintillating of dinner partners, and they had barely sat down before he had his hand on her knee. They wouldn't believe this back in Savannah, or in Richmond either. The British Ambassador was feeling up the wife of the Vice President under the table at a black-tie embassy dinner. She decided to let old Rodney have his fun. He was obviously getting such pleasure out of his little debauchery, and if this was his answer to Edwina's sleeping around, it was harmless enough. The one nice thing about Rodney was that he was so easy to entertain. Sadie was free to turn her attention to Lord Bumbry, since Rodney was perfectly content. She could see Allison was having a rather tough go, working overtime. Lorraine had known Lord Bumbry well when she lived in London and tipped Sadie that he loved a good gossip. She decided that the way to get his attention and charm him was to be slightly titillating. Allison was pumping him about the publishing world with little success.

Bumbry beat her to it.

"Well," he said, as the table finally turned. "You Americans can finally hold your heads up to us at last."

"Why do you say that?"

He was looking at her with considerably more interest than he had at Allison. She was the wife of the Vice President, and since he was not that high-ranking he was flattered to be seated next to her. He suspected, correctly, that Rodney was planning to write his memoirs when he retired from the Foreign Service.

"At last you have a potential scandal right here in your capital that may equal even the best of ours."

"Really?" she said, raising her eyebrows.

He leaned a little closer.

"My dear lady, I have been on the telephone with Lorraine Hadley all day. One never comes to Washington without checking in with Lorraine. She has filled me in on this deliciousness about your good Senator Corwin."

Sadie tried to participate just enough so as not to seem stuffy yet not to want to be indiscreet. She was amused to notice that Allison hadn't missed the fact that Lord Bumbry was enjoying himself immensely. When he finished with the Corwins, they moved onto the safer ground of wonderful British scandals.

Shortly after the guests had retired to the salon for brandy, Lord Bumbry made his way over to Allison, a stricken look on his face, flustered. "My dear girl," he said. "You're Allison Sterling. *The* Allison Sterling, the famous American journalist and White House correspondent." He didn't add that she was the President's goddaughter, but it was written on his face. "My dear, I've been thinking of asking you to write a book about Washington and I didn't even know who you were. Now sit right down here and let's talk about it."

"It's too late," she said, and walked away.

She found Des listening restlessly to Lorraine and Archie Hadley discussing, inevitably, the Corwins. Everyone who was not actually talking to the Corwins was talking about them.

Archie had a deeply somber look as he listened to Lorraine.

Finally, when she stopped speaking, he sighed and, with total sincerity, made his pronouncement.

"Well," he said, "there's only one thing to do."

"What's that, Arch?" asked Des, knowing how he detested being called Arch.

"We must all have them to dinner."

Her father had always said that he and Allison's mother, Kate, had the perfect relationship, although Nana had intimated that Kate had too many career ambitions for her own good. Nana blamed Kate's death, when Allison was two years old, on her ambition. "She certainly never should have gone off on that trip to France when you were so little," Nana would say with nothing but reproach in her voice. "But then, I probably shouldn't say anything."

Even though she had never really known her mother, there were times, like now, when Allison longed for her, missed her almost as much as she missed Sam. She needed a woman to talk to, somebody she could trust, somebody who would understand the feelings she had about Des, the conflicts about the relationship.

This was a real problem between them. Des never wanted to talk about anything that involved the two of them.

The relationship.

It had taken on a huge meaning in their lives. It had acquired all capital letters.

THE RELATIONSHIP.

Before Des her career had come first, second, and third. There was never any room for a serious relationship. She had had affairs, but nothing that would get in her way, tie her down, nothing that demanded any kind of commitment or that would take her away from her work. She had to work on a weekend? Fine. The Saturday-night date got cancelled. Last-minute out-of-town trip? The weekend in New York would have to wait. Late nights to meet a deadline? The dinners would be called off. Now she was surprised, amazed to find herself rearranging her work schedule to be with Des. She found herself begging off good assignments, making excuses for not being able to work late, resenting the trips she'd used to fight for.

It was Friday morning. They lay in bed listening to a quartet, holding hands. They had just made love. Allison was feeling wonderful.

"Do you ever think about us?" she asked.

"Never. I'm here. It would be a waste of time to think about it."

"Ever? I mean, what if we were having a terrible fight?"

"Then I might think about it from time to time during the day."

"About how much time do you figure you'd give to it?"

"Half an hour altogether during the day, usually a couple of minutes at a time. But it isn't productive. It only makes me depressed. As you know, I don't like to be depressed. So how about you?"

"Oh, about the same," she lied. "Maybe a little more. It's just that I like to talk things out more than you do."

"But what good does it do? You ask me to tell you how I feel.

Then I tell you and you get upset. You don't want to know how I feel. You only want to tell me how *you* feel."

"That isn't true. But if you do something to hurt my feelings I think it's better to tell you than keep it to myself. Don't you?"

"Maybe. But it just seems that all I ever do is piss you off or hurt your feelings. I'm always doing something wrong. Sometimes I feel as if I can't do anything right."

"Well, let me ask you this. Don't I ever do anything to make *you* mad or hurt *your* feelings? I must have, but I sure as hell wouldn't know about it."

"I can't think of anything offhand."

"Well, at least you're being honest."

"Sorry."

"You know, that pisses me off even more. What you're saying is that you don't care enough to be hurt by me."

"Jesus, I can't win. I tell you I'm not mad at you, and that means that I don't love you. This is ridiculous. Now you see why I don't like to have this conversation. It's so stupid. Now we won't speak to each other for days all because you wanted to talk about the fucking relationship."

"You never tell me how you feel about anything. I feel angry that I am the one who has to do everything around the house so you can come home from work, put your feet up, and have an Irish whiskey. That is how I feel."

"Okay. You want to know how I feel, Sonny? I feel you are an asshole. That's how I feel."

Against her will, Allison's eyes filled with tears.

"I'm sorry you feel angry," he said finally, after a long silence, "but Sonny, you're not being honest with yourself. You want it both ways. You're hurt that I don't help? Well, I let you do it because I don't give a shit about it. If you didn't care about it, you wouldn't do it, either. Then we wouldn't be arguing about it this morning, and frankly, I don't want to argue about it ever again. I'm bored shitless by this conversation. Okay?"

Des made love to her again that night. The room was so dark she couldn't see even the outline of her hand. Usually he liked the lights on; so did she, though it made it more difficult for her to concentrate. For some reason he had turned them out, and they had lain in bed for a long time in each other's arms without moving, without talking. Allison felt an overwhelming desire to cry. She felt as if a weight were crushing her chest. She almost expected him to start whispering to her, but there was no sound except for the sound of his breathing. Finally she rolled over on top of him and grasped his chest in her arms, trying to make herself a part of him. She wanted to meld into his flesh, attach herself to him in such a way that they could never be separated. She could hear her heart pounding, and she wondered whether this was what they called a panic attack. She had read about panic attacks. People who had phobias got them when they got scared. What was she scared of? If anyone had asked her if she was afraid of anything, she would have had to say no. Yet now she was frantic from fear, and she clutched Des's chest so that he finally grabbed her shoulders. He could feel her body shuddering.

"Hey, hey, what's this about, Sonny? You are in an emotional state tonight, aren't you, babe? What's the matter?"

Her terror made her blurt it out: "Just don't leave me. Don't leave me."

"I don't have any plans to go anywhere. Particularly tonight. For Christ's sake, Sonny, don't be so dramatic."

He hadn't missed the urgency in her voice, but it had scared him too, and he didn't want to acknowledge it. This was not the cool, together, slightly aloof woman he knew. It jarred him. He didn't know whether he liked it or not. He was disturbed that she seemed to have lost control. Her control made him feel secure.

He began to kiss her softly—her cheeks, her ears, her neck, her breasts. This had the effect of a tranquilizer. As long as he was touching her she was fine.

"I love you, I love you, I love you," she murmured over and over as he continued to touch her body, to kiss her and stroke her. With her eyes closed, and in the darkness, she could believe that Des would always be there, that he would never leave her.

That was it. That was what she was afraid of. Being left. Being abandoned. But why now? Her mother had died when she was two; then Chisuko, her beloved Japanese nurse; then Nana; then Sam. Everyone she had ever loved had abandoned her, and it had made her stronger and more independent.

She had survived. She had managed to deal with her loss each time. Now here was Des and he hadn't left her. He was here, in her arms, in her bed. He was here, slowly moving his body over hers, his hands moving over her limbs softly and with such strength and love that she had no reason to doubt him. Yet all she could think of was that he too would leave her. Everyone else had; why shouldn't he? She could understand abandonment. It felt almost comfortable. Des would leave her. Just thinking that gave her a certain satisfaction. She was, much to her amazement, letting herself get off on it, more than the orgasm she was beginning to feel.

Did she need him to leave her?

He was inside her now and she clung to him as hard as she could, squeezing her eyes shut to try to block out all thought, to concentrate only on his body and his love.

"Oh, my God, how I love you, Sonny, how I love you," he moaned. "I could never leave you." She could feel her body as it lifted off the bed and floated away, wrapped, encompassed, consumed by him.

They lay in the dark for a long time afterward as they had before. They were both awake.

"You gave yourself to me," he said finally.

"Yes," she said. "I'm sorry."

"Are you?"

"No."

"Then what are you?"

"Scared."

"Of what?"

"I don't want to talk about it. If I talk about it, it will make me more afraid."

"You're afraid I'll leave you?" He said this with a measure of disbelief.

"Something like that."

"And if I did you'd be in the sack with somebody else in five minutes."

"That's bullshit, Des. That's really bullshit. And you know it is. Don't make fun of me."

"That's hardly what I'm doing. It's just that you're a hell of a lot tougher than you think. In fact, I think you know perfectly well how tough you are. If you're afraid I'll leave you, you're indulging a minor fear. You're a survivor, baby. This is a survivors' town. You'd manage just fine because you've still got ol' number one. Your sense of yourself will get you through anything. Sometimes I wish you weren't quite so strong. Sometimes I wish you really meant it when you said that you need me, that you're afraid I'm going to leave you. But I know you too well, Sonny. You don't need anybody."

She could see he really believed that. She decided it was probably just as well. If he knew how scared she really was, he might not love her anymore. It was her independence and her strength that had attracted him to her in the first place. It was so refreshing, he always said, to have a woman who was not clinging to him all the time, who didn't need him to support her, either financially or emotionally. He felt a great weight off his shoulders, he said. He could finally breathe freely. They were both free agents; they could do as they wanted, unencumbered by obligations, children, money problems. It was perfect. God forbid he should know that she didn't believe she could live without him.

The drive to West Virginia took only two hours. They left on Saturday morning. The little towns of Middleburg and Upperville with their old stone houses and rambling farms looked beautiful under the autumn leaves. The roads were empty, and smoke curled from the chimneys of the houses they passed. Allison felt peaceful. She knew how Des loved his cabin.

"I'm going to disappear for a while, baby," he told her after he'd built a fire. "When I get back, I expect a roast crackling in the oven and fresh biscuits ready to go." He saw her expression and grinned and swatted her on the behind as he strode out the door and into the woods.

"Oh, what the hell," she said out loud, and laughed. She didn't want to fight or be angry with him. She wanted to be happy and to have a nice weekend. She had brought up a big canvas bag full of political articles she ought to read. She fixed herself a cup of tea, went over to the chair by the fire, and propped her feet up. She also had a few books, mostly by pals and colleagues, mostly about politics. She thumbed through them. She got up, turned on the transistor radio to a country-music station, and sat back down again. She stared for a while at the reading pile, then reached into her bag for a novel, but she didn't read that either. She was thinking that she was different from the image people had of her. She looked around the cabin at the way she had cozied it up. She was always struck by how they reverted to roles when she came up here with Des. Since there was nobody around to notice, it didn't bother Allison as it did when they were in town.

She cooked and shopped and planned. Des chopped wood, built fires and did the heavy work outside. Except for an occasional walk, they didn't do much with each other during the day. In the evening they sat by the fire and read or listened to the radio; then they went upstairs and made love. It was a pleasant existence, except that it lulled Allison into complacency.

She didn't want to lower her dukes. It was too relaxing and then it was harder to get them up again. Des always said that she was the most competitive, combative woman he had ever met, and he always said it with a laugh. He liked her that way. She liked it that he liked her that way. Why was she so angry at him and at herself so much of the time?

Was it because something had changed with Des? He just seemed different to her lately, more distant. Or was it her imagination, her perverse need to push him away?

She was still not able to admit to herself that she might eventually want marriage and children, so afraid was she that she might not get them.

But even the subject was taboo for them. Or had been up until now. So when she provoked fights or arguments with him it always had to be about something else.

She had thrown her canvas bag into the car and was sitting in the front seat as Des locked up the cabin and threw the trash and the food container into the back seat.

"This T-bird is not exactly what you would call the ideal woodsman's car," he said. "I can barely get enough wood in the trunk to last a couple of weeks. Not to mention the fact that the bottom nearly gets torn out every time I go over the riverbed. But Jesus, I hate to give this little baby up."

"Well, Des, as long as the cockwagon is imperative to maintaining your image, you simply have no choice."

"Go fuck yourself."

"I would think that I was enough to make you feel good about your image."

"Go fuck yourself."

"Give me a kiss."

"You are such a pain in the ass, do you know that?"

"That must mean you love me."

"My, aren't we in a frisky mood! To what do we owe this mood?"

"I was just thinking," she said, affecting a Southern accent, "how lucky I was to have a great big strong handsome man like you in my life."

"Oh, Christ, do I have to listen to this all the way into town?"

They had crossed over the riverbed and maneuvered their way around the bend in the river and out the rocky road to the highway.

"Fasten your seatbelt, angel," said Allison.

"That has an ominous ring to it."

"This is my favorite part of our weekends. When else have I got you my captive audience, strapped in so that you can't get up and walk out or turn on the TV?"

"I think I'll listen to the Redskins," said Des.

"It doesn't start until four, and they're going to lose. That will put you in a bad mood."

"Better I'm in a bad mood because the Skins lose than because you've pissed me off beyond endurance."

"I want to know why men change after they've gotten involved in a relationship. Why men no longer feel that the relationship is worth working on? Before you say anything I want you to know this is not an argument, nor will it develop into one. I would simply like to have an adult discussion about an interesting sociological situation."

"Bullshit."

"C'mon, Des, you don't even give me a chance."

"A chance? Are you kidding? I'm the one who doesn't have a chance. If there was ever a no-win conversation, this is it. You just love this stuff, don't you? You could go on talking about this all night. Well, forget it. I'm not going to play. Look what happened the other night."

"I promise you that will not happen. I am speaking now strictly out of curiosity. My interest in this subject is not personal. It is purely clinical."

"I don't believe you. In twenty minutes you'll either be calling me a bastard or you'll be crying."

He reached over and turned on the radio full blast.

"First down and nine yards to go. . . ."

Allison reached over and cut off the radio.

They drove in silence for several minutes.

"I have this theory," she said finally.

He didn't answer.

"I have this theory that women are always angry at men."

"Amen."

"Okay—you see? We already agree. Now, the question is, *why* are women angry at men all the time?"

"You find the answer to that one, you make a million bucks."

"Well, I may have found it. Now I want you to stay strapped into your seat there and just look gorgeous while I explain."

"Lay it on me."

"I think that women feel ripped off. They feel ripped off because they are deceived at the beginning of the relationship when they are just the prey and the male is the hunter. In many situations men will carry on a campaign to get the woman they want. They woo her, take her to romantic restaurants, buy her champagne, flowers, presents, promise her everything. But most important, and here is the key to my theory, they listen. They want to know. They make an effort in the conversation to keep her entertained, they want to be alone with her, they flatter, charm, and win."

"So. What's wrong with that?"

"Nothing, dammit. Nothing at all. That's my whole point."

"What's your whole point?"

"Des, how can you be so obtuse? Do you act this dumb in the bureau?"

"You're not making any sense, and don't belittle me. I knew this would end in an argument."

"I'm sorry. I apologize. What I am trying to say is that as soon as they have won, they forget everything as though they'd been lobotomized. They show off their trophy to their colleagues and peers as if they had caught a prizewinning fish or shot a ten-point buck, and then they just forget it. It's as if she were stuffed and mounted and hung up on the wall. Then they go about their business, and except for occasionally glancing at the trophy on the wall and feeling flush at their success for trapping it, they never give it much thought again. That is, unless the woman gets restless and goes off with somebody else and wounds their precious male pride. Then they put the burn on to get her back. If they fail to get her back, they feel wounded for a while and then go after another trophy."

"You thought this up all by yourself?"

"You have to admit it makes sense, doesn't it?"

"I don't suppose there is another side?"

"Well, what is it? I would be most happy to hear your thoughts."

"Have you ever heard the old joke about the Jewish guy who marries this princess, a real piece of ass who has spent the last two years of their courtship blowing him and sucking him and getting him off every way to sunward. Finally, a year later, they are on their honeymoon and she won't get near him and he's begging, 'Just touch it, please, just touch it.'"

This cracks Des up.

"What's your point?"

"My point is that sometimes it works both ways. The poor guy gets sucked off until hell won't have it until he marries the broad and then after she's got her trophy she cuts him off."

"Good thing that isn't going to happen to us."

"Yes. Good thing."

Later that night, as they lay in bed, Allison thought about the drive in from the country. After the requisite amount of time, Des had turned on the game and listened to it the rest of the way to town. By the time they got to her house in Georgetown, they were barely speaking to each other.

He took a shower, fixed the drinks, watched his favorite magazine show, then caught up on the papers.

She heated up a can of tomato soup and fixed some grilled cheese sandwiches and took them upstairs to the study, where he was sitting in front of the fire. He barely acknowledged her as he ate, then ignored the dirty plates, which she took back down to the kitchen and rinsed, slipping them into the dishwasher.

Back in the study, she took some of the papers and announced she was going to read in bed. She had pretended to be asleep when he got into bed. Now he seemed to be asleep too. Even so, she couldn't control her anger. And it seemed to her that she was mad at him too much of the time now. When she got like this he would get distracted and remote, and it drove her crazy. He had been like that last fall. She often wondered after they'd been fighting whether he ever went to bed with other women. There was no evidence, but the possibility sickened her just to think about.

They lay quietly for a while, only the sound of each other's breathing audible.

Then Allison felt a hand reaching over in the dark and stroking her abdomen. She didn't move. The hand moved along her abdomen and up toward her breasts. It stroked both breasts, squeezing each one in a friendly, if somewhat perfunctory, manner.

Detachment was the only sensation she felt as she lay there. Maybe amusement. There was something quite funny about not being sexually involved and watching your beloved try to rip off a piece of ass under your nose. She stayed silent as the hand slowly moved down toward its takeoff point, the abdomen, then continued down to her crotch, easing in between her legs. The fingers of the hand began exploring the inner reaches of her thighs, moving in and out of her in an attempt to excite her. She tried to stifle a giggle. She couldn't decide whether to stay angry or to accommodate. She decided the best approach was one of interested observer.

After the hand had done some relatively good work between her legs, it pulled out and up around her abdomen once more, then moved over to the sheet on the other side of her, where it then rested while the body slid itself over and on top of her. The legs, bony knees as the aggressors, each pushed open one of her legs until she had both legs spread and she could feel him erect on top. Without a single word uttered between them, he entered her and began moving up and down, rhythmically. She could not see his face, but she could feel his breath on her shoulder. The mouth had not attempted to reach hers. This was a routine and pedestrian physical workout. No frills. It really was funny, and before she knew it she had begun to giggle out loud, then to laugh. She tried to stop herself, but she couldn't. At first Des chuckled. Then, as she began to shake, he pulled himself up off her.

"What the hell's the matter with you?"

She couldn't stop laughing then. She was almost shrieking. The tears were welling up in her eyes, and she was nearly choking on her laughter. She tried to tell him, but she couldn't. She was gasping for breath.

Des pulled out of her and reached over behind him to turn on the light. She could see in the light, once she got accustomed to it, that he was bright red, with either fury or embarrassment. She knew there was no way she could begin to explain. She wondered if she should even try, then decided that at least it would be on the record if she did.

"Nothing's the matter," she said. "It's just that you . . ." She broke up again, putting her hand over her mouth as she collapsed in a fit of giggles.

"Goddammit, Allison, I don't think this is very funny. You have been acting like an asshole all weekend, but this really takes the prize. I don't believe you. What are you trying to do?"

She managed to control herself for a minute and sputtered out at him. "When we make love, did it ever occur to you to start at the top and work down? I mean it's not that I'm not sexually attracted to you or anything. It's just that sometimes I need a little work. You know. I think they call it foreplay in the sex manuals."

"Oh, shit. I don't believe this. I tried, for Christ's sake. It was like running a hand over a corpse."

"Shouldn't that have told you something? Or did you take that to be your signal that the coast was clear and you should climb aboard?"

"Jesus, you really fry my ass, you know?"

"You're not answering my question."

"What question?"

"What did you think when I didn't respond? Did you think that was my own special way of showing passion? Or was there somewhere in the farthest reaches of your mind the tiniest suspicion that I might actually not be in the mood or that I might have something on my mind other than fucking? Like maybe what we talked about this afternoon."

"Okay. All right. You have something on your mind. I listened practically all the way home in the car. As far as I was concerned you exhausted the subject. But apparently you didn't. So now that I'm wide awake and we're on the subject and I've achieved the limpest dick in the history of adult life, let's hear it and be done with it."

"Well, let me see if I can clarify it for you, in language you will understand."

"I'm not crazy about your patronizing attitude, but do try to enlighten me."

"Okay. What I'm trying to say is this: No talkee, no fuckee. Translated: If you don't communicate you don't get laid."

With that, Allison smiled sweetly at Des, reached over him to his bedside lamp, turned it off, and rolled over to go to sleep. She hadn't felt so good all day.

But she awoke at dawn not so pleased with herself, worried that she had damaged their relationship. The night before was the first time she had allowed her problems to interfere with their sex life, which had been near perfect up until then and sacrosanct to both. She had humiliated him. She hadn't intended that. She felt that something precious between them had been broken, and she didn't know what to do about it.

She looked over at the clock. Five thirty. She had a lot of work to do. She couldn't afford to lose this morning's sleep. She shivered in the dawn chill and pulled the cashmere blanket up closer around her neck. It was still dark, so she couldn't see him, only hear his breathing beside her. She was overcome with a wave of love for him so strong that she stopped breathing for a moment, unable to feel or do anything else but just be next to him. It was that feeling of love which overwhelmed her from time to time that terrified her and perhaps made her pull these scenes. This morning she was more afraid than she had ever been. Last night she had felt superior that he hadn't really understood. Now she felt despair.

She got up first, crept downstairs, turned up the heat, got the paper, fixed herself some tea, took it upstairs to the study, and lit a fire. She heard him clump around on the third floor, running the water in the bathroom, using his electric razor. She heard him come downstairs and debated whether or not to go to him, put her arms around him, tell him she was sorry. She couldn't. Why should she always be the one? Still, she felt sick, listening to his feet as he kept going downstairs to the first floor. She could hear him down there opening the icebox. He hadn't bothered to see where she was. Then she heard him open the front door and felt the coolness of the air coming up the stairs. He slammed the door shut after him. Now she was frightened. She didn't really believe it was possible to fight and not break up. Yet she had done nothing wrong. He would have to make the first move. Despite her resolve, she began to shake, and her teeth chattered even as the fire crackled.

Much to her surprise, Des had called her for lunch as though nothing had happened. She had spent the morning screwing up her courage to apologize.

Her Bloody Mary had come. She rarely drank at lunch.

They were silent for a while.

"I'm trying to understand how you feel, to see your point of view," she said finally. "I think I have become more aware of the real differences between us, between men and women. I think I understand how pointless it is to expect you to feel the same way I feel, and vice versa. I think it's important for us to respect each other's differences and to try to hear what the other one is saying. I think, for the first time, that maybe men are more tolerant than women. Maybe men love more easily than women. They certainly aren't as critical. I don't know what I think. It's hard when you are so uncommunicative. We make our livings communicating. We're pros. It bugs me that we can't make ourselves understandable to each other."

"It's not as if I haven't been thinking about it myself, you know."

"What can we do?" Her voice was plaintive.

"I know you're trying to understand, and I appreciate that. But there really is a lot of stuff that you don't get. There's a lot of stuff I don't get either."

She fingered her Bloody Mary, playing with the swizzle stick.

"You want total honesty. I'm going to try and be totally honest with you. I think as a man I am probably not investing the same amount of feelings in this relationship as you are right at this moment. I am getting out of a twenty-three-year marriage. The other thing you have to understand is that yes, I am a typical male. It is not traditionally masculine to whine and complain all the time about hurt feelings. Also, it is not in my nature to do that.

"The more you complain about my not talking to you or understanding your feelings, the more superior I feel. It makes me feel as if I am in control, and when you're living with someone as tough as you are, that's no small deal, baby."

She didn't say a word. She felt the way she did when she had a hot source, and the source was spilling a lot of good stuff, and a wrong word might turn it off.

"This is hard for me to say, or even explain, and I have been trying to explore this and get a grasp on it. I think that being with you, a woman who does not really need me in the most primitive sense, makes me less inclined to make an emotional investment."

"But that's—"

"Outrageous? Maybe. You asked me to tell you my honest feelings. This ain't easy, kid. I'm admitting things to you now that I have never even admitted to myself. You have to understand that it's not as if I don't love you. And I like your independence. I have felt tired in my life, dragged down by women who were dependent. Other people's helplessness renders me helpless. So when you start making those kinds of demands on me, I feel a little ripped off and I want to pull away. You're sending me different signals. Do you see what I'm saying? On the one hand you're this tough, ambitious, hard-nosed career woman and then you turn around on me, after I've bought your act, and go helpless and emotional. I'm not prepared for it. And I sort of think you can't have it both ways."

"But that's not true. I mean how can you think . . ."

Allison wasn't sure what she wanted to say. Before she had a chance to go on, he interrupted her.

"Listen. Turn the whole thing around. I assume the same thing is true with you. You are a woman who has chosen a role other than being a wife and mother. You don't have the same nurturing inclinations because of that. God knows you've said enough times how hateful the idea of marriage and children is to you, how you detest the idea, and how you see so many women turn into boring old sows. You don't want that to happen to you. I can understand that, baby. But don't then expect me to turn around and demand a major emotional investment from you. From us. And don't be angry at me. Maybe your investment in this relationship is larger than mine. But it's not as great as if you were my wife and had three of my children."

"And I can thank God for that," she said. "If my commitment is greater than yours and we're not married and don't have three children and I'm working, what in God's name would it be like for me under those circumstances? You would be all I had."

She was almost thinking out loud.

"What do you want from me?" she asked, repeating the question he had asked her earlier.

"I want to eat," he said finally with a grin. "And then I want to go home and get laid."

It was a perfect October day, warm and sunny, the falling leaves rushing in the soft wind. They decided to walk home to Georgetown. It was Monday afternoon. She didn't have a story for the next day. She had finished her profile of the Vice President.

Des usually didn't work long on Mondays. He had gone into the magazine early that morning to check on his mail. They had had Bloody Marys at lunch, and then wine. They were feeling mellow.

There was something anxious about their lovemaking that afternoon, breaking the mellow feeling they had shared on the walk home. It was as if Des were trying to find something in Allison, were asking for something, searching for some answer. It was the same for her. Her passion was urgent. When they finished, neither spoke. If Allison had felt uneasy during lunch, she was even more unquiet now. Des was visibly agitated. Rather than lie in bed chatting or napping the way they normally did, he had got up suddenly and announced that he really had to get down to the office. Allison didn't want to stay alone. She got dressed as quickly as he did and in a quarter of an hour they were in a taxi. She dropped him off on Pennsylvania Avenue. "I don't know what time I'll be through," he said without looking at her. "Maybe we can get a bite at the Class Reunion later. I'll give you a call."

There was something almost embarrassed about the way he tossed it off as he got out and slammed the door. Allison felt more uneasy than she had in a long time. It was not a comfortable feeling. The only thing she could do, she decided, was simply not think about it.

It was Saturday morning, and Aunt Molly had invited her to come over to the White House for tea that afternoon.

She had put on a pair of wool pants, a turtleneck, and a tweed jacket and walked down to the office. She still had to put a few finishing touches on her Grey story, which would run Sunday and which she was afraid was rather more a puff piece than she would have liked. The problem was she just couldn't pin anything on Rosey Grey. He was good at his job, smart about the President, liked by the White House staff, popular with the Democrats around the country. Not to mention that she had really come to like him a lot herself. The only thing she could think of to do to get an edge into the story was to contrast Grey with some of the less efficient members of the President's Administration. That would get her off the hook and give the appearance of fairness.

Aunt Molly was in an agitated state when Allison arrived, about three thirty, at the White House. Allison had learned not to bring up Uncle Roger's health. Aunt Molly always insisted he was fine.

"Oh, this damned place," she said. "Everything is wrong. I don't know why we ever wanted this job in the first place. I tell you, Sonny, I'd be the happiest woman in the world if Roger and I could just pack up and go back home to Colorado. Let some other poor soul who thinks he can do it come in here and handle this job. And I'm afraid of what it's doing to Roger. He's aged a hundred years. Just look at him. I tell you I'm going to do everything I can to talk him out of a second term. That is off the record, just to be safe. Let the Greys have it. He's younger and has more stamina and he seems really to want it. They'd be good at it. I'm not, and neither is Roger, for that matter. I hate even to admit it."

Allison had never heard Molly talk like that. She could be feisty and funny and tough and even downbeat, but she had never heard her so discouraged, so sad. And she had never heard her in any way question Uncle Roger's ability. Allison felt relieved. It had always made her uncomfortable to hear Molly talk about what a great President Roger was, how nobody gave him credit.

"Roger is going to join us for tea," she said. "He's so upset about this Hooker thing. He needs a diversion. You always brighten his day. Will you join me in a drop of rum for your tea?" It was the first time she had smiled since Allison got there.

Allison hadn't seen the President up close for several months. She had seen him at a press conference several weeks before, but she had been in the middle row and he was well made up.

Now he looked pale.

"Goddamn John T. Hooker. Off the record," he said as he

walked in the door. It was automatic now with Allison. "I have a good mind to fire the bastard. He's caused me more trouble than anybody in my entire Administration. I should have listened to the press when they said he would make a lousy Secretary of State. I should have left him in the Foreign Relations Committee to pontificate on his own time. I think the son-of-a-bitch has lost his mind."

"And greetings to you too, Uncle Roger," said Allison, smiling, as she got up to give him a kiss.

"Sorry, honey." He kissed her absentmindedly. "How rude of me. It's just that I have never been so exasperated in my life. The last thing I need is for my Secretary of State to be provoking the Russians. I almost believe he would like some kind of confrontation. He's already managed to stall the arms-control negotiations this time around, for thoroughly petty reasons as far as I can see."

"He's been doing that since he got the job," she said.

"This is strictly off the record, understood?" This time he looked grim. "I can't afford to have this getting out, though I wouldn't put it past John T. to leak it his way. He's decided to link release of several of his favorite dissidents to the outcome of the negotiations. But now the Russians are balking and he's threatening to shut down negotiations. I won't let him, of course, but I may lose a National Security Adviser over this one. That's what I'm really wound up about. Henry Peterson is so mad he's about to resign, and I don't blame him. He thinks Hooker is demented, that he's overcome with megalomania. I know Henry has turned against John T. And I'm not sure he is wrong on this one."

"What are you going to do?"

"The Soviets have given me no choice. If we pursue this course they've threatened to accelerate production of nuclear weapons, claim we lack interest in the negotiations, deploy more weapons in Eastern Europe, which will screw me with NATO, and refuse to go back to the table. They're playing hardball on this one. I called Hooker in this morning and told him if he didn't drop this whole nonsensical business I'd fire him."

"Will you?"

"I don't think he thinks I will. I think he's going to make this a test of wills. If that wasn't enough, Peterson has threatened to quit if I don't fire John T. I can't afford to lose Peterson. He's one of the most valuable people on my staff. I don't know what I'll do even if John T. backs down—about Henry, I mean. I think he'll go if John T. stays. What a hell of a mess."

"If I know John T., he's not going to go happily," said Molly. "He'll battle it out in the press by getting some stooge to take up his cause."

"How did you leave it?" asked Allison.

"He seemed disgruntled, but I got the impression that he was not sure how far I would go with him," said Roger. "It's my own damn fault. It's just that he's such a grandstander I thought it better to let him posture and not spend my life in confrontations with him. Now I'm sorry, because he doesn't know whether or not I'm crying wolf."

"What are you going to do?"

"I told him I wanted to talk to him first thing in the morning. If he hasn't backed down then, I'll just have to fire him."

"Then can I have the story?"

"Here we are locked in a major international incident which could jeopardize world peace and all she cares about is a scoop." He was only half-teasing.

"There's nothing I can do about the situation. There is something I can do about getting the story and getting it right."

"And first?"

"And first."

Allison practically ran back to *The Daily* and found Walt Fineman in his office going over her piece.

"I thought that had moved," she said suspiciously.

"There were a few cuts I thought it needed. You do have a habit of writing long, Sonny," he said.

"Goddammit, Walt, that story has been on your desk since Thursday. I was in here yesterday making fixes, and this morning. It's not fair to wait until I leave and then hack it up."

"I just thought you gushed a little over Grey. I took out some of the compliments. I think you'll be happier with it. You can see for yourself. Besides, I didn't get here until this afternoon. I tried to reach you at home."

She read over his cuts and had to admit he was right. She muttered something about "Okay, that's fine."

"What did bring you back here, anyway?" he asked. "Reporter's instinct that your copy was being butchered?"

"I think the President is about to fire Hooker. He's pushed him up against the wall with the Russians. He'll know tomorrow. I think I can get the story."

"Jesus Christ. We just had a story conference. O'Hara has been over at State all day and he said there was something funny going on but he couldn't get it confirmed. They were all running around there like chickens with their heads cut off. He said it had something to do with the dissidents but there was more to it. He couldn't really get a story out of them, but then neither could anybody else. He's been working on it for days. We just watched the network news and they didn't have any mention. No, wait— let's go in to Warburg with this one. He's already intrigued. He sent O'Hara off to try to find out more."

Allison told them what she knew, emphasizing that it was off the record. Warburg told her to sit down at her machine and type out a memo in story form that they could have ready to go. It was only halfway through that she remembered to call Des. She tried him at home. No answer. She called *The Weekly*. He was still there.

"I've been trying to find you all afternoon," he said. "Where the hell were you?"

She almost told him. "Oh, I went out shopping, then stopped back by the office to make sure they didn't butcher my story. Caught them just in time." She thought she sounded a little bit too casual.

"Listen, sweetheart, we're working on a big story here. I'll tell you about it over dinner . . . on the condition it's embargoed until Monday. Why don't we meet at Germaine's at nine thirty? Can you find something to do until then?"

"Yeah, I'll make Walt take me out for a drink. I think he wants to talk about his love life."

"That fucker. I know what he wants to talk to you about. You want to pick me up in front of the building at nine thirty? I'm pretty sure I'll be finished. I may have to go back after dinner."

"Okay. See you then."

Des was flying as they drove into Georgetown.

"So what's the story? I have a feeling I don't want to hear it."

"You don't. You'll eat your heart out. But your curiosity will get the better of you and you'll beg me to tell you, which I will after you've promised not to tell your desk until we've got it in print. But I don't want to talk about it until I've had an Irish and a couple of spring rolls."

They got a table next to the palm tree in the front room at Germaine's. The place was packed with journalists and politicians.

Des was on a high, and not from booze. "It's that postcoital feeling you get when you've finished writing a good piece on deadline." He held her hand. "You know I really love you, babe," he said. He seemed always to tell her this when he was pleased with himself. He was so up on his story that he "loved" her. It was the opposite with her. She loved him most when he was doing well and she was doing poorly. She felt most insecure then, most needy.

"You know, baby," he said, "I really do think that having both of us in the same profession is the best thing that could happen to a relationship. I didn't think so at first. I thought it might just mean constant conflicts and misunderstandings. But the best part of it is that we understand each other. Like tonight. Well, this whole week, really, where we've both been working odd hours and both understand. Christ, it really works. I never would have believed it."

"All right, tell," said Allison. "I'll kick myself for knowing, but I can't stand it. I won't talk to Walt until Monday morning unless we have the story ourselves."

"If you had it, baby, you wouldn't be sitting here as calmly as you are now, believe me. The story is that John T. and Henry Peterson have finally had a showdown. Hooker gave the Russians some kind of ultimatum in Vienna last week about releasing some of the dissidents and Peterson went up the fucking wall, said John T. was provoking the Russians and endangering the arms-control talks. He was taking a much tougher stand with them than Kimball has or than Peterson has. Peterson was also annoyed because John T. is so flamboyant and has got such a high profile compared to Peterson's zero profile. I guess old Henry was upset that John T. would use the press to get leverage."

Allison felt a little sick. How the hell had Des gotten this story? Of course, he was 100 percent accurate. But Uncle Roger had told her that afternoon that nobody knew anything. And she had promised the President she wouldn't use the story until he decided whether to fire John T., which he probably would do over the weekend. And now she had just promised Des she wouldn't use the story either. What the hell was she going to do? If she was going to go with the story, she would have to tell Des now. She couldn't very well listen to his story, say nothing, and then come out with it Monday morning and say she had known it all along. She felt depressed. She couldn't bear the idea of his becoming angry. She really loved him so. And now, of all times, it seemed as if he loved her as much.

On the other hand, if she told him she knew, he would be upset with her for not telling him, for lying to him earlier that afternoon. She would also be confirming his story, and he would go with it much harder. She decided to listen, to wait until he had finished. But when the waiter brought dinner, she found that she didn't have much of an appetite. Des, on the other hand, wolfed down his food as he talked. She hadn't seen him this turned on by a story in a long time. He always seemed so much turned on by her when he was turned on by a story. Too bad it was this story.

"So what was the upshot?" she asked, afraid of the answer.

"The upshot is that Peterson has submitted his resignation unless the President fires John T. The President called Hooker over to the White House this morning. The President told him to revoke his ultimatum and John T. refused. Said it would be too humiliating for him, for the President and the country for him to back down now. He claimed he would have no bargaining position if he did that, that he would lose his credibility. So he stood his ground. The President insisted. John T. left, so I am told, in a huff. He said he would be forced to resign himself if the President didn't back him up."

Allison was barely able to contain herself. Somebody very much involved had leveled with Des. But who? He had the whole scenario in detail. It had to be Hooker.

"At any rate," continued Des, "after John T. got back to the State Department the President called him on the phone and agreed to several concessions on the condition they remain secret. He also persuaded John T. to stay on the job. So Peterson is going to have to go."

This was the opposite of what the President had told her, and she had left him at six. Des's source was John T., of course, or one of his close aides. Kimball was going to fire John T., and John T.'s people had picked a "stooge," as Aunt Molly had predicted they would, to get the story out, to forestall the President. Dangerous, but clever if it worked.

Now she was in a jam. Des was being made the dupe. If *The Weekly* went with Hooker's version he would look like a fool when the truth came out Monday morning, especially if the truth came out in her paper.

Des ordered another Irish and drank it down. What would he do if he were in her position? Would he let her humiliate herself? In the end, she couldn't keep on thinking that way. She had to choose. She had to warn him.

"Des," she said, "I don't think that is true. I have reason to believe that if anybody goes it will be Hooker. I don't think the President is going to let Henry Peterson go."

The grin disappeared and the blood drained. She knew that he knew right away that she knew. His voice became hard.

"How much do you know?"

"How hard are you going with this story?"

"Pretty hard. We're saying that John T. has won a major battle and the President is keeping him on and letting Peterson go."

"Don't go with it, Des."

"What the fuck are you trying to tell me, Allison? You sit here like a fucking Buddha all the way through dinner listening to me and now you smugly tell me not to go with the story after we've just remade the entire fucking magazine at the last minute to the tune of God knows how much money. This is too important to play games about, Allison. What has your Uncle Roger told you?"

She resented it, but she had to stay calm. She couldn't allow herself to be annoyed with him. She was too confused herself.

"Look, I've already told you more than I should against my own interests. I can't tell you any more than that," she said. "I have made a promise, and I also have my own paper to consider. All I can tell you is that I wouldn't go with it that hard."

"That hard or at all?"

He stared at her for a few minutes. She had never felt such contempt from anyone in her life, such anger.

"Des, what would you do if you were me?"

"I wouldn't be in your situation to begin with. Now, if you'll excuse me, I better get to a phone."

After a long time he returned to the table. His voice was icy, his words measured when he spoke.

"I have just talked to my source. He has confirmed everything he told me this afternoon. There is no doubt in my mind that he is telling me the truth—as far as he knows it, anyway. He says John T. is his source. He is very close to John T. and is with him right now. If you know differently for a fact, then I need to know your source, exactly what your source told you, and when you learned it. And I need to know now. Don't fuck with me on this one, Allison. There's too much at stake here. We're going to have to tear up the bloody magazine, and it's close to midnight."

If she told him, she would be betraying the President. She would be breaking her word to the President and she would be scooping herself. She had already gone further than she thought he would have. He wouldn't do even that for her. She was sure of it.

"I can't tell you any more. If you have doubts, you should just kill the whole story."

"You know perfectly goddamn well there is some truth to it. I'm not going to kill it. We can't do it anyway. It's too late. I think you're just trying to protect your own ass here. It's not a very noble position."

He sat silently for a moment. "You're going with it Monday, aren't you?" She nodded. He jumped to his feet and went back to the phone.

In a call to New York he changed a few lines to protect himself. "Though there are conflicting reports, sources close to the Secretary of State report that . . ." At least now he was laying it at Hooker's feet, so that he wouldn't look like a total jerk if it wasn't true. He could believe John T. would make up the story, but not his second State Department source. It was too dangerous a game. And he didn't believe John T. would mess with him like that. He could do too much damage to Hooker if the Secretary of State was playing with him. He decided that Allison knew something, or some version of it. He didn't exactly feel secure about the whole situation, though. And he really felt like slapping her across the face, she seemed so smug about her own little story when he was facing a problem of crisis proportions.

When he returned to the table he paid the check without a word and they left immediately, not speaking all the way home. They went to bed in silence. The next morning she got up to go into the office early, unable to deal with his anger and resentment. He went off to the *Weekly* office to try to make some sense of what was going on before the magazine finally closed early in the afternoon.

Allison could not get the President on the phone for most of the afternoon. It was early evening before he called and confirmed that he had fired John T. Hooker that afternoon. He ordered her to hold the story from the first edition, otherwise it would make the evening news broadcasts. The White House would announce it the next morning. She would be allowed to insert it into the final edition.

When she finally got home, Des was in the study watching television. She crept up the stairs without speaking to him and got into bed, turning off the light. It was only when he thought she was asleep that he came to bed. Neither spoke. About six o'clock the next morning, having slept not one wink, she got up while he was still asleep, got dressed, and walked the streets of Georgetown for several hours before going to the office. She didn't want to be around when he got the call from New York about her story and heard the announcement from the White House. By this time she was half-terrified and half-angry. She knew perfectly well he would have done the same thing if he were in her position. She also knew that he expected her to behave differently because she was a woman. It made her furious.

She became more and more upset as the realization grew that she had not really helped him. She began to feel even sicker, and yet she had her work, her career. Nobody could take that away from her. She wasn't going to give it away. Somehow, though, it just didn't seem right. If their relationship survived this, which she now doubted, it could never be the same for either of them.

When she got to the office, about ten thirty, all hell was breaking loose. The White House had made the announcement after the final edition of *The Daily* had preempted it. *The Weekly* was out with a different version, and the White House press corps was in a state of confusion. The press secretary had had to deny

The Weekly's story and confirm *The Daily*'s story. Though Allison's byline was not on the story—the decision had been made to let the regular White House guy have it—everybody in the office knew where it had come from.

Walt and Allen Warburg were elated. And Allen was particularly gleeful about *The Weekly*. He had never liked Shaw. He felt Allison's uneasiness, but he couldn't resist rubbing it in a little.

"I'm not sure I'd like to be around for the pillow talk tonight," he said. "But I congratulate you, Allison. You are a journalist first and a 'friend' second."

Allison barely got out of Warburg's office before tears welled in her eyes. Walt saw what was happening and steered her into his office, where he placed her with her back to the glass wall and closed the door.

"Tough, huh?"

She couldn't speak; she was trying hard to contain the tears.

"I know. I can only imagine what you must have gone through. You know he's called several times already, before you got in."

She couldn't speak; she only nodded her head.

"Guts, kid," said Walt. "You got guts. What will he do?"

"I don't know," she whispered.

"Go call him."

She hesitated.

"You might as well get it over with. You're going to have to sometime. I'm here if you need me."

He came on the phone right away. "Congratulations on *The Daily*'s big story," he said pleasantly.

"Des," she began.

"I really called to ask you for dinner tonight. This calls for a celebration."

"Des . . ." she began again. But she was puzzled. She could detect no hostility, resentment, anger—nothing.

"Where would you like to go? How about Tiberio's?" It was one of her favorite places.

She wanted to say so much, but he seemed in a hurry. "I'll pick you up at eight," he said. "See you later, sweetheart."

She couldn't work for the rest of the day. Walt had told her to try to get the President on the phone to follow up, but he had not answered her calls. She hoped he wasn't angry. For some reason she worried that he hadn't quite realized that her story would be out before the White House made its announcement, even though he had agreed to let her use it in the final. Other papers and the wires were calling the paper, and some even asked to speak to her to find out if she had been the source of the story. She refused to talk to anyone and finally had to stop answering her phone. It was not her favorite day, yet she was not relieved when the day was over and it was time to leave. She wished she didn't have to go through with dinner. She had a ghastly feeling.

Des had obviously gone home and shaved and changed. He looked very handsome.

She hadn't changed, but she had gone to the ladies' room and redone her makeup from a little case she kept in her desk for emergencies, brushed her teeth, and reset her hair with her electric curlers. She looked okay, though she hadn't slept and had been up and out since six in the morning. By chance she had worn his favorite peach silk blouse and a pale gray suit with pearls.

"You look beautiful as ever," he said to her as she got into the car, but his kiss was perfunctory.

As they drove to Tiberio's, Des asked politely about the reaction to *The Daily*'s story—what kind of feedback they had had, whether or not she had gotten any follow-up, how Warburg and Fineman were dealing with it. It was all over the networks, he said. He didn't understand why she hadn't allowed them to use her byline when everybody in town knew it was her story. She tried to detect a note of sarcasm in his voice, but it wasn't there.

At Tiberio's he was attentive, complimentary. Allison couldn't quite figure out what was wrong; nothing he said quite rang true. Then, as he poured her a glass of wine from the bottle in the cooler, she realized what it was. He was treating her as though she were a first date, someone he didn't know. The compliments, the attentiveness were uncharacteristic. They had often joked about how he would go through a door first and let it slam in her face and he would tell her it was a compliment. If he really didn't think she was equal, he would treat her with much more care. Tonight he was treating her like a doll.

As they were finishing their dinner, and he was asking her politely if she would like coffee or dessert, a couple walked past them and out the door. It was a well-known man- and a well-known woman-about-town.

Allison was surprised.

"What's Frank Northrup doing with Lizzie?" she asked.

"He left his wife last week."

"I thought they had a great marriage."

"So did everyone, but obviously they didn't."

"I wonder what the problem was."

"From what I can gather," said Des, "they just weren't on the same team."

Before she could answer, he had signaled the waiter for the check and they were leaving.

He was quiet on the short drive back to Georgetown, and she couldn't think of anything to say. Dread had begun to engulf her. She wiped the perspiration off her brow without even realizing she had begun to sweat. All she could think of was that she would be glad when they were in bed together. She had not dared talk about the story or her feelings about it at dinner, though she had wanted to. In bed, she could hold him and kiss him and tell him how afraid she had been, how conflicted she was, how difficult it had been for her. She could make him understand. She would tell him she loved him and how sorry she was. They could make love.

Was she sorry, though? She didn't know yet. She wasn't sure. Nothing had happened to make her sorry.

When he pulled up to her door, she saw a parking place several spaces down and pointed it out to him. "Aren't we lucky?" she said. "I hate walking half a mile to get home at this hour." She could hear the nervousness in her voice.

"I won't be spending the night," he said simply.

She started to ask, then didn't. She knew, and she didn't want him to tell her. For a minute she thought she would faint. Then, when she got her breath, she answered in barely a whisper, "Oh, okay. Fine." She was trying not to let him see how upset she was.

"Well, thank you for a lovely dinner," she said, very formally.

"You're very welcome," he replied.

Then, before she could reply, he had leaned over and kissed her softly on the cheek. "Goodbye, babe," he said. He waited for her to get out of the car. She jumped out and ran to her door. As she turned, she saw him waiting for her to get safely inside. He wasn't smiling. As she unlocked the door he saluted her quickly and drove off.

It was only after he was gone that she realized he had said "Goodbye."

CHAPTER 10

Dear Des:

God, this is a hard letter to write. I've been thinking about it for the last few weeks, wondering whether I should write, deciding that I had to even if I never sent it. I had to try to think out what happened to us. I don't mean that I had to assign blame. What is it they say—half the blame lies with each partner? Okay, I can account for my half. I'm not writing this on deadline, so I've had time to think, but I didn't exactly have page A 1 in mind either, so it's not for publication. You are seeing raw copy, unedited Sterling. So bear with me.

Oh, Des, I hurt so. I can't remember such pain, except, I guess, when Sam died. This isn't all that different. It is death in a way. Somehow it's almost worse. I didn't feel diminished when Sam died because I knew he loved me more than anything in the world. When you died . . . see, look at me . . . I mean when you left, I had to bear the pain of losing you with the pain of rejection.

I want to tell you that I always believed, deep down, that you were not able to handle my independence. I always believed that when you said "your liberation is my liberation" you were lying through your teeth. You may have thought you wanted that from a woman, but in the end your ego demanded that you be the star, the hero, the strong, powerful one in the relationship.

I think you loved me. But I also see now that once I had embarrassed you publicly, or you thought I had, there was no way you could stay with me.

I wish I could talk to you, but that never really worked with us, did it? We couldn't ever talk. It was always a fight. It was always me trying to tell you how I felt and you telling me I was wrong, that I was an asshole. Maybe I don't wish you were here. This way I can write and not have to get that scared feeling in the pit of my stomach that you would get furious with me, put me down, or worse, that you'd tell me to get off your back and walk away.

I'm sorry to say this too, Des, but I do believe that you were jealous that I could be as successful at what I did professionally and that I was the nurturer, that I provided the home, the food, the friends—I'm not talking about money now. Of course you did more than your share . . . I'm talking about the actual thought and work that go with keeping a home, having friends over . . . I'm talking about making sure there are fucking cloth napkins cleaned and pressed and candles, for Christ's sake—and soda. Goddammit, you never saw to it that there was enough soda and you were supposed to be responsible for the bar.

I always got the sense that you resented my competence. That you knew perfectly well if we had gotten married (Ah, now I dare mention the word. What a relief) and if I had had children (another blasphemy I can get out of my system now) that I would have been able to do that one too and you knew you couldn't and that pissed you off.

Do you know what, Desmond Shaw? You don't like me. You love me, but you don't like me one goddamn bit. You don't like me because I don't defer to you. And somehow you got it into your thick Irish skull that if you ever gave in to me, married me, that you would lose your power.

Couldn't you see I didn't want to take your power away, to diminish you in any way? I loved you for the power you had and also for your weaknesses that you were so ashamed of.

If you had been in my position you would have done exactly what I did. And furthermore, you would have expected me to feel proud of you for it. And if you had been me you never would have expected me to break off the relationship for a stupid story. I suppose the feminists would say I should feel great about myself because I didn't let a man stand in the way of my career. But I don't feel great. I feel like shit. That story wasn't all that important to me. You were. And yet the only thing I really have for sure in my life that I can count on is me—and my work. Nobody can take that away from me, and that won't walk away or die, either. The irony is that now that I still have my precious fame, my precious independence, my success, job, career, reputation, whatever you want to call it, it has given me no consolation. Zero. Sometimes I think that I would gladly give up everything if I could have you back, to live with you and take care of you. That is all I have wanted, these last weeks. Or at least all I have thought I wanted.

Oh, Des, I did love you. You will never know how much I loved you. I was always too afraid to show it. Too afraid I would lose you like I've lost everybody I've ever loved. I loved you more than I have ever loved anyone except my father, my beloved Sam. I will never love anyone as much as I loved, no, love—it hasn't gone away yet—you. I've lost you. I've driven you away. Deliberately. I knew what I was doing. I understood the consequences. Now all I have to decide is, was it worth it?

Allison

"Mo and Joe's. It's not going to do my reputation any harm to be seen with Desmond Shaw at Mo and Joe's. But aren't you afraid of the gossip? We'll be linked in the columns by the time lunch is over.'"

"I can't think of anything I'd like better," he said, smiling, as he put his arm around her and gave her a good squeeze.

Jenny Stern had spent hours getting ready for that lunch, carefully putting on makeup, doing her nails, despairing over her sallow complexion, cursing her unmanageable hair, sucking in her stomach. The finished product, she thought, was less than satisfactory.

Jenny was on the national staff of *The Daily* and was well respected in Washington. She wasn't flashy or controversial. There were no spins on her copy, and she wasn't out for impact the way Allison Sterling was. Nor was she nearly as attractive. In fact, Jenny Stern was plain, though she had a rather comfortable, almost *zaftig* quality which made people want to confide in her. She was the perfect best friend. There were many close to Jenny who couldn't understand why Jenny was never jealous or envious of Allison, who seemed, to the public eye, to have it all.

It wasn't that she expected anything. A man like Desmond Shaw would never be interested in her romantically. Jenny protected herself by not hoping he might. Desmond Shaw was meant for beautiful, successful women like Allison.

"How about a drink?"

"Actually, I think I'll have a martini."

"Hey. My kind of gal. Why didn't we ever get together before?"

Jenny wished he wouldn't tease her. She knew he was trying to be affectionate, but men like Shaw never understood how patronizing their little jokes could sound. She looked closely at him. He was swaggering a little too much, laughing a little too hard. His voice had taken on a slightly manic quality. He had waved at practically everybody who came down the main staircase at Mo and Joe's, laughing, quipping. But he seemed strained. The twinkle was gone; the attractive cockiness had disappeared.

He drank his first martini and ordered another. She waved the waiter away when Des offered her another.

"Are you trying to get me drunk?" she asked, and then wanted to kick herself. She had perpetuated his little joke. She knew why she was there.

"So," she said. "To what do I owe the pleasure of this lunch?"

"You know."

"Yes, I guess I do. How are you, Des? I hear you've been out on the town every night. You're the most sought-after extra man in Washington these days."

"I just have to handle it that way. I don't like being alone. If I go out it keeps my mind off of it—her."

"Sooner or later you're going to have to deal with it."

"You're not telling me anything I don't know. Anyway, I'm beside the point. I need some advice. I'm worried about Allison. I've hesitated to ask you, but I don't see any other way. I need somebody to talk to, Jenny. I know you're Allison's closest friend. I know she values your advice and trusts your discretion. I will just have to trust you. I brought something."

He reached into his pocket and pulled out a dog-eared letter. Part of it had been crushed up and then flattened out. The ink was smeared by a glass stain.

"Forgive the condition. It's been read a number of times."

While Jenny read Allison's letter Des ordered a third drink and mumbled something to the waiter about the chicken salad.

The letter was so painful, so personal. Jenny felt she was intruding. "Oh, my God, Des. I never knew she was so vulnerable."

"How the fuck do you think *I* feel?" His voice was heavy from the martinis. "It tore me apart, that letter. And you know what really wiped me out, Jen? She's right about me. I'm a prick. She's goddamn well right. I just couldn't hack it. But shit, you know, she's being unfair to me too. I mean, I'm not going to take all the blame for this one. How was I supposed to know? What drives me crazy about women is that they aren't honest. We cut a deal. We cut a fucking deal and the deal was that we wanted to live together. She was the one who didn't want marriage, who scoffed at the idea of children, who was contemptuous of women who were slaves to their houses, their husbands, their children. Even working women who had children she felt were not as good as their unmarried colleagues. But I mean she talked about it all the time. What am I, some kind of genius that I'm supposed to read her mind and know that it was all a bunch of horseshit? She cut a deal with me and then she changed the deal in the middle of the relationship and she doesn't tell me and then she starts seething and I have to pay.

"How the hell am I supposed to figure that out? I didn't even know what was wrong. I loved her, Jenny. I really, really loved that dame. What the hell. I love her now. But it's too late."

His voice was husky when he spoke, and his eyes were damp. She couldn't bear to see him that way, especially in the middle of Mo and Joe's.

"Hey, Shaw, you old sum-bitch," yelled a voice from the stairway. "No wonder you don't have time for lunch. Now I see why you're so booked up."

Des looked up and smiled, waved a hearty wave, and said, "Yeah, yeah. Maybe next year, old buddy."

The man laughed.

"Des, I'm so sorry. I know how terrible this whole thing is for you both."

"Have you talked to her?"

"She won't talk to anybody. She's been holed up for weeks.

She only comes out to work and then she hardly speaks to any-one. I've told her that I'm there anytime she wants to talk. But she just says she needs to be left alone for a while. She looks like bloody hell. Her eyes look like little black holes."

"Oh, Christ, I'm really thinking of packing it in. Going off somewhere and live on a desert island. I've got enough money to last for a couple of years. Maybe write a novel or something. I guess this is what they call a mid-life crisis. It just seems like everything in my life has gone sour, Jen. I'm too old for this shit. I'm too old to play the game. Journalism is not honorable work for grown-ups. I can't stand chasing any more stories. After a while they all look alike, and you're doing the same story over and over. I can't get it up for a story the way I used to, but I don't know what to do. Maybe I could write books, I don't know; maybe I could go out to pasture, teach journalism at some college . . . shit, I don't know. All I know is that I've had it. I just can't hack it anymore. What the hell."

He ordered another martini. Jenny tried to smile and act casual as she ordered coffee for herself.

"That's ridiculous. Every man in this town envies your suc-cess—both in journalism and with women. And there are a lot of women in this town who find you very attractive."

"Oh, yeah? Name one."

"Present company excluded?"

"Right."

"Well, Adabelle Grey, for one."

"The Vice President's wife?"

"How many Adabelle Greys do you know?"

"Oh, yeah . . . well, she—we, I mean—well, she . . . Jesus Christ, Jenny, she's married, never mind to whom."

"Don't play dumb. I've seen her look at you and I've seen you look at her. So has Allison, for that matter."

"Are you crazy?" He hoped he sounded convincing.

"Des, is it really all over with Allison? Isn't there any way you could see her again, that you two could patch it up?"

"I can't, Jen. I just can't. She cut my fucking nuts off in front of the whole goddamn world. I can't live with that. I can't live with her with that. It's over."

*　*　*

"Okay," said Jenny, her arms crossed, her face creased in a reproachful frown. "You look like hell. Are we not supposed to notice? Or are we not supposed to say anything?"

She was standing over Allison's computer terminal as Allison sat crouched in her seat, staring at the luminous green letters on the screen. She had been staring at the screen for several hours. Her hair was pulled up in a knot. She wore no makeup, and there were circles under her eyes. She had on beige corduroy jeans, boots, a beige cashmere turtleneck, and a heavy beige wool sweater. The monotone made her look washed out.

Jenny snapped her fingers. "Hey, Sonny, snap out of it."

"Huh?"

"Listen, kid, we've got to talk."

"Oh, Jenny, not now. I'm on deadline."

"Is that why you haven't written a word in two solid hours? Don't think everybody in the newsroom hasn't been watching you, Sonny. And besides, I've seen the budget. Your story's not running tomorrow. What is your story, anyway? Do you know?"

"Jenny, I'm not in the mood for jokes—okay? I just need to think."

"Allison, I don't like to see you like this. Neither does anybody else. People are worried about you."

"That is bullshit. People have been waiting for a long time to see Sterling get it. Well, it was worth waiting for."

"Uh-oh, here comes our revered editor, Wiley Turnbull, on his evening rounds. I think we're about to be blessed with a visit."

"I think I have to go to the ladies' room."

"It's too late."

"Well, well, well, I see you gals are having a little coffee klatch over here. How's it going?"

Wiley Turnbull's paunch was pushing against his vest, over which his watch fob jostled insistently. His tie and collar pin pushed his red jowls up. He wore wing-tipped shoes and a gold family-crest ring on his little finger which he liked to show off by pressing all ten of his fingers together and bending his knuckles in and out as he talked. The grin was wide, the chuckle mirthless.

"Fine," said Allison and Jenny in unison.

"That's good, that's good," he said. He paused, then cleared his throat. They weren't helping out any. "So what are you two working on? Allison, you certainly seem to be hard at work here. You look as if you haven't eaten in weeks. I'll have to speak to Warburg about that. We can't browbeat the troops. In fact, Allison, I haven't seen you at any of the fancy gatherings lately. You must be working on something important. Should I know?"

The newsroom had stopped. It was six thirty and the national desk would normally be pandemonium, with stories being finished and editors rushing back and forth with last-minute queries to reporters, but Turnbull's inquisition had created a sudden lull.

"It's nothing really important," said Allison. "Just a sort of roundup story on the White House Congressional liaison office and how effective they have been pushing through their pet items."

Wiley Turnbull had a suspicious frown as he glanced around the room searching out Allen Warburg.

"Hummm," he said finally. "I'd like to see it when you're finished. Well, let's see that pretty face out on the party circuit more, do you hear?" And he pressed his fingers together and moved down the row of computers, scanning the faces to decide whom he would seek out next.

"Asshole," Allison said in a voice loud enough for half the newsroom to hear. Turnbull seemed not to notice.

Before he was across the room, Allen Warburg and Walt Fineman were at Allison's desk.

"What the hell was that all about?" asked Walt.

The deadline din had resumed as reporters went back to their work.

"I think the newsroom is not big enough for both of us," said Allison. "That sexist bastard should not be allowed out alone."

"Don't let him get to you, Allison," said Allen in one of his rare moments of sympathy. "He won't be around that much longer."

"Hey, kid, are you okay?" asked Walt.

"I'm perfectly fine, goddammit," said Allison in a fierce low voice. "And I wish to hell everybody would leave me alone. I'm not a bloody invalid. And I do have this piece to finish."

"Well, I'll leave you people to sort this one out," said Warburg as he shifted uncomfortably, then ambled off toward his office.

"Jesus, that bilious green on this screen is killing my eyes," said Allison. "I feel as if my head is going to burst wide open. I'd love to meet the S.O.B. who designed these machines. He's probably blind by now."

"Listen, Sonny," said Walt. "This story isn't going tomorrow anyway. We decided in story conference to hold it. We've got too much breaking news and we wanted to be able to play it well and let it run the length of what you've written. We could even hold it a couple of days more. Why don't you call it a day? In fact, Jenny, why don't you take Sonny out and get some dinner? My sources tell me you haven't been out of your house in weeks. It will do you good. What do you say, Jen?"

"I say I'm starving and I'm not in the mood to go home and eat Lean Cuisine."

"Oh, shit, now you're going to try to make me feel guilty if I don't have dinner with Jenny."

"You got it," said Walt, and laughed, patting her on the top of the head. "Suckered again."

He could see that though Allison pretended to be miffed, she looked relieved and more enthusiastic than she had in weeks.

"Okay. Let's just play it as a Save Jenny operation. I'll take poor Jenny out and cheer her up. How's that?"

"That sounds great," said Walt.

"Then," said Allison, standing up and grabbing her fur-lined parka, "let's get the hell out of this chicken-shit outfit."

"Oh, and Sonny," said Walt, "put it on the expense account, huh?"

"You bet I will."

Sushi-Ko was a tiny Japanese restaurant across the street from Germaine's. It had only a few tables and a sushi bar. It was not a fancy restaurant by any means—blue jeans were the standard dress—but it served great sushi, and whenever Allison was feeling particularly depressed she would head for it. It was like a Southerner heading for barbecue or a Texan going for Mexican food. It soothed her, reassured her, made her feel secure to eat Japanese food. It reminded her of Chisuko, her nurse and surrogate mother, and her three happy years in Japan with Sam when she was a girl.

Sushi-Ko was a restaurant where women could go alone and feel comfortable. That mattered to Allison.

It was a slow night, so they didn't have to stand outside in the cold and wait for a table. The owner ushered them in immediately and greeted Allison in Japanese, and as she responded in Japanese, he took them to Allison's favorite table and brought them a jug of hot sake.

After a long silence Jenny spoke. "You're really hurting, aren't you, kid?"

Allison looked down at her hands, pressed her lips together, and took some deep breaths.

Jenny couldn't get over how she looked. She was so accustomed to seeing Allison as the invincible golden girl. It spooked her.

Jenny put her hand on Allison's arm. "Talk, Sonny."

The tears welled, and she tried to get control while Jenny studied the menu and lit one cigarette after another.

"I need a cigarette," she said finally. "Maybe then I can stop this stupid crying," and she held out her hand to take it as Jenny offered her one, then lit it for her.

"I feel . . . I feel so frustrated, so angry, so confused," she said at last. "I feel like a third-degree patient in a burn unit. I can't move or blink or speak or even breathe without terrible pain. I'm beyond depression. I can't control my emotions. I'm crying all the time. I don't have any confidence, I don't have any optimism. I'm not comfortable with myself anymore. I feel like shit all the time, and I'm so afraid it's all my fault. That I brought it all on myself."

But even through her tears Allison saw the look of genuine sympathy in Jenny's eyes and she wondered how this woman could always have been so generous and so loyal to her under the circumstances.

Allison had never had many women friends. Women were intimidated by her. Not Jenny. Plain Jenny, with her ordinary job and no man in her life, was always proud of Allison. Jenny was Allison's surrogate mother now. Always supportive. When they were together, it was Allison people approached, Allison they praised and complimented, Allison they admired, feared, sought after. Jenny would beam, full of pleasure and pride. Allison had often thought she would die of jealousy if the situation were the other way around. And yet Jenny had qualities that Allison was coming to appreciate more and more. She was a womanly woman, with a large bosom, a wonderful warm smile, a great sense of humor, and a maternal air that appealed to everyone. She had hundreds of friends, her house was never empty, her icebox always full.

She always had time for other people's problems, always had good advice, always had a spare bed for an out-of-towner. Deadlines and stories took a backseat to her friends if they needed her. Her table at Christmas, Thanksgiving, Easter was packed with strays and singles. Winter weekends her hearth was crowded with friends for brunch, and in summer it was her garden people flocked to on Sundays. Somehow she seemed to come to grips with the fact that she was middle-aged, unmarried, and childless and had managed to put together a pretty good life. Everybody loved Jenny. And it occurred to Allison as she sat at the table that nobody loved her at all. Or everyone who had was gone.

"I don't know, Jenny," Allison said finally. "I just don't know whether or not I did the right thing. I wonder if maybe what I wanted from Des was marriage, even children, and I couldn't allow myself to say it for fear of seeming too vulnerable to him. I felt I had to be tough because that's what he liked about me. Now I think maybe what he wanted was some sign of needing him. But I bent over backwards to show him how tough I was and went too far. At least, this way I have my pride. For what it's worth. Ha."

"Sonny, a long time ago I was very much in love with a man. It turned out when we finally got to the point of intimacy that he was impotent, always had been. I persuaded him to have a thorough physical exam and he found out that nothing was wrong with him. The doctor recommended a psychiatrist. I lived with him for years while he underwent therapy, living without real sex. But we had a wonderful relationship and we were truly in love. He went five days a week for nearly four years and finally he began to show signs of sexual ability and arousal. Then I discovered that he had been seeing other women, that he was successful with them. When I confronted him, he wept and told me that he was going to leave me. He said I reminded him that he needed someone who saw him only as what he had become, a whole man. He left and married and has several children now. I was devastated. I never got over it. And I have been afraid of getting involved ever since."

"God, Jenny."

"After this happened I didn't care whether I lived or died. Finally a friend of mine talked me into going to see a psychiatrist, which I fought for a long time but finally did, and he saved my life. He also made me see where I had gone wrong, what part I had played in what was a sick relationship. I'm not exactly what you would call the perfect picture of mental health right now. And it's too late for me to have children. But I hope, if I keep up my therapy, that one day I'll be able to love somebody again, maybe in a healthy way."

"Oh, for Christ's sake, Jenny, I couldn't go to a shrink. If you go to a shrink in Washington everybody thinks you're crazy, and there's no way you can go without everybody finding out."

"So how come you didn't know *I* was going? I know what you're thinking. You're thinking I'm not famous and nobody cares if I go to a shrink, but people would be very interested if you went. You're right about that, but I think you could keep it a secret if you wanted to."

"I didn't mean that, you know, but I've always thought of going to a shrink as a sign of weakness. I think I should be able to solve my own problems. I can't stand all the trendy crap about shrinks. Besides, I'm not crazy."

"You are if you don't go to one. That's all I can say. If ever I saw a candidate, it's you. Look at it this way. Pretend you're in a pitch-black room full of furniture and you keep bumping into things. You hit your knee and bump your shin, and trip and cut your lip and bruise your ribs. You're not doing that because you're weak. You're doing it because you can't see. Going to a shrink is like turning on a light. Suddenly you can see where all the furniture is and you can walk through the room without hurting yourself. Your problem is that you can't see what your problems are. All a therapist will do is turn on the light for you. If you were physically sick you'd go to a doctor. You're very much a can-do, fix-it kind of person. Give yourself a break. Don't cheat yourself out of the real happiness you deserve."

"But I do know what I want." Her voice was tentative.

"Dammit, Sonny, you just said five minutes ago that you didn't. Okay, so tell me. Because once you've decided, it will be even harder. Then you'll have to admit it, and once you've admitted it, you'll have to do something about it."

"Well, I want to be a successful journalist and have a successful relationship."

"What the hell does that mean? Does that mean marriage? Does that mean children? You don't know. You're too scared to even think about it. But you're at the point now where people are going to stop admiring you and start feeling sorry for you, and you don't have all the time in the world left. You better get your act together."

"You've seen Des, haven't you?"

"What made you ask that?"

"Don't evade, Jenny. I'm a crack journalist, remember? Just tell me."

"Yes, I have talked to Des."

"You know about the letter I wrote him?"

"Yes, I know."

"I won't ask you to betray his trust. I gather by what you just said that he feels sorry for me. Should I go to him? Should I apologize?"

"I don't think anything will do any good now, Sonny."

"What do you mean?"

"He's in real pain. As much pain as you are."

"So maybe we could help each other."

"You're the last person who could help him. He can't do it, Sonny. Any more than you can. You're both about as impotent as my lost love. And the only way you're going to become whole again is to find somebody who can help you."

"I'm going to ask you a question, and I want you to tell me the truth. Okay, Jenny?"

"Okay."

"Is there somebody else?"

"No."

"Jenny?"

"What?"

"You're lying."

"I don't know."

* * *

Allison had reached for the phone a hundred times, had even dialed the number and hung up when she heard the soft voice on the other end.

"Hello? Hello? Who's there, please?"

The last few times, Rachel Solomon had sounded irritated.

It wasn't that Allison didn't want to talk to her. It was just that every time she tried to speak she felt herself falling apart. She simply couldn't get the words out of her mouth. The first time she called it was from the office, and she was horrified by her reaction. The next time, she tried from home. She was embarrassed. It was so uncharacteristic. She had always been under control until this thing with Des. Now she was emotionally incontinent. But she couldn't go on like this. Jenny was right. She was a fix-it person. She would get help, get herself straightened out, solve her problems, and get on with it, goddammit.

This time she would call Rachel Solomon and she would not break down on the phone. It was a Saturday afternoon. She didn't know whether it was okay to call on the weekend, but she was at the point where she didn't think she would make it through until Monday if she didn't get help. She had tried to work most Saturdays, but this morning she had finished her story early and Walt had sent her home. There really wasn't anything for her to do. Her house seemed small and confining. It reminded her of Sam.

It was about four when she practically ran over to the phone and dialed the number, hoping Rachel wouldn't answer.

"Hello?"

"Hello, is this Rachel Solomon?"

She said it in her most forthright voice.

"Yes."

"This is, this is, uh, Allison Sterling." Why was she stuttering? "I'm, uh, I, uh, Jenny Stern suggested I call you."

"Yes, she mentioned you might call."

"Oh, good, then she told you what the problem is."

"No. She just said she had a friend who might call."

"Oh. Well . . ." She was losing her breath again. "I, uh, it's really no emergency or anything. I don't know why I'm bothering you on a Saturday. I mean it's nothing that can't wait, it's just that I, um, I, um . . . Oh, God, Rachel, I need help!" she said, choking back the sobs. But once she had let go she couldn't stop. "Oh, I'm so sorry, I'm so sorry, I didn't mean to do this . . ." She tried to talk, but she couldn't. She was only able to hear the barely audible yet supportive voice on the other end saying, "Yes," "Yes," "I know" while she held on to the receiver as though it were an oxygen mask.

"Actually, I have a couple of hours right now. Would you like to come over?"

"I'd like that very much. I'll be right over."

She decided to drive over, even though it was a sunny day, the kind of crisp late-autumn day she normally would have chosen to walk. She threw on a tweed jacket and splashed some cold water over her face and started to race down the stairs. Then she remembered the letter. She would take a copy and spare herself the painful process of reliving that whole thing. She sat down at her desk and wrote down a number of items to discuss. It would be important to be organized in this session, to keep things in control. She didn't want to waste any time, since she would be seeing Rachel only once, just to help sort things out.

Driving over to Dupont Circle, she reviewed the circumstances.

First of all she would have to look at her recent obsession with her mother. Since she and Des had split up she had been haunted by her. Odd that it was now, when she was practically middle-aged, that Allison missed her mother more than she ever had. She needed her. She was talking to her often, the way she had talked to Sam after he was dead. She had always been fascinated by her mother, or rather her mother's image.

It was just that now it was a grown woman who craved a close relationship with another woman, rather than the star-struck young girl who had nothing but pictures of a movie-star creature on her walls. Katherine Kingsley might well have been a subject for coloring books. She had been a special person, talented, strong, courageous, beautiful. As a child Allison had covered her bedroom walls with pictures of her mother interviewing famous people. She had scrapbooks of all her mother's clippings and stories about her as well. She kept her mother's awards in her room enshrined in a little glass case, as her mother was on the walls, in the scrapbooks, and in Allison's memory. In Allison's mind her mother was a goddess, a perfect woman, the person she aspired to be. From the time she could talk she had wanted to be a journalist. Everyone who came to their house would be grilled by this inquiring young reporter. . . . Had they known Katherine? What was she like? Had they read her stories? She could never get enough. And yet Katherine Kingsley was never real to her.

Only now could she look back on her father's stories about her mother and think that beyond the fantasy of these two beautiful people there really was a woman who had thought and felt and loved and who had had problems and disappointments.

Her parents had met in France during World War II. It was love at first sight. Sam was an intelligence officer in the Army, Katherine a war correspondent for UP. Katherine had become celebrated when she was captured by the Germans.

Allison was born less than a year after they met. Shortly after the war ended.

Two years later, on her first assignment after Allison was born, Katherine had been killed in an automobile accident in France. She'd been assigned to do a story on the final weeks of the war from a woman's point of view. She never wrote the story.

Allison often wondered how her mother had done it—being a journalist forty years ago when sexism was still the rule. If it was bad now, how must it have been then?

Questions were all she had. And the crucial question was, Had her mother had it all? She'd had a fabulous career, she'd had a wonderful marriage, a great husband, and she'd been a terrific mother. And she had died trying to have it all. Did that mean that it was impossible, that one shouldn't try? Was it because she had wanted to have it all that she'd lost everything?

The deaths of her mother and father had obviously affected her relationships, with both men and women. It was always she who had ended every relationship, either directly or forcing the other person to do it.

Now it seemed suddenly as if marriage, a commitment, was what she wanted and needed. She felt a physical emptiness in her belly every time she thought of holding a baby in her arms. Now she was filled with a constant sense of panic. She didn't know who she was anymore. She felt helpless and impotent. She knew she had called Rachel not a moment too soon.

Rachel's office was a small room filled with books and sunlight. There was a pretty blue-and-white tiled fireplace, and pastel watercolors on the walls. The pale rugs were soft and deep, and the chair almost swallowed her up. It was a cozy womb. Rachel was Mother. She too was soft-looking and warm—a bright sunny smile, a soft pastel cashmere sweater, long pale hair, a sweet voice. Whatever reservations Allison had had dissipated when she entered the room and Rachel closed the double doors. She sat opposite Rachel. There was a clock, a box of Kleenex and a pot of tea with two cups on the little corner table. Rachel poured Allison a cup.

"I brought a letter," Allison ventured, after she had had several sips of tea. "I thought it might save a little time."

"Why don't you leave it with me? I'd rather you just told me what's going on for now." Rachel had settled back in her chair, one foot tucked underneath her. She smiled an encouraging smile.

Allison was rattled. Already it wasn't going as she had planned. "Okay," she said, trying to sound in command. "I'll try. I didn't do so well on the phone." She gave Rachel a nervous smile.

"You did just fine."

"Well. The headline is that I've broken up with the man I love. The lead of the story is that I forced the breakup. Let me just give you a few details about how it happened."

Allison got so caught up in the story that she managed to keep her emotions at bay, giving a rather bloodless account. It took nearly an hour. "I'm trying not to leave anything out. I just don't know what you will find significant. This isn't really my field, you understand."

When she had finished, she smiled. "Well, that about wraps it up. Pretty boffo ending, huh? So, Coach, what do you think?"

"What do *you* think?" asked Rachel.

"I think women get fucked is what I think. I think if the situation had been the other way around the same thing would not have happened. I think women and men are totally different. I think women care more. I think I am dying inside and

Des doesn't give a shit. I think I still have my career and that's important to me. I think I've lost the person I love. I think if my father were here he'd give me a lecture about how a woman should never humiliate a man under any circumstances.

"I think if my mother had been here she would have told me . . . what? God. I just don't know what she would have said. And would she have been right, anyway? She didn't fare so well, did she? She tried to be independent, she tried to have her career and her marriage and her husband and her child, and look where it got her. Dead, that's where. She was punished for wanting to and almost having it all. You know what I think? I'll tell you what I think. Bad girls get punished. They do in the movies, they do in real life. They die, they lose everything."

Her voice was building to a pitch. Even Allison could hear the rage in her own words. "I think, I think . . ." She had tried so hard to control her emotion, but now she felt only relief when the tears came. It seemed like forever that she cried while Rachel sat silent, speaking finally when Allison's sobs had diminished.

"Tell me, Allison, what do you think?"

"I . . . oh, God, I can't. . . ."

"It sounds as though it's hard for you to feel dependent," said Rachel.

Allison nodded.

"I'm so lonely. I'm so alone. I have nobody. I have nobody who loves me in my life. I've lost everybody."

"Who have you lost?"

"My mother. She died when I was two. My grandmother, Nana. My nurse, Chisuko; Nick; Sam. And now Des."

"Who's Sam?"

"Sam was my father."

"When did you start calling him Sam?"

"I don't know. I don't remember."

"How did your mother die?"

"She was a journalist. She had covered the war, before I was born. She was covering a story in France a couple of years after the war and she was killed on a French road in an automobile accident. Sam had encouraged her, but Nana had asked her not to go, not to leave me at such a young age. I never really knew her."

"How did Sam die?"

"He was killed one night, coming home from a party, when he surprised a burglar. I was in New York."

"Were you close?"

"We were pals. He wanted me to take her place. He loved my mother so much, and he missed her. He wanted me to be just like her. We did the things together that they had done. I was a good friend to him. A good companion."

"I'm sure you were. Was Sam always there?"

"No, he traveled a lot. He was in the CIA, a spook. He was away on assignment a lot, and then we moved a lot. I was left with Nana a lot of the time."

"It sounds lonely."

"It was; oh, it was so lonely! I missed him. When he came home I tried hard to be gay and witty and charming, just like my mother must have been. I thought if I could charm him he wouldn't go away so much."

"It sounds like you didn't get much chance to be a little girl, to be dependent."

"Sam would have been bored. He wouldn't have come home ever. He liked to have fun, have a good time. I wanted to please him."

"So you had to be grown up?"

"I had to be strong, to be independent. After Nana died, I felt I couldn't count on anybody. I still can't. They all die or leave and then I'm alone. I'm so alone. I have nobody to love. I have nobody who loves me. I'm afraid I'm being sucked into a black hole. I'm scared."

"Are you having a hard time looking at me?"

"I'm embarrassed, so ashamed. . . ." Allison reached into her bag for a piece of notepaper.

"Here," she said. "I've written down a list of questions to ask you. I thought it might help. Number one. If I'm doing what is best for me, why hasn't it worked out? If I'm getting rid of these people for my own reasons, why aren't I happy? Number two. Why is it that women have to give up more? Why do women care more?

"Number three. What makes me any different from some housewife? Number four. Where is my pride? I thought I saved it, so why don't I have it anymore? Number five. Why do I feel ashamed that I long for marriage and children? Number six. Why do I feel so panicked all of a sudden? Number seven. Why do I want to hang on to my old tough-career-girl image? Number eight. Why did I let Nick, then Des go? Number nine. Why do I hurt so? Number ten. Why do I hate myself?"

She paused and looked at Rachel for the first time. "Well," she said with a laugh, "if we can get those questions answered I guess that would about wrap it up, huh? I'm really not interested in any long-term analysis. In fact, I sort of hoped we might get things sorted out today."

She was brisk Sterling again. She pulled herself up straighter. She brushed back a strand of hair, then rubbed her hands over her eyes and tossed a Kleenex into the wastepaper basket. "God, I look a mess. I've really let myself go lately. I want you to know I'm usually a fashion plate." There was a silence, and Allison began to fidget.

"So, I guess I asked you before, what do you think?"

"I think we've got some work to do. I'd like to explore with you a little more about your father and try to see why there is such a split in your mind between the roles of men and women.

"I'd also like to take a look at the idea of dependence versus independence. Why is it so stark? How did it get that way? I'd like to know why your solutions are so absolute. You have to do this, you have to do that. There are no grays. This has to happen, that has to happen. I'd like to explore with you your fear of abandonment, the fact that you don't like to get attached, why you become angry at people when you learn they are someone you can count on. I'd like to see you learn to maintain yourself and still be able to count on others. Now, with your father and mother gone there is a pull to fuse with someone. Without that there is the fear, as you said, of going into a black hole. As a little girl you heard only that you had to be strong and independent, that you could never count on anybody. The idea of therapy is to work through those feelings so that the same things don't happen again. People who have to be adult too early become rigid, absolute. Though they understand intellectually that there is no such thing as perfection, they move toward it anyway. I noticed just as you became really open, just when we were starting to get to the idea of loneliness, you brought out a page of questions in order to control the situation, to take charge. One of the struggles you will have is whether you will be able to be spontaneous or will try to keep the therapy on your terms. You see dependency as something to fear, and independence as the great virtue.

"You've only let me in so far today, Allison, but I feel that you tried, and you've done just fine. I think I'm going to experience being with you as being lonely at first. Our relationship may end as a strong one if we are able to accomplish anything. And from what we've done today, I have no doubts at all that we will." Rachel smiled.

Allison had stopped shaking and her hands had stopped twitching, even though the tears still threatened. Once again she looked Rachel directly in the eye.

"I'm glad Jenny made me call you."

CHAPTER 11

"**Y**OU'VE GOT TO BE KIDDING," SADIE SAID into the telephone. She had been sitting in bed sipping her morning tea and reading *The Daily*. It hadn't taken her very long to get through the Feature section. February in Washington was always the deadest month except for August. Congress usually took off for George Washington's Birthday and everybody else who could afford to went south. "I'm not as stupid as I look, Randy. There is no way I'm going to get up in front of a thousand of the most powerful people in the country and sing. Forget it."

She took a bite of her lasagne and listened to her husband's aide. "I don't really care what Rosey thinks, and I certainly don't give a damn what Everett Dubois thinks. In fact, if Everett thinks I should do it, then I definitely won't."

She listened again and nodded. "Look, Randy, I'm a good political wife, and I'll do most anything to help my husband, but what I will not do is stand up at the Gridiron dinner and sing a song. For one thing, I don't have a great voice, and for another, I'm not particularly crazy about making a fool of myself. But when I do, I like it to be my idea. You can tell my husband and the entire staff that it is out of the question. I will not do it. And that's final."

She put the phone down, smiled, took a sip of tea. "Jesus Christ," she said. "What will they ask me to do next?"

"Rosey, I told Randy I wasn't going to do it. I'm not going to get up at that dinner in front of all those people and sing a song making fun of myself. It's just too big a risk."

"You'll be fabulous, darlin'," Rosey said. "As long as you don't ad-lib. I'm just teasing. They'll fall in love with you, if they haven't already."

It was evening, and Rosey had come home intent on persuading her. They were upstairs in the sitting room off the master bedroom. A fire was lit. Rosey was fixing drinks. A small table had been set up for dinner for two. This was their time to hash over the day, a time Sadie usually enjoyed. It was now less than two years away from the campaign, and Sadie was wondering whether Rosey was running not for the Vice Presidency but for the Presidency. That thought had been creeping up on her. Suddenly she was being judged as a potential First Lady.

"Don't flatter me. It won't work. Besides, I haven't had a decent reason why I should do it. Rosey, I want you to tell me just exactly why you want me to do this."

He stopped his pacing and looked at her. He could see she was serious and that a casual answer would be the wrong one.

"Because," he said finally, "I need you. It would help me if you would do this."

"Forgive me, but just how could my singing at the Gridiron Club help you?"

He sighed with exasperation. "Because the Gridiron Club is one of the oldest institutions in Washington and the journalists who belong will invite other journalists and their publishers to this dinner, not to mention the heavy-hitting politicians, administration types, and ambassadors. And the Supreme Court. If a person does well, appears to have a sense of humor, the word gets out that you're somebody they can deal with, a good guy, somebody they would hesitate to go after unless they had to. Not only that: by accepting we're lending clout, just by being there, and in a way they have to be obligated. We could show we're good sports."

"What do you mean *we*, paleface?" screeched Sadie as she sat up and placed her feet on the floor. "I didn't hear anything about *you* being in the show."

"Well, it's the same thing. You're my wife."

"It's not the same thing. I may be your wife, but I am not the same person. If it's so important to you, why don't *you* sing?"

"Because I'm not the problem."

"Excuse me?"

"I'm not the problem."

"And I am?"

"Well, yes. . . ."

"Just what are you referring to?" She had gotten to her feet and had moved over to the fireplace where Rosey was standing, leaning on the mantel, his back to her. They were speaking in polite, brittle voices.

"You know perfectly well. You talk too much. It could hurt us."

"Wait, let me get this straight. I talk too much and it hurts you so you want me to sing in front of the entire Washington Establishment to help you. Maybe I'm a little slow tonight, but I don't get it."

"I'll go through it with you again." His voice was icy.

"Don't patronize me. Randy did *not* go through it, because I told him not to."

He ignored that.

"The song they want you to do is in response to a song that the Vice President, or rather the actor who plays the Vice President, sings. He will sing a takeoff on 'Why Can't You Behave?' about how his wife shoots off her mouth and is constantly getting her husband in trouble. Then you will come out on stage as a surprise and sing a funny retort, something to the effect that it's not your fault and you're always getting misquoted by the press."

"I see. And how does that solve the problem of my being such a liability to you?"

"It shows that we know you're outspoken and that we think it's funny and that we have a sense of humor about it. A lot of candidates have made a lot of good points at the Gridiron."

"And a lot of them have hurt themselves."

"You won't."

"I'm that much of a liability to you, huh?" She was hurt. She went back to the sofa and sat down.

"Sadie, come on. You're very bright. You know your candor,

if you will, has become a problem to me. You read the papers. It will be more of a problem as Kimball's campaign heats up. I can ask you to try and curb it, but I can't ask you to be another person. And I wouldn't want to. At least this way, if you do continue to speak your mind, the mood will be set for it to be received good-naturedly rather than hostilely."

"You poor man. You really are in a bind, aren't you? Here you are stuck with a wife who can't control herself and gets in deeper every time she opens her mouth, and yet politically it would be just as bad or worse if you dumped her. What a dilemma."

"For God's sake, you're my wife, I love you. Can I help it if I wish that you were a little more cautious?"

"You know, Rosey, I am no different now than I was six years ago as the Governor's wife, or for that matter as the Vice President's wife for the last two years. Why, all of a sudden, is this issue so pressing? Nothing has changed."

"Because the First Lady of the United States cannot say anything she wants to say anytime she wants. She has an obligation to control herself, not just for her husband but for her country."

"The First Lady?"

Rosey bit his lip, then turned and walked over to the bar so he wouldn't have to look at her.

"The First Lady?" she repeated.

She could hear the ice cubes tinkle against his glass and the sound of Scotch pouring.

"Now I see," said Sadie finally, almost to herself. "Well, then, Rosey, if you want me to sing at the Gridiron dinner next month, then I shall be happy to sing at the Gridiron dinner, not just for you but for my country."

"I'm sure you've probably heard, Mr. Rauch, of my reluctance in this matter?"

Though there was a serious tone to her voice, Sadie was smiling. For one thing, she had not expected anyone as attractive as Jed Rauch on her doorstep.

He was six feet tall with reddish-brown hair and blue eyes, a rather ruddy complexion, and a nice grin. He was stocky, strong-looking, just the opposite to Rosey's tall, slim, elegant frame. He carried himself like an athlete. He reminded her of her father. He was direct and cheerful as he came into the small drawing room off the main living room. It was lunchtime, and she had decided to make it as social as possible—anything to keep her mind off the main event.

"Reluctant, hmm?" he said with a smile. "That's what they all say."

She was a little taken aback. It was not exactly the first thing one might say to the wife of the Vice President. On the other hand, it amused her that he was so undeferential. But then, these journalists were. The good ones. They didn't seem to give a hoot about people in power. Half the time they seemed contemptuous of anyone who held public office. It was so different from the deference of the general public and the out-of-town press that it made her feel schizophrenic. Being adored on one front and despised on the other for doing exactly the same thing was confusing. Yet she found herself drawn to the journalists like a stuntman to dangerous scripts. She was surprised to notice that she felt the barest stirrings of attraction to Jed Rauch, AP Bureau Chief. It surprised but amused her.

"This won't hurt a bit, and it will be over before you know it," he said, and laughed. "You should see the look on your face. Now I know they weren't kidding when they said you really didn't want to do this. But you can relax. I have written the lyrics, and if I do say so, they're brilliant. Or at least, brilliant for a Gridiron song. It's a catchy little tune called 'Why Can't You Behave?'"

"I've already been warned."

"Now, you don't sing that one. You sing the answer. I wrote that one too. It's to the tune 'I'm Sorry for the Things I've Done.'"

"Clever."

"They should have sent a lion tamer instead of a poor journalist," Jed said, laughing.

She laughed too in spite of herself. She ran her hand through her hair and smiled at him. She could tell he was admiring her, and she was glad she had worn her blue-green corduroy shirtdress. It made her hair look redder and her eyes brighter.

"I don't mean to be difficult. This all sounds fine, but what if it bombs? You'll be backstage crying into your libretto and my husband will be up at the head table smiling bravely into his program. Has anybody given a thought to poor old Sadie if this falls flat?"

"Frankly, Mrs. Grey—"

"Sadie." She hadn't meant to say it, but now it was too late to take it back.

"Frankly, Sadie, I have. Or rather, I had until I met you. I'm perfectly confident that there is absolutely nothing you can do to ruin this thing. All you have to do is walk on that stage—I thought you might wear black, maybe with sequins and a low back—and you've got them in the palm of your hand. For one thing, yours will be the last number. Those guys will all be on their fifth glass of wine by then and anything will look good to them."

"Thanks."

"Jesus, you're relentless." He laughed. "Now, before we start practicing, let me explain the logistics. We want this to be a surprise. You and the Vice President will be sitting at the head table. I will be sitting directly below you at one of the arms of the table. When it's time, I will look up and nod and you will excuse yourself. The Secret Service will know where to take you backstage. After your number I'll escort you back to your seat."

"You may have to carry me."

"I don't think my date would appreciate that."

"Your date."

"That's right."

"Anyone I know?"

"Somebody I've had my eye on for a long time but she was taken."

Why did Sadie suddenly feel her stomach clutch? She instinctively put her hand on her abdomen.

"Oh?"

"A reporter for *The Daily*, Allison Sterling."

"Ah, yes, we've met." Sadie paused. "She's lovely."

Georges, maître d'hôtel of the Maison Blanche, had led Allison to her table in a little niche under a window facing the middle of the room. It was one of the best tables. She could see and be seen by everyone else. This was a major advantage in Washington, particularly at the Maison Blanche, just across the street from the Executive Office Building and the White House.

Jed wasn't there yet. Normally Allison would have been annoyed, but Jed was a wire-service guy. He had six or eight deadlines a day. Yet this was a good moment to get herself composed. She reached into her bag and pulled out half a pack of cigarettes, lit one, slipped the Maison Blanche matches into her bag, and leaned back.

She took a long, hard drag, then stared down at the cigarette clasped between her two fingers. Her nails were unpainted. She hadn't painted them in a while. Unusual for her to neglect her hands. She had always prided herself on her long, slim fingers, on her perfectly manicured nails carefully painted in Windsor Rose polish. Understated. Most women reporters had chipped polish. It was a professional hazard, typing on those machines. Chipped nail polish seemed to be a trademark.

She lifted her eyes to find that several people were staring at her. They averted their eyes quickly. She had come in staring straight ahead and had failed to greet several friends whom she now spotted. In the center of the room, holding forth at a large round table, was a group of men who were making a lot of noise. They were all friends, high-powered journalists and lawyers who met monthly just to annoy their wives and their women friends.

She could just hear them voting on which woman in the restaurant they would prefer. Allison had been invited once or twice to this lunch when the guys were feeling secure enough to include a woman, and she had witnessed their little games. She knew it annoyed them that she refused to be outraged. They were raising their hands now and they went around the room, pointing to various candidates and shouting at each vote. Finally they came to her. She smiled broadly and gave them the finger as discreetly as she could. They yelled with laughter; then one of them, a columnist, got up from his table and came over.

"You won," he said.

"I'd rather take the vows," she said, laughing. "Besides, every single one of you at that table could be pussy-whipped in a matter of days. It wouldn't be any challenge. You should all be ashamed of yourselves. There are reporters in this room with Administration types, getting fabulous stories, and you are wasting your time playing 'Would Ya.' Just look at Worth Elgin over there kissing the Assistant Secretary of State's ass. Now, there's a real man."

Her friend went back to his table to give a report, which prompted another outburst, raised glasses to Allison, and a bottle of wine from the maître d'. Allison lit another cigarette.

She knew she didn't look her best. In fact, she didn't want to look attractive; she didn't want to attract. She was in retreat. The thought of going to bed with anyone made her sick. Even with someone like Jed Rauch, who was striding across the room.

"Jesus," he said, plunking down beside her on the banquette, "the President nearly fucked us over. We had a story out on the wire saying that he was not going to attend the Gridiron, which he had declined, and now he's changed his mind. It was a little embarrassing because we had put out a story saying he would be in New York meeting with the Soviet Foreign Minister after making a campaign speech at lunch. We were about to go into a great detailed analysis about why he was choosing to skip the Gridiron and what the Soviet meeting portended. We would have looked pretty stupid."

"Well, that's a relief. At least I feel better knowing I was kept waiting for such a momentous story as whether or not the President would or would not attend the Gridiron."

Jed looked a little taken aback at the sharpness in Allison's voice, but he recovered and smiled. She had to admit that he was attractive. There was a vibrant energy about him. He never sat still. Even now he was spinning the crystal ashtray around on the tablecloth. Allison had known Jed for years, but she had just never thought of him in any romantic way. For one thing, he had been married for a long time, and when he got divorced she was already with Des. They had never crossed on the singles circuit. Now he had called her out of the blue for lunch. She hadn't had a date since Des. But lunch. Lunch was something else, especially here. She thought he was probably working on a story on the White House and wanted to pump her.

"Just tell me what more important event than the Gridiron dinner is happening this month, please."

He said it with such a straight face that she had pulled herself up before she realized that he was kidding.

"Jesus, have you ever lost your sense of humor. What ever happened to the happy-go-lucky girl . . . sorry . . . person I used to know on the press bus?"

He hadn't meant to be so frank, but her expression and tone had been almost contemptuous, and it had annoyed him. Now he saw her face fall as she twisted a Maison Blanche postcard into a little roll.

Then she felt Jed's warm hands on hers. "I'm sorry, Sonny. I just had no idea. I guess I shouldn't have called you so soon for a date. Will you forgive me?"

She heard only one word.

"Date?"

"Why did you think I asked you to lunch?"

"I, I, I guess I just didn't think of it." She tried a little laugh.

"He's really a shit, isn't he."

"Don't dump on Des. I did it. I didn't give him any choice."

"That is such bullshit. The guy blew it, Sonny. And don't think he wouldn't have done the same thing, either, sweetheart."

"I didn't realize you were so fond of Des."

"I can't stand the bastard. And it's time he learned a lesson, too."

"And just who's going to teach it to him. You?"

"No. He'll get it. Just watch."

"That's comforting."

"Oh, the hell with it. C'mon, Sonny. I'm here to advance a date with you. We'll decide where and when later. But first, let's order and then get down to business."

"I knew there was something else on your agenda besides romance."

"That's why you're the best reporter in Washington."

"Lot of good that does me."

"Order the mixed-seafood dish and shut up."

"Only if I can have another Bloody Mary first."

They ordered; then Sonny took out another cigarette.

"It's about the Gridiron."

"I can't help you there."

"No, no—I mean, I have been sent by the membership of the Gridiron to feel you out."

"In front of all these people?"

"Knock it off, Sonny; I'm trying to be serious."

"How can you be if you're talking about the Gridiron?"

"Sonny, please. I have been sent by the committee to ask you if you would consider joining if you were asked."

"Why don't they ask and find out?"

"You know perfectly well why they don't. They've been turned down publicly by a rather prominent woman and they don't want it to happen again."

"But Jed, I was dragged bodily out of the Hilton lobby by the police and almost jailed one year when they didn't take women and blacks. How can I possibly join now?"

"Because the reasons for your picketing are over. Besides, they need some attractive young blood. That's you, kid."

"I can't stand the motto. 'There are no journalists present.' What the hell does that mean?"

"Allison, that's perfectly simple. It gets all the high-mucky-mucks to relax and not think every remark they make in private is going to end up in the papers the next morning. That's all."

"You've got answers to everything, haven't you."

"So you'll join?"

"Jed, to tell you the truth, my objections so far have been inconsequential compared to my real problem."

"I give up. What is it?"

"I can't sing."

"Good. As long as it's nothing serious."

"Look, Jed. I'm flattered. But it's just not my scene."

"Have you ever been to a Gridiron dinner?"

"No."

"Then be my date. See what it's like, then decide."

Allison thought about it for a moment. She hadn't been to anything public since Des left, but Rachel had given her back some of her confidence. And the lunch had made her feel quite good. She had actually forgotten about Des for several minutes at a time. And she could tell that Jed liked her. That was something she needed. Maybe going to the Gridiron with Jed would be a good reentry. People would see that she was still a contender.

"I can't think of anything I would like better. I'd be delighted to go to the Gridiron with you, Jed."

"It will be good for you. Not to mention me. My God, my stock will soar when I walk in the door with the fabulous Allison Sterling."

"That may be a slight exaggeration, but I can live with it."

"In fact, I'll have the two most beautiful women in Washington in tow."

"What are you talking about?"

"Off the record? And I mean way off?"

"Sure."

"I'm coaching someone to sing a song I've written for the grand finale of the show."

"Someone?"
"Sadie Grey."

Des saw them at once. He had walked into the Capitol Hilton reception room where cocktails were being served. Most of the white-tie crowd was already assembled, and as it always was in Washington where there was an assembly of power, the air was electric. Most of the Cabinet, the Supreme Court, Congressmen, Senators, the top members of the White House staff, and the Vice President and his wife were already there, surrounded by some of the top publishers, editors, and reporters in the country.

Des straightened his white tie and leaned up against the wall for a minute. He intended to go look for O'Grady, his host for the evening. O'Grady had accepted the invitation to join the club against the good advice of most of his friends and colleagues, who told him the club was Establishment, a stuffed-shirt organization. "Me, a little Mick kid from Boston turning down the Gridiron. Me ol' mother would be turning over in her grave. No, thank you, Desmond laddie. I'll join, just so I can invite you as a guest. I'll need moral support."

Des had promised O'Grady he would be early. But it was Saturday night, and as usual, the queries from New York had started to come in around three that afternoon.

Now here he was in his monkey suit, ready to work the room, and right in front of him, no more than ten feet away, one to the right, the other to the left, stood Allison Sterling and Sadie Grey, each one breathtaking. His head swung back and forth as though he were at a tennis match.

Sadie had on a slim black beaded dress with long, tight sleeves, a boat neck, and a plunging back. Her auburn hair was fluffy and tousled-looking. She wore no jewelry. He had never seen her looking so spectacular, and he could feel his throat tighten with desire.

Allison was in white. It was one-shouldered chiffon, floating, ethereal. She wore a pearl-and-diamond bracelet on the bare-shouldered arm, tiny pearl earrings. Her silvery blond hair was brushed back, slightly waved, and fell loose and flowing down her back. This one he felt in his gut. He still loved Allison, there was no question, but looking at her he was overwhelmed with anger. It would take a long time for that rage to subside.

Love was not a word he associated with Sadie. Lust, certainly. It was the kind of physical longing one has for what is now the unattainable.

They were both surrounded by attentive men. They were both chatting animatedly. Neither saw Des, who was riveted to the spot. He was looking at the two most beautiful women in Washington, and he realized for the first time that he wanted both and that he couldn't have either. It took everything in his power not to turn around and walk out the door.

Des wasn't sure how long he had been standing there when somebody slapped him on the back and he looked around to see the eagle face of Howard Heinrich, the President's top adviser. "Now I understand why you'll never amount to anything in this town, Shaw," said Heinrich.

"You've lost me, as usual, Howard," said Des, laughing. He had no idea what Heinrich was talking about or whether he had missed something. What troubled him was that Heinrich always managed a grain of truth. He was, in fact, afraid that he really had just about had it in Washington, that there was nowhere for him to go.

"Don't act dumb around me, Shaw," said Heinrich, a big grin on his face. "Any man who would come to the Gridiron dinner and mope around over a dame instead of pressing the flesh with the great and near-great is a sure loser in Washington, that's all."

"You've got me wrong, Howard. I was just standing here deciding which group to join. You see, there's the Vice President's group over there, the Supreme Court Justice over there, and, of course, there was the group you were talking to. In fact, I had just decided to join your group. It's my policy to work the group I feel I can cultivate most successfully. But now you've saved me the effort."

"You're pretty fast on your feet, Shaw. I'll hand you that. But if I know you, you hadn't given my group a thought. You had your eye on the Vice President's group, and I don't mean the man himself. You could eat him for breakfast."

"Howard, how unpolitic." Des laughed, playing along. "You would speak of our likely next President that way, cutting off your chances in his Administration. I'm shocked."

"Don't be. He needs me. I'll still be around, so don't get too excited. And don't change the subject. I wasn't talking about Grey and you know it."

"You've got to help me out, Howard."

"I'm talking about our Second Lady, you horny son-of-a-bitch. You know, you surprise me, Des. You're a damn good poker player. I've played with you. But your face is giving you away this time. Every time you look at our Miss Sara Adabelle you're like a starving man at a banquet. It's a pitiful sight." Heinrich was fishing. If Des showed his anger, he would betray his feelings. He forced another smile.

"Well, Howard," he said in his most casual manner, "you're only just a little off. It's more like a man parched with thirst at a bar. And if you don't mind, this is one Mick who could use a wee taste along about now."

"You know, Des," said Heinrich as Des walked toward the bar, "she could be had."

Des was standing at the bar when he saw Jed Rauch walk over to Allison and put his arm around her in what seemed to be a rather proprietary way. Allison, instead of shrugging her arm away, which she had invariably done when Des had shown any public display of affection, smiled up at him. Des had never liked Rauch. Rauch was one of those guys who had built up a reputation based on very little merit. Allison had said so more than once. Now here she was all over him like a tent. Rauch was whispering something to her, and Des watched her face. She got that look that Des knew; she sucked in her upper lip and bit it slightly on the edge.

Rauch put his hand on Allison's waist and steered her toward the middle of the room. Des watched Allison's body stiffen and her face take on a quiet grimace. He used to tease her about that expression. He'd always told her it made her look like she was smelling shit when she put on that expression. "Anybody within twenty miles of you could tell you didn't like the person you were talking to with that look on your face," he used to tell her. He smiled, remembering how they would laugh and she would practice different expressions. He would look at her across a room and signal if she was successful, thumbs up or thumbs down. When they went to parties, Des would walk around with his thumb in the air most of the evening, and they would giggle together behind potted palms. Washington was definitely a thumbs-up, thumbs-down town. He had to suck in his breath; he

hurt all of a sudden. The hurt came on him like that, about Allison. He would go along his way perfectly happy and then,
whomp, right in the gut he could feel the wind go out of him. He
hated it, hated her for being what she was, for doing what she
had done to him, for humiliating him. Yet the irony was that he
liked her for it. He had to admire what she had done because he
knew he would have done the same thing. Allison had balls. He
liked women who had balls.

Then he saw where they were headed. They were moving
slowly toward Vice President Grey and his group. *That* was why
Allison was grimacing.

Just as she approached Sadie, she turned for a split second
toward the bar, and for an instant their eyes locked. Before he
realized what he was doing, Des had raised his fist and signaled
thumbs down at her. Her face broke into a smile for a brief
moment before it started to shatter, and it was only by will that
she managed to compose herself before she turned around. In that
moment of spontaneous joy and grief Des saw everything that he
had loved in Allison.

Sadie had just thrown her head back, responding to a joke
from a worshipful Congressman, when her eyes lit on Allison and
a tight smile replaced the laugh. Des had never seen two stiffer
backs, two tighter mouths.

Before they could greet each other, Des saw Heinrich rush
over, a worried look on his face. He leaned into the group and
spoke so softly that every head in the room turned. All anyone
needed to do in Washington was lower his voice at a cocktail
party and ten reporters would surround him. Des could tell by the
way Howard had his head tilted, his eyebrows knitted, and his
hands circled around the backs of the Vice President and the AP
Bureau Chief that it was something pretty interesting.

He hesitated for a moment before he took the few steps from
the bar to where they were standing. He greeted the Vice President and nodded to the rest of the group before he turned to
Heinrich.

"Howard," he said teasingly in a voice loud enough for everyone to hear. "You can always tell when somebody in this town is
in trouble. They invariably gather a group of heavies around them
and pretend to confide some earth-shattering state secret. Anything to get attention. The next thing we know you'll be rushing
for the phone."

Heinrich looked at Des, a worried expression on his face. "Prick," he whispered to Des as he turned and headed for the phone.

Everyone turned to look at Des, who now stood in Howard's place in the center of the group, between Allison and Sadie.

"So there really is a state secret," he said, laughing in surprise. He was even more surprised at how composed he felt, standing between these two women.

"Mr. Vice President," he said, his voice taking on an edge he hadn't intended, "you can certainly tell *The Weekly*, now that whatever it is is all but out on the AP wire."

Rauch glared at Des.

"The President is going to have to miss the dinner after all," said Rosey Grey, looking uncomfortable. "Problems. Nothing major. We knew this afternoon he probably wouldn't make it."

"Don't try to report it tonight, Shaw," said Rauch. "Remember, there are no journalists present tonight."

"That's bullshit," said Des under his breath, looking at Allison, who refused to meet his eyes. He well knew how she felt about the Gridiron.

"Ah, watch your language. Remember rule two: Ladies are always present," she said, trying to maintain her humor.

There was an uncomfortable silence. The lights began to flicker. Rosey nervously took Sadie's arm as the president of the Gridiron approached to lead them into dinner.

"It seems to me that filing a story of international importance may have a bit more social value than writing lyrics for a show that some asshole is going to get up and sing," whispered Des to Allison, assuming everyone was out of earshot. He knew he was lowering himself into the mud with that one, but he was furious at Rauch's cheap shot.

Rauch overheard. "Unless, of course," he responded angrily under his breath, "that asshole happens to be the wife of the Vice President."

Before Des could answer, Sadie turned from in front of them and smiled at Des; then she raised her wrist and made a thumbs-up gesture, entirely by coincidence, and winked at Des.

The lights flickered again as Rauch tried to steer Allison away.

"Ah, yes, and the third rule of the Gridiron, I believe," said Des, "is that the Gridiron singes but never burns."

The tables in the large ballroom were set in the shape of a gridiron, with one long head table raised a bit from the floor. Directly in front of the head table was the stage where the skits were to take place.

Sadie and Rosey were led to the head table, and both were seated together on the left side of the Gridiron president, directly in front of one of the grids. It was at that point, where the long table was joined by one of the tables shooting off it, that Allison and Jed were seated. Allison found herself looking up at the Greys. The seats to the right of the president of the club were empty. That was where the President and his wife were to have been. The word was out now that they would be arriving for the last skit, but there was still some buzzing in the hall about the empty seats. It required an enormous restraint for most of the journalists not to rush for their phones. Allison had tried to get away from Jed to get to a telephone, but he had held tightly to her, probably suspecting that she might well do just that. Allison knew Des had called *The Weekly*. She had seen him veer off toward the phones after his exchange with Jed. She knew she should probably be on Jed's side, but she was, in fact, furious with him. It had ruined the evening. And now here she was seated under Sadie Grey.

Sadie scanned the room from her perch, searching for Des. She couldn't see him. He must have gone to the telephone. She liked the fact that he was breaking the rules. He was so unlike Rosey. Rosey was the consummate clubman. He had belonged to clubs since he was born. There were the Richmond Country Club and the Men's Club downtown, and of course there had been St. Anthony Hall at the University of Virginia. He had always belonged. His stride, his carriage, his voice, his gestures—everything about him—said, "I'm an insider. I belong here. I am comfortable with myself." William Rosewell Grey III had never not belonged. Here he was, moving to Washington, D.C., the clubbiest, cliquiest town in the country, and he walks in as Vice President and has everybody in the city at his feet. Even his choice of party was brilliant. A Southern Democrat was acceptable even to Republicans. They could all wink at each other and know what they really meant when they said they were Democrats. She turned to look at him in his white tie and tails. She couldn't help thinking of Rosey being delivered by his mother in tiny white tie and tails.

The Vice President was sitting at his seat, at ease, his aquiline nose so perfect, his eyebrows arched to the right degree, his smile one of benign acceptance. It occurred to Sadie that in her husband's mind everyone out there—the entire roomful of important and powerful people—respected him. She envied him that confidence. Here she was sitting at the head table knowing that she was a damn fool for agreeing to sing in this skit tonight.

The room suddenly went pitch-black, and the only thing one could see was the sign of the lighted gridiron over the head table. The voice of the president of the Gridiron Club boomed out over the loudspeakers, welcoming the guests. He concluded with "There are two rules of the Gridiron Club: ladies are always present, reporters are never present. And the Gridiron singes but never burns. Please be seated."

With that, the Marine Band began to blare, and everyone turned to confront the terrapin soup as the first skit got under way. It was the Republicans', since the out party is always first. Each skit had about ten songs, taken from old hits, and to Allison each song seemed longer than the last.

For one thing, since Jed was involved in the program and since they were all hysterical about the logistics of getting Sadie up on the stage without anybody noticing, he was up and down from the table most of the evening, which left Allison sitting with an empty seat on one side and the head of the AP in New York on the other. He was a bore who kept trying to press her for "inside Washington stuff."

Sadie was a wreck. The songs dragged on as she waited for her turn.

At the end of the Republican skit there was the Republican speaker, chosen from among the hopeful Presidential candidates, then more food, then introductions of the Important People just to remind the audience that this was no ordinary political banquet. Then it was on to the Democrats. After several songs Allison was about ready to excuse herself to go to the ladies' room when she noticed that Sadie had done just that. She had glanced in that direction in time to see her almost roll out of her seat and down the back of the platform. It would be too obvious for her to duck out now. Besides, Jed might notice and think she wasn't being a good sport. Most of the guests had more or less given up on the

President, and a wave of disappointment had settled over the room. There was nothing more exciting than waiting for the President to show up. It was not his presence that mattered. In fact, his presence usually slowed things down. It was the waiting.

Then, as people were toying with their baked Alaska, there was a whining of the mike and a voice announced, "Ladies and gentlemen, the President of the United States" and the band struck up "Hail to the Chief." Everyone in the vast hall jumped to his feet as President Kimball appeared at the end of the platform and was suddenly up in front of the assembly, waving his hands in greeting and smiling.

Rosey stood to greet him, jumping to his feet a little too quickly, Allison thought, grasping him by both hands and then more or less escorting him to his seat. Guilt was the way Allison figured it. When people clasped with both hands in Washington, it meant something—guilt, embarrassment, insecurity . . . something, but never affection. Rosey felt guilty. He felt guilty because he was going to run against Roger Kimball or try to persuade Roger Kimball not to run. Allison hadn't really seen it before. She had thought Rosey was a cooler customer than that. She hadn't figured him for a two-handed clasper. Rosey wasn't a grinner, either. The upper classes didn't grin. It was middle-class to grin. Here was Rosey grinning. Yes, he was definitely planning to knock off Roger Kimball.

Kimball was pale and he seemed to be perspiring. His beautiful mane of white hair, which was normally smooth and perfectly combed, had a slightly ruffled quality, and it looked damp. His smile was tentative, and his eyes were darting around as though he were afraid of an enemy, afraid of being assaulted.

Allison knew her godfather well, and she knew that whatever was the matter with him, it was not just work-related stress. There was something else wrong too. Aunt Molly had not accompanied him.

Kimball was still smiling his uneasy smile as the roomful of people remained standing, relieved that the President had actually come. Finally, he sat down, looking grateful. He reached into his pocket and pulled out a rumpled handkerchief. Allison had never seen him so disheveled in public. Of course, she was sitting practically under his nose, so she could see him more closely. At one point he looked out across the table and around the room and caught her eye. She smiled at him and winked, and he seemed to relax a bit. But there was little time for private messages. The last skit was about to begin.

The lights went out and a spotlight focused on one lone man sitting on a tall stool on the stage, his back to the audience. The band struck up and the man turned around, looking astonishingly like Rosey Grey. All eyes turned toward the head table to see if the Vice President was still there. He was, and even he had an astonished look on his face. The man turned to his left and began to sing "Why Can't You Behave?" Then the spotlight focused on the other side of the stage, to the left, where there was another stool. A woman was sitting on the stool, her back to the audience. She had tousled auburn hair and a low-backed black beaded dress. She did not turn around. Every eye in the room looked back at the Vice President, to find the seat next to him empty. The audience broke into uproarious applause. The more the man sang lyrics that made it clear he was Rosey Grey chastising his wife for shooting off her mouth, the louder the audience applauded and laughed. Only after the first stanza was it clear to Allison that the man playing Rosey Grey was Jed Rauch. He had on a wavy light brown wig cut in the slicked-back preppy style in which Rosey wore his hair, and somehow the makeup emphasized his thin nose and made his lips look less full. He was dressed as if he were headed to an Old School Tie reunion, even down to the watch fob, the collar pin, the pin-striped suit with the old-fashioned lapels. And the lyrics were quite funny, referring to Sadie's strong language, her views on planned parenthood, and a recent outspoken attack on Southern Republicans at a Democratic fund-raiser in Savannah.

When "Rosey" finished, Sadie turned on her stool to face the audience.

She had managed to hide her nervousness. Somehow, just being up on the stage had calmed her considerably, and the audience support had buoyed her.

She hadn't realized what a ham she was. She turned to Jed and began to sing in a soft, husky voice:

"I'm sorry for the things I've done. / I know that I'm the foolish one. / I'm sorry for the things I've said . . ."

Her voice was low and husky enough that it camouflaged a lot, and it made her sound sexy and irresistible. By the time she had gotten out her first stanza the audience was on its feet, applauding and yelling, and Sadie was encouraged to ham up the

lyrics that blamed the press for her mishaps. As her song was
ending, Jed got off his stool and came toward her, she got off
hers and walked toward him. They then launched into a duet:
"Why can't you behave?" "I'm sorry for the things I've done."
They ended in the center of the stage hand in hand. When it was
over and the audience was shouting for encores, Sadie blew
Rosey a large kiss from the stage and the audience went wild.

All eyes but Allison's were on the stage. She had turned along
with everyone else to see Rosey's response, but then they had all
looked back at the stage. Only Allison kept her eye on the head
table, where Roger Kimball was quietly propping up his head
with his elbow and wiping his brow. She looked over at the Secret Service agent who was standing directly behind him. She
saw the agent make a move in the darkness to aid the President,
but Kimball waved him back.

The Democratic speaker was Freddy Osgood, a liberal Democratic Senator from New Mexico who had his own eye on the
Presidency. His wife, Blanche, was the tackiest woman in town.
A former country-and-Western singer, she still dressed in sequins
and fringe, and her beehive hairstyle was the only one left in
Washington, probably on the East Coast. Freddy was shrewd,
tough, funny, and an extremely conscientious Senator, however,
and he was much respected. Blanche and Freddy were not exactly
regulars on the Georgetown circuit, but there were those who
thought him a plus for them.

Freddy's speech was witty. When he had finished, the president of the Gridiron Club stood up and raised his glass in the only
toast of the evening.

"Ladies and gentlemen," he said, following tradition: "To the
President of the United States."

Roger Kimball pulled himself up, and the crowd solemnly
stood and saluted him with their glasses raised.

When they were seated, the President spoke in response.

"Ladies and gentlemen," he began. "As you may have noticed, I was a little late and more than a little underdressed tonight for this exalted occasion, but I did get here just in time to
hear our glamorous Mrs. Grey blame it all on the press, and I
couldn't help wishing I had been asked to join her in a medley
instead of the AP Bureau Chief here." There was some laughter.
"Actually, I have a better voice than Jed Rauch does."

That got a real laugh. Then the President looked down at his plate, where he clearly had some written remarks, and repeated them without much spirit. Finally, he raised his glass and toasted the Gridiron and made a special toast to Sadie Grey, who was back at her seat, flushed with success. "If you're looking for something to do, maybe we can find a spot in our press office. There's no reason the Vice President should have all the advantages."

There was a slight rumble in the room. Was the President admitting that he felt some pressure from Rosey Grey? The chatter became louder as the President turned to go. As he came to the edge of the platform, one of his agents reached up to take his elbow, and this time Roger Kimball accepted.

As Jed Rauch and Allison were walking down the hall to the Richmond paper's open-house suite, Allison asked him casually how he thought Roger Kimball had acted.

"Jesus, the guy looked wiped," he said. "I wonder if there's something wrong with him. He was worse than usual."

"That's a cheap shot," said Allison. "He looked as though he felt terrible."

"Well," said Rauch, "if there really is something wrong, that's a story. Will you tell me if you hear anything?"

But once again, Allison didn't care about the story.

Rosey and Sadie didn't stay for any of the after parties, although Sadie had rather wanted to. She was feeling great and would have loved to stay around and accept congratulations. But even though this had been Rosey's idea, he was in a tiny bit of a pout. They rode up Massachusetts Avenue in their limousine in silence. Finally Rosey spoke, almost to himself:

"I wonder what the hell was wrong with Roger. He just didn't look himself tonight."

"I don't know," said Sadie softly, her voice edged with trepidation, "but you may be President sooner than you thought. . . ."

Reynolds and Melanie Durant always had the brunch the day after the Gridiron show. Their McLean estate, Fairview, overlooking the Potomac, was a perfect setting. It was across the river from Washington yet still part of the capital's power center, removed yet central. One could stand back from the fray at Fairview. Durant was an old Gridiron member, and he had been an influential figure in Washington since the days when very few journalists were either socially or professionally acceptable. He had money and power, he had used them judiciously, and he had survived.

Reynolds was tall, slim, white-haired, and genteel and had a Southern accent which could have been produced only in North Carolina. His wife was equally Southern, with short cropped blond hair and pale blue eyes which she used to advantage. Together they managed to make all of their guests feel secure; more than secure: they made their guests feel as if they were at exactly the right place. People never went to the Durants' and wondered if they were missing something better. The Durants' brunch was the social apex of Gridiron weekend. Not everyone was invited. Those who were went. It was that simple. After the brunch there was the Gridiron show late Sunday afternoon downtown for wives and other friends who had not been invited to the big night. It was like going to a Saturday matinee. Sort of warmed-over and flat, but better than nothing. Most of the women were thrilled to be asked, not quite focusing on the fact that now that women were allowed as members and guests, to be invited for Sunday afternoon was a hideous insult.

Most people had had a few Bloody Marys or Bloody Bulls at the Durants', though, so they could plow their way through the Sunday-afternoon show with relatively little pain.

A Bloody Mary was not going to cheer up Allison. She was in a terrible mood. She was depressed and bored and conflicted about everything, and she couldn't for the life of her figure out why she had come to this party. She had been appalled by the show the night before. It was so dumb. How could grown men, and lately a few women, behave that way? Except for the principle of the thing, she couldn't imagine ever having wanted to picket the Gridiron Club. And she had to admit that it hadn't been the greatest of evenings for her. First, seeing Des had been a major setback. It was beginning to dawn on her that he might be attracted to someone else. Then there was Sadie Grey being the big star. Finally, Uncle Roger's queer behavior had worried her terribly. She had tried calling the White House this morning to talk to either Uncle Roger or Aunt Molly, but the butler had told her that they had visitors and couldn't be disturbed. She wondered whom they could be entertaining on a Sunday morning.

There had been nothing on their official schedule; but she relaxed, figuring that if he was well enough to entertain, he must be feeling better.

When Jed had suggested she go with him to the Durants' brunch, she had just laughed. "Enough is enough, Jed."

Jed wouldn't be put off by her sourness. He was still flushed with success. "Sonny, you're not a quitter. You haven't really done the Gridiron unless you've gone to the Durants' brunch. Besides, I hear the President may come. And you're a working girl. You didn't get much done last night. You might be able to pick up something at the lunch."

It was true she hadn't really done any productive work the night before, and the Gridiron was always a good opportunity. The question was, Would going to the Durants' be good for her professionally? Professionally the answer was Yes. "Yes," she had told Jed. "I'll go."

Rosey was in an odd mood. Even though she knew he was proud of her, she wondered if it wasn't hard for him to swallow the fact that his wife had been the center of attention the night before.

"I've got too much work to do to go to this Durant thing," he said. "I've still got all the briefing papers from the meeting with the Russians in New York, and I've got to get that done tomorrow before I see the President."

"How is the President?" asked Sadie, lifting her eyes just slightly over her teacup.

"I called over there," Rosey said, avoiding her eyes. "Or rather I had Everett call over there, on some pretext that if the President would like to discuss the Russian papers with me I was available. I told Everett to tell them the press would be all over us Monday after the strictures of the Gridiron were lifted. Though I can't believe for a moment that 'No journalists are present' actually sticks. Those guys were working that hall the way I work a country barbecue."

"Well, what did they say?"

"Everett says Kimball has visitors this morning and can't be disturbed."

"I'm sure that was bad news for Everett," said Sadie, the sarcasm barely veiled.

"Bad news that he's got visitors?"

"No, bad news that he's well enough to have visitors."

"That is a mean thing to say."

She knew she was provoking him, but she couldn't stop herself. She chose Everett as her instrument.

"Why don't you want to go to the Durants' lunch?"

"What the hell has that got to do with anything, Sadie? You've done nothing but have at me lately."

His tone had become more serious, almost pleading rather than angry. She looked over at him in the easy chair in their upstairs sitting room. He was wearing his pale gray silk pajamas and his gray wool monogrammed bathrobe. His hair wasn't combed and he hadn't shaved yet. They were having their leisurely Sunday-morning breakfast, reading the papers and chatting.

She was guilty. Her attraction to Des had made her want to find fault with Rosey. Rosey was hurt. It made her feel even worse. She got up to go to him. She wrapped her arms around his neck, burying her head in his chest.

"I'm sorry, darlin'," she said. "I'm truly sorry. It's just that you've hurt my feelings recently, implying that I can't do anything right, and your staff, Everett in particular, has done a good job of making me believe that I'm a detriment to you. So now suddenly I've had a little boost and you seemed to resent it. I can't help thinking if you'd made a brilliant speech last night you'd want to go to the Durants' today."

"I didn't realize you felt that way," said Rosey softly. He really was a pushover when she set her mind to it. "Let's make a pact not to hurt each other's feelings anymore—okay, sweetheart?"

"Okay. It's a deal. Now will you go to the Durants'? It's really important to me, Rosey."

He hesitated.

"Nothing will make you look better than to seem to have a good sense of humor. The exasperated husband unable to control the little woman. What man in America, what voter in America wouldn't identify with you?"

It was unseasonably warm for March. The temperature was over seventy degrees, and the sun sparkled over the Durants' terrace and the river below. By the time the Vice President and his wife arrived, the terrace was nearly packed. As they approached, everyone applauded, and Sadie had to cover her eyes from the glare to make sure they were applauding her. Rosey put his arm around her and beamed. In her two years in Washington Sadie had never really felt as if she belonged, but suddenly today she knew she was home. Washington had been a foreign capital. Today she owned it. It felt good.

Allison and Jed arrived late. There had been a query from New York about the bureau's file on Roger Kimball's meeting with the Soviets, and he'd had to get his staff to do some more reporting. He was disappointed to be late to the Durants' brunch. Everybody in town would be there. The rules weren't as strict about "no journalists present" as they were at the Gridiron, and a reporter could get in some good work. He had complained on the way over to the Durants' house, hidden away up a long driveway behind tall trees.

"I hope everybody isn't gone by the time we get there. If there is anybody who knows what the hell is going on with the Soviets I've got to get to them. Our file isn't complete, and nothing is coming out of the White House. The place is like a fucking morgue over there this morning. You can't get through to anybody."

Allison was preoccupied. After she had called the White House she had relaxed a bit, but then she had begun to worry again. The butler had sounded odd. She hadn't really believed the "visitors" story. Just before Jed arrived to pick her up at Olive Street, she had called back. She had asked for Aunt Molly, telling the butler, whom she knew fairly well, that it was rather urgent.

He had sounded agitated and mumbled something about how Mrs. Kimball was unable to come to the phone. He hadn't mentioned visitors.

"Raymond," said Allison, trying to sound as firm as possible. "I want you to tell Aunt Molly"—she deliberately said Aunt Molly—"that I'm worried about Uncle Roger and I'm calling to see if he's all right. I'm going to give you a telephone number where I can be reached if there is any problem. Please tell her to call me as soon as she can."

"Yes, ma'am, Miss Allison," said Raymond, as polite as a thirty-year retainer could be. "I'll surely tell her."

The acknowledgment in his tone of voice scared her, but he had worked at the White House too many years to let on anything. He was discreet. It was that discretion which had kept him his job.

When Allison and Jed arrived at the Durants', most people had gotten their plates and were seated everywhere on the floor, around tables set up on the terrace, and at special tables set up inside. Allison was too worried to eat, but she had not mentioned anything about her phone calls to Jed, who had only inquired in the most perfunctory manner about the President and then lost interest.

Allison spotted the Greys out on the terrace surrounded by admirers. They were among the few who hadn't gotten their plates. Allison decided to stay inside and circulate around the living room.

Reynolds Durant saw her standing by the French doors. He slipped his arm around her waist and whispered, "What's a pretty girl like you standing here all alone for? Won't you let a Southern gentleman fetch you something to drink?"

Allison smiled. Reynolds was one of the few men who could call her a girl and make her smile.

"Oh, thanks, Reynolds," she said, "I think I'll just have plain tomato juice. I had enough wine last night to last me a month. One doesn't really have much choice at the Gridiron, does one?"

She didn't want to offend him either. She said it gently.

"You don't have to be tactful with me, dear girl. The Gridiron is a frightful bore. But how can you abolish an institution that makes so many people feel important in a city where they've come because they need to feel important? If I had my druthers, I'd never go to another bloody Gridiron dinner again. But I guess in my old age I'm just a coward. It's easier to go along than to revolt. But if I were you, dear girl . . ." He smiled, just a hint of mischief in his eyes.

"You. It was you," she said.

"I'm afraid so. Just testing your mettle. Just wondering if you were the woman I thought you were."

"I hope, then, I won't disappoint you when Jed reports back to the committee that I won't be joining up."

"You will delight me and confirm my highest suspicions. That you are a no-nonsense woman."

"And that I can't sing or dance."

"You've done all right so far," he said. That, from Durant, was the highest praise. Her talk with him had made her feel better. She had gone to the Gridiron to break out of her state of self-pity and to give herself confidence, and she had only ended up being hurt by Des and upstaged by Sadie, not to mention disappointed in Jed.

"You know, Allison, you are one of the best reporters in Washington. I know how hard it has been for you the last two years with your godfather as President. It has hindered you a great deal and has caused you a lot of problems. I just want you to know that I'm one person who believes you have handled the situation and yourself impeccably. You have been beyond reproach, and for that you should be commended."

She leaned over and kissed Reynolds Durant. "Oh, Reynolds, you don't know how I needed that. It has been awful. And the irony is that some people envy my position and resent it. You don't know how many times I've wished that he weren't President or even, and it makes me feel guilty even to say it, how I've often hoped he wouldn't run again."

"I don't mean to upset you, Allison," said Durant, "but Roger didn't look at all well last night. I was worried about him. Do you know how his health has been recently?"

"He has seemed very pressured lately," said Allison. "But he's been under a lot of stress. I know Aunt Molly is not holding up well either."

Allison wasn't talking out of school. Durant was an old friend of the Kimballs' and knew more about their problems than Allison did. He made it his business to know Presidents intimately, and he also made it his business to be discreet about them.

"Excuse me, Mr. Durant," the waiter was saying as he leaned toward them, almost whispering. "I'm sorry to interrupt, but there is a call for Miss Sterling. It's from the White House."

Allison could feel her heart in her throat. She didn't say a word for several moments as she tried to catch her breath.

Durant could see the fear on her face. He took her hand and stood up, pulling her up with him. He thanked the waiter, dismissing him with a nod.

"You'll take it upstairs. I'll come with you. Were you expecting a call?" His face had gone white too.

She nodded. They headed up the carpeted stairs and into Durant's upstairs study. "I left this number for Aunt Molly," she muttered, then stood before the phone, staring at the flashing light on the hold button.

Taking a deep breath, she picked it up. A voice told her to hold. Finally Aunt Molly came on the phone.

"Oh, Sonny," she said. Allison thought she was going to faint.

"What is it, Aunt Molly? What's wrong?"

Durant looked ashen now. He put one arm around Allison's shoulder to steady her.

"Roger has just had a stroke. He's paralyzed on one side of his body. They don't know whether or not he's going to make it." She broke down.

"Oh, my God. Oh, my God," said Allison.

"What is it, for God's sake? What's the matter?" said Durant.

"It's Uncle Roger," she gasped. "He's had a stroke. He's paralyzed. They don't know whether he'll live."

"Sweet Jesus," said Reynolds. "Somebody better get to Rosey Grey."

"Do you want me to come over?" said Allison into the phone.

"Yes—oh, please, honey, please come. Come now. The doctors are all here. They're going to have to make an announcement fairly soon. I've tried to persuade them to hold off. They don't know I'm calling you."

"I'll be there as soon as I can," said Allison. "I love you, Aunt Molly."

Durant had rushed down the stairs, almost tripping, he was going so fast. Several guests were leaving and they tried to stop him to thank him for the party, but he brushed them aside, leaving them staring after him. He ran out to the terrace and saw several Secret Service men conferring quietly with the Vice President. Rosey was getting the same message.

"The President, Rosey—it's the President," Durant whispered as Grey looked up at him, stricken. Several people turned toward them, and as they saw the expression on the men's faces they hushed their conversation. "The President," said Durant very softly. Rosey nodded, then walked quickly inside to the telephone as Secret Service agents waited to escort him to the White House.

Rosey turned back to where Sadie had been standing with the rest of the crowd in suspense on the terrace, to see that she was now being brought inside.

"We have to get to the White House right away," he whispered as she approached. "We have to leave now." And he grabbed her by the arm.

"Wait, wait," said Durant to Rosey. "You must take Allison

Sterling. Molly just called her. Molly wants her with her. You must take Allison."

One of the agents went upstairs and got Allison, who was still sitting on the bed, and led her down the stairs and out to the Vice President's limousine.

Allison got in first, then Rosey, then Sadie. They nodded at one another. Then, all three staring out the windows in silence, the limousine sped along Chain Bridge Road, over Chain Bridge, up through Georgetown, down Pennsylvania Avenue, and up to the South Gate of the White House.

CHAPTER 12

It was three in the morning. Again. She still hadn't slept through a single night, and Rosey had been President for two months.

Everything had happened so quickly, and it hadn't been the way she had imagined it. When she had allowed herself to think about it, it had been a remote fantasy—living in the White House, bands playing, flags waving, heads of state in and out, fabulous parties. Instead, it was terrifying and lonely. She couldn't leave the house. Everything was a major production. Shopping? Forget it. You could stop in unannounced with your phalanx of twenty Secret Service, but by the time you had finished greeting the shop owner, nodding and smiling to customers, and being stared at, all you wanted to do was leave. It was easier to get people to bring things to you than to go out. Even going to a restaurant for lunch was a major production.

So she had friends in to lunch. At least, everybody was dying to come to lunch at the White House. After only these few months, she felt so claustrophobic that she woke up in a cold sweat. One night she had wandered through the second-floor hall that served as the family living room, into the oval reception room, and out onto the balcony overlooking the

Washington Monument and the Ellipse. There was a full moon, and the city shimmered with a luminous glow. She had never seen anything more beautiful. She leaned against the tall white pillar on the balcony in her pale peach wrapper and began to weep. She put her arm over her mouth and nearly bit it to muffle her racking sobs. She couldn't remember ever having felt this frightened, this alone. She understood what it must feel like to be imprisoned. It wasn't just the physical confinement. That would have been enough to depress her desperately. It was her relationship with Rosey. Would it be different if she were passionately in love with her husband? She didn't know, but she thought it might at least be bearable. She had once read an article in some women's magazine about a First Lady, she couldn't remember which one. What she loved best about being First Lady, this President's wife said, was the fact that her husband worked right there at the White House. All she had to do was walk down the hall to see him. They had never spent so much time together in their lives, and she had never been happier.

Sadie remembered being envious and wondering if she were telling the truth. They all lied all the time, politicians' wives. You had to lie. You had to pretend and put on a brave face. She wondered if there was anyone in Washington who suspected her marriage wasn't perfect. She thought about it for a moment. Des knew. Allison probably knew. She was a woman. She would know in her gut. And Lorraine. Lorraine could sniff out things like that. She was like a pig to truffles. Even so, those three, for different reasons, wouldn't ever discuss her marriage with others, she was sure of that. She was safe with her lie. Even with Rosey. Rosey was happy working from six in the morning until midnight. She really didn't see him as much as she had before, but he was there. He came "home" for lunch, usually with several staffers. He held meetings after working hours in the family quarters, with a Scotch-and-soda, and most evenings somebody from his staff dined with them. He was there all the time, and he wasn't there. He would seem a devoted husband on the surface, including her in as much as he could, yet she might as well not have been there for all the attention he paid her. At night he was so exhausted that he hardly had the energy to give her a peck on the cheek.

The social aspect of the White House was not exactly a priority with him. Rosey assumed that Sadie was good at parties and teas for Congressional wives, and he had faith that her staff would be good. She dressed well, made a good impression, and to his relief, her confinement meant that she would have less opportunity to shoot off her mouth. He had given her only one command. No interviews, no briefings, no press conferences. Period. If they didn't like it they could lump it. He wasn't going to have his Presidency distracted by some comment Sadie might make as an aside to a hungry young reporter trying to make a name for herself.

So there she was, like a medieval princess in a tower, being "protected" by her powerful king and knight. How many women would envy her! How many women, in Washington alone, were this very night imagining what it must be like to be Queen of the land, to have it all! She had it all. And here she was, her Erno Laszlo pHelityl cream carefully applied under her eyes and around her neck, standing out on the second-floor balcony sobbing. She hated having Rosey be President of the United States. She hated being the First Lady. Now she was trapped.

It had not been the best way to enter the White House, she had to admit, and that could have had something to do with how she felt about the situation. She had liked Roger Kimball. Seeing him paralyzed was horrible. The doctors knew right away that he was going to be paralyzed on the entire right side of his body, if not for life, at least for years. He would require intensive physical therapy and rest. His brain had not been damaged.

Roger Kimball had been a class act. As soon as he heard the doctors' prognosis he had resigned, nearly three years into office, and issued a statement asking the American people to back William Grey to the fullest. Sadie had been too shocked during those first few days really to take in all that was happening, but when she thought back on it she was awed by how well the Kimballs had handled the whole affair. Molly had taken charge. She had rallied to Roger's side, encouraged him to step down, and had received the Greys graciously. She had made arrangements for Roger to return to Colorado with several of the best specialists in the country. If he was to recuperate, she insisted, he should do it in his beloved mountains. Sadie sensed that the Kimballs felt almost relieved leaving Washington, the White House, the Presidency. Their open sense of relief, especially Molly's, filled Sadie with dread. She wanted to ask Molly a million questions, but the time did not seem right.

It didn't matter so much in the beginning because they were literally in mourning after the Kimballs left. It was decided that the smartest and most tasteful thing the Greys could do would be move quietly into the White House and for Rosey to take over quickly and firmly. There would be no social events for at least three months, and certainly Sadie would not talk to the press about anything. They would go to a few political events which had been on Kimball's schedule and which they could not avoid. They would whisk in and out as unobtrusively as possible. No splash, no fanfare, no parties. The image had to be one of a serious President leading the country with a strong hand under the most trying of circumstances.

It was not until the end of June that it was deemed acceptable for the Greys to entertain. A state visit by the President of Brazil had been long scheduled and it was decided that the Greys should go ahead with it. That meant it was time for Sadie to rally. Thank God she had Tilda as her social secretary. Tilda was already versed in Washington protocol. She could relax on that score. But Nan Tyler had declined to make the move, choosing to go into private life. Nan had never quite recovered from Sadie's abortion interview. So she had to choose a press secretary—not an easy task; there was too much information coming out of the White House on the First Lady's side to avoid it. The only two women journalists she knew at all were Sonny Sterling and Jenny Stern, who had made a campaign trip with her to Savannah earlier. Even if she had wanted Sterling, which she most certainly did not, she knew it would be completely inappropriate given her relationship with Roger Kimball.

Jenny Stern was another story. Plain, cozy, sensible Jenny was well liked by her colleagues. Jenny would have the effect of deflecting animosity or hostility that might be directed toward Sadie. The fact that Jenny and Allison were close friends would not pose a problem. Sadie liked and trusted Jenny, and it was obvious from a piece Jenny had written after their trip to Savannah the previous fall that she felt the same. Jenny would be able to sell her product well.

Rosey, however, was hesitant.

"She's Jewish, isn't she?"

"So what?" Sadie was furious.

"So. . . . Nothing. I was just asking."

"For God's sake, Rosey. One of your most trusted advisers is Jewish—Howard Heinrich. Jesus Christ, everybody's Jewish. What's the matter with you?"

"I just thought the First Lady's press secretary should reflect the First Lady."

"Rosewell, you have spent the last two years telling me my image was rotten. Jenny Stern is the perfect person to correct that. Now you're telling me she should reflect my image. I wish you'd make up your mind."

She was surprised to hear herself talk that way. The strain of the past two months had really taken its toll. She had gotten little or no support from Rosey, and now he was criticizing her first proposal, which she believed to be first-rate.

Rosey looked stunned. She never spoke to him that way. They stared at each other for a few minutes; then he put his hand over his forehead and almost slumped down in the chair in the bedroom.

"This hasn't been easy for me either, you know," he said finally, quietly.

She wasn't ready to give in.

"You're as happy as a pig in shit, Rosewell Grey. You have wanted to be President of the United States all your life and now you've got it. Oh, I know it wasn't the way you wanted to get it. You'll have that chance in a year or so. But *I never* wanted it. I never wanted to be First Lady. And what I really don't want is to be put down at every turn by my husband for not being perfect. You're going to get plenty of criticism. You need my support, and you've got it. But I need yours just as much. Maybe more. You'd better understand that."

It was unusual for either of them to speak to the other with so much hostility or so much honesty. They were silent again for a while.

"We can't do it, Rosey," she said finally, "unless we are a team. We need each other now. At least, *I* can't do it." She could feel the tears burning. There was no use even trying to stop them. She had been crying so much lately she was used to it. She was carrying around Kleenex in her pockets, and she reached unconsciously for one and blew her nose.

Rosey's face softened. He got up from where he was sitting and came over to her. She was still standing. He put his arms around her and rocked her slowly in his arms. They stood there and rocked each other back and forth for several minutes without saying a word.

"You're right, darlin'. I apologize. I love you. I've been so preoccupied that I hadn't really focused on how rough it must be on you. Forgive me. From now on we'll be a team."

She had never felt closer to Rosey than she did at that moment, nor would she ever feel as close to him again.

The following week she hired Jenny Stern.

Jenny had been working for Sadie for only two weeks. Already Sadie felt extremely close to her. Jenny made her feel secure. She was a great cheerleader, a wonderful adviser and confidante, a terrific booster. By June the two were practically inseparable. Sadie kept apologizing for hanging on too much, but she needed Jenny's physical presence almost as much as she needed her emotional and psychological support. Naturally, Rosey had plunged back into his work without giving her a second thought. Nor did he ever mention Jenny again. He seemed relieved that Jenny had taken some of the pressure off him.

Jenny had also organized Sadie's life logistically. Sadie hadn't even decided where she wanted to work. Jenny had taken her on a tour the first day she came. It had cheered Sadie tremendously. They had chosen Sadie's office, Jenny's office, and Sadie's small study in the family quarters.

Sadie had taken the office in the East Wing that had been used by Molly Kimball's chief of staff. It was relatively small, but there was room for a sofa and several chairs, and it faced the South Lawn with a view of the garden.

"You've got to start out by making people think you are serious and not some fluff-head who cares only about clothes and parties," Jenny had said firmly. "If you don't have an office it will look as if you're not involved."

"Even if I didn't have any projects," said Sadie, "I would insist on an office. It gives me someplace to go. If I don't have anything to do I'll just go over to my office, close the door, and read fashion magazines."

Jenny winced. "Oh, God, please don't say things like that out loud! That's the kind of thing that shows up in the 'Backstairs at the White House' kind of books."

"But I only said it to *you*," Sadie protested.

"Yes, but I might be the one to write it."

Sadie looked startled for a moment before she burst out laughing.

"I'm not kidding," said Jenny. "Don't assume that anybody can really be trusted. There will always be someone who feels rejected or shortchanged or just plain resentful that you are First Lady and they aren't. Nothing you say or do can be considered private."

"I suppose you're going to tell me that my bathroom is being monitored."

"Well, if I were you I wouldn't take my clothes off before I got into the tub," said Jenny.

Sadie burst out laughing. "What the hell—maybe I should just get it over with and parade nude down Pennsylvania Avenue on a horse."

"Before this is over you'll feel as if you had."

"Thanks a lot, Jenny. You're a real help."

"I'm just trying to prepare you for the worst. If it doesn't happen, you'll be pleasantly surprised. Now, what about your projects?"

"The same. Historic preservation and Planned Parenthood."

"With an emphasis on historic preservation."

"Jenny, I just want to say one thing. I really care about Planned Parenthood. And I am willing to stand up for what I believe in. If it proves difficult for Rosey, then we will just have to deal with it. He doesn't hesitate to ask me to support him in what he believes. If he really believes that the thing I care the most about is too costly for his career, then he can divorce me. I will not give up this issue for him or anybody else. Okay?"

"That's a pretty strong statement."

"That's because I feel strongly about it. Jesus, Jenny, it's not exactly as if I walk around wearing a T-shirt that says 'Kill Babies.' But I do believe in the right to terminate a pregnancy and I will say so publicly."

"These things get pretty specific. Do you believe in it up to the ninth month, and if so, why is that not murder? I'm playing devil's advocate here, you understand."

"I think there should be a cutoff. I think the cutoff should be as long as it takes to get an amniocentesis and diagnosis, which is about five months. Certainly, people should not be allowed to abort after then. That's what I believe."

"Already you're getting into a hornets' nest. But don't worry, I'm not going to let you near the press."

"It's that bad, huh?"

"Let's just say it falls into the Who Needs It? category."

"Frankly, Jenny, if I never see another reporter again it's fine with me."

"What about me?"

"You're not a reporter anymore, remember?"

"That's right—I keep forgetting. I'm a flack now."

"Does that bother you?" Sadie was surprised.

"You want the truth? It does, a little bit. I always thought good reporters didn't do anything else. I feel as if I've sold out on some level. Oh, everybody's been really great about it. But I feel a little uneasy. I guess I always will. But the fact is I wasn't going anywhere much at *The Daily*. I was a reporter on the national staff, I suspect, because I was a woman. I didn't like to admit that to myself. When you asked me to take this job I looked around and thought, Is this what I want to be doing when I'm sixty, slogging away, getting all the shit assignments? The answer is no. It looked like a way out. But you don't get something for nothing. I had to sacrifice my idealistic view of myself as unbuyable."

She could see that Sadie was disturbed by what she was saying.

"Listen," said Jenny, "it has nothing to do with you. You must understand that. This is just about my own inner struggle. I struggled for ten seconds and then accepted the job. It's a great job. And it will put me on the map. When I leave I'll write a best-seller about all the inside dirt at the White House and get a lucrative job as a Washington consultant, have a big office, a staff, maybe a driver. I'll get invited everywhere, I won't have to work really hard, and I'll get a great lecture fee. So you can see the pros outweighed the cons. Rather heavily."

"Just as long as you're not unhappy."

"Believe me, it will give me enormous pleasure to mete out the crumbs of information to the vultures. Not to mention remaking your image."

"What do you mean, remaking my image?"

"I intend to—"

"I know. You intend to turn me from a frivolous blabbermouth into a serious person."

"Well, I would hardly use those words to describe the First Lady."

"Worse have been used, I'm sure."

"Give them time."

Later that week Sadie and Jenny and Tilda met to discuss the first White House party, to be held in July. Sadie couldn't shake her depression. When Rosey finally did appear in the evenings, he was full of White House business. It was impossible, and she knew it could only get worse. She had participated in a few things which Jenny had suggested—chairing a benefit for Children's Hospital, a tea for the American family who had just returned from Russia on a goodwill tour, a meeting sponsored by Amnesty International for Mothers of the Missing in Latin America. She had continued work in a rather desultory fashion on the National Trust for Historic Preservation, and she had turned down a Planned Parenthood request to do television messages. Nothing she did really inspired her, and she was more wary, more afraid of doing anything that might attract controversy.

There were days when she didn't feel like getting dressed, and she would keep a wrapper on most of the morning until Jenny literally came to fetch her and take her down to her office. Some afternoons she slept for several hours and woke up feeling tired.

Lorraine was her lifeline. Lorraine called her every day that she didn't call Lorraine. She didn't dare tell Lorraine how depressed she was, but Lorraine could hear it in her voice.

"Now, darling," she had said one day, "you must pull out of it."

"Out of what?"

"I'm not exactly a mind reader, but I've never heard anyone sound as listless as you do. Your voice is a giveaway. If you want to pretend you're deliriously happy, you'll have to make a better go of disguising your voice."

"Is it that obvious?"

"I'm afraid it is, dearie."

"It's just that I feel so trapped. Is that an awful thing to say? I know I should be thrilled to death about all of this, but I can't help feeling like Rapunzel."

"You know most First Ladies feel that way at some point, don't you? I've known a few of them, or have been close to friends of theirs. It's natural. And particularly now that security is so tight after all the assassination attempts."

Sadie was taken aback by that. How strange that she hadn't even given that a thought. Even with all the security she hadn't thought about the assassination attempts. Perhaps because she and Rosey hardly went anywhere.

"Does it get better?" She realized as she had said it how pathetic she sounded.

"Of course it does, but it won't get better for you if you allow yourself to mope around. You've got to get a hold of yourself, Sadie. You are the First Lady of this country now." There was a stern quality in her voice which Sadie had never heard.

"Worse things have happened to people. You have to get involved in something, get your mind off yourself and onto some project. Plan a party. Even if you can't give one right away, there must be something on the books coming up. It's none too soon to get to work on that right now. You're lucky that you've got some time so you can get it right, do it perfectly and not make any mistakes. Now, what's on the agenda—what's coming up you can really sink your teeth into, ol' girl?"

"There is Brazil coming up," Sadie had said a bit meekly. Lorraine had never talked to her like that before. She knew she was right. She really had needed somebody to shake her, and Lorraine had said just the right thing.

"Brazil. Marvelous. The new President and his wife are so attractive. And the country has so much style. Yet our relations with them are important and serious. We have invested heavily in Brazil. You couldn't be luckier. Oh," she sighed, "how I envy you! There's nothing in the world that perks me up more than planning a party. And here you are in the White House, with all that means at your disposal, able to plan the perfect party and know that everyone will come. What bliss! The more I think of it the more annoyed I am that you have the nerve to be depressed. Now, come on and snap out of it. The country . . . no, the world is waiting for Sadie Grey to put her social stamp on America."

"Oh, God," said Sadie.

"Courage, ma chère," whispered Lorraine, and said goodbye.

Sadie had called the party meeting for the day after her talk with Lorraine. She asked Jenny and Tilda to come to her office at ten thirty. She really did love her office. She couldn't wait to do something with it. She would have to get rid of that hideous government furniture. The old green sofa had rubber cushions that sent the unsuspecting occupant bouncing as if she had sat on a trampoline. She was a fanatic about down-filled everything. She would paint the walls a soft terra cotta. It would be feminine but still look like an office. She would resist flowered chintzes and put in some sort of wonderful ticking stripe on the furniture, and maybe she could get away with fringe and a smart leopard chintz just on the pillows. But here she was decorating again. That was silly. This was a solemn party-planning meeting.

Sadie never quite knew what to wear to her office. It was only one floor and one corridor away from the family quarters, in the same house. She really wanted to wear pants, since she wasn't going out, but somehow it wasn't seemly for the First Lady to wear pants to work. She was afraid people wouldn't think she was serious about working if she came in pants.

This day she chose a pale blue-green cotton dress with a small collar, puffy sleeves to the elbow, and a cummerbund sash. She wore her old standby Chanel shoes and pearl earrings. Very businesslike. It was only the beginning of June, but it was already very hot in Washington and the humidity had begun to settle in.

She arrived at the office first. She decided to walk down the hall to say good morning to those working in the East Wing's office, the calligraphers, the special projects office and the social and press offices. Everyone stood awkwardly and smiled at her.

"Oh, please," Sadie admonished, "please sit down. Don't let me disrupt your work."

She realized that these people were not used to having a First

Lady in the business side of the West Wing. Molly Kimball had never had an office there, and before Molly, the First Lady for eight years had been a clotheshorse who had redone her office in the family quarters into a spa. It would take some time to change all that, create a more serious image, she realized, and she wasn't exactly the feminists' dream of what a First Lady should be. In fact, she didn't know what a First Lady should be.

She went back to her office, closed the door, and sat at her desk. Her back was to the window, but she could see the sun pouring in and hear the magnolia trees brush against the window in response to a merciful breeze across the Ellipse. There was a rather annoying sound which she had been told was excavation work for a bomb shelter underneath the White House basement, and she could hear the ring of the phones from the military office next door. How odd that the office would be on this side of the White House and not on the other. In fact, the White House was odd. One expected everything to be perfect, yet it was really like living in a great big old Southern plantation house. Things went wrong and people were kind of sleepy and slow and various members of the staff had fights and disagreements, and the President and his wife were more or less the patriarch and the matriarch of this great big old family. In that sense it made her feel right at home. It really did remind her of Horace Hall, her family's plantation in Adabelle, Georgia, for which she was named.

Why hadn't she thought of that before? Even though she had been so depressed, she couldn't get over what an odd feeling she had of having lived here before. Now she knew what it was, and she was able to really relax for the first time in the few months that she had been living in the White House. From now on when she got upset or lonely or felt trapped she would just pretend she was at Horace Hall. She knew that would work. And suddenly she knew that she was going to be a good First Lady and that this was going to be an exciting few years.

Tilda and Jenny arrived at ten thirty sharp, surprised to see Sadie sitting at her desk.

"We're supposed to arrive first," said Tilda. "That's protocol.

How can I hold my head up as social secretary if I let the First Lady arrive before I do?"

"You'll learn," said Sadie. She laughed.

Tilda, as usual, was dressed to the teeth. Sadie marveled at how Tilda, after all these years, still managed to look like the consummate Smithie. It was as though she had stepped out of a time capsule, sent twenty-some years before into the modern age. Tilda's blond hair (graying discreetly) was pulled back in a neat shoulder-length pageboy held back with a black velvet ribbon. She wore a perfect little black-and-white short-sleeved silk dress with pearls. She had on white stockings and little low-heeled black-and-white spectators. The black-and-white enamel hoop earrings she would take off when she was on the phone, and she often wore them on her fingers so as not to lose them. Tilda had an upturned nose, pretty blue eyes, high cheekbones, a nice smile, and not one ounce of sex appeal. It had been bred out of her. She also had a sense of humor, but it was limited to things she understood: protocol, manners, social behavior. Sadie had complete faith in Tilda's judgment on these matters, in the same way she had total faith in Jenny's instincts about the press and publicity.

Jenny was hopeless on social matters, and Tilda was even worse about the press. Tilda thought journalists were social inferiors who should be jailed for spelling names wrong or, even better, censored. She was less than enthusiastic about Sadie's idea of hiring a reporter to be her press secretary and had been wary of Jenny at first, but Jenny was such an old shoe that she had managed to win Tilda over almost immediately. What Tilda could not put out of her mind was the way Jenny dressed. The clothes that did fit were baggy, drab, without any style and not very well made. She didn't wear tacky clothes. They just weren't good clothes. And the shoes were always just a little run-down at the heels. Tilda's shoes all looked like patent leather, even the ones that weren't. Tilda's makeup was always perfect. Just a touch of blush, pale lip gloss, the tiniest hint of pale blue eye shadow. Jenny, if she did wear eye makeup, always botched it. Her nose was perpetually shiny, and she managed to eat her lipstick off five minutes after she had put it on.

Jenny's idea of a party was to have a professional exchange. It was an opportunity to work. Her interest did not extend to tablecloths, flowers, and entertainment. Her eyes tended to glaze over when a discussion of china and silverware came up. She secretly thought the idea of having a social secretary was a serious waste of personnel and that it damaged her careful image of a serious person. She was slightly disdainful of what Tilda did for a living, not to mention suspicious of her blond, blue-eyed demeanor, her lockjaw accent, and all that connoted.

It amused Sadie this morning to see the two of them, her own little odd couple, looking at each other as if they had arrived from different planets.

"I have a plan," said Sadie. "I have decided that you two should change jobs for a while. It would be an exercise in understanding the other's responsibilities. A kind of hands-across-the-sea exchange program."

"What?" asked Tilda meekly.

"I think that would be a great idea. Then you would both be ambidextrous, as it were," said Sadie. "In fact, I think it would probably be a good idea to start with this party."

They just sat there staring at her.

"Jenny, why don't you come up with a table-decoration scheme for me—colors, cloths, flowers, china, silver—and don't forget the menu and the wines. Tilda, you write the press release, and be sure to meet with the reporters sometime this week for a briefing. Meeting adjourned."

The two of them sat there with their mouths open for at least a minute.

"How could I possibly have hired such silly asses?" said Sadie finally. "And you can close your mouths now, gals. If you can't figure out when somebody is putting you on, what good are you going to be to me?"

"She's only joking," said Jenny sheepishly.

"I only wanted both of you to realize how demanding and important both of your jobs are. I think I've got the best press secretary and the best social secretary I could have. And together we're going to make a good team. All right, team, let's get on with it. Tilda, why don't you start first. We'll go over details. But Jenny, you're going to have to fill in the details to the press. And you must understand, even though this kind of thing may seem frivolous to you, that international relations are at stake. A tacky table decoration would be noticed by the wife of the Brazilian President, who would point out to her husband that he had been demeaned by the President of the United States. I only wish I were kidding."

Tilda took out her sheaf of notes—already she had sheaves of notes. On top was a white mimeographed paper with THE WHITE HOUSE on top, WASHINGTON underneath. Printed in the left column was OFFICIAL DINNER IN HONOR OF: and DATE OF DINNER: And then lists of arrangements such as tablecloths and napkins, flowers, china, glassware, candlesticks, menu, and music. There were blanks for entertainment and for the press.

She took out her pencil and began going down the list. "Now," she said, "I thought we should eat inside. The weather has been so horrible and humid already."

"We certainly don't want the dignitaries sweating into their soup," said Jenny.

"What a lovely image," said Tilda.

"It has happened, I'm sorry to say," said Sadie. "Last summer at the French Embassy they served dinner out of doors. It was in early July, and it was incredibly hot. The poor Ridgewell's waiters were in those heavy black dinner jackets. They looked like they were about to die, and they were perspiring miserably. We had watercress soup to begin with. I actually saw a waiter, much to the horror of the Ambassador's wife, drip into the soup. I didn't eat a bite, and neither did she . . . I think we should eat inside. But what about the entertainment outside afterwards? Should we risk it?"

"I think so, but we'll get to that in a minute. I would suggest twelve round tables of ten."

"I think I would rather have smaller tables—say, of eight each. I know it hasn't been done before, but with eight you can have a group conversation. One of the problems with these White House dinners is that people don't ever really get to meet or talk to very many people. I want to try to make it as informal as it is possible to feel in the White House."

"I would suggest," said Tilda, "that we work in maybe forty or so after dinner for coffee, liqueurs, and after-dinner dancing."

"Won't they be insulted not to be asked for dinner?" asked Jenny.

"Nobody is ever insulted to be asked to the White House," said Tilda matter-of-factly.

"I absolutely refuse to have anybody come after dinner," said

Sadie. "Either they're good enough to come to dinner or not. It is a terrible bore to get all dressed up in black tie and wait around until ten thirty or eleven to come to the White House. I've always hated having hordes of people piling in after dinner not knowing anyone. It always breaks up the party."

Tilda sniffed, rebuffed.

"If that's what you want . . ." she said finally.

"Come on, Tilda," said Sadie, "you know you agree with me."

Tilda smiled. "I suppose you're right. But it will mean having to have more parties to work all the B- or C-list types in."

"I'll worry about that tomorrow," said Sadie. "Now what about the tent? Can we put a tent on the South Lawn?"

"That's exactly what I propose," said Tilda.

"We can have it all white so it will look cool. We can have white lanterns and white cloths on small tables, like a cabaret, with white flowers. It will look as if everything is floating. People can spill out on the balcony with their champagne glasses after dinner and then just float down to the tent. We can have tiny little bee lights in the greenery to light it. Then we could have a small fountain in the back of the tent to make it seem cooler. Oh, God, I love it."

"Maybe you should be the social secretary," said Tilda.

"Not a bad idea," said Sadie. "You can be the First Lady. You'd probably be a lot better at it than I am. At least you'd be able to keep your mouth shut. She'd be a lot easier to handle— right, Jenny?"

"Ah, yes, but where would be the challenge?" said Jenny, laughing, pleased with her diplomatic response.

"Getting back to the dinner," said Tilda. "What about the dinner itself?"

"I think we should just carry through with the white. Have white cloths, white china, white flowers, everything."

"Won't it look too much like a wedding?" asked Jenny.

"I'll wear a floating green chiffon, instead of white," said Sadie.

"Ah, the mother of the bride," said Jenny.

"I'm too young for that, bitch."

Tilda looked up, surprised.

"Just a Southern term of endearment," said Sadie. "But I guess I'm not allowed to talk that way anymore."

"Just remember what I told you," said Jenny. "Only if you want to read about it later."

"Who would tell?" asked Tilda.

"Well, *you* might, in your White House memoirs," said Jenny.

"I would never think of doing anything like that," said Tilda, genuinely shocked.

Sadie guessed Jenny had touched a nerve.

"I know you wouldn't," said Sadie. "It's just that Jenny and I were joking about it the other day and she told me that nothing was safe in the White House and I should watch everything I say, no matter to whom."

"I certainly go along with that," said Tilda.

"What about the entertainment, Tilda? I have always hated the way the entertainment broke up parties at the White House. Everyone comes out of dinner all full of wine and glowing from a good meal and sometimes, though rarely, a good conversation and then they are dragged into the cold East Room and made to sit on hard-backed chairs if they're lucky enough to get one. Then it's half an hour until the President and his guest come in, and then the entertainment is often dreary, with no drinks. By the time that's over, everybody is catatonic. The well-kept secret of White House dinners is that they are usually excruciatingly boring."

"We're on the same wavelength," said Tilda. "We'll definitely have a cabaret on the South Lawn, with some sort of Brazilian singer. We'll have dancing, and little tables. That way I can ask the President of Brazil and his wife to sit down so they can have somewhere to go instead of standing around. That way we can discreetly delegate two other couples at a time to come over and chat with them. Usually at these things nobody gets to meet the guests of honor and they don't get to meet anybody else. It will tend to cut down on the reporters swarming around too."

"What about food?" asked Jenny.

"Tilda, why don't you ask the chef to propose a menu and we can let him guide us. Give him a little rein and see what he does. Although it would be great to have some sort of light fish mousse, a cold soup, and maybe a cold entrée—veal or something."

"I've called the protocol office at State," said Tilda. "In fact, I've been over there several times. They say the President of Brazil has no allergies or diet restrictions, so we're okay on that.

I suppose that it's none of my business but the President has yet to appoint a chief of protocol."

"I'll talk to Rosey about it. The last woman only cared about where she and her husband were seated at dinners. I heard her tell the King of Norway that they were planning to vacation there and would love to look him up."

"It'll be hard to fill," said Tilda. "It's got to be the worst job in Washington."

"Now what about the guest list?" asked Sadie. "How are we going to decide who to invite? I don't want a lot of famous people standing in corners staring at each other."

"It's not that hard, really," said Tilda. "The hard part we let the office of protocol do. They review the seating. They'll send suggestions over. Naturally I've already got a ten-page sheet of suggestions from them. We'll get a list from the Brazilians. We'll pick several from Congress, the Foreign Relations committees, and then: the arts, musicians, painters, a university president, a scientist, a black, a Hispanic leader, a member of the Joint Chiefs, several corporation presidents, a publisher, and a few reporters. And"—she laughed—"if there's any room left, some friends of yours. I want to warn you that your husband's staff will have some very strong suggestions of particular fund-raisers and friends of theirs. You'll be surprised how many favors we will be asked to do."

"Not at this one, Tilda," said Sadie. "This is my baby. We can start working those others in for the next ones. But I want this party to be just right. I'm not going to have some tobacco-chewing slob from Oklahoma just because somebody on my husband's staff owes him a favor. Is that clear? I want you to be tough about this."

Sadie hadn't said so, but they knew she was talking about Everett Dubois.

"Lorraine Hadley has to be invited. Also, I would like Desmond Shaw on the list. He has been enormously helpful to me. But I suppose he falls into the category of the press. Jenny, we'll get to them in a minute. I have a feeling that will be the hardest part."

"The press, you'll soon learn, is always the hardest part about everything," Jenny said, smiling.

"I think I already have."

"The main thing you have got to decide is how involved you

want the press in the dinner. There are a number of ways to do this."

"The one thing I always hated at the Kimballs' dinners was the way the press came in after dinner and just hung around bombarding the President and his guest of honor with questions," said Sadie.

"Believe me," said Jenny, "the press hates it worse than you do."

"Well, what can we do about it?" asked Sadie.

"Oh, God, I wish there were an easy answer," said Jenny. "But you've got to keep the press behind ropes when the First Family and the guest of honor come down from the family quarters.

"I do think we ought to let the print journalists into the East Room for the receiving line so they can talk to them then. It gives the reporters a head start on their stories, they can meet earlier deadlines, and they aren't so desperate after dinner."

"Brilliant thinking, Jenny," Sadie said. "Also, the guests will be more sober."

"Then you've got all those TV cameras, and they could decapitate any guest who made a wrong move. Most of them will leave after the photo opportunity. But it would be utter chaos without barriers. And we do let them in after dinner for the toasts, but still behind barriers. There's no other way."

"What about during dinner?" asked Sadie.

"I think you've got to do what our predecessors have already done. Invite several journalists as guests. I think we ought to try to fit more in. I'm not saying they can be bought, but for most of them it's a big thrill and it just creates a good atmosphere. Some will accept an invitation and do a hatchet job to prove they haven't been bought. There's nothing you can do about them. Des, by the way," said Jenny to Sadie, "falls into that category."

"I suppose that means that Allison Sterling does too," said Sadie.

"I suppose so. Though she's a little shell-shocked at the moment. Breaking up with Des and then Kimball leaving. She's not really her old self."

"Is she working on something particular at the moment?" asked Sadie, trying not to sound too interested.

"As a matter of fact, she's about to be reassigned to the White House. It was her editor's idea. They felt it would be like falling off a horse. The quicker you get back on, the easier it would be to ride again. Sonny wasn't too crazy about the idea at first. But she was the best White House correspondent *The Daily* ever had. Now she can go back to covering without any conflict."

"That's what worries me," said Sadie.

"Why should that worry you?"

"I don't think she likes me very much."

"That's ridiculous. Look at that great piece she did on your husband when he was Vice President."

"I'm not talking about Rosey. I'm talking about me."

"She's never given me any reason to think so," said Jenny. "And I'm her closest friend."

"Won't she try to pump you?" asked Tilda, her voice darkening with suspicion.

"She's a professional and she knows I'm one too," said Jenny. "She would certainly ask me questions relating to any story she was trying to do, but she would never pry for personal details. She would work the rest of the staff before she would come to me on that. She would never compromise me."

"You reporters have such odd rules," said Tilda. "It's all so arcane and tribal. I just don't understand it and I wonder if I ever will."

"It's really very simple," said Jenny. "There's only one thing to understand. A reporter is always a reporter first. That's it. That's all you have to know."

"Ugh," said Tilda, shrugging. "I just don't know how people can live that way. How could you ever trust your friends?"

"You just trust them a different way," said Jenny. "You trust them to be as good a professional as they are a good friend. You trust them to do what they have to do. You trust them to be honest and straight. You don't trust them to lie or cover up for you. If you're in public life you don't trust them to protect you. You trust them to protect the First Amendment."

"Journalists must live in a state of conflict, then?" asked Sadie, who had been silent for a while.

"Of course," said Jenny, looking surprised to hear something so obvious said aloud.

There was another silence.

Tilda excused herself for a moment to confer with the calligraphers. Sadie wondered if Jenny would mention Des or Allison in the context of trust. She had never forgotten her conversation with Des on the subject. She knew she couldn't ask directly about Allison.

"Tell me," Sadie said finally, "what was it like being a woman on the national staff at *The Daily*? Did you feel that you had to work harder than the men?"

"What brought that up?" Jenny laughed.

"Well, I'm just curious about what it must have been like for a woman on a big-city paper. Did you have to fight for stories? Was there more competition between the women than between you and the men?"

Sadie thought she had slipped that in neatly.

"I guess I just took it for granted and I didn't think about it that much. We all fought for stories, but I don't think I had to fight harder than the others. There were only four women, and two were older and had been around for a long time. The only other woman was Allison. I didn't have any problems with Allison. She's a good friend. Allison had problems. Some of the men were jealous of her, and a few editors gave her a hard time."

"I don't really know her very well," said Sadie. "There was that birthday party..."

"I remember," said Jenny.

"Of course, she's an attractive woman," said Sadie after a pause. "It probably didn't help that she was the President's goddaughter."

"No. This has been a difficult time for Allison."

Jenny was making it easy. They were both playing.

"That's right. I heard that when she and Des Shaw broke up —wasn't it over a story or something?"

Jenny looked at her quizzically. "Well," she said after some hesitation, "it was a little more complicated than that. Allison didn't have any choice, really."

Obviously Jenny thought she knew more about the whole business than she did.

"I don't know, though," said Sadie. "I think it would be awfully hard to do what she did, considering the risks. I mean, I wonder if she thinks now that it was worth it."

Jenny was still trying to figure out where Sadie was going.

"I was brought up to believe that a woman's role is to support her man, to stand by him," said Sadie. "One's perspective must be very different in your profession."

"Honestly, I don't know whether I would have had the courage to do what Allison did either," said Jenny, drawn in by the discussion. "Most of the women I know, professional women, admired Allison tremendously, but I don't think many of them would have done it. The problem was that it was so public. I mean Des was publicly humiliated. Allison insists that if things had been the other way around Des would have done it to her, and I know in my heart that she's right, but still . . . a good man is hard to find. And don't I know it."

"Do you—do you think these things are irrevocable?" asked Sadie.

"I think it's over. I don't think that he will get over being shown up in front of his colleagues that way. Desmond Shaw is a male chauvinist pig. Just because he was living with one of the superwomen of Washington doesn't mean a thing. Allison put up with a lot. Nobody knows. In fact, nobody really knows Allison except for Des and me and a very few other people."

Tilda reappeared and put an end to their conversation.

"So what would you like to do about Allison Sterling at this party?" asked Tilda, picking up her pad and resuming the guest list.

"I would like not to invite her."

"Fine."

She didn't look at Jenny.

"What about serving the covering press some champagne and hors d'oeuvres during the dinner so they will be in a jollier mood?" asked Sadie.

"It's six of one, half a dozen of the other," said Jenny. "It really doesn't matter. What you have to understand is that many of the people who cover the distaff side of the White House are old hacks who couldn't write their way out of a paper bag. They depend on the largess of the White House staff for little tidbits so they can keep their little columns. Serving them champagne and food is not going to make them write any more favorably than they do. The winners, the good reporters, probably wouldn't drink anyway while they're working, and they might feel we were trying to buy them off."

"So, should we do it or not?"

"Sure—why not?"

"Okay," said Sadie, laughing, "so how do we handle the mob scene after dinner when the reporters are let in?"

"As long as one reporter is near the President or head of state, every other reporter will be there too so they won't miss something or get beaten out," said Jenny. "What I would like to do, immediately after dinner, before the entertainment, is to take the President and guest of honor into the Red Room and tell the reporters they can talk to them for a few minutes. Then after that they leave them alone."

"Sounds good to me," said Sadie. "Let's try it."

"Now all I have to worry about is what to wear and what to do with my damn hair," said Sadie. "I have discovered the single most important question and problem that any First Lady must deal with. It's the greatest potential crisis, the make-or-break issue of the East Wing."

"What's that?"

"Hair," said Sadie.

Sadie hadn't been this nervous since the day she was married. Nor would she ever be more on display than she would be this evening. Her palms were sweating. Not just perspiring. They were dripping. She clenched another Kleenex to blot them. How in God's name would she ever be able to shake anybody's hand? What if it got into the gossip columns? The First Lady has sweaty palms. Oh, God. Surely there must be something more highminded to think about than sweaty palms on the night of her first White House party. Perhaps she was focusing on her sweaty palms because it was something concrete to worry about instead of worrying about the unknown disaster that was waiting out there to happen.

She had spent the afternoon tasting food in the kitchen, downstairs in the basement. Chef Stengel had outdone himself with a beautiful cool pastel meal. She had walked over to the White House florist's, just through the basement hallway, and worked hard with Willy on the table arrangements. She had inspected the tables, the china, the tent out on the lawn—everything.

Her dress had been brought down from New York by her own designer and fitted the day before. It was one of the prettiest dresses she had ever seen. It was very pale green chiffon, slim, with a single sleeveless shoulder, the chiffon draped down almost to her elbow, the other arm and shoulder bare. She wore no jewelry except for tiny pearl drop earrings and a pearl-and-diamond bracelet that had belonged to Rosey's grandmother.

Her hair had been given a softer-than-usual set, and she was letting it grow. Ivan had agreed that she would look better with her hair a little longer, framing her face. She had never believed she would be spending so much time with her hairdresser. She and Ivan had always been friendly, but now she might as well be sleeping with him. Her entire schedule and her entire life revolved around her goddamned head. At least Ivan was married with two children, was discreet, sweet, and unbitchy. That made it easier, particularly for the publicity she knew was to come.

Sadie was a little nervous about having invited Desmond Shaw. He was really not a crucial name on the press list. He had never done much for Rosey. But even though she had had almost no contact with him since their encounter, she sensed that he was a friend, a silent ally, and she thought his presence would make her feel more secure. That was what she allowed herself to think when she invited him. Everett and the press secretary had sent over a list of press they thought ought to be invited and his name had not been on it. As Everett explained it, they wanted to "pay off some of the boys who have kissed a little ass" and to ensure that they would continue. Sadie had added Shaw's name, trying to be casual. After all, the *Weekly* Bureau Chief was not a bad friend to make. Nobody really gave her a hard time, and Tilda was delighted because she needed an extra man. Jenny hadn't said a word. She had just looked at Sadie when Sadie suggested it.

Allison Sterling's name was on the list because Rosey had put it there. She had been through so much. They had ridden to the White House together when Roger Kimball collapsed. She had done a fine story on him. She was a nice person. She had just been reassigned to the White House. He had a lot of convincing arguments. Sadie was at a loss. She knew one thing. She would be damned if Sterling was going to be a guest. There was no way. She would have to think of something. She did.

She had countered that it would be bad for Allison to come for all the same reasons Rosey had listed. Her problem had been that she was seen as too close to the White House. If she was invited she couldn't very well refuse gracefully. It would be doing her a favor to let her come as a reporter to cover it if she wanted, to be a professional at the White House again, something she hadn't been for two years. Rosey bought it. Again, Jenny had just looked at her as she got her way.

Ivan was finishing her hair and exclaiming about how beautiful she looked. She told him to knock off the compliments, that she didn't even have her makeup on yet. He laughed. He had sneaked in his makeup lady from the salon, someone Sadie had used for a few formal occasions before and who knew how to do a good, subtle job, something she was incapable of doing herself. She hoped the press wouldn't find out. Jenny had said they would have to admit it if anybody asked, but so far nobody had.

When she had finished, she pulled her robe tightly around her and slipped back across the hall, through the family sitting area in the long hall, to their bedroom. She winced once more at the red-and-yellow flowered print the Kimballs had left. She was going to have to redecorate everything, and the awful part was that Molly had done some things and Molly's predecessor had left the place horribly overdecorated. They would have to use Rosey's money again, too. Raising money from private friends just caused too much trouble. As soon as the summer was over she was determined to do it.

When she got back to the bedroom, Rosey was standing in front of the full-length mirror tying his bow tie. He turned to her and smiled.

"You'd better hurry, sugar; the Da Silveras will be here in a half-hour."

"Oh, are they coming tonight? I forgot," she drawled. "Shall I open a can of chili or should we go out?"

Rosey looked a little surprised for a moment as they both contemplated how impossible either of those suggestions was anymore in their lives.

Suddenly all the excitement and optimism she had begun to feel in the days leading up to the party vanished. She tried to hold the tears back from the mascara, but her eyes welled over and she stood in the middle of the room and watched the birds on the Chinese wallpaper blur into one. She kept waking up in the middle of the night imagining she was in one of those Alfred Hitchcock movies. That would have to go too. Oh, God, what the hell was she thinking about wallpaper for? She was desperate, that's what. She could focus on wallpaper. She could not allow herself to focus on several hundred guests, members of the press, the

Marine Band, and millions of people all over the world just waiting for her to fall on her face. That she could not deal with.
That's what she thought of when she didn't concentrate on her
sweaty palms or her wallpaper.

Rosey stood staring at her as he watched the black streaks run
down her cheeks. He looked stricken. Sadie watched his expression go from exasperation to anger to fear to sympathy. Finally he
walked over to her. He took her by the shoulders and pressed her
close to him. He didn't say anything for the longest time. Sadie
knew he didn't know what to say and was afraid of saying the
wrong thing.

"Help me, Rosey," she said. "You've got to help me. I can't
do it by myself. I've never been so terrified in my life. I need
you. I can't do it without you."

"I, uh, you'll be terrific, darlin'," he said. "I don't know what
you have to worry about. You're beautiful, you're gracious and
charming, you're intelligent. I've seen the tables and the tent. It
all looks just perfect. I've never seen it look prettier. You're a
wonderful hostess. What could you possibly be afraid of?"

"Rosey, aren't *you* afraid? Ever? I mean haven't you been
frightened? Tell me, please. Make me believe I'm not just a
hopeless mess."

She heard his voice speaking very softly and very carefully.
He led her over to their king-size bed and sat her down with
his arm around her. She decided that he was speaking to her
the way a policeman would talk to a nut who was about to
jump off a building or a crazy person who had just taken
twenty hostages.

"Of course I feel self-doubt too," he said slowly. "Everybody
does. I've been more scared these last few months than you'll
ever know. Afraid I wouldn't be up to the job, that I wouldn't be
able to handle it, that I would let the American people down.
That I would let you down."

That was an afterthought. She could tell. But it was a smart
one. It did make her feel better if he really had worried about
what she would think of the job he was doing.

He reached over and rubbed his thumb under her eye.

"I think you're going to need a touch-up, sugar," he said
with a gentle smile. "You've got a little mascara under your
eyes."

He loved her. There was that maddening combination of total

self-absorption—total ambition on the one hand, a dependency and neediness on the other—that drove her crazy. Every time she got fed up with his lack of concern for or interest in her he would turn around and need her, for God's sake. He needed her tonight, she suddenly knew. He needed her as much as she needed him. His coolness and calmness were just his manner. She had been so worried about herself that she hadn't even given that any consideration.

"Oh, wouldn't the ladies of the press love that," she giggled as she dabbed her nose, then under her eyes, with a Kleenex. "I can just see the story now. 'The First Lady, her face red and puffy from crying, her eyes smudged with mascara, carried on next to her husband...'"

"Sadie, don't get worked up."

"My darlin', I am already worked up. Now if you'll excuse me, I'm going to find my makeup lady to see if we can't repair some of the damage." She started out the bedroom door, then turned to face Rosey.

"I'll be fine. I promise. I just needed a little cry. Just think of all the actors and actresses who throw up before they go on stage and then give brilliant performances. Just watch." She turned and sashayed out of the room.

"That's my girl." Rosey laughed, and his face relaxed for the first time in days.

Sadie was just emerging from her touch-up, everything in place, her eyes dried, when the butler informed Rosey that the Da Silveras were leaving Blair House, across the street. They would arrive at the main entrance of the White House and be escorted up the stairs to the family quarters any moment. Rosey was standing in the middle of the family sitting area, twisting a glass of Perrier in his hands, his only sign of nervousness. He looked marvelously handsome as usual in his white dinner jacket, his hair graying perfectly at the temples. "Only WASPs gray at the temples the way your husband does," Desmond Shaw had once joked to her. He looked as if at any minute he would launch into a Fred Astaire routine and begin dancing on the ceiling.

"Promise you'll dance with me once this evening," she said. She was surprised that her lips were sticking to her teeth. And her palms were still wet. She'd heard of an old trick a famous movie star used of putting Vaseline on her teeth so her lips wouldn't stick, but the idea was so repulsive she couldn't bear to try it. She didn't know what to do about her hands. She'd practically gone through a box of Kleenex, wadding up the tissues one after another in her palms. She couldn't very well wipe her hands on her dress. That would be unseemly. She didn't, she was embarrassed to admit, even own a proper handkerchief. Her mother would die if she knew that.

Several members of the staff had arrived. The Da Silveras were on their way up in the elevator at that very moment. The two chiefs of protocol had gathered in the oval room along with the Da Silveras' doctor. Always an ominous sign. Rosey was moving to greet them. She had better pull herself together.

"Ah, Mrs. Grey," said President Da Silvera, after greeting Rosey, "you are even more beautiful than your pictures. Americans are lucky to have such a First Lady."

For some reason that surprised her. She wasn't really feeling very attractive. And even if he was a little corpulent, it made her feel better. Kiki Da Silvera was more attractive than her husband. Compared with him, she was tiny, and once past her fluttery hummingbird nature, she was rather pretty.

"Oh, Mrs. Grey," she said. "Tonio and I are so flattered that you would choose to have your first dinner for us. I must tell you, this is my first visit to the White House and I am so nervous. I wish I had your calm. You look like you have lived here all your life."

"Madame Da Silvera . . ." said Rosey.

"Kiki, please," she said.

"Kiki, you don't realize that you couldn't have said a nicer thing. Sadie had been a little worried about tonight."

"Worried?" The President of Brazil was laughing. "Poor Kiki has been so nervous she hasn't been able to eat for days."

They were both talking rapidly, in heavy accents, good but self-conscious English.

"I didn't know what to wear," said Kiki. "I brought three dresses for tonight. I tried each one on four or five times, modeling them for Tonio." She burst into a barrage of Portuguese, directed at her husband, who burst out laughing, then came over and hugged her reassuringly.

"She is saying that she shouldn't have worn this pink one; it is perhaps a little too bright. Mrs. Grey is so cool-looking in her pale green."

"I think it is too late to go back to Blair House to change, eh?" She looked at Sadie and laughed.

"At least," said Rosey, "we all feel the same way."

"We shall fortify each other," Da Silvera said, laughing again.

"I don't think I will stop being amazed at what life is really like at the White House," said Sadie. "Don't you know that our guests who are arriving downstairs right now are feeling nervous themselves? My husband has a favorite expression: 'It's not what things are but what they appear to be that matters.' It's my impression that we all appear to be totally relaxed and at ease: therefore we are."

"We should think about going down," said Rosey. "I believe I hear the band warming up to my favorite song."

"What is that?" asked the Brazilian President.

" 'Hail to the Chief.' "

Sadie descended on Rosey's arm into the great entrance hallway with the band playing, mobs of press jockeying for position, television cameras grinding away, and the lights so brilliant she was nearly blinded for the first few seconds. The only thing she could remember seeing clearly was Allison Sterling standing behind the ropes. Wasn't it odd that out of all those people in that bright light her eyes had skimmed over the crowd and picked her out as if she had been the only person in the room? Just for a second Sadie felt her confidence slipping, even though by all rights she should clearly be declared the winner in this situation.

Allison was wearing a simple gauzy black cotton dress with a tiered ankle-length skirt, tiny banded waist, straight bodice, and spaghetti straps. Her silver hair grazed her shoulders, her skin had a honeyed tone from just enough sun, and she wore only a thin gold chain around her neck and tiny gold hoop earrings. She looked elegant and sexy. Sadie felt bland and overly cool by comparison.

The press was hemmed in by the red velvet rope that kept them at a determined distance from the President and his wife. Yet despite the considerable jostling and groaning that accompanied any "photo opportunity," Allison, right in the middle of the crowd, looked peculiarly untouched, almost as though she were not aware of them.

In her hand she clutched a tiny reporter's note pad and pen, discreetly. When the Greys and their guests descended the stairs, Sadie thought that should have been one of the most exciting moments of her life. The eyes of the entire world were upon her. This was her moment. She was the queen. But Sadie knew what Allison was thinking. She knew that Allison thought she was a mindless twit.

"She looks beautiful," "exquisite," "spectacular." Sadie hadn't even heard the breathless remarks of the reporters and photographers as she descended the stairs.

"They're talking about you, darlin'," said Rosey, squeezing her hand with pride.

She looked up with amazement to see the faces in front of her, smiling their approval.

Rosey guided her from the hall into the East Room, where the guests were waiting, lined up to shake hands with the First Family and the guests of honor. Sadie had recovered from the cameras, from the approving reception, and regained her poise. Until Desmond Shaw stepped forward.

"Mr. Shaw, Bureau Chief of *The Weekly*," she heard an aide whisper to Rosey.

"Of course," said Rosey. "This man needs no introduction. And you know Sadie, of course." He turned to the next guest in the receiving line.

"Yes, sir. I do indeed."

The evening was perfect. It was hot, but there was almost no humidity—a rarity in this swamp city. After the speeches and the hordes of photographers and cameramen with their hideous lights piling into the dining room—she had tried to get Jenny to persuade Rosey's press office to knock that one off, but they wouldn't hear of it—Sadie and Rosey stood to lead the guests out through the Red Room and down the winding steps onto the South Lawn.

It had been arranged that the Da Silveras would slip off into the Blue Room, where the reporters could speak to them for five to ten minutes. The Greys would join them there. Jenny had gotten the reporters to agree that they would leave them alone at the table if they could see them after dinner for a few minutes.

"I'll believe it when I see it," she had said, which made Sadie a little nervous. "But it's the best deal I could cut."

This would be the first time Sadie had been exposed to the press since she and Rosey had moved into the White House. "Five minutes," she whispered to Jenny as they were walking into the Blue Room. There were about six women reporters, ranging in age from twenty to seventy, and one male.

"Mrs. Grey, that's a lovely dress," began one of the elderly reporters, a rather stout, short lady with white hair. "Whose is it?"

"I made it myself," she said.

There was a gasp. Then, slowly, giggles.

"No, I'm only teasing," she said. "It was designed by Jane Frowirth in New York. She does most of the things I wear. But don't you want to ask something of the Da Silveras?"

"Oh, that's perfectly all right," said President Da Silvera.

"Mrs. Grey, this was your first White House party. Were you nervous?" This from a rather nervous, shy young reporter whose voice shook as she asked the question.

"I was as nervous as you would be if you were covering your first White House dinner," she said with a sympathetic grin. Everyone smiled at the young reporter.

"How involved were you in the guest list?" asked another— this from a very old pro, a veteran White House reporter known for her intense sucking up to First Families, regardless of political ideology.

"Obviously, not as involved as I should have been; otherwise you would have been on it," said Sadie.

Jenny beamed.

The male reporter, a rather smarmy Brit from a disreputable paper, piped up, "President Da Silvera, there was a recent sexual scandal involving a member of your government. How did you handle it, and have you advice for President Grey on how to deal with such problems in his Administration?"

President Da Silvera's portly face fell, and his wife looked at Sadie as though for help. Jenny looked at her watch.

"If I needed any advice on that subject," said Rosey smoothly, a steely smile on his face, "I need only read your newspaper."

It was the reporter's turn to look dejected, and Da Silvera brightened.

"Ah, very good, very good," he said appreciatively to Rosey.

"Thank you very much," said Jenny, moving toward the Presidential party to end the brief "press availability."

"President Grey," came a soft, husky voice from behind one of the taller woman reporters. Sadie had not noticed that Allison Sterling was in the room.

"Yes, Sonny," said Rosey.

"There have been increasing reports of political repression, disappearances, and even torture of opposition-party members in Brazil lately. Do you intend to discuss this with President Da Silvera on this visit, and if so, do you intend to make any American commitments to that region contingent on our approval of their human-rights position?"

Sadie was outraged. This was not the kind of question one should ask at a party; at least, she didn't think so. She shot a look at Jenny, who was refusing to look at her. Madame Da Silvera looked down at the floor. The Brazilian President cleared his throat. There was a horrible moment of silence before Rosey answered.

"Sonny, as you know," he began very slowly and deliberately, "this Administration is very much concerned with the issue of human rights and committed to supporting them in every country." The smiles were off everyone's face now, and the reporters were scribbling.

"This country has always been a friend of Brazil's. It would not be fair of us to draw conclusions or give ultimatums without hearing all sides and having all of the facts. Certainly human rights is one issue which President Da Silvera and I will touch on, and I'm sure he will be able to satisfy me and the American people that we have no reason to be concerned on that issue involving his country. Thank you very much." And with a resolute hand he took the arm of the Brazilian President's wife and led her into the next room and down the stairs toward the garden tent.

The reporters tried to shout a few more questions, but without much enthusiasm. It was clear the President would have no more. When they were out of earshot, Sadie turned to Jenny and muttered through clenched teeth, "What was she trying to do? Who does she think she is?"

"I think," said Jenny, "she thinks she's a journalist."

* * *

Sadie slipped upstairs on the elevator to the bathroom in the private quarters. When she smiled into the mirror, as she always did, she discovered a tiny piece of food caught between her teeth. And to think she had been smiling at President Da Silvera all night. How hideous. It wasn't all that bad, hardly noticeable, but for God's sake, what if it had been spinach? She must remember to tell the chef never to serve spinach at White House dinners. Or anything green ever again. In fact, it would be a lot safer if they had only clear consommé. What did other First Ladies do about this? About going to the bathroom? She had to have the tiniest bladder there ever was. It was a constant source of embarrassment. It was like being perpetually pregnant . . . all this was running through her head as she descended to join the Da Silveras in the Blue Room.

Mrs. Da Silvera was running on about the horrible journalists and why couldn't the Americans control them. "We have nothing like that in Brazil," she was saying. "They would never dare behave like that in Brazil." Sadie had tried to put Sonny's question out of her mind and concentrate on pleasanter things, like bladder control, but it hadn't worked. Didn't the damn Brazilians know that they had no control over the press?

"Don't you know, Kiki, that we have no control over the press?"

"You should. You should do something. This is terrible. I pity you."

Sadie was afraid that the whole evening might have been ruined by that one question from Allison Sterling. She could kill her. And to think of all the time and energy and planning she had put into the table arrangements, the food, the music, the guest list. All for naught. This woman was nearly hysterical.

"Wait till you hear the entertainment," she said with forced enthusiasm to Kiki. "I'll bet you will be surprised," and she led them into the Red Room, where they would descend to the tent.

There was just the slightest breeze wafting up from the Potomac. Not a wind, really, but enough air to cause little wisps of hair to brush against her cheek.

The night sky was perfectly clear, and the full moon shone brilliantly on the Washington Monument and the Capitol. The tent was a pale silhouette as well, placed against the midnight sky, and the gardens were redolent with the scent of spring flowers and the newly mown grass. Garlands of greenery were entwined on the columns holding up the tent, and soft white lilies bedecked the tiny cabaret tables surrounding the dance floor. Tiny votive candles flickered across the space, and the cloths were the softest green, nearly white—Sadie's concession to Jenny's complaint that it would look too much like a wedding. Rum drinks were being offered by the waiters, and a Latin band was playing samba music.

It was as though Sadie were seeing the White House and the grounds for the first time. For a moment she forgot that there was anyone around and she whispered to herself, "Sara Adabelle, honey, you are in tall cotton."

The band had paused when they arrived at the tent and had begun a Brazilian song which Da Silvera immediately pronounced his favorite. "Ah, beautiful lady," he said, "you have thought of everything," and he took Sadie's hand to lead her to the dance floor as Rosey escorted his wife.

As soon as they had been on the floor for a few minutes several of the uniformed White House aides, as instructed by Jenny, made a beeline toward the women reporters and led them to the dance floor.

"Keep them on the dance floor. That way they can't possibly make trouble; and make sure they are never without champagne."

Da Silvera was over six feet tall, with slicked-down black hair laced with gray, a mustache, large lips, small eyes, and several chins to go with his stomach. He looked like an overweight, aging Latin lover, and it was clear he coveted at least half of that image for himself.

No sooner had they hit the dance floor than he held Sadie too close to him and breathed down on her seductively. "I only hope the President understands how lucky he is to have such a beautiful wife."

Sadie couldn't believe he was pulling this on her in the middle of a White House dinner in front of the world, for God's sake.

His hand was pressing her waist, pulling her closer to him, and she could feel his hot breath on her neck. She couldn't imagine what he expected to happen. Were they going to race up to the Lincoln bedroom and get laid? The whole idea of it tickled her so that she began to giggle.

"What is amusing you, dear lady?" whispered Tonio in a forced sexy voice.

"Oh, nothing," she said. "I was just wondering about the sex scandals the reporter mentioned. I wasn't aware of them. Perhaps you could tell me about them when we go sit down." And she stopped dancing and pulled him off the dance floor toward their little cabaret table to the right. She nodded to Jenny, who had arranged for a Brazilian-American investment banker from New York and his wife to join them for a few minutes, then turned to Rosey on the dance floor; he caught her signal and eased Kiki back to the table. Jenny had lined up groups to rotate every ten minutes or so.

Wells Harmon, a tall, well-groomed man with a slightly weak chin, approached Sadie and bowed. "Madame," said the Secretary of State, "may I have the pleasure?"

"Let's make sure they don't play a tango," said Sadie. "I really don't need to make a fool of myself. I can't imagine that I approved this music when this is the one kind of music I cannot dance to."

"Sugar, I think we are about to start the entertainment," said Rosey. "Perhaps afterwards, Wells," he said.

Up on the platform Rosey introduced the singer, who appeared to be an overly seductive Latin type if Sadie had ever seen one, but she had been assured by everyone on the White House staff that he sold more records around the world than any other living singer. He sang several ballads, directing most of his attention to Sadie as though he were making love to her in front of Washington, and all she could do was grit her teeth and smile.

Mercifully, it was over sooner than she had expected and Rosey was again up on the stage, this time clutching her by the hand and telling the singer how terrific he was. Sadie smiled again, amazed that the guests seemed to approve of him.

"Mrs. Grey," said the singer, "this is the thrill of my life to greet you. I have only seen your pictures, but you are even more beautiful in life. Like a painting."

Rosey grinned and Sadie nodded.

President Da Silvera was on his feet clapping and demanding encores. The singer obliged him with one more tune; then the band began to play songs for dancing.

"Sadie," said Tonio, leaning over to her, "it was such a pleasure the first time. If I may, would you honor me with another dance?"

"Mr. President, nothing could delight me more," said Sadie, "but I fear there are so many people here who want to have a chance to chat with you and so many other women who would like to dance with you that we may offend them if you don't give them some time. Besides, if my husband doesn't dance with me, we will read in the press tomorrow that our marriage is in trouble. You know how they are."

"Of course, of course, you are absolutely right," he said quickly. "They are terrible, the press."

"Yes, yes, Tonio," chimed in Kiki, "the President must dance with his wife."

Did she know? God, how humiliating.

"Don't you think that was a little rude?" Rosey said on the dance floor. His voice was curt.

"I did not want to get raped on the dance floor, for one thing," she said, "and I don't think you would have liked it much either."

"What?"

"That man is a disgusting lecher. He was trying to feel me up in front of the entire world."

"Sadie, you're exaggerating as usual."

"Well, Rosey darling, if you don't believe me, then I will simply dance with him again and let you watch, not to mention read about it tomorrow. Shall we go back to the table and get him?"

She started to pull his arm.

"All right, all right, I believe you. It's hard to, but I'll take your word for it. What is going on with you and men tonight, anyway? They're all over you like bees to honey. I've never seen anything like it."

"Does it surprise you?"

"Now, darlin', you know I think you're beautiful. It's just that this sudden attention is unsettling."

"Would you rather no man paid attention to me?"

"Do I have to make a choice?"

"Suppose I said yes?"

"Well, then, if I had to make a choice I suppose I would wish that men found you attractive."

She had not seen his hand tap Rosey's shoulder, only Rosey's startled expression. Before she could say anything she was in his arms. His voice was husky and unnervingly close.

"Your wish is granted, Mr. President," Shaw said.

It took her several seconds to catch her breath. "You're not supposed to cut in on the President, you know."

"I had to do something bold to get your attention. You were obviously so taken with the Brazilian President. Don't think I didn't notice how close you two were dancing."

"Oh, God, was it that obvious? I thought I would die I was so embarrassed. But what could I do?"

"To be honest, I can't blame the poor son-of-a-bitch."

She blushed.

"And now that you're the First Lady, an admirer has no choice but to woo you in public."

"I can't imagine that that will be a problem," she said. She was embarrassed. She could feel that funny sensation she always had when she was losing control.

"I'm afraid it already is."

"What do you mean?" Her voice caught in her throat. She clung to him more tightly than she wanted to, but she wasn't sure her legs wouldn't give way.

"You know what I mean."

"I don't." Why was her mouth so dry? She couldn't even swallow. His face was becoming a blur. She could feel his thighs gently against hers as they danced. She wondered how she was able to move.

"Are we just going to pretend it never happened?"

"No, I . . . yes, we . . ."

"I want to make love to you again, Sadie."

Somehow she would have to keep moving, have to stay on her feet, though she didn't know how she would do that. She tried to speak, but nothing came out of her mouth, so she said nothing and just held on, counting on him to support her. She had the same feeling she usually had at the sight of blood—slightly faint, almost nauseated. Somewhere in the back of her mind she knew she had to get hold of herself or someone would begin to notice that something strange was going on.

"I'm going to request an interview with you for *The Weekly.* We're going to do a cover story on you. I will be in charge of it.

It will require several long interviews. I think the solarium would be a nice private place. . . ."

She could vaguely hear him, as though they were talking long distance and had a bad connection.

If only her heart would stop beating. It occurred to her that it was pointless to worry about what people would think. Nobody would think this. It was the safest place imaginable. As her mind was leaping from one thought to another she couldn't help but be amused by the whole situation.

"Will you agree to it?" she heard him ask.

"What?" she said, focusing on him for the first time. But as she did so she went weak again.

"The interview?" It was the way he said the word "interview" that had started her shaking.

"I don't know," she said, and added quickly, before she had time to think, "I'll have to ask Rosey."

"It's time you started making your own decisions, Sara Adabelle McDougald Grey. Baby, it took guts for me to tell you . . ." His husky voice broke. ". . . that I wanted to make love to you again. I've already been rebuffed once. And I could never have done it if the whole fucking world weren't staring at us. Don't just leave me standing here."

"Sorry, old man, but I'm afraid that's just what I plan to do," said Wells Harmon in his silky Southern accent. He had clearly heard only the last sentence, Sadie noted with relief. "This lovely lady has been eluding me all night and I'm taking the liberty of rescuing her from you."

"Mr. Secretary," said Des with a slight bow, and he released her so quickly she felt as though she would sink. Wells had her in his arms in a moment, and before Sadie could say a word, Des had backed away. As Des headed for a drink, the orchestra broke into a tango, and all her concentration was required not to collapse on the dance floor until the music mercifully came to an end and Wells escorted her back to her table and her husband, the President.

Sadie tried to concentrate on her conversation with President Da Silvera, who had turned to her, his eyes gleaming. This was, he was saying, except for the brief unpleasantness with the reporter, the most enjoyable official dinner he had ever been to: good food, good music, interesting people, and of course, he had never had a more beautiful hostess.

She smiled her polite smile. Thank God Mama had taught her how to do that. She could fake it in the midst of most national disasters if she had to.

But she was on her own now. What if she fainted, which was exactly what she felt like doing? That wouldn't solve anything. She would still be confronted with the problem. The problem? That was when she knew she was in trouble. She was dealing with this situation as though it were a problem. Why hadn't she laughed in his face, told him off, rejected him on the spot? She had rebuffed him before and she wasn't even First Lady then. That was what any normal, sane person in full possession of her faculties would have done.

Da Silvera was telling a story to her and a Brazilian plastic surgeon who had flown up for the party. Normally Sadie would have been interested. She suspected the surgeon had had occasion to work on Kiki, perhaps several times. She did have a slight Oriental cast to her expression. She could see he was eyeing her. He seemed to be the only man in the room who was interested in her face.

She could feel her head nodding as though she were listening. She was trying to digest what Des had said to her. Or rather, asked of her. She couldn't believe that she was actually contemplating granting him a request for the "interview." For one thing, she would have to convince Rosey that she should give an interview. She suspected he would rather, given a choice, have her go to bed with Des than talk to him on the record.

Nothing made any sense to her. She was trying to think rationally when her gut told her she wanted to. She was in love with him. She had never admitted it to herself until now. She was in love with this man who was not her husband and now he wanted her. They could never get away with having a real affair: it was too dangerous; it would jeopardize her marriage, her husband's job, and in some way the stability of the country. The idea of a President's wife having an affair was preposterous.

One of the uniformed White House aides was approaching their table. He came quickly over to her side of the small table and, it seemed to her, waited until the others were not looking at her before he quietly handed her a note beneath the table. She could feel her throat constrict before she even opened it. She brushed her hair back from her face and neck quickly. It was suddenly developing into one of those horrible hot Washington summer nights.

She was perspiring now, and she hadn't even noticed when the weather had turned. She unfolded the note. On a blank piece of paper was a single phrase: "Regrets Only." The aide was standing by, waiting. She dismissed him with a smile, then looked back down at the note. When she looked up she met his gaze across the room. He was standing at the end of the tent, as though he were about to leave. She stared at him for the briefest moment; then, without hesitating any longer, she nodded.

He smiled, turned away, and disappeared into the blackness of the White House lawn.

Why did she feel as if she were about to self-immolate?

"Oh, God, did you see *The Daily*? And look at these other papers! They're all fantastic. With these reviews we could enjoy a very long run," said Tilda. "Oh, Christ, it's just too wonderful. Don't you think so, Jenny?"

"It's great," said Jenny. "I never expected to get such raves. They're unanimous. Even that fascist creep Da Silvera came through all right, miracle of miracles."

"Oh, I thought he was attractive," said Tilda. "He was very debonair. And his wife was adorable."

Jenny backed off. This was not the time to pick a fight.

"Well," said Tilda, changing the subject, "if the President had any doubts about how well you would do, Sadie, he certainly had them laid to rest this morning. They all say you were glamorous, beautiful, and the White House hasn't been this exciting in years."

They were sitting in the West Sitting Hall having coffee, tea, and sweet rolls.

It was only 10 A.M., and Sadie had thrown on a summer cotton shift to join the other two women for breakfast. She was sitting on the sofa, staring out the large Palladian window at the Executive Office Building. She was only vaguely aware of the conversation.

"I must say you certainly didn't lack for gentleman admirers last night," said Jenny, mocking Sadie in a lilting Southern accent.

Sadie didn't respond, but sat slowly sipping her tea.

"Especially one Mr. Desmond Shaw," said Tilda, one eyebrow raised in a slightly disapproving way. "I'm not sure we approved of cutting in on the President. He certainly had his nerve."

Sadie didn't respond.

"Sadie? Sadie? Are you with us? Come in, please; come in, please." Jenny had raised her voice to get Sadie's attention.

"Huh? . . . Oh—what?"

"We just wondered if you would care to join us," said Tilda.

"Oh, I'm sorry. I guess I was just preoccupied. What were you saying?"

"We were saying how awful the coverage was of the party last night and how they all did hatchet jobs on you."

Sadie chuckled absentmindedly. "Oh, is that what you were saying? I guess that means we'll go to war with Brazil and Rosey will drop fifteen points in the polls."

The phone on the table next to Sadie rang and Jenny picked it up.

"You're kidding," she said. "Really? Oh, my God. That's amazing. Okay. Did he say when? Okay, then I'll call him back. Right. Okay. Talk to you later."

"What was that?" asked Tilda. "More news about the party?"

"You're not going to believe this," said Jenny, looking at Sadie. "But Des Shaw has just called to request an interview. It seems *The Weekly* wants to do a cover story on you."

What worried her most was the monitor, the little computer the Secret Service had which kept track of the President and the First Lady no matter where they went. They went to the bathroom—the Secret Service knew about it. They went to have an affair . . .

She was out of her mind, she decided. She should be locked up in St. Elizabeth's instead of the White House. Maybe it was the fact of being locked up that was making her so crazy. She could use that as an excuse when Congress voted to impeach her. She would be elegant, restrained, pathetic at her impeachment hearing. She would wear pastels—pinks and other soft colors—to make her look ethereal, and she would act slightly delirious, maybe even allude to the fact that she had been having her monthlies. That would work now that the feminists had adopted it as an excuse for demented female behavior. "I'm sorry, Mr. Speaker, but I did what I had to do." Maybe a tear or two, but no sobbing. It made men nervous and angry when women cried. A perfectly formed tear sliding down an alabaster cheek was the right touch. Rosey would be furious. Would he win or lose votes? He might get the sympathy vote . . . poor man, how he must have suffered with that bitch, and trying to sail the Ship of State at the same time. On the other hand, he might be regarded as a cuckold —never an attractive image for the macho American male. If he can't handle his wife, how can he handle the country?

The advance on her book would be incredible. Perhaps the highest advance in the history of publishing. Movie rights, first serialization . . .

The movie would open with the hearing. It would be summer. Both Allison and Des would be covering the hearings, and there would be occasional cutbacks to the Oval Office, where the President would be watching, along with millions of hypnotized Americans.

She was crazy. There was no doubt about it. She had to be to even think of enjoying that sick little fantasy. Jesus Christ.

So. Here she was upstairs on the third floor in the solarium waiting for her "interview." It had been set up for two thirty. That way they would have the entire afternoon to talk.

She had not talked to Shaw since the White House dinner. The whole thing had been set up by Jenny. Sadie had asked Jenny to talk to Rosey about it rather than broach it herself. He had been reluctant at first, but Jenny had persuaded him. *The Weekly* was not a hatchet magazine. It would never do a job on a First Lady. Shaw was genuinely fond of Sadie (she said that with a straight face) and admired both the Greys. It wouldn't behoove him to do a number on a new First Lady, particularly one who had come in under such difficult circumstances. Rosey had asked Jenny to sit in on the interview.

"I don't think that's such a good idea, Mr. President," Jenny had said. "Shaw is a first-rate journalist. The really good ones are offended if you have a press person sit in on the interview. They see it as an accusation that you don't trust them. It makes them hostile, and it almost always backfires. I would leave them alone. I think we'll get better results."

Rosey had agreed, finally. Sadie had commended Jenny for

her astute judgment. Did Jenny have any idea? Sadie didn't think so. She certainly didn't act like it.

"I don't need to tell you how important this interview could be for both of us," Rosey had said.

"No, you don't," Sadie answered. Why did everything everyone said these days seem to be a *double entendre*?

She thought she had prepared everything perfectly for the interview. She had looked at the door of the solarium and found to her satisfaction that there was a lock on it. That would have been difficult to order just before the interview. Apparently a former President's daughter used to take her boyfriends upstairs to neck and she had had the lock installed. Not that they would be needing a lock today. Not in the White House.

She had told Jenny that she thought the interview would run at least two hours.

It was funny how one's mind worked. Since the dinner she had not been able to think of anything else. It was like being sixteen again. Sometimes it seemed like the most natural thing in the world. Other times, the implications were too awful. One repressed it because one couldn't deal with the consequences.

What to wear? Her first instinct was something loose. In case he . . . no, that was ridiculous. Not right here in the White House. But certainly not some uptight First Lady suit or anything. Des had told Jenny he was not bringing a photographer. They would set up a photo session after the interview. It was very hot at the end of July, but this particular day it wasn't too humid, and there was a breeze coming across from the Ellipse. She had opened the windows in the solarium, even though the air conditioning was on, so that it was rather tropical and slightly sensual. They were mowing the grass down below and you could smell it upstairs. She had ordered up a large pitcher of pink lemonade and some cookies. There was a small refrigerator, which she had had stocked with drinks, including beer. She must have been up to the solarium a dozen times to check everything out. She had finally decided to wear a pale peach jersey tank dress. Loose, easy, casual, chic, sexy, and, as much as she didn't want to admit it to herself, accessible.

Underneath she had on a pair of flesh-colored bikini underpants and a soft flesh-colored bra. No stockings. It was too hot. She chose a pair of peach leather sling-backed sandals. Her auburn hair was neat but not set. It had taken her hours to get it to look like that. Her makeup was soft: just a little eyeliner and light peach lipstick. No jewelry. She took her purse upstairs with her so she could freshen up if she had to. She had had a small mirror installed over the bar. Everything was perfect. Now where was he? Well, it wasn't two thirty. Jenny had walked her upstairs to the solarium, then gone down to her office. He would be arriving at the West Gate. Now she was alone for a few minutes to think about what she was going to say, to do. One thing she was going to do was get rid of that green-and-white print on the furniture. It was too bold. The "octagonal sky parlor," as it had been called for so many years, was surrounded on three sides by glass, and the view of Washington was spectacular—the Capitol, the Washington Monument, the Lincoln Memorial, the Potomac. There should be soft, subtle solids which would enhance the view. There she was decorating again. Always when she was nervous. Maybe she should divorce Rosey and become an interior decorator. Maybe she could earn her living that way after he was impeached. Her palms were beginning to sweat.

She was beginning to perspire under her arms, and the backs of her knees were damp. She could feel tiny beads of perspiration appearing on her upper lip. She could imagine the lead: "The First Lady was sweating profusely in the swelter of a Washington summer. . . ."

Maybe she had better close the windows and turn up the air conditioning, although she wasn't sure that the temperature was her problem.

"My God, it's hot up here." She heard Jenny's voice and turned to see Jenny and Des standing at the door of the solarium.

"I was just about to close the windows and turn up the air conditioning," she said.

"Good idea," said Des. He smiled at her as she invited him to take off his jacket. He loosened his tie. "We need it."

"Would you like the door shut?" asked Jenny.

"Please." Sadie didn't explain.

Now that he was here, what would he do? She had fantasized. *"Darling,"* he would say, grabbing her and pressing her body close to him as he smothered her with kisses. *"How I have longed for this moment when we would finally be alone again."*

"Pink lemonade?"

"As pink," he would say, *"as your perfectly formed adorable nipples."*

"Do you mind?" asked Des as he poured himself a glass and added several large ice cubes.

"Do you mind," he would say, *"if I press my throbbing member between your velvet thighs?"*

He walked over and sat down on the opposite end of the sofa from where she was sitting. He was wearing a wide-striped shirt in pale green and white and a beige linen tie. His tan summer slacks were wrinkled. His sleeves were rolled up. His skin was deeply tanned the way most men's skin looked in August. His black hair was combed today and slightly wet, like a little boy's, dressed up for a birthday party. There were white wrinkles around his greenish-brown eyes. Every time she saw him, he looked handsomer. He was the kind of man who looked at a woman so directly that she could feel his gaze between her legs. He always wore a smile that seemed to say "Are you game?—because I am."

"You don't look like a First Lady," said Shaw. "But then you didn't look much like a Second Lady either."

"You look like a piece of ass," he would say.

"I don't feel like a First Lady," she said, ignoring his reference.

"I feel like making love to you," she would say.

"Nevertheless, you are one. Which brings me here today."

"For the interview?"

"For the interview."

He was mocking her. But she could give as good as she got.

"Well, then, let's get on with it," she said. "Where would you like to start?" She leaned back in the corner of her end of the sofa and looked at him.

"Start by kissing the back of my neck," she would say. *"And work your way down."*

"Why don't we start by having you tell me how you feel?" he said.

"About being First Lady?"

"About being First Lady."

"I feel . . ." she said.

"You don't mind if I take notes?"

"Notes? Oh, notes. Of course not. After all, that's why you're here."

"Right."

He reached over to the chair where his notebook and pen were protruding from his jacket pocket. She couldn't help noticing, because his legs were spread apart, the large bulge between them.

She unconsciously crossed her breasts with both arms and rubbed her arms protectively, gently, with her hands.

"So," he said as he turned back to her, opened his notebook, then noticed her caressing her arms. He was momentarily distracted.

"Where were we?"

"You were asking me how I feel," she said.

"I feel I want your taut body next to mine," she would say.

She could see him catch his breath as she looked into his eyes; then he glanced down at his notebook, though without anything to write.

She suddenly realized that he would have nothing to write unless she actually did give him an interview. Ultimately, there was going to be a cover story on her in *The Weekly*. He'd have to write something. Rosey would ask her how the interview had gone, and Jenny would want to know every detail.

She wasn't sixteen, and it wasn't funny. She had better get serious if he didn't. He had nothing to lose. She had everything. Or did she? Wasn't it really Rosey who had everything to lose?

"Actually," she said, and the change in her tone of voice made him jerk his head up to look at her. "Actually, I'll tell you how I feel. I feel that it's not as much fun to be First Lady as I thought it would be."

She watched him turn from a potential lover into a journalist so fast that it surprised even her. He began to scribble. He knew a good—no, not good, fabulous—quote when he heard it. She had just given him his lead, maybe even a cover line. She knew it, and he knew it. He realized she had turned this meeting into an interview. She could almost feel his relief. Only then did it occur to her that he had been as scared as she was.

"Why is that?" he asked in a soft voice the way reporters often do when their subject has just opened up a forbidden subject, in the same way a hunter doesn't want to frighten a deer in the forest.

"Because," she said, "I'm married to the President. I can't think of any job in the world that would be more exciting, challenging, more rewarding, more fun than being First Lady as long as you didn't have to have a husband."

Des was writing fast. "Could you explain what you mean?" he asked in that same soft, unobtrusive voice.

She couldn't decide whether to be annoyed or amused. He declares his love, creates an enormous ploy to meet with her, risks her reputation and the downfall of the Democratic Party by coming to her, and all she has to do is throw him a crumb and he forgets totally about her and is preoccupied with his story. His attitude toward her now is one of a psychiatrist with a patient on a couch. He thinks she is going to tell all and he's going to have a scoop. He is, after all, in a no-lose situation. Either way things go this sultry summer afternoon, the son-of-a-bitch is going to score.

"Think of all the things I could do if I didn't have a husband," she said, warming to her subject.

Just as quickly, his eyes looked up at her and she could see he had forgotten his notebook again.

"I'm thinking," he said finally. "I'm thinking."

She was in love. She was forty years old and in love for the third time in her life. Danny, her first love in Savannah; Tag; and now Desmond Shaw. Her life was half over and she had lost the two men she had loved. She didn't have that many good years left. She wasn't going to lose this one. Even if it cost her everything else.

They had been talking for more than an hour and a half. She was musing as carefully as she could about the role of First Lady. He was scratching away in his notebook. Lovers will often tell each other about themselves—a sort of introductory offer—before consummating their relationship. They had done this once before, a year and a half ago. Now they were repeating the ritual. Sadie reflected on her life during the previous months. Des talked about coming to Washington for the first time as the *Weekly* Bureau Chief with much to learn.

"That's when your marriage broke up, isn't it?" she asked.

"It was a time of reassessment, yes," he said. "I was only a little older than you are now. Men are just slower than women at certain things, I guess."

They paused and looked at each other with such longing that it seemed as if nothing could break their gaze.

"We were, uh, talking about my role," said Sadie finally. "I'd just like to say off the record that I didn't mean to be flip when I said it would be wonderful to be First Lady without a husband. I'm deadly serious. A woman can come to this job, if I may call it a job, with all sorts of plans and projects and goals. But everything she does has to be weighed as to how it will affect the President politically. I care about Planned Parenthood. But I can't go all out on it because it's just too controversial. Not to mention abortion. There are so many things I would like to say and do. I care about the problems of the country, the inequities in people's lives, the poverty and the injustice. I'm really not just a redheaded fluff who cares only about decorating and clothes. You get criticized for caring about those things, but they are considered acceptable concerns for a woman. If a First Lady tries to get involved with anything politically substantive, she gets crucified. Just look at the past and see what has fared the best. Beautification, restoration, disabled children—all those areas are safe. But step out of line, say what you think, give an opinion that one American, one voter might disagree with and you get killed. And not just by the churchgoing conservative little ladies, either. Your colleagues have been known to go after any First Lady, or any political wife, for that matter, who sticks her head up above the foxhole, who steps out of line for a second. The First Lady is supposed to be an asset to her husband. Period. It's the toughest job in the country. Tougher than any other job. And I don't know what the answer is. Maybe we should elect First Ladies. Maybe it shouldn't necessarily be the wife of the President. Or maybe we should elect a First Lady and let her husband be President. Or maybe we should leave her alone. Treat every President as if he were a bachelor and let his wife lead her own life without the obligations that a normal First Lady would have to assume. I don't know what the answer is. I only know now, in this era of changing roles for women and feminism, that something in the White House is going to have to change. I'm not sure I'm the one who can do it."

"I think," he said, "you are."

* * *

It happened so quickly that when she was trying to relive it later she couldn't remember how it had begun.

She had gotten up to get some more lemonade. It was still warm in the solarium and she had reopened the window just to let a breeze in, even though the air conditioning was on. When she walked across the room she could feel his eyes on her body. He watched as she slowly poured herself a drink, then made her way back to the sofa.

There was something about his presence that made her want to caress her own body, and she began slowly to move her hand up and down her thigh, almost unconsciously, as she settled into her corner and returned his smile. He didn't say a word, but she could see the perspiration on his forehead, and he had licked his lips as if he were thirsty. He had dropped his notebook to the floor, and his palms were resting lightly on his knees. His hands were strong and masculine, his tanned fingers short and square, but lean, not thick. She became fascinated by them, imagining them on her again, and as she did she moved her own hands slowly up her thigh, across her abdomen, lightly brushing her breasts, and up to her neck, which she rubbed with a deliberate movement while she continued to stare at his hands.

"Don't do that," he whispered, and she could hear his lips crack.

"Don't do what?" she asked, almost absentmindedly, as she looked up at him. She knew immediately when their eyes met that it had been a mistake to return his glance. Now she couldn't look away. Now she would have to acknowledge what they both understood.

Her throat tightened, and when she tried to swallow, she couldn't. She couldn't even get any air into her lungs, even though she gasped. Once, at Tybee Beach, outside Savannah, when she was about ten, she had gone into the ocean alone and had stepped off an underwater ledge and been pulled under by a wave. She remembered later, after she was rescued by a life-guard, seeing flashes of scenes from the beach every time she came up for air, then being dragged under again, until she had nearly lost consciousness, her lungs filled with water. She had never felt so helpless until this moment. She had no power over herself, any more than she had had that summer day at Tybee. Now as she sat there she could see scenes of her life, of Rosey, of the White House, of their children darting into and out of her vision. She had the same certainty, at this moment, of losing everything as she had had then, and she could do nothing about it.

He was moving across the sofa, in a crouch, his eyes fixed on hers. His face bore a look of pain which she understood. It was the kind of pain men feel when they have lost control.

He reached an arm over and grasped one of her arms, brusquely pulling her down on the sofa under him, then pressing his heaviness upon her, knocking the air out of her so that she thought she would faint. She closed her eyes at the same time her mouth opened before she even felt his lips. After that she remembered only one thing.

She gave in as she had finally given in to the waves at Tybee Beach.

This time there was no lifeguard.

CHAPTER 13

N ICK WAS BACK.

She used to wonder what it would feel like. Nick had been the first.

She was at her desk in the White House pressroom when he called from the foreign desk at *The Daily*, just back from the Middle East.

"Sonny?"

She waited for her stomach to drop.

"I'm here."

"So I gather." Her mouth was dry.

"I'd like to see you."

"That's inevitable." Why was she being so cool? It was twelve years.

"Can we make it more specific?"

"How about tonight?" Might as well get it over with. She hadn't meant to sound so bitter. It was as though she were blaming Nick for Des. It was Des. Nick was stirring up the anger she felt toward Des, toward men. This was where they had left off. No point in reviving old hurts. She should be friends with Nick.

"Let me see if I can get out of dinner with Roland. He'll be pissed, but you're more important than the Foreign Editor."

"Oh, that's okay," she said too quickly. "We could do it another night. How long are you going to be here?"

"Several days. I've got plenty of time. I've been hanging around the foreign desk all morning. It just reminds me how much I like being out in the field. I'm not cut out for all the bureaucratic bullshit. I've been on my own too long."

She laughed. She could feel herself relax. She remembered now that she had liked Nick as well as loved him.

"Well, do you want to do it tonight, then?"

"Sure. You pick a restaurant."

"What's your mood?"

"Anything but stuffed grape leaves."

"There's a little French restaurant around the corner from my house in Georgetown . . ."

"Forget little French restaurants. Let's go all out. Roland's buying."

"An important French restaurant, then?"

"Now we're talkin'."

"I'll make reservations at Jean Louis at the Watergate."

"Sounds like a hairdresser."

"Wait till you see the prices."

She got there a little early. She had left the White House after filing a routine story about President Grey and the visiting Japanese Prime Minister and had gone home to change.

In the old days Nick had always liked clothes that were a little far out—anything but the debutante look he had grown up with in Philadelphia. Once he had bought Allison a fringed purple suede tunic. When she wore it she felt like a member of the cast of *Hair*. She chose a sleeveless silk in a cool-looking soft blue-gray—perfect for August—and pearls. Pearls made your skin look younger. At the last minute she had dabbed some wrinkle-disappearing cream under her eyes.

The waiter led her to a banquette in a corner of the mirrored room.

She ordered a kir, very light, and for the first time since Des she allowed herself to think about the possibility of another man. Could there be any chance that she and Nick could make it work again? They had always loved each other. There had never been any question even when they broke it off. Why couldn't they just pick up where they left off, mellower, more experienced, wiser? They had both known some pain and disappointment. They would be better suited to each other now. Maybe she would leave Washington and go with him to the Middle East. It might be nice to get away from Washington. Of course, she couldn't work full time for *The Daily*, but she could string and maybe do some free-lance, write a book. She didn't have a book to write, but she would certainly come up with something. She needed a break. She was getting stale. She was an emotional mess too. Maybe a change of environment would renew her confidence, her enthusiasm, her energy. She could picture herself and Nick in the desert outside Jerusalem in safari clothes, tanned and windblown, looking out over the rolling hills toward Jordan. And she would be away from Des. Why was she thinking of Des if she was going off with Nick?

Dear Nick. The emotion had not come as anticipated. Perhaps when she saw him? It might take a while to uncover the old feelings. She had buried them deep. Dig a hole to China. Throw Des in there with Nick. Cover them up with shovels so full they could never get out. But was there a hole deep enough? All afternoon images of her years with Nick had surfaced, and surprisingly, she was relishing them. It was rather like looking through your old high school yearbook and seeing a picture of the football captain who had jilted you. "Keep your nose clean," he had written.

The first time she had seen Nick he had taken the seat next to her in the back row of the foreign-reporting class at Columbia Journalism School. He was cool, so sure of himself. He seemed not to notice her. She planned a birthday party for one of his closest friends to get him to her apartment. Even then he paid no attention to her. She found herself, toward the end of the evening, staring out at the lights over the Hudson. She didn't notice him come over.

"I'm very flattered you contrived this whole party just to end up with me," he challenged.

"Conceited bastard," she whispered to him.

"Listen, I really dig you."

"I'm going to see if the others need any wine."

He had grabbed her arm. "You started this, you finish it."

He cupped his hand under her chin and pulled her face to him, kissing her gently, just touching her lips with his—a butterfly kiss. "I want you, Allison," he whispered, then let her go. All she could do was steady herself against the wall and let her breath out slowly. She watched him as he motioned to the others, and she said nothing as they all left. When they were gone, he took her by the hand, pulled her down to the sofa, and put his arms around her. "Now" was all he said. She didn't have time to tell him she was a virgin.

"Another kir, madame?"

It was quarter to nine. She felt strangely peaceful.

"Please."

It was all so perfect. Holding hands in the park, foreign movies, Chinese on Sunday nights, wandering through the Village, drives to the Hamptons for walks on winter beaches. Splurges at the Russian Tea Room. "J" school was inconsequential. Love was all that mattered. Making love. It was never going to end. But it did. She ended it. She still couldn't believe it.

Politics was her passion, the war in Vietnam his. He wanted to go, she wanted to stay. The AP wanted them both—her for the political campaigns, him for the war. They both said yes. He asked her to go with him and didn't understand why she didn't want to go. She couldn't believe he expected her to give up everything for him. It was his celebration dinner. She saw the waiter bringing their food and she fled, leaving him sitting in the restaurant. He called all that night and the next day. She couldn't answer the phone. Finally he came over. They sat in silence for a while.

"I don't get it," he said finally. "I've asked you to come with me. I thought you would be so excited. We'll be together. It's the opportunity of my life. You could get some work stringing, I'm sure. What's your problem?"

He really didn't get it. She knew that. "My career, my interests are here," she said. "Would it occur to you to stay here to be with me?"

The look on his face made her laugh even now. He literally couldn't speak. She had uttered the unspeakable. Finally she got up and went to the door. He followed her and opened the door himself.

"I'll call you before I leave," he said finally, embarrassed.

He never did.

Allison sipped her drink and leaned her head against the back of the velvet banquette, trying to feel the pain of that summer just as an exercise. Three months of staring at the ceiling.

"Jesus, Sonny, I'm sorry. I was way out in Chevy Chase and I had to wait forever for a cab. Please forgive me."

"Only if you order a bottle of white wine instantly. I can't drink another kir."

"And a Scotch-and-soda, please." He nodded to the waiter, who went off to fetch a wine list. He turned to her, taking her in with an admiring and frank appraisal.

She tried not to return his stare, curious as she was.

"You look fine, Sonny." As though she had been sick. He was serious at first; then the familiar mischief crept into his gaze. "Nothing a little wrinkle cream couldn't take care of."

"Fuck you."

"Now, there's my Sonny. I'd recognize her anywhere. Sweet, demure, gentle, ladylike."

She remembered why she had loved him.

"How did you know about the wrinkle cream anyway, you bastard?"

"Older women. I had a number of older women. In my youth. Those days are over, though."

"Why?"

"Because I'm too old to be a younger man. Besides, something happens to a woman's skin after a while."

She and Nick were the same age. She unconsciously put her fingers under her eyes as if to smooth the skin away and lifted her chin slightly just in case. At the same time she was thinking how insidious and demeaning it was, particularly since she was tyrannizing herself.

"I'd forgotten what pretty hands you have," he said.

"What is this with you and skin?" she said, taking her hands quickly away from her face. There was an edge to her voice. She had never even thought about her age until she and Des split up. Now she thought about it all the time.

"You're being a little paranoid, Sonny. I was just thinking what graceful hands you had. I didn't say anything about your skin, though I've clearly gotten under it."

"Sorry. I think I had a bad reaction to my last birthday."

"We've both had a lot of birthdays since we saw each other. The few times I've been back you've been out on assignment."

"I know. People thought I was avoiding you."

"Were you?"

"I don't know. Maybe it's coincidence."

"Maybe."

"So why aren't you married with three kids by now? I thought you always wanted to have lots of children."

"I still do. But it's hard traveling so much. There just never seems to be a time to settle down. It isn't fair to your wife or kids. And practically every correspondent I know has split up with his wife. Most of the women correspondents are single. It's just easier."

"I have a shrink friend whose motto is 'You get what you want.' It used to piss me off a lot when she told me that. But she finally persuaded me she was right. If I'm not really happy, it's hard to accept that I'm not really happy because of my own choices. If you really wanted a wife and children, you'd have them. So would I. Have a husband and children."

"Is that why you blew it with Shaw? Did you do that on purpose?"

"What do you know about him?" she asked—almost a challenge.

"I know what everybody else knows. Shit, Sonny, just because I'm in the Middle East doesn't mean I'm cut off from the real world. We're journalists, don't forget—good at reporting, good at trading information. Your breakup was a big story even in Jerusalem. One whole lunch at the American Colony Hotel in East Jerusalem was devoted to a debate over who did the right thing. You are a hero among the women. The men sympathize with Shaw. And they all think he was right to leave."

She was on the verge of tears. She hadn't wanted to discuss Des with Nick. It opened up the old wounds with Nick as well. She could feel the pain engulf her.

"What do *you* think?" She was grateful for the dimness.

"You really want to know?"

"I'm not sure."

"Monsieur, madame, would you like to order?"

She was relieved by the interruption. They joked and laughed over the menu, finally deciding on one forty-dollar meal and one sixty-dollar meal. Plus a good bottle of Meursault. They chatted during the duck salad with radicchio, made light conversation through the quenelle in lobster sauce and the veal with mushrooms, but when dessert came there was a strained silence. Nick finally spoke.

"Do you mind if I indulge in a little amateur psychology?"

"I do, but I'm too curious to stop you."

"It wasn't all that different from what happened between us, Sonny."

She started to speak.

"Please, let me finish. You had a choice between your man and your career and you chose your career. I think—no, I'm sure—that in our case you did the right thing. I wasn't ready to settle down. I was obsessed with my work then too. It would have been a disaster. But we're fifteen years older now. You have your career. Jesus Christ, do you have your career. You're the most famous woman journalist in America. And the most respected. You have nothing more to prove. And even so, you've let one of the best guys around slip through your fingers. This time, Sonny, you made the wrong choice. *That's* what I think."

She had had just enough wine that she couldn't stop the tears when they started. She sat there quietly and let them run down her cheeks.

Nick didn't say anything either, but he put his arm around her and held her for a while.

All those sessions with Rachel hadn't hit home the way Nick's words had. He was right. She had made the wrong decision about Des and she had been defending it ferociously ever since. The more she came to doubt it, the more staunchly she defended it. This time she hadn't gotten what she wanted because she hadn't known what she wanted. Now she knew it and it was too late.

"Let's blow this joint," he said. She searched for a handkerchief, finally, in desperation, relying on the large pink napkin which was already wet with perspiration.

"I'm coming home with you. I'm not leaving you alone in this shape," he said once she was behind the wheel.

"Oh, Nick, I don't think—"

"Shut up and drive."

She found a place to park and they walked the block and a half in the balmy August night arm in arm.

On the ground-floor entrance level she stopped at the kitchen and turned to Nick.

"Why don't I fix some coffee, and we can take it up to the roof?"

"Oh, fuck coffee, Sonny. We're both half shit-faced as it is; we might as well go all the way."

She shrugged, pretending not to catch his *double entendre*, and got a bottle of white wine out of the refrigerator. They walked up past the third floor and out onto the tiny railed observation roof, where they could see most of the city. The lights were brilliant against the clear night sky, and it was unusually cool and dry for August. For a long time they sipped their wine, looked out at the view, and said nothing.

"I still love you, Sonny."

She drew a breath.

"Do you think we could try again?"

She still said nothing.

"I'd like to throw my hat in the ring."

She felt drained. Somehow this evening was Nick's responsibility. It was up to him to keep it going. Whatever he wanted was okay with her as long as she didn't have to do anything about it.

He sensed that and moved closer to her. She didn't move. He put his arms around her, pulled her to him, and kissed her gently on the lips. She did not resist. She wanted to be taken. She didn't want to have to make any decisions. She wanted to be done to.

Nick took her by the hand and led her downstairs to her bedroom. He laid her on the bed and slowly undressed her, then himself. Now he was kneeling over her, caressing her breasts and her thighs, just looking at her.

"Oh, God, you're more beautiful than I remembered," he whispered, and she sighed and said nothing.

Now he was on top of her, kissing her body and holding her, fondling her, and she sighed again because it felt so good to be held again. She didn't want him ever to stop holding her; but she couldn't say anything, she couldn't even lift her arms or her legs to receive him when he came into her. He was kissing her neck and shoulders and hair and ears and whispering loving things to her and she was sad and grateful and touched. She wanted to love him back, but she didn't have the energy. He seemed not to mind, and when she sighed he would whisper, "Oh, yes, my love," and she knew it was all right.

When he came with a shudder it was familiar, even after all those years, and it made her feel secure.

Still, she couldn't control the sobs once they began—this time not quiet tears but from deep inside her body, from a hurt that was still new and an old hurt that would always be remembered.

They held on to each other for a long time.

She cried forever and he kept on holding her, and when she stopped she saw there were tears in his eyes. She could see them shining in the darkness.

"Sonny?"

"Yes, Nick?"

"It's gone, isn't it?"

"Yes."

"It just ain't no mo'."

"I'm so sorry."

"Oh, so am I, babe. So am I. But it's okay. It really is. We'll be all right, both of us. Because we still care about each other. We're still friends. We've still got each other to hold on to. That's not all bad."

He caressed her cheek, kissing her gently on the forehead, the eyelids, the chin.

"And I still do love you, for what it's worth."

"I love you too, Nick. And it's worth a lot. Now will you shut up and hold me? It seems to me that you've been doing an awful lot of talking tonight and I've hardly said a word. In fact, all I've done is cry."

"I was wondering when you were going to notice." He laughed as he got up and turned on the light. "I need a cigarette. Do you mind?" He rummaged around in his coat pocket and found a half-empty pack of Marlboros. "I know, I know, I'm trying to quit. It's just that it's not easy to give up the hard-drinking, hard-smoking, hard-driving, shit-kicking foreign-correspondent image. I'll make it, though. I'm a tough mother."

He was standing in the middle of the room with nothing on, and she gazed at his perfect, beautiful slim body, so different from Des's stocky Irish build.

"What are you looking at?"

"Not a bad piece o' meat," she said. "I was just having second thoughts about us. Maybe it isn't over."

"Forget it. It's too late. Besides, I can't take myself off the market yet anyway. There are too many women who would be devastated. I'm going to have to ease my way off. Let them down slowly."

"Speaking of other women, we haven't discussed any of your girlfriends, past or present. Why don't we start with present and work back?"

"Do you want to start with Jerusalem, Tel Aviv, Damascus, Beirut, Cairo, Riyadh, or maybe Rome?"

"You conceited bastard. Now I remember why it would be impossible with you. You're not a legend for nothing, you know."

"Legend, am I? I'm just a poor reporter trying to do my job, and if I get a little pussy on the side now and then, why, that's just an added bonus."

"Actually, that's pretty much the way I see it." She laughed. "You know, you're no less a legend than I am."

"What have we got to show for it?"

"Well, we're both pretty good lays."

"Be serious."

"A lot of dead clips and an empty heart."

"You've got one more thing."

"What's that?"

"A friend who loves you."

He put his arms around her and they just held on.

Lorraine really couldn't bear to have people think she was crass. No matter how successful a Washington hostess might be, it never did to be thought a social climber. And it was a very fine line— oh, was it fine— to walk. The problem was that she had been hearing whispers about herself. Not that Claire Elgin understood the meaning of the word whisper. Nevertheless, Claire had let her know that there were certain people around Washington who felt that Lorraine had dropped Allison like a hot potato after Roger Kimball had a stroke and Desmond Shaw had walked out on her. To make matters worse, they were suggesting that she was sucking up to Sadie Grey. Well, the facts were that she had invited Allison dozens of times since all of that happened and Allison had turned her down each time and didn't seem inclined to continue their friendship. Lorraine was a bit hurt by that. Also, she and Sadie Grey had been very good friends before Rosey Grey was President. It was just that now that Sadie was First Lady her activities were more publicized and everyone knew and cared if she and Sadie had lunch together. Still, if they thought she had abandoned Allison and befriended Sadie, even if it was untrue and unfair, it was the appearance that mattered. Lorraine would not have all her hard work go down the drain with something like this. She wanted to be admired as a hostess, not condemned as a social climber. She would have to take matters in hand. She would have to have another party. In September. A party to kick off the season. A party for Allison.

Whom to invite? That was the problem. Should she have Desmond Shaw? It didn't seem like a very good idea, but how could she not? Besides, he was a great catch. She'd have to consult Allison about whether she could have a party. Lorraine had gotten ahead of herself. She found she was like a great artist. Once she had conceived the idea for a party, her imagination began to race and she couldn't stop. This one was beginning to form in her mind. She would invite as many attractive bachelors as she could find, and as many pretty women and have—although she would never dare say the word—a glorified singles party. She would make sure everyone was someone in power, and she would even import if she had to. Ironically, it would be single women she would have to import. There were always plenty of attractive and powerful single men running loose in Washington. Contrary to myth, it was the easiest thing in the world to find an extra man. The women were the big problem. She already knew which men she would have, all ostensibly to meet Allison. Ali Habib was the new Ambassador from Oman. He was the Sultan's closest friend, confidant, and adviser. He was not an Omani at all: rather, he carried four passports. Oxford-and-Harvard-educated, he was brilliant, sophisticated, and sexy. And rich beyond words. He had already bought "his" country a newly restored mansion on Decatur Place for its embassy residence, complete with gym, screening room, ballroom, pool, and enough security for a President of the United States.

Ali Habib would be mad for Allison. He understood perfectly that one did not want a woman who was an accessory. In New York, London, Paris, perhaps. Not in Washington.

Earl Downs, the maverick Senator from Florida, might as well be a bachelor because his wife never came to Washington. Not very attractive, but hugely powerful, having replaced John T. Hooker as chairman of the Foreign Relations Committee, he had a commmanding personality and was an addition to any hostess' salon. Lorraine just happened to know that Jones Barrett, the actor who was the new head of the National Endowment for the Arts, would be in town.

She would fly in her beauties from New York, invite enough people from the Administration to make it work, and *voilà!* another *succès fou.* It wouldn't hurt that *The Weekly* had just done a takeout on reporters who cover the White House. They had featured Allison quite heavily throughout the piece as the glamour queen of the White House press corps, returned after a two-year exile while her godfather was President. Lorraine suspected Jerry Mendelsohn had had something to do with the spread. She had heard that Desmond Shaw had not been involved.

Of course, the spread in *The Weekly* had nothing to do with Lorraine's wanting to have a party for Allison. It was coincidence. She was worried, however, when she called, that Allison might think so.

Allison smiled when Lorraine told her why she was calling. She really liked Lorraine. She was a game old broad. Allison loved her for caring so much. Sometimes she wished she had as much dedication these days to her career as Lorraine had to hers. There came a time when you saw the same old stories going by for the hundredth time and you just didn't give a damn. Lorraine would care desperately about her parties until they carried her out of Dumbarton Street in a box.

"Why not?" she said. "I want you to invite every attractive bachelor you can think of so they can fawn all over me." She laughed. "I need a little ego massage these days."

"What a good idea," said Lorraine, but she was already thinking that she would start with Ezio's wonderful vegetable pâté. This one would be seated. Three tables of twelve. Allison between Ali Habib and Jones Barrett. Lorraine would keep Senator Downs for herself. She would wear her new caftan, a simple column of leopard chiffon.

"Lorraine, are you still there?"

"Oh, yes, darling. What is it?"

"You're not going to invite . . . ?"

"Of course not. I never even considered it."

* * *

It had been a long time since Allison had been to Lorraine's house. She felt recharged after her night with Nick, almost ready to go out again, almost ready for men. She hadn't made love with anyone since Des, until Nick, and it was only then that she realized how much she had missed not only the sex but the holding. She needed that. She had a feeling that something good was going to happen at Lorraine's.

Lorraine had asked her to come a bit early, and she was happy to do so. She wanted to seem in command, and receiving would make her feel that way. She had decided to look sexy rather than chic. Her hair would be parted on one side and hanging over the other, a little longer than shoulder length. Veronica Lake. The white silk-and-cashmere dress had a high neck, long sleeves, a plunging back line, and a body-molding fit. Des would have said she looked as if she were on the prowl. Fuck Des.

Lorraine was dazzled, possibly miffed.

"Darling," she said, brushing the air with her scarlet lips, "you look positively ravishing."

Allison smiled.

"Doesn't she, Archie?"

"Ravishing. You'll have to beat them away with sticks, eh?" Archie chuckled at his own little joke.

"Archie, you always say just the right thing," Allison said to annoy Lorraine. "Now tell me about the bachelors. Who am I going to let take me home?"

Lorraine knew that the party would be a success. She had had some doubts earlier. Allison had insisted on her inviting dreary Walt Fineman. She was adamant about that and adamant about the fact that Allen Warburg not be invited, even though rumors were heavy that he was about to be named editor and Wiley Turnbull was on his way out.

"It's my turf, Lorraine," Allison had said. "I don't like Allen Warburg. If he gets to be the editor I'll live with it, but he's not my friend."

"All right, Sonny, if you insist," Lorraine had sighed, "but there are a few friends of mine I really can't exclude."

"Don't tell me. Claire and Worth, Edwina and Rodney."

"Well, yes. I'm sorry, but . . ."

"You don't have to apologize, Lorraine. Besides, a little competition will keep me on my toes, which of course I will have to be to talk to Edwina anyway."

"Now, Sonny."

"I shouldn't have said that. I know she and Claire are your bosom buddies. Speaking of bosoms, Claire—"

"Sonny!"

"My guess is that Edwina will go for Ali and Claire will come on to Jones Barrett, unless, of course, she thinks she can do Worth some good by going for someone more politically well placed. . . ."

"Sonny, I really don't—"

"You think it's the other way around?"

"No, but . . ." Lorraine was exasperated.

"Come on, Lorraine, you know I'm telling the truth. But just because they're both horse's asses doesn't mean they're not good at what they do. By the way, what *do* they do?"

"Sonny, I absolutely will not listen to one more word. You're being positively vicious."

"And you love every minute of it."

"That's unfair."

"Who said anything about fair?"

Howard Heinrich was the first to arrive. Good old Howard had managed to hang in as counsel to the President after Rosewell Grey took over. He was more powerful than ever. And being an attractive bachelor, he was on every hostess' list. Allison suspected that Lorraine had a slight sneaker for him and might even have done something about it if she hadn't taken her hostess' vow of chastity.

Allison also suspected that Howard didn't like her, though he was too political to show it. He had never made the slightest pass at her, either during Kimball's Administration or after, when she had gone back to covering the White House full time. He spent a lot of time talking about how he was sure every man who met her wanted to go to bed with her. He talked about it too much. But he was a great source, and she particularly liked him because she suspected he disliked Sadie Grey.

"Lorraine, my sweet, as usual you look lovely and your house is perfect." He kissed Lorraine on both cheeks, then turned to

Allison. He surveyed her carefully, taking in the whole effect, then whistled.

"My, my, this is quite a coming-out party," he said. "There's not a man in this room who will be able to keep his hands off you."

"That's what I'm counting on, Howard," said Allison. "And I wish you especially would try to keep yours under control."

Lorraine looked stricken. This was the counsel to the President. But before she could say anything, Howard had his arms around Allison in a bear hug, laughing.

"If it weren't for the inhuman demands on me because of my job, Allison, you know I'd be on your front doorstep every night."

The doorbell rang. It was the Elgins and the Abel-Smiths.

"Ahhhhh," said Lorraine, her arms widening in a welcoming gesture, "my favorite people. Now the party can begin."

"You are more beautiful than even your pictures."

Ali Habib's eyes were sparkling with admiration as he turned to Allison once they had sat down. He was as good-looking as his pictures: tall, with coal-black hair swept back, deep black eyes, interminable eyelashes, sensual lips, and a perfect desert tan. His accent was Oxford, his suit Savile Row, his shirt Turnbull and Asser. The only thing that marred his perfection was the slight fullness in his cheeks and the hint of rings under his eyes which gave him a rather debauched look. Too many nights in the Casbah.

Despite his attractiveness and obvious come-on, Allison couldn't help introducing politics into the conversation. She was, as usual, blunt. She found that she got more that way. If you caught people off guard, they responded, more out of surprise than anything else.

"I hear you've been working over several people in the Administration," she said, a smile on her face. "I'm told you're a pretty good persuader. Have you gotten what you want from the President yet?"

She was right. He looked stunned. He had been concentrating on sex and she had caught him off guard.

"How do you know that?" he asked. He wasn't smiling any longer.

"It's my job to know that. You want technology, a guarantee of protection, and a Palestinian homeland. That's a tall order. But you should be able to get the first two. Oman is in a pretty good negotiating position."

"I'm afraid it's not as simple as you might think."

"I didn't say it was simple." She bristled at the insinuation. "I said you're in a pretty good negotiating position. Besides, President Grey is a lot more pro-Arab than Roger Kimball was."

"Unfortunately, as I'm sure you know, there are a few obstacles in our path."

He was either trying to tell her something or challenging her knowledge, and she didn't know what he was talking about.

"Doesn't the challenge make it more interesting for you?" She was teasing him. She wanted him off balance; she intended the *double entendre*.

He couldn't tell whether she was coming on or not. "I'm afraid the challenge is not very attractive. The opposition to our interests comes from someone very close to the President." He paused, then zapped her back: "But I'm sure you know all of that."

Who in Rosey Grey's inner circle could be anti-Oman and so influential? Why?

"What I don't know," she said, still faking, "but what you could enlighten me about, is what his motives are."

"You're the reporter; you find out. Frankly, I find it most baffling."

Allison didn't know whether he knew she didn't know whom he was talking about.

"I have an idea," she said. "Why don't you have a party in his honor at the embassy? Dancing, caviar, champagne, music—that sort of thing. Soften him up a bit."

Ali grimaced in spite of himself.

"This man would never be interested in a party of that sort."

So it was Everett Dubois. The President's special assistant. How odd. As far as she knew, Everett was in tight with the Arabs and the oil companies. Suspiciously so. It didn't make any sense. But it would be fun to find out. Allison loathed Everett. He was a sleaze.

Ali was looking at Allison trying to determine whether she had understood. He seemed to want her to know something without having to tell her.

"Of course—you're absolutely right," she said. "I have a better idea. Why don't you assign one of your most beautiful spies to seduce him?"

Ali laughed delightedly. "How do I know you are not an agent for the CIA assigned to seduce me?"

"You don't."

"I promise you it will be the easiest assignment of your life."

She smiled, but she was unnerved. She looked away and took a sip of wine.

"Why don't you start working me over, as you say, when I take you home tonight?"

"I'm hurt that you haven't asked me for an interview," said Jones Barrett, turning to Allison. He was turning the table himself, forcing Ali to turn to the woman on his left. Lorraine had seated them both next to "wives." Now Jones looked liberated and Ali resigned.

"What would you like to talk about?" she asked. "Your latest picture?" He was sexy, there was no question about that.

"How about the Presidential campaign?"

Her instinct was to put him down. On second thought, though, she figured most women would have that reaction. A secure woman would be charming and appreciative. She decided to change her tack.

"It's true," she said.

"What's true?"

"You *are* sexy."

"I don't believe you said that."

"Why?"

"Well, your reputation is . . . I mean, isn't it a bit uncharacteristic for you to say that?" But he was clearly pleased.

"I'm a reporter. My job is to discover truth and report it."

"How about investigating a little deeper?"

"Are you sure you want that? I'm pretty thorough."

"You're pretty sexy yourself."

They were both pleased with their little game. His hair was deliberately uncombed. He looked as if he had just gotten out of bed. He focused on her as if she were the only woman he had ever seen. She decided she would definitely like to make love, probably this evening. Ali would have to wait. Besides, Ali was too complicated. And he had a story she needed.

"I could always interview you," she said, "but then we'd have a problem."

"Let's skip the interview," he said quickly, and grinned his adorable grin.

"I could make you famous, put your name in lights. I was thinking of a three-part series for the A section on 'The Politicalization of Jones Barrett.' I'd go back and interview all your old girlfriends, get them to remember when you first got interested in politics."

Jones smiled and leaned over to her so that his mouth was almost touching her neck. "I really want to fuck you," he said. She could feel his breath touching her neck. All she could think of was how to get through the rest of the evening so they could leave and go home to bed. Several people at the table had stopped talking and were looking at them. It did appear that Jones was about to kiss her. He straightened up quickly. She looked at him solemnly and said with a sincere voice, "I quite agree. Isn't it a coincidence that we both feel the same way about an issue on which I am normally quite conservative?"

"Politics does make strange bedfellows," he said.

Archie was the worst toast-giver in Washington. It was legendary. This was no exception. He managed to insult Allison by announcing that she had been in hiding for almost a year, but now she was back on the market. "And she looks like she's doing pretty well for herself tonight," said Archie, leering at Allison. "To Sonny!"

Allison had had just enough wine and was just giddy enough that she started to giggle as she stood to respond.

"I would like to thank Archie and Lorraine for launching me tonight. And as I look to my left and to my right there is no question that I could not have done better myself. It's wonderful to be at a party inspired by friendship alone." Did anybody believe that one? "Where everyone is here simply to have a good time." She knew nobody believed that, but Lorraine beamed. "I've had the best time I've had at a party in years, and the only thing that mars the evening is that Archie is not available." She paused for the appreciative laughter and Lorraine's shriek of pleasure. "A toast to our host and hostess!"

It wasn't until after dinner, when Allison was perched on one of Lorraine's love seats talking office politics with Walt Fineman, that Senator Earl Downs made his approach. Downs had always repelled Allison with his pudgy little body and squinty little eyes.

"Why, Miss Allison," he said, "I hope you don't mind if I join you. Unfortunately I was not lucky enough to sit by your side at dinner."

Walt jumped in. "Please do, Senator. We were just talking about the predicament in Oman."

Downs's face dropped. This was not what he had hoped to discuss.

"Ah, yes," he said carefully. "You were sitting next to Habib."

Allison heard the caution in his voice and glanced quickly at Walt. As Chairman of the Foreign Relations Committee, Downs would know what was going on. He knew as well as Allison that the only thing that mattered was that one knew what was going on. In Washington knowledge was the hot commodity.

"I gather that Everett Dubois is causing the Omanis some trouble," said Allison, testing.

"He said that?"

She smiled. Downs took that as an affirmative. "Well, hell, if Habib's talking about it . . . Frankly, we don't understand what Dubois's problem is, but I'll be goddamned if he doesn't have the President's ear on this thing."

Allison didn't know what "this thing" was, but she wasn't about to quit now. She could see Walt looking at her with amusement. He loved watching her do her number.

"Senator," said Allison, "I don't believe I've introduced you and Walt Fineman. As you know, Walt is the National Editor at *The Daily.*"

"Glad to meet you, Walt," said Downs. "Of course I know of you." He had had a bit to drink, Allison thought.

"It's always been a mystery to me what President Grey sees in Everett Dubois," said Allison.

"He's one shrewd son-of-a-bitch, that's for sure," said Downs.

"Darling, I see you got a chance to talk to the Senator," said Lorraine. "But you mustn't let him take all your time. And Walt, office gossip is not allowed. Allison, your toast was adorable. Archie will never get over it."

"Hell, Archie thought he'd died and gone to heaven," chuckled Downs, looking down at his glass. "Look at me—I'm empty." And he stood up and headed toward the bar.

Allison glanced at Walt. It was probably for the best. She wasn't exactly sober. She would do better to interview him later.

Allison glanced across the room and noticed with amusement that Edwina was all over Jones Barrett and Claire was practically in Ali's lap. She looked at Lorraine pointedly, then back at the two women.

"All right," said Lorraine. "You were right. Don't rub it in."

"What do those women want?" said Allison, suddenly serious.

"Anything but what they have, my dear."

"But they have what they wanted."

"Ask your friend Ali. There's an old Arab saying I picked up in London. 'You get what you want and you pay for it.'"

Allison thought for a moment of Des. "And pay and pay and pay," she said quietly to herself.

"I believe," said Jones, who was approaching the two with a wicked grin, having pried himself away from Edwina, "that you wanted a ride home."

"Yes," said Allison. She had almost forgotten.

He crooked his arm and looked down at her.

"Whatever the lady wants the lady gets."

The next morning, shortly after Jones had left, the doorbell rang. Allison threw on her robe and ran down the two flights of stairs. The man at the door was dressed in a black chauffeur's uniform.

Double-parked in front of her house was a shiny new dark blue Mercedes with a beige leather interior. The man handed her a thick ecru envelope.

"What is it?" she asked.

"A Mercedes, madame," he replied in a heavy accent, and turned and walked quickly down Olive Street, disappearing around the corner.

Inside the envelope were a set of car keys and a note. In strong, heavy black ink was scrawled: "Now you won't have to depend on the kindness of strangers for a ride home. Ali."

Was he serious? Could he possibly have intended to give her this car? No. It was not possible. But here was this bloody Mercedes in the middle of the street. What the hell was she supposed to do? And the note. She actually had sort of sneaked out with Jones because she had pretty much agreed to let Ali take her home before Jones made his move. She closed the door and turned to the phone on the counter in her tiny kitchen. She got the number of the embassy through Information, then explained patiently to the secretary that she had to speak to the Ambassador immediately.

"Ah, Cinderella, good morning." His voice was cheery.

"Ali," she said, trying to be calm, "there's a brand-new blue Mercedes double-parked in front of my house."

"Is it blocking your car?"

"My Fiat is parked around the corner."

"I see."

"Ali, what am I supposed to do with this Mercedes?"

"I would suggest you park it before the neighbors call the police and have it towed."

"And then what am I supposed to do with it?"

"Drive it with pleasure. Frankly, I cannot bear the idea of a beautiful woman like yourself driving around in a pathetic little Fiat which you told me yourself is always breaking down. What if you stalled in the middle of the night on a dark street?"

"My mechanics' bill would be considerably less than if it happened in a Mercedes."

"I don't want you to worry about the mechanics' bill. I will take care of it."

"Ali!"

"Yes?" His voice was innocent.

"For Christ's sake, will you send somebody over and get this car immediately!"

"Why? It's yours."

"Don't be naive, Ali. You know perfectly well that I cannot accept a car from you."

"Why not?"

"Because I'm a journalist and you are a potential source and it would be a conflict of interest. That's why."

"Then I will never discuss business with you again."

"That's not the point and you know it. I can't accept gifts, period. That's a rule."

"You mean reporters cannot accept gifts from people they go out with, not even birthday and Christmas presents?"

"That's different."

"Frankly, Sonny, you are offending me, whether you know it or not. I consider myself a potential suitor, not a potential source.

In my country it is the custom to give presents to people we admire. By refusing my gift you are insinuating that I am trying to buy you off in some way, and that is the worst possible insult. You question my sincerity, my generosity, my motivations."

The humor was gone from his voice. He really was offended.

"Listen, Ali, it's just that we have different customs in this country, and the appearance of conflict, even if it wasn't the case, could ruin my career—don't you understand that?"

"No, I don't. Why don't you try to explain it to me a little better over dinner tonight? I will pick you up at eight thirty. We will eat at the embassy. Goodbye."

He hung up.

"Shit," she said out loud. "What am I going to do with this fucking Mercedes?"

But before she had even finished her sentence she knew perfectly well what she was going to do with the Mercedes. She was going to drive it.

The drive over to the Omani Embassy was bliss. She had put the sliding roof back, and the warm September air blew her hair across her eyes as she glided down P Street and up Florida Avenue toward Decatur Place. God, what a fabulous car!

She could feel the wave of depression come over her as she pulled through the black iron gates and into the brick courtyard of the embassy. She jumped out and rang the doorbell. A uniformed man came to the door, and she plunked the keys into his hand and walked quickly away before he had a chance to say anything.

Walt Fineman was in his office when she arrived at the paper.

"Well, it's finally happened," he said. He had a rather smug look on his face.

"What?"

"Wiley got canned this morning. They've found some obscure company to offer him a job. Allen is his replacement."

"Jesus—I'm away from a phone for twenty minutes and I miss the biggest event in the last ten years. When did this happen?"

"In the last twenty minutes."

"How's Wiley handling it?"

"He resigned citing personal reasons. He is thrilled to have been offered the new job, anxious for the new challenge, anticipating making new strides, blah blah blah."

"Allen must be wetting his pants. If I know him, he's already moved poor old Wiley out of his office."

Walt nodded toward the glass office where Wiley had held forth. Allen was standing in the middle of the room, his arms full of books and papers, and Wiley was directing him as to where to put them.

"God, what a killer. He actually makes me feel sorry for Wiley."

"Spare yourself the emotion. Wiley's an asshole."

"So who takes over as Managing Editor?" Before she finished the question, she caught the grin on his face and threw her arms around him. "Oh, Walt, that's fabulous. I was afraid to ask. I just knew they were going to give it to Worth Elgin."

"You don't have enough faith in me."

"It's not enough to be the best editor: you have to be a good politician too. Worth is always working overtime—not to mention Claire. And Allen is so hard-nosed. I never saw you as his type."

"First of all, I have a feeling it was gently suggested to Allen. Secondly, Allen is at least smart enough to recognize the fact that he's not Mr. Congeniality. I'm a good balance for him, and I'm no threat. He knows that."

"You could be."

"You sound like Claire Elgin."

"Go fuck yourself."

"Which reminds me: I am the Managing Editor now and I would appreciate a little more respect from my reporters."

"It depends on how you define respect. I never once told Wiley Turnbull to go fuck himself."

"In that case all is forgiven. But let's move on to more important things than my ascent to the top."

"Next to the top."

"Excuse me. I seem to have had an attack of ambition."

"See, with a little coaching from me you might be able to ease Allen out of his job."

Walt burst out laughing. "If I got to be the editor, would you marry me?"

"Sorry, Walt darling, I'm saving myself for Earl Downs, the distinguished Senator from Florida."

"That's exactly what I wanted to talk to you about."

"Don't worry—I'm still intact."

"I *am* worried. That guy is hot for you. But we need him. I think you ought to do a follow-up interview."

"You should be more worried about Ali Habib."

"How so? I thought you went home with Jones." He wrinkled his nose. He was always jealous of her men.

"I did, but ungrateful wretch that he is, he just fucked and ran. Ali, on the other hand, is going the opposite route. This is a man who knows how to woo."

"Don't tell me, let me guess. This morning the doorbell rang and it was a tall, mysterious Arab at the door with . . . fill in the blanks . . . a diamond necklace; caviar; the keys to a Rolls-Royce."

Allison was truly shocked.

"How the hell did you know?"

It was Walt's turn to be shocked.

"You mean he gave you a Rolls-Royce? Jesus."

"No, you asshole, it was only a Mercedes."

"A Mercedes! What did you do with it?"

"I drove it, you idiot; what else?"

"Wait a minute, Sonny. We have a rule—"

"Right: you can't accept gifts unless it's something you can eat, drink, fuck, or drive within twenty-four hours."

She could see Walt wasn't finding this amusing.

"What's he buying?"

"He would be deeply offended by that remark. We've already had the conversation. And you can relax. I drove it back to the embassy. Boy, was that a sacrifice. You should have seen me, Walt. I looked real good in that baby."

"Now what?"

"I don't know. I'm going to need him for the Oman story. So I've got to stay on his good side, at least for the time being. We'll just have to keep the conflict-of-interest problem under control. He really doesn't get it, either. This will be a neat trick. I know he wants to go to bed with me."

"Well, you're certainly not going to do that. As your editor, I can strongly advise you against it."

"Gimme a break, Walt."

"Well, shit, I'm not going to sit here and watch you throw your career down the drain."

"I took the car back. What do you want?"

"You know what I want."

She started to blush. She knew he wanted her.

"I want the bloody story. That's what I want."

"I'll call Earl Downs's office right now and see if I can set up an interview. I'll probably wait a couple of days before I hit up Ali on this story. Meanwhile I'll see what I can pick up at the White House. Although everyone is pretty close-mouthed when it comes to Everett Dubois. They're all scared of him. He apparently can be one mean son-of-a-bitch."

"So go call."

She smiled at Walt, who sat hunched over his desk. He looked defeated, even in victory.

"I'm very proud of you," she said.

He smiled back at her and she thought he looked as if he were going to cry.

Her desk was a mess. One day she was going to clean it up. It would be nice to be able, at least, to find the Rolodex at will. She didn't trust the computer enough to put all her numbers on it. The computer was always going down at the most crucial moment. Things disappeared in the machine as if it were quicksand, never to be found again. The Rolodex had to be there somewhere, unless another reporter had borrowed it and forgotten to put it back. That was not unusual. Allison had the hottest Rolodex at the office.

She finally gave up and dialed the number of the Capitol.

CA 4-3121. That number was engraved on every reporter's brain—that and 456-1414, the White House.

She got Senator Downs's appointments secretary right away.

"Ah, yes. Senator Downs was expecting your call."

"I'd like to set up an interview with the Senator. He knows what the subject is to be."

"The Senator asked me to explain to you that he would be happy to talk to you but he will be unable to see you during the day. He is booked up with meetings and out-of-town constituents. He wanted to know if we could set up something in the evening later this week."

Allison was thrown. She had felt smug when the secretary said she was expecting her call. Now she could see he was putting one over on her. She wanted to sound firm, but all she could say was "Uh—I, uh, had hoped I might be able to catch him for breakfast."

"I'm sorry." The secretary's voice was as firm as Allison wanted to be. "It will have to be after eight P.M. The Senator suggests you meet him when he comes off the floor."

The little fucker. He had her. What could she say? Her male colleagues had had dinner with Earl Downs. His wife was never around. They thought nothing of it. It was a convenient way to get a source relaxed. Dinners were preferable to rushed breakfasts and lunches. A few drinks and people opened up. She, on the other hand, would have to contend with rumors, appearances, not to mention the fact that he would be trying to get into her pants all the way through the interview.

"That will be fine," said Allison. "Dinner will be fine." She hoped she sounded casual. "But I would prefer to meet the Senator at the restaurant."

"The Senator has some documents in his office he would like to show you. He thought you might like to meet him when he comes off the floor. He hoped tomorrow night would be convenient."

"Fine."

After she hung up she felt like an ass. She picked up the phone and made a reservation at Duke Zeibert's. A lot of journalists and politicians hung out at Duke's. If she took him to Duke's, put her notebook on the table, and took notes through dinner, there would be no mistaking what they were doing.

Allison went straight to Downs's office instead of meeting him when he came off the floor. She didn't like the way the Senator's receptionist looked at her when she walked into the office. She was asked to have a seat in the outer office. When the Senator finally appeared, he was dripping with perspiration, mopping his brow with a damp handkerchief.

"Kinda hot, isn't it," he drawled. "You look like you could use a nice cool drink as bad as I could. C'mon in." He motioned her into his inner sanctum, the walls filled, as she might have expected, with the Senator and every famous person he had ever met.

"Senator, your secretary mentioned some documents you wanted to show me."

"Documents?" He looked surprised. "Well, honey, I was expecting to get some documents from the Senator from Louisiana, but I haven't had any luck in getting him to turn them over to me."

He mopped his pink face once more, and Allison's skin crawled.

"I had reservations made at the Prime Rib," he said.

The Prime Rib piano bar was where the out-of-town lobbyists took their bimbos.

"Oh, dear," she said. "The bar is so loud and distracting. I was thinking of someplace quieter where we could do the interview. I took the liberty of making a reservation at Duke's."

"Forget Duke's. Every journalist in Washington will be there. I don't want to be nailed as your source. I'm about to give you some pretty confidential stuff, honey." He winked.

"Let's compromise," he said. "We'll go to the Intrigue. Nice and quiet, and no interruptions. We can talk in privacy to our hearts' content."

One-upped again. She couldn't believe he was getting the better of her every time. She must be out of practice. But he had something she wanted. She was going to get it, but she was going to have to work for it. The Intrigue was quiet, dark, with little alcoves and cubbyholes. It was not the place you wanted to go with someone other than your spouse unless you had motives. It wasn't worth fighting this time. She would have to be very much on her guard.

The Senator was well known at the restaurant. His table was in the rear, secluded. The service was discreet.

"Does everyone tell you how beautiful you are?" he whispered the moment they had been seated.

"I understand your wife is very beautiful."

He looked sour. "Let's order drinks. I'll have a margarita. How about you?"

"Kir, very light, please."

"What's that?"

"It's white wine with a touch of cassis in it. It was named after a priest who was Mayor of Dijon."

"Boy, honey, you don't miss a trick, do you?" He smirked.

He called the waiter "Garçon," mispronouncing it, and fumbled with the wine list.

The minute their dinner came, Allison whipped out her notebook and slapped it on the table. Squinting in the gloom, she began asking questions.

"You don't look nearly as pretty when you're serious," he said.

"I'm sorry to disappoint you, Senator, but I'm afraid I'm going to be serious for the rest of the evening."

"Call me Earl."

"I couldn't. Senator just seems to suit you better."

"I've ordered crêpes Suzette for dessert. I hope you like it." The waiter was opening a second bottle of expensive wine. Allison was still nursing her first glass.

She was so close to walking out, she almost put her pad and pencil away. Yet something inside her managed to keep her distance. It was almost as though she were watching his behavior through a one-way mirror. If every reporter, male or female, walked away from a source because he felt insulted, the copy flow would be severely diminished. Ultimately she would get the better of him, and if she had to put up with him for a while, then she would. Besides, he was getting drunk. He would talk.

"Put that goddamned notebook away," he said. He was slurring his words. "Put it away"—he gestured again—"or I won't tell you what I'm going to tell you."

She took it off the table and pretended to put it into her purse, resting it instead on the banquette beside her. Reporters can take notes in the dark.

"I think I know what has motivated our friend Everett Dubois into putting the kibosh on the Omanis."

His eyes were gleaming in the candlelight. This was it. He thought he could buy her with this information. She looked up and caught his stare. She quickly looked down. She didn't want to seem too interested. It might scare him. She said nothing.

"Ol' Everett, it seems, got sumpthin goin' with some Louisiana"—he said Looziana—"offshore oil company. The Omanis made some deal with a British company and Everett's pals didn't get the contract. I'm not saying Everett was going to get anything out of it, y'hear. All I'm sayin' is that some folks think it's mighty coincidental that Everett's turned sour on the Omanis right after the Louisiana contract fell through."

Allison nodded to indicate she was listening. She didn't want to cut him off before he finished; but he stopped talking.

"What was the name of the company?"

"That, I'm afraid, you'll have to look up. I don't have it right here at my fingertips. I don't know the name of the British company either. In fact, little lady, I don't know anything more than what I told you. How about a brandy?"

"No, thank you. How much influence in this matter do you think Everett has with the President?"

"Lots. Everett's field is oil. He worked for that oil company in Louisiana long before he went to work for the Governor of Oklahoma. The President thinks Everett knows everything about oil deals and he trusts his judgment."

"Do you think the President knows about Everett's connection to the Louisiana oil company?"

"Hell, no. Rosewell Grey is the biggest candy-ass I ever met. He wouldn't know a kickback deal if it hit him in the face. Now, that's about all I have to say on this subject. If you won't have a brandy, how about coming back to my place for a nightcap?"

Allison had what she needed, and she figured he really didn't know any more. She put her notebook into her purse and stood up. He jumped up and tried to pull her back down. "Wait a second—I haven't paid yet," he said.

"It's all taken care of, monsieur," said the maître d'hôtel, who had stopped by their table. He nodded toward Allison. Allison had paid on her way to the ladies' room earlier.

Even in the dark she could see the Senator's face turn red.

"Hell, no, I'm not lettin' some girl pay my way."

She was walking toward the door, not even turning around to see him. She stepped out onto New Hampshire Avenue just in time to see a cab heading toward the Kennedy Center. She hailed it and jumped in, breathing a sigh. The sigh was premature. Earl Downs was in the seat next to her before the cab could pull away.

"Sure you don't want a little nightcap?" His voice was pleading.

She stared out the window.

Then she felt his hand. She looked down and watched horrified as he put his paw on her thigh at the same time he was making a smacking noise with his mouth. It was the same sensation as watching a tarantula crawl over her.

"Get your hands off me," she said in a quiet, deadly voice, "or I will have the cabdriver take us directly to the police station, where I will have you charged with attempted rape." Then she turned to him and looked him directly in the eye. "And don't think I don't mean it."

He moved his small, round frame over to his corner of the car and sulked as the cab drove down Pennsylvania Avenue to M Street, then turned right on Twenty-eighth. She could hear his heavy breathing, and his boozy breath filled the taxi, making her slightly nauseated. The cab pulled up in front of her house. She quickly opened the door and had begun to get out when she heard his raspy voice say in almost a whisper, "If you didn't want to go to bed with me, why did you have dinner?" His expression registered utter confusion, and for a moment she almost felt sorry for him. Instead, she burst out laughing and ran inside her house.

Later, when she went to close a window, she noticed the dark blue Mercedes parked out in front.

Allison was still smarting from her dinner with Earl Downs and her latest conversation—or rather, argument—with Ali. She had at last won out with her insistence that she could not accept the car. It had taken several dinners alone with him at the Omani Embassy. She would drive over in the car and leave the keys. He would have it delivered the next morning. The third evening at the embassy, she lost her temper.

"If you cared at all about me, and you say you do, then you have got to take this car back and never give me another present. Please try to understand that our rules are different and you are hurting me by giving me presents, which I believe is the opposite of what you want to do."

Ali seemed convinced finally.

At first she had thought she might have trouble with his trying to make a pass at her. But he never once tried to touch her or even insinuate that they might end up in bed. He was a perfect gentleman, and delightful company.

He received her on the second floor in the garden room, a light, airy high-ceilinged room with French doors which gave onto a beautiful, private second-floor-level garden. It was a tiny oasis, with lush trees, fall flowers, a small grassy area, and a diminutive swimming pool lined in mosaics. There was a ceramic lion's head which spat water into one end of the pool, creating the sound of a fountain burbling quietly in the background.

The garden-room walls were covered in pale lemon-yellow damask, as were the draperies and the plump down-filled sofas. The rugs were soft rose Orientals, the French watercolors in pastel hues. Fresh-cut flowers were on the mantel in front of the mirror, and from somewhere Debussy was playing. It was still warm enough for the doors to be open, and when twilight came Ali turned down the lights and lit candles around the room for a gentle glow.

She wondered why she was not sexually attracted to him. He had to be one of the best-looking men she had ever seen in her life. He was witty, intelligent, and well mannered. Yet there was something neuter about him to her, much to her relief. She didn't dwell on it. Sex would only have interfered with her agenda. Everett Dubois.

It became clear to Allison only gradually that the reason he was as anxious as she not to be seen out in public was that he didn't want to be identified as her source. At least now she felt free to pursue the matter of Everett. She brought it up casually over caviar. She had done her research and knew a lot more than when she'd dined with Earl Downs.

"I'm rather curious as to why you chose to grant the offshore leasing contract to Marble Arch instead of Rittman. Rittman, from everything I can see, presented a much better bid, and they have a flawless reputation in Louisiana. Marble Arch has had so many problems with the North Sea drilling."

He cocked an eyebrow.

"I don't believe anything has been announced. Where did you get your information?"

"Well, it seemed the obvious place to go was Everett Dubois."

She had not gone to Dubois, but then, that wasn't exactly a lie, either. She hadn't said she had, and it was the obvious thing.

"Indiscretion will only hurt him, not Oman."

"He can hurt Oman?"

"He already has."

"So why didn't you play along with him? Give his company the contract? Even if he were going to get a kickback, that's not your problem. You have different customs—or need I remind you?"

"Ah, that such a beauty could be so cruel!"

"You didn't answer my question."

He looked at her long and hard, then lowered his eyes and almost whispered, "The demands were greater than we found acceptable. At least with the British company there were no strings. He's playing a dangerous game, that man."

"It gets more dangerous for him as we talk." She probably shouldn't have said that, but Ali didn't seem deterred.

He smiled, and his teeth clenched together as he said conspiratorially, "We didn't talk."

CHAPTER 14

SHE HAD TO TELL JENNY. THERE WAS NO choice, really. If it was going to work, she had to have an accomplice. And she was determined to make it work. It was going to save her sanity.

She had asked Jenny to come upstairs for lunch in her tiny office in the family quarters. It was where she did her correspondence, paid bills, dealt with household matters. It was one of her favorite places in the White House because of its intimacy and its view of Lafayette Park and the gardens. It was her window on the real world.

Sadie was standing by the window looking out at the demonstrators in front of the White House, trying to figure out how to tell her, when Jenny knocked on the door. Jenny had a questioning look as she walked in.

"What on earth is going on? You sounded mysterious on the phone. And why are we meeting in here?"

Sadie hadn't realized how nervous she was. She had twisted one curl at the back of her head so hard that strands of auburn hair were beginning to come out in her hand. She smiled feebly.

"Why don't you sit down, Jenny."

Jenny sat down on the little chintz love seat against the wall and looked expectant. "So?"

"Well . . ." she began, walking the floor.

"Are you all right?"

"I'm just fine. I have something to discuss with you."

"You're not happy with my work, you'd like to look for another press secretary. Look, Sadie, if you don't think I'm right for you, then—"

"Oh, for God's sake," said Sadie, laughing in spite of herself.

"What is it, then? You're acting like a deranged person."

"As a matter of fact, when you hear what I'm about to tell you you'll think I am."

"Come on. Out with it."

Sadie paced a few minutes, then plopped onto the chair facing Jenny. She took a breath.

"I'm having an affair."

Jenny stared at her.

"I'm having an affair."

Then, as if she had no energy left, she collapsed against the cushion and waited for a response.

Jenny still didn't say anything, and Sadie didn't have the energy to say any more.

Finally Jenny whispered, "Holy shit." Then she leaned back and put her hand on her head.

"I think you need a new press secretary," she said quietly. And then, raising her voice: "Are you out of your mind?"

"I told you you would think I'm deranged."

"Does the President know about this?"

"Now it's my turn to ask you if *you're* out of your mind."

"Do you mind if I ask a few questions like who, what, how, when, and where? Especially how?"

"That's why I'm telling you. I need your help."

"What? I'm supposed to help you with this suicide? No, thank you. I don't even want to know about it. Let's pretend you didn't tell me."

"Jenny, I'm serious. I'm having an affair. I'm very much in love, I plan to continue seeing him, and I need to find a way. I need you to figure out a way."

"Jesus. On the *oy vay* scale of one to ten, this is definitely a ten."

"Will you?"

"I have an idea," said Jenny. "Why don't you meet in the press room? That way it will save the reporters a few days' work and it will get the whole thing over with in no time."

"Come on, Jenny. Be serious."

"You want serious? I'll give you serious. This affair must stop immediately. It is insane. You cannot do it. You will be found out and you will destroy your husband, not to mention the welfare of the nation. Sadie, I'm not kidding, you have got to put your country first. And that's all there is to it."

It was as if Sadie were watching her body sitting calmly in the chair as her spirit drifted up to the ceiling and gazed down dispassionately at the scene. She felt nothing. No fear, no guilt, no remorse, no frustration.

"It's not negotiable, Jenny," she said with utter calm. "Either you help me find a way to do it secretly or I'll have to find a way myself. I think you'll agree that with your help we have less chance of being found out."

"You never answered my question. Who's the other half of 'we'?"

Sadie looked at her with a straightforward glance.

"Desmond Shaw."

Jenny could feel her stomach drop out.

"Holy shit," she said.

"You already said that."

"This time I mean it."

Sadie lay in bed that night thinking. Rosey had long since been asleep. He always went to sleep the minute he kissed her good night and put his head on the pillow. They made love even less often now. Every six weeks or so. He was so busy, so preoccupied, so tired. It was a relief. Shortly after she and Des had made love Rosey had wanted to and she had put him off. She knew in a few weeks she would have to. It upset her but if she was going to continue with Des she would have to learn to compartmentalize the two. She couldn't keep Rosey at bay if she wanted to keep him from being suspicious.

She had finally persuaded Jenny. It was her implacable stance that had won her over. Jenny was stunned. She had obviously thought she could talk Sadie out of it. And too, Sadie knew that

Jenny must hurt for Allison. Not to mention the guilt she obviously felt about her complicity.

It had taken them most of the day to figure out how it might work. Jenny had called down to her office to tell her people to hold calls and Sadie had rung the butler for lunch. For some reason she was ravenous. Being able to talk about it and make plans had given her a sense of exhilaration. Jenny ate scarcely a bite. She sent down for some cigarettes and drank a dozen cups of black coffee. But she had come through.

The plan was this: "Lagoon" would have to take an office. Lagoon was the Secret Service name for Sadie. Rosey was "Hilltop." Des, they decided, would be "Canyon."

Lagoon would tell Hilltop that she needed another office away from the White House where she could write. Hilltop knew that Lagoon had been longing to get back to her writing. But it was difficult because both in her East Wing office and in her private office off the West Sitting Room, there were constant interruptions. There was an office over in the Executive Office Building, the hideaway of a former President, which had remained vacant. Jenny knew about it because Everett Dubois was trying to secure it for his private use and Hilltop's staffers were trying to discourage that. All Lagoon had to do was open her mouth and it would be hers. Hilltop was already feeling guilty about not spending enough time with her, and he would do anything to make her happy.

It wasn't entirely a subterfuge. She really did want to get back to her writing. Canyon had been very encouraging. Even though she had enough to do to keep her busy, none of it gave her a sense of accomplishment or fulfillment. Writing was something she did for herself. She was bored and lonely sitting around the West Sitting Room talking on the phone in her spare time. Still, even with this private office, Canyon would not be able to visit her often. She would, in fact, have a place to write in peace.

The tricky part was going to be getting Canyon into and out of the EOB. There was a guard at the main entrance behind electronic gates who checked everyone's credentials, signed people in and out, and called whomever they were to visit before letting them in. Jenny was going to have to befriend one of the guards in the afternoon shift. She would confide in him that the First Lady was writing a novel, that it was ultrasecret, and that her editor would be visiting her occasionally to work with her on the book.

Jenny would tell Toby Waselewski, Lagoon's private agent, and she would get Toby to check with the guard each time Canyon was coming. Canyon would have to come at a specified time so that only one of the guards would be aware of him.

Jenny thought it might work. For a while.

"Des?"

"Hi, beauty. I thought you'd never call."

"Sorry. I've had the kids from Children's Hospital here all afternoon for a concert. I couldn't get away until now."

"Jesus, it's so frustrating not to be able to call you."

"I've fixed that."

"What do you mean?"

"I've had a private, unmonitored telephone put in. It doesn't go through the White House switchboard. I've had it installed in my office off the West Sitting Room. I've given instructions that nobody is allowed to answer it but me."

"That's genius. How did you pull that off?"

"I told you. Rosey is so worried about my mental and emotional health that he will do anything to make me happy, with the exception of giving up the Presidency."

"So when do we continue with our interview? And where?"

"I told Jenny."

"Christ. How did she take it?"

"Not too well at first. In fact, rather badly. But I told her if she didn't help me I'd have to figure out a way to do it on my own."

"And?"

"She's on the case. I must say, once she puts her mind to it she really is amazing. She's already figured out the whole strategy."

"Are you going to let me in on this or am I the last to know?"

"No, no. Here's the plan. You know Rosey's gone down to New Orleans to speak to some offshore-oil types—something Everett got him into. Anyway, he has agreed to give me an old office over in the EOB. It was used by President Norton. I haven't seen it, but Jenny says it's wonderful. She and I are going to do a walk-through tonight, since Rosey's out of town, and sort of fix it up a little bit. Then Jenny will give you your marching instructions."

"You two don't waste any time, do you?"

"Jenny has this shrink who always used to tell her, You get

what you want. The trick is to know what it is that you do want. I know. That's why I'm not wasting any time. Oh, by the way, you're not going to be interviewing me anymore."

"No? I got the idea you kind of liked to be interviewed by me."

"I loved being interviewed by you, and I'm going to love even more being edited by you."

"Edited?"

"Yes, on a longtime basis. You see, I'm writing a novel. And this novel is going to take at least two years to finish. I foresee burning a lot of midnight oil."

"Well, I think it sounds like a great idea. I would be honored to be your editor, but I must warn you . . . I have a relentless pencil."

"I feel like a schoolgirl sneaking out after curfew."

Sadie was dressed in beige slacks and a beige string sweater set. Jenny was still in her office clothes. Sadie had a notebook and a tape measure. They might need some more furniture or some other things from the warehouse.

"What on earth have you got in that bag?" said Jenny, looking at Sadie's large leather satchel. "We're only going next door."

"It's a surprise. You'll see. But we'd better go. It's late enough, don't you think?"

"It's after nine. I'm sure most everybody will have left their offices by now. For one thing, the President's not here, so the suck-ups don't have that much reason to stay late."

"It's almost like walking through a plan to escape from a prison camp. In fact, that's pretty much what it is."

"Just always be aware that the minute we step off that elevator on the ground floor the monitor in the ushers' office is going to pick up Lagoon, and they'll know where you are every second."

"What a way to live. Why would anyone in their right mind choose to live this way?"

Jenny sighed.

The elevator door opened and they were on the ground floor facing the diplomatic entrance. Portraits of former First Ladies were hung up and down the red-carpeted hall.

"One day," said Sadie, "my portrait will hang here with the

rest of them . . . or will it? Maybe I will go down in infamy, scratched from the history books."

"Don't talk like that," said Jenny. "This is going to remain a secret even if *I* have to start having an affair with Des to cover up."

"Forget it."

"Actually, that's not such a bad idea."

They both laughed.

They turned right and walked down the corridor.

"We'll have to get the ushers to pull these red linen screens out so that we can walk behind them," mused Jenny. "We'll just call down before we come."

They followed the corridor down the stairs and past the Oval Office, down by the Xerox machines, past the door to the press office, through the colonnade, by the west garden room, down some more stairs to the Lower West Hall office, past the White House mess, and out the door and across the parking lot to the Executive Office Building.

"There must be a tunnel or something to the EOB so that I don't have to go outside in front of everyone in the cold and rain," said Sadie. "I can't believe there isn't."

"I've asked the Secret Service and they swear there isn't," said Jenny. "The fact is that there is no way you can get over to the EOB without having everybody in the White House, including the entire press corps, know it. So you better think that one over. God, you've practically got to walk through the bloody pressroom to get over here."

Sadie started to say something, but Jenny stopped her.

"Please, no suggestions about wigs and dark glasses. I can just see the front page of *The Daily* now . . . 'First Lady dashes to clandestine rendezvous' . . . Forget it. In fact, I'm going to have a little briefing on your activities and tell them that you are taking a small office in the EOB for your own personal writing. I'll tell them you have been writing poetry and short stories ever since you left *The Gotham* after you got married and that you have decided to do so for your own pleasure and relaxation."

"What if they ask if I'm going to publish anything?"

"Just say no, at least not while your husband is President. That's the truth, isn't it? Always tell the truth, even if you have to commit a few sins of omission. The fuckers will find out anyway and then you really will be in trouble. Besides, this is no big deal. It will probably play well anyway, the idea that the First Lady actually has a life of her own outside her official duties. It will appeal to women, and it won't threaten men the way it might if you were into, say, bodybuilding."

"Don't give me any ideas."

They were walking across the driveway between the EOB and the White House, but it was dark enough so that the few people who were getting into their cars didn't notice them. They hurried in the darkness to the freight entrance and went inside to the basement of the EOB and turned right to the elevator. There was nobody in sight as they got off the elevator on the second floor and turned right again. Immediately there was a large door which Jenny quickly opened. They were standing in a small, high-ceilinged room with a desk and a chair and a large window almost to the floor. The room had beautiful moldings and was painted a pale yellow. Sadie looked slightly disappointed.

"This isn't it," said Jenny. "This is the outer office. This is my office. This is where the watchdog sits. The inner sanctum is here." She pulled out a key and unlocked the adjoining door and flung it open almost as though she were showing a young bride her new home.

Sadie gasped. It was a fabulous room. On the left-hand wall, facing the White House, there were two large windows and a pair of French doors which gave onto a small balcony. The room was painted a soft beige, with off-white heavy linen curtains that matched the beautiful woodwork and moldings. Underneath one of the windows was a huge sofa in a soft beige linen with large pillows in various shades of off-white, cream, and beige. A large mocha rug carpeted the floor, and there were armchairs and antique end tables with small lamps around the room.

Facing the windows and the sofa was a large oak desk with a swing armchair behind it and a standing lamp over the typewriter table to the side. To the right of the desk was an imposing fireplace with moldings to match the crown moldings and chair rails. Around the room were paintings of historic American scenes in muted colors and one Gilbert Stuart portrait. It couldn't have been better if she had done it herself. It clearly hadn't been used for quite a while, yet one had almost the feeling that someone had just gotten up and walked away. It didn't look decorated. The neutral colors gave it a soft, cozy feeling. It was a room you could take your shoes off in. Or your clothes. . . .

"Oh, God, Jenny, it's perfect. I love it. Are you sure it's okay, that I can really have it?"

"I'm sure. Rosey requested it. He is, after all, the President. You haven't finished yet. There's another room through that door next to the fireplace."

Sadie walked over to the door and pulled it open. It was a tiny room with a love seat, two end tables with lamps, and next to it a small bathroom.

Sadie looked at the sofa, and Jenny, seeing the look on her face, said, "It's a sofa bed."

Sadie blushed.

"Come back in here," Jenny said quickly. "You didn't notice this console. It's a TV set. And there's a small bar with a refrigerator and sink in that closet on the other side of the fireplace."

"Maybe I'll just move in here," said Sadie. "It's got everything I want. Oh, Jenny"—and with that she reached over and embraced her friend, squeezing her so tightly that Jenny finally gave a little cough of embarrassment and pulled away.

"I think we should talk about logistics. You do realize that every time Canyon comes there will be people who will notice. That means that you absolutely cannot meet more than once a week, and even that's a bit heavy. I would suggest once every two weeks."

She saw Sadie's face fall.

"Sadie, sit down." She waited until Sadie was seated. "Now listen. You know I am not happy about this whole thing. As far as I'm concerned this is a suicide mission. There is no way, in my opinion, that you and Des are not going to be found out eventually. You're caught up in the moment, so you're not thinking clearly. I'm not going to try to change your mind. But you have got to start thinking realistically about this. You will be found out. I repeat that. There is no such thing anymore as a First Lady or a President being able to keep a secret about their activities. So you have got to decide how you are going to handle it. Because I am way out of my league on this one. Way out. It is simply beyond me even to contemplate the statement we will have to make when the shit hits the fan. And believe me, as sure as your name is Sara Adabelle McDougald Grey, it will."

Sadie looked thoughtful for a moment, then reached into her large bag and pulled out a bottle of Roederer Cristal champagne.

She uncorked it and poured two glasses. She held one aloft. "Cheers," she said.

Jenny sounded strangely distant on the phone.

"Jen, I'm depressed. I need a friend."

"Oh? What's the problem?" She sounded rushed.

"Nothing specific. Just 'it.' You're the smartest person I know. I need to talk to you. I need to figure some things out. Not on the phone," she added quickly. "I was thinking we could have dinner."

"When?"

"Tonight."

"Oh, jeez, I promised . . ." She paused. "I don't know. This is a killer week. The Greys are having a big dinner for the new Supreme Court Justice before the Court goes into session and Sadie's parents and brother are coming up and I've got so much shit to do."

"How about this weekend sometime?"

"Well, I don't know. I've got a dinner date Saturday night." She laughed a little nervously. "Saturday, it seems, is my only night off these days. Nobody told me the truth about this job. It's like taking the vows."

Allison knew she was being put off, but she couldn't figure out why, and she felt so hurt by Jenny's tone that she almost said goodbye. Normally so perceptive, she didn't catch the pain in Jenny's voice.

"I don't envy you," she said instead. "Well, don't worry about it. Maybe we could get together next week sometime."

"Next week would be great, terrific," said Jenny, relieved. "I should be out from under by then."

"Jen?"

"Yeah?"

"Who're you going out with Saturday night? You got some hot new flame you're not telling me about?"

"Not really—it's just that I, uh . . ."

"Jenny, it's me—Allison," she teased. "Crack reporter. You might as well tell me. You know I'm going to find out anyway."

"I know." Jenny wasn't laughing.

"So who is it?"

"It's Des."

* * *

"Do be careful, darling."

"I don't know what you're talking about, Lorraine." Sadie was munching on a piece of wheat toast without butter, a soft-boiled egg with no salt, half a pink grapefruit with no sugar, and tea with no skim milk or honey. She felt noble and deprived, but she had a renewed sense of purpose about her thighs since the affair with Des had begun.

She settled back against her Porthault pillows and shifted a bit uncomfortably. She knew Lorraine would lecture her before she unloaded any dirt, and she would have to listen. But she had already worked out what she wanted to say. She was innocent.

"Yes, you do. Desmond Shaw is a very attractive man. And, I might add, he's on the loose. And let's be honest. You weren't exactly ignoring him at that party for the Brazilians."

"First of all, Lorraine, you're projecting. In case you don't understand that, it's shrink talk for accusing me of something *you're* thinking of. I think Des is quite marvelous. I also think he is bad news. I think any woman who would get involved with him should have her head examined."

"That's not what I'm talking about. Everyone is talking about that cover story he did on you in *The Weekly*. A valentine if I ever saw one. He's trying to soften you up. And from the tone of your voice, he did a pretty good job."

"Oh, don't be ridiculous. That piece couldn't have been more helpful to me—or to Rosey, for that matter. I can use Des too. It works both ways."

"Don't ever deceive yourself about that. Listen, Sadie, I've told you this before and I'm going to tell it to you again. Des doesn't trust anyone and you shouldn't trust him. He is a reporter. He needs you. You are a source. First, last, and always. He may find you attractive. He most certainly does. But that means nothing. I have lived in this town for a long time and I want you to listen to me because I am right. Never, never trust a reporter. Everyone who does gets burned. You are no exception. Desmond Shaw would just as soon burn you as look at you if it meant a good story. And it seems to me that what happened between him and Allison is a good lesson for all of us. She would destroy the only decent relationship she's ever had, she would give up the love of her life, humiliate the man she adored—for what?—for a story. And as they like to say themselves, they will wrap the fish in it tomorrow. I'm not going to tell you this again. Do not trust the press, and particularly do not trust Desmond Shaw. Do, and you'll be sorry."

"Look, Sadie, your parents are one thing. Your brother is another."

Rosey was furious. He didn't turn red when he got mad the way most people did; he turned white. "A white rage" was what he called it when he was really angry. There were very few things that sent him into a white rage. One of them was Sadie's brother, Outland McDougald.

Rosey was standing in their bedroom next to the sofa by the fireplace. He had just taken a shower, and he was wearing his navy cashmere robe with the maroon monogram and the monogrammed needlepoint slippers Sadie had made for him several Christmases ago. He was glaring at her in a way he rarely did.

Sadie had just gotten ready for bed herself. She was still perspiring from her long soak in the tub, and she had put on a heavy terry-cloth robe over her damp skin. Her hair was brushed away from her face, and she had already creamed under her eyes.

"Oh, Rosey, what am I supposed to do? I've already invited him. Besides, it's not like it's a state dinner or anything. It's just a dinner for a new Supreme Court Justice whom Outland even approves of. Raleigh Foster is Southern and fairly conservative. Outland will behave himself. I know he will. He wouldn't do anything to embarrass me. Or you, for that matter. He gets along with G and Miz G. The kids will be here. I just thought it would be a good time to work the whole family in and get it over with in October so we won't have to worry about the holidays. I can't think of a better opportunity."

"Please don't 'Oh, Rosey' me. Your brother has caused me more embarrassment already than any of those fools ever caused Roger Kimball. He has done nothing but blast me and my policies since I've been in the White House. If he weren't your bloody brother nobody would give a damn what he wrote in his column for that worthless college-town paper. . . . I'm sorry. It's not acceptable."

He had alarmed her at first, he was so angry, and she had pleaded with him. Now she was mad.

"Oh, come off it, Rosey. You are enough of a politician to see the advantages in all of this, and don't think I'm so stupid I don't. There is a large faction in the Democratic Party that thinks you're too conservative. This is the best ammunition you could have. A right-wing brother-in-law who rails against you for being too liberal. And not only that, but every man in the country with a brother-in-law will sympathize with you. And especially that you would be gracious enough to welcome him into your home after what he has written and said about you. It makes you look bigger than all that pettiness."

"Sara Adabelle, I have had my say. As far as I'm concerned the subject is closed. Now will you kindly not discuss it any more. I have some briefs to go over for the NATO Economic Ministers' meetings and I don't need any more distractions."

It was Sadie who went white this time. She stood perfectly still as Rosey walked over to the king-size bed, carefully took off his robe and spread it over the side chair, placed his slippers beside his bed, climbed in between the sheets in his pajamas, put on his reading glasses, and calmly began going over his papers.

After a few minutes standing there without being taken notice of, she walked over to her side of the bed and perched on the edge of it, leaning slightly toward her husband.

"Don't you ever dismiss me like that again," she said evenly in a murderous tone. "Do you hear me?"

Rosey looked up, startled.

"Huh?"

"You heard what I said."

He started to respond.

"I am not finished yet ... Mr. President. I have one more thing to say to you. I did not want to be the First Lady of the United States, and I particularly do not want to campaign for the job. However, out of loyalty to you and nothing more, I have been planning to do everything I can to get you reelected so that I can spend another four years in boredom, fear, and misery. I have already sacrificed one year of my life and I have got five more to look forward to. There is nothing in it for me. Nothing but confinement. I loathe every minute of it. That is a lot to ask of another person. When one asks something like that of another person, then one must expect to give something in return. I do not ask you for much. The few things I do ask you for I expect to get. I asked you for an office and I got it. I asked you for a private telephone line and I got it. Each one of those favors required a phone call from your chief of staff. I am now asking for my brother to be invited to the White House for the first time in a year. I can understand your reluctance. But he is my brother and I love him very much. It means a lot to me. This is, as I understand it, our house, not your house. Therefore I will feel free to invite him or anyone else I wish to this house anytime I wish. If you try to stop me I will refuse to campaign for you, or fulfill any of the expected duties of the First Lady. That is only the most minor of my threats.

"Why do you think all of those political wives whose husbands are screwing everything in sight stay with them and campaign for them when they run? I'll tell you why. Because it's the first time in their lives that those women have total power over their husbands. They can destroy them with one sentence. All they have to do is open their mouths. After years of being beaten down and taken advantage of that's mighty enticing. Well, I don't want power. I just want to live what little life I have of my own the way I want to live it. And if I have to blackmail you to be able to do that, then so be it. I can start giving press conferences and say exactly what I think on every subject and you can't stop me. I can walk out on you and you can't stop me. I'm not going to do either of those things unless I'm pushed to the wall. But if you don't think I'm capable of it, then you just watch my stuff."

Rosey stared at her for the longest time. She returned his gaze. Neither of them spoke. Finally he took his glasses off and looked down at his hands in contemplation. After a while he looked up at her again.

"That was quite a speech," he said. There was no sarcasm in his voice.

She nodded as though that were the recognition she sought.

She took off her terry-cloth robe, flung it on the floor, and climbed into bed nude, her back to him.

"Good night, Rosey," she said as she turned out her light.

"Good night, sugar . . . " he said, then paused, a lilt in his voice. "Walk out on me if you have to. But please don't give a press conference."

* * *

"Lorraine, I don't care what you say. I'm tired of ass-kissing." Sadie was frustrated and angry. She was beginning to hate this dinner party for the new Justice, particularly since he was an old friend of the Greys'. Now Lorraine was telling her she had to start wooing the Washington insiders—the journalists, lawyers, lobbyists, Lorraine's Georgetown inner sanctum. It was getting close to the election, and though Rosey had no real opposition from the Republicans it would be foolish to take victory for granted.

"Darling, what on earth do you think politics is all about?" Lorraine was exasperated at Sadie's recalcitrance. "Have you forgotten these people were your friends? They can't help you, but they can hurt you. I don't have to tell you all this, Sadie. You know it as well as I do. They love you but they've always been suspicious of Rosey. They all talk a lot, and either they are the opinion-makers or they socialize with them. They're not going to lose Rosey the election. But it's better to have them on your side. And it's so easy. All you have to do is invite them to the White House for dinner. That always throws them off guard. It makes them a little less likely to bad-mouth Rosey. It's money in the bank. Goodwill. Whatever you want to call it."

"I did that in the Vice President's house at your suggestion. It didn't stop them from criticizing Rosey."

"They're never going to stop criticizing. That's what they do for a living. Besides, you don't know what they would have said and written had you not invited them. The White House is different from the Vice President's house. Believe me. Once you move in here you start a new slate. You've got to invite them again."

"I just feel it's hypocritical. They'll see through it."

"Of course they'll see through it. Everybody in Washington always sees right through everything. It's only the stupid or the unsuccessful who resent or are offended by using or being used. Really, Sadie, I can't think what has gotten into you. You've always loved to play. Don't tell me you've lost your taste for it."

"Maybe I have. I don't know. It just seems like it's not so much fun anymore. You know, you really can't play when you're President. We don't go anywhere anymore. Not only do we not get invited, but when we do try to go anywhere it is such a nightmare it's not worth it. Look what happened when we went to your house. My God, Lorraine, there were sharpshooters on your roof, and a doctor waiting upstairs in your bedroom in case Rosey keeled over or was shot."

"It was the most exciting night of my life."

"Well, not mine. I don't want to live that way. I'll tell you, it makes it a lot less attractive to accept a dinner invitation knowing you may get assassinated going or coming. We take our lives in our hands every time we set foot out of this prison."

"Dear girl, you *are* down in the dumps, aren't you?"

"I'm upset about this party, with both our parents and my brother and the kids all there. And then you tell me I have to start inviting the vipers, and I'm just not in the mood to be amused. Sometimes I wish Rosey would lose the election and we could all go back to normal life again."

"Don't ever"—Lorraine's voice was stern—"say that to anyone else but me."

"So. I'm sitting at the table with Judge Foster."

Outland was perched on the pale yellow silk sofa in the yellow oval room. He was looking at Sadie, who was ignoring him. He had had a glass of champagne and was signaling the butler for another. She couldn't believe that he would embarrass her at the dinner, but she didn't like the tone of his voice. Rosey had just glanced at her, but it was clear he had decided to divorce himself from the problem. Despite his joke, their little talk had had the desired effect. Sadie supposed that she had actually scared him. He had been unusually deferential to her since then.

The family had gathered in the oval room to await the Judge.

Sadie could not wait until this night was over. She was filled with a sense of dread. Asking all the family had been a mistake. But they were all friendly with Judge Foster, and it had seemed right at the time. Already Miz G had been busily putting her mother down, asking her about her friends in Savannah who were not close friends of Sadie's parents.

Rosey's father always managed to affect a British accent when he was around her parents. They almost never were together: weddings, christenings, funerals were about it. When Rosey and Sadie had lived in Richmond and her parents had come to visit she had rarely had G and Miz G over. And then only for the most formal occasions.

Sadie usually managed to contain herself at these quiet confrontations. She couldn't bear scenes. Tonight, however, she was almost enough on the edge to lash out. She managed to stay quiet, but she couldn't quite conceal her dislike for the Greys.

Miz G pursed her lips as she observed Sadie. Now that Sadie was First Lady, she was in awe of her and desperate to maintain at least cordial relations. It was a nightmare to kowtow to this cheeky girl from Savannah whom Rosey should never have married in the first place.

G, looking pale, was rubbing his long, pointed fingernails, as he always did when he was nervous. He too was afraid of Sadie now that she was the President's wife. Sadie's mother and father took courage from her demeanor. They had always been intimidated by the Greys.

But Outland was adding to the tension, drinking a little too fast and joshing, and finally making a toast to Rosey. "I would like to drink to our President. Here is a perfect example of someone, shall we say, to the manner born, who has reached out to the people, has embraced everyone of all creeds, races, and colors, who is truly an aristocrat. And a true Democrat."

Why did everything Outland said sound sarcastic?

"Why, thank you, Outland; what a nice compliment. I accept it with pleasure," said Rosey, raising his glass of Perrier to Outland. He never drank at big dinners. In fact, he had never been very much interested in alcohol since college, and since becoming President he drank almost nothing. Sadie had never drunk more. She didn't have a problem. It was just that there were too many mornings when she wished she hadn't had that last glass of wine.

G and Miz G could hardly disguise their unhappiness. They knew Rosey was more liberal than they were, but they couldn't bear to hear it.

Sadie was about to speak when she heard the butler in the West Hall and turned to see Judge Foster. She rushed to him with her arms outstretched as though she were welcoming him home from war.

"Oh, Judge Foster. I mean Mr. Justice. You don't know how glad I am to see you!" She gave him a hug and a kiss, much more than she normally would.

"Why, Miss Sadie," he said, in a thick Southern accent. "I

reckon this is the nicest greetin' a po' ol' judge could evah hope for."

The Justice took his wife's arm and led her into the oval room. "Why, honey, look at this," he said with delight. "It's the Greys and the McDougalds, and all the chillen. What a surprise. And what a happy family y'all do make."

Sadie had put her brother at her table, along with the guest of honor. That way she could keep an eye on him. She was horrified at the way he was drinking, though nobody else seemed to notice. She hadn't seen him since her trip to Savannah the year before, and he had put on weight. His beautiful eyes were puffy. His stomach strained at his belt, and even his once-slender brown hands were fleshy. There was something soft about him where he had once seemed lean and hard. This person was not the brother she had once adored—and would always love in spite of everything. This person had been writing vitriolic columns about her husband's Administration which had torn at her and which she had refused to condemn until now. She had meant to talk to him earlier, but he had arrived late and there was so much else going on that there hadn't been time. The only thing giving Sadie any pleasure was that her brother was taking out after Everett Dubois and his Louisiana connections in a big way. Anything that made Everett look bad was a plus from Sadie's point of view.

The six round tables were set for ten and were decorated for fall with dried fruits and vegetables interspersed with chrysanthemums. It was pretty, if not particularly imaginative, but Sadie had been too preoccupied to make a real effort for this party. She had left it to Tilda, and because it was a relatively small party and not a state dinner with some foreign leader to offend, she had felt comfortable doing so. The guest list included members of Congress and the Supreme Court and friends of Judge Foster, mostly Southerners. She had given one table to Vice President Osgood, and another to his wife, Blanche.

Rosey had chosen Freddy Osgood as his Vice President out of the House. Osgood was an immensely popular liberal Democrat from New Mexico, and Blanche, with her dyed hair and strapless gown and sling-back high heels, was a character, if nothing else. They had no class and a lot of heart. They were, as one says in politics, the perfect balance for William and Sara Adabelle Grey.

Sadie had placed G next to Blanche and Miz G next to Freddy. It was sure to be a disaster—which pleased her immensely. At her own table, Justice Foster was on Sadie's right and Abigail Sohier, as a ranking Senator's wife, was on his other side. He was bound to be pleased. Abigail was bright, clever, decent, and she worked very hard at these evenings. She was the perfect guest.

Sadie thought she had insulated Outland between the attractive young wife of a right-wing Republican who served on the House Judiciary Committee and a woman columnist who wrote for a rather conservative chain of newspapers.

Halfway through dinner Sadie began to relax. Things seemed to be going well. She glanced over at Rosey and he nodded his approval. She had been charming Judge Foster, who was glowing, and now Abigail was working him over while she concentrated on the Chief Justice on her other side, a rather innocuous man who liked to talk about himself. It was toward the end of the main course that she began to notice that Outland's voice was growing louder. His conversation was directed at the Judge and the Chief Justice, though they were seated opposite him and he was talking to the columnist.

"As far as I can see," he was pronouncing, "the Supreme Court has been a bastion of liberalism for the past few Administrations. Judge Foster's appointment is a welcome sign."

Judge Foster overheard, though he had been pretending to listen to Blanche, who was regaling him with an update on her favorite soap operas. He glanced at Sadie, who wiped her mouth daintily with her napkin—a ploy to pretend that she hadn't heard. When she looked up, she saw the Chief Justice wince. The fold of skin hanging over his collar had turned noticeably red.

Before she could think of a way to interrupt, Outland addressed the Chief Justice and the table went silent.

"What do you say, Mr. Chief Justice?" he asked. "Do you think the arrival of Judge Foster on the Court will turn the Court in a new direction?"

The Chief Justice looked helpless.

"I'm a journalist and I represent the people, the readers. And I'm sure the people of this country would like to know in what direction the Supreme Court is going. Only the Supreme Court is in a position to put us back on the right track by espousing true American values."

Sadie sucked in her breath.

"I'm sure Brother Outland here means no disrespect to the Chief Justice," said Judge Foster, an edge to his gentle Southern voice. "Do you, Outland boy?"

The Judge had spoken so softly that the harsh tone was all the more effective.

Outland looked stunned for a moment, tried to smile, which quickly faded when he finally had the courage to look at Sadie. She nodded to him, and after a pause, he excused himself.

Sadie looked down at her plate for the merest moment, then around the table. She could see that everyone was looking to her to rescue the situation.

"I apologize for my brother," she said to the Chief Justice, very quietly.

"We all have relatives," said Abigail Sohier.

Everyone giggled with relief.

Sadie smiled a grateful smile at Abigail, then felt Judge Foster's hand on hers.

"That boy is in real trouble, honey," he said quietly to her. "Unless you do something about him soon, he's bound to hurt somebody real bad. Or hurt himself. He's in real trouble."

Now here he was standing inside her bedroom the next morning. He had knocked perfunctorily, then had shut the door behind him. He stood looking at her. She could smell the stale odor of booze still seeping from his pores from the night before. She said nothing. She could hear him breathing heavily.

"I wouldn't blame you if you never wanted to see me again."

"Good."

"I know I was inexcusable."

"Yes."

"I've been under a lot of pressure."

"Yes."

"I had too much to drink."

"I'm sorry."

"I love you. You're the only one."

There were tears on his face, and he was kneeling at her bedside.

"Outland," she burst out, "you have done everything in your power in the last year to force me to abandon you. You have criticized my husband and therefore hurt me, and our marriage. You have caused me embarrassment, and you have sorely tried my patience and tested my love. It seems to me as if you have been begging me to cut you off. You're hurting yourself more than me. Why are you doing this? I don't understand." She was crying now too. "What have I done to you?"

"I know it's been hard, but there are things happening in my life that have made me do things that I never would have done before. Things I can't talk about now. And there are things going on here with people close to your husband that could hurt him. Things you don't know about. I'm trying to help you."

"Outland, it's me, your sister. I know you too well. I'm afraid you just like to snipe, particularly if it gets you attention. And that you have gotten. Unfortunately, there are consequences."

"What do you mean?"

He looked so sad. It made her sad. But she was angry too.

"I mean that you're losing me. I have put up with your criticisms in that newspaper for over a year and I have listened to Rosey complain about it and I have never said a word because I didn't want to question your integrity. As for last night, I don't know what to say. Why couldn't you just sit down with me and tell me why you're angry at me, why do you try to hurt me by putting down my husband, by embarrassing my guests?"

She didn't look at him.

Outland didn't say a word. He continued to kneel on the floor next to her bed, but she could hear him stifle his sobs.

"Do you remember how we used to go out to the smokehouse when we lived at Horace Hall in Adabelle?" she said. "And remember you used to light candles, and then you would take out Daddy's revolver. And you would put one bullet in it and then you would spin it around and point it to your head and pull the trigger? I didn't know until long afterward that you only pretended to put bullets in."

"Uh-huh," mumbled Outland. He looked up at her with an eerie expression on his face.

"I used to be so scared, but so in awe of you. I thought you were the bravest, most courageous person I had ever known; but I was really so young then that I didn't truly understand what you were pretending to do. Well, Outland, you've been gambling all your life. And one day your luck's going to run out."

* * *

They had made love three times. Her face was raw, her hair tangled; her body was tingling.

"Not bad for an old goat like me." He flexed his ample muscle at her in a mock gesture of strength. "Wait till the guys back at the office hear about this."

"You wouldn't!" she gasped in feigned horror.

"I can't wait. 'Hey, Rocky, hey, Charlie. I just had the sweetest piece in all D.C.' And they'll say, 'Oh, yeah? Who?' And I'll say, 'Oh, nobody you know. Just the First Lady.' And they'll say, 'The first lady of what?' And I'll say, 'The First Lady of the land, you asshole.' . . ."

She jabbed him in the ribs. Just as quickly as they had started to laugh they stopped, and he pulled her to him, pinning her arms above her head. She could smell him. He started to kiss her again, nibbling at her lips. "I don't believe we're doing this again," she tried to say.

This time, afterward, he said it. She almost missed it.

"What?"

"I love you." He cleared his throat. He was staring at the ceiling.

She didn't look at him.

"I love you, Sara Adabelle McDougald Grey."

"I love you too, Des."

He reached over and took her hand.

"Jesus H. Christ," he said finally. "What are we going to do?"

"That's the woman's question, not the man's."

"You're right. See, I'm already losing my identity. I knew this whole thing was a mistake."

"How can you say it was a mistake? Don't you think I'm a good writer?"

"Pulitzer Prize material, but you're changing the subject."

"That's what girls say. When *men* don't want to talk about the relationship."

"Yes, but you still haven't dealt with the question."

"We're going to do nothing. What can we do? We'll continue to meet here and work on my novel. Don't you think it's definitely a novel, not a short story?"

"I think we should talk about the novel when we have our

clothes on. I'm not at my best when I'm lying nude with a hard-on next to a great-looking broad."

"Well, then, Mr. Shaw, you are certainly not at your best at this moment."

"That's why I think we should talk about us."

They made love again.

"I think that was only about fifty minutes between takes. This has got to be a world record." Shaw was feeling very pleased with himself.

"I've certainly never heard of a man doing it this often," she said softly. Flattery came instinctively. It was her way of dealing with men. She didn't know any other way. And it was always successful. Although it was the truth, now.

"How many men have you known?"

"You say that as though you don't think I've had any experience at all."

She was only slightly annoyed.

"I can't see how you've had much, since you were married almost immediately after you left college."

"I never told you about Tag."

"I give up. Who's Tag?"

"College. He taught me everything I know about sex."

"So why aren't you married to him now? Why aren't you making love to him this very moment if he was so fantastic?"

Des had gotten up off the sofa bed and got a glass of ginger ale from the small table near the window. He took a sip, but the ice had melted and it was warm. He grimaced, then got back into the bed, sitting up this time.

"I was too young. I hadn't even finished Smith. So I went to New York brokenhearted. Then I met Rosey at a coming-out party in Richmond, and that was that."

"That was that? So the fabulous Tag was your only lover before me—not counting the President, of course."

"The President. God. We're talking about my husband."

"I know. I feel that we have to remind ourselves every now and then just who your husband is."

"Not me. I just repress it."

"Anyhow. Tag. Was he the only one?"

"Actually, no. I had an affair."

"I'm not sure I want to know about this."

He was sitting up against the back of the sofa bed very straight, looking as indignant as anybody can with no clothes on.

"You should know about this. It was while Rosey was Governor."

He looked at her stunned, as though she had slapped him.

"His name was Stuart Cortwright. The tobacco Cortwrights."

Des got up and felt around in his jacket pocket for a cigarette. "Shit," she heard him mumble as he lit up. He climbed back into bed, putting the ashtray between them, his own little barrier. She knew there was something perverse about her insistence on telling him this. Yet his displeasure pleased her.

"I got caught. I was turning out of the drive of Stuart's house onto the main road when a car sideswiped me. The police showed up and I had to get Everett to come get me."

"Did Rosey ever find out?"

"Everett told him. It nearly broke up our marriage. It might have if Roger Kimball hadn't asked him to run."

"What about Cortwright?" He asked this hesitantly.

"I never saw him again."

"That's not what I mean."

"I never loved him."

She looked over at Des, sitting there being like a big little boy pouting, and she leaned over and kissed him on the cheek. He sort of shrugged her away halfheartedly. She snuggled up to him, put her head on his shoulder, and began playing with his chest hairs.

"It's true, Des. I was just using Stuart. I wanted Rosey to find out so that he would pay more attention to me. I was still trying to make our marriage better. It didn't work. I tried to explain. But he was so hurt. He cried a lot. He really loves me, you know."

"Is that what you're doing now?"

"What?"

"Using me?"

She realized he was serious. She couldn't give him a glib answer. She sat up and looked at him directly.

"Des," she said finally, "I've never loved anybody in my life the way I love you."

He took it in, stroking her hair with his hands, looking at her solemnly.

"So what are we going to do about it?"

She laughed. "We're going to make love. What else?"

* * *

Monday. That was their day. Lagoon and Canyon. Jenny had said no more than once every two weeks, only in the afternoon. They couldn't stay apart that long. Monday. Every Monday. Jenny had alerted the morning guard at the Executive Office Building.

Des stayed all day. Sadie informed her office. Beautiful, lovely, wonderful, anything-but-blue Monday. Only they never had enough time. They were always rushing out at the end of the day, at twilight, and twilight was getting earlier and earlier. Departure was a scene. Kissing, and getting dressed, and "Where is my goddamn shoe?" and "You've got lipstick on your shirt," and "Is my hair messed?" and "How are you going to explain that bite on your neck?"

Sometimes they worked on her book. She was writing, or trying to write. Mostly she daydreamed. Des would read what she had written and comment very seriously. He was always complimentary, always supportive, so much so that sometimes she got suspicious. He was pushing her to work on a short story that he could arrange to have published under an assumed name.

"But it's not as though I need the money or the recognition."

"Ah, but someday you might."

That sort of oblique comment made her as uneasy as his persistent encouragement.

"Do I detect a Pygmalion?" she asked one day. "Are you trying to make me into another Allison?"

She saw his jaw tighten.

"You two are so different, it's ridiculous even to talk like that."

"How are we different?"

She had been waiting so long for an opening in all these months. She had to broach it herself.

"I'm not going to fall into that trap."

"What do you mean?"

"If I ever heard a no-win question, that's it. What the hell am I supposed to say? . . . Well, let's see now. Allison is beautiful, sexy, talented, smart . . . Forget it."

"Well, I told you about my other men. Why can't you tell me something about Allison?"

"I don't want to hear another word about any of those guys

again, and I don't understand why you would want to hear about Allison. That's in the past."

"Is it?"

"Of course it is. I'm here, aren't I?"

"Mondays."

"Well, sweetheart, if that's not good enough for you I'll be happy to meet with you seven days a week. You just say the word."

"You know I can't."

"Exactly. So what the hell am I supposed to do seven nights and six days a week? I don't take out any women except for Jenny."

"I just wonder what it is about Allison that keeps you away. She is all those things you said she was. So what's wrong with her?"

She knew she shouldn't pursue the subject. But she needed to hear it from him. The more she knew about the women he had loved, the more she knew him. Knowledge was power, and even though she didn't quite admit it to herself, it was power she wanted. She had pumped him dry about the other women and he had never seemed to mind, though he would occasionally get bored and ask her why she wanted to know so much. He didn't even mind talking about Chessy. He rather liked unloading on her. "You really love this stuff, don't you?"

Allison was different. That was why she went about this one more delicately, because he didn't want to talk. But something made her think that he might actually talk about Allison this time. Maybe he had decided he might as well get it over with.

"Sonny," he said slowly, softly, "Sonny is a woman who doesn't know what she wants. I got chewed up in her confusion. It's hard to know what you want from a woman who doesn't know what she wants. I like things to be clear. Not unsettled. Things were always unsettled around her. If she ever figures out what it is that she does want she'll be one helluva dame. But she's got a long way to go."

This was not the answer she wanted. It made her sick with fear. Sonny was wonderful in every way except that she wasn't sure she wanted him. What if she decided she did want him? They were sitting in the main office. They had decided to have a drink before he left, and they had gotten dressed and started a fire. Now they were both sitting on the sofa, Sadie in her usual sweater and slacks, Des in corduroys and shirt sleeves. She knew for her own good she should change the subject, but the will was not there.

"So how are we different?"

"Jesus," he said. "There's no comparison. If ever I saw a woman who knew who she was and what she wanted, it's you. You are a man's woman. You like men. You know how to please men. You like to be protected and taken care of by men. You don't seem to need power over a man the way some of these feminists do. You understand that a relationship isn't a power play."

She was about to protest, but he cut her off.

"You have things in perspective. You're not seething inside. You know who and what you are, what you want, and you're happy about it. That is what I call the perfect woman. And that, my beauty, is you."

"Desmond. I like your name. Des-monnd." She drew it out on her tongue. "I like men's names with *n*'s in them. I think I will call you Desmond. I like it when you call me Adabelle, too." She paused. "Did you always call her Sonny?"

She was trying to sound casual.

"Mostly." He didn't look up.

"What did she call you?"

"Prick, more than likely."

"Oh, come on."

They had been working on the book, and she had actually finished a chapter. Des had had to go out of town, so they had missed a week. Her schedule had been light, and she had managed to do quite a bit of writing. He was sitting at the desk reading. She was lounging on the sofa. The fire was going, as usual. It was getting colder outside; November was in the air. She had tried to concentrate on a magazine while he read, but she couldn't, and now she was trying to distract him, get his attention away from her manuscript.

"Let's change the subject."

"Okay. What do you want to talk about?"

"Politics. Let's talk about politics. What's going on in the White House? Why don't you give me a scoop?"

"I thought you said real journalists never use the word scoop. That it's a joke word."

"It is. I did. I'm joking."

"Okay, then. Let's talk about politics. Why don't you explain to me why most journalists are liberals."

"Is that what you think?"

"Well, it certainly seems that way. And Rosey is always complaining that you can't get a fair shake from the press if you're conservative because they're all left-wing. Do you think it's true?"

"Christ, I don't know. I think there's a difference between reporters and editors, and I think age makes a big difference."

"How do you mean?"

"Well, there's an old saying that reporters should wake up angry. Most reporters are young. They start out with an idealistic zeal which mellows as they get older. In the beginning there are only good guys and bad guys, right and wrong, black and white. There's no gray for a young reporter—and that's probably not all bad. They cover everything, people from all walks of life, and they see misery and injustice up close. They see it prevail and they believe they can change it, can make a difference."

"What happens when they get older?"

"Me. I'm what happens. It doesn't mean you don't care. It just means that you're more realistic, that you have to know what's possible and what's not, what you can change and what you can't. And as you get older, things are never as simple as they once seemed. That's why editors are generally less ideological than reporters. They have to listen to all sides. But I guess Rosey probably has a point. Journalists generally sympathize with the underdog, and that is seen to be a liberal position."

"I'm a liberal."

"Of course you are."

"What makes you say that? My husband is a Southern conservative."

"I've made love to you. I can always tell a woman's politics by the way she makes love."

"Desmond Shaw, you are so full of shit."

"Do you want me to finish reading your manuscript or not?"

"No, I want you to test my politics."

Now when they made love it was slow and satisfying, not the frenzy they had been in in the early months. Now that they were

getting used to each other, they could actually have a conversation. The passion was still there; it was just a little more in control. It was like being in a space capsule and sent off to Pluto.
They were completely confined to their own environment. They
could pretend that they were the only ones alive. Occasionally
Jenny would buzz in to ask Sadie a question or to refer something
to her, sometimes passing a message from Rosey. But everyone
had been told that her writing time was sacred, and it had become
more or less an accomplished fact over at the West Wing. Even
Rosey had been made to feel reticent about interrupting. So far
there had been no suspicions. The few times he had run into
people he knew at the EOB, he had been with Jenny. And even
she was beginning to be a little easier about it than she had been.
At least for the time being, things seemed to be working out.

"My dear, it was too preposterous. Even I, in all my years in
London and Washington, have never seen anything so absurd."

"I don't get it, Lorraine. Why did anybody go?"

"Sweetie, when the wife of the editor of the View section of
The Daily has a musicale, everyone goes. It's that simple. People
are just scared. It's an investment. Worth Elgin has a lot of power
in this town, and Claire counts on it."

"Was everybody making fun of her?" Sadie was curled up on
the love seat in her private office, sipping tea. It was late afternoon, and she had finished with most of her First Lady chores.
Now it was time for one of her favorite pastimes. A gossip session with Lorraine.

"Of course. Nobody could keep a straight face. But Claire
simply refused to acknowledge it. She stood at the door chatting
everyone up and talking about how thrilling and 'delightfully un-
Washington' it was to have a musicale."

"Well, that's for sure. What did she wear?"

"She had on a long-sleeved green velvet dress to the floor, so
décolleté that even she didn't dare lean over."

Sadie could imagine the Elgins' spacious Georgetown house.
Nobody could figure out where they had gotten the money. Some
old lover of Claire's was the gossip. Although it seemed that
everybody in Washington managed to live better than they
should.

"Claire's house is a little ratty-looking, though I have to admit she is clever with candlelight. It hides some of the rough edges."

"Some of her rough edges too," cackled Lorraine. "She lies about her age, you know. And she's had at least one face lift. She's the kind of woman who's chosen her face over her figure, though she does manage to drape those dresses rather cleverly."

"Who all was there?" Sadie wanted to move on. Lorraine would have been content to cut up her best friend for the rest of the afternoon.

"The usual crowd. The perfect assortment of diplomatic, Administration, Capitol Hill, and journalists. But it didn't matter. She only had eyes for Des."

"Des?" Sadie sat up, her body suddenly stiffening. Des had told her laughingly about the invitation to the musicale, but he'd said he wasn't going to go.

"Oh, my darling, you wouldn't have believed it. Claire was all over him. Laughing up at him flirtatiously, leading him around by the arm before the 'entertainment,' and then, it was so awful, after a few *Lieder* she actually sang several love songs to him. In front of *le tout* Washington, not to mention her own husband."

Sadie tried to sound casual. "Oh, well, Worth is sort of a silly fop anyway."

"I must say Claire has certainly advanced since the old days of feeling up other people's husbands under the dinner table. This was one of the most extraordinary sights I've ever seen.

"Worth was flitting around the drawing room as if she'd just sung a love song to him. And at the end he said loudly after leading the applause, 'Well, the old girl's still got it in her.'"

"And how did Des . . ." She hesitated, afraid to ask. "How did he take it?"

"I must admit he did look a bit uncomfortable when she turned to him and started singing. But he was rather good-natured about it. After all, it goes with the territory."

"What do you mean?"

"Don't you know about him and Claire?"

They were sitting in the EOB office. She in a chair. Isolated. He on the sofa. They had been making small talk for a while. He could tell there was something wrong. Between the long silences the only sound was the fire crackling. She did not look happy. She wouldn't look him in the eye.

"I've only had lunch with her," he said finally.

"What?"

"I said, I've only had lunch with her, nothing more."

She tried to look puzzled.

"Don't pretend you don't know what I'm talking about. Lorraine Hadley couldn't keep her mouth shut if she tried. I'm only helping Claire out. She's of an age where she doesn't feel attractive anymore and she's always afraid she's going to lose Worth to some young heiress. When she gets desperate she likes to have lunch. She likes to go to places that are obvious, like the Maison Blanche, Le Lion d'Or, or the Jockey Club. It makes people talk and keeps her in the running. It also keeps Worth on his toes. It turns him on to think other men are interested in her. I don't know why people don't figure out that if we were having an affair we certainly wouldn't eat lunch together."

She didn't know what to say, so she said nothing.

"You're right," he said. "She went overboard when she sang to me. It got old Worth all het up, but it made me feel ridiculous. I told her. No more lunches. She can make a fool of herself if she wants to, but not of me."

"Why would it make a fool out of you? You're single. You don't have anything to worry about."

"So I am. So I am. It's funny, but I keep forgetting that."

"Do you like being single?" She tried to make the question seem not loaded.

"You want the truth?" He sobered, stared down at his hands, then looked back at her. "I hate it. It's cold and lonely. I don't like coming home to an empty bed at night, and I never did like filling my bed with people I didn't care about. It's always been easy to get laid. It's never been easy to get loved. Full time. Not by a good woman, at any rate."

"You had a good woman." She held her breath when she said it. She just couldn't stay away from the subject of Allison no matter how hard she tried.

"Yep, I sure as hell did. She was a fabulous woman. But she blew it. No, I take that back. Maybe I blew it. Or"—he looked at her again—"maybe you could say we both blew it."

Sadie didn't say anything. She was scared to have him go on, scared to have him stop.

"You wanted to talk about this," he said. "So now I'm talking about it."

"Do you miss her?"

"When we broke up I never thought I could miss anyone as much as I missed her. I never thought I could feel so much pain over a woman."

Sadie was near tears now. But something made her go on.

"Why can't you get back together?" She could feel her fingers grow icy.

"No. It's over. It's irrevocable. Something died for us when it happened. I'm sure you've heard the details by now, and I'd just as soon not go into them. . . ." He could see her eyes misting over and the stricken look on her face. He reached over to the chair where she was sitting, grabbed her hands, and pulled her over to the sofa where he was sitting. He put his arm around her and held her to him. He could feel her body trembling slightly.

"Sadie," he said finally, in a whisper.

"Yes?"

"I'm only telling you this because I love you."

"I wonder how much difference a President's wife really can make. I think not much. Look at what happened before the Kimballs came. Eight years of the Nortons wiped out everything Mrs. Garvey had done before her. It just seems so superficial, so phony, to 'pick a project'—something to keep the pretty little thing occupied for four years, knowing that four years later some air-head will come along and choose 'Children in Space' or 'Communicating Underwater.'"

They were sitting up in the sofa bed now. Sadie was eating a juicy ripe pear that Des had brought her from a fruit stand in West Virginia. The pear was dripping on her breasts, and Des licked the pear juice off. She brushed him away. "I want to be serious. This is a serious subject."

"Excuse me," said Des. "Okay, let's be serious. But why are we serious today?"

"I don't know. I have a lot of time by myself to think, you know, that here I am in this potentially powerful position and all I do is moon over you, make love, and occasionally try to write a novel, and shouldn't I be doing more with my life?"

"C'mon, Sadie, you're doing a lot. You've got two major

projects going. Planned Parenthood and the National Trust for Historic Preservation, both of which are important and to which you have contributed an enormous amount. You work your ass off for both of them."

"I don't think it's very earthshaking. And now that we're only a year away from the elections, his staff has seriously curtailed my Planned Parenthood activities. They think it's too controversial. And I can only fight them so much. I care about the National Trust, but it's not about whether people live or die. I'm preoccupied with how much I hate being here and with how much I love you, and I haven't been able to concentrate on anything else. I feel guilty."

"Well, what do you want to do?"

"I don't know. My problem is that Rosey and I differ on really important political issues. He's against abortion. And he doesn't really believe in prayer in the schools, but he's not using it as an issue either. And I'm supposed to support his positions. I feel like such a bloody hypocrite."

"You're really on a tear, aren't you, baby?" said Des, kissing her fingers.

"Don't patronize me, Des. I swear I won't stand for it. I'm trying to tell you something that's important to me. I'm living a lie. And I don't know what to do about it. I can't say any of the things I believe because they differ from my husband's political positions and it would hurt him in the campaign. Not to mention the fact that I'm having an affair. It's my fault and nobody else's. But I'm really disgusted with myself. I don't feel very good about anything."

Des looked at her in a way she had never seen him look at her. It was as though a light had dawned, as though he were looking at her and seeing her for the first time instead of a glamorous First Lady with whom he was having a clandestine affair.

"I'm sorry. I had no intention of being patronizing; it's the last thing I want to do. I just didn't realize. But if you feel the way you say you do, then you ought to do something. What do you want to do?"

"You just asked me that, and I told you I didn't know. That's my problem. I don't think there's anything I can do."

"Sure there is."

"What, for instance?"

"Run away and marry me."

"Don't be ridiculous, Des. I told you I was serious, and now you're making fun of me again."

She suddenly noticed the strange look on his face and the way he shrugged. She did not chide him about smoking when he got up quickly and lit a cigarette.

"I'm sorry," she said. "I shouldn't burden you with my problems. It's just that Jenny and you are really the only people I can talk to, and I know Jenny feels a little stymied by my situation because she and I see eye to eye on most political issues. But I suppose you two get a chance to discuss this on your own time. God, you must be sick of me! Let's change the subject. Tell me about the real world. Jenny says you two went to Lady Mallory's brunch Saturday. Did you have a good time?"

"Jesus H. Christ, are you kidding? It was a killer. Everybody in Washington I didn't want to see. The place was a fucking minefield. Everywhere you stepped you were in trouble. All I wanted to do was get to the country, and Jenny kept wanting to stay. I got stuck with half the bores and assholes in town. It was a disaster."

"That's not what Jenny said," said Sadie, laughing. "She said it was great fun and terrific people-watching."

"Maybe I'm getting old. Or sick of this town, or something. But I'll tell you, nobody in this city has any morals. As long as you've got a name, got power, even money, you're accepted. If Adolf Hitler were in town and Lady Mallory had a dinner for him, everybody would show up, believe me. Nobody lives by principles anymore. If you do, people think you're either stupid or a wimp."

"My, you're certainly on a tear," she said.

"Now it's my turn, goddammit, to tell you not to patronize me. There were people at that brunch who are criminals, amoral people. And there was everyone just kissing their asses. Celebrity and publicity are all that matters. Now, I do have an excuse. I'm a journalist and this is work. I look upon these occasions as work, and therefore all of these people are subjects, not friends. Still, I don't like it. I would rather have been out chopping wood at the cabin. As it was, I didn't get there until nearly sundown. Wasted a perfectly beautiful day."

"We make quite a pair of malcontents, don't we?"

"So what do you want to do about it?"

"Why don't we run off to your cabin in West Virginia and live happily ever after?"

"Now, why didn't I think of that?"

It was the Monday before Christmas, and Sadie had had Jenny get a small Christmas tree and set it up in her office with a few lights and pretty decorations. They were going to have a small Christmas party, she and Des, and she had invited Jenny too. They would drink champagne and have Christmas cakes and little sandwiches. All of this Jenny had to produce. Sadie didn't want the White House chef to get too suspicious, and Jenny felt a little strange preparing the food in her own kitchen and then dragging it over in a shopping bag. She wasn't at all sure she should come, but Sadie insisted. She wanted company.

"We're getting a little claustrophobic in there," she said. "It's unreal. We've started our lives together; now we need something more. We need somebody to confirm that this is actually happening. We need to be a couple. We can't be a couple if there isn't another person there."

"What does Des say?"

"Des thinks it's fine. Although it will be a little strange for him, since Des is beginning to think *you* and he are a couple."

"I must admit I'm getting awfully used to it myself."

Did Sadie detect a little wistfulness?

Sadie got Christmas-music tapes for the tape deck and wore a green cashmere sweater dress. She was more excited about her little party than she had been about any social event in a long time. She and Des, after six months alone, were actually going to sit in front of a fire and drink and talk with a person from the outside world.

Sadie arrived before Des as usual, to finish the tree, start the fire, and get her tapes going. She checked the mirror ten times to see that she looked all right. Her auburn hair was now shoulder length and layered around the top to frame her face—a look that was softer than her old shorter, tousled look, and a little less chic, but Des adored it. She powdered her nose again and sprayed a little breath spray down her throat and pinched her cheeks.

Jenny brought Des in from downstairs. He was red from the cold and walked immediately over to the fire to warm his hands. They looked at each other awkwardly, then finally Des reached out and squeezed her hand in greeting. She blushed. They both looked down.

"Why don't you take off your coat?" she asked, her voice a little high.

"Good idea," he said. He took it off and hung it up on a coat stand by the door. Then there was silence.

"God, if it's going to be this awkward with me around I better leave now," said Jenny.

They both laughed and went to hug Jenny at the same time.

"You're right, Jen, this is ridiculous," said Des. "Let's break out the champagne."

Before too long they were eating sandwiches, drinking their second bottle of champagne, and telling stories of Christmases past and laughing.

"Wonder what we'll all be doing next year this time," said Sadie.

"Well, Rosey will have just won the election, judging from the pathetic group the Republicans have put forward so far," said Des.

"Is that what you want?" Jenny asked Sadie.

Things had turned suddenly serious.

"Why is everybody always asking me what I want?" said Sadie. "I can't answer that simply. I think Rosey is a good President, though we do disagree on certain things. I think he would be a better President than any of the others. I think it would be better for the country. As for me, I couldn't really answer that. But one thing is for sure. If he does win, I won't have to make any decisions about what I want. Everything will have been decided."

"I don't want to get personal, as if I can help it, but you two know you're in a fools' paradise, if you'll pardon me for being trite."

"We know it, Jenny," said Sadie. "It's just that we haven't wanted to think about it. What can we do? There's nothing to do except stop, which we can't do."

"I've never been in a situation like this in my life," said Des. "It makes me feel helpless, and I don't like to feel helpless."

"I wish we could look into the future," said Sadie.

"We could always call Millicent," said Jenny. "Though I'm sure now that she and John T. Hooker are married, she's too grand to be telling fortunes."

"God, I forgot about Millicent," said Sadie. "She told me I would have an affair. 'This affair shakes you to the roots,' she told me, and I stormed out and slammed the door on her."

"Jesus, you never told me that," said Des. "What the hell else did she tell you? Did she tell you what would happen?"

"No. As I remember, she couldn't really say—it wasn't clear. I just remember the part about the affair."

"Well, shit, call her up and get her to read the rest."

"No way," said Sadie. "She'd tell everybody in town, and Rosey would go crazy."

"So how are we going to find out what happens?" asked Des. "Does the guy get the gal? Does everybody live happily ever after?"

"Does the press secretary get her ass in a sling?" asked Jenny.

"I believe that what's meant to be will be," said Sadie, turning serious. "I don't think we can change the way things are supposed to be. I was angry at Millicent for telling me that I didn't have a great marriage and that I would take a lover. But I knew she was right. That it was fated to be. I've always believed that since I was a small child. And it certainly was true of my namesake Adabelle."

"Oh, great, the famous story," said Jenny. "Well, when I first started working for you, Sadie, I was a real skeptic. But after six months in this job I'll believe anything. Tell away. We've got all afternoon."

Des got up and threw another log on the fire as Jenny refilled everyone's champagne glass.

"Adabelle McDougald was the most beautiful girl in all of Georgia," she began. "She had flaming red hair and turquoise eyes and had more beaux than she could count. But she always said she would never marry because she was going to die by the time she was twenty-one.

"Then she met a very handsome dark-haired Yankee..." Sadie and Des smiled at each other. "...and fell in love. They became engaged, and her family planned a huge wedding at their Horace Hall plantation near Statesboro.

"The night before the wedding there was a splendid dinner dance, and after everyone was in bed, the sound of chains rattling up and down the great hall could be heard throughout the house. But when they came to look, the only sign of the chains was the scratch marks on the floor where they had been dragged from one end to the other.

"The next morning Adabelle was in a trance, talking to no one as she dressed for her wedding. Guests came from miles around to see her married, and as they gathered at the foot of the grand staircase to wait for the bride, the organ music began to play.

"Just then, Adabelle, looking ravishing, appeared at the top of the stairs on the arm of her proud father.

"As she took the first step forward, her foot caught on the veil and she began to tumble down the stairs. All anyone could remember afterwards was the profusion of white lace and veils and auburn hair as her lithe body cascaded down the stairs, landing at the foot in a heap, her pale, slim neck dangling to one side. She was dead."

"Jesus, Mary!" said Des, catching his breath. "What an image."

"Didn't they name the town after Adabelle?" asked Jenny.

"They did. And my mother was the first person in the family to dare name a daughter after her. Everyone else thought it was a jinx."

The fire crackled in the silence. Sadie took a sip of her champagne and stared into the flames.

"Maybe . . . " she said, almost to herself. "Maybe they were right."

"My darling precious sister," the letter began. Sadie could barely read it.

"I am writing you this letter because you are the only one who will understand what I have done. And why I have done it. I also know that you will have forgiven me for my transgressions at your dinner. I was under enormous stress at the time, stresses I can now tell you about. I know I should have written to you before this, but I just didn't have the proper words or the proper deeds. Only know that I had no intention, though it may seem hard to believe, of hurting or embarrassing you. Anyway, if the pundits are right, I have helped your husband with the liberals in his party. This is by way of rationalization, but I never wrote anything I didn't believe. As you know, I disagree with Rosey on many issues. Had it not been for the situation, however, I might not have written it. Sometimes from a distance, looking at the

great and mighty, it is hard to realize that they are real. From
where I sit, you and Rosey seem invincible. It never occurred to
me that anything I might write in my obscure little paper might
have the slightest effect on either of you. If it did, and I now
believe it did, I am eternally sorry.

"But I digress. I guess I don't want to tell you this, but I must.
And you must know it.

"As you may have noticed if you read my columns, I have
alluded to some oil deals off the coast of Louisiana. I never came
out and said anything specific because I didn't want to hurt
Rosey. However, now I can tell you what I know.

"For the past several years I have been involved in a high-
stakes weekly poker game in Atlanta. And when I say high
stakes, I mean high stakes. These boys don't fool around. Most
of them are big-time businessmen, deal makers. One of them is
in oil. I know, I know, you and Mama and Daddy have always
warned me about my gambling, but I can't control it. Never have
been able to. As you may be able to guess, I used stock in my
newspaper as collateral, and yes, I lost a lot. Every time I kept
hoping I would win big and be able to get back in the black. As
they owned more and more of me, they wanted more say in the
editorial position of the paper, hence the rough columns about
Rosey and the Administration. To call them conservative would
be an understatement. They think Rosey is a Communist. Everett
Dubois started coming down hard on me, as well he should have.
But I gave him no quarter. I had no choice. Then, through my
'friend' in oil I discovered some unsavory dealings on Everett's
part.

"According to my source, your husband's special assistant
Everett Dubois has a secret deal with the Rittman Oil offshore-
drilling company. He was to get the Omanis to accept Rittman's
bid for offshore drilling off their own coast in return for a kickback. My source hears, but cannot prove, that Everett was personally involved with the Omanis and was making personal
demands of them as well as the Rittman people, trying to double-
deal them both. Apparently the Omanis balked and eventually
chose a British company, Marble Arch, even though they didn't
come up with as good a bid. It appears that Everett is trying to
punish the Omanis by convincing your husband that they should
not be given military aid and other help that they have counted on
from the United States. Rosey doesn't know any of this, but it

could all explode in his face. That's when I began alluding to Everett in the column. Everett didn't know how much I knew. He called me several times to get me to lay off, naturally denying everything.

"When I refused, Everett put a private detective on me, and he hit pay dirt. He found out about my gambling and also that my paper was in fact not my paper but that it belonged to this right-wing crowd who appeared to be dictating their anti-Administration editorial views to me. He threatened to expose me if I didn't stop writing about him. As you can imagine, Everett's concern was not really about the President. He just wanted to save his own ass.

"Darling Sadie. I knew all this when I came up to Washington for the dinner, and I almost told you several times. I knew then that it would only be a matter of time before you found out. At any rate, I wanted to tell you before that bastard Everett did. And I also want you and Rosey to know that I have signed over the paper to my poker companions. It became clear to me that they were allowing me to hang on to it and run it simply to attack Rosey with more credibility, and that I could not countenance.

"I know you will think I'm weak, maybe contemptible. But you must believe one thing. You are the dearest thing in the world to me. Please forgive me. That is all I ask. I know Rosey will never understand, but I ask his forgiveness as well. And do what you must do for your own happiness. There is so little of it. You deserve it more than anyone I know. I love you.

"Your brother, Outland."

As Sadie read the letter over, she wept. This time she was sitting in her office with Des, and when she finished it she handed it to him, her head in her hands, while she waited for him to read it.

"Holy Mary, Mother of God," he said slowly as he came to the end. "I don't believe it. When did you get this letter? Has Rosey seen it?"

"Yesterday. And yes, I showed it to Rosey. He's the only one who knows what happened."

"Well, what did he say?"

She sighed. "He read it, flung it down, muttered something about Everett, and walked out. Later he came back. He said he had called Everett and Everett had hit the roof. Denied everything. He said it was preposterous, and as for the gambling thing, everybody in Georgia knew about it and there was no point in trying to blackmail somebody about something like that. He said Everett told him he called Outland a number of times about his columns, just as any loyal member of the staff would do. He was only trying to protect the President, and Outland resented it and said he was going to get Everett. . . . He said Outland had no concrete proof and it sounded like sour grapes. Rosey believes Everett."

Des came over to the sofa and sat down next to her.

"Maybe I shouldn't have been so hard on him. He is my brother and he was crying out for help and I just didn't see it. How could I have been so stupid? I failed him. He has been changing, withdrawing, and I never noticed any of the signs. I was too preoccupied with my own problems, with my own life, to see it. I wonder if Outland's right. He always tells me I'm a Pollyanna. He laughs at me for my dreams. I've always thought he was cynical. But maybe he isn't wrong. I don't know anything anymore."

"You can't blame yourself," said Des. "Outland is a troubled guy. He has his own demons he can't live with."

"Well, I can certainly blame Everett. He ruined my brother. I'll get him if it's the last thing I do."

"Do you mind if I look into this?" he said.

"Oh, Des, you can't. I don't want anyone to hurt Outland any more, or his family. Please, promise me you won't."

"Calm down, sweetheart," he said. "I'm not talking about the gambling. I'm talking about the Rittman oil deal and Everett. If this story is true, it is a real scandal. I always knew that little fucker was crooked. You can see it in his face."

"But that will hurt Rosey. Oh, Des, please. I knew I shouldn't have shown you that letter."

"Listen, Sadie, I would never do anything with this if you told me not to. But don't you see this will be much more hurtful to Rosey if it is allowed to fester and grow? If the Rittman people are talking, then it's only a matter of time. And if the Omanis are getting screwed, you can bet they won't waste any time leaking it to the press. It has tremendous international ramifications. If I can just check some of it out and use it in *The Weekly,* maybe it will get Rosey to realize he's got a problem on his hands and deal with it before it gets out of control."

"Well, maybe you're right." She was hesitant. "One thing is for sure. Rosey will never guess where the leak came from."

The following Monday, Des couldn't make it. He was in Louisiana with a *Weekly* reporter. Sadie went to her office and tried to write. Finally, she called Jenny, who was over in her West Wing office, and begged her to come join her for tea. Jenny arrived looking a bit nervous and irritated.

"I'm beginning to get questions on your writing," she said. "People want to know what it is, whether it will be published, who are you writing for—all that kind of thing. I'm trying to be vague, but the vaguer you are the more they get suspicious. Pretty soon you're going to have them camping on your doorstep. So you better start thinking of something. I can't keep them at bay forever."

"What if I published something?"

"You're kidding! You mean you're actually writing?"

"Oh, go screw yourself, Jenny," she said. "Of course I am. What do you think I do over here when Des isn't here?"

"Think about Des."

"Well, I do some of that. But I do write. And Des thinks some of it's all right. It started as a short story about a friend in Savannah, the one I told you about, who left her husband for the tennis pro. Now I think it may end up being a novel. Anyway, Des thinks part of it could be excerpted. He was thinking of submitting it for me to *The Gotham*."

"Do you mind if I see what he's interested in having you publish?"

"I guess it's okay. He didn't tell me not to show it to you."

"For Christ's sake, Sadie, it's me—your press secretary. I'm the only one who's going to have to deal with this issue. I might as well know what we're in for. Besides, I've never seen you like this. You're letting Des run your life, tell you what to do. I thought you wanted to be your own person. That's what you're always complaining about. But you've just given yourself up to this man as though you were some kind of mindless doll."

"You've never talked to me like that before." Her voice was very quiet.

"I'm sorry," said Jenny. "I didn't mean to. It's just that I've watched you turn into a lump of jelly in the past six months.

Rather than take control, you're giving up control. Frankly, I think that's maybe what Des thinks he wants now, under these circumstances, particularly after Allison, but it's not what he wants in the long run."

"Who said anything about the long run?"

They looked at each other with surprise.

"I mean, well, what kind of future could there be for us?" stammered Sadie. "I just can't think in those terms."

"Well, I've got news for you. Des thinks in those terms."

"What are you talking about?"

"Des thinks the two of you have got a future together. I don't think he's thought it out, but I think he sees you eventually leaving Rosey and going off with him."

Sadie wouldn't look at Jenny. She was sitting behind her desk, which put a convenient barrier between them, as Jenny stalked up and down the floor waving her arms.

"Don't tell me you haven't thought about it," said Jenny when Sadie didn't answer.

"Of course I've thought about it."

"And . . . ?"

"I don't know."

"Do you love him?"

"I'm in love with him, more than I ever thought possible. I love him more than I've ever loved anybody in my life except for my own children."

"Too bad you're not clear about how you feel."

"It doesn't make any difference how I feel."

"I would think it would make everything very simple. You stick with Rosey until after he's won the election and then you leave him for Des."

Her sarcastic tone annoyed Sadie.

"Don't even talk like that," she said sharply.

"Well, what in God's name do you think will happen? Look, Sadie, I'm not exactly wild about that scenario. I lose a job. But if you keep on like this you're bound to be found out. And I lose my job anyway."

Sadie couldn't help laughing.

"So this has become an unemployment problem."

"Sadie, all I'm saying is if you love Des as much as you say you do, you're going to have to do something. You'll either have to leave Rosey or give Des up. You have no other options."

"Jenny, you're forgetting one minor problem. Desmond Shaw has not asked me to leave my husband and run off with him."

"He will . . . and when he does, what will you say?"

"Jenny, you're the only person I have to talk to and I need to talk to you about this and I know you see a lot of Des. I have got to ask you to promise me that you will not tell him what I say. Okay?"

"Okay."

"I'm terrified. I've suspected that Des wants to ask me to leave. I've always pretended it was a joke. He's preparing me for the outside world by making me write and encouraging me. He obviously wants me to be able to work when we're together on the outside. But I've never worked, except for that year in New York, and I was just biding my time until I found somebody suitable to marry, and besides, my parents were supporting me. I've always been Rosey's wife. I don't know how to work or to support myself, and it scares me. And Des doesn't have any money. I've always had some money. If I left Rosey I wouldn't get much alimony, and the children will be grown soon. And what if it didn't work out? What if I leave Rosey and then Des decides he's still in love with Allison and leaves me? Then where will I be? What if I can't make a go of it and can't support myself? Then I'll be helpless. Des is in love with me, but I don't know whether it's me or who I am. He's only known me since I've been the wife of the Vice President or the President. He thinks it's glamorous and exciting that he's having an affair under these circumstances, and he's challenged by the idea that he could get a woman away from the President. A woman he really can't have. But if he wins, if I leave Rosey to go to him, then where will be the glamour? Then he'll be saddled with a helpless woman. I'll have no power. I think Des would like to have a son. I'm almost forty. Do I want to start another family? If I did that, it would set me back even further, make me even more dependent. I know he says he likes the fact that I'm feminine, that I know how to please a man; but if that's all I am, he'll get bored after a while."

Jenny had stopped pacing and was now sitting in the armchair by the fire, listening quietly.

"I guess you have given it some thought. And the thing that amazes me is that you've never let on any of this to Des."

"We haven't really gotten to a point where we have to make a decision. I suspect you're right, though. If I were to leave, and I simply can't imagine it, it would probably have to be right after Rosey's won. If he loses, it would make things simpler. But I don't suppose he will lose, will he?"

"Probably not, but you can't count on anything these days. Let me just ask you a hypothetical question. Suppose you submitted your novel to a publisher and you got a huge advance and a contract on a movie deal. Would you feel different? What would you want to do then?"

"If I thought I could be successful and not just earn a living but make a lot of money at it and be self-sufficient and have a real identity of my own?"

"Yep."

"I'd leave Rosey in a minute—after the election."

"Hey, gorgeous, am I glad to see you!"

Des hadn't even taken off his trench coat, but he ran into her office and scooped her up in his arms, squeezing the air out of her.

He nuzzled her neck, pretended to bite it, then pulled back and looked at her, at the same time grabbing her behind in both his hands.

"Sometimes I forget just what a fabulous piece of ass you really are."

"Oh, Des," she said, barely able to breathe, "I'm so glad you're back. God, I've missed you so." And to her surprise her eyes welled up with tears.

"Hey, baby, it's not like I've been off at war." Laughing, he reached over and wiped the tears off her cheeks with his cold hands.

"Your hands are freezing," she said, pulling back slightly. "Take your coat off and come over by the fire."

He threw off his coat and dropped it on the corner of a chair in a crumpled wad, then put his arm around her and walked her over to the fire with him. He looked down at her, kissing her nose, her forehead, her lips, then pulled her to him. They embraced—a long, fierce embrace.

"You're so beautiful I can't stop looking at you, my lovely Adabelle Grey," he said to her after a while.

She was wearing black. Black pants and a black turtleneck

sweater. No jewelry. Very little makeup. It was useless to wear makeup around Des anyway.

"I've made martinis," she said.

"Not only is she beautiful but she knows how to take care of her man," he said, kissing her again. He went to the bar and poured himself a martini.

It was lunchtime, and he had brought sandwiches in his brief-case. They sat by the fire and ate. Outside it was sleeting and cold and gray. Inside was their private world, their warm, cozy cocoon.

"So tell," he said as he sipped his martini. "How did they take our story on the Rittman oil deal?"

"I can't tell. I asked Rosey, and all he said was that *The Weekly* didn't really have much of a story."

"Shit, we had people at Rittman talking about the fact that they didn't get the contract and saying they thought somebody in the White House was out to screw them. We didn't mention Everett's name because we don't have it hard enough. We can't get anybody to nail him on the record. But you'd think Rosey..."

"Rosey is extremely loyal. A person on his staff is innocent until proved guilty. And when you've got a clever liar like Everett saying it's not true, what are you going to do? Everett is the most convincing liar I've ever seen, and Rosey can't conceive of anybody actually lying to him. He has to believe him. He knows I dislike Everett, so what I say about him doesn't carry much weight. He just clams up or says something insulting like 'Some of the best minds in this Administration think you're wrong.'"

"How can you stand it?" he asked, losing interest in his story for a moment.

"I can't."

He didn't say anything.

"Anyway, Rosey thinks the Omani Ambassador is crying over their loss of aid and trying to pin the blame on somebody."

"That's probably true."

"He didn't spill it to you, I did."

"No, but I'm worried. Ali has been putting a big burn on Allison. She's been seeing a lot of him lately, quietly. She's bound to get onto the Everett story soon enough. And when she sees that I'm onto it, it will make her want to beat me. That does seem to be her goal in life."

He was too angry for someone who didn't care anymore. It made Sadie afraid again. She decided not to pursue the subject. She didn't want to have to deal with Allison now.

"I wish I knew what was the right thing to do. I wonder if my telling you all this will hurt Rosey more than help him. I'm scared, Des. I would not forgive myself if I've betrayed my husband . . ." She paused and turned away from Des. ". . . this way."

"Baby, I would never do anything to hurt Rosey. For one thing, it would hurt you, and that would hurt us. If we can get enough into print to arouse suspicions about Everett, we can make him resign or get Rosey to fire him before this thing blows up into a big scandal and really causes problems. I just don't understand why your husband is putting it off. He's got to know the son-of-a-bitch is guilty. He better do it soon, though. Too many people are getting onto the story. Everybody smells blood."

"Rosey is very upset about the part of the story which says that he is blind to the faults of his staff and would never consider anyone on his team to have been involved in anything like this. He kept saying, 'Who could they have talked to? Who would tell *The Weekly* anything like this? You don't think Jenny is talking to her friend Shaw, do you? I understand there's a romance going on there.' "

"What did you say?"

"I told him that Jenny was the most trustworthy person I had ever known and she would never leak anything to anyone. That just wasn't her style. And if she did, she certainly wouldn't leak it to you because it would be too obvious."

"Good work, baby."

"Rosey kept saying at dinner last night, right after they called him with what *The Weekly* would say today, he kept saying, 'How could they have heard of this? I only heard it last week, through Outland's letter. Do you think he wrote somebody on *The Weekly*?' I just acted more surprised than he was."

"You know what surprises me? The fact that we haven't made love yet."

He pulled her up off the sofa and carried her into their little bedroom, where they made love for most of the afternoon. It was only later, when they were lying in each other's arms, that she turned to him.

"And now for the bad news," she said.

"Oh, Jesus, now what?"

"I have to go off the pill."

"When?"

"At the end of this cycle."

"Why?"

"Because I have something called mitral-valve prolapse."

"Christ, what's that?"

"It's the new chic heart condition. It's not serious, but because I'm almost forty and should have been off the pill when I was thirty-five, my doctor is making me quit now."

"So what will you do?"

"I love it. Suddenly it's *my* problem."

"Well, what am *I* supposed to do—have a vasectomy? Forget it. I'm not having anybody mess with my tallywacker. No way. Besides, I read somewhere that it causes hardening of the arteries."

"I didn't say anything about a vasectomy. There are such things as condoms, you know."

"That's bullshit. Those things are out of the question. Why don't you try an IUD?"

"Because I can't. With mitral-valve prolapse you're too susceptible to infection. He advises against it."

"So what are *we* going to do?"

"Well, I have considered foams, sponges, jellies, and suicide and I have decided I'm going to try the diaphragm."

"Great idea."

"I'm glad you like it. I think it's horrible. It's a mess, with all that jelly, and it's so undignified. Yuk."

"It's not as if we're together that much. You'll only have to use it once a week."

She didn't say anything. He looked at her. His jaw tightened. She looked away.

"Maybe more than once a week. Ah, yes, I forgot, you're a married woman."

"You know I have no choice."

"Choice you have, sweetheart. It's just that you won't make it."

"I don't remember being asked to make it."

They looked at each other for a long time.

He leaned over and kissed her, finally, caressing her face, her neck, her breasts; brushing her gently with his mouth, then kissing her fully on the lips.

"We have a lot to talk about when I get back."

"Get back? You just got back. Where are you going?"

"I'm going with the President on his trip to the Middle East."

"Oh, no. I thought you weren't going."

"I tried to get out of it, but New York really wants me on it for some reason. Besides, I may be able to nail Everett on this one. Why aren't *you* going?"

"It's only for five days, and it's a working trip. None of the wives are going, and there are no big social events. What do they need a bubble-head like me along for?"

"The President ought to have *his* head examined for not taking you with him. If you were my woman I'd chain you to my side." He leaned over and began kissing her again.

She knew they were going to make love again, but something made her pull away from him and ask a question she did not want the answer to.

"Who's going from *The Daily*?"

"Allison. Who else?"

CHAPTER 15

T HEY WERE SO CLOSE THEY WERE ALMOST touching. Allison could feel his rough tweed sleeve against her arm through her silk blouse. She was typing in her seat; he was kneeling in the aisle playing his tape recorder.

"I can't hear the last word," Des said. "I think it's renege. Here, you listen."

"It's renege," she said. "Okay, I've got it. We're almost finished. I suppose we've got to say that they served bad fish on *Air Force One*? Manolas will be pissed."

"Fuck Manolas. He's the one who's been joking around about being sure to remember our dysentery pills and not to drink the water. Now the entire plane, including the President, is about to land in Israel with the runs."

"You know, if we put it in it's going to be everyone's lead." Allison was giggling. "I love it. Especially after they trooped our revered Secretary of State back here to brief us on the importance of President Grey celebrating the involvement of Jordan in the peace process. 'January 27. The President, yesterday, suffering from intestinal upset reportedly caused by eating contaminated fish on *Air Force One*, met with Israeli Prime Minister Itsak Ensellem for the beginning of . . .'"

The two wire-service reporters and the television correspondent laughed.

"In fact, why don't we make it the lead of the pool report? They always hate it so when we don't lead with what they want us to. I think they dragged poor Wells Harmon back here to throw us off the fish story."

"Let's just wrap it up with the fish, if you'll pardon the expression. I want to get this fucking thing done so we can have a drink. Besides, you know that Manolas will be back again to brief us on arrival time and logistics. Let's just give this to Congdon the next time he comes back here to pee and he can take it up and get it run off now."

Allison finished typing the last few sentences and pulled it out of the typewriter, handing it to Des:

POOL REPORT #1

The President never left the front of the plane for the whole trip, not even to take a walk at Lajes in the Azores. Manolas was asked if the President would come back to talk to us, and he said he "would see," but nothing ever materialized.

Before we reached the Azores, a high government official (not the National Security Adviser or the Secretary of Defense) talked to us on background about the President's hopes for the trip. He said that things were tenuous because they never knew what to expect from the Israelis. The reason the Jordanians had agreed to join the peace process in the first place was because the Israelis had agreed to begin to phase out the West Bank settlements. But the various factions in Israel are arguing about it, and there is some fear that they may renege on their agreement, which might foil the talks altogether. The President was made aware of this possibility only a day ago, but decided to stick with his plans anyway and risk the pullout of the Jordanians. He would still continue his talks with the Israelis and the Egyptians in any case. He denied that the purpose of the trip had anything to do with the campaign, and Manolas ended our briefing when we asked that question. The high government official then disappeared to the front of the plane to join the other notables, who included the Secretary of Defense, the National Security Adviser, the Chief of

Protocol, Everett Dubois, the President's Communications Director, and the President's Chief of Staff, who will be departing soon to work on the campaign.

Manolas then admitted that the President, as were most of his staff, was feeling a bit queasy in the stomach from the bad fish that was served for lunch at the beginning of the flight. Manolas downplayed the ramifications of the fish story and encouraged us to concentrate on the briefing by the high government official, hinting that he might produce other such officials later in the flight. Otherwise uneventful.

Your Pool
Sterling and Shaw

"Here comes Congdon now," said Des. He grabbed the pool report and gave it to the President's aide.

"God, this sucks," said Des. "The reason I hate these trips is that I know I'll always end up in the frigging pool. You'd think traveling on *Air Force One* would be luxurious. But here we are in the ass end of the plane, next to the galley, in the narrow, hard seats which don't recline, with every turkey on the plane coming back and forth to the john. I don't know why I let New York talk me into this."

Des was standing up now, shaking his knees out where he had been kneeling next to Allison. She was sitting in Des's seat, one of four seats that faced each other across a table. As the newspaper correspondent, she was odd person out and had been seated across the aisle next to an airman.

"Here, you can have your seat back now, Des," said Allison, getting up from his aisle seat, which faced backward toward the wall and the galley behind it.

"Oh, no, I don't mind; why don't you stay there, and I'll sit here across the aisle."

He didn't say it, but the reason he didn't want his seat back was that on the wall behind the two wire-service seats was a large picture of Sadie, smiling down at him. It was a beautiful picture, but there was something accusatory about her expression, and it made him nervous. Allison had been open and friendly and not at all hostile as he might have imagined. He suspected that it might be an act, but if it was, she was doing a good job. Jenny had told him that Sonny was seeing the Omani and some movie star and that she seemed in good shape, but he hadn't expected her to be in this good shape. She was treating him the way she treated the television cameraman, who was a big, friendly sheepdog. It irritated him that she was uninterested in him, but it made it easier for them to do the pool together. She looked great. She was wearing a plum-colored cashmere sweater dress and a cardigan that matched. Her hair was cut shorter, soft and curly, not as severe as before.

"I have a better idea," said Des. "Why don't I see if the airman will trade with me? Then we can sit together."

The other three reporters exchanged glances as the airman moved over and Allison and Des sat down across the aisle. Des lit his cigarette with White House matches and took several drags before he looked at her. They had been so busy that they hadn't had a chance to focus on each other. Now here they were next to each other, with a long flight ahead of them.

"You shouldn't smoke."

"I know."

"Sorry—I didn't mean to sound preachy."

"You look fabulous."

"I know."

"Well, kiss my ass."

"Your hair is going gray."

"I know."

"It looks very distinguished."

"I don't want to look distinguished."

"Does Jenny like it?"

"Jenny?"

"Yes, Jenny Stern."

Des was thrown by this. Nobody had ever quizzed him about his relationship with Jenny. They went to parties together and everyone took it for granted that they were a pair.

He didn't know what to answer. He couldn't tell how much she knew. She was a good reporter; nothing would surprise him. If anybody in the White House press corps got on to the fact that he was having an affair with Sadie, it would be Allison. But she was so calm. He didn't sense anything in her questioning.

"Oh, well, Jenny's great. I love her dearly. And she is easy to be with. She kind of grows on you."

"Are you in love with her?"

"Jesus, Sonny, gimme a break. I don't want to get into that kind of thing. I like her a lot. Let's leave it at that."

"I gather it's mutual. Jenny doesn't seem to have much time these days for her old friends."

"I don't think that's a problem. I mean, I think she's just busy. She works her ass off over at the White House. That's a tough job. There isn't a lot left over for anybody else, even me."

"I gather she and Sadie Grey have become very tight."

This was not at all what Des wanted to talk about, but Allison was relentless. When there was something she wanted to talk about, she wouldn't give up. It was what made her both such a good reporter and so hard to live with sometimes.

"They have a good working relationship. Yeah, they get along fine."

"I have to tell you I feel quite hurt by Jenny. I mean, she was my closest friend and now she doesn't even have time to talk to me on the phone. Every time I call her she sounds guilty, and it's making me suspicious. Maybe she's involved or the White House is involved in something that she doesn't want me to know about. Is there something going on she doesn't want me to know about?"

"I think Jen is just up to here with work, and she does see a lot of me, and she has just kind of let things slide. I wouldn't worry about it."

He was trying to sound casual. He wasn't succeeding.

Allison looked at him curiously.

"Why are you being so defensive?"

"For Christ's sake, Sonny, lay off. I'm not the President of Brazil."

She had pushed him too far. She laughed.

"Sorry. I apologize. It's really none of my business."

She picked up a newspaper, trying to feign indifference.

"Oh, God, I think that's worse. Having you pretend you're not interested."

She looked at him slyly; then they both cracked up.

"Okay, it's my turn."

"Your turn at what?"

"What's with you and the Sheik of Araby?"

"I can't imagine what you're talking about."

"The Desert Fox. I hear you've been seen cruising around town in a blue Mercedes."

"He's a great lay."

"What about Mr. Hollywood?"

"One of the best."

"And Nick?"

It didn't sound like jesting.

"Nick is a close friend. I adore Nick. Besides, Nick lives in the Middle East and I live in Washington."

"Are you going to see him?"

"I don't think I like being interviewed. I like it the other way around. But I guess not all of your subjects feel that way. I never got to tell you I thought your cover on Sadie Grey was the most incredible puff job I have ever read in my life. What did she do, go down on you?"

He tried to smile.

"Why don't we agree to cut the third degree? Let's talk about our work—a nice, safe subject."

"Great," she said. "I gather you're onto Dubois. I saw the bit in *The Weekly* about Rittman Oil not getting the Omani bid and I heard you were in Louisiana that same week. Nice work." She added it reluctantly.

"My, aren't we gracious." He laughed. "But what makes you think Everett Dubois is involved?"

"For one thing, the look on your face. You were always a lousy poker player."

"You working on it too? . . . But of course you would be. Ali Baba would have turned you around three times and pointed you in Everett's direction. Be careful with that one. It's not as obvious as you might think. Don't let him use you."

"I can't be used any more than you can."

"What's that supposed to mean?"

"Just what I said."

"I forgot. You were always a terrific poker player."

POOL REPORT #2

The President was greeted at the plane by Prime Minister Itsak Ensellem, and the two men embraced. President Grey was then led to a waiting limousine and proceeded to the King David Hotel. There was no ceremonial arrival because of the late hour. There will be a welcoming ceremony tomorrow at the Knesset.

The motorcade from the airport was without incident. There were a few people with placards along the way which our Israeli driver told us were anti-giving-up-the-settlements. They were not loud or disruptive. The President went immediately to his suite. Grey would answer no questions as he entered the hotel. Manolas said he might after the ceremony at the Knesset but was making no promises. Manolas said the President is feeling better, but we suspect the beginnings of a cover-up on the fish story. Stay tuned.

Sterling and Shaw

"I need a drink."

"I think we've been here before."

"How's your stomach?"

"Much better. I'm starved."

"Good. Let's go eat."

"Are you asking me for a date, Shaw?"

"Why not? Two old friends. Get together, reminisce, have a few drinks, a few laughs."

There was a nervousness in his voice that she had not heard before. He seemed almost insecure. It was odd how she was suddenly the one who was in control. Probably it was her attitude of amiable nonchalance that had intrigued him. She hadn't intended to behave that way. In fact, when she had learned that she and Des were assigned to the pool, she'd tried to get out of it. The only reason she was stuck with it was that nobody else wanted to make the uncomfortable flight in the back of *Air Force One*.

She had summoned every ounce of self-control to manage to be friendly and casual when she met him at Andrews Air Force Base. As they began working together, it had seemed natural and familiar, and she had relaxed. Still, being around Des made her throat go dry. He was so strong, so masculine. There was something in him that was lacking in the other men she had been seeing. He was Lancelot. All the things that used to annoy her seemed to appeal to her now . . . the shirt sleeves rolled up under his jacket; the top button of his shirt never buttoned; the jacket with the hem coming unraveled; his hair never properly combed; ink stains on his shirt pocket. He looked like a journalist. He had always said she was trying to pussy-whip him into dressing like an investment banker. She would reply that she only wanted him to look handsome. But of course, he already did. She liked it that his hair had grayed. She liked the crinkles around his eyes. She liked his straight white teeth and his crooked smile. She liked everything about him, dammit. In fact, she loved him. Still. She would never let him know it. She had to be cool.

"I hear there's a fabulous new place near the Old City."

"What's it called?"

"It's called 'The Only Decent Food in Jerusalem.'"

"I'll believe it when I see it. Nick says . . ."

She saw him flinch then. She stopped in mid-sentence.

"Well, what are we waiting for?"

The restaurant was perfect. Built of old pale pink sandstone, it had a *cave*-like quality. There were half-oval windows overlooking the lighted wall of the Old City, small tables in quiet corners, everything lit by candlelight. They were given a table with a view, and the waiter took their drink orders before he left. When he brought them back, Des picked up his martini and held it up in the air.

"Cheers," he said.

She took her glass and touched his gently, then took a long sip of wine.

They looked into each other's eyes for the first time since they had boarded the plane. Allison was overwhelmed by a sense of loss. How could she have given this man up? What kind of jerk had she been to think that a story was worth losing him? She could feel the tears in her eyes and was grateful for the dimness of the room. She cleared her throat and decided that she wanted to die. All that glib talk on the plane. This man she loved more than anyone in the world. He was a part of her. They were right for each other. They were meant to be together, not separately playing out their pride. Was it too late? A sense of terror overtook her.

Now she was admitting it to herself. That made it so much harder. It was easier to deal with if she didn't have to face it. Now that she allowed herself to acknowledge she loved him and wanted him, she would have to do something. But what? She had absolutely no idea what he felt for her anymore.

Des smiled tentatively and reached cross the table, putting his hand on top of hers.

He was overwhelmed by a sense of confusion. Looking at Allison now, he loved her so much that he could barely restrain his impulse to take her in his arms. He had always loved never stopped loving her really. Yet how could he have fooled himself all this time? He had truly believed he was in love with Sadie. Was it possible to love two women at once? Just thinking of Sadie made him perspire. But the idea of never seeing her again did not cause him the same pain as he'd had when he lost Allison. When he left Allison, he had left his soul behind. Now he recognized that feeling of numbness he had been living with as a bereavement. Sadie excited him. Sadie was beautiful and giving. But Allison's and his lives were entwined. They were part of each other. It was Allison he loved, Allison he wanted, Allison he must have.

"Oh, Des," she said under her breath.

"Where've you been, baby?"

"I, uh, I . . . waiting for you."

She hadn't meant to say it. How stupid of her. She realized a moment later that she had been holding her breath, and she let it out like a diver surfacing.

"The wait's over." She reached out her other hand, and he took both her hands in his. "Jesus," he said. "What a couple of fools we've been." His voice cracked.

She could see that his eyes were as bright as hers felt. She was afraid to say anything for fear she would cry.

They were both afraid of letting go.

"Are you ready to order?"

The waiter's voice startled them.

"In a moment," said Des, distractedly. Then he looked back at Allison.

"Let's get the hell out of here," he said.

"Oh, God, Sonny. I'd forgotten. I'd forgotten how good it was with you, my precious Sonny. I've missed you so. Let me hold you."

Both his arms were around her, and as she always had been with Des when they made love, she was consumed by him. That power he had had over her when they were in bed together had always frightened and irritated her before. Now she felt comforted by it. It always amazed her how a man as strong as he was could be so tender and gentle. Now he was stroking her hair and her face, kissing her neck and her ears, her lips and her hands as though he would starve without her. There was a desperateness to his need. He hadn't let her go since they had gotten back to her room at the King David. They had not even turned on the lights. He had just led her to the bed and undressed her, the way he had done when they first met at the Democratic convention nearly four years ago. There wasn't anything to say. They just had to hold on.

Allison hurt with joy. She had never expected this of Des. She didn't know what she had actually expected: maybe some sexual attraction, or as he had said, a few drinks, a few laughs. She was afraid to respond in kind, though it was hard to hold back.

Now he was on top of her again and he was in her and she could feel his weight and she didn't want to think about anything at all. She just wanted him, and for the first time in a year and a half she had him.

It was only at dawn, when they were both exhausted, that she realized he hadn't told her that he loved her. Of course, she hadn't told him either; but somehow that was up to him, after what had happened. Though why should she expect him to make that kind of commitment again so soon? Those things take time. And Des was never effusive about his feelings. It had taken him months to say it the first time, and she had known from the first moment he kissed her that he loved her. Now she knew it again. Or did she? She wasn't as sure of herself as she had been four years ago. Wiser maybe. Not surer.

"What time is the Knesset circus supposed to start?" he asked, rolling over and grabbing her breast.

She turned her back to him and curled up in the hollow of his body, clasping his hand that held her breast, her head on the pillow, facing away.

"Ten. But Ensellem is arriving for breakfast at eight thirty and then he'll escort Grey over there. Are you going?"

"I guess so. It's going to be nothing but a ceremony, but what the hell. Pick up a little color. Since it's Monday, I don't have to file anything until I get back. Then I spend the weekend working my ass off. God, I'm beginning to hate weekends. One of these days I'm going to retire to my cabin in West Virginia and write a book."

"That sounds like not a bad idea. Need a housekeeper?"

"It's essential. But I don't think I can advertise the job description in the *Daily* classifieds."

"I'll look around for you. What are the requirements?"

"Weekends, nights. Must cook, must write, must fuck."

"Benefits?"

"Baby, you've got the benefits between your legs right now."

"Salary?"

"She should pay *me*."

Allison groaned. "Time? Two years, three years?"

"If it works out, forever."

She caught her breath. They lay silently, breathing together. She could feel both their hearts.

"Do you have to file today?" he asked finally, when their hearts had slowed.

"No. Nick is doing the daily stuff. Which is fine with me. I hate all that rushing around. I'm doing an overall piece on the Jerusalem part of the trip for Thursday."

"So you'll have to hook up with him at some point?"

"At some point."

"You in any pools today?"

"Not that I know of, but that could change. How about you?"

"I'm not sure. I haven't checked yet."

"So we'll probably run into each other during the day. There's the helicopter flight up to the settlements. We probably ought to go down to the filing room and see what's going on."

"So what are you up to after the banquet tonight?"

She had to laugh. He was acting like a shy sixteen-year-old asking a girl for a date the first time.

"Oh, nothing much. What about you?"

"Cunt."

"What? Why me?"

"Because you know what I'm asking."

"Well, it's hard to decipher. It's just not the old Des."

"What would the old Des have said?"

"'Wanna get laid?'"

"And what would the old Sonny have said?"

"'You bet your sweet ass I do.'"

He laughed delightedly as he swung back the covers and sprang out of bed. He looked like a happy man. And once again, Allison nearly gasped at how gorgeous he was, what a great body he had.

He unzipped her suitcase, pulled a razor and some shampoo out of her makeup kit, and went into the bathroom.

Sonny had been waiting for him to leave the room. She had been desperate with curiosity ever since they had stopped at the desk for keys and messages the night before. The desk clerk had handed him a message from his box. Des had glanced at it quickly, but she couldn't help being surprised by his reaction. He had closed his eyes and let out a soft groan, then folded it up and stuffed it into his jacket pocket.

Now she couldn't stand it any longer. She went over to the bathroom door to make sure the shower was on, then walked quickly over to the chair where he had tossed his jacket. She reached into one pocket, then the other, fingering the crumpled paper. Something told her not to take it, and for a second she hesitated, pulling her hand halfway out of the pocket. Then she grabbed the note and smoothed it out. It said, "Jenny says please call Lagoon."

She crumpled the note again and stuffed it back into the pocket, then quickly jumped into the bed as he opened the bathroom door to let the steam out. Vaguely she heard him humming as he shaved and combed his hair. Everything was swimming in her head so fast that she could barely make sense of it. Lagoon was Sadie's Secret Service name. Why on earth would he be calling Sadie? What kind of relationship could he have with her that he would call her from halfway around the world, and why would Jenny call? Why wouldn't her secretary call? And why would Jenny use that name? Why didn't she just leave a message to call her?

The only thing Allison could think of was the look on Des's face at the White House dinner the night he had cut in on Sadie. She had seen then that he was infatuated with her. She knew from Lorraine that he had been especially attentive at parties right after they had broken up, particularly when Rosey was out of town. He had always thought Sadie was sexy and pretty and funny and bright. It used to enrage her. It was part of the reason she had never really liked Sadie. Because Des did. But this? Could it be that he was in love with her, that they were having an affair? It was impossible. How could the First Lady have an affair? But then she began to remember hearing people say Des was over at the EOB a lot. And then she thought about Des and Jenny and how she knew in her gut that they had never been to bed together. And she knew Des well enough to know he had to get laid. And since a few months after they had broken up, she had never heard a single word about Des seeing anybody but Jenny. Could Jenny be the beard? It was all so improbable. But then, Des hadn't told her he loved her. He would have if he did. This time he would have. He didn't tell her he loved her because he couldn't. Because he was in love with somebody else. He was in love with the fucking First Lady and they were having an affair. That note could mean nothing else. It was suddenly so obvious, so clear. She had been so baffled by him and Jenny all year. Now she felt foolish.

Des loved Sadie. Des did not love her. Then how could he have done this? How could he have made love to her knowing that he was in love with another woman? Her teeth began to chatter in anger, and she pulled the covers over her head and curled her body up in a fetal position. She was too hurt, too angry to cry. She took several quick breaths for fear of suffocating. She heard Des come out of the bathroom.

"What a great piece of ass you are, Sterling," he was saying, and she knew she had to get herself together, not let him know. She had to play it cool, but she wasn't sure she could manage. She couldn't move.

"What's the matter, baby? Are you okay?"

"I'm okay," she managed. "I think I'm having another fish attack, that's all. I just suddenly doubled over with stomach cramps."

"Oh, no. I'm so sorry. Is it really bad? Should I get the house doctor?"

"No, no. I'll be all right. But I think I'll stay here for a while. I don't feel like getting up. Why don't you go on down to the filing room."

"You sure?"

"Positive."

"Well, let me get one more look at that beautiful face," he said, sitting down on the edge of the bed and pulling the sheet away.

"Jesus, you really do look pale. Promise me you'll call a doctor if you don't feel better in a while."

"I promise," she said weakly.

"Great." He kissed her cheek. "You're one hell of a woman, Sonny Sterling," he said softly. "And you know, I really do think you've changed since we were together. You seem to know what you want now, and I like that. I'll see you tonight."

* * *

Betrayal, hurt had turned to fury. She had been angry at him when he left her, but she had been more angry at herself. Now she was sick with rage that he had humiliated her this way. She avoided him all day, staying away from several events so that she wouldn't have to see him, and she stuck close to Nick. Wonderful, dear Nick. They had embraced so warmly that she had nearly cried. She needed to see Nick, to see somebody who cared about her genuinely. If he hadn't been around, she wouldn't have made it through the day. She hadn't figured out what to do about that night until she ran into Everett Dubois. It occurred to her that she could solve two problems at once. Make a dinner date with Everett, or an after-banquet date, and have a legitimate excuse for getting out of meeting Des. It was ironic that once again her way of dealing with him was to beat him out of a story. She knew Everett was a womanizer, and with a little prodding he would probably tell her some things he didn't mean to.

Everett fell for it.

She left a note in Des's box that she was meeting Everett later and wouldn't be able to see him.

Her meeting with Everett was disappointing. He knew she was seeing Ali and was very cagey. Still, she felt she had made some connection and that a few more lunches or dinners and she might get something out of him. He was indiscreet.

When she returned to the hotel, she found a note from Des in her box:

"I don't get it."

"And you never will," she said to herself under her breath.

She didn't sleep. All she could do was imagine Des and Sadie in bed together, imagine him caressing Sadie the way he caressed her, calling Sadie precious, and angel, and enveloping her with kisses. It was unbearable. She tried to erase the thoughts. But she was obsessed. She hated Des now more than she had ever hated anyone, and she was amazed that her feelings could reverse so quickly and so totally. She didn't want him to know that she was angry or why. She couldn't. There was no way she could confront him. For one thing, she didn't have enough evidence; for another, he would deny it; and for a third, what right had she anyway? She would simply have to stay away from him, even, in this case, if it meant hurting her story. Today she would be writing anyway, so that she wouldn't be doing much traveling around with the President.

She got dressed and went downstairs for breakfast, then headed toward the filing room to pick up the press releases.

The President was leaving the hotel for a private meeting with President Ensellem, and the motorcade was just lining up.

"Sonny! Jesus, am I glad I saw you," shouted a voice, and she felt someone grab her by the arm. She turned, annoyed, to find Jay Herbert from the New York paper. "Listen, Sonny, I've just been asked to file an analysis piece for tomorrow and I've got to start writing today. I'm supposed to be in this pool and I really need you to fill in for me. Please. I'm desperate."

Sonny was about to say no, then remembered that Herbert had given her a fill the year before on a trip when she had overslept. She saw the frantic look in his eyes.

"Sure, Herbert," she said finally. "I'll take the ride for you."

"Great. They want you in that car over there," he said, and pulled her in the direction of a large station wagon which was already jammed. The front cars in the motorcade had already started up and were slowly pulling out. Herbert shouted at the station wagon to hold it, and Sonny ran toward it without looking as the press aide stood holding the door and waving her toward it.

"You'll have to sit on his lap," said the press aide brusquely as he pushed her into the car and slammed the door. As the car pulled out, she looked up and saw that she was inches away from Des's face. His arm moved possessively around her waist, and his hand grabbed her ass.

He feigned a dignified, solemn look as he greeted her.

"Good morning, Sterling," he said. "Are you feeling better?"

His hand, which was on the door side of the car and could not be seen by its other occupants, continued to caress her behind. She was so stunned by this turn of events that she had no choice but to nod automatically as the rest of the reporters in the car looked at her.

"Uh, fine," she said.

The smell in the car within several minutes was of hot breath and sweat, but it didn't block out the distinctive scent of Des, a scent which only two nights before had sent her into a swoon. She tried to turn her head so that she was looking at the driver of the car, but it only meant that his breath was on her neck, and he had slipped his hand up under her jacket so that he could reach her breast without anybody noticing. He didn't say anything more on the fifteen-minute drive, just continued to look solemn and stroke her body until she thought she would explode with rage and humiliation. Yet she had to keep a straight face. She at least could refuse to look at him.

When the motorcade finally arrived and they untangled themselves from the car, she dashed ahead to where the other reporters were standing to get a glimpse of the President and the Prime Minister greeting each other. When they had gone inside and left the press outside to wait, Des walked over to her. She could see the confused look on his face.

"Don't I deserve an explanation?" he asked.

"For what?" She was trying not to show her anger.

"For last night. We had plans. I get back to the hotel and get this cryptic note that you're meeting Everett Dubois after the banquet. Okay. Fair enough. I've been around this track with you before, but I'm older and wiser and more secure, so I can handle it. But I expected you to give me a call when you got back to your room. I left a note in your box. What the hell is going on?"

She started to say "Nothing." Then she couldn't help herself.

"I was with Nick." Her face was stony.

"All night?" He looked stunned.

"Yes." There was no explanation, no apology in her voice.

For a minute she thought he might cry. She saw the agony on his face and the profound hurt in his eyes. Then his jaw tightened and he matched her stony look.

He started to walk away, then hesitated, then turned back to her, his own rage welling up in his voice.

"Well, then, fuck you," he said, and turned to walk away from her once again.

Sadie looked at the pile of bills on the small desk in her office off the West Hall and sighed. One of the most boring jobs of being First Lady was paying bills. Bills for living in the White House. The idea that the President should have to pay for all the meals on the second floor of the White House, plus small personal toiletries, was absurd. It would seem that the American people could foot that bill. It wasn't as if the Greys couldn't afford it. But there were First Families who didn't have much money. And it upset her further that she had to pay for her own transportation in *Air Force One*. First-class fare plus one dollar. But there was no point in seething about it. That was the rule, and they above all were not the ones to try to change it. She pushed the pile of bills away from her as if that would solve the problem, then turned and looked out at Lafayette Square. She could see the various demonstrators out in front waving their placards and pacing up and down in front of the gate. They were such a familiar sight that she scarcely noticed them anymore. The bright red tulips were out in full bloom in the park, and the tiny pale green buds had begun to appear on the trees. It was unseasonably warm for April, and people were lying on the grass in the sun or sitting there eating their lunches. Sadie had an uncontrollable urge to run downstairs and outside, past the gate and out into the park.

She wanted to take off her shoes and romp around, flop down on the grass, talk to people, walk down the street, window-shop, walk into a restaurant, eat lunch, see friends. The desire was so overwhelming that she lost her breath for a moment thinking about it. Nearly two years of being a prisoner was really getting to her. Sometimes she thought, in the middle of some ceremony on the South Lawn, that she would just scream out loud, "Get me out of here." She knew what it must feel like to be a hostage with a gun to your head telling the police at the door that there was nothing wrong. She had to smile and pretend she was happy and in love with her husband when she was an inmate. She was sure that four more years of this kind of life in a straitjacket and she would be truly nuts. The only thing that kept her going was the thought that she might write a decent book about it. There was no doubt that it would be a best-seller. She and Des had joked about the title. Something along the lines of *Bananas: A First Lady Freaks Out* had appealed to them. More and more, though, neither one of them was finding the situation very funny.

Des had been in an odd mood when he returned from the Middle East in February. Sadie had tried to find out whether he had spent time with Allison. But he had cut her off so abruptly that she was afraid to probe.

She pumped Jenny, but Jenny appeared not to know anything. The only thing she could figure was that they had had a falling-out over something to do with Everett. Des had been beating Allison out on the story at every turn, and Sadie had to admit it gave her a certain incentive to keep on leaking. In the time they had been back Allison had had several stories on the Rittman-Omani situation, trying to catch up to the *Weekly* stories. She had alluded once to the fact that certain Washington insiders felt that Everett might have been involved. Rosey had dug in his heels. He was besieged by his advisers to get rid of Everett, and for some reason he had decided to remain Mr. Loyal. Sadie could not persuade him, so she continued to pass on any little anti-Everett tidbits to Des.

Whatever the problem with Allison, Sadie was not worried about her any longer. Des was more loving, more attentive than ever, almost to the point of frightening her. She knew that they were heading for a confrontation, for some kind of decision, and she didn't want to think about it. He had a rather desperate air about him, something she had not seen before. Each time she saw him, she expected it to be the time when he would explode, demand that she leave Rosey or he would not see her anymore.

"Hard at work, I see," said Jenny, smiling, as she walked into Sadie's office. "That stack is as high as it was last week when you resolutely announced you were not leaving here until you had paid them all."

"Jenny," Sadie cried out, her voice almost a shriek, "I have got to get out of here. I can't stand it another minute. I have got to get out of here. Get me out of here, Jenny. Please. Before I do something unthinkable."

"Excuse me for reminding you," said Jenny, "but you are already doing something unthinkable. Every Monday, to be exact. I hate to think what you'll come up with for an encore."

"You don't understand," said Sadie, a frantic note in her voice. "I have to get out. We've got to go somewhere. We've just got to get out of here instantly."

"Where do you want to go?"

"I don't care. Anywhere except Camp David. That place is giving me the willies too. It's just a bigger prison. What about East Hampton? We could open up the house there. You could come with me. Rosey's going to be on a campaign swing next weekend. Without me. He'd be delighted to have me go up there. Why don't we go there? Nobody's up there this time of year. We could walk on the beach and eat pizza from Sam's."

"I smell a rat."

"No, you don't, Jenny. I swear. I've just had it up to here with this place, and if I don't get out soon I'm going to take off all my clothes and run down Pennsylvania Avenue. How about that for an encore?"

"We'll go. How about this afternoon? How fast can you pack?"

Sadie burst out laughing. "You know what I like about you, Jenny? There are no flies on your head."

"And you know what I like about you? You know how to get what you want."

Sadie loved East Hampton in the off season. The endless stretches of beautiful white beach were deserted. You could walk for miles and not see anybody. The house was right at the beach, behind the dunes, with a little hidden path through the privet hedge to a tiny cottage right on the beach at the top of the dune. Sadie could walk from her house to the cottage anytime in privacy, and she could sit on the little deck on the dune without anybody noticing. It was perfect. Des could stay in the cottage. He could pull his car into the parking lot by the Coast Guard station and then walk over the dune. Naturally, Sadie had not told Jenny the plan. She would never have approved. But once she got up there she wouldn't have any choice. Des would just show up. She'd have only one Secret Service agent with her. Toby was the only one besides Jenny who knew. He had to. Rosey wanted her to take more agents with her to East Hampton, but she persuaded him that she really didn't need anybody else.

They would take the small military jet to the East Hampton airport, and they could stay a week. Then come back the same way. Des could spend several days in the cottage, and they would have a chance to be alone outside their little EOB rooms for the first time. It would be heaven.

The day she arrived the weather had changed from unseasonably warm to unseasonably cold, but the sun was shining and the sky and sea were sparkling. The caretaker had opened the house, and it was spanking-clean and warm and cozy with a big fire in the wood-burning stove in the kitchen. There were groceries in the icebox and flowers on the table, and Sadie wanted to sing and dance and cry, she was in such ecstasy to be out of chains and back into the real world. She and Jenny, with Toby not far behind, couldn't wait to get out on the beach, and they walked for hours until it was past lunchtime and their noses were red from the wind.

Later that night Sadie and Jenny sat in front of the fire and talked.

"Des is coming up, isn't he?"

"How did you know?"

"You already paid me the ultimate Southern compliment by telling me there were no flies on my head. How could I not know? You're both human. It would have been a shock to me if he weren't coming."

"I guess I should have told you."

"No, no. You did me a favor. Now I'm not responsible. . . . So when's he arriving?"

"Tomorrow morning."

They sat and stared at the fire for a while.

"You know you're going to have to make a decision, don't you?"

"I'm trying not to think about it."

"You have to. This particular excursion is especially dangerous. A few more of these and it's bound to get out. I suspect you know that and you are unwittingly trying to be found out so that you will be forced to do something. At least, that's what Rachel would say. But that is not the smartest thing to do. You've got to think this out, Sadie. It's not fair to Rosey. Or to yourself, for that matter. Or Des. You can't actually have focused in on what a tremendous scandal it would be and how hurtful to everyone, including the country. If you are even vaguely contemplating leaving Rosey, you have got to start planning it now. You can't do it until after he's elected, but then you really will have no choice. If you really can't do it then, and I know it will be hard, you are going to have to break it off with Des. I am not being your malleable, cooperative press secretary now. I am telling you what has to be done. I have given this a lot of thought. And I have decided that if you don't do one or the other by the election, then I will have to quit. Assuming, of course, that the shit hasn't hit the fan before that."

Sadie felt her stomach fall out. She closed her eyes for a moment to make sure she had her bearings. Then she looked at Jenny closely. But Jenny wasn't smiling. She meant it.

"Oh, Jen," she whispered. "Please don't say that. Please. I couldn't function without you. You're my lifeline."

"I know that, Sadie. Which is why this has not been an easy decision for me. But I have made up my mind, and I know I have no choice. Neither do you, really. I love you a lot. And the only way I know how to make you realize the consequences of what you are doing is to give you an ultimatum. I hope you understand that."

Sadie nodded, blinking back the tears, and minutes later excused herself. She lay awake most of the night listening to the wind blow the branches of the cherry tree against the porch roof and the waves pound the beach. At dawn she fell asleep and dreamed about Des. Des was lying on the bed with her, holding her in his strong arms. She dreamed he was kissing her and stroking her, gently, tenderly, telling her he loved her. Even if it hadn't been clear in her waking mind what she must do, she was now without doubts. There was no way that she could let this man go. She had never loved anyone this way, and she never would, or could. She would have to leave Rosey. She would tell Jenny today. But she didn't want to wake up because the dream was so good.

"I love you," he was whispering to her. "I adore you. Please, stay with me."

She wanted it to be like this always, just the two of them. Alone. In a real bed. Together.

"Des, I love you too," she murmured back. And then he was kissing her again, this time less gently, and she was afraid he would wake her with his passion. Now he had his hand beneath the sheets and he had pulled up her nightgown and was caressing her abdomen, then her breasts.

"Oh, God," she said, "don't stop, don't stop." Even though she knew if he didn't stop she would awaken. He didn't stop, he kept on and on, pulling her nightgown up around her neck and she could feel his body as he eased it on top of her and she could feel the heat of her skin as it tingled and she could feel his breath on her neck and she could feel him pounding away at her and she didn't ever want to wake up and she could hear him cry out her name as he came and she could feel her own body flush all over and then she felt her body heave with shudders and she grasped his back with her hands and said, "I love you, I love you, I love you" over and over until she had quieted down and her body was still. Then she opened her eyes and it was Des. He was there. She was awake and he had been there all along. And then the tears came again, rolling down her cheeks, and she clung to him so tightly that he gasped and laughed. But his eyes were tearing too.

"I need you, baby," he said. "I've got to have you."

"You do," she said, wiping her tears away with the edge of her sheet and closing her eyes again. "You do, forever."

"If" had changed to "when."

"When we're together," he would say to her, "we'll go to La Samanna for a vacation. It's a fabulous resort in the Caribbean, the most romantic place I've ever been."

"When we're together, we'll spend weekends in the log cabin in West Virginia by the fire. We'll walk in the woods, and I'll make love to you on the rocks in the river."

"When we're together, we'll get a house in Georgetown and you can decorate it to your heart's desire and make it cozy, and we'll both have our offices there."

"When we're together, we can sleep in the same bed and I'll hold on to you all night long and never let you go."

"When? When will we be together?"

"After the election. I'll tell Rosey after the election."

They were walking arm in arm down the beach. It was late afternoon, and though the wind had subsided, it was still brisk. They were wearing heavy sweaters and windbreakers, and though the beach was deserted, Sadie was wearing a scarf and dark glasses which partially disguised her face. They hadn't meant to be walking arm in arm. They had started off very carefully, walking apart. But once they had seen that there was no one on the beach, they had relaxed and started horsing around.

He chased her part of the way until she tripped and fell into the dunes, and they lay in the tall dune grasses and kissed for a while, then picked themselves up and wrapped their arms around each other as they continued on down toward the Beach Club, a series of old lockers and showers on an open-air boardwalk.

"You've got to tell him before then. You have to prepare him. It's going to be hard on the poor bastard. You can't just spring it on him like that. He's got to get used to the idea, make plans, learn to deal with it. He's got to have time to hate you before you leave him. Then it will be easier for both of you."

"You didn't do that with Sonny."

He stiffened and pulled away slightly.

"That was different. I wasn't leaving her for another woman."

"I'm sorry," she said, pulling closer. "I shouldn't have brought her up. I know it was different."

Even now the mention of Allison's name caused him pain. But it was pain he was going to have to either learn to live with or get over. He would not allow her to dominate his thoughts or ruin his life. She had hurt him terribly in Jerusalem, worse than he had ever thought he could be hurt by a woman, and he would never allow that to happen again. He would never allow himself to be so vulnerable again. He had pushed his love for Allison out of his mind as much as he could and determined to concentrate on his feelings for Sadie. And he did love her. He loved her warmth and humor, her femininity, her sexiness, her willingness to please, her deference to him. There were things about her which Allison lacked. Sadie was a man's woman. And he was a man who needed a woman. He loved Sadie, there was no question of that. He cared for her deeply. And Sadie loved him. But more than that, he needed her. He needed her to help him forget Allison.

They walked in silence, his arm around her, but she could tell the mention of Sonny had changed his mood. She wanted to get him out of it.

"Let's go look at the Beach Club. I love old dilapidated boardwalks on deserted beaches," she said, pulling him up the rickety gray wood steps.

"Let's play Hide and Seek. You close your eyes and I'll hide. If you find me, you get a prize," she said, giggling. She was in a zany mood, and she could tell by his expression that he had picked up her mood and was ready to play.

She ran off down the maze of old wooden lockers.

"Ready or not, here I come," she heard him call, "if you'll pardon the expression." She was trying hard not to laugh as she stood squeezed inside the musty locker with cobwebs brushing her face. She could hear Des walking up and down the next row of lockers opening and closing doors at random. Then his footsteps got closer and closer to where she was. She could hear him standing nearly beside the door of her locker. Then, for some reason, he started moving off to the side. She heard him pull open a door and there was a startled shriek—not Des's voice— and then he cried out, "My God!"

Frantic, Sadie pushed open the door to her locker and saw Des, a few feet away, standing in front of one of the shower stalls, his hand on the door. He was staring speechless into the stall. Sadie rushed to where he was standing. Inside the shower stall, partially dressed, stood the very married Catholic Mayor of New York City with the wife of a well-known television correspondent. Sadie was so taken aback that it didn't immediately occur to her that the two of them, once they had recovered from their own embarrassment, might notice the wife of the President of the United States. Of course they knew each other, all four of them. And so there they stood, in shock and embarrassment, until Des spoke.

"We never saw each other," he said quietly, and without another word he took Sadie's arm and pulled her away toward the beach.

All Sadie could think about was whether or not Lorraine had seen the item. Lorraine had acted perfectly normal when Sadie arrived at the Jockey Club for lunch. Lorraine was waiting for her at one of the corner banquettes in the front room. They kissed on both cheeks, complimented each other on how they looked, ordered Perriers with a twist of lime, and cased the place before turning to talk.

Sadie had wanted to cancel the lunch, but Jenny had told her to "tough it out" when the item appeared in the New York gossip column that morning.

"Cancelling your lunch with Lorraine would be like holding a press conference and announcing you're having an affair," said Jenny. "You've got to go. And then you've got to tell Rosey. Somebody's going to bring it to his attention. And by someone, I mean Everett. It's now or never, kiddo."

"I don't think I can do it, Jenny."

"Do what? Have lunch with Lorraine or tell Rosey?"

"Either. I think I'll just go take some pills and quietly go to sleep forever."

"I think you will not do that. I think you will go to lunch with Lorraine, act perfectly natural, smile and wave at your friends and admirers, and then come home and tell your husband you're leaving him for another man."

"Is the item that obvious?" Sadie's voice was trembling. The worst was happening and she still wasn't able to absorb it.

"Anastasia is not known for being the subtlest gossip columnist in New York. Let me just read it over to you once more in case you haven't memorized it:

"'Here's a tough one, darlings.... What wife of a very very, very high-up government official was seen frolicking about a certain nearby beach resort with what high-powered Washington journalist? We'll let you stew over that one for now, but here's a clue. She was not wearing a red wig. It's going to be a delicious spring, gossipwise.'"

"Okay. Okay. It's pretty obvious. Do you think Lorraine will have seen it?" She was trying to keep calm, but her heart was beating so quickly that she could feel her body twitching.

"Does McDonald's have golden arches? Come on, Sadie. We're talking All-Pro gossip here. Of all the people you could be having lunch with, she is either the worst or the best, depending on how you play it. You have got to be so cool today that Lorraine will get on the horn and start denying it the minute lunch is over."

"What if she brings it up? What will I say?"

"Repeat after me: 'What item in Anastasia's column?' Now repeat: 'Oh, good—some fresh dirt. I'm starved for it. Tell me every detail. I knew you were the perfect person to have lunch with.' And then you say, 'How delicious! Do you think it could possibly be Helene Corwin?'"

Sadie laughed in spite of herself.

"Oh, you are so evil. I couldn't do it."

"The fate of our nation rests on the fact that you can."

"You certainly have a way of putting things in perspective."

"I'm only half-kidding."

"I've never heard of Helene Corwin screwing around."

"She doesn't. You do. Remember? We're just trying to throw sand in Lorraine's eyes."

Sadie ignored her.

"Poor Helene. I feel so sorry for her. She's kept up such a brave face all the way through those censure hearings. I don't see how she stood it. At least he didn't get thrown out of the Senate."

"Well, if he wins this fall it'll be a miracle."

"Maybe it would be better for Helene if he lost. Then she could get out of that dreadful marriage. I don't think she'll have the courage to if he wins again."

"Sounds familiar."

"You're being awfully tough on me today, Jen." Her voice was shaky.

"I'm sorry. I don't mean to be." She came over to where Sadie was sitting and gave her a hug. She could hear Sadie stifle a sob.

"Okay, kid, I want you to come out of the corner fighting. You're having lunch with a world heavyweight today."

Sadie could tell Lorraine had something on her mind because she kept being distracted from her conversation. And she kept looking curiously at Sadie for any sign that everything wasn't perfect.

Lorraine had that wonderful attribute without which any serious power maven was crippled: multiple pairs of eyes. She could monitor the comings and goings of everyone in the room while holding down an intimate and seemingly riveting one-on-one conversation. Sadie was awed. It was a busy day at the Jockey Club and there was a lot to keep track of. Edwina was having lunch with Claire Elgin. Bud Corwin and Earl Downs were commiserating, and Allison Sterling was in the opposite corner from Sadie and Lorraine with Everett Dubois. Allison pretended not to notice Sadie, and Sadie felt suddenly sick to her stomach, surrounded by this motley cast of characters. And though she was the President's wife and therefore a natural object of attention, she couldn't help thinking that most of them were staring at her a little too obviously. She remembered the nightmare she had had when she had first come to Washington in which she was walking through an amusement park and everyone was distorted and grotesque. It made her dizzy, and she kept having to blink to get people's faces back into focus.

"Are you all right, dear?" asked Lorraine. Sadie closed her eyes again. She could feel the beads of sweat appear on her forehead and on her upper lip. She knew she had to get control of herself. She certainly couldn't faint in the middle of the Jockey Club, though she couldn't imagine how she was ever going to get out of there if it wasn't on a stretcher.

Finally the wave of nausea dispersed and she sat upright and took a sip of her water.

"I don't know, Lorraine. I feel as if I'm coming down with the flu. I seem to be a little feverish."

Lorraine raised an eyebrow but said nothing.

"Well, as I was saying," said Lorraine, "we might as well enjoy ourselves this spring season because when the fall comes and everyone's off on the campaign, Washington will simply close down. I just loathe this town in the autumn of an election year. Nobody entertains. Either they're afraid they won't be able to get any stars because they're out on the road, or they're afraid they'll waste all their time and money on people who won't be in power after January. Of course"—and Lorraine smiled ingratiatingly at Sadie—"that won't be the case this year. Everyone knows Rosey will be elected. But still . . . people don't like to take chances, put their eggs in one basket."

"It won't make any difference to me. Being in the White House is never very entertaining."

"Oh, you don't know. The election-year blahs even fall on the White House, my dear. You just don't realize it because you've never lived there during a Presidential campaign. I can't begin to tell you how dreary it is until Thanksgiving. It makes one want to stay at the beach until the election is over."

Lorraine had not brought up the beach by accident. She looked at her, but Lorraine didn't bat an eyelid. She just kept on talking.

"Don't you wish you could use your beach house in the Hamptons more?"

Sadie swallowed. Here it comes.

She was trying to remember what Jenny had told her to say.

"I've always loved the beach out of season. This is my favorite time at Fishers Island," Lorraine continued.

Sadie felt another wave of nausea coming on.

"You didn't happen to see that item in Anastasia's column about the wife of a high-up government official, did you? I don't suppose you would have. It was in that New York rag. But she is an amusing writer. Apparently—"

"Oh, yes," said Sadie, too quickly, "I think I know the one you mean. Jenny told me about it this morning."

She couldn't imagine that she was being convincing. Her mouth was so dry her lips were cracking. She tried to muster a giggle. It was pathetic.

"We decided it had to be Helene Corwin. Poor thing. What a time she's had of it. Well, I don't blame her. She deserves to have something nice happen to her. I hope it's somebody decent and not somebody who's trying to take advantage of her."

Lorraine started to say something, but the maître d'hôtel was approaching their table. Sadie had hardly touched her filet of sole. They both nodded when he asked if everything was satisfactory.

"I want to tell you a story," Lorraine said, after she had picked at her crab dijonnaise for a few moments without looking at Sadie. Sadie was surprised. She had not expected to get off this easily. Lorraine had clearly been boring in on her.

"There was a young Jewish girl from Kansas City in the early forties. Her name was Naomi Goldman. She came from a poor but honest family. Her father was a tailor's assistant, her mother a seamstress. She learned how to sew and after high school got a job in a dress shop doing alterations. She became a salesgirl and finally ended up running the shop. She had, she felt, too much style to be in Kansas City, so she moved to New York and got a job as a receptionist at a small magazine. She had her nose fixed and changed her name to Lorraine Gordon. After several years she ended up at *Fashion* and was made an editor. Her success took her to London as fashion editor there, and she met and married a very old, very right British lord, who died soon after their marriage. In the meantime she had set up a celebrated salon, and eventually she married a rich American diplomat."

Sadie had been staring at Lorraine, a puzzled expression on her face, but now her eyes widened in recognition.

"You? But Archie . . ."

"I know. Archie is the most anti-Semitic person you've ever met. And Archie does not know that I am Jewish. Nobody knows. I'm as elusive as our own favorite Howard Heinrich, who has a similar background.

"The irony is that here I am in Washington at a time when everybody who's anybody is Jewish and I'm still trying to pass."

She laughed bitterly. "If Archie didn't have so much money and if I hadn't become addicted to my career as hostess, I would have left him years ago. And if he ever found out that I was Jewish, I have no doubt that he would leave me."

"Why are you telling me this?"

"Because I just wanted you to know that every day of my life I have lived in fear. In fear of being discovered. And I wanted to tell you that it is no way to live. I am trusting you with this secret because I care about you and I don't want you to suffer the way I have. And I would like you to know that if I had a choice, I would never, ever do it again."

Lorraine had been staring down at her plate, twisting her napkin, but when she looked up at Sadie, there were tears in her eyes and an imploring look on her face.

"Do you understand what I am saying to you, my darling girl?"

"Excuse me," said Sadie. "I think I'm going to be sick."

She quickly left the table and, followed by her Secret Service agents, found her way to the ladies' room, where she threw up.

"Lorraine knows."

"How can you be sure?"

Sadie had called Des as soon as she got back to the White House and told him what had happened.

"I'm telling you, she wouldn't have told me for nothing. Especially after she'd brought up the beach. There's no doubt in my mind. But if she knows, then everybody else must at least suspect."

"Shit."

"Exactly."

"That son-of-a-bitch Mayor. I'll get his ass. The idea that he would have the nerve to spread this around considering his own compromising position."

"Oh, come on, Des. It wasn't him. It was her. She doesn't have that much to lose. Her husband isn't in office or anything. And besides, she's a journalist. You know how—"

"How are they?"

She laughed, a bit nervously. "I didn't mean it that way."

"Yes, you did. You meant you can't trust us with a good story, and you're right. I would have done exactly what she did, except I care too much about you. She obviously doesn't give a damn about him. Poor fucker."

"I'm scared, Des."

"Has Rosey said anything to you?"

"No. But he has seemed awfully preoccupied. I don't know whether he knows anything. Maybe I should try the Helene Corwin gambit on him, bring it up first."

"Forget it. If he doesn't know it won't hurt him, and if he does, then let him bring it up."

"I can't believe Allison and Everett weren't discussing it."

"They were there?" He said it quickly, abruptly.

"Yes. At the corner table opposite us."

"Shit."

It didn't have the same ring when he said it this time.

"I just can't believe this is happening."

"It's happening, baby. It's happening. What you've got to come to terms with is that you're going to have to sit down with him fairly soon and tell him you're going to leave him. Just do me one favor."

"What's that?"

"Wait till my interview with him is over."

"What interview?"

"I'm interviewing him next week. We're doing a cover story on him. The peg is other Presidents who have inherited the office and what their chances are of getting elected for the first time."

"So you want me to wait until after that?"

"I think you should tell him immediately after the interview."

She could feel the perspiration begin to appear on her forehead again.

"I think I'm going to be sick."

"Mr. President."

"Des."

The President got up from his desk in the Oval Office and walked around it with his hand extended toward Des as he was escorted in.

The door to the garden beyond was open, and a late-May breeze was wafting into the room.

"Sit down, please, sit down," said Grey as he motioned toward a seat on the comfortable sofa near the fireplace.

"How about some coffee or tea?"

Des nodded, and the President motioned to the steward who was entering the room. He had a few words with Manolas, who had brought Des in, while Des looked around the room. He had not been in the Oval Office since Roger Kimball had left the Presidency, and he could see Sadie's handiwork everywhere. Her presence was so strong through her taste that he could almost feel her plumping up the pillow behind him and straightening a picture on the wall. It was one of the things he liked most about her, the way she could make a man feel comfortable, cozy, and he had an enormous sense of irony sitting here in the Oval Office with the President of the United States knowing that he was fucking his wife.

"Well," said Rosey, a friendly if reserved smile on his face. "What can I help you with today, sir?"

"As you know, sir, we're doing a cover on those Presidents who have inherited the office and how they fared. I'd like to talk to you a little bit today about what specific difficulties you encountered and how you think it might have been different had you been elected to office the first time around."

Des could see Rosey relax. This one was a soft ball. Rosey wasn't quite sure where Des was going with the interview, and he had no way of knowing that under the circumstances Des wouldn't think of hitting hard. All Des could think about was the fact that doing this interview was probably the grossest example of conflict of interest that he had ever been involved in in his life. Except possibly for the interview with Sadie. But New York had ordered it up. What the hell.

"There is no question," said Rosey, "that I was far better prepared than most elected Presidents, having been Vice President and having been so closely involved with every aspect of the job, thanks to Roger Kimball. That, I think, was my greatest asset. And too, there was a staff already in place. A new President has to appoint an entire government, and sometimes that takes months to get off the ground. I was able to hit the ground running, as they say. I also feel that I was elected. After all, I ran with the President on the same ticket. By voting for that ticket, I feel the American people were giving me a vote of confidence as well."

He was being so serious. Could he be nervous? Des couldn't see why. Normally President Grey had a wry sense of humor. But today he was uninspired and flat. Des could see what would drive Sadie crazy about living with Rosey. He couldn't imagine the guy relaxing, having fun, making love. He didn't want to, either. This was certainly not going to be a major-impact interview, but then, he hadn't expected it to be. He and Rosey continued in the same vein, with Rosey answering the questions with predictable answers, politely but without much enthusiasm. Des hadn't planned to bring up Everett in his interview with the President because it really wasn't relevant to the story, but about halfway through the allotted hour he felt the need to jolt Grey out of his recording pattern.

"Mr. President," he said, "you must be aware by now of the building problem regarding your special counsel, Everett Dubois?"

"Of course I am aware of it," he said, nearly jumping from his seat. "The poor man is being persecuted by the press. Not a day goes by that he doesn't have to defend himself against these accusations, and it is taking its toll on him, believe me. Allison Sterling in *The Daily* has been particularly hard on him, and I regret to say, so has your journal."

"You are absolutely convinced that Everett Dubois was not involved in a kickback scheme with Rittman Oil? That he pressured the Omanis until they gave the contract to another company and that now he is lobbying to limit aid to Oman?"

Rosey's voice was calm. "This is an outrageous claim, sir, if I do say so. This is a decent and loyal human being who has served me long and well. And even though he may be tried and convicted by the media, until a special prosecutor finds him guilty he is innocent in my book."

"Aren't you afraid that this scandal may hurt your campaign?" Des hadn't meant to get this tough, but he was turned off by Rosey's blind loyalty to Everett when he didn't know the facts, and his instinct was to go for the jugular.

"If being loyal to a trusted aide who has been proved guilty of nothing can cost me the election, then I'd be shocked."

The politician in him got the better after a moment.

"But make no mistake about it, mister, it won't. I'm going to win this thing and I'm going to win it big."

Des sensed that it would be useless to pursue the story further. Rosey was not angry anymore. He wasn't going to play.

"We were discussing the assets in having inherited the job of President," asked Des. "Are there any detriments?"

"I didn't finish listing my assets, actually," said Rosey. He paused and leaned back in his chair as if he were contemplating them. He rested both elbows on the arms of the chair and clasped his hands under his chin. He didn't say anything for a while, just stared at Des with a strange look until Des could feel himself squirming uncomfortably.

Finally he spoke.

"My greatest asset, and one that cannot be measured, is my

wife. Sadie. She has been my strength and my support, not only since I've had this job but through our entire marriage. She is a rare and beautiful person, and without her I could not—no, would not—function in this job."

Sadie couldn't keep her eyes open. She had been trying to write all morning and she kept getting drowsier and drowsier. She had been so tired lately, it seemed she was exhausted most of the time. She knew it had to be psychosomatic. She was just so upset that all she wanted to do was sleep. Even though it was Monday, Des was working. He had interviewed Rosey the Friday before, and the piece on the Presidents wasn't due until the end of the week. Still, he wanted to get it just right, and he wasn't taking any chances on letting anybody else mess with it. Des had promised her he would get over to see her later in the afternoon, and she was desperately trying to stay awake. She was losing the battle, and finally she gave up.

She walked over to the big sofa and stretched out, her eyelids drooping before she even settled in. The air was warm and the French doors to her balcony were open and somewhere in the distance as she drifted off to sleep she could hear a lawn mower droning.

"Wake up, Sleeping Beauty."

His voice was loud and gruff, and it woke her up abruptly.

"Unless, of course, you want a repeat performance of East Hampton. Is that it?"

"Ummmm," she said, still half-asleep. "What time is it?"

He came over to the sofa and sat down on the edge next to her.

"A little after four. I could use a beer, actually."

He got up and walked over to the bar, where he took out a Heineken from the small refrigerator, opened it, took a sip, and then came over to sit in the chair next to the sofa, putting his feet on the coffee table.

"I'll tell you. If they thought the piece I did on you was a puff job, just wait till they get a load of the one on your husband."

"Who thought it was a puff job?"

She had pulled herself to a sitting position and was smoothing her hair back as she looked at him in surprise.

He hesitated for a moment, then replied, "Oh, some of my

colleagues. You know they're never satisfied unless you take a pound of flesh."

"Well, thank God you're not doing that to Rosey. He doesn't deserve it."

"Yeah, especially after what's going to happen to him this weekend. He'll need this."

"What's happening to him this weekend?"

"You're going to tell him you'll leave him, remember? You have suddenly started developing a mental block about this."

"Oh, yes." She looked down at the sofa, then pulled out a tissue and dabbed her nose.

"No, no. It's just my nose. I'm having trouble with my sinuses, I guess, and I can't breathe. I've got the sniffles. I feel a little crampy, too. I always feel this way when I'm getting my period."

Des shrugged. He was not particularly interested in this conversation, she could see. He didn't react well when other people were depressed or feeling down. She had noticed this first when Outland got into trouble. Des was not as supportive as she had hoped and seemed to want to distance himself from her problems. He had even called her a basket case at one point. It had given her pause a number of times. But she knew he loved her and she loved him, and that was what mattered.

"I think we ought to talk logistics," he said, taking another sip of beer. "This will be the last time we see each other until you tell Rosey. I think Sunday would be the best time. That way he'll have the whole day to deal with it, to get used to the idea."

"Then what do I tell him?"

She had slumped back on the sofa and was watching Des listlessly. He was being very businesslike and matter-of-fact.

"I think you might say that you and I are in love, that we've been meeting for almost a year, and that we feel that it can't go on like this any longer—it's too risky—and that therefore, as soon as the election is over, you will leave him and move out of the White House. It's that simple."

"And then what?"

"And then we'll live happily ever after. What do you mean?"

"I mean, he's going to say 'And then what?' and I'm going to want to be able to answer. Are we going to get married? Will we live here? What will *I* do? What about my children? There are a lot of questions that we haven't resolved, Des. I think we ought to talk about them."

"That's what we're doing right now."

He sounded testy. She knew she sounded a bit whiny.

"You can tell him we are going to get married. We've talked about that before. But first you have to get divorced. I'm going to rent a house in Georgetown within the next month or two, with Jenny's help. She will take pictures and you will approve of it. You will continue to write, presumably best-selling novels that will be made into TV miniseries. I—well, it's hard for me to know what I'm going to do. I have created such a serious conflict of interest here, interviewing both you and the President, that I may have to quietly resign my position. I just don't know how badly what I have done will be received, but I know I'm going to take a lot of shit. And well deserved."

"But why? What could you have done? The only way you could have gotten out of doing what you did was to tell New York about us. You can't be Washington Bureau Chief and refuse to interview the President. You had no choice."

"I did. I could have resigned then. But I didn't, and I may have to take the consequences."

"But Des, what will you do? How will we live? You don't have any money." Her voice was high-pitched, and she knew she sounded frantic.

"Relax, baby. We'll be all right. I can still stay at the magazine and be a columnist and do all the talk shows. Like it or not, I'll be famous when this happens. I might as well capitalize on it. And you will be even more. We'll do better than we can even imagine right now."

"What about the kids?" She didn't sound convinced.

"The kids will be fine. We'll get a house big enough so they can stay with us if they want to when they're home. I don't imagine that will be often."

She laughed a little bitterly. "Not for my Outland—not while Rosey's President. Annie Laurie will quit St. Tim's and enroll in National Cathedral just so she can live in the White House with her daddy and be his little hostess. God, she'll be in seventh heaven."

"How does that make you feel?" he asked softly.

"I don't know. I just . . . it just . . ." She couldn't finish her sentence. All she could do was weep.

Des got up and came to her, taking her in his arms.

"It's just that it's all so scary," she said when her tears subsided. "I never realized how hard it would be. I love you so. And I'm so miserable the way things are right now. I know what I'm doing is right. It's just that I'm scared. And I can't bear the idea of hurting Rosey."

"You have nothing to be scared of because I'm here, my beauty, and we'll have each other. Besides, it will be easier for him than you think. The man is obsessed with his job. And it's not going to get any better in a second term. And don't forget, he's eligible to run again after this. You could be looking at eight more years. You wouldn't survive that, Sadie. And you know it. Rosey is committed to being President, which is a noble commitment. But it doesn't leave enough for you. And my guess is that if the guy had to choose his country or you, he'd choose his country."

She didn't say anything for a while. She just sat on the sofa and cried silently. Then she looked up at Des—an imploring look.

"Did he—did he say anything about me in your interview?"

Des paused for a moment and then looked directly back at Sadie.

"Nothing that I remember."

She couldn't do it at breakfast. Sunday breakfast was his favorite meal. He had pancakes and eggs and bacon and coffee and fruit, and then he settled back to read the papers. It always took him most of the morning to read the papers. It was the one day he allowed himself the luxury. Every other day he read the news summary. Sundays he insisted on reading at least the two major papers himself.

She sat at the table with him trying to read the papers herself, but it was impossible to concentrate. She had been up all night trying to work out how she would tell him. Nothing seemed right. She took a sip of tea and looked around the room. Her eyes rested on the beautiful Daniel Webster sideboard and the soft blue French wallpaper. Certainly there was nothing in this room that she would change. She couldn't wait, however, to get her hands on the West Hall and the President's bedroom. She had barely been able to stand it, not redecorating instantly, but Rosey had told her that they should wait until he was elected. She knew exactly how she was going to do everything. What was she thinking? She wasn't going to do anything. She was leaving. She felt her stomach drop. She was so short of breath that she kept having to force herself to take big gulps of air from time to time just so she wouldn't suffocate. She had been eying the cigarette box on the breakfast table which was always kept full for various aides of Rosey's. She hadn't had a cigarette herself since before she left Richmond, but now she had an overwhelming desire for one. She reached over, took a Marlboro, and picked up the book of matches that read THE PRESIDENT'S HOUSE. That was the whole problem. It didn't have anything to do with her.

It was that little reinforcement that she needed, and she used it to make herself angry, to give herself courage, to make it easier. She lit the cigarette and took a long drag, glaring resentfully at an unsuspecting Rosey, taking a gulp of his coffee as he turned the pages of *The Daily*. Well, he could live here in *his* house for the next eight years. She would be somewhere else living in *her* house.

She took another drag and blew it out noisily, trying to attract his attention. He hated it when she smoked.

Finally she got his attention.

"Smoking again?" he asked casually.

"What does it look like?"

"You know you shouldn't. It's not good for you."

He turned back to his paper. "I think I'll go get dressed," she said as she got up from the table and walked out into the West Hall.

She hurried into her bedroom, trying not to think of the red-flowered chintz in the West Sitting Room, only to be confronted with the birds. Lately, the birds on the wallpaper had been making her dizzy, even nauseated. She kept waking up in the middle of the night and thinking that the birds were attacking her. And she had five more months of it. Des would never know what a sacrifice she was making for him.

She was giving up the most fabulous decorating project in the world. And the pity was that she had already decorated it in her mind. The yellow oval room was going to be painted the most beautiful soft rosy red. The pain of it all was nearly too much. Maybe Des would agree to let her stay on just long enough . . .

In the dressing room she stood in front of her wardrobe. Her clothes were tagged with the dates of when and for what occasions she had worn them. What was proper to wear for telling one's husband one was leaving him? She looked at the tag on the peach jersey dress as she took it off the hanger: "Interview with Desmond Shaw of *The Weekly*." Her liberation dress. She would wear it.

Rosey asked for lunch in his study. He had some work to do. She waited until the butler had taken away his tray. He was poring through a magazine. She sat down in an armchair opposite his desk. She hadn't thought of anything else for days and now here she was and she still didn't know how she would say it. Rosey had only nodded to her when she came in and had gone back to his *Diplomatic Affairs* magazine as though she weren't there. She could sense that he knew something was coming. He was going to let her begin. Since her outburst over Outland he had treated her rather gingerly.

She tried to say something, but the words wouldn't come out. She sat there for almost five minutes, gripping the arms of the chair with her fingers for moral support.

"Rosey, I . . ." she blurted finally.

"What is it, sweetheart?" He pulled his reading glasses down his nose and looked over them at her with an affectionate smile.

Don't smile at me, she thought. Don't be nice.

"I can tell you've got something on your mind," he said with a patience in his voice she hadn't heard in a long time. "Why don't we talk?"

This was not in the script.

"Look, why don't we take the helicopter to Camp David for a walk, then come back and I'll take you out to dinner."

"Rosey, what are you talking about? We can't just do that."

"Why the hell not?"

With that he jumped up, came around his desk and pulled her out of the chair.

"We can't, Rosey."

"Just give me a reason why."

"I'm leaving you."

She hadn't meant to say it. The stunned look on his face mirrored her own. After the words were out, there was no recall.

"I'm leaving you, Rosey." It was almost a plea. This time she began to cry.

She sat in the chair burying her head in her hands, his knees in front of her head almost touching her as he stood quietly, absorbing what she had just said to him.

"I'm leaving you," she said a third time, her voice so quiet that he barely heard her. She needed to keep saying it, as though it would reinforce her resolve if she heard it herself.

Slowly he let himself down in the armchair next to hers. She could feel him let the air out of his body as he sank back in the chair and his body went limp.

She didn't dare look at him, not really believing that she had done this.

"I don't understand," he said finally.

"I'm in love with someone else."

"Who?"

"Desmond Shaw."

She could hear the air as he let out his breath.

"But how? How can you know you love him? What chance have you had—"

"We've been having an affair for nearly a year."

"Oh, my God."

She finally got her courage to look at him. His head was resting on the back of the chair and he had his hands over his eyes.

She reached into her pocket and pulled out a Kleenex. She seemed always to have tissues with her these days. She wiped her eyes and blew her nose. The motions were comforting. They gave her something to do.

Rosey stood up. "Do you know what could have happened if you were found out?" He was angry now.

"I do. So you can understand how strongly I must have felt to do it." She was surprised at how calm she sounded. She was trying to regain control.

"Who knows about this?"

"Jenny and Toby Waselewski."

"No one else?"

"No."

"Well, we'll have to keep it that way. Now . . ."

Rosey was suddenly very businesslike. He had taken charge, swung into action as if he were forced to make sudden funeral plans and had no time to grieve for the dead.

His manner made it easier for her.

"I thought I should tell you now so we could prepare for me to leave immediately after the election."

"Jenny. Of course. How stupid of me. The children?" He was talking to himself.

"Outland will be away till you leave office. Annie Laurie will be thrilled."

"Why did you decide to tell me now? Today?"

"For one thing, I couldn't stand living a lie anymore. And then there was that item."

"What item?"

"The one in Anastasia's column in the New York paper about the high-powered government official's wife and the journalist."

"That was you?"

"You saw it?"

"Everett showed it to me. Asked me who I thought it could be. I didn't know. Hell, that's not my field. I told him to ask you. You were the one who would know. He just smiled."

"That son-of-a-bitch. I'll get him if it's the last thing I do."

"You don't have to. He's leaving."

"He what? I thought he could do no wrong in your eyes."

"He was persecuted by the press."

"Spare me."

"It's an election year and he's hurting me. I fired him."

"Finally."

"I know he's never been one of your favorites, but I'm going to miss him."

Sadie couldn't believe they were having this conversation at this particular moment. She had just told her husband that she was leaving him and there they were arguing about one of his aides.

Rosey stood up to face her.

"I think I'll go down to the Oval Office. I have some thinking and planning to do."

He squeezed her arm as he walked past her out the door and to the elevator. She watched him from his study as he got on the elevator, looking down, and pressed the button. The door closed slowly, and she thought as she watched his face disappear what a dignified, distinguished-looking man he was.

She couldn't wait to get to the phone. She rushed into her tiny office next to the dining room and called Des at home.

"I told him."

"Christ, I thought you'd never call. I've been sitting here waiting since eight this morning. I'm about to jump out of my bloody skin."

"Don't you want to know what happened?"

"What happened?"

"It was easy. He didn't take it badly at all. He was very calm and thoughtful."

"You sound disappointed."

"No—well, yes, I guess I am, a little. But I'm more relieved than anything else. It was harder on me than it was on him. I'm a little wrung out."

"I can't believe this. The guy's wife tells him she's leaving him for another man and he's calm and thoughtful. Baby, you are doing the right thing, that's all I can say. It sounds like he's planning a fucking transition like he went through with Roger Kimball. It blows my mind."

"Well, what would *you* do?" She sounded defensive.

"I'd cut the guy's nuts off. That's what. All I can tell you is I wouldn't be calm and thoughtful."

"How do you know he's not on his way over to your house right now?"

"You mean he's not there?"

"No. He went down to the Oval Office to think and plan."

"Jesus."

"Everett knows."

"How do you know?"

"Because he showed Rosey the item in Anastasia's column. Rosey didn't get it, but obviously Everett did."

"That sleazy little son-of-a-bitch. I'm going to get his ass."

"You already have."

"What do you mean?"

"Rosey fired him. The story will be that he resigned, quote unquote, yesterday, that he and Rosey agreed it was hurting the campaign too much. They'll blame it on the press, say they were persecuting him."

"Hey, that's a story. Listen, I'll talk to you later. I want to get on this one. And Sadie . . ."

"Yes?"

"You did good, baby."

* * *

It was late afternoon and Rosey was still in the Oval Office. She had no idea when he would come back up. Sadie thought she would go crazy if she had to stay in the White House another minute.

She had tried to reach Jenny at home, but there was no answer. She hadn't told Jenny that she was going to tell Rosey. She tried Lorraine, but she was out too. Finally, desperate, she called her mother. She chatted with her for a while but broke off short, afraid that she would break down.

She thumbed through several decorating and fashion magazines but was unable to concentrate. She tried to watch an old movie on TV, but she switched it off after twenty minutes. She turned on the music in her dressing room and did exercises for forty-five minutes, working up a sweat. But even that didn't relax her. She went into her office and took out a notebook. She should write all of this down for her novel. She had to remember what Des had said once: "Everything is copy."

The Sunday-night movie was a tearjerker about a marriage splitting up. She had had a tray sent up to her room. Still no word from Rosey.

She cried all the way through and finally, when it was over, she switched off the light, exhausted, and lay in the dark trying to imagine what it would all be like. Would the publicity be awful? Yes, she knew that. Would she and Des be truly happy? She had to believe it would all be worth it in the end. Otherwise nothing was worth the pain of losing one's husband, one's home, one's security, even, to some extent, one's family.

It was about eleven thirty when Rosey came in. She pretended to be asleep. He went into the bathroom and she could hear the shower. He came back into the bedroom and got into bed, lying close enough to her so that she could feel his body's presence.

She knew he knew she was awake. It didn't surprise her, for some reason, when Rosey reached out and took her hand. They lay there in silence for a long time.

"I'm losing you and it makes me very sad," he said in a soft, hushed tone of voice.

"It makes me sad too," she said.

He didn't say anything. He tried to muffle a sob, but he failed, and soon his body was racking. She had never heard anyone cry like that. She couldn't bear it. She squeezed his hand and he squeezed hers back until she thought he would break her hand, and still he sobbed until she couldn't hold back her own tears, and together they lay side by side in the dark and wept for the longest time. Then he pulled her to him and held her tightly in his arms.

"Don't leave me, Sadiebelle," he said in an exhausted whisper when their sobs had subsided. "Please don't leave me. I love you so much. I can't do it without you. I need you. I know you don't realize how important you are to me. But don't you see? I'm the President. I have to be a good President. It's an overwhelming responsibility. Nobody can do this job without support and love. It's hard on you, I know. But I'll make it up to you for the rest of our lives. If you leave me, I won't run again."

"You can't mean that, Rosey."

"I've never been more serious in my life."

They were in her little office off the West Sitting Room. It was Monday morning. Sadie was so tired she didn't have the energy to sit up. Jenny was sitting facing her. She sat on the edge of her chair when Sadie broke the news.

"This one is off the scale, Jen." Sadie managed a weak smile.

"What are you going to do?"

"I don't know. I care for him. But I love Des. I really don't think I can live without him. I don't think I could bear the idea of living in this place for another four years without Des. And I can't go on seeing him like this. It's driving us both insane. I just have to be with him, Jenny. I don't have a choice."

"Do you really believe that Rosey won't run?"

"I don't know what I believe anymore. I don't see how he can mean it. He's the most dedicated person I've ever known, and he cares deeply about this country. I know he feels he is by far the most qualified to run it. I can't imagine that he would give it up. And for what? For a wife who has left him? Besides, he's paid so little attention to me lately that it's hard for me to believe he loves me so much he would give up everything he ever cared about even if I leave him. It just doesn't make any sense. Still, he was very convincing. I just don't know what to tell you."

"Have you told Des?"

"I called him yesterday after I'd told Rosey. But Rosey was so calm in the beginning. None of this happened until late last night. Des doesn't know about his threat."

"Sadie, do you have any doubts about Des—about spending the rest of your life with him, about giving up this place and your husband for him? Because if you do, you better articulate them now, face them before it's too late. This decision you're making is irrevocable."

"Oh, God. Of course I have doubts. I've tried to talk to Des about them, but he doesn't take me seriously. He keeps saying we have each other and he loves me and that's all that matters. But I'm terrified. I'm not sure Des knows me, knows who I am. I'm so scared that he's just enticed by the fact that I'm the First Lady, and when I leave the White House I'll be just another nifty dame. Des is used to being with a woman who has a career and is totally independent. I'm not like that. I am a dependent. I don't know anything else. I have my writing, but I've never made a penny out of it. I think Des expects me to suddenly become a successful writer overnight, that he's banking on the fact that my name will sell books or stories. I can't support myself and I don't want to have to. My idea of romance is having someone take care of me. That may be a cop-out, but it's the honest truth. I know I'm always annoyed with Rosey because he never tells me how much money he has, and he's so tight with it anyway. I always feel like we're broke, even though I know he's worth millions. He's broke unless *he* wants to spend it. Then his money appears miraculously. Sometimes I feel kept with him, as though I am not my own person. But in the end I feel more comfortable living that way than being totally responsible for myself."

"I think those fears are well founded. Des is an independent man, and he has never had to support a woman. Chessy was loaded. He bought his own clothes and paid for dinner when they went out, but that was about it. Sonny is the most independent woman I know, or at least she would like everyone, particularly Des, to think she is. It will be a change for him."

"But will it be a welcome change? I don't know. That's what scares me. And I'll tell you honestly, Jenny. It scares me that Des won't talk to me about it. One of the things that drives me crazy about Rosey is that he will never talk to me about how he feels about anything. The reason I fell for Des in the first place is that he was so open with me about how hurt and lonely he was. He showed me his vulnerability. Now he's closed up again. I have absolutely no idea in the world what he's thinking or feeling. Whether he has any doubts or fears about this whole thing. Whether he still has any feeling for Allison. Those are big worries. Maybe there's no such thing as a man who talks. Maybe it's just that I'm only attracted to the ones who don't. But I feel a little bit as if I'm jumping from the frying pan into the fire, if you'll pardon the cliché. Des and Rosey are a lot alike in many ways, except that Des is sexy and Rosey is not. The question is, is that enough?"

"You've got a lot to think about. And you don't have any time. If Rosey is serious, he's going to have to announce before the convention that he's taking himself out of the race. It's now the beginning of June. That leaves him six weeks before the convention in San Francisco."

"I know what *I'm* going to do."

"What?"

"I'm going to leave Rosey and go with Des. I have no choice. Otherwise I'm in the land of the living dead. And if Rosey wants to give up the Presidency, then that's his problem. I'll not let him lay it on me."

Sadie said this with such resolve that there was no doubt in Jenny's mind that that was exactly what she intended to do. She was amazed at how calm Sadie seemed as she sat up and leaned over to pour herself another cup of tea from the tray the butler had brought in earlier.

The phone rang on Sadie's desk—the regular phone. Jenny picked it up.

"Mrs. Grey's office. Oh, yes, right. Will you hold one moment, please." She turned to Sadie. "It's Dr. Williams."

"Oh, great. It will be just my luck if I have to have an artificial-heart transplant." She took the phone from Jenny.

"Yes?" There was an anxious note to her voice.

"Right? Yes. Good! Yes? What? Oh, no." Her face turned ashen and she grasped her stomach. "Oh, no."

Jenny jumped up.

"Okay, yes, I will. Right. Thank you very much, Dr. Williams. Yes. Right. Goodbye." Her voice was shaking as she hung up and slowly turned to Jenny.

"What in God's name is it, Sadie?" she practically shouted.

"I'm pregnant."

She paused to let the news sink in, then looked at Sadie sharply.

"Who's the father?"

"I don't have any idea."

She couldn't, wouldn't tell Des. Nor had she told Rosey. She had made love to Rosey the night she returned from East Hampton. Or rather, he had made love to her. He had been out campaigning and was glad to see her after a week. He had approached her after they'd gone to bed. Twice, the time with Des in East Hampton and that night, had been spontaneous and unexpected and she had neglected to use a diaphragm. She hated it, anyway. It was inconvenient and messy, and she had been so used to the ease of the pill that somewhere in her brain she hadn't really thought she would get pregnant again.

But she was pregnant, with either Des's baby or Rosey's baby, and they would both know, when they found out, that she couldn't know who the father was. The baby was due in January.

She wanted Des badly, needed him more than she had ever needed anyone, and yet she knew she couldn't tell him. In a way she was relieved that they wouldn't be able to see each other for two weeks. He was in Louisiana all this week, so they would miss their Monday. Then she was going out on a long-promised campaign swing with Rosey the following week. The staff were getting anxious that she hadn't been out that much, and there had been a few inquiries from the press. By the time she and Des met again, it would be only three weeks until the convention. She talked to him regularly on the phone, whispering the usual "I love you's" and the "You know what I'm going to do to you when I finally get my hands on you's," and she tried to be as jolly as possible, not giving her anguish away.

Although she hadn't actually said anything to him, it was obvious from the way Rosey was acting that he thought she had decided to stay. The threat of stepping down was serious, and she would find it very hard to let him do that. He was treating her like a queen—being terribly solicitous, letting her have anything at all she wanted.

What Sadie really wanted to do was get drunk and stay drunk, and now here she was six weeks pregnant, the convention only a month away, and unable even to have a glass of wine or an aspirin or a Valium or anything that would put her out of her misery.

She had nobody to talk to but Jenny, and she clung to her like a life preserver.

"What's the matter, baby?"

Des pulled her away from him and looked down at her pale, unsmiling face.

"Don't you feel well?"

He had just walked into her office in the EOB, so excited to see her after their two-week separation, so ebullient about their plans, that he hadn't noticed at first how drawn and sallow she appeared. It was only when he held her to him that he could feel her limp body and the slightly feverish perspiration on her brow.

Now he was studying her with concern.

"As a matter of fact, I feel really lousy," she said, giving him another weak hug before she went and collapsed against the pillows of the sofa.

"I think I'm coming down with the flu. It might even be pneumonia. It's probably psychosomatic."

She managed a weak smile.

"I always get pneumonia during campaigns. I hate them so, and it gives me an out. I've got a sore throat and a slight fever and I feel rather weak and dizzy. I shouldn't even have come here today for fear of infecting you. The last thing you need now, in the middle of the campaign, is to get sick yourself. With me it doesn't really matter. I can stay in bed. Nobody misses me."

Her plan had been to lie to him about not feeling well to cover up for her anguish over being pregnant, but as it turned out she really was feeling sick, and worse than that, she was feeling terribly sorry for herself.

"I miss you, my love. I miss you every second we're apart."

Sometimes she couldn't tell whether he meant it or whether he was being facetious. He had that funny twinkle in his eye which usually meant he was teasing, only she wasn't in the mood to be teased. She didn't ask if he was serious. She wanted—needed—to believe him.

Why was it that now, when she was agonizing over her decision, both Des and Rosey were making it more difficult for her by acting so loving? If only one of them would behave abominably it would make things so much easier.

She had waited to tell Des about Rosey's threat in person, because she wanted to see his face, make sure he understood how much she loved him, before he responded.

"Des," she began hesitantly, after he had joined her on the sofa.

"Yes?"

"I don't think he means it. I mean, you never can tell. But I can't believe he would do it, but . . ."

"What are you talking about?"

"Rosey. He says he'll refuse the nomination if I leave him." She blurted it out.

"Bullshit." He burst out laughing.

"Well, I don't see what's so funny."

"Are you kidding me? That guy is the most dedicated S.O.B. I've ever met. If you left him, he would have to have the Presidency. He wouldn't have anything else."

"But how do we know that?"

"Believe me, sweetheart. I'm a man. I know what's going through his head. He's not going to lose the thing that means the most to him and give up the other at the same time. It just doesn't make sense. This is not an emotional man. This is a very clever politician. And this is a very clever ploy to shame you into staying with him. In fact, it kind of pisses me off for him to use you like that. He's not going anywhere. I can promise you that."

"I wish I were as sure of that as you are. You weren't there. You didn't hear the desperation in his voice."

"So tell him you won't leave him, then."

"You mean lie to him?"

"That's what I mean."

"But it wouldn't be fair."

"On the contrary. It would give him a great sense of confidence throughout the campaign. And it would guarantee that he would stay on and get reelected, which would be a patriotic act. And it would ensure that he would in fact have his job after you left him. I think it is a truly noble thing to do."

"Being noble has many faces," she said.

"What?"

"Oh, nothing. I was just talking out loud."

* * *

Des had put his arms around her and was caressing her body slowly and softly. He kissed her on the neck and on the head, pulling her closer to him as he did.

"I want to make love to you. It's been two weeks. That's too long, baby. It will never be that long again after we're together."

"Oh, Des, I really feel so rotten."

"I'll make you feel better, my beautiful Sadie."

He picked her up and carried her into their small bedroom in back, put her down on the open sofa bed, and began to stroke her and caress her as he climbed on top of her and held her to him.

Des was right. He made her forget that she felt bad, and miraculously, as he made love to her, all of her fears seemed to evaporate. Nothing else mattered except for her and Des. If only she could have him around all the time, she knew she wouldn't be plagued with indecision. It was only when they were apart that she couldn't make up her mind about anything.

"You are mine now," he whispered as he pressed his body to her. "Oh, God. Oh, hold me, baby, hold me." He was coming now, and his ferocity overwhelmed her, so that when she came she could feel herself slipping into a faint, and the last thing she remembered was Des's breath on her shoulder and his voice crying out in passion.

Rosey had been in great spirits since Sadie had told him she would stay with him and give up Des.

Somehow, even though Des had made it sound so right, she had felt guilty about lying to him again. It was the deception before which she had despised so. And it was the deception that had caused her to tell him she was leaving him in the first place. Now she had signed on for nearly four more months of it. Not that she was actually thinking rationally about any of this. Jenny had told her that these last few weeks, she was certifiable.

"Delirious is what my doctor calls it," said Sadie, smiling weakly. She didn't really feel like smiling. She felt so sick she could barely sit up in bed. She hadn't been able to eat in a week, and then only clear soups and tea. She had refused all calls from Des. Her private phone was in her study, and she was too sick to go in there anyway. She had asked Jenny to tell him that she was too sick and too confused to talk and that she needed some time alone to think. She had in fact come down with pneumonia, as she always did when she was under tremendous stress. She couldn't have been more relieved. She did exactly what she had wanted to do: she went to bed and stayed there. Rosey slept in the Lincoln bedroom to avoid getting sick. He came to see her briefly each evening when he wasn't on the road, but he was busy and preoccupied, and she was glad when their short visits ended.

Jenny was her constant companion, either perched on the edge of their king-size bed or curled up in an armchair she had dragged over close to Sadie so they could hear each other better.

"Jesus," said Jenny. "It's a good thing Allison's not around. She'd be on to this in five minutes."

"What do you mean? Where is she?"

"You *are* out of it, aren't you? If you'd been reading *The Daily* you'd know that she's off the White House beat and covering the Republican candidates."

"Wonder why she did that."

"On your list of worries, my dear, I'd say that was at the very bottom."

"What's at the top? Remind me. I've forgotten."

Jenny ignored her attempt at humor.

"You haven't told either of them?"

"Now who's certifiable? Are you kidding? Exactly how would you suggest I phrase it: 'Oh, by the way, I'm pregnant'?"

"Something like that."

"Oh, Jenny, I'm so terrified. Don't make fun of me."

"Des called again this morning."

"I can't bear it."

"You've really got to talk to him. It isn't fair."

"I don't know what to say. Ever since my meeting with him I've just been racked with doubts and misgivings. You know Des has a way of making everything sound so simple, so that when I'm with him I agree, and then I get away from him and I'm all confused again. Besides, all the advice he has given me is without knowing that I'm pregnant. Don't you see how awful this is for me? Whichever one I decide to stay with will have to accept a child which might not be his. It's an intolerable situation. I don't see how I can rightly stay with either of them."

"You're delirious."

"Well, Jenny, just think about it."

"Think about it, she tells me. Do you think I have thought of anything else this past year? We could be in the midst of a nuclear war and I wouldn't know it."

"That's not a bad idea. Maybe Rosey will accidentally push the wrong button and blow us all away and then I won't have to deal with this. I think I'll speak to him about it. He said he'd do anything to get me to stay."

"I can't help thinking there's a simpler solution."

"Abortion?"

"Well . . ."

"Oh, God."

"It's certainly the most viable solution. After all, you are forty and you've got two practically grown children. And don't forget your heart condition. Giving birth could endanger your health."

"I could never keep it a secret."

"Yes, you could. Say you're having a D and C."

"Rosey would find out. Somebody would find out. I just don't think it would work."

"Is that the only reason?"

"Yes."

Jenny looked at her.

"No . . . What if it's Des's baby? It would be my love child. And what if it were Rosey's? It would be a brother or sister of Outland's. Rosey gave me my beloved Outland. How could I do away with another Outland? I just couldn't."

"So what are your alternatives?"

"I can tell Des it's his, leave Rosey after the nomination, and go into seclusion. But that might cost Rosey the election. I can leave the White House and go off somewhere to Europe to stay with Outland and write and have my baby there. I can stay with Rosey and go into seclusion here claiming I'm sick until the election. Then leave him. I can stay with Rosey pretending the baby is his and remain a prisoner in the White House for the next four years."

"None of them sound very attractive—or very realistic, for that matter."

"They all sound horrible."

"You could lie to Rosey and tell him you used a diaphragm with Des. He'll never know. For that matter, you could lie to Des and say you used one with Rosey. But the fact is that you will be showing before the election, and if you are showing you will have to stay with Rosey. If you want to go with Des, you have only one choice."

"What's that?"

"Have an abortion."

Sadie closed her eyes and lay back on her pillow. She could feel her heart pounding in her chest, and though she thought it must be her imagination, she could have sworn that she felt the baby's heartbeat as well. Whatever it was, she felt a quickening in her body, and she instinctively put her arms around her belly to protect her child within.

"Jenny," she had finally said, "you've got to do something for me. I can't bear to talk to Des. I don't know what to say to him. I'm too afraid to tell him I'm pregnant for fear of what he'll say. You've got to tell him for me that I am not sure anymore of what I'm going to do. That the decision is harder than I had thought it would be. And that he must try to understand what I am going through and how difficult it is for me. Please tell him that for me, Jenny. Tell him I will let him know what I decide as soon as I am well and can think properly. Please don't tell him I'm pregnant. I'll have to find a way to tell him myself. Oh, and Jen? Tell him I love him."

Monday was the first day she had actually gotten dressed. She had called Ivan, her hairdresser, to go with her on *Air Force One* to San Francisco, and he had brought his makeup specialist with him. Ivan had worked her over for what seemed like hours before they were to leave the White House, trying to make her look healthy.

"Mrs. Grey," he had said, "you are still very sick. Are you sure you should go with the President? Why don't you stay in Washington and fly out Thursday for the acceptance speech? You really are not well enough to go today, and frankly, if I may speak the truth, you do not look well. Three more days and you would look more like yourself."

She still did feel extremely weak, and she didn't see how she would be able to handle the appearances she would be expected to make if she did go out with Rosey that afternoon. And too, she would have to deal with the jet lag, which always knocked her for a loop.

The Weekly had called and asked her to be its special guest of honor at a luncheon on Wednesday of that week. Jenny had approached her with that message. She still hadn't responded. Jenny didn't know whether Des had been responsible for the invitation or not.

When Ivan suggested she not go, she called Jenny and asked her to come up to her dressing room right away. She presented her with the argument that she not go until Thursday, and Jenny, seeing the desperation in her eyes, agreed and called Rosey to tell him she was still too weak to go with him.

Rosey was nothing but solicitous. He came from finishing last-minute preparations in the Oval Office and took her into the bedroom with him and shut the door.

"I am so sorry you're still feeling poorly, sugar," he said. "I'll miss you very much, but I think you're doing the right thing. The suite will be a zoo, with people running in and out, and I'll be busy meeting with people, so I won't have any time to concentrate on you. Besides, I want you feeling wonderful and looking like my beautiful bride for Thursday night when I accept the nomination. I promise you that Friday afternoon, you and I are heading up to East Hampton, and we'll stay there at least two weeks, and I plan to concentrate on you and you alone. I love you, my darling Sadiebelle. I love you more than life itself. And I promise you that you have made the right decision."

Sadie kissed him goodbye, went into the bathroom, and ran a hot tub, turning the water on full blast so that nobody would hear her cry.

The weather in San Francisco was perfect. Clear and warm, without a trace of fog, and fifteen degrees cooler than the scorching heat across the Bay.

Sadie had arrived at about four in the afternoon—just enough time, really, to get dressed and made up and have Ivan do her hair. She had chosen a white knit suit with a white silk blouse and ropes of pearls. The irony of wearing white while she was pregnant with one of two men's baby appealed to her in a macabre way.

The backdrop in the San Francisco convention hall was bright blue and red, and she thought that the white would not only complement the colors but also stand out against them. It also did wonderful things for her auburn hair, and it didn't make her look as washed-out as a bright color would, considering that she had been sick for so many weeks.

The Presidential Suite at the Huntington was soft and elegant, with beautiful flowers everywhere and a spectacular view of the Bay. But it was so crowded with staff and aides that Sadie was delighted to have arrived only at the last minute.

Rosey rushed to greet her, and the two disappeared into the bedroom for a moment alone.

"You're going to be proud of me tonight, sugar. As proud of me as I am of you. I have a surprise for you. I'm not going to tell you what it is, but I think you'll like it. I've got to go over the speech one more time. I'll leave you alone now to get dressed. I love you." And he looked fondly down at her and kissed her lightly on the nose, squeezing both of her hands in support.

"Good luck" was all she could say as he walked out of the bedroom to meet with his waiting staff.

Ivan really had worked miracles, as had his makeup person. She not only looked healthy, she looked radiant. She couldn't believe it was her own image in the mirror that she was seeing. The transformation from a pale, wan, sickly creature to vibrant, glowing beauty was extraordinary.

She practically held her breath in the limousine going over to the convention hall, where she would take her place in the family box next to the podium and wait for Rosey to appear. Jenny was with her in the car. She was her life-support system. Taking Jenny away from her would be like pulling the plug.

"Will he be there?"

"Of course. He's a journalist."

"Where will he be sitting?"

"On the other side of the podium from where you're sitting. The press is on the opposite side."

"Will I be able to see him?"

"Not from where you're sitting. You can see him when you join Rosey on the podium. He'll be to your left."

"How is he, Jen?"

"Frantic."

"Oh, God."

"He can't believe you might change your mind. And he's really angry that you won't talk to him."

"I don't know what to say."

"That's why he's frantic."

"I can't bear it."

"You can't cry, Sadie—you'll smudge your makeup."

"To hell with my makeup."

"Listen, the networks are going to interview you when you're in the family box, and they're going to be doing close-up shots. Now, I've got you out of any interviews in the network booths. They all know you've been sick. But you can't look like you've been crying. Please, Sadie, pull yourself together."

"What am I going to do, Jenny?"

"You're going to make up your mind. And you're going to tell Des one way or the other—that's what. I can't live this way any longer. It's tearing me apart. And I can imagine how Des feels. Do you have any idea what that man has been going through the last few weeks? You can't do this to him. Or yourself, for that matter. You're going to have to decide, Sadie. And you're going to have to do it now."

They were escorted to the holding room behind the podium from where they would then be taken to their seats in the box. Sadie felt as though she were walking in a daze as they came up in the elevator and then climbed the blue-carpeted stairs to enter a series of small, windowless rooms with a narrow hall. Looking at her white clothes, she suddenly imagined herself an Aztec maiden being led to the top of the pyramid to be sacrificed. She could imagine blood on her dress and herself crying out, as she had so many times in her feverish dreams of the last few weeks. Her urge to break away and run back down the ramp and out of the hall was overwhelming, but somehow she managed the polite smiles and handshakes that were required of a First Lady.

As she walked into the tiny holding room behind the podium, she saw her son, Outland, standing tall and straight and smiling at her as he held out his arms.

"Outland! Oh, my baby, my baby, Outland!" she cried as she threw herself into his arms and held on as tightly as she could, not wanting to ever let go.

"Hi, Mama," he said, laughing at her tears. "Hey, calm down. It's a surprise. I'm coming, not leaving."

"Sadie, here," said Jenny. "Ivan gave me a little extra makeup in case of emergencies. I would say this is an emergency. I told the President this surprise was not a good idea. But he wanted Outland to be here and not have you know about it. It's a get-well present, he said."

Sadie saw Annie Laurie, standing behind Outland, and turned to give her a hug. At least now, with her family here, she knew she could make it through the evening. She let Jenny fix her makeup and calmed herself down as much as she could under the circumstances, then proceeded out to the family box, flanked by her two children, to tremendous applause. She stood and waved for minutes while the band played "Sweet Georgia Brown," and then, when the demonstrating had died down, the three of them sat down. No sooner had they been seated than she heard others come into the box and she turned to see her parents, G, and Miz G. She almost burst into tears when she saw her mother, but Miz G's presence there helped her to control herself.

"It's a surprise, darlin'," said her mother. "Rosey said you'd been so sick he didn't want to bother you with plans. He just wanted us all to be here, the family—to be with you."

Sadie couldn't decide whether she should be angry at Rosey or sympathetic. Obviously he had gathered the whole family around as reinforcement for her, for him, for them, their marriage.

"Mrs. Grey, Mrs. Grey." The network correspondents were converging upon the family box with their earphones in place, their microphones held high toward her face.

"How are you feeling after your bout with pneumonia?" one of them shouted.

"I feel much better. I had a good three weeks in bed and enough time to recuperate because I wanted to be sure I could be here tonight."

"Didn't you get pneumonia during the last weeks of the campaign four years ago?"

"That's right."

"Is this your way of getting out of campaigning?"

She was an ace by now at turning potentially hostile questions into jokes.

"Funny, you're not the first one to suggest that. My husband asked me the same question." And she laughed a disarming laugh.

"How do you feel about your husband getting nominated tonight?"

"Well, I know he feels that he has done a lot so far in this job, but there are so many things that he's started he'd like to see finished. He's hoping to get that chance."

"What about you, Mrs. Grey? Are you looking forward to another four years in the White House?"

For a moment she thought she was going to lose her composure, but she managed to smile and look enthusiastic before she could come up with an answer.

"Four years is a long time," she started to say, and then caught herself before she continued that thought. "You can get a lot accomplished in four years. My husband will need that time to do what needs to be done, and I look forward to seeing someone of his quality elected to carry out the programs that he and his Administration have begun."

"Thank you, Mrs. Grey."

Her neck was getting stiff; she found it difficult to turn her head all the way either way. She scanned the floor while her friend Senator Malcolm Sohier was addressing the convention to see if she could find Des, but he wasn't down there. Once she saw Allison talking to one of the network floor reporters, but she vanished back up on the other side of the podium to the press section before Sadie could get a good look at her.

Mercifully, Rosey had been introduced and had appeared on the podium, to tumultuous applause. The demonstration went on forever, and Rosey looked ecstatic standing there waving to the crowds. He really did belong there, Sadie knew. He belonged in that office. He *should* be President. The country needed him. The question was did the country need her?

Just as he began to speak, he found her in the family box and nodded just the slightest secret smile to her.

His speech was electrifying. He had always been an effective speaker, but this was the best speech she had ever heard him give, and she was truly mesmerized by his words. As he was concluding, he remarked on the importance in America of the stability and the viability of the family.

"And nowhere is that more true than in my own life. I readily admit to you that the support and love of those around us is of utmost importance. Without the love and support of my own family and particularly of my wife, Sadie, I would not be able to carry on."

By the time he finished, the crowds were on their feet, some clapping and cheering, others sobbing at the emotionally charged tenor of his speech.

Rosey summoned Sadie to join him, and she walked quickly toward the lectern where he was standing, followed by the family. As she was approaching her husband, Toby Waselewski, her Secret Service agent, pressed something into her hand.

"Jenny asked me to give you this," he whispered.

She walked into Rosey's embrace, and as she did he leaned down and kissed her on the lips, and the crowd went even wilder.

They stood for several minutes smiling and waving, Rosey's arm continuously around her.

It was only when he reached over to embrace Freddy and Blanche Osgood that she was able to glance down at the tiny note folded in her hand. As she opened it up and read it, she could feel the tears well up in her eyes and the dizziness come over her. The note was very simple. It said:

"Regrets Only."

She glanced over to her left, to where the press was sitting, not having dared before. He was there in *The Weekly*'s section, looking directly at her. Several feet away in *The Daily*'s section stood Allison Sterling. She was watching Des.

Sadie stared at Des. She could feel his dark eyes boring into hers and still she couldn't take hers away. She was only vaguely aware that the noise was dying down as the two of them continued to look at each other as though if they let go of their gaze, like one person holding another from falling off a ledge, they would both plunge to their deaths.

Finally Des moved, and with the subtlest of motions, unable to hide his apprehension, he raised his shoulders in a questioning gesture.

She looked at him for what seemed an eternity before she shook her head back and forth slowly, unable to keep the tears from sliding down her cheeks.

She watched Des's face as anguish engulfed him, watched him pick up his jacket and quickly make his way to the exit.

Allison's eyes met Sadie's and Sadie could see that Allison understood.

"h, look at Sadie, poor darlin'," she heard her mother say.

"'s so emotional. She always cries when she's happy."

"turned back to where Sadie was standing and put his

her again, giving her a reassuring squeeze as he

waved to the adoring crowds and sparked a new round of applause and cheering.

Sadie took that opportunity to glance back to the press section.

She saw Des at the exit. And as he was turning to walk out, following him with her eyes, was Allison.

ABOUT THE AUTHOR

Sally Quinn was for many years a political reporter for *The Washington Post*, famous for her coverage of the social scene as well as national politics. Quinn was also co-anchor of the CBS Morning News, an experience she described in *We're Going to Make You a Star*. She lives in Washington, D.C., with her son, Quinn, and husband, Benjamin C. Bradlee, Executive Editor of *The Washington Post*.